THE KNIGH'
CROS
or, KRZYZACY

Historical Romance

By HENRYK
SIENKIEWICZ

Translated By Samuel A.
Binion

HON. WILLIAM T. HARRIS, LL.D.

Commissioner of Education

My Dear Doctor:—

This translation, of one of the greatest novels of Poland's foremost modern writer, Henryk Sienkiewicz, I beg to dedicate to you. Apart for my high personal regard for you, my reason for selecting you among all my literary friends, is: that you are a historian and philosopher, and can therefore best appreciate works of this kind.

SAMUEL A. BINION,

New York City.

To the Reader.

Here you have, gentle reader—old writers always called you gentle—something very much more than a novel to amuse an idle hour. To read it will be enjoyable pastime, no doubt; but the brilliant romance of the brilliant author calls upon you for some exercise of the finest sympathy and intelligence; sympathy for a glorious nation which, with only one exception, has suffered beyond all other nations; intelligence, of the sources of that unspeakable and immeasurable love and of the great things that may yet befall before those woes are atoned for and due punishment for them meted out to their guilty authors.

Poland! Poland! The very name carries with it sighings and groanings, nation-murder, brilliance, beauty, patriotism, splendors, self-sacrifice through generations of gallant men and exquisite women; indomitable endurance of bands of noble people carrying through world-wide exile the sacred fire of wrath against the oppressor, and uttering in every clime a cry of appeal to Humanity to rescue Poland.

It was indeed a terrible moment in history, when the three military monarchies of Europe, Russia, Austria and Prussia, swooped down upon the glorious but unhappy country, torn by internal trouble, and determined to kill it and divide up its dominions. All were alike guilty, as far as motive went. But Holy Russia—Holy!—since that horrible time has taken upon herself by far the greatest burden of political crime in her dealings with that noble nation. Every evil passion bred of despotism, of theological hatred, of rancorous ancient enmities, and the ghastliest official corruption, have combined in Russian action for more than one hundred and fifty years, to turn Poland into a hell on earth. Her very language was proscribed.

This is not the place to give details of that unhappy country's woes. But suffice it to say, that Poland, in spite of fatuous prohibitions, has had a great literature since the loss of her independence, and that literature has so kept alive the soul of the nation, that with justice Poland sings her great patriotic song:

"Poland is not yet lost
As long as we live…."

The nation is still alive in its writers and their works, their splendid poetry and prose.

It is a pity that so few of these great writers are widely known. But most people have heard of Jan Kochanowski, of Mikolaj Rey, of Rubinski, of Szymanowicz, of Poland's great genius in this century, one of the supreme poets of the world, Adam Mickiewicz, of Joseph Ignac, of Kraszewski, who is as prolific in literary and scientific works as Alexander von Humboldt, and of hundreds of others in all branches of science and art, too numerous to mention here.

And it is remarkable that the author of this book, Henryk Sienkiewicz, should of late have attained such prominence in the public eye and found a place in the heart of mankind. It is of good omen. Thus, Poland, in spite of her fetters, is keeping step in the very van of the most progressive nations.

The romance of Sienkiewicz in this volume is perhaps the most interesting and fascinating he has yet produced. It is in the very first rank of imaginative and historical romance. The time and scene of the noble story are laid in the middle ages during the conquest of Pagan Lithuania by the military and priestly order of the "Krzyzacy" Knights of the Cross. And the story exhibits with splendid force the collision of race passions and fierce, violent individualities which accompanied that struggle. Those who read it will, in addition to their thrilling interest in the tragical and varied incidents, gain no little insight into the origin and working of the inextinguishable race hatred between Teuton and Slav. It was an unfortunate thing surely, that the conversion of the heathen Lithuanians and Zmudzians was committed so largely to that curious variety of the missionary, the armed knight, banded in brotherhood, sacred and military. To say the least, his sword was a weapon dangerous to his evangelizing purpose. He was always in doubt whether to present to the heathen the one end of it, as a cross for adoration, or the other, as a point *to kill with*. And so, if Poland *was* made a Catholic nation, she was also made an undying and unalterable hater of the German, the Teutonic name and person.

And so this noble, historical tale, surpassed perhaps by none in literature, is commended to the thoughtful attention and appreciation of the reader.

SAMUEL A. BINION.

NEW YORK, May 9, 1899.

KNIGHTS OF THE CROSS.

PART FIRST

CHAPTER I.

In Tyniec,[1] in the inn under "Dreadful Urus," which belonged to the abbey, a few people were sitting, listening to the talk of a military man who had come from afar, and was telling them of the adventures which he had experienced during the war and his journey.

He had a large beard but he was not yet old, and he was almost gigantic but thin, with broad shoulders; he wore his hair in a net ornamented with beads; he was dressed in a leather jacket, which was marked by the cuirass, and he wore a belt composed of brass buckles; in the belt he had a knife in a horn scabbard, and at his side a short traveling sword.

Near by him at the table, was sitting a youth with long hair and joyful look, evidently his comrade, or perhaps a shield-bearer, because he also was dressed as for a journey in a similar leather jacket. The rest of the company was composed of two noblemen from the vicinity of Krakow and of three townsmen with red folding caps, the thin tops of which were hanging down their sides to their elbows.

The host, a German, dressed in a faded cowl with large, white collar, was pouring beer for them from a bucket into earthen mugs, and in the meanwhile he was listening with great curiosity to the military adventures.

The burghers were listening with still greater curiosity. In these times, the hatred, which during the time of King Lokietek had separated the city and the knighthood, had been very much quenched, and the burghers were prouder than in the following centuries. They called them still *des allerdurchluchtigsten Kuniges und Herren* and they appreciated their readiness *ad concessionem pecuniarum*, therefore one would very often see in the inns, the merchants drinking with the noblemen like brothers. They were even welcome, because having plenty of money, usually they paid for those who had coats of arms.

Therefore they were sitting there and talking, from time to time winking at the host to fill up the mugs.

"Noble knight, you have seen a good piece of the world!" said one of the merchants.

"Not many of those who are now coming to Krakow from all parts, have seen as much," answered the knight.

"There will be plenty of them," said the merchant. "There is to be a great feast and great pleasure for the king and the queen! The king has ordered the queen's chamber to be upholstered with golden brocade, embroidered with pearls, and a canopy of the same material over her. There will be such entertainments and tournaments, as the world has never seen before."

"Uncle Gamroth, don't interrupt the knight," said the second merchant.

"Friend Eyertreter, I am not interrupting; only I think that he also will be glad to know about what they are talking, because I am sure he is going to Krakow. We cannot return to the city to-day at any rate, because they will shut the gates."

"And you speak twenty words, in reply to one. You are growing old, Uncle Gamroth!"

"But I can carry a whole piece of wet broadcloth just the same."

"Great thing! the cloth through which one can see, as through a sieve."

But further dispute was stopped by the knight, who said:

2

"Yes, I will stay in Krakow because I have heard about the tournaments and I will be glad to try my strength in the lists during the combats; and this youth, my nephew, who although young and smooth faced, has already seen many cuirasses on the ground, will also enter the lists."

The guests glanced at the youth who laughed mirthfully, and putting his long hair behind his ears, placed the mug of beer to his mouth.

The older knight added:

"Even if we would like to return, we have no place to go."

"How is that?" asked one of the nobles.

"Where are you from, and what do they call you?"

"I am Macko of Bogdaniec, and this lad, the son of my brother, calls himself Zbyszko. Our coat of arms is Tempa Podkowa, and our war-cry is Grady!"

"Where is Bogdaniec?"

"Bah! better ask, lord brother, where it was, because it is no more. During the war between Grzymalczyks and Nalenczs,[2] Bogdaniec was burned, and we were robbed of everything; the servants ran away. Only the bare soil remained, because even the farmers who were in the neighborhood, fled into the forests. The father of this lad, rebuilt; but the next year, a flood took everything. Then my brother died, and after his death I remained with the orphan. Then I thought: 'I can't stay!' I heard about the war for which Jasko of Olesnica, whom the king, Wladyslaw, sent to Wilno after he sent Mikolaj of Moskorzowo, was collecting soldiers. I knew a worthy abbot, Janko of Tulcza, to whom I gave my land as security for the money I needed to buy armor and horses, necessary for a war expedition. The boy, twelve years old, I put on a young horse and we went to Jasko of Olesnica."

"With the youth?"

"He was not even a youth then, but he has been strong since childhood. When he was twelve, he used to rest a crossbow on the ground, press it against his chest and turn the crank. None of the Englishmen, whom I have seen in Wilno, could do better."

"Was he so strong?"

"He used to carry my helmet, and when he passed thirteen winters, he could carry my spear also."

"You had plenty of fighting there!"

"Because of Witold. The prince was with the Knights of the Cross, and every year they used to make an expedition against Lithuania, as far as Wilno. Different people went with them: Germans, Frenchmen, Englishmen, who are the best bowmen, Czechs, Swiss and Burgundians. They cut down the forests, burned the castles on their way and finally they devastated Lithuania with fire and sword so badly, that the people who were living in that country, wanted to leave it and search for another land, even to the end of the world, even among Belial's children, only far from the Germans."

"We heard here, that the Lithuanians wanted to go away with their wives and children, but we did not believe it."

"And I looked at it. Hej! If not for Mikolaj of Moskorzowo, for Jasko of Olesnica, and without any boasting, if not for us, there would be no Wilno now."

"We know. You did not surrender the castle."

"We did not. And now notice what I am going to say, because I have experience in military matters. The old people used to say: 'furious Litwa'[3]—and it's true! They fight well, but they cannot withstand the knights in the field. When the horses of the Germans are sunk in the marshes, or when there is a thick forest—that's different."

"The Germans are good soldiers!" exclaimed the burghers.

"They stay like a wall, man beside man, in their iron armor. They advance in one compact body. They strike, and the Litwa are scattered like sand, or throw themselves flat on the ground and are trampled down. There are not only Germans among them, because men of all nations serve with the Knights of the Cross. And they are brave! Often before a battle a knight stoops, stretches his lance, and rushes alone against the whole army."

"Christ!" exclaimed Gamroth. "And who among them are the best soldiers?"

3

"It depends. With the crossbow, the best is the Englishman, who can pierce a suit of armor through and through, and at a hundred steps he will not miss a dove. Czechowie (Bohemians) cut dreadfully with axes. For the big two-handed sword the German is the best. The Swiss is glad to strike the helmets with an iron flail, but the greatest knights are those who come from France. These will fight on horseback and on foot, and in the meanwhile they will speak very brave words, which however you will not understand, because it is such a strange language. They are pious people. They criticise us through the Germans. They say we are defending the heathen and the Turks against the cross, and they want to prove it by a knightly duel. And such God's judgment is going to be held between four knights from their side, and four from our side, and they are going to fight at the the court of Waclaw, the Roman and Bohemian king."[4]

Here the curiosity so increased among the noblemen and merchants, that they stretched their necks in the direction of Macko of Bogdaniec and they asked:

"And who are the knights from our side? Speak quickly!" Macko raised the mug to his mouth, drank and then answered:

"Ej, don't be afraid about them. There is Jan of Wloszczowa, castellan of Dobrzyn; there's Mikolaj of Waszmuntow; there are Jasko of Zdakow and Jarosz of Czechow: all glorious knights and sturdy fellows. No matter which weapons they choose,—swords or axes—nothing new to them! It will be worth while for human eyes to see it and for human ears to hear it—because, as I said, even if you press the throat of a Frenchman with your foot, he will still reply with knightly words. Therefore so help me God and Holy Cross they will outtalk us, but our knights will defeat them."

"That will be glory, if God will bless us," said one of the nobles.

"And Saint Stanislaw!" added another. Then turning toward Macko, he asked him further:

"Well! tell us some more! You praised the Germans and other knights because they are valiant and have conquered Litwa easily. Did they not have harder work with you? Did they go against you readily? How did it happen? Praise our knights."

But evidently Macko of Bogdaniec was not a braggart, because he answered modestly:

"Those who had just returned from foreign lands, attacked us readily; but after they tried once or twice, they attacked us with less assurance, because our people are hardened and they reproached us for that hardness: 'You despise,' they used to say,'death, but you help the Saracens, and you will be damned for it.' And with us the deadly grudge increased, because their taunt is not true! The king and the queen have christened Litwa and everyone there tries to worship the Lord Christ although not everyone knows how. And it is known also, that our gracious lord, when in the cathedral of Plock they threw down the devil, ordered them to put a candle before him—and the priests were obliged to tell him that he ought not to do it. No wonder then about an ordinary man! Therefore many of them say to themselves:

"'The *kniaz*[5] ordered us to be baptized, therefore I was baptized; he ordered us to bow before the Christ, and I bowed; but why should I grudge a little piece of cheese to the old heathen devils, or why should I not throw them some turnips; why should I not pour the foam off of the beer? If I do not do it, then my horses will die; or my cows will be sick, or their milk will turn into blood—or there will be some trouble with the harvest.' And many of them do this, and they are suspected. But they are doing it because of their ignorance and their fear of the devils. Those devils were better off in times of yore. They used to have their own groves and they used to take the horses which they rode for their tithe. But to-day, the groves are cut down and they have nothing to eat—in the cities the bells ring, therefore the devils are hiding in the thickest forest, and they howl there from loneliness. If a Litwin[6] goes to the forest, then they pull him by his sheep-skin overcoat and they say: 'Give!' Some of them give, but there are also courageous boys, who will not give and then the devils catch them. One of the boys put some beans in an ox bladder and immediately three hundred devils entered there. And he stuffed the bladder with a service-tree peg, brought them to Wilno and sold them to the Franciscan priests, who gave him twenty *skojcow*[7] he did this to destroy the enemies of Christ's name. I have seen that bladder with my own eyes; a dreadful stench came from it, because in that way those dirty spirits manifested their fear before holy water."

"And who counted them, that you know there were three hundred devils," asked the merchant Gamroth, intelligently.

"The Litwin counted them, when he saw them entering the bladder. It was evident that they were there, because one would know it from the stench, and nobody wished to take out the peg to count them."

"What wonders, what wonders!" exclaimed one of the nobles.

"I have seen many great wonders, because everything is peculiar among them. They are shaggy and hardly any *kniaz* combs his hair; they live on baked turnips, which they prefer to any other food, because they say that bravery comes from eating them. They live in the forests with their cattle and snakes; they are not abstinent in eating nor drinking. They despise the married women, but greatly respect the girls to whom they attribute great power. They say that if a girl rubs a man with dried leaves, it will stop colic."

"It's worth while to have colic, if the women are beautiful!" exclaimed Uncle Eyertreter.

"Ask Zbyszko about it," answered Macko of Bogdaniec.

Zbyszko laughed so heartily that the bench began to shake beneath him.

"There are some beautiful ones," he said. "Ryngalla was charming."

"Who is Ryngalla? Quick!"

"What? you haven't heard about Ryngalla?" asked Macko.

"We have not heard a word."

"She was Witold's sister, and the wife of Henryk, Prince Mazowiecki."

"You don't say! Which Prince Henryk? There was only one Prince Mazowiecki, elect[8] of Plock, but he died."

"The same one. He expected a dispensation from Rome, but death gave him his dispensation, because evidently he had not pleased God by his action. Jasko of Olesnica sent me with a letter to Prince Witold, when Prince Henryk, elect of Plock, was sent by the king to Ryterswerder. At that time, Witold was tired of the war, because he could not capture Wilno, and our king was tired of his own brothers and their dissipation. The king having noticed that Witold was shrewder and more intelligent than his own brothers, sent the bishop to him, to persuade him to leave the Knights of the Cross, and return to his allegiance, for which he promised to make him ruler over Litwa. Witold, always fond of changing, listened with pleasure to the embassy. There were also a feast and tournaments. The elect mounted a horse, although the other bishops did not approve of it, and in the lists he showed his knightly strength. All the princes of Mazowsze are very strong; it is well known, that even the girls of that blood can easily break horseshoes. In the beginning the prince threw three knights from their saddles; the second time he threw five of them. He threw me from my saddle, and in the beginning of the encounter, Zbyszko's horse reared and he was thrown. The prince took all the prizes from the hands of the beautiful Ryngalla, before whom he kneeled in full armor. They fell so much in love with each other, that dining the feasts, the *clerici*[9] pulled him from her by his sleeves and her brother, Witold, restrained her. The prince said: 'I will give myself a dispensation, and the pope, if not the one in Home, then the one in Avignon, will confirm it, but I must marry her immediately—otherwise I will burn up!' It was a great offence against God, but Witold did not dare to oppose him, because he did not want to displease the embassador—and so there was a wedding. Then they went to Suraz, and afterward to Sluck, to the great sorrow of this youth, Zbyszko, who, according to the German custom, had selected the Princess Ryngalla to be the lady of his heart and had promised her eternal fidelity."

"Bah!" suddenly interrupted Zbyszko, "it's true. But afterward the people said that Ryngalla regretted being the wife of the elect (because he, although married, did not want to renounce his spiritual dignity) and feeling that God's blessing could not be over such a marriage, poisoned her husband. When I heard that, I asked a pious hermit, living not far from Lublin, to absolve me from that vow."

"He was a hermit," answered Macko, laughing, "but was he pious? I don't know; we went to him on Friday, and he was splitting bear's bones with an axe, and sucking the marrow so hard, that there was music in his throat."

"But he said that the marrow was not meat, and besides he had received permission to do it, because after sucking marrow, he used to have marvelous visions during his sleep and the next day he could prophesy until noontime."

"Well, well!" answered Macko. "And the beautiful Ryngalla is a widow and she may call you to her service."

"It would be in vain, because I am going to choose another lady, whom I will serve till death, and then I will find a wife."

"You must first find the girdle of a knight."

"*Owa!*[10] There will be plenty of tournaments. And before that the king will not dub a single knight. I can measure myself against any. The prince could not have thrown me down, if my horse had not reared."

"There will be knights here better than you are."

Here the noblemen began to shout:

"For heaven's sake! Here, in the presence of the queen, will fight not such as you, but only the most famous knights in the world. Here will fight Zawisza of Garbow and Farurej, Dobko of Olesnica, Powala of Taczew, Paszko Zlodzie of Biskupice, Jasko Naszan and Abdank of Gora. Andrzej of Brochocice, Krystyn of Ostrow, and Jakob of Kobylany! Can you measure your sword against the swords of those, with whom neither the knights here, nor of the Bohemian court, nor of the Hungarian court can compete? What are you talking about? Are you better then they? How old are you?"

"Eighteen," answered Zbyszko.

"Everyone of them could crush you between his fingers."

"We will see."

But Macko said:

"I have heard that the king rewarded those knights munificently who returned from the Lithuanian war. Speak, you belong here; is it true?"

"Yes, it is true!" answered one of the nobles. "The king's munificence is known to the world; but it will be difficult to get near him now, because the guests are swarming to Krakow; they are coming to be in time for the queen's confinement and for the christening, wishing to show reverence to our lord and to render him homage. The king of Hungary is coming; they say the Roman emperor will be here also, and plenty of princes, counts and knights, will come because not one of them expects to return with empty hands. They even say that Pope Boniface, himself will arrive, because he also needs favor and help from our lord against his adversary in Avignon. Therefore in such a crowd, it will be difficult to approach the king; but if one would be able to see him and bow at his feet, then he will liberally reward him who deserves it."

"Then I will bow before him, because I have served enough, and if there is another war, I shall go again. We have taken some booty, and we are not poor; but I am getting old, and when one is old, and the strength has left his bones, one is pleased to have a quiet corner."

"The king was glad to see those who returned from Litwa with Jasko of Olesnica; and they feast well now."

"You see I did not return at that time; I was still at the war. You know that the Germans have suffered because of that reconciliation between the king and *Kniaz* Witold. The prince cunningly got the hostages back, and then rushed against the Germans! He ruined and burned the castle and slaughtered the knights and a great many of the people. The Germans wanted revenge, as did also Swidrygello, who went to them. There was again a great expedition started. The grand master Kondrat himself went with a great army; they besieged Wilno, and tried from their towers to ruin the castles; they also tried to capture the city by treachery—but they did not succeed! While retreating there were so many killed, that even half of them did not escape. Then we attacked Ulrich von Jungingen, the grand master's brother, who is bailiff in Swabja. But the bailiff was afraid of the *kniaz* and ran away. On account of this flight there is peace, and they are rebuilding the city. One pious

6

monk, who could walk with bare feet on hot iron, has prophesied since that time, that as long as the world exists, no German soldier will be seen under the walls of Wilno. And if that be so, then whose hands have done it?"

Having said this, Macko of Bogdaniec, extended his palms, broad and enormous; the others began to nod and to approve:

"Yes, yes! It's true what he says! Yes!"

But further conversation was interrupted by a noise entering through the windows from which the bladders had been taken out, because the night was warm and clear. From afar thrumming, singing, laughing and the snorting of horses were heard. They were surprised because it was quite late. The host rushed to the yard of the inn, but before the guests were able to drink their beer to the last drop, he returned shouting:

"Some court is coming!"

A moment afterward, in the door appeared a footman dressed in a blue jacket and wearing a red folding cap. He stopped, glanced at the guests, and then having perceived the host, he said:

"Wipe the tables and prepare lights; the princess, Anna Danuta, will stop here to-night."

Having said this, he withdrew. In the inn a great commotion began; the host called his servants, and the guests looked at one another with great surprise.

"Princess Anna Danuta," said one of the townsmen, "she is Kiejstutowna,[11] Janusz Mazowiecki's wife. She was in Krakow two weeks, but she went to Zator to visit Prince Waclaw, and now she is coming back."

"Uncle Gamroth," said the other townsman, "let us go to the barn and sleep on the hay; the company is too high for us."

"I don't wonder they are traveling during the night," said Macko, "because the days are very warm; but why do they come to the inn when the monastery is so near?"

Here he turned toward Zbyszko:

"The beautiful Ryngalla's own sister; do you understand?"

And Zbyszko answered:

"There must be many Mazovian ladies with her, hej!"

CHAPTER II.

At that moment the princess entered. She was a middle-aged lady with a smiling face, dressed in a red mantle and light green dress with a golden girdle around her hips. The princess was followed by the ladies of the court; some not yet grown up, some of them older; they had pink and lilac wreaths on their heads, and the majority of them had lutes in their hands. Some of them carried large bunches of fresh, flowers, evidently plucked by the roadside. The room was soon filled, because the ladies were followed by some courtiers and young pages. All were lively, with mirth on their faces, talking loudly or humming as if they were intoxicated with the beauty of the night. Among the courtiers, there were two *rybalts*,[12] one had a lute and the other had a *gensla*[13] at his girdle. One of the girls who was very young, perhaps twelve years old, carried behind the princess a very small lute ornamented with brass nails.

"May Jesus Christ be praised!" said the princess, standing in the centre of the room.

"For ages and ages, amen!" answered those present, in the meanwhile saluting very profoundly.

"Where is the host?"

The German having heard the call, advanced to the front and kneeled, in the German fashion, on one knee.

"We are going to stop here and rest," said the lady. "Only be quick, because we are hungry."

The townsmen had already gone; now the two noblemen, and with them Macko of Bogdaniec and young Zbyszko, bowed again, intending to leave the room, as they did not wish to interfere with the court.

But the princess detained them.

"You are noblemen; you do not intrude, you are acquainted with courtiers. From where has God conducted you?"

Then they mentioned their names,[14] their coats of arms, their nicknames and the estates from which they received their names. The lady having heard from *wlodyka*[15] Macko that he had been to Wilno, clapped her hands, and said:

"How well it has happened! Tell us about Wilno and about my brother and sister. Is Prince Witold coming for the queen's confinement and for the christening?"

"He would like to, but does not know whether he will be able to do so; therefore he sent a silver cradle to the queen for a present. My nephew and I brought that cradle."

"Then the cradle is here? I would like to see it! All silver?"

"All silver; but it is not here. The Basilians took it to Krakow."

"And what are you doing in Tyniec?"

"We returned here to see the procurator of the monastery who is our relative, in order to deposit with the worthy monks, that with which the war has blessed us and that which the prince gave us for a present."

"Then God gave you good luck and valuable booty? But tell me why my brother is uncertain whether he will come?"

"Because he is preparing an expedition against the Tartars."

"I know it; but I am grieved that the queen did not prophesy a happy result for that expedition, and everything she predicts is always fulfilled."

Macko smiled.

"Ej, our lady is a prophetess, I cannot deny; but with Prince Witold, the might of our knighthood will go, splendid men, against whom nobody is able to contend."

"Are you not going?"

"No, I was sent with the cradle, and for five years I have not taken off my armor," answered Macko, showing the furrows made by the cuirass on his reindeer jacket; "but let me rest, then I will go, or if I do not go myself then I will send this youth, my nephew, Zbyszko, to Pan[16] Spytko of Melsztyn, under whose command all our knights will go."

Princess Danuta glanced at Zbyszko's beautiful figure; but further conversation was interrupted by the arrival of a monk from the monastery, who having greeted the princess, began to humbly reproach her, because she had not sent a courier with the news that she was coming, and because she had not stopped at the monastery, but in an ordinary inn which was not worthy of her majesty. There are plenty of houses and buildings in the monastery where even an ordinary man will find hospitality, and royalty is still more welcome, especially the wife of that prince from whose ancestors and relatives, the abbey had experienced so many benefits.

But the princess answered mirthfully:

"We came here only to stretch our limbs; in the morning we must be in Krakow. We sleep during the day and we travel during the night, because it is cooler. As the roosters were crowing, I did not wish to awaken the pious monks, especially with such a company which thinks more about singing and dancing than about repose."

But when the monk still insisted, she added:

"No. We will stay here. We will spend the time well in singing lay songs, but we will come to the church for matins in order to begin the day with God."

"There will be a mass for the welfare of the gracious prince and the gracious princess," said the monk.

"The prince, my husband, will not come for four or five days."

"The Lord God will be able to grant happiness even from afar, and in the meanwhile let us poor monks at least bring some wine from the monastery."

"We will gladly repay," said the princess.

When the monk went out, she called:

"Hej, Danusia! Danusia! Mount the bench and make our hearts merry with the same song you sang in Zator."

Having heard this, the courtiers put a bench in the centre of the room. The *rybalts* sat on the ends, and between them stood that young girl who had carried behind the princess the lute ornamented with brass nails. On her head she had a small garland, her hair falling on her shoulders, and she wore a blue dress and red shoes with long points. On the bench she looked like a child, but at the same time, a beautiful child, like some figure from a church. It

8

was evident that she was not singing for the first time before the princess, because she was not embarrassed.

"Sing, Danusia, sing!" the young court girls shouted.

She seized the lute, raised her head like a bird which begins to sing, and having closed her eyes, she began with a silvery voice:

"If I only could get
The wings like a birdie,
I would fly quickly
To my dearest Jasiek!"

The *rybalts* accompanied her, one on the *gensliks*, the other on a big lute; the princess, who loved the lay songs better than anything else in the world, began to move her head back and forth, and the young girl sang further with a thin, sweet childish voice, like a bird singing in the forest:

"I would then be seated
On the high enclosure:
Look, my dear Jasiulku,
Look on me, poor orphan."

And then the *rybalts* played. The young Zbyszko of Bogdaniec, who being accustomed from childhood to war and its dreadful sights, had never in his life heard anything like it; he touched a Mazur[17] standing beside him and asked:

"Who is she?"

"She is a girl from the princess' court. We do not lack *rybalts* who cheer up the court, but she is the sweetest little *rybalt* of them all, and to the songs of no one else will the princess listen so gladly."

"I don't wonder. I thought she was an angel from heaven and I can't look at her enough. What do they call her?"

"Have you not heard? Danusia. Her father is Jurand of Spychow, a *comes*[18] mighty and gallant."

"Hej! Such a girl human eyes never saw before!"

"Everybody loves her for her singing and her beauty."

"And who is her knight?"

"She is only a child yet!"

Further conversation was stopped by Danusia's singing. Zbyszko looked at her fair hair, her uplifted head, her half-closed eyes, and at her whole figure lighted by the glare of the wax candles and by the glare of the moonbeams entering through the windows; and he wondered more and more. It seemed to him now, that he had seen her before; but he could not remember whether it was in a dream, or somewhere in Krakow on the pane of a church window.

And again he touched the courtier and asked in a low voice:

"Then she is from your court?"

"Her mother came from Litwa with the princess, Anna Danuta, who married her to Count Jurand of Spychow. She was pretty and belonged to a powerful family; the princess liked her better than any of the other young girls and she loved the princess. That is the reason she gave the same name to her daughter—Anna Danuta. But five years ago, when near Zlotorja, the Germans attacked the court,—she died from fear. Then the princess took the girl, and she has taken care of her since. Her father often comes to the court; he is glad that the princess is bringing his child up healthy and in happiness. But every time he looks at her, he cries, remembering his wife; then he returns to avenge on the Germans his awful wrong. He loved his wife more dearly than any one in the whole Mazowsze till now has loved; but he has killed in revenge a great many Germans."

In a moment Zbyszko's eyes were shining and the veins on his forehead swelled.

"Then the Germans killed her mother?" he asked.

"Killed and not killed. She died from fear. Five years ago there was peace; nobody was thinking about war and everybody felt safe. The prince went without any soldiers, only with the court, as usual during peace, to build a tower in Zlotorja. Those traitors, the Germans, fell upon them without any declaration of war, without any reason. They seized the prince himself, and remembering neither God's anger, nor that from the prince's ancestor, they had received great benefits, they bound him to a horse and slaughtered his people. The prince was a prisoner a long time, and only when King Wladyslaw threatened them with war, did they release him. During this attack Danusia's mother died."

"And you, sir, were you there? What do they call you? I have forgotten!"

"My name is Mikolaj of Dlugolas and they call me Obuch.[19] I was there. I saw a German with peacock feathers on his helmet, bind her to his saddle; and then she died from fear. They cut me with a halberd from which I have a scar."

Having said this he showed a deep scar on his head coming from beneath his hair to his eyebrows.

There was a moment of silence. Zbyszko was again looking at Danusia. Then he asked:

"And you said, sir, that she has no knight?"

But he did not receive any answer, because at that moment the singing stopped. One of the *rybalts*, a fat and heavy man, suddenly rose, and the bench tilted to one side. Danusia tottered and stretched out her little hands, but before she could fall or jump, Zbyszko rushed up like a wild-cat and seized her in his arms.

The princess, who at first screamed from fear, laughed immediately and began to shout:

"Here is Danusia's knight! Come, little knight and give us back our dear little girl!"

"He grasped her boldly," some among the courtiers were heard to say.

Zbyszko walked toward the princess, holding Danusia to his breast, who having encircled his neck with one arm, held the lute with the other, being afraid it would be broken. Her face was smiling and pleased, although a little bit frightened.

In the meanwhile the youth came near the princess, put Danusia before her, kneeled, raised his head and said with remarkable boldness for his age:

"Let it be then according to your word, my gracious lady! It is time for this gentle young girl to have her knight, and it is time for me to have my lady, whose beauty and virtues I shall extol. With your permission, I wish to make a vow and I will remain faithful to her under all circumstances until death."

The princess was surprised, not on account of Zbyszko's words, but because everything had happened so suddenly. It is true that the custom of making vows was not Polish; but Mazowsze, being situated on the German frontier, and often being visited by the knights from remote countries, was more familiar with that custom than the other provinces, and imitated it very often. The princess had also heard about it in her father's court, where all eastern customs were considered as the law and the example for the noble warriors. Therefore she did not see in Zbyszko's action anything which could offend either herself or Danusia. She was even glad that her dear girl had attracted the heart and the eyes of a knight.

Therefore she turned her joyful face toward the girl.

"Danusia! Danusia! Do you wish to have your own knight?"

The fair-haired Danusia after jumping three times in her red shoes, seized the princess by the neck and began to scream with joy, as though they were promising her some pleasure permitted to the older people only.

"I wish, I wish——!"

The princess' eyes were filled with tears from laughing and the whole court laughed with her; then the lady said to Zbyszko:

"Well, make your vow! Make your vow! What will you promise her?"

But Zbyszko, who preserved his seriousness undisturbed amidst the laughter, said with dignity, while still kneeling:

"I promise that as soon as I reach Krakow, I will hang my spear on the door of the inn, and on it I will put a card, which a student in writing will write for me. On the card I will proclaim that Panna Danuta Jurandowna is the prettiest and most virtuous girl among all living in this or any other kingdom. Anyone who wishes to contradict this declaration, I will fight until one of us dies or is taken into captivity."

"Very well! I see you know the knightly custom. And what more?"

"I have learned from Pan Mikolaj of Dlugolas that the death of Panna Jurandowna's mother was caused by the brutality of a German who wore the crest of a peacock. Therefore I vow to gird my naked sides with a hempen rope, and even though it eat me to the bone, I will wear it until I tear three such tufts of feathers from the heads of German warriors whom I kill."

Here the princess became serious.

"Don't make any joke of your vows!"

And Zbyszko added:

"So help me God and holy cross, this vow I will repeat in church before a priest."

"It is a praiseworthy thing to fight against the enemy of our people; but I pity you, because you are young, and you can easily perish."

At that moment Macko of Bogdanice approached, thinking it proper to reassure the princess.

"Gracious lady, do not be frightened about that. Everybody must risk being killed in a fight, and it is a laudable end for a *wlodyka*, old or young. But war is not new nor strange to this man, because although he is only a youth, he has fought on horseback and on foot, with spear and with axe, with short sword and with long sword, with lance and without. It is a new custom, for a knight to vow to a girl whom he sees for the first time; but I do not blame Zbyszko for his promise. He has fought the Germans before. Let him fight them again, and if during that fight a few heads are broken, his glory will increase."

"I see that we have to do with a gallant knight," said the princess.

Then to Danusia, she said:

"Take my place as the first person to-day; only do not laugh because it is not dignified."

Danusia sat in the place of the lady; she wanted to be dignified, but her blue eyes were laughing at the kneeling Zbyszko, and she could not help moving her feet from joy.

"Give him your gloves," said the princess.

Danusia pulled off her gloves and handed them to Zbyszko who pressed them with great respect to his lips, and said:

"I will fix them on my helmet and woe to the one who stretches his hands for them!"

Then he kissed Danusia's hands and feet and arose. Then his dignity left him, and great joy filled his heart because from that time the whole court would consider him a mature man. Therefore shaking Danusia's gloves, he began to shout, half mirthfully, half angrily:

"Come, you dog-brothers with peacock's crests, come!"

But at that moment the same monk who had been there before entered the inn, and with him two superior ones. The servants of the monastery carried willow baskets which contained bottles of wine and some tidbits. The monks greeted the princess and again reproached her because she had not gone directly to the abbey. She explained to them again, that having slept during the day, she was traveling at night for coolness; therefore she did not need any sleep; and as she did not wish to awaken the worthy abbot nor the respectable monks, she preferred to stop in an inn to stretch her limbs.

After many courteous words, it was finally agreed, that after matins and mass in the morning, the princess with her court would breakfast and rest in the monastery. The affable monks also invited the Mazurs, the two noblemen and Macko of Bogdaniec who intended to go to the abbey to deposit his wealth acquired in the war and increased by Witold's munificent gift. This treasure was destined to redeem Bogdaniec from his pledge. But the young Zbyszko did not hear the invitation, because he had rushed to his wagon which was guarded by his servants, to procure better apparel for himself. He ordered his chests carried to a room in the inn and there he began to dress. At first he hastily combed his hair and put it in a silk net ornamented with amber beads, and in the front with real pearls. Then he put on a "*jaka*" of white silk embroidered with golden griffins; he girded himself with a golden belt from which was hanging a small sword in an ivory scabbard ornamented with gold. Everything was new, shining and unspotted with blood, although it had been taken as booty from a Fryzjan knight who served with the Knights of the Cross. Then Zbyszko put on beautiful trousers, one part having red and green stripes, the other part, yellow and purple, and both ended at the top like a checkered chessboard. After that he put on red shoes with long points. Fresh and handsome he went into the room.

In fact, as he stood in the door, his appearance made a great impression. The princess seeing now what a handsome knight had vowed to Danusia, was still more pleased. Danusia jumped toward him like a gazelle. But either the beauty of the young man or the sounds of admiration from the courtiers, caused her to pause before she reached him, drop her eyes suddenly and blushing and confused, begin to wring her fingers.

After her, came the others; the princess herself, the courtiers, the ladies-in-waiting, the *rybalts* and the monks all wanted to see him. The young Mazovian girls were looking at him as at a rainbow, each regretting that he had not chosen her; the older ones admired the costly dress; and thus, a circle of curious ones was formed around him. Zbyszko stood in the centre with a boastful smile on his youthful face, and turned himself slightly, so that they could see him better.

"Who is he?" asked one of the monks.

"He is a knight, nephew of that *wlodyka*" answered the princess, pointing to Macko; "he has made a vow to Danusia."

The monks did not show any surprise, because such a vow did not bind him to anything. Often vows were made to married women, and among the powerful families where the eastern custom was known, almost every woman had a knight. If a knight made a vow to a young girl, he did not thus become her fiancé; on the contrary he usually married another; he was constant to his vow, but did not hope to be wedded to her, but to marry another.

The monks were more astonished at Danusia's youth, and even not much at that, because in those times sixteen year old youths used to be castellans. The great Queen Jadwiga herself, when she came from Hungary, was only fifteen years old, and thirteen year old girls used to marry. At any rate, at that moment they were more occupied looking at Zbyszko than at Danusia; they also listened to Macko's words, who, proud of his nephew, was telling how the youth came in possession of such beautiful clothes.

"One year and nine weeks ago," said he, "we were invited by the Saxon knights. There was another guest, a certain knight, from a far Fryzjan nation, who lived there on the shores of a sea. With him was his son who was three years older than Zbyszko. Once at a banquet, that son began to taunt Zbyszko because he has neither moustache nor beard. Zbyszko being quick tempered, was very angry, and immediately seized him by his moustache, and pulled out all the hair. On account of that I afterward fought until death or slavery."

"What do you mean?" asked the Pan of Dlugolas.

"Because the father took his son's part and I took Zbyszko's part; therefore we fought, in the presence of the guests, on level ground. The agreement was, that the one who conquered, should take the wagons, horses, servants and everything that belonged to the vanquished one. God helped us. We killed those Fryzes, although with great labor, because they were brave and strong. We took much valuable booty; there were four wagons, each one drawn by two horses, four enormous stallions, ten servants, and two excellent suits of armor which are difficult to find. It is true we broke the helmets in the fight, but the Lord Jesus rewarded us with something else; there was a large chest of costly clothing; those in which Zbyszko is now dressed, we found there also."

Now the two noblemen from the vicinity of Krakow, and all the Mazurs began to look with more respect on both the uncle and the nephew, and the Pan of Dlugolas, called Obuch, said:

"I see you are terrible fellows, and not lazy."

"We now believe that this youngster will capture three peacocks' crests."

Macko laughed, and in his face there really appeared an expression similar to that on the face of a beast of prey.

But in the meanwhile, the servants of the monastery had taken the wine and the dainties from the willow baskets, and the servant girls were bringing large dishes full of steaming boiled eggs, surrounded by sausage, from which a strong and savory smell filled the whole room. This sight excited everybody's appetite, and they rushed to the tables.

But nobody sat down until the princess was seated at the head of the table; she told Zbyszko and Danusia to sit opposite her and then she said to Zbyszko:

"It is right for you both to eat from one dish; but do not step on her feet under the table, nor touch her with your knees, as the other knights do to their ladies, because she is too young."

To this he answered:

"I shall not do it, gracious lady, for two or three years yet, until the Lord Jesus permits me to accomplish my vow, and then this little berry will be ripe; as for stepping on her feet, even if I would like to do it I can not, because they do not touch the floor."

"True," answered the princess; "but it is pleasant to see that you have good manners."

Then there was silence because everybody was busy eating. Zbyszko picked the best pieces of sausage, which he handed to Danusia or put directly into her mouth; she was glad that such a famous knight served her.

After they had emptied the dishes, the servants of the monastery began to pour out the sweet-smelling wine—abundantly for the men, but not much for the ladies. Zbyszko's gallantry was particularly shown when they brought in the nuts which had been sent from the monastery. There were hazel nuts and some very rare nuts imported from afar, called Italians; they all feasted so willingly, that after awhile there was heard no sound in the whole room but the cracking of shells, crushed between the jaws. But Zbyszko did not think only about himself; he preferred to show to the princess and Danusia his knightly strength and abstinence. Therefore he did not put the nuts between his jaws, as the others did, but he crushed them between his fingers, and handed to Danusia the kernels picked from the shells. He even invented for her an amusement; after having picked out the kernel, he placed his hand near his mouth and, with his powerful blowing, he blew the shells to the ceiling. Danusia laughed so much, that the princess fearing that the young girl would choke, was obliged to ask him to stop the amusement; but perceiving how merry the girl was, she asked her:

"Well, Danusia, is it good to have your own knight?"

"Oj! Very!" answered the girl.

And then she touched Zbyszko's white silk "*jaka*" with her pink finger, and asked:

"And will he be mine to-morrow?"

"To-morrow, and Sunday, and until death," answered Zbyszko.

Supper lasted a long time, because after the nuts, sweet cakes with raisins were served. Some of the courtiers wished to dance; others wished to listen to the *rybalts* or to Danusia's singing; but she was tired, and having with great confidence put her little head on the knight's shoulder, she fell asleep.

"Does she sleep?" asked the princess. "There you have your 'lady.'"

"She is dearer to me while she sleeps than the others are while they dance," answered Zbyszko, sitting motionless so as not to awaken the girl.

But she was awakened neither by the *rybalts'* music nor by the singing. Some of the courtiers stamped, others rattled the dishes in time to the music; but the greater the noise, the better she slept.

She awoke only when the roosters, beginning to crow, and the church bell to ring, the company all rushed from the benches, shouting:

"To matins! To matins!"

"Let us go on foot for God's glory," said the princess.

She took the awakened Danusia by the hand and went out first, followed by the whole court.

The night was beginning to whiten. In the east one could see a light glare, green at the top, then pink below, and under all a golden red, which extended while one looked at it. It seemed as though the moon was retreating before that glare. The light grew pinker and brighter. Moist with dew, the rested and joyous world was awakening.

"God has given us fair weather, but there will be great heat," said the courtiers.

"No matter," answered the Pan of Dlugolas; "we will sleep in the abbey, and will reach Krakow toward evening."

13

"Sure of a feast."

"There is a feast every day now, and after the confinement and tournaments, there will be still greater ones."

"We shall see how Danusia's brave knight will acquit himself."

"Ej! They are of oak, those fellows! Did you hear what they said about that fight for four knights on each side?"

"Perhaps they will join our court; they are consulting with each other now."

In fact, they were talking earnestly with each other; old Macko was not very much pleased with what had happened; therefore while walking in the rear of the retinue, he said to his nephew:

"In truth, you don't need it. In some way I will reach the king and it may be he will give us something. I would be very glad to get to some castle or *grodek*[20]—— Well we shall see. We will redeem Bogdaniec from our pledge anyhow, because we must hold that which our forefathers held. But how can we get some peasants to work? The land is worth nothing without peasants. Therefore listen to what I am going to tell you: if you make vows or not to anyone you please, still you must go with the Pan of Mielsztyn to Prince Witold against the Tartars. If they proclaim the expedition by the sound of trumpets before the queen's confinement, then do not wait either for the lying-in, or for the tournaments; only go, because there will be found some profit. Prince Witold is munificent, as you know; and he knows you. If you acquit yourself well, he will reward you liberally. Above all, if God help you, you will secure many slaves. The Tartars swarm in the world. In case of victory, every knight will capture three-score of them."

At this, Macko being covetous for land and serfs, began to fancy:

"If I could only catch fifty peasants and settle them in Bogdaniec! One would be able to clear up quite a piece of forest. You know that nowhere can you get as many as there."

But Zbyszko began to twist his head.

"Owa! I will bring hostlers from the stables living on horse carrion and not accustomed to working on the land! What use will they be in Bogdaniec? Then I vowed to capture three German crests. Where will I find them among the Tartars?"

"You made a vow because you were stupid; but your vow is not worth anything."

"But my honor of *wlodyka* and knight? What about that?"

"How was it with Ryngalla?"

"Ryngalla poisoned the prince, and the hermit gave me absolution."

"Then in Tyniec, the abbot will absolve you from this vow also. The abbot is greater than a hermit."

"I don't want absolution!"

Macko stopped and asked with evident anger:

"Then how will it be?"

"Go to Witold yourself, because I shall not go."

"You knave! And who will bow to the king? Don't you pity my bones?"

"Even if a tree should fall on your bones, it would not crush them; and even if I pity you, I will not go to Witold."

"What will you do then? Will you turn *rybalt* or falconer at the Mazowiecki court?"

"It's not a bad thing to be a falconer. But if you would rather grumble than to listen to me, then grumble."

"Where will you go? Don't you care for Bogdaniec? Will you plow with your nails without peasants?"

"Not true! You calculated cleverly about the Tartars! You have forgotten what the Rusini[21] told us, that it is difficult to catch any prisoners among the Tartars, because you cannot reach a Tartar on the steppes. On what will I chase them? On those heavy stallions that we captured from the Germans? Do you see? And what booty can I take? Scabby sheep-skin coats but nothing else! How rich then I shall return to Bogdaniec! Then they will call me *comes*!"

Macko was silent because there was a great deal of truth in Zbyszko's words; but after a while he said:

"But Prince Witold will reward you."

"Bah, you know; to one he gives too much, to another nothing."

"Then tell me, where will you go?"

"To Jurand of Spychow."

Macko angrily twisted the belt of his leather jacket, and said:

"May you become a blind man!"

"Listen," answered Zbyszko quietly. "I had a talk with Mikolaj of Dlugolas and he said that Jurand is seeking revenge on the Germans for the death of his wife. I will go and help him. In the first place, you said yourself that it was nothing strange for us to fight the Germans because we know them and their ways so well. *Secundo*, I will thus more easily capture those peacock's crests; and *tercio*, you know that peacock's crests are not worn by knaves; therefore if the Lord Jesus will help me to secure the crests, it will also bring booty. Finally: the slaves from those parts are not like the Tartars. If you settle such slaves in a forest, then you will accomplish something."

"Man, are you crazy? There is no war at present and God knows when there will be!"

"How clever you are! The bears make peace with the bee-keepers and they neither spoil the beehives, nor eat the honey! Ha! ha! ha! Then it is news to you, that although the great armies are not fighting and although the king and the grand master stamped the parchment with their seals, still there is always great disturbance on the frontiers? If some cattle are seized, they burn several villages for one cow's head and besiege the castles. How about capturing peasants and their girls? About merchants on the highways? Remember former times, about which you told me yourself. That Nalencz, who captured forty knights going to join the Knights of the Cross, and kept them in prison until the grand master sent him a cart full of *grzywien*,[22] did he not do a good business? Jurand of Spychow is doing the same and on the frontier the work is always ready."

For a while they walked along silently; in the meanwhile, it was broad daylight and the bright rays of the sun lighted up the rocks on which the abbey was built.

"God can give good luck in any place," Macko said, finally, with a calm voice; "pray that he may bless you."

"Sure; all depends on his favor!"

"And think about Bogdaniec, because you cannot persuade me that you go to Jurand of Spychow for the sake of Bogdaniec and not for that duck's beak."

"Don't speak that way, because it makes me angry. I will see her gladly and I do not deny it. Have you ever met a prettier girl?"

"What do I care for her beauty! Better marry her, when she is grown up; she is the daughter of a mighty *comes*."

Zbyszko's face brightened with a pleasant smile.

"It must be. No other lady, no other wife! When your bones are old, you shall play with the grandchildren born to her and myself."

Now Macko smiled also and said:

"Grady! Grady![23]—— May they be as numerous as hail. When one is old, they are his joy; and after death, his salvation. Jesus, grant us this!"

CHAPTER III.

Princess Danuta, Macko and Zbyszko had been in Tyniec before; but in the train of attendants there were some courtiers who now saw it for the first time; these greatly admired the magnificent abbey which was surrounded by high walls built over the rocks and precipices, and stood on a lofty mountain now shining in the golden rays of the rising sun. The stately walls and the buildings devoted to various purposes, the gardens situated at the foot of the mountain and the carefully cultivated fields, showed immediately the great wealth of the abbey. The people from poor Mazowsze were amazed. It is true there were other mighty Benedictine abbeys in other parts of the country; as for instance in Lubusz on Odra, in Plock, in Wielkopolska, in Mogila and in several other places: but none of them could compare with the abbey in Tyniec, which was richer than many principalities, and had an income greater than even the kings of those times possessed.

Therefore the astonishment increased among the courtiers and some of them could scarcely believe their own eyes. In the meanwhile, the princess wishing to make the journey

15

pleasant, and to interest the young ladies, begged one of the monks to relate the awful story about Walgierz Wdaly which had been told to her in Krakow, although not very correctly.

Hearing this, the ladies surrounded the princess and walked slowly, looking in the rays of the sun like moving flowers.

"Let Brother Hidulf tell about Walgierz, who appeared to him on a certain night," said one of the monks, looking at one of the other monks who was an old man.

"Pious father, have you seen him with your own eyes?" asked the princess.

"I have seen him," answered the monk gloomily; "there are certain moments during which, by God's will, he is permitted to leave the underground regions of hell and show himself to the world."

"When does it happen?"

The old monk looked at the other monks and became silent. There was a tradition that the ghost of Walgierz appeared when the morals of the monastic lives became corrupted, and when the monks thought more about worldly riches and pleasures than was right.

None of them, however, wished to tell this; but it was also said that the ghost's appearance portended war or some other calamity. Brother Hidulf, after a short silence, said:

"His appearance does not foretell any good fortune."

"I would not care to see him," said the princess, making the sign of the cross; "but why is he in hell, if it is true as I heard, that he only avenged a wrong?"

"Had he been virtuous during his whole life," said the monk sternly, "he would be damned just the same because he was a heathen, and original sin was not washed out by baptism."

After those words the princess' brows contracted painfully because she recollected that her father whom she loved dearly, had died in the heathen's errors also.

"We are listening," said she, after a short silence.

Brother Hidulf began thus:

During the time of heathenism, there was a mighty *grabia*[24] whose name was Walgierz, whom on account of his great beauty, they called Wdaly.[25] This whole country, as far as one can see, belonged to him, and he lead all the expeditions, the people on foot and a hundred spearmen who were all *wlodykas*; the men to the east as far as Opule, and to the west as far as Sandomierz, were his vassals. Nobody was able to count his herds, and in Tyniec he had a towerful of money the same as the Knights of the Cross have now in Marienburg."

"Yes, they have, I know it!" interrupted the princess.

"He was a giant," continued the monk. "He was so strong he could dig up an oak tree by the roots, and nobody in the whole world could compare with him for beauty, playing on the lute or singing. One time when he was at the court of a French king, the king's daughter, Helgunda, fell in love with him, and ran away with him to Tyniec, where they lived together in sin. No priest would marry them with Christian rites, because Helgunda's father had promised her to the cloister for the glory of God. At the same time, there lived in Wislica, Wislaw Piekny,[26] who belonged to King Popiel's family. He, while Walgierz Wdaly was absent, devastated the county around Tyniec. Walgierz when he returned overpowered Wislaw and imprisoned him in Tyniec. He did not take into consideration this fact: that every woman as soon as she saw Wislaw, was ready immediately to leave father, mother and even husband, if she could only satisfy her passion. This happened to Helgunda. She immediately devised such fetters for Walgierz, that that giant, although he could pluck an oak up by its roots, was unable to break them. She gave him to Wislaw, who took and imprisoned him in Wislica. There Rynga, Wislaw's sister, having heard Walgierz singing in his underground cell, soon fell in love with him and set him at liberty. He then killed Wislaw and Helgunda with the sword, left their bodies for the crows, and returned to Tyniec with Rynga."

"Was it not right, what he did?" asked the princess.

Brother Hidulf answered:

"Had he received baptism and given Tyniec to the Benedictines, perhaps God would have forgiven his sins; but he did not do this, therefore the earth has devoured him."

16

"Were the Benedictines in this kingdom at that time?"

"No, the Benedictines were not here; only the heathen lived here then."

"How then could he receive baptism, or give up Tyniec?"

"He could not; and that is exactly why he was sent to hell to endure eternal torture," answered the monk with authority.

"Sure! He speaks rightly!" several voices were heard to say.

In the meanwhile they approached the principal gate of the monastery, where the abbot with numerous monks and noblemen, was awaiting the princess. There were always many lay people in the cloister: land stewards, barristers and procurators. Many noblemen, even powerful *wlodykas*, held in fief from the monastery numerous estates; and these, as "vassals," were glad to pass their time at the court of their "suzerain," where near the main altar it was easy to obtain some gift and many benefits. Therefore the "*abbas centum villarum*"[27] could greet the princess with a numerous retinue.

He was a man of great stature, with a thin, intelligent face; his head was shaved on the top with a fringe of grey hair beneath. He had a deep scar on his forehead, which he had evidently received during his youth when he performed knightly deeds. His eyes looked penetratingly from beneath dark eyebrows. He wore a monk's dress similar to that worn by the other monks, but over it he wore a black mantle, lined with purple; around his neck was a gold chain from which was hanging a gold cross set with precious stones. His whole figure betrayed a proud man, accustomed to command and one who had confidence in himself.

But he greeted the princess affably and even humbly, because he remembered that her husband belonged to the family of the princes of Mazowsze, from which came the kings, Wladyslaw and Kazimierz; and that her mother was the reigning queen of one of the most powerful kingdoms in the world. Therefore he passed the threshold of the gate, bowed low, and then having made the sign of the cross over Anna Danuta and over her court, he said;

"Welcome, gracious lady, to the threshold of this poor monastery. May Saint Benedictus of Nursja, Saint Maurus, Saint Bonifacius, Saint Benedictus of Aniane and also Jean of Tolomeia—our patrons living in eternal glory,—give you health and happiness, and bless you seven times a day during the remainder of your life."

"They would be deaf, if they did not hear the words of such a great abbot," said the princess affably; "we came here to hear mass, during which we will place ourselves under their protection."

Having said this she stretched her hand toward him, which he falling upon one knee, kissed in knightly manner. Then they passed through the gate. The monks were waiting to celebrate mass, because immediately the bells were rung; the trumpeters blew near the church door in honor of the princess. Every church used to make a great impression on the princess who had not been born in a Christian country. The church in Tyniec impressed her greatly, because there were very few churches that could rival it in magnificence. Darkness filled the church except at the main altar where many lights were shining, brightening the carvings and gildings. A monk, dressed in a chasuble, came from the vestry, bowed to the princess and commenced mass. Then the smoke from the fragrant incense arose, veiled the priest and the altar, and mounted in quiet clouds to the vaulted ceiling, increasing the solemn beauty of the church. Anna Danuta bent her head and prayed fervently. But when an organ, rare in those times, began to shake the nave with majestic thunderings, filling it with angelic voices, then the princess raised her eyes, and her face expressed, beside devotion and fear, a boundless delight; and one looking at her would take her for some saint, who sees in a marvelous vision, the open heaven.

Thus prayed Kiejstut's daughter, who born in heathenism, in everyday life mentioned God's name just as everybody else did in those times, familiarly; but in the Lord's house she used to raise her eyes with fear and humility, toward his secret and unmeasurable power.

The whole court, although with less humility, prayed devoutly. Zbyszko knelt among the Mazurs, and committed himself to God's protection. From time to time he glanced at Danusia who was sitting beside the princess; he considered it an honor to be the knight of such a girl, and that his vow was not a trifle. He had already girded his sides with a hempen rope, but this was only half of his vow; now it was necessary to fulfill the other half which was more difficult. Consequently now, when he was more serious than when in the inn

17

drinking beer, he was anxious to discover how he could fulfill it. There was no war. But amidst the disturbances on the frontier, it was possible to meet some Germans, and either kill them or lay down his own life.

He had told this to Macko. But he thought: "Not every German wears peacock or ostrich feathers on his helmet. Only a few among the guests of the Knights of the Cross are counts, and the Knights of the Cross themselves are only *comthurs*, and not every one of them is a *comthur* either. If there be no war, then years may pass before I shall get those three crests; I have not been knighted yet and can challenge only those who are not knights like myself. It is true I expect to receive the girdle of a knight from the king's hands during the tournaments, which have been announced to take place during the christening, but what will happen then? I will go to Jurand of Spychow; he will help me kill as many *knechts*[28] as possible; but that will benefit me little. The *knechts* are not knights, with peacock feathers on their heads."

Therefore in his uncertainty, seeing that without God's special favor, he could do nothing, he began to pray:

"Jesus, grant a war between the Knights of the Cross and the Germans who are the foes of this kingdom and of all other nations confessing Your Holy Name. Bless us; but crush them who would rather serve the *starosta*[29] of hell, than serve you; they have hatred in their hearts against us, being angry because our king and queen, having baptized the Lithuanians, forbade them cut your Christian servants with the sword. For which anger punish them!"

"And I, Zbyszko a sinner, repent before you and from your five wounds beseech for help, that in your mercy you permit me to kill as soon as possible three Germans having peacock feathers on their morions. These crests I promised upon my knightly honor to Panna Anna Danuta, Jurand's daughter, and your servant."

"If I shall find any booty on those defeated Germans, I shall faithfully pay to holy church the tithe, in order that you also, sweet Jesus, may have some benefit and glory through me; and also that you may know, that I promise to you with a sincere heart. As this is true, so help me, amen!"

But as he prayed, his heart softened under the influence of his devotions and he made another promise, which was that after having redeemed Bogdaniec from its pledge, he would give to the church all the wax which the bees could make during the whole year. He hoped that his Uncle Macko would not make any opposition to this, and that the Lord Jesus would be especially pleased with the wax for the candles, and wishing to get it, would help him sooner. This thought seemed to him so right, that joy filled his soul; and he was almost sure that his prayer would be heard and that the war would soon come, so that he could accomplish his vow. He felt such might in his legs and in his arms, that at that moment he would have attacked a whole army. He even thought that having increased his promises to God, he would also add for Danusia, a couple of Germans! His youthful anger urged him to do it, but this time prudence prevailed, as he was afraid to exhaust God's patience by asking too much.

His confidence increased, however, when after mass and a long rest, he heard the conversation between the abbot and Anna Danuta.

The wives of the reigning kings and princes, both on account of devotion as well as on account of the magnificent presents, sent them by the Master of the Order, were very kindly disposed toward the Knights of the Cross. Even the pious Jadwiga, as long as she lived, restrained her husband's anger against them. Anna Danuta alone, having experienced dreadful wrongs from the knights hated them with her whole soul. Therefore when the abbot asked her about Mazowsze and its affairs, she began to complain bitterly against the Order:

"Our affairs are in a bad condition and it cannot be otherwise with such neighbors! Apparently it is the time of peace; they exchange ambassadors and letters, but notwithstanding all that nobody can be sure of anything. The one who lives on the borders of the kingdom, never knows when he goes to bed in the evening, whether he will awaken in fetters, or with the blade of a sword in his throat, or with a burning ceiling over his head. Neither oaths, nor seals, nor parchment will protect from treachery. Thus it happened at

Zlotorja where during the time of peace, they seized the prince and imprisoned him. The Knights of the Cross said that our castle was a menace to them; but the castles are repaired for defence not for an onset; and what prince has not the right to build and repair in his own land? Neither the weak nor the powerful can agree with the Order, because the knights despise the weak and try to ruin the mighty. Good deeds they repay with evil ones. Is there anywhere in the world another order which has received as many benefits from other kingdoms as the knights have received from Polish princes? And how have they repaid? With threats, with devastation of our lands, with war and with treachery. And it is useless to complain, even to our apostolic capital, because they do not listen to the Roman pope himself. Apparently they have sent an embassy now for the queen's confinement and the expected christening, but only because they wish to appease the anger of this mighty king for the evil deeds they performed in Litwa. But in their hearts they are always plotting means to annihilate this kingdom and the whole Polish nation."

The abbot listened attentively with approval and then said:

"I know that Comthur Lichtenstein came to Krakow at the head of the embassy; he is very much respected in the Order for his bravery and intelligence. Perhaps you will see him here soon, gracious lady, because he sent me a message yesterday, saying that as he wished to pray to our holy relics, he would pay a visit to Tyniec."

Having heard this, the princess began to complain again:

"The people say—and I am sure rightly—that there will soon be a great war, in which on one side will be the kingdom of Poland and all the nations speaking a language similar to the Polish tongue, and on the other side will be all the Germans and the Order. There is a prophecy about this war by some saint."

"Bridget," interrupted the scholarly abbot; "eight years ago she was canonized. The pious Peter from Alvastra and Matthew from Linköping have written her revelations, in which a great war has been predicted."

Zbyszko shuddered at these words, and not being able to restrain himself, asked: "How soon will it be?"

But the abbot being occupied with the princess, did not hear, or probably did not wish to hear, the question.

The princess spoke further:

"Our young knights are glad that this war is coming, but the older and prudent ones speak thus: 'We are not afraid of the Germans, although their pride and power are great, but we are afraid of their relics, because against those all human might is powerless.'"

Here Anna Danuta looked at the abbot with fear and added in a softer voice:

"They say they have a true piece of the holy cross; how then can one fight against them?"

"The French king sent it to them," answered the abbot.

There was a moment of silence, then Mikolaj of Dlugolas, called Obuch, a man of great experience, said:

"I was in captivity among the Knights of the Cross; I saw a procession in which they carried this great relic. But beside this, there are many other relics in the monastery in Oliva without which the order would not have acquired such power."

The Benedictines stretched their necks toward the speaker, and began to ask with great curiosity:

"Tell us, what are they?"

"There is a piece of the dress of the Most Holy Virgin," answered the *wlodyka* of Dlugolas; "there is a molar tooth of Marya from Magdala and branches from the bush in which God the Father revealed himself to Moses; there is a hand of Saint Liberjus, and as for the bones of other saints, I cannot count them on the fingers of both hands and the toes of both feet."

"How can one fight them?" repeated the princess, sighing.

The abbot frowned, and having thought for awhile, said:

"It is difficult to fight them, for this reason; they are monks and they wear the cross on their mantles; but if they have exceeded the measure of their sins, then even those relics will refuse to remain with them; in that case they will not strengthen the knights, but will take their strength away, so that the relics can pass into more pious hands. May God spare Christian blood; but, if a great war should come, there are some relics in our kingdom also which will succor us."

"May God help us!" exclaimed Zbyszko.

The abbot turned toward the princess and said:

"Therefore have confidence in God, gracious lady, because their days are numbered rather than yours. In the meanwhile, accept with grateful heart this box, in which there is a finger of Saint Ptolomeus, one of our patrons."

The princess extended her hand and kneeling, accepted the box, which she immediately pressed to her lips. The courtiers shared the joy of the lady. Zbyszko was happy because it seemed to him that war would come immediately after the Krakowian festivals.

CHAPTER IV.

It was in the afternoon that the princess left hospitable Tyniec and went toward Krakow. Often the knights of those times, coming into larger cities or castles to visit some eminent person, used to put on their entire battle armor. It is true it was customary to take it off immediately after they arrived at the gates; in fact it was the custom for the host himself to invite them to remove it in these words: "Take off your armor, noble lord; you have come to friends!" This entrance was considered to be more dignified and to increase the importance of the knight. To conform with this ostentatious custom Macko and Zbyszko took with them those excellent suits of armor and shoulder-bands—won from the conquered Fryzjan knights,—bright, shining and ornamented on the edges with a gold band. Mikolaj of Dlugolas, who had seen the world and many knights, and was very expert in judging war things, immediately recognized that the suits of armor had been made by a most famous armorer of Milan; armor which only the richest knights could afford; each of them being worth quite a fortune. He concluded that those Fryzes were mighty lords among their own people, and he looked with more respect on Macko and Zbyszko. Their helmets, although not common ones, were not so rich; but their gigantic stallions, beautifully caparisoned, excited envy and admiration among the courtiers. Macko and Zbyszko, sitting on very high saddles, could look down proudly at the whole court. Each held in his hand a long spear; each had a sword at at his side and an axe at the saddlebow. For the sake of comfort they had left their shields in the wagons, but even without them, both men looked as though they were going to battle and not to the city.

Both were riding near the carriage, in which was seated the princess, accompanied by Danusia, and in front of them a dignified court lady, Ofka, the widow of Krystyn of Jarzombkow and the old Mikolaj of Dlugolas. Danusia looked with great interest at the two iron knights, and the princess, pulling from time to time the box with the relics of Saint Ptolomeus from her bosom, raised it to her lips.

"I am very anxious to see what bones are inside," said she, "but I will not open it myself, for I do not want to offend the saint; the bishop in Krakow will open it."

To this the cautious Mikolaj of Dlugolas answered:

"Ej, it will be better not to let this go out of your hands; it is too precious a thing."

"May be you are right," said the princess, after a moment of reflection; then she added:

"For a long time nobody has given me such pleasure, as this worthy abbot has by this present; and he also calmed my fears about the relics of the Knights of the Cross."

"He spoke wisely and well," said Macko of Bogdaniec. "At Wilno they also had different relics, and they wanted to persuade the guests that they were at war with the heathen. And what? Our knights noticed that if they could only make a blow with an axe, immediately the helmet gave way and the head fell down. The saints help—it would be a sin to say differently—but they only help the righteous, who go to war justly in God's name. Therefore, gracious lady, I think that if there be another war, even if all Germans help the Knights of the Cross, we will overcome them, because our nation is greater and the Lord Jesus will give us more strength in our bones. As for the relics,—have we not a true particle of the holy cross in the monastery of Holy Cross?"

"It is true, as God is dear to me," said the princess. "But ours will remain in the monastery, while if necessary they carry theirs."

"No matter! There is no limit to God's power."

"Is that true? Tell me; how is it?" asked the princess, turning to the wise Mikolaj of Dlugolas; and he said:

"Every bishop will affirm it. Rome is distant too, and yet the pope rules over the whole world; cannot God do more!"

These words soothed the princess so completely that she began to converse about Tyniec and its magnificence. The Mazurs were astonished not only at the riches of the abbey, but also at the wealth and beauty of the whole country through which they were now riding. All around were many flourishing villages; near them were orchards full of trees, linden groves, storks' nests on the linden trees, and beneath the trees were beehives with straw roofs. Along the highway on both sides, there were fields of all kinds of grain. From time to time, the wind bent the still greenish sea of grain, amidst which shone like the stars in the sky, the blue heads of the flowers of the bachelor button, and the light red wild poppies. Far beyond the fields appeared the woods, black in the distance but bathed in sunlight; here and there appeared moist meadows, full of grass and birds flying round the bushes; then appeared hills with houses; again fields; and as far as one could see, the country appeared to flow not only with milk and honey but also with quiet and happiness.

"That is King Kazimierz' rural economy," said the princess; "it must be a pleasure to live here."

"Lord Jesus rejoices to see such a country," answered Mikolaj of Dlugolas; "and God's blessing is over it; but how can it be different; when they ring the bells here, there is no corner where they cannot be heard! And it is known that no evil spirit can endure the ringing of the bells, and they are obliged to escape to the forests on the Hungarian frontier."

"I wonder," said Pani Ofka, the widow of Krystyn of Jarzombkow, "how Walgierz Wdaly, about whom the monk was talking, can appear in Tyniec, where they ring the bells seven times a day."

This remark embarrassed Mikolaj for a moment, who after thinking, quietly said:

"In the first place, God's decrees are not well known; and then you must remember that every time he appears he has had special permission."

"At any rate, I am glad that we shall not pass the night in the monastery. I would die from fear if I saw such an infernal giant."

"Hej! I doubt it, because they say, he is very handsome."

"If he were very beautiful, I would not want a kiss from such a man, from whose mouth one could smell sulphur."

"I see that when the conversation is even about devils, you are still thinking about kisses."

At these words the princess, Pan Mikolaj and both *wlodykas* of Bogdaniec began to laugh. Danusia laughed also, following the example of the others. But Ofka of Jarzombkow turned her angry face toward Mikolaj of Dlugolas, and said:

"I should prefer him to you."

"Ej! Don't call the wolf out of the forest;" answered the merry Mazur; "the ghost often wanders on the high road, between Krakow and Tyniec, especially toward night; suppose he should hear you and appear to you in the form of a giant!"

"Let the enchantment go on the dog!" answered Ofka.

But at that moment Macko of Bogdaniec, who being seated on a high stallion, could see further than those who were in the carriage, reined in his horse, and said:

"O, as God is dear to me, what is it?"

"What?"

"Some giant of the forest is coming!"

"And the word became flesh!" exclaimed the princess. "Don't say that!"

But Zbyszko arose in his stirrups and said:

"It is true; the giant Walgierz; nobody else!"

At this the coachman reined in the horses, but not dropping the reins, began to make the sign of the cross, because he also perceived on an opposite hill the gigantic figure of a horsemen.

The princess had risen; but now she sat down, her face changed with fear. Danusia hid her face in the folds of the princess' dress. The courtiers, ladies and *rybalts*, who were on horseback behind the carriage, having heard the ill-omened name, began to surround the carriage. The men tried to laugh, but there was fear in their eyes; the young girls were pale; only Mikolaj of Dlugolas maintained his composure and wishing to tranquilize the princess, said:

"Don't be frightened, gracious lady. The sun has not yet set; and even if it were night, Saint Ptolomeus will manage Walgierz."

In the meanwhile, the unknown horseman, having mounted the top of the hill, stopped his horse and stood motionless. In the rays of the setting sun, one could see him very distinctly; his stature seemed greater than ordinary human dimensions. The space separating him from the princess' retinue was not more than three hundred steps.

"Why is he stopping?" asked one of the *rybalts*.

"Because we stopped," answered Macko.

"He is looking toward us as if he would like to choose somebody," said another *rybalt*; "if I were sure he was a man and not an evil spirit, I would go and give him a blow on the head with the lute."

The women began to pray aloud, but Zbyszko wishing to show his courage to the princess and Danusia, said:

"I will go just the same. I am not afraid of Walgierz!"

Danusia began to scream: "Zbyszko! Zbyszko!" But he went forward and rode swiftly, confident that even if he did meet the true Walgierz, he could pierce him through and through with his spear.

Macko who had sharp sight, said:

"He appears like a giant because he is on the hill. It is some big man, but an ordinary one, nothing else! Owa! I am going also, to see that he does not quarrel with Zbyszko."

Zbyszko, while riding was debating whether he should immediately attack with the spear, or whether first take a close view of the man standing on the hill. He decided to view him first, and immediately persuaded himself that it was the better thought, because as he approached, the stranger began to lose his extraordinary size. He was a large man and was mounted on a large horse, which was bigger than Zbyszko's stallion; yet he did not exceed human size. Besides that he was without armor, with a velvet cap shaped like a bell on his head; he wore a white linen dust cloak, from beneath which a green dress could be seen. While standing on the hill he was praying. Evidently he had stopped his horse to finish his evening devotions.

"It is not Walgierz," thought the boy.

He had approached so close that he could touch the unknown man with his spear. The man who evidently was a knight, smiled at him benevolently, and said:

"May Jesus Christ be praised!"

"For ages and ages."

"Is that the court of the Princess of Mazowsze below?"

"Yes, it is!"

"Then you come from Tyniec?"

But he did not receive any answer, because Zbyszko was so much surprised that he did not even hear the question. For a moment he stood like a statue, scarcely believing his own eyes, for, behold! about half a furlong behind the unknown man, he perceived several soldiers on horseback, at the head of whom was riding a knight clad in full armor, with a white cloth mantle with a red cross on it, and with a steel helmet having a magnificent peacock tuft in the crest.

"A Knight of the Cross!" whispered Zbyszko. Now he thought that God had heard his prayers; that he had sent him the German knight for whom he had asked in Tyniec. Surely he must take advantage of God's kindness; therefore without any hesitation,—before all these thoughts had hardly passed through his head, before his astonishment had diminished,—he bent low on the saddle, let down his spear and having uttered his family shout: "Grady! Grady!" he rushed with the whole speed of his horse against the Knight of the Cross.

22

That knight was astonished also; he stopped his horse, and without lowering his spear, looked in front of him, uncertain whether the attack was against him or not.

"Lower your spear!" shouted Zbyszko, pricking his horse with the iron points of the stirrups.

"Grady! Grady!"

The distance separating them began to diminish. The Knight of the Cross seeing that the attack was really against him, reined in his horse and poised his spear. At the moment that Zbyszko's lance was nearly touching his chest, a powerful hand broke it like a reed; then the same hand reined in Zbyszko's horse with such force, that the charger stopped as though rooted to the ground.

"You crazy man, what are you doing?" said a deep, threatening voice; "you are attacking an envoy, you are insulting the king!"

Zbyszko glanced around and recognized the same gigantic man, whom he had taken for Walgierz, and who had frightened the princess and her court.

"Let me go against the German! Who are you?" he cried, seizing his axe.

"Away with the axe! for God's sake! Away with the axe, I say! I will throw you from your horse!" shouted the stranger more threateningly. "You have offended the majesty of the king and you will be punished."

Then he turned toward the soldiers who were riding behind the Knight of the Cross. "Come here!"

"At this time Macko appeared and his face looked threatening. He understood that Zbyszko had acted like a madman and that the consequences of this affair might be very serious; but he was ready to defend him just the same. The whole retinue of the stranger and of the Knight of the Cross contained only fifteen men, armed with spears and crossbows; therefore two knights in full armors could fight them with some hope of being victorious. Macko also thought that as they were threatened with punishment, it would be better perhaps to avoid it, by overcoming these men, and then hiding somewhere until the storm had passed over. Therefore his face immediately contracted, like the jaws of a wolf ready to bite, and having pushed his horse between Zbyszko and the stranger's horse, he began to ask, meanwhile handling his sword:

"Who are you? What right have you to interfere?"

"My right is this," said the stranger, "that the king has intrusted to me the safety of the environs of Krakow, and they call me Powala of Taczew."

At these words, Macko and Zbyszko glanced at the knight, then returned to their scabbards the half drawn swords and dropped their heads, not because they were frightened but in respect for this famous and very well-known name. Powala of Taczew, a nobleman of a powerful family and a mighty lord, possessor of large estates round Radom, was at the same time one of the most famous knights in the kingdom. *Rybalts* sang about him in their songs, citing him as an example of honor and gallantry, praising his name as much as the names of Zawisza of Garbow and Farurej, Skarbek of Gora, Dobek of Olesnica, Janko Nanszan, Mikolaj of Moskorzowo, and Zandram of Maszkowic. At this moment he was the representative of the king, therefore to attack him was to put one's head under the executioner's axe.

Macko becoming cooler, said with deep respect:

"Honor and respect to you, sir, to your fame and to your gallantry."

"Honor to you also, sir," answered Powala; "but I would prefer to make your acquaintance under less serious circumstances."

"Why?" asked Macko.

Powala turned toward Zbyszko.

"What have you done, you youngster? You attacked an envoy on the public highway in the king's presence! Do you know the consequences of such an act?"

"He attacked the envoy because he was young and stupid; therefore action was easier for him than reflection," said Macko. "But you will not judge him so severely, after I tell you the whole story."

"It is not I who will judge him. My business is only to put him in fetters."

"How is that?" said Macko, looking gloomy again.

23

"According to the king's command."

Silence followed these words.

"He is a nobleman," said Macko finally.

"Let him swear then upon his knightly honor, that he will appear at the court."

"I swear!" exclaimed Zbyszko.

"Very well. What do they call you?"

Macko mentioned the name and the coat of arms of his nephew.

"If you belong to Princess Janusz' court, beg her to intercede for you with the king."

"We are not with her court. We are returning from Litwa, from Prince Witold. Better for us if we had never met any court! This misfortune has come from that."

Here Macko began to tell about what had happened in the inn; he spoke about the meeting with the princess and about Zbyszko's vow. Then suddenly he was filled with anger against Zbyszko, whose imprudence had caused their present dreadful plight; therefore, turning toward him, he exclaimed:

"I would have preferred to see you dead at Wilno! What have you done, you young of a wild boar!"

"Well," said Zbyszko, "after the vow, I prayed to the Lord Jesus to give me some Germans; I promised him a present; therefore when I perceived the peacock feathers, and also a mantle embroidered with a cross, immediately some voice cried within me: 'Strike the German! It is a miracle!' Well I rushed forward then; who would not have done it?"

"Listen," interrupted Powala, "I do not wish you any evil. I see clearly that this youngster sinned rather from youthful giddiness than from malice. I will be only too glad to ignore his deed and go forward as if nothing had happened. But I cannot do this unless that *comthur* will promise that he will not complain to the king. Beseech him; perhaps he also will pity the lad."

"I prefer to go before the courts, than to bow to a *Krzyzak*!"[30] exclaimed Zbyszko. "It would not be befitting my dignity as a *wlodyka*."

Powala of Taczew looked at him severely and said:

"You do not act wisely. Old people know better than you, what is right and what is befitting a knight's dignity. People have heard about me; but I tell you, that if I had acted as you have, I would not be ashamed to ask forgiveness for such an offence."

Zbyszko felt ashamed; but having glanced around, answered:

"The ground is level here. Instead of asking him for forgiveness, I would prefer to fight him on horseback or on foot, till death or slavery."

"You are stupid!" interrupted Macko. "You wish then to fight the envoy?"

Here he turned to Powala:

"You must excuse him, noble lord. He became wild during the war. It will be better if he does not speak to the German, because he may insult him. I will do it. I will entreat him to forgive. If this *comthur* be willing to settle it by combat, after his mission is over, I will meet him."

"He is a knight of a great family; he will not encounter everybody," answered Powala.

"What? Do I not wear a girdle and spurs? Even a prince may meet me."

"That is true; but do not tell him that, unless he mentions it himself; I am afraid he will become angry if you do. Well, may God help you!"

"I am going to humiliate myself for your sake," said Macko to Zbyszko; "wait awhile!"

He approached the Knight of the Cross who had remained motionless on his enormous stallion, looking like an iron statue, and had listened with the greatest indifference to the preceding conversation. Macko having learned German during the long wars, began to explain to the *comthur* in his own language what had happened; he excused the boy on account of his youth and violent temper, and said that it had seemed to the boy as though God himself had sent the knight wearing a peacock tuft, and finally he begged forgiveness for the offence.

The *comthur's* face did not move. Calm and haughty he looked at Macko with his steely eyes with great indifference, but also with great contempt. The *wlodyka* of Bogdaniec noticed this. His words continued to be courteous but his soul began to rebel. He talked with increasing constraint and his swarthy face flushed. It was evident that in the presence of this haughty pride, Macko was endeavoring to restrain his anger.

Powala having noticed this, and having a kind heart, determined to help Macko. He had learned to speak German while seeking knightly adventures at the Hungarian, Burgundian and Bohemian courts, when he was young. Therefore he now said in that language in a conciliatory but jesting tone:

"You see, sir, the noble *comthur* thinks that the whole affair is unimportant. Not only in our kingdom but in every country the youths are slightly crazy; but such a noble knight does not fight children, neither by sword nor by law."

Lichtenstein touched his yellow moustache and moved on without a word, passing Macko and Zbyszko.

A dreadful wrath began to raise the hair under their helmets, and their hands grasped their swords.

"Wait, you scoundrel!" said the elder *wlodyka* through his set teeth; "now I will make a vow to you. I will seek you as soon as you have finished your mission."

But Powala, whose heart began to bleed also, said:

"Wait! Now the princess must speak in favor of the boy; otherwise, woe to him!"

Having said this, he followed the Knight of the Cross, stopped him and for a while they talked with great animation. Macko and Zbyszko noticed that the German knight did not look at Powala so proudly as he had at them; this made them still more angry. After a while, Powala returned and said to them:

"I tried to intercede for you, but he is a hard man. He said that he would not complain to the king if you would do what he requires."

"What?"

"He said thus: 'I will stop to greet the Princess of Mazowsze; let them come, dismount, take off their helmets, and standing on the ground with uncovered heads, ask my forgiveness.'"

Here Powala looked sharply at Zbyszko, and added:

"I know it will be hard for people of noble birth to do this; but I must warn you, that if you refuse no one knows what you may expect,—perhaps the executioner's sword."

The faces of Macko and Zbyszko became like stone. There was silence.

"What then?" asked Powala.

Zbyszko answered quietly and with great dignity as though during this conversation he had grown twenty years older:

"Well, God's might is over all!"

"What do you mean?"

"I mean, that even if I had two heads and the executioner was going to cut off both, still I have only one honor which I will not stain."

Powala became grave and turning toward Macko, asked:

"And what do you say?"

"I say," answered Macko gloomily, "that I reared this youth from childhood. On him depends our family, because I am old; but he cannot do what the German asks, even if he must perish."

Here his grim face began to quiver and finally his love for his nephew burst forth with such strength, that he seized the boy in his arms, and began to shout:

"Zbyszku! Zbyszku!"[31]

The young knight was surprised and having returned his uncle's embrace, said:

"Aj! I did not know that you loved me so much."

"I see that you are both true knights," said Powala; "and as the young man has promised me upon his knightly honor, that he will appear at the court, I will not imprison him; one can trust such people as you. No more gloomy thoughts! The German intends to stay in Tyniec a day or two; therefore I will have an opportunity to see the king first, and I will try to tell him about this affair in such a way that his anger will not be aroused. I am glad I succeeded in breaking the spear in time,—great luck, I tell you!"

But Zbyszko said:

"Even if I had to lay down my life, I would like at least to have the satisfaction of breaking his bones."

"It surprises me that you who know how to defend your own honor, do not understand that you would thus disgrace our whole nation!" impatiently answered Powala.

"I understand it very well," said Zbyszko; "but I regret my disability just the same."

Powala turned toward Macko:

"Do you know, sir, that if this lad succeeds in escaping the penalty for his offence, then you ought to put a cowl like a hawk's on his head! Otherwise he will not die a natural death."

"He will escape if you, sir, will not say anything to the king about the occurrence."

"And what shall we do with the German? We cannot tie his tongue."

"That is true! That is true!"

Talking thus, they went back toward the princess' retinue. Powala's servants followed them. From afar one could see amidst the Mazovian caps, the quivering peacock feathers of the Knight of the Cross and his bright helmet shining in the sun.

"Strange is the nature of a *Krzyzak*," said the knight of Taczew. "When a *Krzyzak* is in a tight place, he will be as forbearing as a Franciscan monk, as humble as a lamb and as sweet as honey; in fact, it would be difficult to find a better man. But let him feel power behind him; then nobody will be more arrogant and merciless. It is evident that God gave them stones for hearts. I have seen many different nations and I have often witnessed a true knight spare another who was weaker, saying to himself; 'My fame will not increase if I trample this fallen foe.' But at such a time a *Krzyzak* is implacable. Hold him by the throat, otherwise woe to you! Such a man is that envoy! He wanted not only an apology, but also your humiliation. But I am glad he failed."

"He can wait!" exclaimed Zbyszko.

"Be careful not to show him that you are troubled, because then he would rejoice."

After these words they approached the retinue and joined the princess' court. The envoy of the *Krzyzaks*, having noticed them, immediately assumed an expression of pride and disdain; but they ignored him. Zbyszko stood at Danusia's side and began to tell her that from the hill one could see Krakow; at the same time Macko was telling one of the *rybalts* about the extraordinary strength of the Pan of Taczew, who had broken the spear in Zbyszko's hand, as though it were a dry stem.

"And why did he break it?" asked the *rybalt*.

"Because the boy in fun attacked the German."

The *rybalt*, being a nobleman, did not consider such an attack a joke; but seeing that Macko spoke about it lightly, did not take it seriously either. The German was annoyed by such conduct. He glanced at Macko and Zbyszko. Finally be realized that they did not intend to dismount and that they did not propose to pay any attention to him. Then something like steel shone in his eyes, and he immediately began to bid the princess adieu.

The Lord of Taczew could not abstain from deriding him and at the moment of departure he said to him:

"Go without fear, brave knight. The country is quiet and nobody will attack you, except some careless child."

"Although the customs of this country are strange, I was seeking your company and not your protection," answered Lichtenstein; "I expect to meet you again at the court and elsewhere."

In the last words a hidden menace rang; therefore Powala answered gravely:

"If God will permit."

Having said this, he saluted and turned away; then he shrugged his shoulders and said in an undertone, but loud enough to be heard by those who were near:

"Gaunt! I could lift you from the saddle with the point of my spear, and hold you in the air during three *pater-nosters*."[32]

Then he began to talk with the princess with whom he was very well acquainted. Anna Danuta asked him what he was doing on the highway. He told her that the king had commanded him to keep order in the environs while there were so many wealthy guests going to Krakow. Then he told her about Zbyszko's foolish conduct. But having concluded that there would be plenty of time to ask the princess to protect Zbyszko, he did not put any stress on the incident, not wishing to spoil the gaiety. The princess laughed at the boy, because he was so anxious to obtain the peacock tuft; the others, having learned about the breaking of the spear, admired the Lord of Taczew very much, especially as he did it with one hand only.

And he, being a little vain, was pleased because they praised him. Finally he began to tell about some of the exploits which made his name famous; especially those he performed in Burgundia, at the court of Philip the Courageous. There one time, during a tournament, he seized an Ardenian knight, pulled him out of the saddle and threw him in the air, notwithstanding that the knight was in full armor. For that exploit, Philip the Courageous presented him with a gold chain and the queen gave him a velvet slipper, which he wore on his helmet.

Upon hearing this, all were very much amazed, except Mikolaj of Dlugolas, who said:

"In these effeminate times, there are not such strong men as there were when I was young. If a nobleman now happens to shatter a cuirass, to bend a crossbow without the aid of the crank, or to bend a cutlass between his fingers, he immediately considers himself a very strong man. But in times of yore, girls could do such deeds."

"I don't deny that formerly there were stronger people," answered Powala; "but even now there are some strong men. God did not stint me in strength, but I do not consider myself the strongest in this kingdom. Have you ever seen Zawisza of Garbow? He can surpass me."

"I have seen him. He has shoulders broad like a rampart."

"And Dobko of Olesnica? Once at the tournament given in Torun by the Knights of the Cross, he defeated twelve knights for his own and our nation's glory."

"But our Mazur, Staszko Ciolek, was stronger, sir, than you or your Zawisza and Dobko. They say that he took a peg made from green wood in his hand and pressed the sap out of it."[33]

"I can press the sap out myself," said Zbyszko. And before anyone could ask him to prove it, he broke a branch which he pressed so strongly, that really the sap began to ooze from it.

"Aj, Jesus!" exclaimed Ofka of Jarzombkow; "don't go to the war; it would be a pity if such an one should perish before his marriage."

"It would indeed be a pity!" replied Macko, suddenly becoming sorrowful.

But Mikolaj of Dlugolas laughed as did also the princess. The others, however, praised Zbyszko's strength, and as in those times might was appreciated more than any other quality, the young girls cried to Danusia: "Be glad!" She was glad although she could not then understand what benefit she would receive from that piece of compressed wood. Zbyszko having forgotten all about the *Krzyzak* now looked so proud, that Mikolaj of Dlugolas wishing to curb his pride, said:

"There are better men than you; therefore do not be so proud of your strength. I did not see it, but my father was a witness of something more difficult which happened at the court of Charles, the Roman emperor. King Kazimierz went to pay him a visit and with him went many courtiers. Among these courtiers was Staszko Ciolek, son of *Wojewoda*[34] Andrzej, who was noted for his strength. The emperor began to boast that he had a Czech who could strangle a bear. They had an exhibition and the Czech strangled two bears in succession. Our king not wishing to be outdone, said: 'But he cannot overcome my Ciolek.' They agreed that they should fight in three days' time. Many ladies and famous knights came, and the Czech and Ciolek grappled in the yard of the castle; but the contest did not last long; hardly had they come together before Ciolek broke the backbone of the Czech, crushed all his ribs, and left him dead to the great glory of the king.[35] They have called him since then Lomignat.[36] Once he placed without help, a bell which twelve men could not move from its place."[37]

"How old was he?" asked Zbyszko.

"He was young!"

In the meantime, Powala of Taczew, while riding at the princess' right hand, bent toward her and told her the truth about the importance of Zbyszko's adventure, and asked her to speak to the king in Zbyszko's behalf. The princess being fond of Zbyszko, received this news with sadness and became very uneasy.

"The Bishop of Krakow is a friend of mine," said Powala; "I will ask him and also the queen to intercede; but the more protectors he has, the better it will be for the lad."

"If the queen will promise to say one word in his favor, not a hair will fall from his head," said Anna Danuta; "the king worships her for her piety and for her dowry, and especially now, when the shame of sterility has been taken from her. But the king's beloved sister, Princess Ziemowit lives in Krakow; you must go to her. For my part I will do anything I can; but the princess is his own sister, and I am only his first cousin."

"The king loves you also, gracious lady."

"Ej, but not as much," she answered with a certain sadness; "for me a link, for her a whole chain; for me a fox skin, for her a sable. He loves none of his relations as dearly as he loves Alexandra."

Thus talking, they approached Krakow. The highway which was crowded on the road from Tyniec, was still more crowded here. They met countrymen going with their servants to the city, sometimes armed and sometimes in summer clothing and straw hats. Some of them were on horseback; some traveled in carriages, with their wives and daughters, who wished to see the long looked for tournaments. In some places the whole road was crowded with merchants' wagons which could not pass Krakow until the toll was paid. They carried in these wagons wax, grain, salt, fish, skins, hemp and wood. Others came from the city loaded with cloth, barrels of beer and different merchandise. One could now see Krakow very well; the king's gardens, lords' and burghers' houses surrounded the city; beyond them were the walls and the towers of the churches. The nearer they came to the city the greater was the traffic and at the gates it was almost impossible to pass.

"What a city! There is no other like it in the world," said Macko.

"It is always like a fair," answered one of the *rybalts*, "how long since you were here, sir?"

"A very long time ago. I wonder at it just as much as if I saw it now for the first time, because we are returning from a wild country."

"They say that Krakow has grown very much since the time of King Jagiello."

This was true; after the grand duke of Litwa ascended the throne, enormous Lithuanian and Russian countries were opened for commerce; because of this the city had increased in population, richness and buildings, and had become one of the most important cities in the world.

"The cities of the Knights of the Cross are very beautiful also," said the larger *rybalt*.

"If only we could capture one of them," said Macko. "Worthy booty we could get!"

But Powala of Taczew was thinking about something else; namely, of Zbyszko, who was in peril because of his stupid blind fury. The Pan of Taczew, fierce and implacable in the time of war, had in his powerful breast, however, the heart of a dove; he realized better than the others what punishment awaited the offender; therefore he pitied him.

"I ponder and ponder," said he again to the princess, "whether to tell the king of the incident or not. If the *Krzyzak* does not complain, there will be no case; but if he should complain, perhaps it would be better to tell the king everything beforehand, so that he will not become angry."

"If the *Krzyzak* has an opportunity to ruin somebody, he will do it," answered the princess; "but I will tell that young man to join our court. Perhaps the king will be more lenient to one of our courtiers."

She called Zbyszko, who having had his position explained to him, jumped from his horse, kissed her hands and became with the greatest pleasure one of her courtiers, not so much for greater safety, as because he could now remain nearer Danusia.

Powala asked Macko:

"Where will you stay?"

"In an inn."

"There is no room in any inn now."

"Then we will go to merchant Amylej, he is an acquaintance of mine, perhaps he will let us pass the night in his house."

"Accept hospitality in my house. Your nephew can stay with the princess' courtiers in the castle; but it will be better for him not to be near the king. What one does in the first paroxysm of anger, one would not do afterward. You will be more comfortable and safe with me."

Macko had become uneasy because Powala thought so much about their safety; he thanked Powala with gratitude and they entered the city. But here they both as well as Zbyszko forgot for a while about danger in the presence of the wonders they saw before them. In Lithuania and on the frontier, they had only seen single castles, and the only city of any importance which they knew was Wilno, a badly built and ruined town; but here many of the merchants' houses were more magnificent than the grand duke's palace in Lithuania. It is true that there were many wooden houses; but even these astonished them by the loftiness of their walls and roofs; also by the windows, made of glass balls, set in lead which so reflected the rays of the setting sun, that one would imagine that there was fire in the houses. In the streets near the market place, there were many highly ornamented houses of red brick, or of stone. They stood side by side like soldiers; some of them, broad; others, narrow; but all lofty with vaulted halls, very often having the sign of the Passion of our Lord Jesus Christ or an image of the Most Holy Virgin over the door. There were some streets, on which one could see two rows of houses, over them a stripe of blue sky, between them, a road paved with stones; and on both sides as far as one could see stores and stores. These were full of the best foreign goods, at which being accustomed to war and the capture of booty, Macko looked with a longing eye. But both were still more astonished at the sight of the public buildings; the church of Panna Maryia on the square; the *sukiennice*;[38] the city hall with its gigantic cellar, in which they were selling beer from Swidnica; other churches, depots of broadcloth, the enormous "*mercatorium*," devoted to the use of foreign merchants; then a building in which were the public scales, bath houses, cooper works, wax works, silver works, gold works, breweries, the mountains of barrels round the so-called Schrotamto,—in a word, riches which a man not familiar with the city, even though a well-to-do possessor of a *grodek*, could not even imagine.

Powala conducted Macko and Zbyszko to his house situated on Saint Anna Street, assigned a large room to them, recommended them to his shield-bearers, and then went to the castle, from which he returned for supper quite late at night.

A few friends accompanied him, and they enjoyed the plentiful repast of wine and meat. The host alone was sorrowful. When finally the guests departed, he said to Macko:

"I spoke to a canon, able in writing and in the law, who says, that an insult to an envoy is a capital offence. Therefore pray God, that the *Krzyzak* may not complain."

Hearing this, both knights, who, during the feast had exceeded the other guests in mirth, retired with sorrowful hearts. Macko could not even sleep and after a while when they were in bed, he said to his nephew:

"Zbyszku?"

"What?"

"I have considered everything and I do not think they will execute you."

"You do not think so?" asked Zbyszko, in a sleepy voice.

Having turned toward the wall, he fell sound asleep, because he was very weary.

The next day, both *wlodykas* of Bogdaniec, went with Powala to morning mass in the cathedral, for devotion and also to see the court and the guests who had arrived at the castle. In fact, on the way Powala met many acquaintances, and among them several knights famous at home and abroad. At these Zbyszko looked with admiration, promising himself that if he escaped death for the insult to Lichtenstein, he would try to rival them in gallantry and in all knightly virtues. One of these knights, Toporczyk, a relative of the castellan of Krakow, told them that Wojciech Jastrzembiec had returned from Rome, where he had been sent to Pope Bonifacius IX. with the king's invitation to the christening at Krakow. Bonifacius accepted the invitation; and although it was doubtful whether he would be able to come personally, he authorized the envoy to stand godfather for the coming child in his name; and he asked that the name Bonifacius or Bonifacia be given to the child as a proof of his particular love for the king and the queen.

They also spoke of the arrival of the Hungarian king, Sigismundus; they expected him positively, because he always came, invited or not, whenever there was an opportunity for feasts and tournaments. Of these he was very fond, because he desired to be famous the world over as a ruler, a singer and the first among knights. Powala, Zawisza of Garbow, Dobko of Olesnica, Naszan and others of the same rank, recollected with a smile that during Sigismundus' first visit, King Wladyslaw requested them privately not to attack him very fiercely, but to spare "the Hungarian guest," whose vanity, known throughout the world, used to make him cry in case of defeat. But the most interest was excited among the knights by Witold's affairs. They told marvelous tales about the magnificence of that cradle, made of sterling silver, which the Lithuanian princes and *bojars*[39] had brought as a present from Witold and his wife, Anna. Macko told about the proposed enormous expedition against the Tartars. The expedition was almost ready, and a great army had already gone eastward toward Rus'. If it were successful, it would extend the king's supremacy over almost half the world, to the unknown Asiatic countries, to the frontier of Persia and to the shores of the Aral. Macko, who formerly served under Witold and knew his plans, could tell about them so accurately and even so eloquently, that before the bells were rung for mass, a large circle of curious people had formed around him. He said that the question was simply about a crusade. "Witold himself," he said, "although they call him a grand duke, rules over Litwa by Jagiello's authority; he is only viceroy, therefore the renown will be the king's. What fame it will be for the newly baptized Lithuanians and for the might of Poland, when the united armies carry the cross to those countries where, if they mention the Saviour's name at all, it is only to blaspheme! When the Polish and Lithuanian armies restore Tochtamysh to the throne of Kapchak, he will acknowledge himself "the son" of King Wladyslaw, and he has promised to bow to the cross with the whole Zlota Orda."

The people listened to Macko with great attention; but many did not thoroughly understand what people Witold intended to help nor against whom he intended to fight; therefore some one asked:

"Tell exactly with whom is the war to be?"

"With whom? With Tymur the Lame!" replied Macko.

There was a moment of silence. It is true the eastern knights often heard the names of Golden, of Blue, of Azovian and of other Ords; but they were not familiar with the civil wars of the Tartars. Nevertheless there was not one man in Europe, who had not heard about the terrible Tymur the Lame, or Tamerlan. This name was heard with no less fear than of old was the name of Attila. He was "lord of the world" and "lord of ages;" the ruler over twenty-seven conquered states: the ruler of Moskiewskoy Russia; ruler of Siberia and of China as far as the Indies; of Bagdad, of Ispahan, of Alep, of Damascus—whose shadow was falling over the sands of Arabia, on Egypt, and on Bosphorus in the Greek empire; he was the exterminator of mankind; the terrible builder of pyramids composed of human skulls; he was the conqueror in all battles, never conquered in any, "lord of souls and of bodies."

Tochtamysh had been placed by him on the throne of the Golden and the Blue Ords,[40] and acknowledged as "the son." But when his sovereign authority extended from Aral to Crimea, over more lands than were in the rest of Europe, "the son" wanted to be an independent ruler. For this he was deposed from his throne with "one finger" of the terrible father; he escaped to the Lithuanian governor and asked him for help. Witold decided to restore him to his throne; but to do this it was necessary to vie with the world-ruling Tymur the Lame.

For these reasons his name made a great impression on the audience, and after a short silence, one of the oldest knights, Kazko of Jaglow, said:

"A difficult business!"

"And for a trifle," said the prudent Mikolaj of Dlugolas. "What difference will it make to us, whether Tochtamysh or some Kutluk rules over the sons of Belial who dwell beyond the tenth-land?"

"Tochtamysh will turn to the Christian faith," answered Macko.

"He will or he will not! Can you trust dog-brothers, who do not confess Christ?"

"But we are ready to lay down our lives for Christ's name," answered Powala.

"And for knightly honor," added Toporczyk, the relative of the castellan; "there are some among us however who will not go. The Lord *Wojewoda, Spytko of Melsztyn* has a young and beloved wife, but he has already joined *Kniaz* Witold."

"No wonder," added Jasko Naszan; "no matter how hideous a sin you have on your soul, pardon and salvation are sure for those who fight in such a war."

"And fame for ages and ages," said Powala of Taczew. "Let us then have a war, and it will be better if it be a great war. Tymur has conquered the world and has twenty-seven states under him. It will be an honor for our nation if we defeat him."

"Why not?" answered Toporczyk, "even if he possesses a hundred kingdoms, let others be afraid of him—not us! You speak wisely! Let us gather together ten thousand good spearmen, and we will pass round the world."

"And what nation should conquer The Lame, if not ours?"

Thus the knights conversed. Zbyszko was sorry now because he did not go with Witold to the wild steppes. But when he was in Wilno, he wanted to see Krakow and its court and take part in the tournaments; but now he fears that he will find disgrace here at the court, while there on the steppes even at the worst, he would have found a glorious death.

But the aged Kazko of Jaglow, who was a hundred years old, and whose common sense corresponded to his age, discouraged the zealous knights.

"You are stupid!" said he. "Is it possible that none of you have heard that Christ's image spoke to the queen? If the Saviour himself condescend to such familiarity, then why will the Holy Ghost, who is the third person of the Trinity, be less kind to her. Therefore she sees future events, as if they were passing before her, and she has thus spoken:"

Here he stopped for a while, shook his head, and then said:

"I have forgotten what she prophesied, but I will soon recollect."

He began to think, and they waited silently, because the popular belief was that the queen could see the future.

"Aha!" said he, finally, "I remember now! The queen said, that if every knight went with Witold against The Lame-Man, then heathenish power would be destroyed. But all cannot go because of the dishonesty of Christian lords. We are obliged to guard the boundaries from the attacks of the Czechs and the Hungarians and also from the attacks of the Order, because we cannot trust any of them. Therefore if Witold go with only a handful of Polish warriors, then Tymur the Lame, or his *wojewodas*, coming with innumerable hosts, will defeat him."

"But we are at peace now," said Toporczyk, "and the Order will give some assistance to Witold. The Knights of the Cross cannot act otherwise, if only for the sake of appearances, and to show to the holy father that they are ready to fight the pagans. The courtiers say that Kuno von Lichtenstein came not entirely for the christening, but also to consult with the king."

"Here he is!" exclaimed the astonished Macko.

"True!" said Powala, turning his head. "So help me God, it is he! He did not stay long with the abbot."

"He is in a hurry," answered Macko, gloomily.

Kuno von Lichtenstein passed them. Macko and Zbyszko recognized him by the cross embroidered on his mantle; but he did not recognize either of them because he had seen them before with their helmets on. Passing by, he nodded to Powala of Taczew, and to Toporczyk; then with his shield-bearers, he ascended the stairs of the cathedral, in a majestic and stately manner.

At that moment the bells resounded, frightening flocks of doves and jackdaws, and announcing that mass would soon begin. Macko and Zbyszko entered the church with the others, feeling troubled about Lichtenstein's quick return. The older *wlodyka* was very uneasy, but the young one's attention was attracted by the king's court. He was surrounded by noted men, famous in war and in counsel. Many of those by whose wisdom the marriage of the grand duke of Lithuania with the young and beautiful queen of Poland, had been planned and accomplished, were now dead; but a few of them were still living, and at these, all looked with the greatest respect. The young knight could not admire enough the magnificent figure of Jasko of Tenczyn, castellan of Krakow, in which sternness was united with dignity and honesty; he admired the wise countenances of the counsellors and the powerful faces of the knights whose hair was cut evenly on their foreheads, and fell in long curls on their sides and backs. Some of them wore nets, others wore bands to keep the hair in order. The foreign guests, Hungarian and Austrian, and their attendants, were amazed at the great elegance of the costumes; the Lithuanian princes and *bojars*, notwithstanding the summer heat, were dressed for the sake of pompous display in costly furs; the Russian princes wore large stiff dresses, and in the background they looked like Byzantine pictures. With the greatest curiosity Zbyszko awaited the appearance of the king and the queen. He advanced toward the stalls behind which he could see the red velvet cushions near the altar, on which the king and the queen kneeled during mass.

He did not wait long; the king entered first, through the vestry door, and before he reached the altar one could have a good look at him. He had long, dark, disheveled hair; his face was thin and clean shaven; he had a large pointed nose and some wrinkles around his mouth. His eyes were small, dark, and shining. His face had a kind but cautious look, like that of a man who having risen by good luck to a position far beyond his expectations, is obliged to think continually whether his actions correspond to his dignity and who is afraid of malicious criticism. This also was the reason why in his face and in his movements there was a certain impatience. It was very easy to understand that his anger would be sudden and dreadful. He was that prince, who being angered at the frauds of the Knights of the Cross, shouted after their envoy: "Thou comest to me with a parchment, but I will come to thee with a spear!"

But now this natural vehemence was restrained by great and sincere piety. He set a good example, not only to the recently converted Lithuanian princes, but even to the Polish lords, pious for generations. Often the king kneeled, for the greater mortification of the flesh, on bare stones; often having raised his hands, he held them uplifted until they dropped with fatigue. He attended at least three masses every day. After mass he left the church as if just awakened from slumber, soothed and gentle. The courtiers knew that it was the best time to ask him either for pardon, or for a gift.

Jadwiga entered through the vestry door also. Seeing her enter, the knights standing near the stalls, immediately kneeled, although mass had not begun, voluntarily paying her homage as to a saint. Zbyszko did the same; nobody in this assembly doubted that he really saw a saint, whose image would some time adorn the church altars. Besides the respect due to a queen, they almost worshipped her on account of her religious and holy life. It was reported that the queen could perform miracles. They said that she could cure the sick by touching them with her hand; that people who could not move their legs nor their arms, were able to do it, after they put on a dress which the queen had worn. Trustworthy witnesses affirmed that they had heard with their own ears, Christ speak to her from the altar. Foreign monarchs worshipped her on their knees and even the Order of the Knights of the Cross respected her and feared to offend her. Pope Bonifacius IX. called her the pious and chosen daughter of the church. The world looked at her deeds and remembered that this child of the Andegavian[41] house and Polish Piasts[42], this daughter of the powerful Louis, a pupil of the most fastidious of courts, and also one of the most beautiful women on earth, renounced happiness, renounced her first love and being a queen married a "wild" prince of Lithuania, in order to bring to the cross, by his help, the last pagan nation in Europe. That which could not be accomplished by the forces of all the Germans, by a sea of poured out blood, was done with one word from her. Never did the glory of an apostle shine over a younger and more charming forehead; never was the apostleship united with equal self-denial; never was the beauty of a woman lighted with such angelic kindness and such quiet sadness.

Therefore minstrels sang about her in all the European courts; knights from the remotest countries came to Krakow to see this "Queen of Poland;" her own people loved her, as the pupil of the eye and their power and glory had increased by her marriage with

Jagiello. Only one great sorrow hung over her and the nation; for long years this child of God had had no issue.

But now this sorrow had passed away and the joyful news of God's blessing on the queen sped like lightning from the Baltic to the Black Sea, also to Karpaty[43] and filled with joy all peoples of this powerful kingdom. In all foreign courts, except in the capital of the Knights of the Cross, the news was received with pleasure. In Rome "Te Deum" was sung. In the provinces of Poland the belief was firmly established, that anything the "Saint lady" asked of God, would be granted.

Therefore there came to her people to beseech her, that she ask health for them; there came envoys from the provinces and from other countries, to ask that she pray according to their need, either for rain, or for fair weather for harvesting; for lucky moving time; for abundant fishing in the lakes or for game in the forests.

Those knights, living in castles and *grodeks* on the frontier, who according to the custom learned from the Germans, had become robbers or waged war among themselves, at the command of the queen, put their swords in their scabbards, released their prisoners without ransom, restored stolen herds and clasped hands in friendship. All kinds of misery, all kinds of poverty crowded the gates of her castle in Krakow. Her pure spirit penetrated human hearts, softened the hard lot of the serfs, the great pride of the lords, the unjust severity of the judges, and hovered like a dove of happiness, like an angel of justice and peace, over the whole country.

No wonder then that all were awaiting with anxious hearts for the day of blessing. The knights looked closely at the figure of the queen, to see if they could ascertain how long they would be obliged to wait for the future heir to the throne. The *ksiondz*[44] bishop of Krakow, Wysz, who was also the ablest physician in the country, and famous even abroad, had not announced when the delivery would occur. They were making some preparation; but it was the custom at that time to begin all festivals as early as possible, and to prolong them for weeks. In fact the figure of the lady, although a little rounded, had retained until now its former grandeur. She was dressed with excessive simplicity. Formerly, having been brought up at a brilliant court, and being more beautiful than any of the contemporary princesses, she was fond of costly fabrics, of chains, pearls, gold bracelets and rings; but now and even for several years past, she not only wore the dress of a nun, but she even covered her face, fearing that the thoughts of her beauty might arouse in her worldly vanity. In vain Jagiello, having learned of her condition, in a rapture of joy ordered her sleeping apartment to be decorated with brocade and jewels. Having renounced all luxury, and remembering that the time of confinement is often the time of death, she decided that not among jewels, but in quiet humility she ought to receive the blessing which God had promised to send her.

Meanwhile the gold and jewels went to establish a college and to send the newly converted Lithuanian youths to foreign universities.

The queen agreed only to change her monastical dress, and from the time that the hope of maternity was changed to positive certainty, she did not veil her face, thinking that the dress of a penitent was no longer proper.

Consequently everybody was now looking with love at that beautiful face, to which neither gold, nor precious stones could add any charm. The queen walked slowly from the vestry door toward the altar, with uplifted eyes, holding in one hand a book, in the other a rosary. Zbyszko saw the lily-like face, the blue eyes, and the angelic features full of peace, kindness and mercy, and his heart began to throb with emotion. He knew that according to God's command he ought to love the king and the queen, and he did in his way; but now his heart overflowed with a great love, which did not come by command, but burst forth like a flame; his heart was also filled with the greatest worship, humility and desire for sacrifice. The young *wlodyka* Zbyszko was impetuous; therefore a desire immediately seized him, to show in some way that love and the faithfulness of a knight; to accomplish some deed for her; to rush somewhere, to conquer some one and to risk his own life for it all. "I had better go with *Kniaz* Witold," he said to himself, "because how can I serve the holy lady, if there is no war here." He did not stop to think that one can serve in other ways as well as with sword or spear or axe; he was ready to attack alone the whole power of Tymur the Lame. He wanted to jump on his charger immediately after mass and begin something. What? He did not know himself. He only knew, that he could not hold anything, that his hands were burning and his whole soul was on fire.

He forgot all about the danger which threatened him. He even forgot about Danusia, and when he remembered her, having heard the children singing in the church, he felt that this love was something different. He had promised Danusia fidelity; he had promised her three Germans and he would keep his promise. But the queen is above all women. While he was thinking how many people he would like to kill for the queen, he perceived regiments of armors, helmets, ostrich feathers, peacocks' crests, and he felt that even that would be small in proportion to his desire.

He looked at her constantly, pondering with overflowing heart, how he could honor her by prayer, because he thought that one could not make an ordinary prayer for a queen. He could say: *Pater noster, qui es in coelis, sanctificetur nomen Tuum*, because a certain Franciscan monk taught him this in Wilno; but it may be that the Franciscan himself did not know more; it may be that Zbyszko had forgotten; but it is certain that he could not recite the whole "Our Father." But now he began to repeat these few words which in his soul had the following meaning: "Give our beloved lady good health, long life and great happiness; care for her more than for anyone else."

As this was repeated by a man over whose head punishment was suspended, therefore there was no more sincere prayer in the whole church.

CHAPTER V.

After mass Zbyszko thought that if he could only fall upon his knees before the queen and kiss her feet, then he did not care what happened afterward. But after the first mass, the queen went to her apartments. Usually she did not take any nourishment until noontime, and was not present at the merry breakfast, during which jugglers and fools appeared for the amusement of the king. The old *wlodyka* of Dlugolas came and summoned Zbyszko to the princess.

"You will serve Danusia and me at the table as my courtier," said the princess. "It may happen that you will please the king by some facetious word or deed, and the Krzyzak if he recognize you, will not complain to the king, seeing that you serve me at the king's table."

Zbyszko kissed the princess' hand. Then he turned to Danusia; and although he was more accustomed to battles than to the manners of the court, still he evidently knew what was befitting a knight, when he sees the lady of his thoughts in the morning; he retreated, and assuming an expression of surprise, and making the sign of the cross, exclaimed:

"In the name of the Father and of the Son and of the Holy Ghost!"

Danusia, looking at him with her blue eyes, asked:

"Why do you make the sign of the cross, Zbyszko, after mass is ended?"

"Because your beauty increased so much, during last night, that I am astonished!"

Mikolaj of Dlugolas, who did not like the new, foreign customs of chivalry, shrugged his shoulders and said:

"Don't lose time talking to her about her beauty! She is only a bush hardly grown up from the soil."

At this Zbyszko looked at him with rancor.

"You must be careful about calling her a 'bush,'" said he, turning pale with anger; "if you were younger, I would challenge you immediately and would fight until either you or I were dead!"

"Keep quiet, you beardless boy! I can manage you even to-day!"

"Be quiet!" said the princess. "Instead of thinking about your own danger, you are seeking a quarrel! I would prefer to find a more steady knight for Danusia. If you wish to foam, go where you please; but we do not need you here."

Zbyszko felt abashed at the princess' words and began to apologize. But he thought to himself that if Pan Mikolaj of Dlugolas had a grown-up son, then sometime he would challenge the son and would not forgive Mikolaj for calling her "bush." Now he determined to be quiet while in the king's castle and not to provoke anybody, only in case of absolute necessity.

The blowing of horns announced that breakfast was ready; therefore the Princess Anna taking Danusia by the hand, went to the king's apartments, where the lay-dignitaries and the knights, stood awaiting her arrival. Princess Ziemowita entered first, because being the king's sister, she occupied a higher seat at the table. Soon the hall was filled with guests, dignitaries and knights. The king was seated at the upper end of the table, having near him Wojciech Jastrzembiec, bishop of Krakow, the bishop, although inferior in rank to the other priests wearing mitres, was seated at the right hand of the king because he was the pope's envoy. The two princesses took the next places. Near Anna Danuta, the former archbishop of Gniezno, Jan, was comfortably seated in a large chair. He was a descendant of the Piasts of Szlonsk and the son of Bolko, Prince of Opole. Zbyszko had heard of him at the court of Witold; and now while standing behind the princess and Danusia, he recognized the archbishop by his abundant hair which being curled, made his head look like a *kropidlo*.[45] At the courts of the Polish princes, they called him "Kropidlo," for this reason; and the Knights of the Cross gave him the name of "Grapidla." He was noted for his gaiety and giddy manners. Having received the nomination for the archbishopric of Gniezno, against the king's wish, he took possession of it by military force; for this act he was deprived of his rank. He then joined the Knights of the Cross who gave him the poor bishopric of Kamieniec in Pomorze. Then he concluded that it was better to be friendly with the mighty king; he craved his pardon, returned to the country and was now waiting for a vacancy to occur, hoping that the good hearted lord would let him fill it. He was not mistaken as the future proved. In the meantime he was trying to win the king's heart by merry frolics. But he still liked the Knights of the Cross. Even now, at the court of Jagiello where he was not greatly welcomed by the dignitaries and knights, he sought Lichtenstein's company and gladly sat beside him at the table.

Zbyszko, standing behind the princess' chair, was so near to the Krzyzak, Lichtenstein, that he could have touched him with his hand. In fact, his fingers began to twitch, but he overcame his impetuosity and did not permit himself any evil thoughts. But he could not refrain from looking eagerly at Lichtenstein's head and shoulders, trying to decide whether he would have a hard fight with him, if they met either during the war, or in single combat. He concluded that it would not be difficult to conquer the German. The Krzyzak's shoulder bones appeared quite large under his dress of grey broadcloth; but he was only a weakling compared with Powala or with Paszko Zlodziej of Biskupice, or with both of the most famous Sulimczyks, or with Krzon of Kozieglowy or with many of the other knights, sitting at the king's table.

At these knights Zbyszko looked with admiration and envy; but his attention was also attracted by the actions of the king, who at this moment gathered his hair with his fingers and pushed it behind his ears, as if he was impatient because breakfast was not served. His eyes rested for a moment on Zbyszko, and at that the young knight felt afraid, fearing that perhaps he would be obliged to face the angry king. This was the first time he had thought seriously about the consequences of his rash action. Until now it had seemed to him to be something remote, therefore not worthy of sorrow.

The German did not know that that youth who dad attacked him so boldly on the highway, was so near. The breakfast began. They brought in caudle, seasoned so strongly with eggs, cinnamon, cloves, ginger and saffron, that the fragrance filled the whole room. In the meanwhile the fool Ciaruszek, sitting on a chair in the doorway, began to imitate the singing of a nightingale, of which the king was very fond. Then another jester went around the table, stopped behind the guests and imitated the buzzing of a bee so well, that some of them began to defend their heads. Seeing this, the others burst with laughter. Zbyszko had served the princess and Danusia diligently; but when Lichtenstein began to clap his baldhead, he again forgot about his danger and began to laugh. The young Lithuanian *kniaz*, Jamut, who was standing beside him, also laughed at this very heartily. The Krzyzak having finally noticed his mistake, put his hand in his pocket, and turning to the bishop, Kropidlo, said a few words to him in German; the bishop immediately repeated them in Polish.

"The noble lord says to you," said he, turning toward the fool, "that you will receive two *skojce*; but do not buzz too near, because the bee is driven away, but the drones are killed."

The fool took the two *skojce* given to him by the Krzyzak, and taking advantage of the license granted at all courts to the fools, answered:

"There is plenty of honey in the province of Dobrzyn;[46] that is why it is beset with the drones. Drive them, King Wladyslaw!"

"Here is a penny from me, because you have said a clever thing," said Kropidlo, "but remember that if the rope break, the beehive keeper break his neck.[47] Those drones from Malborg, by whom Dobrzyn is beset, have stings, and it is dangerous to climb to the beehives."

"Owa!" exclaimed Zyndram of Maszkow, the sword bearer of Krakow, "one can smoke them out!"

"With what?"

"With powder."

"Or cut the beehive with an axe," added the gigantic Paszko Zlodziej of Biskupice.

Zbyszko's heart was ready to leap with joy, because he thought that such words betokened war. Kuno von Lichtenstein understood what was said, because during his long sojourn in Torun and Chelmno, he learned the Polish language; but he would not use it on account of pride. But now, being irritated by the words of Zyndram of Maszkow, he looked at him sharply with his grey eyes and said:

"We shall see."

"Our fathers saw at Plowce[48] and at Wilno," answered Zyndram.

"*Pax vobiscum!*" exclaimed Kropidlo. "*Pax, pax!* If only the *ksiondz*[49] Mikolaj of Kurow, will give up his Kujawian bishopric, and the gracious king appoint me in his place, I will preach you such a beautiful sermon about the love between Christian nations, that you will sincerely repent. Hatred is nothing but *ignis* and *ignis infernalis* at that; such a dreadful fire that one cannot extinguish it with water, but is obliged to pour wine on it. Give us some wine! We will go on *ops*,[50] as the late Bishop Zawisza of Kurozwenki used to say!"

"And from *ops* to hell, the devil says," added the fool Ciaruszek.

"Let him take you!"

"It would be more amusing for him to take you. They have not yet seen the devil with Kropidlo, but I think we shall all have that pleasure."

"I will sprinkle you first. Give us some wine and may love blossom among the Christians!"

"Among true Christians!" added Kuno von Lichtenstein, emphatically.

"What?" exclaimed the Krakowian bishop Wysz, raising his head; "are you not in an old Christian kingdom? Are not our churches older than yours in Malborg?"[51]

"I don't know," answered the Krzyzak. The king was especially sensitive where any question about Christianity arose. It seemed to him that the Krzyzak wished to make an allusion to him; therefore his cheeks flamed immediately and his eyes began to shine.

"What!" said he, in a deep voice, "am I not a Christian king?"

"The kingdom calls itself a Christian one," coolly answered the Krzyzak; "but its customs are pagan."

At this many angry knights arose; Marcin of Wrocimowice, whose coat of arms was Polkoza, Florian of Korytnica, Bartosz of Wodzinek, Domarat of Kobylany, Zyndram of Maszkow, Powala of Taczew, Paszko Zlodziej of Biskupice, Jaxa of Targowisko, Krzon of Kozieglowy, Zygmunt of Bobowa and Staszko of Charbimowice, powerful and famous knights, victorious in many battles and in many tournaments. Alternately blushing and turning pale from anger, gnashing their teeth, they began to shout:

"Woe to us! He is a guest and we cannot challenge him!"

Zawisza Czarny, Sulimczyk, the most famous among the famous, "the model of knighthood," turned to Lichtenstein with a frown on his forehead and said:

"I do not recognize you, Kuno. How can you, a knight, insult a mighty nation, when you know that, being an envoy, you cannot be punished for it."

But Kuno quietly sustained the threatening look, and answered slowly and precisely:

"Our Order, before it came to Prussia, fought in Palestine; even there the Saracens respected the envoys. But you do not respect them; that is the reason I called your customs pagan."

At these words the uproar increased. Round the table again were heard shouts: "Woe! Woe!"

But they subsided when the king, who was furious, clasped his hands in the Lithuanian fashion. Then the old Jasko Topor of Tenczyn, castellan of Krakow, venerable, grave and dreaded on account of the importance of his office, arose and said:

"Noble Knight of Lichtenstein, if you, an envoy, have been insulted, speak, and severe punishment will be given quickly."

"It would not have happened to me in any other Christian country," answered Kuno. "Yesterday on the road to Tyniec I was attacked by one of your knights, and although he could very easily recognize by the cross on my mantle who I was, he attempted my life."

Zbyszko, having heard these words, became very pale and involuntarily glanced at the king, whose anger was terrible. Jasko of Tenczyn was surprised, and said:

"Can it be possible?"

"Ask the Pan of Taczew, who was a witness of the incident."

"All eyes turned toward Powala, who stood for a while gloomy, and with lowered eyelids; then he said:

"Yes, it is so!"

Hearing this the knights began to shout: "Shame! Shame! The earth will devour such a man!" Because of this disgrace some of them began to strike their chests with their hands, and others to rap the silver dishes, not knowing what to do.

"Why did you not kill him?" shouted the king.

"Because his head belongs to the court," answered Powala.

"Have you put him in prison?" asked the castellan, Topor of Tenczyn.

"No. He is a *wlodyka*, who swore on his knightly honor, that he would appear."

"But he will not appear!" ironically exclaimed Kuno, raising his head.

At that moment a young voice resounded behind the Krzyzak:

"I did it; I, Zbyszko of Bogdaniec!"

After these words the knights rushed toward the unhappy Zbyszko; but they were stopped by a threatening nod from the king who began to shout in an angry voice, similar to the rattling of a carriage rolling over the stones:

"Cut his head off! Cut his head off! Let the Krzyzak send it to Malborg to the grand master!"

Then he cried to the young Lithuanian prince standing near.

"Hold him, Jamont!"

The frightened Jamont put his trembling hands on Zbyszko's shoulders.

But the white-bearded castellan of Krakow, Topor of Tenczyn, raised his hand as a sign that he wished to speak; when everybody was quiet, he said:

"Gracious king! Let this *comthur* be convinced that not only your impetuous anger, but our laws will punish with death any who insult an envoy. Otherwise he will think that there are no Christian laws in this country. To-morrow I will judge the offender."

The last words he said quietly and as though no one could change his decision. Then he said to Jamont:

"Shut him in the tower. As for you, Pan of Taczew, you will be a witness."

"I will tell about the offence of this lad," answered Powala, looking at Lichtenstein.

"He is right!" immediately said some knights. "He is only a lad! Why should the shame be put on us all!"

There was a moment of silence, and angry looks were cast at the Krzyzak. In the meanwhile Jamont conducted Zbyszko to the court-yard of the castle and intrusted him to the archers. In his young heart he pitied the prisoner, and this pity was increased by his natural hatred of the Germans. But he was a Lithuanian, accustomed to fulfill blindly the orders of the grand duke; being himself afraid of the king's wrath, he began to whisper to the young knight, with kindly persuasion:

37

"Do you know, what I would do if in your place? Hang myself! It will be the best! The *korol*[52] is angry; they will cut off your head. Why should you not make him joyful? Hang yourself, *druh*.[53] Such is the custom in my country."

Zbyszko, half dazed with shame and fear, at first did not seem to understand the words of the *kniazik*;[54] but finally he understood them and then he was amazed:

"What do you say?"

"Hang yourself! Why should they judge you. You will only afford pleasure for the king!" repeated Jamont.

"Hang your own self!" exclaimed the young *wlodyka*. "They have baptized you but your heathen skin remains on you. Do you not know that it is a sin for a Christian to kill himself?"

The *kniaz* shrugged his shoulders:

"It will not be according to your will. They will cut off your head just the same."

These words angered Zbyszko, and he wondered if it would be proper to challenge the *bojarzynek*[55] for a fight either on horseback or on foot, with swords or with axes; but he stifled this desire. He dropped his head sadly and surrounded by the archers, went silently to the tower.

In the meanwhile everybody's attention in the dining hall was turned to Danusia, who became pale with fright. She stood motionless like a wax figure in a church. But when she heard that they were going to execute Zbyszko, then she was seized with great fear; her mouth quivered and at once she began to cry so loudly and so pitifully, that all faces turned toward her and the king himself asked her:

"What is the matter with thee?"

"Gracious king!" said the Princess Anna, "she is the daughter of Jurand of Spychow and this unhappy knight made a vow to her. He promised her to tear three peacock tufts from the helmets of the Germans, and having noticed such a tuft on the helmet of this *comthur*, he thought that God himself had sent the Krzyzak. He did not attack him, lord, through malice, but through stupidity; therefore be merciful and do not punish him, we beseech you on our knees!"

Having said this she arose, seized Danusia by the hand, and rushed with her toward the king, who seeing this began to retire. But both kneeled before him and Danusia began to cry;

"Forgive Zbyszko, king, forgive Zbyszko!"

Because she was afraid, she hid her fair head between the folds of the king's dress, kissed his knees and trembled like a leaf. Anna Ziemowitowa kneeled on the other side and having clasped her hands, looked at the king on whose face there was visible great perplexity. He retired toward the chair, but did not push Danusia back, only waved his hands.

"Do not trouble me!" he cried. "The youth is guilty; he has brought disgrace on the country! They must execute him!"

But the little hands clung closer and closer to his knees and the child cried more and more pitifully:

"Forgive Zbyszko, king, forgive Zbyszko!"

Now the voices of some knights were heard to exclaim:

"Jurand of Spychow is a famous knight, and the cause of awe to the Germans."

"And that youth fought bravely at Wilno!" added Powala.

But the king excused himself further, although he pitied Danusia.

"He is not guilty toward me and it is not I who can forgive him. Let the envoy of the Order pardon him, then I will pardon him also; but if the envoy will not, then he must die."

"Forgive him, sir!" exclaimed both of the princesses.

"Forgive, forgive!" repeated the voices of the knights.

Kuno closed his eyes and sat with uplifted forehead, as if he was delighted to see both princesses and such famous knights entreating him. Then his appearance changed; he dropped his head, crossed his hands on his breast and from a proud man became a humble one, and said with a soft, mild voice:

"Christ, our Saviour, forgave his enemies and even the malefactor on the cross."

"He is a true knight!" said Bishop Wysz.

"He is, he is!"

"How can I refuse to forgive," continued Kuno, "being not only a Christian, but also a monk? Therefore I forgive him with all my heart, as Christ's servant and friar!"

"Honor to him!" shouted Powala of Taczew.

"Honor!" repeated the others.

"But," said the Krzyzak, "I am here among you as an envoy and I carry in me the majesty of the whole Order which is Christ's Order. Whosoever offends me, therefore, offends the Order; and whosoever offends the Order, offends Christ himself; and such an offence, I, in the presence of God and the people, cannot forgive; and if your law does not punish it, let all Christian lords know."

After these words, there was a profound silence. Then after a while there could be heard here and there the gnashing of teeth, the heavy breathing of suppressed wrath and Danusia's sobbings.

By evening all hearts were in sympathy with Zbyszko. The same knights who in the morning were ready to cut him into pieces, were now considering how they could help him. The princesses determined to see the queen, and beseech her to prevail upon Lichtenstein to withdraw his complaint; or if necessary to write to the grand master of the Order, and ask him to command Kuno to give up the case. This plan seemed to be the best because Jadwiga was regarded with such unusual respect that if the grand master refused her request, it would make the pope angry and also all Christian lords. It was not likely that he would refuse because Konrad von Jungingen was a peaceable man. Unfortunately Bishop Wysz of Krakow, who was also the queen's physician, forbade them to mention even a word about this affair to the queen. "She never likes to hear about death sentences," he said, "and she takes even the question of a simple robber's death too seriously; she will worry much more if she hear about this young man who hopes to obtain mercy from her. But such anxiety will make her seriously ill, and her health is worth more to the whole kingdom than ten knightly heads." He finally said that if anyone should dare, notwithstanding what he had said, to disturb the queen, on that one he would cause the king's anger to rest and then he threatened such an one with excommunication.

Both princesses were frightened at such menace and determined to be silent before the queen; but instead to beseech the king until he showed some mercy. The whole court and all the knights sympathized with Zbyszko. Powala of Taczew declared that he would tell the whole truth; but that he would also speak in favor of the young man, because the whole affair was only an instance of childish impetuousness. But notwithstanding all this, everybody could see, and the castellan, Jasko of Tenczyn made it known, that if the Krzyzak was unrelenting, then the severe law must be fulfilled.

Therefore the knights were still more indignant against Lichtenstein and they all thought and even said frankly: "He is an envoy and cannot be called to the lists; but when he returns to Malborg, God will not permit that he die a natural death." They were not talking in vain, because a knight who wore the girdle was not permitted to say even one word without meaning it, and the knight who vowed anything, was obliged to accomplish his vow or perish. Powala was the most implacably angry because he had a beloved daughter of Danusia's age in Taczew, and Danusia's tears made his heart tender.

Consequently, that same day, he went to see Zbyszko, in his underground cell, commanded him to have hope, and told him about the princesses' prayers and about Danusia's tears. Zbyszko having learned that the girl threw herself at the king's feet for his sake, was moved to tears, and wishing to express his gratitude, said, wiping his tears with his hand:

"Hej! may God bless her, and permit me as soon as possible to engage in a combat, either on horseback or on foot, for her sake! I did not promise Germans enough to her! To such a lady, I ought to vow as many as she has years. If the Lord Jesus will only release me from this tower, I will not be niggardly with her!" He raised his eyes, full of gratitude.

"First promise something to some church," advised the *Pan* of Taczew; "if your promise is pleasing, you will surely soon be free. Now listen; your uncle went to see

Lichtenstein, and I will go see him also. It will be no shame for you to ask his pardon, because you are guilty; and then you do not ask for pardon of Lichtenstein, but an envoy. Are you ready?"

"As soon as such a knight as your grace tells me it is proper, I will do it. But if he require me to ask him for pardon in the same way he asked us to do it, on the road from Tyniec, then let them cut off my head. My uncle will remain and he will avenge me when the envoy's mission is ended."

"We shall hear first what he says to Macko," answered Powala.

And Macko really went to see the German; but he returned as gloomy as the night and went directly to the king, to whom he was presented by the castellan, himself. The king received Macko kindly because he had been appeased; when Macko kneeled, he immediately told him to arise, asking what he wished.

"Gracious lord," said Macko, "there was an offence, there must be a punishment; otherwise, there would be no law in the world. But I am also guilty because I did not try to restrain the natural impetuosity of that youth; I even praised him for it. It is my fault, gracious king, because I often told him: 'First cut, and then look to see whom you have hurt.' That was right in war, but wrong at the court! But he is a man, pure as gold, the last of our family!"

"He has brought shame upon me and upon my kingdom," said the king; "shall I be gracious to him for that?"

Macko was silent, because when he thought about Zbyszko, grief overpowered him; after a long silence, he began to talk in a broken voice:

"I did not know that I loved him so well; I only know it now when misfortune has come. I am old and he is last of the family. If he perish—we perish! Merciful king and lord, have pity on our family!"

Here Macko kneeled again and having stretched out his arms wasted by war, he spoke with tears:

"We defended Wilno; God gave us honest booty; to whom shall I leave it? If the Krzyzak requires punishment, let punishment come; but permit me to suffer it. What do I care for life without Zbyszko! He is young; let him redeem the land and beget children, as God ordered man to do. The Krzyzak will not ask whose head was cut off, if there is one cut. There will be no shame on the family. It is difficult for a man to die; but it is better that one man perish than that a family should be destroyed."

Speaking thus clasped the king's legs; the king began to wink his eyes, which was a sign of emotion with him; finally he said:

"It can not be! I cannot condemn to death a belted knight! It cannot be! It cannot be!"

"And there would be no justice in it," added the castellan. "The law will crush the guilty one; but it is not a monster, which does not look to see whose blood is being shed. And you must consider what shame would fall on your family, if your nephew agreed to your proposal. It would be considered a disgrace, not only to him, but to his children also."

To this Macko replied:

"He would not agree. But if it were done without his knowledge, he would avenge me, even as I also will avenge him."

"Ha!" said Tenczynski, "persuade the Krzyzak to withdraw the complaint."

"I have asked him."

"And what?" asked the king, stretching his neck; "what did he say?"

"He answered me thus: 'You ought to have asked me for pardon on the road to Tyniec; you would not then; now I will not.'"

"And why didn't you do it?"

"Because he required us to dismount and apologize on foot."

The king having put his hair behind his ears, commenced to say something when a courtier entered to announce that the Knight of Lichtenstein was asking for an audience.

Having heard this, Jagiello looked at Jasko of Tenczyn, then at Macko. He ordered them to remain, perhaps with the hope that he would be able to take advantage of this opportunity and using his kingly authority, bring the affair to an end.

Meanwhile the Krzyzak entered, bowed to the king, and said:

"Gracious lord! Here is the written complaint about the insult which I suffered in your kingdom."

"Complain to him," answered the king, pointing to Jasko of Tenczyn.

The Krzyzak, looking directly into the king's face, said:

"I know neither your laws nor your courts; I only know, that an envoy of the Order can complain only to the king."

Jagiello's small eyes flashed with impatience; he stretched out his hand however, and accepted the complaint which he handed to Tenczynski.

The castellan unfolded it and began to read; but the further he read, the more sorrowful and sad his face became.

"Sir," said he, finally, "you are seeking the life of that lad, as though he were dangerous to the whole Order. Is it possible that the Knights of the Cross are afraid even of the children?"

"The Knights of the Cross are not afraid of anyone," answered the *comthur*, proudly.

And the old castellan added:

"And especially of God."

The next day Powala of Taczew testified to everything he could before the court of the castellan, that would lessen the enormity of Zbyszko's offence. But in vain did he attribute the deed to childishness and lack of experience; in vain he said that even some one older, if he had made the same vow, prayed for its fulfillment and then had suddenly perceived in front of him such a crest, would also have believed that it was God's providence. But one thing, the worthy knight could not deny; had it not been for him, Zbyszko's spear would have pierced the Krzyzak's chest. Kuno had brought to the court the armor which he wore that day; it appeared that it was so thin that Zbyszko with his great strength, would have pierced it and killed the envoy, if Powala of Taczew had not prevented him. Then they asked Zbyszko if he intended to kill the Krzyzak, and he could not deny it. "I warned him from afar," said he, "to point his lance, and had he shouted in reply that he was an envoy, I would not have attacked him."

These words pleased the knights who, on account of their sympathy for the lad, were present in great numbers, and immediately numerous voices were heard to say: "True! Why did he not reply!" But the castellan's face remained gloomy and severe. Having ordered those present to be silent, he meditated for a while, then looked sharply at Zbyszko, and asked:

"Can you swear by the Passion of our Lord that you saw neither the mantle nor the cross?"

"No!" answered Zbyszko. "Had I not seen the cross, I would have thought he was one of our knights, and I would not have attacked one of ours."

"And how was it possible to find any Krzyzak near Krakow, except an envoy, or some one from his retinue?"

To this Zbyszko did not reply, because there was nothing to be said. To everybody it was clear, that if the *Pan* of Taczanow had not interposed, at the present moment there would lie before them not the armor of the envoy, but the envoy himself, with pierced breast—an eternal disgrace to the Polish nation;—therefore even those who sympathized with Zbyszko, with their whole souls, understood that he could not expect a mild sentence.

In fact, after a while the castellan said:

"As you did not stop to think whom you were attacking, and you did it without anger, therefore our Saviour will forgive you; but you had better commit yourself to the care of the Most Holy Lady, because the law cannot condone your offence."

Having heard this, Zbyszko, although he expected such words, became somewhat pale; but he soon shook his long hair, made the sign of the cross, and said:

"God's will! I cannot help it!"

Then he turned to Macko and looked expressively at Lichtenstein, as if to recommend him to Macko's memory; his uncle nodded in return that he understood and would remember. Lichtenstein also understood the look and the nod, and although he was as courageous as implacable, a cold shiver ran through him—so dreadful and ill-omened was the face of the old warrior. The Krzyzak knew that between him and that knight it would be a question of life or death. That even if he wanted to avoid the combat, he could not do it; that when his mission was ended, they must meet, even at Malborg.[56]

Meanwhile the castellan went to the adjoining room to dictate the sentence to a secretary. Some of the knights during the interruption came near the Krzyzak, saying:

"May they give you a more merciful sentence in the great day of judgment!"

But Lichtenstein cared only for the opinion of Zawisza, because he was noted all over the world for his knightly deeds, his knowledge of the laws of chivalry and his great exactness in keeping them. In the most entangled affairs in which there was any question about knightly honor, they used to go to him even from distant lands. Nobody contradicted his decisions, not only because there was no chance of victory in a contest with him, but because they considered him "the mirror of honor." One word of blame or praise from his mouth was quickly known by the knighthood of Poland, Hungary, Bohemia (Czech) and Germany; and he could decide between the good and evil actions of a knight.

Therefore Lichtenstein approached him as if he would like to justify his deadly grudge, and said:

"The grand master himself, with the chapter, could show him clemency; but I cannot."

"Your grand master has nothing to do with our laws; our king can show clemency to our people, not he," answered Zawisza.

"I as the envoy was obliged to insist upon punishment."

"Lichtenstein, you were first a knight, afterward an envoy!"

"Do you think that I acted against honor?"

"You know our books of chivalry, and you know that they order us to imitate two animals, the lamb and the lion. Which of the two have you, imitated in this case?"

"You are not my judge!"

"You asked me if you had committed an offence, and I answered as I thought."

"You give me a hard answer, which I cannot swallow."

"You will be choked by your own malice, not by mine."

"But Christ will put to my account, the fact that I cared more about the dignity of the Order, than about your praise."

"He will judge all of us."

Further conversation was interrupted by the reappearance of the castellan and the secretary. They knew that the sentence would be a severe one, and everyone waited silently. The castellan sat at the table, and, having taken a crucifix in his hand, ordered Zbyszko to kneel.

The secretary began to read the sentence in Latin. It was a sentence of death. When the reading was over, Zbyszko struck himself several times on the chest, repeating; "God be merciful to me, a sinner!"

Then he arose and threw himself in Macko's arms, who began to kiss his head and eyes.

In the evening of the same day, a herald announced at the four corners of the market place with the sound of trumpets, to the knights, guests and burghers assembled, that the noble Zbyszko of Bogdaniec was sentenced by the castellan's court to be decapitated by the sword.

But Macko obtained a delay of the execution; this was readily granted, because in those days they used to allow prisoners plenty of time to dispose of their property, as well as to be reconciled to God. Lichtenstein himself did not wish to insist upon an early execution of the sentence, because he understood, that as long as he obtained satisfaction for the offended majesty of the Order, it would be bad policy to estrange the powerful monarch, to whom he was sent not only to take part in the solemnity of the christening, but also to attend to the negotiations about the province of Dobrzyn. But the chief reason for the delay was the queen's health. Bishop Wysz did not wish even to hear about the execution before her delivery, rightly thinking, that it would be difficult to conceal such an affair from the lady. She would feel such sorrow and distress that it would be very injurious to her health. For these reasons, they granted Zbyszko several weeks, and perhaps more, of life, to make his final arrangements and to bid his friends farewell.

Macko visited him every day and tried to console him. They spoke sorrowfully about Zbyszko's inevitable death, and still more sorrowfully about the fact that the family would become extinct.

"It cannot be otherwise, unless you marry," Zbyszko said once.

"I would prefer to find some distant relative," answered the sorrowful Macko. "How can I think about women, when they are going to behead you. And even if I am obliged to marry, I will not do it, until I send a knightly challenge to Lichtenstein, and seek to avenge your death. Do not fear!"

"God will reward you. I have at least that joy! But I know that you will not forgive him. How will you avenge me?"

"When his duty as an envoy has ended, there may be a war! If there be war, I will send him a challenge for single combat before the battle."

"On the leveled ground?"

"On the leveled ground, on horseback or on foot, but only for death, not for captivity. If there be peace, then I will go to Malborg and will strike the door of the castle gates with my spear, and will order the trumpeter to proclaim that I challenge Kuno to fight until death. He cannot avoid the contest!"

"Surely he will not refuse. And you will defeat him."

"Defeat? I could not defeat Zawisza, Paszko, nor Powala; but without boasting, I can take care of two like him. That scoundrel Krzyzak shall see! That Fryzjan knight, was he not stronger? And how I cut him through the helmet, until the axe stopped! Did I not?"

Zbyszko breathed with relief and said:

"I will perish with some consolation."

They both began to sigh, and the old nobleman spoke with emotion:

"You mustn't break down with sorrow. Your bones will not search for one another at the day of judgment. I have ordered an honest coffin of oak planks for you. Even the canons of the church of Panna Marya could not have any better. You will not perish like a peasant. I will not permit them to decapitate you on the same cloth on which they behead burghers. I have made an agreement with Amylej, that he furnish a new cloth, so handsome that it would be good enough to cover king's fur. I will not be miserly with prayers, either; don't be afraid!"

Zbyszko's heart rejoiced, and bending toward his uncle's hand, he repeated:

"God will reward you!"

Sometimes, however, notwithstanding all this consolation he was seized with a feeling of dreadful loneliness; therefore, another time when Macko came to see him, as soon as he had welcomed him, he asked him, looking through the grate in the wall:

"How is it outside?"

"Beautiful weather, like gold, and the sun warms so that all the world is pleased."

Hearing this, Zbyszko put both his hands on his neck, and raising his head, said:

"Hej, Mighty God! To have a horse and to ride on fields, on large ones!
It is dreadful for a young man to perish! It is dreadful!"

"People perish on horseback!" answered Macko.

"Bah! But how many they kill before!"

And he began to ask about the knights whom he had seen at the king's court; about Zawisza, Farurej, Powala of Taczew, about Lis of Targowisko and about all the others; what they were doing; how they amused themselves; in what honest exercises they passed the time? And he listened with avidity to Macko who told him that in the morning, the knights dressed in their armor, jumped over horses, broke ropes, tried one another's skill with swords and with axes having sharp ends made of lead; finally, he told how they feasted and what songs they sang. Zbyszko longed with heart and soul to be with them, and when he learned that Zawisza, immediately after the christening, intended to go somewhere beyond Hungary, against the Turks, he could not refrain from exclaiming:

"If they would only let me go! It would be better to perish among the pagans!"

But this could not be done. In the meanwhile something else happened. Both princesses of Mazowsze had not ceased to think about Zbyszko, who had captivated them by his youth and beauty. Finally the Princess Alexandra Ziemowitowna decided to send a

43

letter to the grand master. It was true that the grand master could not alter the sentence, pronounced by the castellan; but he could intercede with the king in favor of the youth. It was not right for Jagiello to show any clemency, because the offence was an attempt on the life of the envoy; but if the grand master besought the king, then the king would pardon the lad. Therefore hope entered the hearts of both princesses. Princess Alexandra being fond of the polished monk-knights, was a great favorite with them also. Very often they sent her from Marienburg, rich presents and letters in which the master called her venerable, pious benefactress and the particular protectress of the Order. Her words could do much; it was probable that her wishes would not be denied. The question now was to find a messenger, who would be zealous enough to carry the letter as soon as possible and return immediately with the answer. Having heard this, the old Macko determined without any hesitation to do it.

The castellan promised to delay the execution. Full of hope, Macko set himself to work the same day to prepare for the journey. Then he went to see Zbyszko, to tell him the good news.

At first Zbyszko was filled with as great joy, as if they had already opened the door of the tower for him. But afterward he became thoughtful and gloomy, and said:

"Who can expect anything from the Germans! Lichtenstein also could ask the king for clemency; and he could get some benefit from it because he would thus avoid your vengeance; but he will not do anything."

"He is angry because we would not apologize on the road to Tyniec. The people speak well about the master, Konrad. At any rate you will not lose anything by it."

"Sure," said Zbyszko, "but do not bow too low to him."

"I shall not. I am going with the letter from Princess Alexandra; that is all."

"Well, as you are so kind, may God help you!"

Suddenly he looked sharply at his uncle and said:

"But If the king pardon me, Lichtenstein shall be mine, not yours. Remember!"

"You are not yet sure about your neck, therefore don't make any promises. You have enough of those stupid vows!" said the angry old man

Then they threw themselves into each other's arms. Zbyszko remained alone. Hope and uncertainty tossed his soul by turns; but when night came, and with it a storm, when the uncovered window was lighted by ill-omened lightnings and the walls shook with the thunder, when finally the whistling wind rushed into the tower, Zbyszko plunged, into darkness, again lost confidence; all night he could not close his eyes.

"I shall not escape death," he thought; "nothing can help me!"

But the next day, the worthy Princess Anna Januszowna came to see him, and brought Danusia who wore her little lute at her belt. Zbyszko fell at their feet; then, although he was in great distress, after a sleepless night, in woe and uncertainty, he did not forget his duty as a knight and expressed his surprise about Danusia's beauty.

But the princess looked at him sadly and said:

"You must not wonder at her; if Macko does not bring a favorable answer, or if he does not return at all, you will wonder at better things in heaven!"

Then she began to weep as she thought of the uncertain future of the little knight. Danusia wept also. Zbyszko kneeled again at their feet, because his heart became soft like heated wax in the presence of such grief. He did not love Danusia as a man loves a woman; but he felt that he loved her dearly. The sight of her had such an effect on him that he became like another man, less severe, less impetuous, less warlike. Finally great grief filled him because he must leave her before he could accomplish the vow which he had made to her.

"Poor child, I cannot put at your feet those peacock crests," said he. "But when I stand in the presence of God, I will say: 'Lord, forgive me my sins, and give *Panna* Jurandowna of Spychow all riches on earth.'"

"You met only a short time ago," said the princess. "God will not grant it!"

Zbyszko began to recollect the incident which occurred in Tyniec and his heart was melted. Finally he asked Danusia to sing for him the same song which she was singing when he seized her from the falling bench and carried her to the princess.

Therefore Danusia, although she did not feel like singing, raised her closed eyes toward the vault and began:

"If I only could get
The wings like a birdie,
I would fly quickly
To my dearest Jasiek!
I would then be seated
On the high enclosure:
Look my dear Jasiulku——"

But suddenly the tears began to flow down her face, and she was unable to sing any more. Zbyszko seized her in his arms, as he had done in the inn at Tyniec and began to walk with her around the room, repeating in ecstasy:

"If God release me from this prison, when you grow up, if your father give his consent, I will take you for my wife! Hej!"

Danusia embraced him and hid her face on his shoulder. His grief which became greater and greater, flowed from a rustic Slavonic nature, and changed in that simple soul almost to a rustic song:

"I will take you, girl!
I will take you!"

CHAPTER VI.

An event now happened, compared with which all other affairs lost their importance. Toward evening of the twenty-first of June, the news of the queen's sudden illness spread throughout the castle. Bishop Wysz and the other doctors remained in her room the whole night. It was known that the queen was threatened with premature confinement. The castellan of Krakow, Jasko Topor of Tenczyn, sent a messenger to the absent king that same night. The next day the news spread throughout the entire city and its environs. It was Sunday, therefore the churches were crowded. All doubt ceased. After mass the guests and the knights, who had come to be present at the festivals, the nobles and the burghers, went to the castle; the guilds and the fraternities came out with their banners. From noontide numberless crowds of people surrounded Wawel, but order was kept by the king's archers. The city was almost deserted; crowds of peasants moved toward the castle to learn some news about the health of their beloved queen. Finally there appeared in the principal gate, the bishops and the castellan, and with them other canons, king's counselors and knights. They mingled with the people telling them the news, but forbidding any loud manifestation of joy, because it would be injurious to the sick queen. They announced to all, that the queen was delivered of a daughter. This news filled the hearts of all with joy, especially when they learned, that, although the confinement was premature, there was now no danger, neither for the mother nor for the child. The people began to disperse because it was forbidden to shout near the castle and everybody wished to manifest his joy. Therefore, the streets of the city were filled immediately, and exulting songs and exclamations resounded in every corner. They were not disappointed because a girl had been born. "Was it unfortunate that King Louis had no sons and that Jadwiga became our queen? By her marriage with Jagiello, the strength of the kingdom was doubled. The same will happen again. Where can one find a richer heiress than our queen. Neither the Roman emperor nor any king possesses such dominion, nor so numerous a knighthood! There will be great competition among the monarchs for her hand; the most powerful of them will bow to our king and queen; they will come to Krakow, and we merchants will profit by it; perhaps some new domains, Bohemian or Hungarian, will be added to our kingdom."

Thus spoke the merchants among themselves, and their joy increased every moment. They feasted in the private houses and in the inns. The market place was filled with lanterns and torches. Almost till daybreak, there was great life and animation throughout the city.

During the morning, they heard more news from the castle.

They heard that the *ksiondz* Bishop Peter, had baptized the child during the night. On account of this, they feared that the little girl was not very strong. But the experienced townswomen quoted some similar cases, in which the infants had grown stronger immediately after baptism. Therefore they comforted themselves with this hope; their confidence was greatly increased by the name given to the princess.

"Neither Bonifacius nor Bonifacia can die immediately after baptism; the child so named is destined to accomplish something great," they said. "During the first years, especially during the first weeks, the child cannot do anything good or bad."

The next day, however, there came bad news from the castle concerning the infant and the mother, and the city was excited. During the whole day, the churches were as crowded as they were during the time of absolution. Votive offerings were very numerous for the queen's and princess' health. One could see poor peasants offering some grain, lambs, chickens, ropes of dried mushrooms or baskets of nuts. There came rich offerings from the knights, from the merchants and from the artisans. They sent messengers to the places where miracles were performed. Astrologers consulted the stars. In Krakow itself, they ordered numerous processions. All guilds and fraternities took part in them. There was also a children's procession because the people thought that these innocent beings would be more apt to obtain God's favor. Through the gates new crowds were coming.

Thus day after day passed, with continual ringing of bells, with the noise of the crowds in the churches, with processions and with prayers. But when at the end of a week, the beloved queen and the child were still living, hope began to enter the hearts of the people. It seemed to them impossible, that God would take from the kingdom the queen who, having done so much for it, would thus be obliged to leave so much unfinished. The scholars told how much she had done for the schools; the clergy, how much for God's glory; the statesmen, how much for peace among Christian monarchs; the jurisconsults, how much for justice; the poor people, how much for poverty. None of them could believe that the life so necessary to the kingdom and to the whole world, would be ended prematurely.

In the meanwhile on July thirteenth, the tolling bells announced the death of the child. The people again swarmed through the streets of the city, and uneasiness seized them. The crowd surrounded Wawel again, inquiring about the queen's health. But now nobody came out with good news. On the contrary, the faces of the lords entering the castle, or returning to the city, were gloomy, and every day became sadder. They said that the *ksiondz* Stanislaw of Skarbimierz, the master of liberal sciences in Krakow, did not leave the queen, who every day received holy communion. They said also, that after every communion, her room was filled with celestial light. Some had seen it through the windows; but such a sight frightened the hearts devoted to the lady; they feared that it was a sign that celestial life had already begun for her.

But everybody did not believe that such a dreadful thing could happen; they reassured themselves with the hope that the justice of heaven would be satisfied with one victim. But on Friday morning, July seventeenth, the news spread among the people that the queen was in agony. Everybody rushed toward Wawel. The city was deserted; even mothers with their infants rushed toward the gates of the castle. The stores were closed; they did not cook any food. All business was suspended; but around Wawel, there was a sea of uneasy, frightened but silent people.

At last at the thirteenth hour from noontime, the bell on the tower of the cathedral resounded. They did not immediately understand what it meant; but the people became uneasy. All heads and all eyes turned toward the tower in which was hung the tolling bell; its mournful tones were soon repeated by other bells in the city: by those at Franciscans, at Trinity, and at Panna Marya. Finally the people understood; then their souls were filled with dread and with great grief. At last a large black flag embroidered with a death's head, appeared on the tower. Then all doubt vanished: the queen had rendered her soul to God.

Beneath the castle walls resounded the roar and the cries of a hundred thousand people and mingled with the gloomy voices of the bells. Some of the people threw themselves on the ground; others tore their clothing or lacerated their faces; while others looked at the walls with silent stupefaction. Some of them were moaning; some, stretching their hands toward the church and toward the queen's room, asked for a miracle and God's mercy. But there were also heard some angry voices, which on account of despair were verging toward blasphemy:

"Why have they taken our dear queen? For what then were our processions, our prayers and our entreaties? Our gold and silver offerings were accepted and we have nothing in return for them! They took but they gave us nothing in return!" Many others weeping, repeated: "Jesus! Jesus! Jesus!" The crowds wanted to enter the castle, to look once more on the face of their queen.

This they were not permitted to do; but were promised that the body would soon be placed in the church where everyone would be allowed to view it and to pray beside it. Consequently toward evening, the sorrowing people began to return to the city, talking about the queen's last moments, about the future funeral and the miracles, which would be performed near her body and around her tomb. Some also said that immediately after her burial, the queen would be canonized, and when others said that they doubted if it could be done, many began to be angry and to threaten to go to the pope in Avignon.

A gloomy sorrow fell upon the city, and upon the whole country, not only on the common people, but on everybody; the lucky star of the kingdom was extinguished. Even to many among the lords, everything looked black. They began to ask themselves and others, what would happen now? whether the king had the right to remain after the queen's death and rule over the country; or whether he would return to Lithuania and be satisfied with the throne of the viceroy? Some of them supposed—and the future proved that they thought correctly—that the king himself would be willing to withdraw; and that, in such an event the large provinces would separate from the crown, and the Lithuanians would again begin their attacks against the inhabitants of the kingdom. The Knights of the Cross would become stronger; mightier would become the Roman emperor and the Hungarian king; and the Polish kingdom, one of the mightiest until yesterday, would be ruined and disgraced.

The merchants, for whom waste territories in Lithuania and in Russia had been opened, forseeing great losses, made pious vows, hoping that Jagiello might remain on the throne. But in that event, they predicted a war with the Order. It was known that the queen only could restrain his anger. The people recollected a previous occasion, when being indignant at the avidity and rapacity of the Knights of the Cross, she spoke to them in a prophetic vision: "As long as I live, I will restrain my husband's hand and his righteous anger; but remember that after my death, there will fall upon you the punishment for your sins."

In their pride and folly, they were not afraid of a war, calculating, that after the queen's death, the charm of her piety would no longer restrain the wish for affluence of volunteers from eastern countries, and that then thousands of warriors from Germany, Burgundia, France and other countries, would join the Knights of the Cross.

The death of Jadwiga was an event of such importance, that the envoy Lichtenstein, could wait no longer for the answer of the absent king; but started immediately for Marienburg, in order to communicate as soon as possible to the grand master and to the chapter the important, and in some ways, threatening news.

The Hungarian, the Austrian and the Bohemian envoys followed him or sent messengers to their monarchs. Jagiello returned to Krakow in great despair. At first he declared to the lords, that he did not wish to rule without the queen and that he would return to Litwa. Afterward, on account of his grief, he fell into such a stupor, that he could not attend to any affairs of state, and could not answer any questions. Sometimes he was very angry with himself, because he had gone away, and had not been present at the queen's death to bid her farewell and to hear her last words and wishes. In vain Stanislaw of Skarbimierz and Bishop Wysz explained to him that the queen's illness came suddenly, and that according to human calculations he would have had plenty of time to go and return if the confinement had occurred at the expected time. These words did not bring him any consolation; did not assuage his grief. "I am no king without her," he answered the bishop; "only a repentant sinner, who can receive no consolation!" After that he looked at the ground and no one could induce him to speak even one word.

Meanwhile preparations for the queen's funeral occupied all minds. From all over the country, great crowds of lords, nobles and peasants were going to Krakow. The body of the queen was placed in the cathedral on an elevation, so arranged that the end of the coffin in which the queen's head rested, was much higher than the other end. It was so arranged purposely, to enable the people to see the queen's face. In the cathedral continual prayers were offered; around the catafalque thousands of wax candles were burning. In the glare of the candles and among the flowers, she lay quiet and smiling, looking like a mystic rose. The people saw in her a saint; they brought to her those possessed with devils, the crippled and the sick children. From time to time there was heard in the church, the exclamation of some mother who perceived the color return to the face of her sick child; or the joyful voice of some paralytic man who at once was cured. Then human hearts trembled and the news spread throughout the church, the castle, and the city, and attracted more and more of such human wretchedness as only from a miracle could expect help.

CHAPTER VII.

During this time Zbyszko was entirely forgotten. Who in the time of such sorrow and misfortune, could remember about the noble lad or about his imprisonment in the tower of the castle? Zbyszko had heard, however, from the guards, about the queen's illness. He had heard the noise of the people around the castle; when he heard their weeping and the tolling of the bells, he threw himself on his knees, and having forgotten about his own lot, began to mourn the death of the worshipped lady. It seemed to him, that with her, something died within him and that after her death, there was nothing worth living for in this world.

The echo of the funeral—the church bells, the processional songs and the lamenting of the crowd,—was heard for several weeks. During that time, he grew gloomier, lost his appetite, could not sleep and walked in his underground cell like a wild beast in a cage. He suffered in solitude; there were often days during which the jailer did not bring him food nor water. So much was everybody engaged with the queen's funeral, that after her death nobody came to see him: neither the princess, nor Danusia, nor Powala of Taczew, nor the merchant Amylej. Zbyszko thought with bitterness, that as soon as Macko left the city, everybody forgot about him. Sometimes he thought that perhaps the law would forget about him also, and that he would putrefy in the prison till death. Then he prayed for death.

Finally, when after the queen's funeral one month passed, and the second commenced, he began to doubt if Macko would ever return. Macko had promised to ride quickly and not to spare his horse. Marienburg was not at the other end of the world. One could reach it and return in twelve weeks, especially if one were in haste. "But perhaps he has not hurried!" thought Zbyszko, bitterly; "perhaps he has found some woman whom he will gladly conduct to Bogdaniec, and beget his own progeny while I must wait here centuries for God's mercy."

Finally he lost all trace of time, and ceased altogether to talk with the jailer. Only by the spider web thickly covering the iron grating of the window, did he know that fall was near at hand. Whole hours he sat on his bed, his elbows resting on his knees, his fingers in his long hair. Half dreaming and stiff, he did not raise his head even when the warden bringing him food, spoke to him. But at last one day the bolts of the door creaked, and a familiar voice called him from the threshold;

"Zbyszku!"

"Uncle!" exclaimed Zbyszko, rushing from the bed.

Macko seized him in his arms, and began to kiss his fair head. Grief, bitterness and loneliness had so filled the heart of the youth, that he began to cry on his uncle's breast like a little child.

"I thought you would never come back," said he, sobbing.

"That came near being true," answered Macko.

Now Zbyszko raised his head and having looked at him, exclaimed:

"What was the matter with you?"

He looked with amazement at the emaciated and pallid face of the old warrior, at his bent figure and his gray hair.

"What was the matter with you?" he repeated.

Macko sat on the bed and for a while breathed heavily.

"What was the matter?" said he, finally.

48

"Hardly had I passed the frontier, before the Germans whom I met in the forest, wounded me with a crossbow. *Raubritters!* You know! I cannot breathe! God sent me help, otherwise you would not see me here."

"Who rescued you?"

"Jurand of Spychow," answered Macko.

There was a moment of silence.

"They attacked me; but half a day later he attacked them and hardly half of them escaped. He took me with him to the *grodek* and then to Spychow. I fought with death for three weeks. God did not let me die and although I am not well yet, I have returned."

"Then you have not been in Malborg?"

"On what would I ride? They robbed me of everything and they took the letter with the other things. I returned to ask Princess Ziemowitowa for another; but I have not met her yet, and whether I will see her or not, I do not know. I must prepare for the other world!"

Having said this, he spit on the palm of his hand and stretching it toward Zbyszko, showed him blood on it, saying:

"Do you see?"

After a while he added:

"It must be God's will."

They were both silent for a time under the burden of their gloomy thoughts; then Zbyszko said:

"Then you spit blood continually?"

"How can I help it; there is a spear head half a span long between my ribs. You would spit also! I was a little better before I left Jurand of Spychow; but now I am very tired, because the way was long and I hastened."

"He; I why did you hasten?"

"Because I wished to see Princess Alexandra and get another letter from her. Jurand of Spychow said 'Go and bring the letter to Spychow. I have a few Germans imprisoned here. I will free one of them if he promise upon his knightly word to carry the letter to the gland master.' For vengeance for his wife's death, he always keeps several German captives and listens joyfully when they moan and their chains rattle. He is a man full of hatred. Understand?"

"I understand. But I wonder that you did not recover the lost letter, if Jurand captured those who attacked you."

"He did not capture all of them. Five or six escaped. Such is our lot!"

"How did they attack you? From ambush?"

"From behind such thick bushes that one could see nothing. I was riding without armor, because the merchants told me that the country was safe, and it was warm."

"Who was at the head of the robbers? A Krzyzak?"

"Not a friar, but a German. Chelminczyk of Lentz, famous for his robberies on the highway."

"What became of him?"

"Jurand chained him. But he has in his dungeons two noblemen, Mazurs, whom he wishes to exchange for himself."

There was a moment of silence.

"Dear Jesus," Zbyszko said, finally; "Lichtenstein is alive, and also that robber from Lentz; but we must perish without vengeance. They will behead me and you will not be able to live through the winter."

"Bah! I will not live even until winter. If I could only help you in some way to escape."

"Have you seen anybody here?"

"I went to see the castellan of Krakow. When I learned that Lichtenstein had departed, I thought perhaps the castellan would be less severe."

"Then Lichtenstein went away?"

"Immediately after the queen's death, he went to Marienburg. I went to see the castellan; but he answered me thus: 'They will execute your nephew, not to please

Lichtenstein, but because that is his sentence. It will make no difference whether Lichtenstein be here or not. Even if he die, nothing will be changed; the law is according to justice and not like a jacket, which you can turn inside out. The king can show clemency; but no one else.'"

"And where is the king?"

"After the funeral he went to Rus'."

"Well, then there is no hope at all."

"No." The castellan said still further: "I pity him, because the Princess Anna begs for his pardon, but I cannot, I cannot!"

"Then Princess Anna is still here?"

"May God reward her! She is a good lady. She is still here, because Jurandowna is sick, and the princess loves her as her own child."

"For God's sake! Then Danusia is sick! What is the matter with her?"

"I don't know! The princess says that somebody has thrown a spell over her."

"I am sure it is Lichtenstein! Nobody else,—only Lichtenstein—a dog-brother!"

"It may be he. But what can you do to him? Nothing!"

"That is why they all seemed to have forgotten me here; she was sick."

Having said this, Zbyszko began to walk up and down the room; finally he seized Macko's hand, kissed it, and said:

"May God reward you for everything! If you die, I will be the cause of your death. Before you get any worse, you must do one thing more. Go to the castellan and beg him to release me, on my knightly word, for twelve weeks. After that time I will return, and they may behead me. But it must not be that we both die without vengeance. You know! I will go to Marienburg, and immediately send a challenge to Lichtenstein. It cannot be otherwise. One of us must die!"

Macko began to rub his forehead.

"I will go; but will the castellan permit?"

"I will give my knightly word. For twelve weeks——I do not need more."

"No use to talk; twelve weeks! And if you are wounded, you cannot return; what will they think then?"

"I will return if I have to crawl. But don't be afraid! In the meanwhile the king may return and one will be able to beseech him for clemency."

"That is true," answered Macko.

But after awhile he added:

"The castellan also told me this: 'On account of the queen's death, we forgot about your nephew; but now his sentence must be executed.'"

"Ej, he will permit," answered Zbyszko, hopefully. "He knows that a nobleman will keep his word, and it is just the same to him, whether they behead me now, or after St. Michael's day."

"Ha! I will go to-day."

"You better go to Amylej to-day, and rest awhile. He will bandage your wound, and to-morrow you can go to the castellan."

"Well, with God then!"

"With God!"

They hugged each other and Macko turned toward the door; but he stopped on the threshold and frowned as if he remembered something unpleasant.

"Bah, but you do not yet wear the girdle of a knight; Lichtenstein will tell you that he will not fight with you; what can you do then?"

Zbyszko was filled with sorrow, but only for a moment, then he said:

"How is it during war? Is it necessary that a knight choose only knights?"

"War is war; a single combat is quite different."

"True, but wait. You must find some way. Well, there is a way! Prince Janusz will dub me a knight. If the princess and Danusia ask him, he will do it. In the meantime I will fight in Mazowsze with the son of Mikolaj of Dlugolas."

"What for?"

"Because Mikolaj, the same who is with the princess and whom they call Obuch, called Danusia, 'bush.'"

Macko looked at him in amazement. Zbyszko, wishing to explain better about what had occurred, said further:

"I cannot forgive that, but I cannot fight with Mikolaj, because he must be nearly eighty years old."

To this Macko said:

"Listen! It is a pity that you should lose your head; but there will not be a great loss of brains, because you are stupid like a goat."

"Why are you angry?"

Macko did not answer, but started to leave. Zbyszko sprang toward him and said:

"How is Danusia? Is she well yet? Don't be angry for a trifle. You have been absent so long!"

Again he bent toward the old man who shrugged his shoulders and said mildly:

"Jurandowna is well, only they will not let her go out of her room yet. Good-bye!"

Zbyszko remained alone, but he felt as if he had been regenerated. He rejoiced to think that he might be allowed to live three months more. He could go to remote lands; he could find Lichtenstein, and engage in deadly combat with him. Even the thought about that filled him with joy. He would be fortunate, to be able to ride a horse, even for twelve weeks; to be able to fight and not perish without vengeance. And then—let happen what would happen—it would be a long time anyhow! The king might return and forgive him. War might break out, and the castellan himself when he saw the victor of the proud Lichtenstein, might say: "Go now into the woods and the fields!"

Therefore a great hope entered his heart. He did not think that they would refuse to grant him those three months. He thought that perhaps they would grant hem more. The old *Pan* of Tenczyn would never admit that a nobleman could not keep his word.

Therefore when Macko came to the prison, the next day toward evening, Zbyszko, who could hardly sit quiet, sprang toward him and asked:

"Granted?"

Macko sat on the truckle-bed, because he could not stand on account of his feebleness; for a while he breathed heavily and finally said:

"The castellan said: 'If you wish to divide your land, or attend to your household, then I will release your nephew for a week or two on his knightly word, but for no longer.'"

Zbyszko was so much surprised, that for a while he could not say a word.

"For two weeks?" asked he, finally. "But I could not even reach the frontier in two weeks! How is it? You did not tell the castellan why I wished to go to Marienburg?"

"Not only I, but the Princess Anna begged for you."

"And what then?"

"What? The old man told her that he did not want your head, and that he pitied you. 'If I could find,' said he, 'some law in his favor, or only a pretext, I would release him altogether; but I cannot. There would be no order in a country in which the people shut their eyes to the law, and acted according to friendship; I will not do it; even if it were Toporczyk, who is a relative of mine, or even my own brother, I would not. Such hard people are here!' And he said still further; 'We do not care about the Knights of the Cross; but we cannot bring reproach on ourselves. What would they think of us, and all our guests, coming from all parts of the world, if I release a nobleman sentenced to death, in order to give him a chance to fight? Would they believe that he will be punished, and that there is some law in our country? I prefer to order one head cut off, than to bring contempt on the king and the kingdom.' The princess told him that that was strange justice, from which even a king's relative could not obtain anything by her prayer; but the old man answered: 'The king may use clemency; but he will not tolerate lawlessness.' Then they began to quarrel because the princess grew very angry; 'Then,' said she, 'don't keep him in the prison!' And the castellan replied to this: 'Very well! To-morrow I will order a scaffold built on the market square.' Then they departed. Only the Lord Jesus can help you."

There was a long moment of silence.

"What?" he said, gloomily. "Then it will be immediately?"

"In two or three days. There is no help. I have done what I could. I fell at the castellan's knees; I implored him for mercy, but he repeated: 'Find a law, or a pretext.' But what can I find? I went to see the *ksiondz* Stanislaw of Skarbimierz, and I begged him to come to you. At least you will have this honor, that the same priest who heard the queen's confession will hear yours. But I did not find him home; he had gone to Princess Anna."

"Perhaps for Danusia!"

"Not at all. The girl is better. I will go see him to-morrow early in the morning. They say that if he bears one's confession, salvation is as sure as if you had it in your pocket."

Zbyszko put his elbows on his knees and dropped his head so that his hair covered his face entirely. The old man looked at him a long time and finally began to call him softly:

"Zbyszku! Zbyszku!"

The boy raised his head. His face had an expression of anger and of cold hatred, but not of weakness.

"What?"

"Listen carefully; perhaps I have found a way of escape."

Having said this, he approached and began to whisper:

"Have your heard about Prince Witold, who at one time, being imprisoned by our king in Krewo, went out from the prison disguised in a woman's dress. There is no woman who will remain here instead of you, but take my *kubrak*.[57] Take my cowl and go—understand? They will not notice. It is dark behind the door. They will not flash a light into your eyes. They saw me yesterday going out; but they did not look at me closely. Be quiet and listen. They will find me here to-morrow—and what then? Will they cut my head off? That will be no satisfaction, because I will die anyhow in three or four weeks. And you, as soon as you are out of here, to horse, and go straight to Prince Witold. You will present yourself to him; you will bow before him; he will receive you and you will be as safe with him as if you were sitting at God's right hand. They say here that the *kniaz*'s armies have been defeated by the Tartars, because the late queen prophesied defeat. If it be true, the *kniaz* will need soldiers and he will welcome you. You must remain with him, because there is no better service in the world. If our king were defeated in a war, it would be his end; but there is such an amount of shrewdness in *Kniaz* Witold, that after a defeat he grows still more powerful. And he is liberal also, and he loves our family. Tell him everything that happened. Tell him that you wanted to go with him against the Tartars; but you could not because you were imprisoned in the tower. If God permit, he will give you some land and peasants; he will dub you a knight and he will intercede for you with the king. He is a good protector—you will see!—What?"

Zbyszko listened silently, and Macko, as if he was excited by his own words, spoke further:

"You must not perish young, but return to Bogdaniec. And when you return, you must immediately take a wife so that our family does not perish. Only when you have children, may you challenge Lichtenstein to fight until death; but before that, you must abstain from seeking vengeance. Take my *kubrak* now, take my cowl and go, in God's name."

Having said this, Macko stood up and began to undress; but Zbyszko arose also, stopped him and said:

"I will not do it, so help me God and Holy Cross."

"Why?" asked Macko, astonished.

"Because I will not!"

Macko became pale with anger.

"I wish you had never been born!"

"You told the castellan," said Zbyszko, "that you would give your head in exchange for mine."

"How do you know that?"

"The *Pan* of Taczew told me."

"What of it?"

52

"What of it? The castellan told you that disgrace would fall on me and on all my family Would it not be a still greater disgrace, if I escaped from here, and left you to the vengeance of the law?"

"What vengeance? What can the law do to me, when I must die just the same? Have common sense, for God's mercy!"

"May God punish me if I abandon you now when you are old and sick. Tfu! shame!"

There was silence; one could only hear the heavy, hoarse breathing of Macko, and the archers' calls.

"Listen," Macko said, finally, in broken tones, "it was not shameful for *Kniaz* Witold to escape from Krewo; it would not be for you, either."

"Hej!'" answered Zbyszko, with sadness "You know! *Kniaz* Witold is a great *kniaz*; he received a crown from the king's hand, also riches and dominion; but I, a poor nobleman, have only my honor."

After a while he exclaimed in a sudden burst of anger:

"Then you do not understand that I love you, and that I will not give your head instead of mine?"

At this, Macko stood on his trembling feet, stretched out his hands, and although the nature of the people of those days, was hard, as if forged of iron, he cried suddenly in a heartbroken voice:

"Zbyszku!"

CHAPTER VIII.

The next day, the court servants began to make preparations in the market square, to build the scaffold which was to be erected opposite the principal gate of the city hall.

The princess, however, was still consulting with Wojciech Jastrzembiec, Stanislaw of Skarbimierz and other learned canons, who were familiar with the written laws and also with the laws sanctioned by custom.

She was encouraged in these efforts by the castellan's words, when he said, that if they showed him "law or pretext," he would free Zbyszko. Therefore they consulted earnestly, to ascertain if there were any law or custom that would do. Although the *ksiondz* Stanislaw, had prepared Zbyszko for death and administered the last sacraments, he went directly from the prison to the consultation, which lasted almost till daybreak.

The day of execution arrived. From early morning, crowds of people had begun to gather on the market square, because the decapitation of a nobleman excited more curiosity than that of a common criminal. The weather was beautiful. News of the youth and great beauty of the sentenced man, spread among the women. Therefore the whole road leading to the castle, was filled with crowds of townswomen, dressed in their best; in the windows on the market square, and on the balconies, could be seen velvet bonnets, or the fair heads of young girls, ornamented only with wreaths of lilies and roses. The city councilors, although the affair did not belong in their jurisdiction, all appeared, in order to show their importance and placed themselves near the scaffold. The knights, wishing to show their sympathy for the young man, gathered in great numbers around the elevation. Behind them swarmed the gayly dressed crowd, composed of small merchants and artisans dressed in their guild costumes. Over this compact mass of human heads, one could see the scaffold which was covered with new broadcloth. On the elevation stood the executioner, a German, with broad shoulders, dressed in a red *kubrak* and on his head a cowl of the same color; he carried a heavy two-edged sword; with him were two of his assistants with naked arms and ropes at their girdles. There were also a block and a coffin covered with broadcloth. In Panna Maryia's tower, the bells were ringing, filling the town with metallic sounds and scaring the flocks of doves and jackdaws. The people looked at the scaffold, and at the executioner's sword protruding from it and shining in the sun. They also looked at the knights, on whom the burghers always gazed with respect and eagerness. This time it was worth while looking at them. The most famous knights were standing round the elevation. They admired the broad shoulders and dark hair, falling in abundant curls of Zawisza Czarny; they admired the short square figure of Zyndram of Maszkow as well as the gigantic stature of Paszko Zlodziej of Biskupice; the threatening face of Wojciech of Wodzinek and the great beauty of Dobko of Olesnica, who at the tournament in Torun had defeated twelve knights; they

53

looked admiringly at Zygmunt of Bobowa, who became equally famous in Koszyce in a fight with the Hungarians, at Krzon of Koziegłowy, at Lis of Targowisko, who was victorious in duels, and at Staszko of Charbimowice who was able to catch a running horse.

General attention was also attracted by the pale face of Macko of Bogdanice; he was supported by Floryan of Korytnica and Marcin of Wrocimowice. It was generally thought that he was the sentenced man's father.

But the greatest curiosity was aroused by Powala of Taczew who, standing in front, was holding Danusia, dressed in white, with a wreath of green rue resting on her fair hair. The people did not understand what it meant, nor why this young girl was present to look at the execution. Some of them thought she was a sister; others, that she was the knight's lady; but none were able to explain the meaning of her dress or of her presence at the scaffold. The sight of her fair face covered with tears, aroused commiseration and emotion. The people began to criticise the castellan's stubbornness, and the severity of the laws. Those criticisms gradually changed to threats. Finally, here and there, some voices were heard to say, that if the scaffold were destroyed, then the execution would be postponed.

The crowd became eager and excited. They said that if the king were present, he would surely pardon the youth.

But all became quiet when distant shoutings announced the approach of the king's archers, escorting the prisoner. The procession soon appeared in the market square. It was preceded by a funeral fraternity, the members of which were dressed in long black cloaks, and were covered with veils of the same color, which had openings cut for the eyes. The people were afraid of these gloomy figures and became silent. They were followed by a detachment of soldiers, armed with crossbows, and dressed in elk-skin jerkins; these were the king's Lithuanian guards. Behind them one could see the halberds of another detachment of soldiers. In the centre, between the clerk of the court, who was going to read the sentence, and the *ksiondz* Stanislaw of Skarbimierz who was carrying a crucifix, walked Zbyszko.

All eyes now turned toward him, and at all the windows and from all the balconies, women's heads protruded. Zbyszko was dressed in his white "*jaka*," embroidered with golden griffins and ornamented with gold galoon; in these magnificent clothes he looked like a young prince, or the page of a wealthy court. His broad shoulders and chest and his powerful haunches indicated that he was already a full-grown man; but above that strong figure of a man, appeared a childish face with down on the upper lip. It was a beautiful face like that of a king's page, with golden hair cut evenly over the eyebrows and falling on the shoulders. He walked erect, but was very pale. From time to time he looked at the crowd as if he was dreaming; he looked at the church towers, toward the flocks of jackdaws, and at the bells, ringing his last hour; then his face expressed amazement when he realized that the sobbing of the women, and all this solemnity was for him. Finally, he perceived the scaffold and the executioner's red figure standing on it. Then he shivered and made the sign of the Cross; the priest gave him the crucifix to kiss. A few steps further, a bouquet of roses thrown by a young girl, fell at his feet. Zbyszko stooped, picked up the bouquet and smiled at the girl who began to cry. But evidently he thought that, amidst these crowds and in the presence of these women, waving their kerchiefs from the windows, he must die courageously and at least leave behind him the reputation of "a brave man;" therefore he strained his courage and will to the utmost. With a sudden movement, he threw his hair back, raised his head still higher and walked proudly, almost like a conqueror, whom, according to knightly custom, they conduct to get the prize. The procession advanced slowly, because the crowd was dense and unwillingly made way. In vain the Lithuanian guard, marching in front, shouted: "*Eyk szalin! Eyk szalin!* go away!" The people did not wish to understand these words, and surrounded the soldiers more closely. Although about one-third of the burghers of Krakow were Germans, still there were heard on all sides, threats against the Knights of the Cross: "Shame! Shame! May they perish, those wolves! Must they cut off children's heads for them! Shame on the king and on the kingdom!" The Lithuanians seeing the resistance, took their crossbows from their shoulders, and menaced the crowd; but they did not dare to attack without orders. The captain sent some men to open the way with their halberds and in that manner they reached the knights standing around the scaffold.

They stepped aside without any resistance. The men with halberds entered first, and were followed by Zbyszko, accompanied by the priest and the clerk of the court. At that moment something happened which nobody had expected. From among the knights, Powala stepped forward with Danusia in his arms and shouted: "Stop!" with such a powerful voice, that the retinue stopped at once, as if rooted to the ground. Neither the captain, nor any of the soldiers dared to oppose the lord and knight, whom they were accustomed to see every day in the castle and often in confidential conversation with the king. Finally, other knights, equally distinguished, also began to shout with commanding voices:

"Stop! Stop!" In the meantime, the *Pan* of Taczew approached Zbyszko and handed Danusia to him.

Zbyszko caught her in his arms and pressed her to his chest, bidding her farewell; but Danusia instead of nestling to him and embracing him, immediately took her white veil from her head and wrapped it around Zbyszko's head, and began to cry in her tearful, childish voice:

"He is mine! He is mine!"

"He is hers!" shouted the powerful voices of the knights. "To the castellan!"

A shout, like the roar of thunder, answered: "To the castellan! To the castellan!" The priest raised his eyes, the clerk looked confused, the captain and his soldiers dropped their arms; everybody understood what had happened.

There was an old Polish and Slavonic custom, as strong as the law, known in Podhale, around Krakow, and even further. If a young girl threw her veil on a man conducted to death, as a sign that she wished to marry him, by so doing she saved his life. The knights, farmers, villagers and townsmen all knew this custom; and the Germans living in the old cities and towns, had heard about it. The old man, Macko, almost fainted with emotion; the knights having pushed away the guards, surrounded Zbyszko and Danusia; the joyful people shouted again and again: "To the castellan! To the castellan!"

The crowd moved suddenly, like the waves of the sea. The executioner and his assistants rushed down from the scaffold. Everybody understood that if Jasko of Tenczyn resisted the custom, there would be a riot in the city. In fact the people now rushed to the scaffold. In the twinkling of an eye, they pulled off the cloth and tore it into pieces; then the beams and planks, pulled by strong arms, or cut with axes, began to crack, then a crash, and a few moments later there was not a trace left of the scaffold.

Zbyszko, holding Danusia in his arms, was going to the castle, but this time like a true victor,—triumphant. With him were marching joyfully the most noted knights in the kingdom; thousands of men, women and children were shouting and singing, stretching their arms toward Danusia and praising the beauty and courage of both. At the windows the townswomen were clasping their hands, and everywhere one could see faces covered with tears of joy. A shower of roses, lilies, ribbons and even gold rings were thrown to the lucky youth; he, beaming like the sun, with his heart full of gratitude, embraced his sweet lady from time to time and sometimes kissed her hands. This sight made the townswomen feel so tender, that some of them threw themselves into the arms of their lovers, telling them that if they encountered death, they also would be freed. Zbyszko and Danusia became the beloved children of the knights, burghers and common people. Macko, whom Floryan of Korytnica and Marcin of Wrocimowice were assisting to walk, was almost beside himself with joy. He wondered why he had not even thought about this means of assistance. Amidst the general bustle, Powala of Taczew told the knights that this remedy had been discovered by Wojciech Jastrzembiec and Stanislaw of Skarbimierz, both experts in the written laws and customs. The knights were all amazed at its simplicity, saying among themselves, that nobody else would have thought about that custom, because the city was inhabited by Germans, and it had not been used for a long time.

Everything, however, still depended on the castellan. The knights and the people went to the castle, which was occupied by *Pan* Krakowski during the king's absence. The clerk of the court, the *ksiondz* Stanislaw of Skarbimierz, Zawisza, Farurej, Zyndram of Maszkow and Powala of Taczew explained to him the power of the custom and reminded him of what he had said himself, that if he found "law or pretext," then he would release the prisoner immediately. And could there be any better law, than the old custom which had never been abolished?

The *Pan* of Tenczyn answered that this custom applied more to the common people and to robbers, than to the nobles; but he knew the law very well, and could not deny its validity. Meanwhile he covered his silvery beard with his hand and smiled, because he was very much pleased. Finally he went to the low portico, accompanied by Princess Anna Danuta, a few priests and the knights.

Zbyszko having perceived him, lifted Danusia again; the old castellan placed his hand on her golden hair, and gravely and benevolently inclined his hoary head. The assembled people understood this sign and shouted so that the walls of the castle were shaken: "May God preserve you! Long life, just lord! Live and judge us!"

Then the people cheered Zbyszko and Danusia when a moment later, they both went to the portico, fell at the feet of the good Princess Anna Danuta, who had saved Zbyszko's life, because she, together with the scholars, had found the remedy and had taught Danusia how to act.

"Long life to the young couple!" shouted Powala of Taczew.

"Long life!" repeated the others. The castellan, hoary with age, turned toward the princess and said:

"Gracious princess, the betrothal must be performed immediately, because the custom requires it!"

"The betrothal will take place immediately," answered the good lady, whose face was irradiated with joy; "but for the wedding, they must have the consent of Jurand of Spychow."

END OF PART FIRST.
PART SECOND.
CHAPTER I.

In merchant Amylej's house, Macko and Zbyszko were deliberating what to do. The old knight expected to die soon, and Father Cybek, a Franciscan friar who had experience in treating wounds, predicted the same, therefore he wanted to return to Bogdaniec to die and be buried beside his forefathers in the cemetery in Ostrow.

But not all of his forefathers were buried there. In days of yore it had been a numerous family of *wlodykas*. During the war their cry was: "Grady!" On their shields, because they claimed to be better *wlodykas* than the others who had no right to a coat of arms, they had emblazoned a Tempa Podkowa. In 1331, in the battle of Plowce, seventy warriors from Bogdaniec were killed in the marshes by German archers. Only one Wojciech, called Tur, escaped. After this defeat by the Germans, the king, Wladyslaw Lokietek, granted him a coat of arms and the estate of Bogdaniec as a special privilege. Wojciech returned home, only to discover the complete annihilation of his family.

While the men of Bogdaniec were perishing from German arrows, the *Raubritters* of Szlonsk fell upon their homes, burned their buildings, and slaughtered or took into slavery the peasants. Wojciech remained alone, the heir of a large but devastated tract of land, which formerly belonged to the whole family of *wlodykas*. Five years afterward he married and he begot two sons, Jasko and Macko. Afterward he was killed in a forest by an urus.[58]

The sons grew up under the mother's care. Her maiden name was Kachna of Spalenica. She was so brave that she conducted two successful expeditions against the Germans of Szlonsk to avenge former wrongs; but in the third expedition she was killed. Before that, however, she built with the help of the slaves, a *grodek*[59] in Bogdaniec; on account of that, Jasko and Macko, although from their former estates of *wlodykas* were called *wlodykas*, now became men of importance. When Jasko became of age, he married Jagienka of Mocarzew, and begot Zbyszko; Macko remained unmarried. He took care of his nephew's property as far as his war expeditions permitted.

But when during the civil war between Grzymalits and Nalenczs, Bogdaniec was again burned and the peasants scattered, Macko could not restore it, although he toiled for several years. Finally he pledged the land to his relative, the abbot, and with Zbyszko who was small, he went to Lithuania to fight against the Germans.

But he had never forgotten about Bogdaniec. He went to Litwa hoping to become rich from booty so as to return to Bogdaniec, redeem the land from his pledge, colonize it with slaves, rebuild the *grodek* and settle Zbyszko on it. Therefore now, after Zbyszko's lucky deliverance, they were discussing this matter at the house of the merchant, Amylej.

They had money enough to redeem the land they possessed quite a fortune gathered from the booty, from the ransoms paid by the knights captured by them, and from Witold's presents. They had received great benefit from that fight with the two Fryzjan knights. The suits of armor alone, were worth what was considered in those times quite a fortune; beside the armor, they had captured wagons, people, clothes, money and rich implements of war. The merchant Amylej had just purchased many of these things, and among them two pieces of beautiful Flemish broadcloth. Macko sold the splendid armor, because he thought that he would have no use for it. The merchant sold it the next day to Marcin of Wrocimowice, whose coat of arms was Polkoza. He sold it for a large sum, because in those times the suits of armor made in Milan were considered the best in the world and were expensive. Zbyszko regretted very much that they sold it.

"If God give you back your health," said he, to his uncle, "where will you find another like it?"

"There, where I found this one; on some German," answered Macko. "But I shall not escape death. The head of the spear will not come out from my body. When I tried to pull it out with my hands, I pushed it in further. And now there is no help."

"You must drink two or three pots of bear's grease."

"Bah! Father Cybek also said that would be a good thing. But where can I get it here? In Bogdaniec one could very easily kill a bear!"

"Then we must go to Bogdaniec! Only you must not die on the road."

Old Macko looked at his nephew with tenderness.

"I know where you would like to go; to the Prince Janusz's court, or to Jurand of Spychow, and fight the Germans of Chelminsko."

"I will not deny it. I would be glad to go to Warszawa with the princess' court, or to go to Ciechanow; and I would remain as long as possible with Danusia, because now she is not only my lady, but my love also. I tremble when I think of her! I shall follow her even to the end of the world; but now you are first. You did not desert me, therefore I will never abandon you. We must go to Bogdaniec."

"You are a good man," said Macko.

"God would punish me, if I were not mindful of you. Look, they are getting ready! I ordered one wagon to be filled with hay. Amylejowna has made us a present of a feather bed, but I am afraid it will be too warm for you. We will travel slowly, in company with the princess' court, so that you may have good care. When they turn toward Mazowsze, we will turn toward home; may God help us!"

"If I can only live long enough to rebuild the *grodek*!" exclaimed Macko. "I know that after my death, you will not think anything more about Bogdaniec."

"Why will I not?"

"Because your head will be filled with thoughts of battles and of love."

"Did you not think yourself about war? I have planned what I must do; in the first place, I will rebuild the *grodek*."

"Do you mean to do that?" asked Macko, "Well, and when the *grodek* is finished?"

"When the *grodek* is rebuilt, then I will go to Warszawa to the prince's court, or to Ciechanow."

"After my death?"

"If you die soon, then after your death; but before I go, I will bury you properly; if the Lord Jesus restore your health, then you will remain in Bogdaniec. The princess promised me that I should receive my knightly girdle from the prince. Otherwise Lichtenstein will not fight with me."

"Then afterward you will go to Marienburg?"

"To Marienburg, or even to the end of the world to reach Lichtenstein."

"I do not blame you for it! Either he or you must die!"

"I will bring his girdle and his gloves to Bogdaniec; do not be frightened!"

"You must look out for treachery. There is plenty among them."

"I will bow to Prince Janusz and ask him to send to the grand master for a safe conduct. There is peace now. I will go to Marienburg, where there are always many knights. Then you know? In the first place, Lichtenstein; then I will look for those who wear peacock's tufts, and I will challenge them in turn. If the Lord Jesus grant me victory, then I will fulfill my vow."

Speaking thus, Zbyszko smiled at his own thoughts; his face was like that of a lad who tells what knightly deeds he will perform when he is a man.

"Hej!" said Macko; "if you defeat three knights belonging to great families, then you will not only fulfill your vow, but you will bring some booty!"

"Three!" exclaimed Zbyszko. "In the prison I promised myself, that I would not be selfish with Danusia. As many knights as I have fingers on both hands!"

Macko shrugged his shoulders.

"Are you surprised?" said Zbyszko. "From Marienburg I shall go to Jurand of Spychow. Why should I not bow to him, he is Danusia's father? With him I shall attack the Germans of Chelminsko. You told me yourself that in the whole of Mazowsze there was no greater ware-wolf against the Germans."

"And if he will not give you Danusia?"

"Why not? He is seeking his vengeance. I am searching for mine. Can he find a better man? And then, the princess has given her consent for the betrothal; he will not refuse."

"I see one thing," said Macko, "you will take all the people from Bogdaniec in order to have a retinue, as is proper for a knight, and the land will remain without hands to till it. As long as I live, I will not let you do it; but after my death, I see, you will take them."

"The Lord God will help me to get a retinue; Janko of Tulcza is a relation of ours and he will help me also."

At that moment the door opened, and as though to prove that the Lord God would help Zbyszko get a retinue, two men entered. They were dark-complexioned, short, dressed in Jewish-like yellow caftans, red caps and very wide trousers. They stopped in the doorway and touched their fingers to their foreheads, to their mouths, and then to their chests; then they bowed to the ground.

"Who are these devils?" asked Macko. "Who are you?"

"Your slaves," answered the newcomers in broken Polish.

"For what reason? Where from? Who sent you here?"

"*Pan* Zawisza sent us here as a present to the young knight, to be his slaves."

"O for God's sake! two men more!" exclaimed Macko, joyfully.

"Of what nationality are you?"

"We are Turks!"

"Turks?" repeated Zbyszko. "I shall have two Turks in my retinue. Have you ever seen Turks?"

And having jumped toward them, he began to turn them around and to look at them curiously. Macko said:

"I have never seen them; but I have heard, that the *Pan* of Garbow has Turks in his service whom he captured while fighting on the Danube with the Roman emperor, Zygmunt. How is it? Are you heathens, your dog-brothers?"

"The lord ordered us to be baptized," said one of the slaves.

"Did you have no money for ransom?"

"We are from far lands, from Asiatic shores, from Brussa."

Zbyszko, who always listened gladly to war stories, and especially when there was anything told about the deeds of the famous Zawisza of Garbow, began to inquire how they were captured. But there was nothing extraordinary in their narration; Zawisza attacked them in a ravine, part of them perished and part were captured; and he sent the prisoners as presents to his different friends. Zbyszko and Macko's hearts were throbing at the sight of such a noble gift, especially as it was difficult to get men in those days and the possession of them constituted true wealth.

In the meanwhile, Zawisza himself accompanied by Powala and Paszko Zlodzie; of Biskupice arrived. As they had all worked hard to free

58

Zbyszko, they were pleased when they succeeded; therefore everyone of them gave him some present as a souvenir. The liberal *Pan* of Taczew gave him a beautiful large caparison embroidered with gold; Paszko, a Hungarian sword and ten *grzywiens*.[60] Then came Lis of Targowisko, Farurej and Krzon of Kozieglowy, with Marcin of Wrocimowice and finally Zyndram of Maszkow; everyone brought rich presents.

Zbyszko welcomed them with a joyful heart, feeling very happy on account of the presents and because the most famous knights in the kingdom were showing him their friendship. They asked him about his departure and Macko's health, recommending to the latter, different remedies which would miraculously heal wounds.

But Macko recommended Zbyszko to their care, being ready himself for the other world. He said that it was impossible to live with an iron spear head between the ribs. He complained also that he spit blood and could not eat. A quart of shelled nuts, a sausage two spans long and a dish of boiled eggs were all he could eat at once. Father Cybek had bled him several times, hoping in that way to draw out the fever from around his heart, and restore his appetite; but it had not helped him any.

But he was so pleased with the presents given to his nephew, that at that moment he was feeling better, and when the merchant, Amylej, ordered a barrel of wine brought in honor of such famous guests, Macko drank with them. They began to talk about Zbyszko's deliverance and about his betrothal with Danusia. The knights did not doubt that Jurand of Spychow would give his consent, especially if Zbyszko avenged the death of Danusia's mother and captured the peacock tufts.

"But as for Lichtenstein," said Zawisza, "I do not think he will accept your challenge, because he is a friar, and also one of the officers in the Order. Bah! The people of his retinue told me that perhaps he would be elected grand master!"

"If he refuse to fight, he will lose his honor," said Lis of Targowisko.

"No," answered Zawisza, "because he is not a lay knight; and a friar is not permitted to fight in single combat."

"But it often happens that they do fight."

"Because the Order has become corrupt. The knights make different vows; but they often break them, thus setting a bad example to the whole Christian world. But a Krzyzak, especially a *comthur*, is not obliged to accept a challenge."

"Ha! Then only in war can you reach him."

"But they say, that there will be no war," said Zbyszko, "because the Knights of the Cross are afraid of our nation."

To this Zyndram of Maszkow said:

"This peace will not last long. There cannot be a good understanding with the wolf, because he must live on the goods of others."

"In the meantime, perhaps we will be obliged to fight with Tymur the Lame," said Powala. "Prince Witold was defeated by Edyga; that is certain."

"Certain. *Wojewoda* Spytko will not return," said Paszko Zlodziej of Biskupice.

"The late queen prophesied it would be so," said the *Pan* of Taczew.

"Ha! Then perhaps we will be obliged to go against Tymur."

Here the conversation was tunned to the Lithuanian expedition against the Tartars. There was no doubt that Prince Witold, that able commander being rather impetuous, had been badly defeated at Worskla, where a great number of the Lithuanian *bojars* and also a few Polish knights were killed. The knights now gathered in Amylej's house, pitied especially Spytek of Melsztyn, the greatest lord in the kingdom, who went with the expedition as a volunteer; and after the battle he was lost—nobody knew where. They praised his chivalrous deed, and told how he, having received from the commander of the enemy a protective *kolpak*,[61] would not wear it during the battle, preferring honorable death to life granted him by the ruler of a heathen nation. But it was not certain yet, whether he had perished, or was in captivity. If he were a prisoner, he could pay his ransom himself, because his riches were enormous, and he also held in fief the whole Podole from King Wladyslaw.

But the defeat of Witold's army might prove ruinous to the whole of Jagiello's empire. Nobody knew when the Tartars, encouraged by the victory over Witold, might now invade the lands and cities belonging to the grand dukedom. In that case the kingdom of Poland would be involved in a war. Therefore many knights, who like Zawisza, Farurej, Dobko and even Powala, were accustomed to seek adventures and fights in foreign countries, remained in Krakow not knowing what might soon happen. In case Tamerlan, who was the ruler of twenty-seven states, moved the whole Mongolian world, then the peril to the kingdom would be great.

"If it be necessary, then we will measure our swords with the Lame. With us it will not be such an easy matter as it was with those other nations, which he conquered and exterminated. Then the other Christian princes will help us."

To this Zyndram of Maszkow, who especially hated the Order, said bitterly:

"I do not know about the princes; but the Knights of the Cross are ready to become friends even with the Tartars and attack us from the other side."

"Then we shall have a war!" exclaimed Zbyszko. "I am against the Krzyzaks!"

But the other knights began to contradict Zyndram. "The Knights of the Cross have no fear of God, and they seek only their own advantage; but they will not help the pagans against Christian people. And then Tymur is at war somewhere in Asia, and the commander of the Tartars, Edyga, lost so heavily in the battle, that he is afraid even of victory. Prince Witold is a man full of expedients, and you may be sure he took precautions; and even if this time the Lithuanians were not successful, at any rate it is not a new thing for them to overcome the Tartars."

"We have to fight for life and death; not with the Tartars but with the Germans," said Zyndram of Maszkow, "and if we do not crush them, our peril will come from them."

Then he turned toward Zbyszko:

"And in the first place Mazowsze will perish. You will always find plenty to do there; be not afraid!"

"Hej! if my uncle were well, I would go there immediately."

"God help you!" said Powala, raising a glass.

"Yours and Danusia's health!"

"To the destruction of the Germans!" added Zyndram of Maszkow.

Then they began to say farewell. At that moment one of the princess' courtiers entered with a falcon on his arm; and having bowed to the knights who were present, he turned with a peculiar smile to Zbyszko:

"The lady princess wished me to tell you," said he, "that she will stay in Krakow over night, and will start on the journey to-morrow."

"That is well," said Zbyszko; "but why? Is anybody sick?"

"No. But the princess has a visitor from Mazowsze."

"The prince himself?"

"Not the prince, but Jurand of Spychow," answered the courtier.

Having heard this, Zbyszko became very much confused, and his heart began to throb as it did when they read the sentence of death to him.

CHAPTER II.

Princess Anna was not much surprised at the arrival of Jurand of Spychow. It used to happen, that during the continual attacks and fights with neighboring German knights, a sudden longing for Danusia seized him. Then he would appear unexpectedly in Warszawa, in Ciechanow, or wherever Prince Janusz's court was situated for the time being.

Every time he saw the child, his grief burst forth anew because Danusia looked like her mother. The people thought that his iron heart filled with feelings of vengeance, would become softer through such grief. The princess often tried to persuade him to abandon his bloody Spychow, and remain at the court near Danusia. The prince himself, appreciating his bravery and importance, and at the same time wishing to spare him the fatigue inevitable in the quarrels on the frontier, offered him the office of sword bearer. It was always in vain. The sight of Danusia opened the old wounds in his heart. After a few days he always lost his appetite, could not sleep, and became silent. Evidently his heart began to bleed, and finally he would disappear from the court and returned to the marshes of Spychow, in order to drown in blood his grief and anger. Then the people used to say: "Woe to the Germans! It is true they are not sheep; but they are sheep to Jurand, because he is a wolf to them." In fact, after a time, the news would spread about the volunteers who, going to join the Knights of the Cross, were captured on their journey; about burned towns, and captured peasants; or about deadly fights from which the terrible Jurand always emerged victorious. On account of the rapacious disposition of the Mazurs and of the German knights who were holding the land and the strongholds from the Order, even during the greatest peace between the prince of Mazowsze and the Order, continual fighting was going on near the frontier. Even when cutting wood in the forests or harvesting in the fields, the inhabitants used to carry their arms. The people living there felt no certainty for the morrow; were in continual readiness for war, and were hard-hearted. Nobody was satisfied with defence only; but for pillage repaid with pillage; for conflagration, with conflagration; for invasion, with invasion. It often happened that while the Germans were stealing through the forest, to attack some stronghold and to seize the peasants or the cattle, at the same time, the Mazurs were doing the same. Sometimes they met, then they fought; but often only the leaders challenged each other for a deadly fight, after which the conqueror took the retinue of his defeated adversary. Therefore, when complaints were received at the Warsavian court about Jurand, the prince used to reply with complaints about the attacks made by the Germans. Thus both sides asked for justice, but neither was willing to grant it; all robberies, conflagrations and invasions went unpunished.

But Jurand dwelling in Spychow, surrounded by marshes overgrown with rushes, and being filled with an unquenchable desire for vengeance, was so dreaded by his German neighbors, that finally their fear became greater than their courage. The lands bordering upon Spychow, were lying fallow; the forests were overgrown with wild hops and the meadows with reeds. Several German knights tried to settle in the neighborhood of Spychow; but everyone of them after a time, preferred to abandon his estate held in fief, his herds and his peasants, rather than live near this implacable man. Very often the knights planned a common expedition against Spychow; but everyone ended in defeat. They tried different means. One time they brought from the province of Mein, a knight noted for his strength and cruelty, and who had always been victorious in all fights. He challenged Jurand. But as soon as they entered the lists, the German was so frightened at the sight of the dreadful Mazur, that he wheeled his horse intending to flee; Jurand pierced his defenceless back with a spear, and in that way dishonored him forever. After that still greater fear filled the neighbors, and if a German perceived even from afar Spychowian smoke, he immediately crossed himself and began to pray to his patron in heaven. It was generally believed that Jurand had sold his soul to the evil one for the sake of vengeance.

The people told dreadful tales about Spychow: they said that the path leading to it through the quaggy marshes which were overgrown with duck weed and had bottomless depths, was so narrow that two men on horseback could not ride abreast; that on each side there were many Germans' bones, and that during the night, the heads of drowned men were seen walking on spiders' legs, howling and drawing travelers on horses into the depths. They also said that the gate in the *grodek* was ornamented with skeletons. These stories were not true. But in the barred pits dug under the house in Spychow, there were always many groaning prisoners; and Jurand's name was more dreadful than those tales about the skeletons and drowned people.

Zbyszko having learned of Jurand's arrival, hastened to him, but with a certain uneasiness in his heart because he was Danusia's father. Nobody could forbid him choose Danusia for the lady of his thoughts; but afterward the princess had betrothed them. What will Jurand say to that? Will he consent? What will happen if he refuse his consent? These questions filled his heart with fear, because he now cared for Danusia more than for anything else in the world. He was only encouraged by the thought that perhaps Jurand would praise him for having attacked Lichtenstein, because he had done it to avenge Danusia's mother; and in consequence had nearly lost his own head.

In the meantime he began to question the courtier, who had come to Amylej's for him:

"Where are you conducting me?" asked he; "to the castle?"

"Yes, to the castle. Jurand is with the princess' court."

"Tell me, what kind of a man he is, so that I may know how to talk with him!"

"What can I tell you! He is a man entirely different from other men. They say that he was mirthful before his blood became seared in his heart!"

"Is he clever?"

"He is cunning; he robs others but he does not let others rob him. Hej! He has only one eye, because the other was destroyed by the thrust of a German crossbow; but with that one, he can look a man through and through. He loves no one except the princess, our lady; and he loves her because his wife was a lady from her court, and now his daughter is with her."

Zbyszko breathed.

"Then you think that he will not oppose the princess' will?"

"I know what you would like to learn, and therefore I will tell you what I heard. The princess spoke to him about your betrothment, because it would not be proper to conceal it from him; but it is not known what he said in reply."

While thus speaking, they arrived at the gate. The captain of the archers, the same who had conducted Zbyszko to the scaffold, now saluted them. After having passed the guards, they entered the court-yard and turned to the left toward the part of the castle occupied by the princess.

The courtier meeting a servant in the doorway, asked:

"Where is Jurand of Spychow?"

"In the '*krzywy*[62] room' with his daughter."

"It is there," said the courtier, pointing at the door.

Zbyszko crossed himself, raised the curtain in the doorway, and entered with throbbing heart. But he did not perceive Jurand and Danusia at once, because the room was not only "crooked" but dark also. But after a while he saw the fair head of the girl, who was sitting on her father's lap. They did not hear him when he entered; therefore e stopped near the door, and finally he said:

"May He be blessed!"

"For ages and ages," answered Jurand, rising.

At that moment Danusia sprang toward the young knight and having seized him with both hands, began to scream:

"Zbyszku! *Tatus*[63] is here!"

Zbyszko kissed her hands; then he approached Jurand, and said:

"I came to bow to you; you know who I am."

And he bent slightly, making a movement with his hands as if he wished to seize Jurand by his knees. But Jurand grasped his hand, turned him toward the light and began to look at him.

Zbyszko had already regained his self-possession; therefore he looked with curiosity at Jurand. He beheld before him a gigantic man with fallow hair and moustache, with a face pitted with smallpox and one eye of iron-like color. It seemed to him as if this eye would pierce him, and he again became confused. Finally, not knowing what to say, but wishing to say something to break the embarrassing silence, he asked:

"Then you are Jurand of Spychow, Danusia's father?"

But the other only pointed to an oaken bench, standing beside the chair on which he sat himself and continued to look at Zbyszko, who finally became impatient, and said:

"It is not pleasant for me to sit as though I were in a court."

Then Jurand said:

"You wanted to fight with Lichtenstein?"

"Yes!" answered Zbyszko.

In the eye of the Lord of Spychow shone a strange light and his stern face began to brighten. After awhile he looked at Danusia and asked;

"And was it for her?"

"For no other! My uncle told you that I made a vow to her to tear the peacock tufts from German heads. But now there shall be not only three of them, but at least as many as I have fingers on both hands. In that way I will help you to avenge the death of Danusia's mother."

"Woe to them!" answered Jurand.

Then there was silence again. But Zbyszko, having noticed that by showing his hatred of the Germans, he would capture Jurand's heart, said:

"I will not forgive them! They nearly caused my death."

Here he turned to Danusia and added:

"She saved me."

"I know," said Jurand.

"Are you angry?"

"Since you made a vow to her, you must serve her, because such is the knightly custom."

Zbyszko hesitated; but after awhile, he began to say with evident uneasiness:

"Do you know that she covered my head with her veil? All the knights and also the Franciscan who was with me holding the cross, heard her say: 'He is mine!' Therefore I will be loyal to her until death, so help me God!"

Having said this, he kneeled, and wishing to show that he was familiar with the customs of chivalry, he kissed both of Danusia's shoes with great reverence. Then he arose and having turned to Jurand, asked him:

"Have you ever seen another as fair as she?"

Jurand suddenly put his hands behind his head, and having closed his eyes, he said loudly:

"I have seen one other; but the Germans killed her."

"Then listen," said Zbyszko, enthusiastically; "we have the same wrong and the same vengeance. Those dog-brothers also killed my people from Bogdaniec. You cannot find a better man for your work. It is no new thing for me! Ask my uncle. I can fight either with spear or axe, short sword or long sword! Did my uncle tell you about those Fryzjans? I will slaughter the Germans for you like sheep; and as for the girl, I vow to you on my knees that I will fight for her even with the *starosta* of hell himself, and that I will give her up neither for lands nor for herds, nor for any other thing! Even if some one offered me a castle with glass windows in it but without her, I would refuse the castle and follow her to the end of the world."

Jurand sat for awhile with his head between his hands; but finally he awakened as from a dream, and said with sadness and grief:

"I like you, young man, but I cannot give her to you; she is not destined for you, my poor boy."

Zbyszko hearing this, grew dumb and began to look at Jurand with wondering eyes.

But Danusia came to his help. Zbyszko was dear to her, and she was pleased to be considered not "a bush" but "a grown-up girl." She also liked the betrothal and the dainties which the knight used to bring her every day; therefore when she understood that she was likely to lose all this, she slipped down from the arm chair and having put her head on her father's lap, she began to cry:

"*Tatulu, Tatulu!*"[64] He evidently loved her better than anything else, for he put his hand softly on her head, while from his face disappeared all trace of deadly grudge and anger; only sadness remained.

In the meantime Zbyszko recovered his composure, and now said:

"How is it? Do you wish to oppose God's will?"

To this Jurand replied:

"If it be God's will, then you will get her; but I cannot give you my consent. Bah! I would be glad to do it, but I cannot."

Having said this, he arose, took Danusia in his arms, and went toward the door. When Zbyszko tried to detain him, he stopped for a moment and said:

"I will not be angry with you if you render her knightly services; but do not ask me any questions, because I cannot tell you anything."

And he went out.

CHAPTER III.

The next day Jurand did not avoid Zbyszko at all; and he did not prevent him from performing for Danusia, during the journey, those different services which, being her knight, he was obliged to render her. On the contrary, Zbyszko noticed that the gloomy *Pan* of Spychow looked at him kindly, as if he were regretting that he had been obliged to refuse his request. The young *wlodyka* tried several times to have some conversation with him. After they started from Krakow, there were plenty of opportunities during the journey, because both accompanied the princess on horseback; but as soon as Zbyszko endeavored to learn something about the secret difficulties separating him from Danusia, the conversation was suddenly ended.

Jurand's face became gloomy, and he looked at Zbyszko uneasily as if he were afraid he would betray himself.

Zbyszko thought that perhaps the princess knew what the obstacle was; so having an opportunity to speak to her privately, he inquired; but she could not tell him anything.

"Certainly there is some secret," she said. "Jurand himself told me that; but he begged me not to question him further, because he not only did not wish to tell what it was, but he could not. Surely he must be bound by some oath, as so often happens among the knights. But God will help us and everything will turn out well."

"Without Danusia I will be as unhappy as a chained dog or a bear in a ditch," answered Zbyszko. "There will be neither joy nor pleasure, nothing but sorrow and sighing; I will go against the Tartars with Prince Witold and may they kill me there. But first I must accompany uncle to Bogdaniec, and then tear from German heads the peacock's tufts as I promised. Perhaps the Germans will kill me; and I prefer such a death rather than to live and see some one else take Danusia."

The princess looked at him with her kind blue eyes, and asked him, with a certain degree of astonishment:

"Then you would permit it?"

"I? As long I have breath in my nostrils, it will not happen, unless my hand be paralyzed, and I be unable to hold my axe!"

"Then you see!"

"Bah! But how can I take her against her father's will?"

To this the princess said, as to herself:

"Does it not happen that way sometimes?"

Then to Zbyszko:

"God's will is stronger than a father's will. What did Jurand say to you? He said to me 'If it be God's will, then he will get her.'"

"He said the same to me!" exclaimed Zbyszko.

"Do you not see?"

"It is my only consolation, gracious lady."

"I will help you, and you can be sure of Danusia's constancy. Only yesterday I said to her: 'Danusia, will you always love Zbyszko?' And she answered: 'I will be Zbyszko's and no one else's.' She is still a green berry, but when she promises anything, she keeps her word, because she is the daughter of a knight. Her mother was like her."

"Thank God!" said Zbyszko.

"Only remember to be faithful to her also; man is inconstant; he promises to love one faithfully, and afterward he promises another."

"May Lord Jesus punish me if I prove such!" exclaimed Zbyszko energetically.

"Well, remember then. And after you have conveyed your uncle to Bogdaniec, come to our court; there will be some opportunity for you to win your spurs; then we will see what can be done. In the meanwhile Danusia will mature, and she will feel God's will; although she loves you very much even now, it is not the same love a woman feels. Perhaps Jurand will give his consent, because I see he likes you. You can go to Spychow and from there can go with Jurand against the Germans; it may happen that you will render him some great service and thus gain his affection."

"Gracious princess, I have thought the same; but with your sanction it will be easier."

This conversation cheered Zbyszko. Meanwhile at the first baiting place, old Macko became worse, and it was necessary to remain until he became better. The good princess,

Anna Danuta, left him all the medicine she had with her; but she was obliged to continue her journey; therefore both *wlodykas* of Bogdaniec bid those belonging to the Mazovian court farewell. Zbyszko prostrated himself at the princess' feet, then at Danusia's; he promised her once more to be faithful and to meet her soon at Ciechanow or at Warszawa; finally he seized her in his strong arms, and having lifted her, he repeated with a voice full of emotion:

"Remember me, my sweetest flower! Remember me, my little golden fish!"

Danusia embraced him as though he were a beloved brother, put her little cheek to his face and wept copiously.

"I do not want to go to Ciechanow without Zbyszko; I do not want to go to Ciechanow!"

Jurand saw her grief, but he was not angry. On the contrary, he bid the young man good-bye kindly; and after he had mounted, he turned toward him once more, and said:

"God be with you; do not bear ill will toward me."

"How can I feel ill will toward you; you are Danusia's father!" answered Zbyszko cordially; then he bent to his stirrup, and the old man shook hands with him, and said:

"May God help you in everything! Understand?"

Then he rode away. But Zbyszko understood that in his last words, he wished him success; and when he went back to the wagon on which Macko was lying, he said:

"Do you know I believe he is willing; but something hinders him from giving his consent. You were in Spychow and you have good common sense, try to guess what it is."

But Macko was too ill. The fever increased so much toward evening, that he became delirious. Therefore instead of answering Zbyszko, he looked at him as if he were astonished; then he asked:

"Why do they ring the bells?"

Zbyszko was frightened. He feared that if the sick man heard the sound of bells, it was a sign that death would soon come. He feared also that the old man might die without a priest and without confession, and therefore go, if not to hell, then at least for long centuries to purgatory; therefore he determined to resume their journey, in order to reach, as soon as possible, some parish in which Macko could receive the last sacraments.

Consequently they started and traveled during the night. Zbyszko sat in the wagon on the hay, beside the sick man and watched him till day-break. From time to time he gave him wine to drink. Macko drank it eagerly, because it relieved him greatly. After the second quart he recovered from his delirium; and after the third, he fell asleep; he slept so well that Zbyszko bent toward him from time to time, to ascertain if he was still alive.

Until the time of his imprisonment in Krakow, he did not realize how dearly he loved this uncle who replaced, for him, father and mother. But now he realized it very well; and he felt that after his uncle's death, life would be very lonesome for him, alone, without relatives, except the abbot who held Bogdaniec in pledge, without friends and without anyone to help him. The thought came to him that if Macko died, it would be one more reason for vengeance on the Germans, by whose means he had nearly lost his head, by whom all his forefathers had been killed, also Danusia's mother and many other innocent people, whom he knew or about whom he had heard from his acquaintances—and he began to say to himself:

"In this whole kingdom, there is no man who has not suffered some wrong from them, and who would not like to avenge those wrongs." Here he remembered the Germans with whom he fought at Wilno, and he knew that even the Tartars were less cruel.

The coming dawn interrupted his thoughts. The day was bright but cold. Evidently Macko felt better, because he was breathing more regularly and more quietly. He did not awaken until the sun was quite warm; then he opened his eyes and said:

"I am better. Where are we?"

"We are approaching Olkusk. You know, where they dig silver."

"If one could get that which is in the earth, then one could rebuild Bogdaniec!"

"I see you are better," answered Zbyszko laughing. "Hej! it would be enough even for a stone castle! We will go to the *fara*,[65] because there the priests will offer us hospitality and you will be able to make your confession. Everything is in God's hands; but it is better to have one's conscience clear."

"I am a sinner and will willingly repent," answered Macko. "I dreamed last night that the devils were taking my skin off. They were talking German. Thanks be to God that I am better. Have you slept any?"

"How could I sleep, when I was watching you?"

"Then lie down for a while. When we arrive, I will awaken you."

"I cannot sleep!"

"What prevents you?"

Zbyszko looked at his uncle and said:

"What else can it be, if not love? I have pain in my heart; but I will ride on horseback for a while, that will help me."

He got down from the wagon, and mounted the horse, which his servant brought for him; meanwhile, Macko touched his sore side; but he was evidently thinking about something else and not about his illness, because he tossed his head, smacked his lips and finally said:

"I wonder and wonder, and I cannot wonder enough, why you are so eager for love, because your father was not that way, and neither am I."

But Zbyszko, instead of answering, stretched himself on the saddle, put his hands on his hips, gave his head a toss and sang:

"I cried the whole night, cried in the morning,
Where have you been, my sweet girl, my darling!
It will not help me, if I mourn for thee,
Because I am quite sure, you will not see me."

"Hej!"

This "hej" resounded in the forest, reverberated against the trunks of the trees, finally reëchoed in the far distance and then was lost in the thickets.

Again Macko felt his side, in which the German spearhead had lodged and said, moaning a little:

"Formerly the people were wiser!"

Then he became thoughtful, as if recollecting the old times; and he added:

"Although even then some of them were stupid also."

But, in the meantime, they emerged from the forest, behind which they perceived the miners' sheds, and further walls, built by King Kazimierz, and the tower of the *fara* erected by Wladyslaw Lokietek.

The canon of the *fara* heard Macko's confession and offered them hospitality; they remained there over night, and started the next morning. Beyond Olkusk, they turned toward Szlonsk,[66] and on its boundaries, they proposed to ride toward Wielkopolska. The road was laid out through a large forest, in which there was heard toward sunset, the roaring of the urus and of the bison, and during the night the eyes of wolves were seen shining behind the thick hazelnut trees. But the greatest danger which threatened the traveler on this road, was from the German and Germanized knights of Szlonsk, whose castles were erected here and there near the boundaries. It is true, that because of the war with the Opolczyk, Naderspraw, whom the Silesians were helping against King Wladyslaw, the majority of these castles had been destroyed by Polish hands; it was necessary, however, to be watchful, and especially after sunset, and to have one's weapons ready.

They were riding so quietly, however, that Zbyszko found the journey tedious; when they were about one day's journey from Bogdaniec, they heard the snorting and trampling of horses behind them.

"Some people are following us," said Zbyszko.

Macko, who was awake, looked at the stars and answered like an experienced traveler:

"Day-break is near. Robbers do not attack toward the end of the night."

Zbyszko stopped the wagon; however, placed the men across the road, facing the advancing horses, and waited.

In fact, after a certain time he perceived in the dusk, several horsemen. One of them was riding ahead, and it was evident that he did not wish to hide, because he was singing.

66

Zbyszko could not hear the words of the song; but the gay "hoc! hoc!" with which the stranger ended each refrain, reached his ears.

"Our people!" he said to himself.

After a while he shouted, however:

"Stop!"

"And you sit down!" answered a joyous voice.

"Who are you?"

"And you?"

"Why do you follow us?"

"And why do you obstruct the road?"

"Answer, our crossbows are bent."

"And ours,—thrust out,—aimed!"

"Answer like a man, otherwise woe to you!"

To this a merry song was given, as an answer to Zbyszko.

"One misery with another
They are dancing on the crossway.
Hoc! Hoc! Hoc!
What use have they of dancing?
It's a good thing, anyhow.
Hoc! Hoc! Hoc!"

Zbyszko was amazed at hearing such an answer; meantime, the song stopped and the same voice asked:

"And how is the old man Macko? Does he still breathe?"

Macko rose in the wagon and said:

"For God's sake, they are some of our people!"

Zbyszko rushed forward.

"Who asks about Macko?"

"A neighbor. Zych of Zgorzelice. I have looked for you for a week and inquired about you from all on the road."

"*Rety!*[67] Uncle! Zych of Zgorzelice is here!" shouted Zbyszko.

They began to greet each other joyfully because Zych was really their neighbor, and also a good man of whom everybody was very fond on account of his mirth.

"Well, how are you?" asked he, shaking hands with Macko. "Still *hoc*, or no more *hoc*?"[68]

"Hej, no more *hoc*!" answered Macko. "But I see you gladly. Gracious God, it is as if I were already in Bogdaniec."

"What is the matter with you; I heard that the Germans had wounded you?"

"They did, dog-brothers! I A head of a spear stuck between my ribs."

"You see!" said Zbyszko, "everybody advises the grease of a bear. As soon as we reach Bogdaniec, I will go with an axe to the *barcie.*"[69]

"Perhaps Jagienka has some."

"What Jagienka? Your wife's name was Malgochna," said Macko.

"O! Malgochna is no more! It will be three years on St. Michael's day since Malgochna was buried in the priests' field. She was a sturdy woman; may the Lord make his face shine upon her soul! Jagienka is exactly like her, only younger."

"Behind a ravine, there is a mount,
As was mother, such is daughter.
Hoc! Hoc!"

"I told Malgochna not to climb the pine tree because she was no longer young. But she would climb it. The branch broke; she fell and was badly hurt; within three days, she died."

"Lord, make your face shine upon her soul!" said Macko. "I remember, I remember! When she was angry, the farm boys used to hide in the hay. But she was clever. So she fell from a pine tree!"

"She fell down like a cone. Do you know, after the funeral I was so stupefied with grief, that for three days they could not arouse me. They thought I was dead. Afterward, I wept for a long time. But Jagienka is also clever. She takes care of everything."

"I can scarcely remember her. She was not as large as the helve of an axe when I went away. She could pass under a horse without touching its body. Bah! that is a long time ago, and she must have grown."

"She was fifteen the day of St. Agnes; but I have not seen her for more than a year."

"Why have you not seen her? Where have you been?"

"To the war. I do not need to stay home; Jagienka takes care of everything."

Macko, although ill, began to listen attentively when the war was mentioned, and asked:

"Perhaps you were with *Kniaz* Witold at Worskla?"

"Yes, I was there," answered Zych of Zgorzelice gaily. "Well, the Lord God did not send him good luck; we were dreadfully defeated by Edyga. First they killed our horses. A Tartar will not attack you openly like a Christian knight, but throws his arrows from afar. You attack him and he flees, and then again throws his arrows. What can you do with such a man? In our army the knights boasted and said: 'We do not need to lower our spears, nor draw our swords; we will crush the vermin under our horses' feet.' So they boasted; but when the arrows began to twange, it grew dark they were so numerous, and the battle was soon over. Hardly one out of ten survived. Will you believe it? More than half of the army were slain; seventy Lithuanian and Russian princes lay dead on the battlefield; and one could not count in two weeks' time, the *bojars* and other courtiers, whom they call *otroks*, that were killed."

"I heard about it," interrupted Macko. "Many of our knights perished also."

"Bah! even ten Knights of the Cross were killed, because they were obliged to serve in Witold's army. Many of our people perished, because they, you know, never run away. *Kniaz* Witold had the greatest confidence in our knights and he wanted a guard of them round him during the battle, exclusively Poles. Hi! Hi! Great havoc was made among them; but he was not touched! *Pan* Spytko of Mielsztyn was killed, also the sword bearer, Bernat, Judge Mikolaj, Prokop, Przeclaw, Dobrogost, Jasko of Lazewice, Pilik Mazur, Warsz of Michow, *Wojewoda* Socha, Jasko of Dombrowa, Pietrko of Miloslaw, Szczepiecki, Oderski and Tomko Lagoda. Who can enumerate all of them! Some of them had been hit with so many arrows, that after death they looked like porcupines; it was awful to look at them!"

Here he laughed as if he were telling a most amusing story, and at once he began to sing:

"You have learned what is a Tartar,
When he beat you and flew afar!"

"Well, and what then?" asked Zbyszko.

"Then the grand duke escaped; but he was as courageous as he usually is. The more you press him, the farther he jumps, like a hazelnut stick. We rushed to the Tavanian ford to defend those crossing over. There were with us a few knights from Poland. The second day, Edyga came with a swarm of Tartars; but he could not do a thing. Hej! When he wanted to pass the ford, we fought him so hard he could not do it. We killed and caught many of them. I myself caught five Tartars, and I sent them to Zgorzelice. You will see what dogheads they have."

"In Krakow, they say that the war may reach Poland also."

"Do they think Edyga is a fool! He knows well what kind of knights we have; and he also knows that the greatest knights remained home, because the queen was not pleased when Witold began the war on his own authority. Ej, he is cunning, that old Edyga! He understood at Tavania that the prince's army had increased and had gone far beyond the tenth-land!"

"But you returned?"

"Yes, I returned. There is nothing to do there. In Krakow I heard about you, and that you had started a little ahead of me."

Here he turned to Zbyszko:

"Hej! my lord, the last time I saw you, you were a small boy; and now, although there is no light, I suppose you are large like an urus. And you had your crossbows ready! One can see you have been in the war."

"War has nurtured me since childhood. Let my uncle tell you if I am lacking in experience."

"It is not necessary for your uncle to tell me anything; in Krakow, I saw the *Pan* of Taczew who told me about you. But I understand that the Mazur does not want to give you his daughter. I have nothing against you; but I like you. You will forget about that one when you see my Jagienka. She is a wonder!"

"I shall not forget, even if I see ten such as your Jagna."

"She will get the estate of Moczydoly for her dowry. Many will ask me for Jagna, do not fear?"

Zbyszko wanted to answer: "But not I!" But Zych of Zgorzelice began to sing:
"I will bend to your knees
And you for that, will give me the girl,
    Give me the girl!"

"You are always happy and singing," said Macko.

"Well, and what do the blessed do in heaven."

"They sing."

"Well, then! And the damned cry. I prefer to go to those who sing rather than to those who cry; and St. Peter will say thus: 'We must let him into paradise; otherwise he will sing in hell, and that will not be right.' Look, the day breaks!"

In fact, daylight was coming. After awhile they arrived at a large glade. By the lake covering the greater part of the glade, some people were fishing; but seeing the armed men, they left their nets and immediately seized their picks and staffs and stood ready for battle.

"They thought we were robbers," said Zych, laughing. "Hej, fishermen! To whom do you belong?"

They stood for a while silently, looking distrustfully; but finally one of them having recognized that they were knights, answered:

"To the *ksiondz*, the abbot of Tulcza."

"Our relative," said Macko, "the same who holds Bogdaniec in pledge. These must be his forests; but he must have purchased them a short time ago."

"He did not buy them," answered Zych. "He was fighting about them with Wilk of Brzozowa and it seems that the abbot defeated Wilk. A year ago they were going to fight on horseback with spears and long swords for this part of the forest; but I do not know how it ended because I went away."

"Well, we are relatives," said Macko, "he will not quarrel with us."

"Perhaps; he is a chivalrous abbot who knows how to wear a helmet; but he is pious and he sings the mass beautifully. Don't you remember? When he shouts at mass, the swallows nested under the ceiling, fall from their nests. In that way God's glory increases."

"Certainly I remember! At ten steps he could blow the candles at the altar out. Has he been in Bogdaniec?"

"Yes, he was there. He settled five peasants on the land. He has also been at my house at Zgorzelice, because, as you know, he baptized Jagienka, of whom he is very fond and calls her little daughter."

"God will bless him if he be willing to leave me the peasants," said Macko.

"*Owa!* what will five peasants amount to! Then Jagienka will ask him and he will not refuse her."

Here the conversation stopped for a while, because over the dark forest and from the pink down, the bright sun had risen and lighted the environs. The knights greeted it with the customary: "May it be blessed!" and then having made the sign of the cross, they began their morning prayers.

Zych finished first and said to his companions:

"I hope to see you well soon. Hej! you have both changed. You, Macko, must regain your health. Jagienka will take care of you, because there is no woman in your house. One can see that you have a piece of iron between your ribs."

Here he turned toward Zbyszko:

"Show yourself also. Well, mighty God! I remember you when you were small and used to climb on the colts by the help of their tails; and now, what a knight! The face looks like that of a little lord; but the body like that of a sturdy man. Such can wrestle even with a bear."

"A bear is nothing for him!" said Macko. "He was younger than he is to-day, when that Fryzjan called him a beardless youth; and he resenting it, immediately pulled out the Fryzjan's mustaches."

"I know," interrupted Zych, "and you fought afterward, and captured their retinue. *Pan* of Taczew told me all about it:"

"There came a German very proud,
He was buried with sore snout;
Hoc! Hoc!"

Zbyszko wondered at Zych's long thin figure, at his thin face with its enormous nose and at his laughing round eyes.

"O!" said he, "with such a neighbor there will be no sadness, if God only restore my uncle's health."

"It is good to have a joyful neighbor, because with a jolly fellow there will be no quarrel," answered Zych. "Now listen to what I tell you. You have been away from home a long time, and you will not find much comfort in Bogdaniec. I do not say in the farming, because the abbot has taken care of that; he dug up a large piece of the forest and settled new peasants. But as he went there very often, you will find the larder empty; even in the house, there is hardly a bench or a bunch of straw to sleep on; and a sick man needs some comforts. You had better come with me to Zgorzelice. I will be glad to have you stay a month or two. During that time, Jagienka will take care of Bogdaniec. Rely on her and do not bother yourselves with anything. Zbyszko can go there, from time to time, to inspect the farming; I will bring the abbot to Zgorzelice, and you can settle your account with him. The girl will take good care of you, as of a father, and during illness, a woman's care is the best. Well, my dear friends, will you do as I ask you?"

"We know that you are a good man and you always were," answered Macko with emotion; "but don't you see, if I must die on account of this wound, I prefer to die in my own home. Then when one is home, although he is old, he can inquire about different things, can inspect and do many other things. If God order me to go to the other world, well, then I cannot help it! I cannot escape it even with better care. As for inconvenience, we are accustomed to that at the war. Even a bunch of straw is pleasant to that one who, during several years, has slept on the bare ground. But I thank you for your kind heart and if I be not able to show you my gratitude, God will permit Zbyszko to do it."

Zych of Zgorzelice, who was noted for his kind heart and readiness to oblige, began to insist: but Macko was firm: "If I must die, it will be better to die in my own courtyard!"

He had longed to see Bogdaniec for several years, therefore now, when he was so near it, he must go there, even if it were his last night. God was merciful, having permitted him who was so ill, to reach here.

He brushed away the tears gathered under his eyelids, with his hand, looked around and said:

"If these are the woods of Wilk of Bizozowa we will be home this afternoon."

"They do not belong to Wilk of Bizozowa any longer; but to the abbot," said Zych.

Macko smiled and said after awhile:

"If they belong to the abbot, then sometime, they may belong to us."

"Bah! awhile ago you were talking about death," said Zych joyfully, "and now you wish to outlive the abbot."

"No, I will not outlive him; but Zbyszko may."

Further conversation was interrupted by the sound of horns in the forest.

Zych stopped his horse and began to listen.

70

"Somebody is hunting," said he. "Wait."

"Perhaps it is the abbot. It would be pleasant to meet him here."

"Keep quiet!"

Here he turned to his retinue.

"Stop!"

They halted. The horns resounded nearer, and soon afterward the baying of dogs was heard.

"Stop!" repeated Zych. "They are coming toward us."

Zbyszko jumped from his horse and began to shout:

"Give me the crossbow! The beast may attack us! Hasten! Hasten!"

Having seized the crossbow from the servant's hands, he rested it against the ground, pressed it against his abdomen, bent, stretched his back like a bow, and having seized the string with the fingers of both hands, he pulled it on to the iron hook; then placed an arrow and sprang into the woods.

"He stretched it without a crank!" whispered Zych, astonished at such great strength.

"Ho, he is a strong boy!" answered Macko, proudly.

Meanwhile, the sound of horns and the barking of dogs stole nearer; all at once, at the right side of the forest, a heavy trampling resounded, accompanied by the crackling of broken branches and bushes—then out of the thicket rushed an old bearded urus, with his gigantic head lowered, with bloody eyes and panting tongue, breathless and terrible. Coming to a small ravine, he leaped it, but fell on his forelegs; but immediately he arose, and a few seconds later he would have disappeared in the thicket on the other side of the road, when the string of the crossbow twanged, the whistling of the arrow resounded, the beast reared, turned, roared dreadfully and fell on the ground as if he were struck by a thunderbolt.

Zbyszko leaped from behind a tree, again stretched the crossbow, and approached the bull who was pawing the ground with his hind feet.

But having glanced at it, he turned quietly toward the retinue, and began to shout from afar:

"I hit him so hard that he is severely wounded!"

"You are a strong boy!" said Zych, riding toward him, "with one arrow only!"

"Bah, it was near, and the speed was great. Come and see; not only the iron, but even the shaft has disappeared under the left shoulder bone."

"The huntsmen must be near; they will claim the beast."

"I will not give it to them!" answered Zbyszko. "It was killed on the road, and the road is not private property."

"But if it belong to the abbot?"

"Well, then he may have it."

Meanwhile, several dogs came out of the forest. Having perceived the animal, they rushed on him.

"Soon the huntsmen will appear," said Zych. "Look! There they are, but they do not see the beast yet. Stop! Stop! Here, here! Killed! Killed!"

Then he became silent, and sheltered his eyes with one hand; after a while, he said:

"For God's sake! what has happened? Have I become blind, or does it only seem so to me?"

"There is some one on a piebald horse in the front," said Zbyszko.

Then Zych exclaimed at once:

"Dear Jesus! It must be Jagienka!"

And he began to shout:

"Jagna! Jagna!"

Then he rushed forward; but before he could make his horse gallop, Zbyszko perceived a most wonderful spectacle; he beheld a girl sitting like a man, on a swift piebald horse, rushing toward them; she had a crossbow in one hand and a boar-spear on her shoulders. Her floating hair was full of hop strobiles; her face was bright like the dawn. Her shirt was opened on the bosom, and she wore a *serdak*.[70] Having reached them, she reined in her horse; for a while, her face expressed surprise, hesitation, joy; finally, being scarcely able to believe her own eyes, she began to cry in a childish voice:

71

"*Tatulo,*[71] *tatus*[71] dearest!"

In the twinkling of an eye, she jumped from her horse, and Zych dismounted also to welcome her; she threw her arms around his neck. Fora long time, Zbyszko heard only the sounds of kisses and these two words: "*Tatulo!* Jagula! *Tatulo!* Jagula!" repeated in a joyful outburst.

Both retinues now approached, and Macko arrived also; they continued to repeat: "*Tatulo!* Jagula!" and still kissed each other. Finally Jagienka asked:

"Then you decided to return from the war? Are you well?"

"From the war. Why should I not be well? And you? And the boys? Are they well also? Yes, otherwise you would not run in the forest. But, my girl, what are you doing here?"

"Don't you see that I am hunting?" answered Jagienka, laughing.

"In somebody else's woods?"

"The abbot gave me permission. He even sent me experienced huntsmen and a pack of hounds."

Here she turned to the servants:

"Chase the dogs away, they will tear the skin!"

Then to Zych:

"Oj, how glad I am to see you!" And they again kissed each other. When they were through, Jagna said:

"We are far from home; we followed the beast. I am sure it must be more than ten miles; the horses are exhausted. What a large urus! Did you notice? He must have at least three of my arrows in him; the last one killed him."

"He was killed by the last, but it was not yours; this knight killed him."

Jagienka threw her hair back and looked at Zbyszko sharply, but not very friendly.

"Do you know who he is?" asked Zych.

"I do not know."

"No wonder you do not recognize him, because he has grown. Perhaps you will recognize old Macko of Bogdaniec?"

"For God's sake! is that Macko of Bogdaniec?" exclaimed Jagienka.

Having approached the wagon, she kissed Macko's hand.

"It is you?"

"Yes, it is I; but I am obliged to ride in the wagon, because the Germans wounded me."

"What Germans? The war was with the Tartars?"

"There was a war with the Tartars, but we were not in that war; we fought in the war in Lithuania, Zbyszko and I."

"Where is Zbyszko?"

"Then you did not recognize Zbyszko?" said Macko smiling.

"Is that man Zbyszko?" exclaimed the girl, looking again at the young knight.

"Yes, it is he."

"You must give him a kiss, because he is an old acquaintance of yours," said Zych, mirthfully.

Jagienka turned gaily toward Zbyszko; but suddenly she retreated, and having covered her eyes with her hand, she said:

"I am bashful."

"But we have known each other since we were children," said Zbyszko.

"Aha! we know each other well. I remember when you made us a visit with Macko about eight years ago, and my *matula*[72] gave us some nuts with honey; you being the elder, struck me with your fist and then ate all the nuts yourself."

"He will not act like that now!" said Macko. "He has been with *Kniaz* Witold, and with the court in Krakow, and he has learned courtly manners."

But Jagienka was now thinking about something else; turning toward Zbyszko, she asked:

"Then you killed the urus?"

"Yes."

"We must see where the arrow is."

72

"You cannot see it; it disappeared under the shoulder bone."

"Be quiet; do not dispute," said Zych. "We all saw him shoot the urus, and we saw something still better; he bent the bow without a crank."

Jagienka looked at Zbyszko for the third time, but now with astonishment.

"You bent the crossbow without a crank?"

Zbyszko, detecting some doubt in her voice, rested the crossbow on the ground, and bent it in the twinkling of an eye; then wishing to show that he was familiar with knightly manners, he kneeled on one knee and handed the bow to Jagienka. But the girl, instead of taking it from him, suddenly blushed—she did not know why herself, and began to fasten the shirt, which, during the swift riding, had become opened on her bosom.

CHAPTER IV.

The next day after their arrival at Bogdaniec, Macko and Zbyszko began to look around their old home; they soon realized that Zych of Zgorzelice was right when he told them that at first they would be uncomfortable.

With the farming they could get along quite well. There were several fields cultivated by the peasants whom the abbot had settled there. Formerly there had been much cultivated land in Bogdaniec; but after the battle at Plowce[73] where the family Grady perished, there was a scarcity of working hands; and after the invasion of the Germans from Szlonsk and after the war of Nalenczs with Grzymalits, the formerly rich fields became overgrown with trees. Macko could not help it. In vain he tried for several years to bring farmers from Krzesnia and rent the land to them; they refused to come, preferring to remain on their own strips of land rather than to cultivate some one else's. His offer however attracted some shelterless men; in the different wars, he captured several slaves whom he married and settled in the houses; and in that way he populated the village. But it was hard work for him; therefore as soon as he had an opportunity, Macko pledged the whole of Bogdaniec, thinking that it would be easier for the powerful abbot to settle the land with peasants, and that the war would bring to him and to Zbyszko some people and money. In fact, the abbot was energetic. He had increased the working force of Bogdaniec with five peasant families; he increased the stock of cattle and horses; then he built a barn, a stable and a cow house. But as he did not live in Bogdaniec, he did not repair the house. Macko, who had hoped to find the *grodek* surrounded with a ditch and hedge when he returned, found everything just as he had left it, with this difference only, that the walls were more crooked and seemed to be lower, because they had settled deeper in the earth.

The house contained an enormous hall, two large rooms with alcoves, and a kitchen. In the rooms there were windows made of bladders; and in the centre of each room, there was a fireplace made of lime, and the smoke escaped through a hole in the ceiling. From the ceilings now blackened from smoke, during former times used to hang the hams of boars, bears and deer, rumps of roes, sides of beef and rolls of sausages. But now the hooks were empty as well as the shelves fastened to the walls, on which they used to put the tin and earthen dishes. The walls beneath the shelves were no longer empty, however, because Zbyszko had ordered his servants to hang helmets, cuirasses, long swords and short swords on them; and further along boar-spears and forks, caparisons and saddles. The smoke blackened the weapons, and it was necessary to clean them very often. But Macko, who was careful, ordered the servants to put the costly clothes in the alcove in which his bed stood.

In the front rooms there stood near the windows, pine tables and benches of the same, on which the lords used to sit during the meals, with all their servants. People accustomed to war were easily satisfied; but in Bogdaniec there was neither bread nor flour and no dishes. The peasants brought what they could; Macko expected that the neighbors, as was then customary, would help him; and he was not mistaken, at least as far as Zych of Zgorzelice was concerned.

The second day, when the old *wlodyka* was sitting on a log in front of the house, delighted with the bright autumn day, Jagienka came, riding a black horse; she dismounted and approached Macko, out of breath on account of fast riding, and rosy as an apple; she said:

"May you be blessed! *Tatulo* sent me to inquire about your health."

"I am no worse," answered Macko; "and at least I have slept in my own house."

"But you cannot be comfortable at all, and a sick person needs some care."

"We are hardened people. It is true that at first there was no comfort; but we were not hungry. We ordered an ox and two sheep killed, so there is plenty of meat. The women brought some flour and eggs; the worst is that we have no dishes."

"Well, I ordered my servants to load two wagons. On one there are two beds and dishes, and on the other different provisions. There are some cakes and flour, some salt pork and dried mushrooms; there is a barrel of beer and one of mead; in fact a little of everything we had in the house."

Macko, who was grateful for this kindness, caressed Jagienka's head, and said:

"May God reward your father and you. When our housekeeping improves, we will return the provisions."

"How clever you are! We are not like the Germans, who take back what they give."

"Well, so much more may God reward you. Your father told us what a good housekeeper you are, and that you had taken care of Zgorzelice the whole year?"

"Yes! If you need anything else, send somebody; but send some one who will know what is needed, because a stupid servant never knows what he has been sent for."

Here Jagienka began to look round, and Macko having noticed it, smiled and asked:

"For whom are you looking?"

"I am looking for no one!"

"I will send Zbyszko to thank you and your father. Do you like Zbyszko?"

"I have not looked at him."

"Then look at him now, because he is just coming."

In fact Zbyszko was coming from the stable. He was dressed in a reindeer jacket and round felt cap like those worn under the helmets; his hair was without a net, cut evenly over his eyebrows and hung in golden curls on his shoulders; he walked swiftly, having noticed the girl; he was tall and graceful, looking like the shield-bearer of a rich nobleman.

Jagienka turned toward Macko as if to show that she came only to see him; but Zbyszko welcomed her joyfully, and having taken hold of her hand, raised it to his mouth, notwithstanding her resistance.

"Why do you kiss my hand?" asked she. "Am I a priest?"

"Such is the custom; you must not resist."

"Even if he had kissed both your hands," said Macko, "it would not be enough for all that you have brought us."

"What have you brought?" asked Zbyszko, looking around the court-yard; but he did not see anything except the black horse tied to the post.

"The wagons have not come yet; but they will soon be here," answered Jagienka.

Macko began to enumerate what she had brought; but when he mentioned the two beds, Zbyszko said:

"I am satisfied to sleep on the urus' skin; but I thank you because you thought about me also."

"It was not I; it was *Tatulo*," answered the girl, blushing. "If you prefer to sleep on the skin, you can do it."

"I prefer to sleep on what I can. Sometimes after a battle, I slept with a dead Krzyzak instead of a pillow under my head."

"You do not mean to tell me that you have ever killed a Krzyzak? I am sure you have not."

Zbyszko, instead of answering, began to laugh. But Macko exclaimed:

"For heaven's sake, girl, you do not know him yet! He has never done anything else, but kill the Germans. He can fight with an axe, a spear or with any weapon; and when he sees a German from afar, one must tie him with a rope, or else he will rush against him. In Krakow he wanted to kill the envoy, Lichtenstein, and for that he barely escaped execution. Such a man! I will tell you also about the two Fryzes, from whom we took their retinues and so much rich booty, that one could redeem Bogdaniec with half of it."

Here Macko began to tell about his duel with the Fryzjans; also about other adventures which had happened to them, and about the deeds they had performed. How they had fought from behind the walls and in the open fields, with the greatest knights living in foreign lands; how they had fought Germans, Frenchmen, Englishmen and Burgundians. He also told her what they had seen! They had seen German castles of red brick, Lithuanian wooden *grodze*[74] and churches, more beautiful than one could see around Bogdaniec; also large cities and the dreadful wilderness in which during the nights Lithuanian gods cried, and many different, marvelous things; and everywhere, in any fight, Zbyszko was victorious, so that even the greatest knights were astonished at him.

Jagienka, who was sitting on the log beside Macko, listened with open mouth to that narrative, tossing her head and looking at the young knight with increasing admiration and amazement. Finally when Macko was through, she sighed and said:

"I am sorry I was not born a boy!"

But Zbyszko, who during the narration had been looking at her attentively, evidently was thinking about something else, because he suddenly said:

"What a beautiful girl you are now!"

Jagienka answered, half in displeasure and half in sadness:

"You have seen many more beautiful than I am."

But Zbyszko could truly answer her that he had not seen many as pretty as she, because Jagienka was beaming with health, youth and strength. The old abbot used to say that she looked like a pine tree. Everything was beautiful in her; a slender figure, a broad bosom that looked as if it were cut out of marble, a red mouth, and intelligent blue eyes. She was also dressed with more care than when in the forest with the hunting party. Around her neck she had a necklace of red beads; she wore a fur jacket opened in front and covered with green cloth, a homespun skirt and new boots. Even old Macko noticed this beautiful attire, and having looked at her for a moment, asked:

"Why are you dressed as if you were going to church?"

But instead of answering, she exclaimed:

"The wagons are coming!"

In fact the wagons now appeared and she sprang toward them, followed by Zbyszko. The unloading lasted quite a long time to the great satisfaction of Macko who looked at everything, and praised Jagienka all the time. It was dusk when the girl started home. While she was getting ready to mount her horse, Zbyszko suddenly caught her, and before she was able to say a word, lifted her into the saddle. Then she blushed like the dawn and turning her head toward him, said with emotion in her voice:

"What a strong boy you are!"

But he, not having noticed her confusion nor her blushes because it was dark, laughed and said:

"Are you not afraid of wild beasts? It is night!"

"There is a boar-spear in the wagon. Give it to me."

Zbyszko went to the wagon, took the boar-spear and handed it to Jagienka; then he said:

"Be in good health!"

"Be in good health!" she answered.

"May God reward you! To-morrow, or the day after, I will be in Zgorzelice to thank Zych and you for your kindness."

"Come! You will be welcome!"

Having touched her horse, she disappeared among the bushes growing on the sides of the road.

Zbyszko returned to his uncle.

"You must go inside."

But Macko answered, without moving from the log:

"Hej! I what a girl! I She made the court-yard brighter!"

"That is true!"

There was a moment of silence. Macko seemed to be thinking about something while looking at the stars; then he said, as if he were speaking to himself:

"She is pretty and a good housekeeper, although she is not more than fifteen years old."

"Yes!" answered Zbyszko. "Therefore old Zych loves her dearly."

"And he said that the estate of Moczydoly will be her dowry; and there on the pastures is a herd of mares with many colts."

"Are there not a great many marshes in the Moczydlowski estate?"

"Yes; but in those marshes there are plenty of beavers."

There was silence again. Macko looked intently at Zbyszko for a while, and finally he asked, "About what are you thinking?"

"Seeing Jagienka reminded me of Danusia, and something pricked me in the heart."

"Let us go into the house," answered the old *wlodyka*. "It is getting late."

Having risen with difficulty, he leaned on Zbyszko, who conducted him to the alcove.

The next day Zbyszko went to Zgorzelice, because Macko urged him. He also insisted that he take two servants with him for ostentation, and that he dress in his best clothes, to show respect and gratitude to Zych. Zbyszko did as he was asked and went attired as if for a wedding, in his *jaka* made of white satin, bordered with gold fringe and embroidered with gold griffins. Zych received him with open arms, with joy and with singing; as for Jagienka, when she entered, she stopped as if she were rooted to the ground and almost dropped the bucket of wine which she was carrying; she thought that a son of some king had arrived. She became timid and sat silently, rubbing her eyes from time to time as if she would like to awaken from a dream. The inexperienced Zbyszko thought that, for some reason unknown to him, she did not wish to talk to him; therefore he conversed only with Zych, praising his munificence and admiring the house at Zgorzelice, which in fact was quite different from that in Bogdaniec.

Everywhere comfort and wealth were evident. In the rooms there were windows with panes made of horn, cut in thin slices and polished so that it was as transparent as glass. Instead of fireplaces in the centre, there were large chimneys in the corners. The floors were made of larch tree planks, while on the walls were hung suits of armor and many polished dishes, also silver spoons. Here and there were costly rugs brought from the wars. Under the tables there were enormous urus' skins. Zych showed his riches willingly, saying that it was Jagienka's household. He conducted Zbyszko to the alcove, fragrant with rosin and peppermint, in which were hanging from the ceiling, large bunches of wolf skins, fox skins, beaver skins and marten skins. He showed to him the provisions of cheese, honey, wax, barrels of flour, pails of dried bread, hemp and dried mushrooms. Then he went with him to the granaries, barns, stables, cow houses, and to the sheds filled with plenty of hunting implements and nets. Zbyszko was so dazzled by all this wealth that during supper, he could not refrain from admiration.

"What a pleasure to live in Zgorzelice!" exclaimed he.

"In Moczydoly, there is almost the same wealth," answered Zych. "Do you remember Moczydoly? It is not far from Bogdaniec. Formerly our forefathers quarreled about the boundaries and challenged each other; but I shall not quarrel."

Here he filled Zbyszko's goblet with mead and said:

"Perhaps you would like to sing?"

"No," answered Zbyszko; "but I shall listen to you with pleasure."

"Zgorzelice will belong to the young bears."

"What do you mean by 'young bears?'"

"Why, Jagienka's brothers."

"Hej! they will not have to suck their paws during the winter."

"No; but Jagienka will also have plenty in Moczydoly."

"That is true!"

"Why don't you eat and drink? Jagienka, pour for him and for me."

"I am drinking and eating as much as I can."

"Ungird your belt; then you will be able to eat and drink more. What a beautiful girdle you have! Yon must have taken rich booty in Lithuania!"

"We cannot complain," answered Zbyszko, gladly seizing the opportunity to explain that the heirs of Bogdaniec were no longer *wlodykas*. "A part of our booty, we sold in Krakow and received forty silver *grzywiens* for it."

"You don't say so! Why, one can buy an estate for that."

76

"Yes. There was one Milanese armor which my uncle, expecting to die, sold for a good price."

"I know! Well, it is worth while to go to Lithuania. I wanted to go there also; but I was afraid."

"Of what? Of the Knights of the Cross?"

"Ej, who would be afraid of Germans? I was afraid of those heathenish gods or devils. It seems there are plenty of them in the woods."

"They do not have any other place for shelter, because their temples have been burned. Formerly they were well-to-do; but now they live on mushrooms and ants."

"Did you see them?"

"No, I did not see any myself; but I heard of people who had seen them. Sometimes one of them sticks out a hairy paw from behind a tree and shakes it, begging for something."

"Macko told me the same," answered Jagienka.

"Yes! He told me about it on the road," said Zych. "Well, no wonder! In our country also, although it has been a Christian country for a long time, one can hear laughter in the marshes; and although the priests scold about it in the churches, it is always good policy to put a dish filled with something to eat, for the little devils; otherwise they will scratch on the walls so much that one can hardly sleep. Jagienka, my dearest! put a dish at the threshold."

Jagienka took an earthen porringer full of noodles and cheese, and placed it at the threshold. Zych said:

"The priests scold! But the Lord Jesus will not be angry about a dish of noodles; and a god, as soon as his hunger is satisfied, will protect one from fire and from thieves."

Then he turned to Zbyszko:

"But will you not ungird yourself and sing a little?"

"You had better sing, or perhaps *Panna*[75] Jagienka will sing."

"We will sing by turns," exclaimed Zych. "We have a servant who will accompany us on a wooden fife. Call the boy!"

They called the servant who sat down on the bench and put the fife to his mouth, waiting to learn whom he was to accompany.

None of them wanted to be first. Finally Zych told Jagienka to begin; therefore Jagienka, although bashful because Zbyszko was present, rose from the bench and having put her hands under her apron, began:

"If I only could get
The wings like a birdie,
I would fly quickly
To my dearest Jasiek."

Zbyszko opened his eyes wide; then he jumped up and shouted:

"Where did you learn that song?"

Jagienka looked at him astonished.

"Everybody sings that. What is the matter with you?"

Zych thinking that Zbyszko was a little intoxicated, turned his jovial face toward him and said:

"Ungird! It will relieve you!"

But Zbyszko stood for a while with astonishment on his face; then, having recovered from his emotion, said to Jagienka:

"Excuse me, I suddenly remembered something. Sing further."

"Perhaps it makes you sad?"

"Ej, not at all!" he answered, with a quivering voice. "I could listen to it the whole night."

Then he sat down, covered his face with his hand, and listened.

Jagienka sang another couplet; but when she finished, she noticed a big tear rolling down Zbyszko's fingers.

Then she sat down beside him, and began to touch him with her elbow.

"What is the matter with you? I do not want to make you cry. Tell me what is the matter with you?"

"Nothing! Nothing!" answered Zbyszko, sighing. "I could tell you much. But it is over. I feel merry now."

"Perhaps you would like to have some sweet wine?"

"Good girl!" exclaimed Zych. "Call him 'Zbyszko,' and you call her 'Jagienka.' You have known each other since you were children."

Then he turned toward his daughter:

"Do not mind because he struck you when you were children. He will not do it now."

"I will not!" answered Zbyszko, mirthfully. "If she wishes, she may beat me now for it."

Then Jagienka, wishing to cheer him up, began to play that she was striking him with her little fist.

"Give us some wine!" shouted the merry *Pan* of Zgorzelice.

Jagienka sprang to the closet and brought out a jug of wine, two beautiful silver goblets, engraved by a silversmith of Wroclaw[76] and a couple of cheese.

Zych, being a little intoxicated, began to hug the jug and said to it as if he were talking to his daughter:

"Oj, my dear girl! What shall I do, poor man, when they take you from Zgorzelice; what shall I do?"

"And you must give her up soon!" said Zbyszko.

Zych began to laugh.

"Chy! Chy! The girl is only fifteen; but she is already fond of boys! When she sees one of them, she begins immediately to rub knee with knee!"

"*Tatusiu*[77] if you don't stop, I will leave you," said Jagienka.

"Don't go! It's better with you here." Then he continued to say to Zbyszko:

"Two of them visit us. One of them is young Wilk, the son of old Wilk of Bizozowa; the other is Cztan[78] of Rogow. If they meet you here, they will gnash their teeth, as they do at each other."

"Owa!" said Zbyszko. Then he turned to Jagienka and asked:

"Which do you prefer?"

"Neither of them."

"Wilk is a great boy," said Zych.

"Let him go in another direction!"

"And Cztan?"

Jagienka began to laugh:

"Cztan," said she, turning toward Zbyszko, "he has hair on his face like a goat; one can hardly see his eyes; and he has as much grease on him as a bear."

Zbyszko now touched his head with his hand as if he had just remembered something important, and said:

"I must ask you for one thing more; have you any bear's grease? I want to use it for medicine for my uncle; and I could not find any in Bogdaniec."

"We used to have some," answered Jagienka; "but the boys have used some to grease their bows, and the dogs have eaten the rest."

"Is there none left?"

"Not a bit!"

"Well, then, I must find some in the forest."

"Have a hunting party for bears; there are plenty of them; and if you want some hunting implements, we will lend you some."

"I cannot wait. I will go some night to a *barcie*."

"Take a few men with you."

"No, I shall not do that, for they will frighten the beast."

"But you will take a crossbow!"

"What can I do with a crossbow during the night? There is no moon now! I will take a fork and a strong axe, and I will go alone to-morrow."

Jagienka was silent for awhile; but great uneasiness was reflected on her face.

"Last year," said she, "the huntsman, Bezduch, was killed by a bear. It is dangerous, because as soon as the bear sees a man near the *barcie*, he immediately stands up on his hind feet."

"If he ran away, I could not get him," answered Zbyszko.

At that moment Zych who had been dozing, suddenly awakened and began to sing:

"Thou Kuba, of toil
I Maciek of pleasure,
Go then in the morning with the yoke in the field,
While I amuse myself with Kasia."

Then he said to Zbyszko:

"You know? There are two of them, Wilk of Brzozowa and Cztan of Rogow; and you?"

But Jagienka being afraid that Zych would say too much, swiftly approached Zbyszko, and began to inquire:

"When are you going? To-morrow?"

"To-morrow after sunset."

"And to which *barcie*?"

"To ours in Bogdaniec, not far from your boundaries, near the marshes of Radzikow. They tell me it is very easy to get a bear there."

CHAPTER V.

Zbyszko went for the bear as he proposed, because Macko became worse. At first when he reached Bogdaniec, he was sustained by joy and the first cares about the house; but on the third day, the fever returned, and the pain was so great that he was obliged to go to bed. Zbyszko went to the *barcie* during the day, and while there he perceived that there were the footprints of a bear in the mud. He spoke to the beehive keeper, Wawrek, who slept in a shed not far away, with his two faithful Podhalan[79] dogs; but he intended to return to the village on account of the cold.

They destroyed the shed, and Wawrek took the dogs with him. But first they smeared the trees here and there with honey, so that the smell of it would attract the animal. Zbyszko returned home and began to prepare for the expedition. He dressed himself in a warm reindeer jacket without sleeves; on the top of his head, he put a bonnet made of iron wire; finally he took a strong fork and a steel axe. Before sunset he had taken his position; and having made the sign of the cross, he sat down and waited.

The red beams of the setting sun were still shining between the branches of the gigantic pines. In the tops of the trees, the crows were flying, croaking and beating the air with their wings; here and there the hares were leaping toward the water, making a noise on the dried leaves; some times a swift marten passed by. In the thickets, the chirping of the birds was at first heard—but gradually ceased.

After sunset the noises of the forest began. Immediately a pack of boars passed near Zbyszko with a great bustle and snorting; then elks galloped in a long row, each holding his head on the tail of the one in front of him. The dried branches crackled under their feet and the forest resounded; but on they rushed toward the marshes where during the night, they were cool and safe. Finally the twilight was reflected on the sky, and the tops of the pine trees illuminated by it seemed to burn, as if on fire; then little by little everything began to be quieted. The forest was still. Dusk was rising from earth toward the gleaming twilight, which began finally to grow fainter, then gloomy, blacker and then was quenched.

"Now, everything will be quiet, until the wolves begin to howl," thought Zbyszko.

He regretted that he had not taken his crossbow, because he could easily have killed a boar or an elk. In the meanwhile, from the marshes came muffled sounds similar to heavy panting and whistling. Zbyszko looked toward that marsh with some apprehension, because the peasant, Radzik, who used to live here in an earth-hut, disappeared with his whole family, as if devoured by the earth. Some people said they were seized by robbers; but there were others who saw some strange footprints, neither human nor of beasts, round the cabin. The people shook their heads very much about that, and they even spoke about bringing a priest from Krzesnia, to bless the hut. But they did not do it because nobody was willing to live in that hut, which from that time, had an evil reputation. It is true that the beehive keeper, Wawrek, did not pay any attention to these reports.

Zbyszko being armed with the fork and axe, was not afraid of the wild beasts; but he thought with some uneasiness about the evil forces, and he was glad when that noise stopped.

The last reverberation ceased, and there was complete silence. The wind stopped blowing and there was not even the usual whispering in the tops of the pine trees. From time to time, a pine cone fell, making quite a noise amidst the deep silence; but in general, everything was so quiet that Zbyszko heard his own respirations.

Thus he sat quietly for a long time, thinking first about the bear, and then about Danusia. He recollected how he seized her in his arms when bidding the princess farewell, and how she cried; he remembered her fair head and bright face, her wreaths of bachelor buttons, her singing, her red shoes with long tips, and finally everything that happened from the moment he first saw her. Such a longing to see her, filled his heart, that he forgot that he was in the forest waiting for the bear; instead of that he began to talk to himself:

"I will go to see you, because I cannot live without you."

He felt that he must go to Mazowsze; that if he remained in Bogdaniec, he would become good for nothing. He recollected Jurand and his strange opposition; then he thought that it was even more necessary he should go, and learn what that obstacle was, and if a challenge to combat could not remove it. Finally it seemed to him that Danusia stretched her bands toward him and cried:

"Come, Zbyszku! Come!" How could he refuse?

He was not sleeping, but he saw her as distinctly as in a dream. There she was, riding beside the princess, thrumming on her little lute, humming and thinking of him. Thinking that she would soon see him, and perhaps looking back.

Hero Zbyszko aroused himself and listened, because he heard a rustling behind him. Then he grasped the fork in his hand more tightly, stretched his neck and listened again.

The rustling approached and then it became very distinct. Under some careful foot, the dried branches were crackling, the fallen leaves were rustling. Something was coming.

From time to time the rustling ceased, as if the beast halted beneath the trees; then there was such quietude that Zbyszko's ears began to ring; then again slow, careful steps were heard. That approach was so cautious that Zbyszko was surprised.

"I am sure 'the old'[80] must be afraid of the dogs which were here in the shed," said he to himself; "but it may be a wolf that has scented me."

Now the footsteps were no longer heard. Zbyszko, however, was sure that something had stopped twenty or thirty feet behind him.

He turned around once or twice; but although he could see the trunks of the trees quite well, he could not perceive anything else. He was obliged to wait.

He waited so long, that he was surprised a second time.

"A bear would not come here to stop under the *barcie*; and a wolf would not wait until morning."

Suddenly a shiver ran through his body as he thought:

"Suppose it is something dreadful that comes from the marshes and is trying to surprise me from the rear! Suppose the slippery arms of a drowned man seize me, or the green eyes of a ghost look into my face; suppose a blue head on spider's legs comes out from behind the tree and begins to laugh!"

He felt his hair begin to rise under his iron bonnet.

But after a while, a rustling sounded in front of him, more distinct this time than formerly. Zbyszko breathed more freely; he thought that the same "wonder" had gone around him, and now approached from the front; but he preferred that. He seized his fork firmly, arose quietly and waited.

Now he noticed over his head the rustling of the pine trees, and he felt the wind blow in his face, coming from the marsh, and he smelt the bear.

There was not the slightest doubt that a *mys*[81] was coming!

Zbyszko was afraid no longer, and having bent his head, he strained to the utmost his hearing and his sight. Heavy, distinct steps were coming; the smell grew stronger; soon the snore and groaning were heard.

"I hope there are not two of them!" thought Zbyszko.

But at that moment, he perceived in front of him the large, dark form of the animal, which was walking in the same direction from which the wind was blowing, and could not get the scent of him; its attention was also attracted by the smell of the honey on the trees.

"Come, uncle!" exclaimed Zbyszko, coming out from beneath the pine tree.

The bear roared shortly as if frightened by an unexpected apparition; but he was too near to seek safety in flight; therefore, in a moment he reared and separated his forelegs as if for a hug. This was exactly what Zbyszko was waiting for; he gathered himself together, jumped like lightning and with all the strength of his powerful arms and of his weight, he drove the fork into the animal's chest.

The whole forest resounded now with the fearful roaring. The bear seized the fork with his paws, and tried to pull it out, but the incisions made by the points were too deep; therefore, feeling the pain, he roared still more fearfully. Wishing to reach Zbyszko, he leaned on the fork and thus drove it into his body still further. Zbyszko, not knowing that the points had entered so deeply, held on to the handle. The man and the animal began to struggle. The forest again resounded with the roaring in which wrath and despair were mingled.

Zbyszko could not use his axe until after he could drive the sharpened end of the fork into the ground. The bear having seized the handle, was shaking it as well as Zbyszko, and notwithstanding the pain caused by every movement of the points imbedded in his breast, he would not let it be "underpropped." In this way the terrible struggle continued, and Zbyszko finally felt that his strength would soon be exhausted. If he fell, then he would be lost; therefore, he gathered all his strength, strained his arms to the utmost, set his feet firmly and bent his back like a bow, so as not to be thrown backward; and in his enthusiasm he repeated through set teeth:

"You or I will die!"

Such anger filled him that he really preferred at that moment to die, rather than to let the beast go. Finally his foot caught in the root of a tree; he tottered and would have fallen, if at that moment a dark figure had not appeared before him, and another fork "underpropped" the beast; and in the meanwhile, a voice shouted near his ear:

"Use your axe!"

Zbyszko, being excited by the fight, did not wonder even for a moment from whence came the unexpected help; but he seized the axe and cut with all his might. The fork cracked, broken by the weight and by the last convulsion of the beast, as it fell. There was a long silence broken only by Zbyszko's loud respirations. But after a while, he lifted his head, looked at the form standing beside him and was afraid, thinking that it might not be a man.

"Who are you?" asked he, with uneasiness.

"Jagienka!" answered a thin, womanly voice.

Zbyszko became dumb from astonishment; he could not believe his own eyes. But his doubts did not last long, because Jagienka's voice again resounded:

"I will build a fire."

Immediately the clatter of a fire steel against a flint sounded and the sparks began to fall; by their glittering light, Zbyszko beheld the white forehead, the dark eyebrows and the red lips of the girl who was blowing on the tinder which began to burn. Not until then did he realize that she had come to the forest to help him, and that without her aid, he would have perished. He felt such gratitude toward her, that he impulsively seized her around the waist and kissed her on both cheeks.

The tinder and the steel fell to the ground.

"Let me be!" she began to repeat in a muffled voice; but she allowed him to kiss her and even, as if by accident, touched Zbyszko's lips with her mouth. He released her and said:

"May God reward you. I do not know what would have happened without your help."

Then Jagienka, while searching for the tinder and fire steel, began to excuse herself:

"I was worried about you, because Bezduch also went with a fork and an axe, but the bear tore him to pieces. If you met with such a misfortune, Macko would be very desolate, and he hardly breathes now. So I took a fork and came."

"Then it was you whom I heard there behind the pines?"

"Yes."

"And I thought it was an evil spirit."

"I was very much frightened, because it is dangerous to be without fire here around the Radzikowski marshes."

"Then why did you not speak to me?"

"Because I was afraid you would send me away."

Having said this, she again began to strike sparks from the steel, and put on the tinder a bundle of hemp which began to burn.

"I have two resinous pieces of wood," said she; "you bring some dried branches quickly, and we will soon have a fire."

In fact, after a while a bright fire was burning, and lighted the enormous, brown body of the bear which was lying in a pool of blood.

"Hej, a dreadful beast!" said Zbyszko, boastfully.

"You split his head entirely open! O, Jesus!"

Then she leaned over and felt of the bear's body, to ascertain whether the beast was fat; then she arose with a bright face, and said:

"There will be plenty of grease for two years."

"But the fork is broken, look!"

"That is too bad; what shall I tell them at home?"

"About what?"

"*Tatus* would not let me come into the forest, therefore I was obliged to wait until everybody had retired."

After a moment she added:

"You must not tell that I was here, because they will laugh at me."

"But I will go with you to your house, because I am afraid the wolves will attack you, and you have no fork."

"Very well!"

Thus they sat talking for a while beside the bright fire, looking like two young forest creatures.

Zbyszko looked at the girl's pretty face, lighted by the flames, and said with involuntary admiration:

"There is not another girl in this world as brave as you are. You ought to go to the war!"

She looked into his face and then she answered, almost sadly:

"I know; but you must not laugh at me."

CHAPTER VI.

Jagienka herself melted a large pot of bear's grease. Macko drank the first quart willingly, because it was fresh, and smelt good. Jagienka put the rest of it in a pot. Macko's hope increased; he was sure he would be cured.

"That is what I needed," said he. "When all parts inside of me become greasy, then that dog's splinter will slip out."

But the next quarts did not taste as well as the first; but he continued to drink it and Jagienka encouraged him, saying:

"You will get well. Zbilud of Ostrog had the links of a coat of mail driven into his neck; but they slipped out because he drank grease. But when your wound opens, you must put some grease of a beaver on it."

"Have you some?"

"Yes, we have. But if it be necessary to have it fresh, we will go with Zbyszko and get a beaver. Meanwhile it would not do any harm, if you promised something to some saint, who is the patron for wounds."

"I was thinking about that, but I do not know to whom I should make the promise. Saint George is the patron of knights; he protects the warrior from any accident and always

82

gives him victory, and it is said that sometimes he fights personally for the one who is right. But a saint who fights willingly, does not heal willingly; and for that, there must be another saint with whom he would not want to interfere. It is known that every saint has his specialty. But they will not interfere with one another; because that would cause quarrels, and it is not proper to fight in heaven. There are Kosma and Damian to whom all doctors pray, that illness may exist; otherwise the doctors would not have anything to eat. There is Saint Apolonia for the teeth and Saint Liborius for stone; but they will not do for me. The abbot, when he comes, will tell me whom I must ask. Every *clericus* does not know all celestial secrets and everyone of them is not familiar with such things, but the abbot is."

"Suppose you make a vow to the Lord Jesus himself?"

"Of course he is over all of them. But suppose your father had injured my servant, and I went to Krakow to complain to the king; what would the king tell me? He would say thus: 'I am monarch over all the country, and you complain to me about one of your peasants! Do you not have my officials in your part of the country; why did you not go to the castellan?' So the Lord Jesus is the ruler over the whole universe; but for smaller affairs, he employs the saints."

"Then I will tell you what to do," said Zbyszko, who entered just now; "make a vow to our late queen, that if she intercede for you, you will make a pilgrimage to Krakow. Why should you search after strange saints, when we have our own lady, who is better than they?"

"Bah! if I only knew that she would intercede for wounds!"

"No matter! There is no saint who would dare to show her an angry face; or if he dared, Lord God would punish him for it, because she was not an ordinary woman, but a Polish queen."

"Who converted the last heathen country to the Christian faith! That is right," said Macko. "She must have a high place in God's council and surely none would dare to oppose her. Therefore I will do as you say."

This advice pleased Jagienka, who admired Zbyszko's common sense very much. That same evening, Macko made a vow and drank with still greater hope, the bear's grease. But after a week, he began to lose hope. He said that the grease was fermenting in his stomach, and that a lump was growing on his side near the last rib. At the end of ten days Macko was worse, and the lump grew larger and became inflamed. The sick man again had fever and began to make preparations for death.

But one night he awakened Zbyszko, and said:

"Light a piece of resinous wood; there is something the matter with me, but I do not know what."

Zbyszko jumped up and lighted a piece of pine wood.

"What is it?"

"What is it! Something has pierced the lump on my side. It must be the head of the spear! I had hold of it, but I cannot pull it out."

"It must be the spearhead! Nothing else. Grasp it well and pull."

Macko began to turn and to twist with pain; but he pushed his fingers deeper and deeper, until he seized a hard substance which finally he pulled out.

"O, Jesus!"

"Have you pulled it out?" asked Zbyszko.

"Yes. I am in a cold perspiration all over; but I have it; look!"

Having said this, he showed to Zbyszko a long splinter, which had separated from the spear and remained in his body for several months.

"Glory be to God and to Queen Jadwiga! Now you will get well."

"Perhaps; I am better, but it pains me greatly," said Macko, pressing the wound from which blood and pus began to flow. "Jagienka said that now I ought to dress the wound with the grease of a beaver."

"We will go to-morrow and get a beaver."

Macko felt considerably better the next day. He slept till morning, and when he awoke, immediately asked for something to eat. He would not even look at the bear's grease; but they cooked twenty eggs for him. He ate them voraciously, also a big loaf of bread, and drank about four quarts of beer; then he demanded that they call Zych, because he felt jovial.

Zbyszko sent one of the Turks, given to him by Zawisza, after Zych who mounted a horse and came in the afternoon when the young people were ready to go to the Odstajny lake to catch a beaver. At first there was plenty of laughter and singing, while they drank mead; but afterward the old *wlodykas* began to talk about the children, each praising his own.

"What a man Zbyszko is!" said Macko; "there is no other like him in the world. He is brave and as agile as a wild-cat. Do you know that when they conducted him to the scaffold in Krakow, all the girls standing at the windows were crying, and such girls;—daughters of knights and of castellans, and also the beautiful townswomen."

"They may be beautiful and the daughters of castellans, but they are not better than my Jagienka!" answered Zych of Zgorzelice.

"Did I say they were better? It will be difficult to find a better girl than Jagienka."

"I do not say anything against Zbyszko either; he can stretch a crossbow without a crank."

"He can underprop a bear also. Did you see how he cut the bear? He cut the head and one paw off."

"He cut the head off, but he did not underprop it alone. Jagienka helped him."

"Did she? He did not tell me about that."

"Because he promised her not to tell anyone. The girl was ashamed because she went into the forest alone at night. She told me all about it; she never hides the truth. Frankly speaking, I was not pleased because who knows what might have happened. I wanted to scold her, but she said, 'If I be not able to preserve my wreath myself, how can you preserve it, you *tatulu*; but do not fear, Zbyszko knows what knightly honor is.'"

"That is true. They have gone alone to-day also."

"They will be back in the evening. But during the night, the devil is worse and the girl does not feel ashamed because of the darkness."

Macko thought for a while; then he said as if to himself:

"But they are fond of each other."

"Bah! it is a pity he made a vow to another!"

"That is, as you know, a knightly custom. They consider the one who has no lady, a churl. He also made a vow to capture some peacocks' tufts, and those he must get because he swore by his knightly honor; he must also challenge Lichtenstein; but from the other vows, the abbot can release him."

"The abbot is coming soon."

"Do you expect him?" asked Macko; then he said again: "And what does such a vow amount to; Jurand told him positively that he could not give the girl to him! I do not know whether he had promised her to some one else, or whether he had destined her for God."

"Have I told you that the abbot loves Jagienka as much as if she were his own? The last time I saw him he said: 'I have no relations except those from my mother's side; and they will receive nothing from me.'"

Here Macko looked at Zych suspiciously and after awhile he answered:

"Would you wrong us?"

"Jagienka will get Moczydoly," said Zych evasively.

"Immediately?"

"Immediately. I would not give it to another; but I will do it for her."

"Half of Bogdaniec belongs to Zbyszko, and if God restore my health, I will improve the estate. Do you love Zbyszko?"

Zych began to wink and said:

"When anybody mentions Zbyszko's name in the presence of Jagienka, she immediately turns away."

"And when you mention another?"

"When I mention another, she only laughs and says: 'What then?'"

"Well, do you not see. God will help us and Zbyszko will forget about the other girl. I am old and I will forget also. Will you have some more mead?"

"Yes, I will."

"Well, the abbot is a wise man! You know that some of the abbots are laymen; but this abbot, although he does not sit among the friars, is a priest just the same; and a priest

84

can always give better advice than an ordinary man, because he knows how to read, and he communes with the Holy Ghost. I am glad that Jagienka is going to have the estate of Moczydoly. As for me, as soon as the Lord Jesus restores my health, I will try to induce some of the peasants living on the estate of Wilk of Brzozowa, to settle on my land. I will offer them more land, I have plenty of it in Bogdaniec. They can come if they wish to, for they are free. In time, I will build a *grodek* in Bogdaniec, a worthy castle of oaks with a ditch around it. Let Zbyszko and Jagienka hunt together. I think we shall soon have snow. They will become accustomed to each other, and the boy will forget that other girl. Let them be together. Speak frankly; would you give Jagienka to him or not?"

"I would. Did we not decide a long time ago that they should marry, and that Moczydoly and Bogdaniec would be our grandchildren's?"

"*Grady!*" exclaimed Macko, joyfully. "God will bless us and their children will be as numerous as hail. The abbot shall baptize them."

"If he will only be quick enough!" exclaimed Zych. "I have not seen you so jolly as you are to-day for a long time."

"Because I am glad in my heart. Do not fear about Zbyszko. Yesterday when Jagienka mounted her horse, the wind blew. I asked Zbyszko then: 'Did you see?' and his eyes shone. I have also noticed that although at first they did not speak much to each other, now when they go together, they are continually turning their heads toward each other, and they talk— talk! Have some more mead?"

"Yes, I will."

"To Zbyszko and Jagienka's health!"

CHAPTER VII.

The old *wlodyka* was not mistaken when he said that Zbyszko and Jagienka were fond of each other, and even that they longed for each other. Jagienka pretending that she wanted to visit the sick Macko, went very often to Bogdaniec, either alone or with her father. Zbyszko also went often to Zgorzelice. In that way, after a few days a familiarity and friendship originated between them. They grew fond of each other and talked about everything that interested them. There was much mutual admiration in that friendship also. The young and handsome Zbyszko, who had already distinguished himself in the war, had participated in tournaments and had been in the presence of kings, was considered by the girl, when she compared him with Cztan of Rogow or Wilk of Brzozowa, a true courtly knight and almost a prince; as for him, he was astonished at the great beauty of the girl. He was loyal to Danusia; but very often when he looked suddenly at Jagienka, either in the forest or at home, he said involuntarily to himself: "Hej! what a girl!" When, helping her to mount her horse, he felt her elastic flesh under his hands, disquietude filled him and he shivered, and a torpor began to steal over him.

Jagienka, although naturally proud, inclined to raillery, and even aggressive, grew more and more gentle with him, often looking in his eyes to discover how she could please him; he understood her affection; he was grateful for it and he liked to be with her more and more. Finally, especially after Macko began to drink the bear's grease, they saw each other almost every day; when the splinter came out of the wound, they went together to get some fresh beaver's grease, necessary for the healing of the wound.

They took their crossbows, mounted their horses and went first to Moczydoly, destined for Jagienka's dowry, then to the edge of the forest, where they entrusted the horses to a servant and went on foot, because it was impossible to pass through the thicket on horseback. While walking, Jagienka pointed to the large meadow covered with reeds and to the blue ribbon of forest and said:

"Those woods belong to Cztan of Rogow."

"The same man who would like to take you?"

She began to laugh:

"He would if he could!"

"You can defend yourself very easily, having for your defence the Wilk[82] who, as I understand, gnashes his teeth at Cztan. I wonder that they have not challenged each other to fight until death."

"They have not because *tatulo* before he went to the war said to them: 'If you fight about Jagienka I do not want to see you any more.' How could they fight then? When they are in Zgorzelice they scowl at each other; but afterward they drink together in an inn in Krzesnia until they are drunk."

"Stupid boys!"

"Why?"

"Because while Zych was away one of them should have taken you by force. What could Zych do, if when he returned he had found you with a baby on your lap?"

At this Jagienka's blue eyes flashed immediately.

"Do you think I would let them take me? Have we not people in Zgorzelice, and do I not know how to manage a crossbow or a boar-spear? Let them try! I would chase them back home and even attack them in Rogow or Brzozowa. Father knew very well that he could go to the war and leave me home alone."

Speaking thus, she frowned, and shook the crossbow threateningly, so that Zbyszko began to laugh, and said:

"You ought to have been a knight and not a girl."

She becoming calmer, answered:

"Cztan guarded me from Wilk and Wilk from Cztan. Then I was also under the abbot's tutelage, and it is well for everyone to let the abbot alone."

"Owa!" answered Zbyszko. "They are all afraid of the abbot! But I, may Saint George help me to speak the truth to you, I would neither be afraid of the abbot, nor of your peasants, nor of yourself; I would take you!"

At this Jagienka stopped on the spot, and fixing her eyes on Zbyszko, asked in a strange, soft, low voice:

"You would take me?"

Then her lips parted and blushing like the dawn, she waited for his answer.

But he evidently was only thinking what he would do, were he in Cztan or Wilk's position; because after a while, he shook his golden hair and said further:

"A girl must marry and not fight with the boys. Unless you have a third one, you must choose one of these two."

"You must not tell me that," answered the girl, sadly.

"Why not? I have been away from home for a long time, therefore I do not know whether there is somebody around Zgorzelice, of whom you are fond or not."

"Hej!" answered Jagienka. "Let it be!"

They walked along silently, trying to make their way through the thicket which was now much denser because the bushes and the trees were covered with wild hop vines. Zbyszko walked first, tearing down the green vines, and breaking the branches here and there; Jagienka followed him with a crossbow on her shoulder, looking like a hunting goddess.

"Beyond that thicket," said she, "there is a deep brook; but I know where the ford is."

"I have long boots on, reaching above my knees; we can cross it," answered Zbyszko.

Shortly afterward, they reached the brook. Jagienka being familiar with the Moczydlowski forests, very easily found the ford; but the water was deeper than usual, the little brook being swollen by the rains. Then Zbyszko without asking her permission, seized the girl in his arms.

"I can cross by myself," said Jagienka.

"Put your arms around my neck!" answered Zbyszko.

He walked slowly through the water, while the girl nestled to him. Finally when they were near the other shore, she said:

"Zbyszku!"

"What?"

"I care neither for Cztan, nor for Wilk."

As he placed her on the shore, he answered excitedly:

"May God give you the best I He will not be wronged."

The Odstajny lake was not far away now. Jagienka walking in front, turned from time to time, and putting a finger on her lips, ordered Zbyszko to be silent. They were walking amidst the osiers and gray willows, on low, damp ground. From the left side, were heard the voices of birds, and Zbyszko was surprised at that, because it was time for the birds to migrate.

"We are near a morass which is never frozen," whispered Jagienka; "the ducks pass the winter there; even in the lake the water freezes only near the shores. See how it is steaming."

Zbyszko looked through the willows and noticed in front of him, something like a bank of fog; it was the Odstajny lake.

Jagienka again put a finger to her lips, and after a while they reached the lake. The girl climbed on an old willow and bent over the water. Zbyszko followed her example; and for a long time they remained quiet, seeing nothing in front of them, on account of the fog; hearing nothing but the mournful puling of lapwings. Finally the wind blew, rustled the osiers and the yellow leaves of the willows, and disclosed the waters of the lake which were slightly ruffled by the wind.

"Do you see anything?" whispered Zbyszko.

"No. Keep quiet!"

After a while, the wind ceased and complete silence followed. Then on the surface of the lake appeared one head, then another; finally near them a big beaver entered the water from the shore, carrying in his mouth a newly cut branch, and began to swim amidst the duck-weed and marigold holding his mouth out of the water and pushing the branch before him. Zbyszko lying on the trunk beneath Jagienka, noticed that her elbow moved quietly and that her head was bent forward; evidently she had aimed at the animal which, not suspecting any danger, was swimming close by, toward the clear water.

Finally the string of the crossbow twanged and at the same moment Jagienka cried:

"I hit him! I hit him!"

Zbyszko instantly climbed higher and looked through the thicket toward the water; the beaver plunged into the water, then reappeared on the surface, turning somersets.

"I hit him hard! He will soon be quiet!" said Jagienka.

The movements of the animal grew slower, and then before one had time sufficient to recite one "*Ave Maria*," he was floating on his back on the surface of the water.

"I will go and get him," said Zbyszko.

"No, do not go. Here, near the shore, there is, deep slime. Anyone who does not know how to manage, will surely drown."

"Then how will we get him?"

"He will be in Bogdaniec this evening, do not worry about that; now we must go home."

"You hit him hard!"

"Bah! It is not the first one!"

"Other girls are afraid to even look at a crossbow; but with you, one can go to the forest all his life."

Jagienka smiled at such praise, but she did not answer; they returned the same way they came. Zbyszko asked her about the beavers and she told him how many of them there were in Moczydoly, and how many in Zgorzelice.

Suddenly she struck her hip with her hand and exclaimed:

"Well, I left my arrows on the willow. Wait!"

Before he could say that he would return for them, she jumped back like a roe and disappeared. Zbyszko waited and waited; at last he began to wonder what detained her so long.

"She must have lost the arrows and is searching for them," he said to himself; "but I will go and see whether anything has happened to her."

He had hardly started to return before the girl appeared with her bow in her hand, her face smiling and blushing, and with the beaver on her shoulders.

"For God's sake!" cried Zbyszko, "how did you get him?"

"How? I went into the water, that is all! It is nothing new for me; but I did not want you to go, because the mud drags anyone down who does not know how to swim in it."

"And I waited here like a fool! You are a sly girl."

"Well, could I undress before you?"

"Bah! If I had followed you, then I would have seen a wonder!"

"Be silent!"

"I was just starting, so help me God!"

"Be silent!"

After a while, wishing to turn the conversation, she said:

"Wring my tress; it makes my back wet."

Zbyszko caught the tress in one hand and began to wring with the other, saying:

"The best way will be to unbraid it, then the wind will soon dry it."

But she did not wish to do that on account of the thicket through which they were obliged to make their way. Zbyszko now put the beaver on his shoulders. Jagienka walking in front of him, said:

"Now Macko will soon be well, because there is no better medicine for a wound than the grease of a bear inside, and the grease of a beaver outside. In about two weeks, he will be able to ride a horse."

"May God grant that!" answered Zbyszko. "I am waiting for it as for salvation, because I cannot leave the sick man, and it is hard for me to stay here."

"Why is it hard for you to stay here?" she asked him.

"Has Zych told you nothing about Danusia?"

"He did tell me something. I know that she covered you with her veil. I know that! He told me also that every knight makes some vow, to serve his lady. But he said that such a vow did not amount to anything; that some of the knights were married, but they served their ladies just the same. But Danusia, Zbyszko; tell me about her!"

Having come very close to him, she began to look at his face with great anxiety; he did not pay any attention to her frightened voice and looks, but said:

"She is my lady, and at the same time she is my sweetest love. I have not spoken about her to anybody; but I am going to tell you, because we have been acquainted since we were children. I will follow her beyond the tenth river and beyond the tenth sea, to the Germans and to the Tartars, because there is no other girl like her. Let my uncle remain in Bogdaniec, and I will go to her. What do I care about Bogdaniec, the household, the herds, or the abbot's wealth, without her! I will mount my horse and I will go, so help me God; I will fulfill that which I promised her, or I will die."

"I did not know," answered Jagienka, in a hollow voice.

Zbyszko began to tell her about all that had happened; how he had met Danusia in Tyniec; how he had made a vow to her; about everything that happened afterward; about his imprisonment, and how Danusia rescued him; about Jurand's refusal, their farewell and his loneliness; finally about his joy, because as soon as Macko became well, he would go to his beloved girl. His story was interrupted at last by the sight of the servant with the horses, waiting on the edge of the forest.

Jagienka immediately mounted her horse and began to bid Zbyszko good-bye.

"Let the servant follow you with the beaver; I am going to Zgorzelice."

"Then you will not go to Bogdaniec? Zych is there."

"No. *Tatulo* said he would return and told me to go home."

"Well, may God reward you for the beaver."

"With God."

Then Jagienka was alone. Going home through the heaths, she looked back for a while after Zbyszko; when he disappeared beyond the trees, she covered her eyes with her hands as if sheltering them from the sunlight. But soon large tears began to flow down her cheeks and drop one after another on the horse's mane.

CHAPTER VIII.

After the conversation with Zbyszko, Jagienka did not appear in Bogdaniec for three days; but on the third day she hurried in with the news that the abbot had arrived at Zgorzelice. Macko received the news with emotion. It is true he had money enough to pay the amount for which the estate was pledged, and he calculated that he would have enough to induce settlers to come, to buy herds and to make other improvements; but in the whole transaction, much depended on the disposition of the rich relation, who, for instance, could take or leave the peasants settled by him on the land, and in that way increase or diminish the value of the estate.

Therefore Macko asked Jagienka about the abbot; how he was; if he was in a good humor or gloomy; what he had said about them; when he was coming to Bogdaniec? She gave him sensible answers, trying to encourage and tranquillize him in every respect.

She said that the abbot was in good health and gay; that he was accompanied by a considerable retinue in which, besides the armed servants, there were several seminarists and *rybalts;* that he sang with Zych and that he listened gladly not only to the spiritual but to the worldly songs also. She had noticed also that he asked carefully about Macko, and that he listened eagerly to Zych's narration of Zbyszko's adventure in Krakow.

"You know best what you ought to do," finally the clever girl said; "but I think that Zbyszko ought to go immediately and greet his elder relative, and not wait until the abbot comes to Bogdaniec."

Macko liked the advice; therefore he called Zbyszko and said to him:

"Dress yourself beautifully; then go and bow to the abbot, and pay him respect; perhaps he will take a fancy to you."

Then he turned to Jagienka:

"I would not be surprised if you were stupid, because you are a woman; but I am astonished to find that you have such good sense. Tell me then, the best way to receive the abbot when he comes here."

"As for food, he will tell you himself what he wishes to have; he likes to feast well, but if there be a great deal of saffron in the food, he will eat anything."

Macko hearing this, said:

"How can I get saffron for him!"

"I brought some," said Jagienka.

"Give us more such girls!" exclaimed the overjoyed Macko. "She is pretty, a good housekeeper, intelligent and good-hearted! Hej! if I were only younger I would take her immediately!"

Here Jagienka glanced at Zbyszko, and having sighed slightly, she said further:

"I brought also the dice, the goblet and the cloth, because after his meal, the abbot likes to play dice."

"He had the same habit formerly, and he used to get very angry."

"He gets angry sometimes now; then he throws the goblet on the ground and rushes from the room into the fields. Then he comes back smiling, and laughs at his anger. You know him! If one does not contradict him, you cannot find a better man in the world."

"And who would contradict him; is he not wiser and mightier than others?"

Thus they talked while Zbyszko was dressing in the alcove. Finally he came out, looking so beautiful that he dazzled Jagienka, as much as he did the first time he went to Zgorzelice in his white *jaka.* She regretted that this handsome knight was not hers, and that he was in love with another girl.

Macko was pleased because he thought that the abbot could not help liking Zbyszko and would be more lenient during their business transaction. He was so much pleased with this idea, that he determined to go also.

"Order the servants to prepare a wagon," said he to Zbyszko. "If I could travel from Krakow to Bogdaniec with an iron in my side, surely I can go now to Zgorzelice."

"If you only will not faint," said Jagienka.

"Ej! I will be all right, because I feel stronger already. And even if I faint, the abbot will see that I hastened to meet him, and will be more generous."

"I prefer your health to his generosity!" said Zbyszko.

But Macko was persistent and started for Zgorzelice. On the road he moaned a little, but he continued to give Zbyszko advice; he told him how to act in Zgorzelice, and especially recommended him to be obedient and humble in the presence of their mighty relative, who never would suffer the slightest opposition.

When they came to Zgorzelice, they found Zych and the abbot sitting in front of the house, looking at the beautiful country, and drinking wine. Behind them, near the wall, sat six men of the abbot's retinue; two of them were *rybalts*; one was a pilgrim, who could easily be distinguished by his curved stick and dark mantle; the others looked like seminarists because their heads were shaved, but they wore lay clothing, girdles of ox leather, and swords.

When Zych perceived Macko coming in the wagon, he rushed toward him; but the abbot, evidently remembering his spiritual dignity, remained seated, and began to say something to his seminarists. Zbyszko and Zych conducted the sick Macko toward the house.

"I am not well yet," said Macko, kissing the abbot's hand, "but I came to bow to you, my benefactor; to thank you for your care of Bogdaniec, and to beg you for a benediction, which is most necessary for a sinful man."

"I heard you were better," said the abbot, placing his hand on Macko's head; "and that you had promised to go to the grave of our late queen."

"Not knowing which saint's protection to ask for, I made a vow to her."

"You did well!" said the abbot, enthusiastically; "she is better than all the others, if one only dare beseech her!"

In a moment his face became flushed with anger, his cheeks filled with blood, his eyes began to sparkle.

They were so used to his impetuosity, that Zych began to laugh and exclaimed: "Strike, who believes in God!"

As for the abbot, he puffed loudly, and looked at those present; then laughed suddenly, and having looked at Zbyszko, he asked:

"Is that your nephew and my relation?"

Zbyszko bent and kissed his hand.

"I saw him when he was a small boy; I did not recognize him," said the abbot. "Show yourself!" And he began to look at him from head to foot, and finally said:

"He is too handsome! It is a girl, not a knight!"

To this Macko replied:

"That girl used to go to dancing parties with the Germans; but those who took her, fell down and did not rise again."

"And he can stretch a crossbow without a crank!" exclaimed Jagienka.

The abbot turned toward her:

"Ah! Are you here?"

She blushed so much that her neck and ears became red, and answered:

"I saw him do it."

"Look out then, that he does not shoot you, because you will be obliged to nurse yourself for a long time."

At this the *rybalts*, the pilgrim and the seminarists broke out with great laughter, which confused Jagienka still more; the abbot took pity on her, and having raised his arm, he showed her his enormous sleeve, and said:

"Hide here, my dear girl!"

Meanwhile Zych assisted Macko to the bench and ordered some wine for him. Jagienka went to get it. The abbot turned to Zbyszko and began to talk thus:

"Enough of joking! I compared you to a girl, not to humiliate you, but to praise your beauty, of which many girls would be proud. But I know that you are a man! I have heard about your deeds at Wilno, about the Fryzes, and about Krakow. Zych has told me all about it, understand!"

Here he began to look intently into Zbyszko's eyes, and after a while he said:

"If you have promised three peacocks' tufts, then search for them! It is praiseworthy and pleasing to God to persecute the foes of our nation. But, if you have promised something else, I will release you from the vow."

"Hej!" said Zbyszko; "when a man promises something in his soul to the Lord Jesus, who has the power to release him?"

Macko looked with fear at the abbot; but evidently he was in an excellent humor, because instead of becoming angry, he threatened Zbyszko with his finger and said:

90

"How clever you are! But you must be careful that you do not meet the same fate that the German, Beyhard, did."

"What happened to him?" asked Zych.

"They burned him on a pile."

"What for?"

"Because he used to say that a layman could understand God's secrets as well as the clergy."

"They punished him severely!"

"But righteously!" shouted the abbot, "because he had blasphemed against the Holy Ghost. What do you think? Is a layman able to interpret any of God's secrets?"

"He cannot by any means!" exclaimed the wandering seminarists, together.

"Keep quiet, you *shpilmen*!" said the abbot; "you are not ecclesiastics, although your heads are shaved."

"We are not '*shpilmen*,' but courtiers of Your Grace," answered one of them, looking toward a large bucket from which the smell of hops and malt was filling the air.

"Look! He is talking from a barrel!" exclaimed the abbot. "Hej, you shaggy one! Why do you look at the bucket? You will not find any Latin at the bottom of that."

"I am not looking for Latin, but for beer; but I cannot find any."

The abbot turned toward Zbyszko, who was looking with astonishment at such courtiers as these, and said:

"They are *clerici scholares*,[83] but every one of them prefers to throw his books aside, and taking his lute, wander through the world. I shelter and nourish them; what else can I do? They are good for nothing, but they know how to sing and they are familiar with God's service; therefore I have some benefit out of them in my church, and in case of need, they will defend me, because some of them are fierce fellows! This pilgrim says that he was in the Holy Land; but I have asked him in vain about some of the seas and countries; he does not know even the name of the Greek emperor nor in what city he lives."

"I did know," said the pilgrim, in a hoarse voice; "but the fever I caught at the Danube, shook everything out of me."

"What surprises me most is, that they wear swords, being wandering seminarists," said Zbyszko.

"They are allowed to wear them," said the abbot, "because they have not received orders yet; and there is no occasion for anyone to wonder because I wear a sword even though I am an abbot. A year ago I challenged Wilk of Brzozowa to fight for the forests which you passed; but he did not appear."

"How could he fight with one of the clergy?" interrupted Zych.

At this the abbot became angry, struck the table with his fist, and exclaimed:

"When I wear armor, then I am not a priest, but a nobleman! He did not come because he preferred to have his servants attack me in Tulcza. That is why I wear a sword: *Omnes leges, omniaque iura vim vi repellere cunctisque sese defensare permittunt!* That is why I gave them their swords."

Hearing the Latin, Zych, Macko and Zbyszko became silent and bent their heads before the abbot's wisdom, because they did not understand a word of it; as for the abbot, he looked very angry for a while, and then he said:

"Who knows but what he will attack me even here?"

"Owa! Let him come!" exclaimed the wandering seminarists, seizing the hilts of their swords.

"I would like to have him attack me! I am longing for a fight."

"He will not do that," said Zych. "It is more likely that he will come to bow to you. He gave up the forests, and now he is anxious about his son. You know! But he can wait a long time!"

Meanwhile the abbot became quieted and said:

"I saw young Wilk drinking with Cztan of Rogow in an inn in Krzesnia. They did not recognize us at once, because it was dark; they were talking about Jagienka."

Here he turned to Zbyszko:

"And about you, too."

91

"What do they want from me?"

"They do not want anything from you; but they do not like it that there is a third young man near Zgorzelice. Cztan said to Wilk: 'After I tan his skin, he will not be so smooth.' And Wilk said: 'Perhaps he will be afraid of us; if not, I will break his bones!' Then they assured each other that you would be afraid of them."

Hearing this Macko looked at Zych, and Zych looked at him; their faces expressed great cunning and joy. Neither of them was sure whether the abbot had really heard such a conversation, or whether he was only saying this to excite Zbyszko; but they both knew, and Macko especially, that there was no better way to incite Zbyszko to try to win Jagienka.

The abbot added deliberately:

"It is true, they are fierce fellows!"

Zbyszko did not show any excitement; but he asked in a strange tone that did not sound like his voice:

"To-morrow is Sunday?"

"Yes, Sunday."

"You will go to church?"

"Yes!"

"Where? to Krzesnia?"

"That is the nearest!"

"Well, all right then!"

CHAPTER IX.

Zybszko, having joined Zych and Jagienka, who were accompanying the abbot and his retinue to Krzesnia, rode with them, because he wanted to show the abbot that he was afraid neither of Wilk of Brzozowa, nor of Cztan of Rogow. He was again surprised at Jagienka's beauty. He had often seen her in Zgorzelice and Bogdaniec, dressed beautifully; but never had she looked as she did now when going to church. Her cloak was made of red broadcloth, lined with ermine; she wore red gloves, and on her head was a little hood embroidered with gold, from beneath which two braids fell down on her shoulders. She was not sitting on the horse astride, but on a high saddle which had an arm and a little bench for her feet, which scarcely showed from beneath her long skirt. Zych permitted the girl to dress in a sheepskin overcoat and high-legged boots when at home, but required that for church she should be dressed not like the daughter of a poor *wlodyczka*,[84] but like the *panna* of a mighty nobleman. Two boys, dressed like pages, conducted her horse. Four servants were riding behind with the abbot's seminarists, who were armed with swords and carried their lutes. Zbyszko admired all the retinue, but especially Jagienka, who looked like a picture. The abbot, who was dressed in a red cloak, having enormous sleeves, resembled a traveling prince. The most modest dress was worn by Zych, who requiring magnificent display for the others, for himself cared only for singing and joy.

Zych, Zbyszko, Jagienka and the abbot rode together. At first the abbot ordered his *shpilmen* to sing some church songs; afterward, when he was tired of their songs, he began to talk with Zbyszko, who smiled at his enormous sword, which was as large as a two-handed German sword.

"I see," said he gravely, "that you wonder at my sword; the synod permits a clergyman to wear a sword during a journey, and I am traveling. When the holy father forbade the ecclesiastics to wear swords and red dresses, most assuredly he meant the men of low birth, because God intended that noblemen should wear arms; and he who would dare to take this right from a nobleman, would oppose His eternal will."

"I saw the Mazovian Prince Henryk, when he fought in the lists," said Zbyszko.

"We do not censure him, because he fought," answered the abbot, raising his finger, "but because he married and married unhappily; *fornicarium* and *bibulam* had taken *mulierem*, whom *Bachum* since she was young *adorabat*, and besides that she was *adultera*, from whom no one could expect any good." He stopped his horse and began to expound with still greater gravity:

"Whoever wishes to marry, or to choose *uxorem* must ascertain if she is pious, moral, a good housekeeper and cleanly. This is recommended not only by the fathers of the church, but also by a certain pagan sage, called Seneca. And how can you know whether you have chosen well, if you do not know the nest from which you take your life companion? Because another sage has said: *Pomus nam cadit absque arbore.* As is the ox, so is the skin; as is the mother, so is the girl. From which you, a sinner, must draw this moral,—that you must look for your wife not far away, but near; because if you get a bad one, you will cry as did the philosopher, when his quarrelsome wife poured *aquam sordidam* on his head."

"*In saecula saeculorum*, amen!" exclaimed in unison the wandering seminarists, who when responding to the abbot, did not always answer properly.

They were all listening very attentively to the abbot's words, admiring his eloquence and his knowledge of the Scriptures; he apparently did not speak directly to Zbyszko; but on the contrary, he turned more toward Zych and Jagienka, as if he wished to edify them. But evidently Jagienka understood what he was trying to do, because from beneath her long eyelashes, she looked at Zbyszko, who frowned and dropped his head as if he were seriously thinking about what the abbot had said.

After this the retinue moved on silently; but when they came near Krzesnia, the abbot touched his girdle and then turned it so that he could seize the hilt of his sword more easily, and said:

"I am sure that old Wilk of Brzozowa will come with a good retinue."

"Perhaps," replied Zych, "but I heard that he was not well."

"One of my seminarists heard that he intends to attack us in front of the inn after the service is over."

"He will not do that without a challenge, and especially after holy mass."

"May God, bring him to reason. I do not seek a quarrel with anybody and I bear my wrongs patiently."

Here he looked at the *shpilmen*, and said:

"Do not draw your swords, and remember that you are spiritual servants; but if they attack us first, then strike them!"

Zbyszko, while riding beside Jagienka, said to her:

"I am sure that in Krzesnia we will meet young Wilk and Cztan. Show me them from afar, so that I may know them."

"Very well, Zbyszku," answered Jagienka.

"Do they not meet you before the service and after the service? What do they do then?"

"They serve me."

"They will not serve you now, understand?" And she answered again, almost with humility:

"Very well, Zbyszku."

Further conversation was interrupted by the sound of the wooden knockers, there being no bells in Krzesnia. After a few moments they arrived at the church. From the crowd in front, waiting for mass, young Wilk and Cztan of Rogow came forward immediately; but Zbyszko jumped from his horse, and before they could reach her, seized Jagienka and lifted her down from her horse; then he took her by the hand, and looking at them threateningly, conducted her to the church.

In the vestibule of the church, they were again disappointed. Both rushed to the font of holy water, plunged their hands in, and then stretched them toward the girl. But Zbyszko did the same, and she touched his fingers; then having made the sign of the cross, she entered the church with him. Then not only young Wilk, but Cztan of Rogow also, notwithstanding his stupidity, understood that this had been done purposely, and both were very angry. Wilk rushed out of the vestibule and ran like a madman, not knowing where he was going. Cztan rushed after him, although not knowing why.

They stopped at the corner of the inclosure where there were some large stones ready for the foundation of the tower which was to be built in Krzesnia. Then, Wilk wishing to assuage the wrath which raged in his breast, seized one of these stones, and began to shake it; Cztan seeing him do this, seized it also, and both began to roll it toward the church gate.

The people looked at them with amazement, thinking that they had made some vow, and that in this way they wished to contribute to the building of the tower. This effort gave them relief and they came to their senses; then they stood, pale from their exertion, puffing and looking at each other.

Cztan of Rogow was the first to break the silence.

"What now?" asked he.

"What?" answered Wilk.

"Shall we attack him immediately?"

"How can we do that in the church?"

"Not in the church, but after mass."

"He is with Zych and the abbot. And have you forgotten that Zych said that if there were a fight, he would refuse to let either of us visit at Zgorzelice. But for that, I would have broken your ribs long ago."

"Or I, yours!" answered Cztan, clinching his powerful fists.

And their eyes began to sparkle threateningly; but soon they both realized that now, more than ever, they needed to have a good understanding. They often fought together; but after each fight, they always became reconciled, because although they were divided by their love for Jagienka, they could not live without each other. Now they had a common foe and they understood that the enemy was a dangerous one.

After a while Cztan asked:

"What shall we do? Shall we send him a challenge?"

Wilk, although he was wiser, did not know what to do. Fortunately the knockers resounded to notify the people that mass would begin. When he heard them he said:

"What shall we do? Go to church now and after that, we will do whatever pleases God."

Cztan of Rogow was pleased with this answer.

"Perhaps the Lord Jesus will send us an inspiration," said he.

"And will bless us," added Wilk.

"According to justice."

They went to church, and having listened devoutly to the mass, they grew more hopeful. They did not lose their temper after mass, when Jagienka again accepted holy water from Zbyszko. In the church-yard they bowed to Zych, to Jagienka and even to the abbot, although he was an enemy of Wilk of Brzozowa. They scowled at Zbyszko, but did not attempt to touch him, although their hearts were throbbing with grief, anger and jealousy; never before had Jagienka seemed to them to be as beautiful as she was then. When the brilliant retinue moved on and when from afar they heard the merry song of the ambulant seminarists, Cztan began to wipe the perspiration from his hairy cheeks and to snort like a horse; as for Wilk, he said, gnashing his teeth:

"To the inn! To the inn! Woe to me!" Afterward remembering what had relieved them before, they again seized the stone and rolled it back to its former place.

Zbyszko rode beside Jagienka, listening to the abbot's *shpilmen* singing merry songs; but when they had traveled five or six furlongs, he suddenly reined in his horse, and said:

"Oh! I intended to pay for a mass to be said for uncle's health and I forgot it; I must return."

"Do not go back!" exclaimed Jagienka; "we will send from Zgorzelice."

"No, I will return, and you must not wait for me. With God!"

"With God," said the abbot. "Go!" And his face brightened; when Zbyszko disappeared, he touched Zych with his elbow and said:

"Do you understand?"

"What?"

"He will surely fight in Krzesnia with Wilk and Cztan; but I wished for it and I am glad."

"They are dreadful boys! If they wound him, then what of it?"

"What of it? If he fight for Jagienka, then how can he afterward think about that other girl, Jurandowna? From this time, Jagienka will be his lady, not the other girl; and I wish it because he is my relative and I like him."

"Bah! What about his vow?"

94

"I will give him absolution in the twinkling of an eye! Have you not heard that I promised to absolve him?"

"Your head is wise about everything," answered Zych.

The abbot was pleased with this praise; then he approached nearer Jagienka and asked:

"Why are you so sad?"

She leaned on the saddle, seized the abbot's hand and lifted it to her mouth:

"Godfather, could you not send your *shpilmen* to Krzesnia?"

"What for? They will get drunk in the inn—that's all."

"But they may prevent a quarrel."

The abbot looked into her eyes and then said sharply:

"Let them even kill him."

"Then they must kill me also!" exclaimed Jagienka.

The bitterness which had accumulated in her bosom since that conversation about Danusia with Zbyszko, mingled with grief, now gushed forth in a stream of tears. Seeing this, the abbot encircled her with his arm, almost covering her with his enormous sleeve, and began to talk:

"Do not be afraid, my dear little girl. They may quarrel, but the other boys are noblemen; they will attack him only in a chivalrous manner; they will call him up on the field, and then he can manage for himself, even if he be obliged to fight with both of them at once. As for Jurandowna, about whom you have heard, I will tell you this: there is no wood growing for a bed for the other girl."

"If he prefers the other girl, then I do not care about him," answered Jagienka, through her tears.

"Then why do you, weep?"

"Because I am afraid for him."

"Woman's sense!" said the abbot, laughing.

Then having bent toward Jagienka's ear, he said:

"You must remember, dear girl, that even if he take you, he will be obliged to fight just the same; a nobleman must be a knight." Here he bent still closer and added:

"And he will take you, and before long, as God is in heaven!"

"I do not know about that!" answered Jagienka.

But she began to smile through her tears, and to look at the abbot as if she wished to ask him how he knew it.

Meanwhile, Zbyszko having returned to Krzesnia, went directly to the priest, because he really wished to have a mass read for Macko's health; after having settled about that, he went to the inn, where he expected to find young Wilk of Brzozowa, and Cztan of Rogow.

He found both of them there, and also many other people, noblemen, farmers and a few "madcap fellows" showing different German tricks. At first he could not recognize anybody, because the windows of the inn being made of ox bladders, did not let in a good light; but when the servant put some resinous wood on the fire, he noticed in the corner behind the beer buckets, Cztan's hairy cheeks, and Wilk's furious face.

Then he walked slowly toward them, pushing aside the people; when he reached them, he struck the table so heavily with his fist that the noise resounded throughout the whole inn.

They arose immediately and began to turn their girdles; but before they could grasp the hilts of their swords, Zbyszko threw down a glove, and speaking through his nose, as the knights used to speak while challenging, he said these words which were unexpected by everybody:

"If either of you, or any other knightly person here present, deny that the most beautiful and most virtuous girl in the world is *Panna* Danuta Jurandowna of Spychow, that one I will challenge to combat, on horseback or on foot, until the first kneeling, or until the last breath."

Wilk and Cztan were astonished as much as the abbot would have been, had he heard Zbyszko's words; and for a while they could not say a word. Who was this *panna*? They cared about Jagienka and not about her; and if this youth did not care for Jagienka, then what did he wish? Why had he made them angry in the church-yard? What did he return for, and why did he wish to quarrel with them? These questions produced such confusion in their minds, that they opened their mouths widely and stared at Zbyszko as if he were not a man, but some German wonder.

But the more intelligent Wilk, who was a little familiar with chivalrous customs and knew that often a knight served one lady, but married another, thought that this must be a similar case, and that he must seize the opportunity, to defend Jagienka.

Therefore he came out from behind the table, and coming close to Zbyszko, asked threateningly:

"Then, you dog-brother, you mean to say that Jagienka Zychowna is not the most beautiful girl in the world?"

Cztan followed him; and the people surrounded them, because they understood that it would not end in words.

CHAPTER X.

When Jagienka reached home, she immediately sent a servant to Krzesnia to learn whether there had been a fight in the inn, or whether there had been a challenge. But the servant having received a *skojec*,[85] began to drink with the priest's servants, and did not hasten. Another servant who had been sent to Bogdaniec to inform Macko that the abbot was going to pay him a visit, returned, having fulfilled the commission and reported that he had seen Zbyszko playing dice with the old man. This partly soothed Jagienka, because knowing by experience how dexterous Zbyszko was, she was not so much afraid about a regular duel, as she was about some unexpected accident in the inn. She wanted to accompany the abbot to Bogdaniec, but he was not willing. He wished to talk with Macko about the pledge and about some other important business; and then he wanted to go there toward night. Having learned that Zbyszko had returned home safe, he became very jovial and ordered his wandering seminarists to sing and shout. They obeyed him so well that the forest resounded with the noise, and in Bogdaniec, the farmers came out from their houses, and looked to see whether there was a fire or an invasion of the enemy. The pilgrim riding ahead, quieted them by telling them that a high ecclesiastical dignitary was coming; therefore when they saw the abbot, they bowed to him, and some of them even made the sign of the cross on their chests; he seeing how they respected him, rode along with joyful pride, pleased with the world and full of kindness toward the people.

Macko and Zbyszko having heard the singing, came to the gate to meet him. Some of the seminarists had been in Bogdaniec before with the abbot; but others of them having joined the retinue lately, had never seen it until now. They were disappointed when they saw the miserable house which could not be compared with the large mansion in Zgorzelice. But they were reassured when they saw the smoke coming out from the thatched roof of the house; and they were greatly pleased when upon entering the room, they smelt saffron and different kinds of meats, and noticed two tables full of tin dishes, empty as yet, but enormous. On the smaller table which was prepared for the abbot, shone a silver dish and also a beautifully engraved silver cup, both taken with the other treasures from the Fryzes.

Macko and Zbyszko invited them to the table immediately; but the abbot who had eaten plentifully in Zgorzelice, refused because he had something else on his mind. Since his arrival he had looked at Zbyszko attentively and uneasily, as if he desired to see on him some traces of the fight; but seeing the quiet face of the youth, he began to be impatient; finally he was unable to restrain his curiosity any longer.

"Let us go into the chamber," said he, "to speak about the pledge. Do not refuse me; that will make me angry!"

Here he turned to the seminarists and shouted:

"You keep quiet and do not listen at the door!"

Having said this, he opened the door to the chamber and entered, followed by Zbyszko and Macko. As soon as they were seated on the chests, the abbot turned toward the young knight:

"Did you go back to Krzesnia?" asked he.

"Yes, I was there."

"And what?"

"Well, I paid for a mass for my uncle's health, that's all."

The abbot moved on the chest impatiently.

"Ha!" thought he, "he did not meet Cztan and Wilk; perhaps they were not there, and perhaps he did not look for them. I was mistaken."

But he was angry because he was mistaken, and because his plans had not been realized; therefore immediately his face grew red and he began to breathe loudly.

"Let us speak about the pledge!" said he. "Have you the money? If not, then the estate is mine!"

Macko, who knew how to act with him, rose silently, opened the chest on which he was sitting, and took out of it a bag of *grzywien*, evidently prepared for this occasion, and said:

"We are poor people, but we have the money; we will pay what is right, as it is written in the 'letter' which I signed with the mark of the holy cross. If you want to be paid for the improvements, we will not quarrel about that either; we will pay the amount you say, and we will bow to you, our benefactor."

Having said this, he kneeled at the abbot's knee and Zbyszko did the same. The abbot, who expected some quarrels and arguing, was very much surprised at such a proceeding, and not very much pleased with it; he wanted to dictate some conditions and he saw that he would have no opportunity to do so.

Therefore returning the "letter" or rather the mortgage which Macko had signed with a cross, he said:

"Why are you talking to me about an additional payment?"

"Because we do not want to receive any presents," answered Macko cunningly, knowing well that the more he quarreled in that matter the more he would get.

At this the abbot reddened with anger:

"Did you ever see such people? They do not wish to accept anything from a relative! You have too much bread! I did not take waste land and I do not return it waste; and if I want to give you this bag, I will do it!"

"You would not do that!" exclaimed Macko.

"I will not do it! Here is your pledge! Here is your money! I give it because I want to, and had I even thrown it into the road, it would be none of your affairs. You shall see if I will not do as I wish!"

Having said this, he seized the bag and threw it on the floor so hard that it burst, and the money was scattered.

"May God reward you! May God reward you, father and benefactor!" exclaimed Macko, who had been waiting for this; "I would not accept it from anyone else, but from a relation and a spiritual father, I will accept it."

The abbot looked threateningly at both of them, and finally he said:

"Although I am angry, I know what I am doing; therefore hold what you have, because I assure you that you shall not have one *skojeo* more."

"We did not expect even this."

"You know that Jagienka will inherit everything I have."

"The land also?" asked Macko, simply.

"The land also!" shouted the abbot.

At this Macko's face grew long, but he recovered himself and said:

"Ej, why should you think about death! May the Lord Jesus grant you a hundred years or more of life, and an important bishopric soon."

"Certainly! Am I worse than others?" said the abbot.

"Not worse, but better!"

These words appeased the abbot, for his anger never lasted long.

"Well," said he, "you are my relations, and she is only my goddaughter; but I love her, and Zych also. There is no better man in the world than Zych and no better girl than Jagienka, also! Who can say anything against them?"

He began to look angry, but Macko did not contradict; he quickly affirmed that there was no worthier neighbor in the whole kingdom.

"And as for the girl," said he, "I could not love my own daughter any more than I love her. With her help, I recovered my health and I shall never forget it until my death."

"You will both be punished if you forget it," said the abbot, "and I will curse you. But I do not wish to wrong you, therefore I have found a way by which, what I will leave after my death, can belong to you and to Jagienka; do you understand?"

"May God help us to realize that!" answered Macko. "Sweet Jesus! I would go on foot to the grave of the queen in Krakow or to Lysa Gora[86] to bow to the Holy Cross."

The abbot was very much pleased with such sincerity; he smiled and said:

"The girl is perfectly right to be particular in her choice, because she is pretty, rich and of good family! Of what account are Cztan or Wilk, when the son of a *wojewoda* would not be too good for her! But if somebody, as myself for instance, spoke in favor of any particular one, then she would marry him, because she loves me and knows that I will advise her well."

"The one whom you advise her to marry, will be very lucky," said Macko.

But the abbot turned to Zbyszko:

"What do you say to this?"

"Well, I think the same as my uncle does."

The face of the abbot became still more serene; he struck Zbyszko's shoulder with his hand so hard that the blow resounded in the chamber, and asked:

"Why did you not let Cztan or Wilk approach Jagienka at church?"

"Because I did not want them to think that I was afraid of them, and I did not want you to think so."

"But you gave the holy water to her."

"Yes, I did."

The abbot gave him another blow.

"Then, take her!"

"Take her!" exclaimed Macko, like an echo.

At this Zbyszko gathered up his hair, put it in the net, and answered quietly:

"How can I take her, when before the altar in Tyniec, I made a vow to Danusia Jurandowna?"

"You made a vow about the peacock's tufts, and you must get them, but take Jagienka immediately."

"No," answered Zbyszko; "afterward when Danusia covered me with her veil, I promised that I would marry her."

The blood began to rush to the abbot's face; his ears turned blue, and his eyes bulged; he approached Zbyszko and said, in a voice muffled with anger:

"Your vows are the chaff and I am the wind; understand! Ot!"

And he blew on Zbyszko's head so powerfully, that the net fell off and the hair was scattered on his shoulders. Then Zbyszko frowned, and looking into the abbot's eyes, he said:

"In my vows is my honor, and over my honor, I alone am the guardian!"

At this, the abbot not being accustomed to opposition, lost his breath to such a degree, that for a time he could not speak. There was an ill-omened silence, which finally was broken by Macko:

"Zbyszku!" exclaimed he, "come to your wits again! What is the matter with you?"

Meanwhile the abbot raised his hand and pointing toward the youth, began to shout:

"What is the matter with him? I know what is the matter; he has not the heart of a nobleman, nor of a knight, but of a hare! That is the matter with him; he is afraid of Cztan and Wilk!"

But Zbyszko, who had remained cool and calm, carelessly shrugged his shoulders and answered:

"Owa! I broke their heads when I was in Krzesnia."

"For heaven's sake!" exclaimed Macko.

The abbot stared for a while at Zbyszko. Anger was struggling with admiration in him, and his reason told him that from that fight, he might derive some benefit for his plans.

Therefore having become cooler, he shouted to Zbyszko:

"Why didn't you tell us that before?"

"Because I was ashamed. I thought they would challenge me, as it is customary for knights to do, to fight on horseback or on foot; but they are bandits, not knights. Wilk first took a board from the table, Cztan seized another and they both rushed against me! What could I do? I seized a bench; well—you know!"

"Are they still alive?" asked Macko.

"Yes, they are alive, but they were hurt. They breathed when I left."

The abbot, rubbing his forehead, listened; then he suddenly jumped from the chest, on which he had seated himself to be more comfortable and to think the matter over, and exclaimed:

"Wait! I want to tell you something!"

"What?" asked Zbyszko.

"If you fought for Jagienka and injured them for her sake, then you are really her knight, not Danusia's; and you must take Jagienka."

Having said this, he put his hands on his hips and looked at Zbyszko triumphantly; but Zbyszko smiled and said:

"Hej! I knew very well why you wanted me to fight with them; but you have not succeeded in your plans."

"Why? Speak!"

"Because I challenged them to deny that Danusia Jurandowna is the prettiest and the most virtuous girl in the world; they took Jagienka's part, and that is why there was a fight."

Having heard this, the abbot stood amazed, and only the frequent movement of his eyes indicated that he was still alive. Finally he turned, opened the door with his foot, and rushed into the other room; there he seized the curved stick from the pilgrim's hands and began to strike the *shpilmen* with it, roaring like a wounded urus.

"To horse, you rascals! To horse, you dog-faiths! I will not put my foot in this house again! To horse, he who believes in God, to horse!"

Then he opened the outer door and went into the court-yard, followed by the frightened seminarists. They rushed to the stable and began to saddle the horses. In vain Macko followed the abbot, and entreated him to remain; swore that it was not his fault. The abbot cursed the house, the people and the fields; when they brought him a horse, he jumped in the saddle without touching the stirrups and galloped away looking, with his large sleeves filled by the wind, like an enormous red bird. The seminarists rushed after him, like a herd following its leader.

Macko stood looking after them for some time; but when they disappeared in the forest, he returned slowly to the room and said to Zbyszko, shaking his head sadly:

"See what you have done?"

"It would not have happened if I had gone away; and it is your fault that I did not."

"Why?"

"Because I did not wish to leave you when you were sick."

"And what will you do now?"

"Now I shall go."

"Where?"

"To Mazowsze to see Danusia; and after that to search for peacock's tufts among the Germans."

Macko was silent for a moment, then he said:

"He returned the 'letter,' but the mortgage is recorded in the mortgage-book at the court. Now the abbot will not give us even a *skojec*."

"I do not care. You have money, and I do not need anything for my journey. I will be received everywhere and my horses will be fed; if I only had a suit of armor on my back and a sword in my hand, I would need nothing else."

Macko began to think about everything that had happened. All his plans and wishes had been frustrated. He had wished with his whole heart that Zbyszko would marry Jagienka; but he now realized that this wish would never be fulfilled; and considering the abbot's anger, the behavior of Zbyszko toward Jagienka and finally the fight with Cztan and Wilk, he concluded it would be better to allow Zbyszko to go.

"Ha!" said he, finally, "if you must seek for the peacock's feathers on the heads of the Knights of the Cross, go then. Let the Lord Jesus' will be accomplished. But I must go immediately to Zgorzelice; perhaps I will succeed in appeasing their wrath if I implore pardon of the abbot and of Zych; I care especially for the friendship of Zych."

Here he looked into Zbyszko's eyes and asked:

"Do you not regret Jagienka?"

"May God give her health and the best of everything!" answered Zbyszko.

END OF PART SECOND.

PART THIRD.

CHAPTER I.

Macko waited patiently for several days, hoping to receive some news from Zgorzelice, or to hear that the abbot's anger had been appeased; finally he became impatient and determined to go personally to see Zych. Everything had happened contrary to his wishes, and now he was anxious to know whether Zych was angry with him. He was afraid that the abbot would never be reconciled with Zbyszko and him. He wanted, however, to do everything he could, to soften that anger; therefore while riding, he was thinking what he would say in Zgorzelice, to palliate the offence and preserve the old friendship with his neighbor. His thoughts, however, were not clear, therefore he was glad to find Jagienka alone; the girl received him as usual with a bow and kissed his hand,—in a word, she was friendly, but a little sad.

"Is your father home?" asked he.

"He went out hunting with the abbot. They may be back at any moment."

Having said this, she conducted him into the house, where they both sat in silence for a long time; the girl spoke first, and said:

"Are you lonely now in Bogdaniec?"

"Very lonely," answered Macko. "Then you knew that Zbyszko had gone away?"

Jagienka sighed softly:

"Yes, I knew it the very same day; I thought he would come here to bid me good-bye, but he did not."

"How could he come!" said Macko. "The abbot would have torn him to pieces; neither would your father have welcomed him."

She shook her head and said:

"Ej! I would not allow anybody to injure him."

Upon this Macko hugged the girl and said:

"God be with you, girl! You are sad, but I also am sad. Let me tell you that neither the abbot nor your own father loves you more than I do. I wish that Zbyszko had chosen you, and not another."

There came upon Jagienka such a moment of grief and longing, that she could not conceal her feelings, but said:

"I shall never see him again, or if I see him, it will be with Jurandowna, and then I will cry my eyes out."

She raised her apron and covered her eyes, which were filled with tears.

Macko said:

"Stop crying! He has gone, but with God's grace, he will not come back with Jurandowna."

"Why not?" said Jagienka, from behind her apron.

"Because Jurand does not want to give him the girl."

Then Jagienka suddenly uncovered her face, and having turned toward Macko, said to him:

"Zbyszko told me that; but is it true?"

"As true as that God is in heaven."

"But why?"

"Who knows why. Some vow, or something like that, and there is no remission for vows! He liked Zbyszko, because the boy promised to help him in his vengeance; but even that was useless. Jurand would listen neither to persuasion, nor to command, nor to prayers. He said he could not. Well, there must be some reason why he could not do it, and he will

100

not change his mind, because he is stern and unyielding. Don't lose hope but cheer up. Rightly speaking, the boy was obliged to go, because he had sworn in the church to secure three peacocks' crests. Then, also, the girl covered him with her veil, which was a sign that she would take him for her husband; otherwise they would have beheaded him; for that, he must be grateful to her—one cannot deny it. With God's help, she will not be his; but according to the law, he is hers. Zych is angry with him; the abbot has sent a plague upon him, so that his skin shivers; I am angry also, but if one thinks carefully, what else could he do? Since he belonged to the other girl, he was obliged to go. He is a nobleman. But I tell you this; if the Germans do not kill him, then he will come back; and he will come back not only to me an old man, not only to Bogdaniec, but to you, because he was very fond of you."

"I don't believe he was!" said Jagienka.

But she drew near Macko, and having touched him with her elbow, she asked: "How do you know it? I am sure that is not true."

"How do I know?" answered Macko. "I saw how difficult it was for him to go away. When it was decided that he must go, I asked him: 'Do you not regret Jagienka?' and he said: 'May God give her health and the best of everything.' Then immediately he began to sigh."

"I am sure that it is not true!" said Jagienka, softly; "but tell me again."

"As God is dear to me, it is true! After seeing you, he will not care for the other girl, because you know yourself that there is no girl more beautiful than you in the whole world. He has felt God's will toward you—do not fear—perhaps even more than you have felt it toward him."

"Not at all!" exclaimed Jagienka. Then she again covered her face, which was as rosy as an apple, with her sleeve; Macko smiled, passed his hand over his moustache and said:

"Hej! if I were only younger; but you must comfort yourself, because I see how it will be. He will get his spurs at the Mazowiecki court, because that is near the boundary and it is not difficult to kill a Krzyzak there. I know that there are good knights among the Germans; but I think that it will take a very good one to defeat Zbyszko. See how he routed Cztan of Rogow and Wilk of Brzozowa, although they are said to be dreadful boys and as strong as bears. He will bring his crests, but he will not bring Jurandowna."

"But when will he return?"

"Bah I if you are not willing to wait, then you will not be wronged. Repeat what I have told you to the abbot and to Zych; perhaps they will not be so angry with Zbyszko."

"How can I tell them anything? *Tatus* is more sorrowful than angry; but it is dangerous even to mention Zbyszko's name to the abbot. He scolded me because I sent Zbyszko a servant."

"What servant?"

"We had a Czech, whom *tatus* captured at Boleslawiec, a good, faithful boy. His name was Hlawa. *Tatus* gave him to my service, because he was a *wlodyka*; I gave him a worthy armor and sent him to Zbyszko, to serve and protect him. I also gave him a bag of money for the journey. He promised me that he would serve Zbyszko faithfully until death."

"My dear girl! may God reward you! Was Zych opposed to your doing it?"

"Yes, at first *tatus* did not want to let me do it; but when I began to coax him, then he consented. When the abbot heard about it from his seminarists, he immediately rushed out of the room swearing; there was such a disturbance, that *tatus* escaped to the barn. Toward evening, the abbot took pity on my tears and even made me a present of some beads."

"As God is dear to me, I do not know whether I love Zbyszko any better than I love you; but he had a worthy retinue. I also gave him money, although he did not want to take it. Well, the Mazurs are not beyond the seas."

The conversation was interrupted by the barking of dogs, by shouting and by the sounds of brass trumpets in front of the house. Having heard this, Jagienka said:

"*Tatus* and the abbot have returned from hunting. Let us go outside; it will be better for the abbot to see you there, and not to meet you unexpectedly in the house."

Having said this, she conducted Macko out-of-doors; in the courtyard, on the snow they perceived a throng of men, horses and dogs, also elks and wolves pierced with spears or shot with crossbows. The abbot saw Macko before he dismounted, and hurled a spear toward him, not to strike him, but to show in that way, his great anger against the inhabitants of Bogdaniec. But Macko uncovered and bowed to him as if he noticed nothing unusual; Jagienka, however, had not noticed the abbot's action, because she was very much surprised to see her two wooers in the retinue.

"Cztan and Wilk are here!" she exclaimed; "I presume they met *tatus* in the forest."

Immediately the thought ran through Macko's mind, that perhaps one of them would get Jagienka, and with her Moczydoly, the abbot's lands, forests and money. Then grief and anger filled his heart, especially when he perceived what occurred. Behold, Wilk of Brzozowa, although only a short time before the abbot wanted to fight with his father, sprang to the abbot's stirrups, and helped him to dismount; and the abbot leaned in a friendly manner on the young nobleman's shoulder.

"In that way, the abbot will become reconciled with old Wilk," thought Macko, "and he will give the forests and the lands with the girl."

His sad thoughts were interrupted by Jagienka who said:

"They are soon cured after Zbyszko's beating; but even if they come here every day, it will not benefit them!"

Macko looked and saw that the girl's face was red with anger, and that her blue eyes sparkled with indignation, although she knew very well that Cztan and Wilk had taken her part in the inn, and had been beaten on her account.

Therefore Macko said:

"Bah! you will do as the abbot commands."

She immediately retorted:

"The abbot will do what I wish."

"Gracious Lord!" thought Macko, "and that stupid Zbyszko left such a girl!"

CHAPTER II.

Zbyszko had left Bogdaniec with a sad heart indeed. In the first place he felt strange without his uncle, from whom he had never been separated before, and to whom he was so accustomed, that he did not know how he would get along without him during the journey, as well as in the war. Then he regretted Jagienka. Although he was going to Danusia whom he loved dearly, still he had been so comfortable and happy with Jagienka, that now he felt sad without her. He was surprised himself at his grief, and even somewhat alarmed about it. He would not have minded if he longed for Jagienka only as a brother longs for a sister; but he noticed that he longed to embrace her, to put her on horseback, to carry her over the brooks, to wring the water from her tress, to wander with her in the forest, to gaze at her, and to converse with her. He was so accustomed to doing all this and it was so pleasant, that when he began to think about it, he forgot that he was going on a long journey to Mazury; instead of that, he remembered the moment when Jagienka helped him in the forest, when he was struggling with the bear. It seemed to him as though it happened only yesterday; also as though it were only yesterday when they went to the Odstajny lake for beavers. Then he recalled how beautifully she was dressed when going to church in Krzesnia, and how surprised he was that such a simple girl should appear like the daughter of a mighty lord. All these thoughts filled his heart with uneasiness, sweetness, and sadness.

"Had I only bid her good-bye," he said to himself, "perhaps I would feel easier now."

Finally he became afraid of these reminiscences, and he shook them from his mind like dry snow from his mantle.

"I am going to Danusia, to my dearest," he said to himself.

He noticed that this was a more holy love. Gradually his feet grew colder in the stirrups, and the cold wind cooled his blood. All his thoughts now turned to Danusia Jurandowna. He belonged to her without any doubt; but for her, he would have been beheaded on the Krakowski square. When she said in the presence of the knights and burghers: "He is mine!" she rescued him from the hands of the executioners; from that time, he belonged to her, as a slave to his master. Jurand's opposition was useless. She alone could drive him away; and even then he would not go far, because he was bound by his vow. He imagined, however, that she would not drive him away; but rather that she would follow him from the Mazowiecki court, even to the end of the world. Then he began to praise her to himself to Jagienka's disadvantage, as if it were her fault, that temptations assailed him and his heart was divided. Now he forgot that Jagienka cured old Macko; he forgot that without her help, the bear would have torn him to pieces; and he became enraged with her, hoping in this way to please Danusia and to justify himself in his own eyes.

At this moment the Czech, Hlawa, sent by Jagienka, arrived, leading a horse.

"Be blessed!" said he, with a low bow.

Zbyszko had seen him once or twice in Zgorzelice, but he did not recognize him; therefore he said:

"Be blessed for ages and ages! Who are you?"

"Your servant, famous lord."

"What do you mean? These are my servants," said Zbyszko, pointing to the two Turks, given to him by Sulimczyk Zawisza, and to two sturdy men who sitting on horseback, were leading the knight's stallions; "these are mine; who sent you?"

"*Panna* Jagienka Zychowna of Zgorzelice."

"*Panna* Jagienka?"

A while ago, Zbyszko had been angry with her and his heart was still full of wrath; therefore he said:

"Return home and thank the *panna* for the favor; I do not want you."

But the Czech shook his head.

"I cannot return. They have given me to you; besides that, I have sworn to serve you until death."

"If they gave you to me, then you are my servant."

"Yours, sir."

"Then I command you to return."

"I have sworn; although I am a prisoner from Boleslawiec and a poor boy, still I am a *wlodyczka*."[87]

Zbyszko became angry:

"Go away! What; are you going to serve me against my will? Go away, before I order my servants to bend their crossbows."

But the Czech quietly untied a broadcloth mantle, lined with wolf-skins, handed it to Zbyszko and said:

"*Panna* Jagienka sent you this, also, sir."

"Do you wish me to break your bones?" asked Zbyszko, taking a spear from an attendant.

"Here is also a bag of money for your disposal," answered the Czech.

Zbyszko was ready to strike him with the lance, but he recollected that the boy, although a prisoner, was by birth a *wlodyka*, who had remained with Zych only he did not have money to pay his ransom; consequently Zbyszko dropped the spear.

Then the Czech bent to his stirrups and said:

"Be not angry, sir. If you do not wish me to accompany you, I will follow you at a distance of one or two furlongs; but I must go, because I have sworn to do so upon the salvation of my soul."

"If I order my servants to kill you or to bind you?"

"If you order them to kill me, that will not be my sin; and if you order them to bind me, then I will remain until some good people untie me, or until the wolves devour me."

Zbyszko did not reply; he urged his horse forward and his attendants followed him. The Czech with a crossbow and an axe on his shoulder, followed them, shielding himself with a shaggy bison skin, because a sharp wind carrying flakes of snow, began to blow. The storm grew worse and worse. The Turks, although dressed in sheepskin coats, were chilled with cold; Zbyszko himself, not being dressed very warmly, glanced several times at the mantle lined with wolf-fur, which Hlawa had brought him; after a while, he told one of the Turks to give it to him.

Having wrapped himself with it carefully, he felt a warmth spreading all over his body. He covered his eyes and the greater part of his face with the hood of the mantle, so that the wind did not annoy him any more. Then, involuntarily, he thought how good Jagienka had been to him. He reined in his horse, called the Czech, and asked him about her, and about everything that had happened in Zgorzelice.

"Does Zych know that the *panna* sent you to me?" he said.

"He knows it," answered Hlawa.

"Was he not opposed to it?"

"He was."

"Tell me then all about it."

"The *pan* was walking in the room and the *panna* followed him. He shouted, but the *panienka* said nothing; but when he turned toward her, she kneeled but did not utter one word. Finally the *panisko*[88] said: 'Have you become deaf, that you do not answer my questions? Speak then; perhaps I will consent.' Then the *panna* understood that she could do as she wished and began to thank him. The *pan* reproached her, because she had persuaded him, and complained that he must always do as she wished; finally he said: 'Promise me that you will not go secretly to bid him good-bye; then I will consent, but not otherwise.' Then the *panienka* became very sorrowful, but she promised; the *pan* was satisfied, because the abbot and he were both afraid that she would see you. Well, that was not the end of it; afterward the *panna* wanted to send two horses, but the *pan* would not consent; the *panna* wanted to send a wolf-skin and a bag of money, but the *pan* refused. His refusal did not amount to anything, however! If she wanted to set the house on fire, the *panisko* would finally consent. Therefore I brought two horses, a wolf-skin and a bag of money."

"Good girl!" thought Zbyszko. After a while he asked:

"Was there no trouble with the abbot?" The Czech, an intelligent attendant, who understood what happened around him, smiled and answered:

"They were both careful to keep everything secret from the abbot; I do not know what happened when he learned about it, after I left Zgorzelice. Sometimes he shouts at the *panienka*; but afterward he watches her to see if he did not wrong her. I saw him myself one time after he had scolded her, go to his chest and bring out such a beautiful chain that one could not get a better one even in Krakow, and give it to her. She will manage the abbot also, because her own father does not love her any more than he does."

"That is certainly true."

"As God is in heaven!"

Then they became silent and rode along amidst wind and snow. Suddenly Zbyszko reined in his horse; from the forest beside the road, there was heard a plaintive voice, half stifled by the roar of the wind:

"Christians, help God's servant in his misfortune!"

Thereupon a man who was dressed partly in clerical clothing, rushed to the road and began to cry to Zbyszko:

"Whoever you are, sir, help a fellow-creature who has met with a dreadful accident!"

"What has happened to you, and who are you?" asked the young knight.

"I am God's servant, although not yet ordained; this morning the horse which was carrying my chests containing holy things, ran away. I remained alone, without weapons; evening is approaching, and soon the wild beasts will begin to roar in the forest. I shall perish, unless you succor me."

"If I let you perish," answered Zbyszko, "I will be accountable for your sins; but how can I believe that you are speaking the truth. You may be a highway robber, like many others wandering on the roads!"

"You may believe me, sir, for I will show you the chests. Many a man would give a purse full of gold for what is in them; but I will give you some of it for nothing, if you take me and the chests with you."

"You told me that you were God's servant, and yet you do not know that one must give help, not for earthly recompense, but for spiritual reward. But how is it that you have the chests now if the horse carried them away?"

"The wolves devoured the horse in the forest, but the chests remained; I brought them to the road, and then waited for mercy and help."

Wishing to prove that he was speaking the truth, he pointed to two chests made of leather, lying under a pine tree. Zbyszko still looked at him suspiciously, because the man did not look honest, and his speech indicated that he came from a distant part of the country.

He did not refuse to help him, however, but permitted him to ride the horse led by the Czech and take the chests, which proved to be very light.

"May God multiply your victories, valiant knight!" said the stranger.

Then, seeing Zbyszko's youthful face, he added softly:

"And the hairs of your beard, also."

He rode beside the Czech. For a time they could not talk, because a strong wind was blowing, and roaring in the forest; but when it decreased, Zbyszko heard the following conversation behind him.

"I don't deny that you were in Rome; but you look like a beer drunkard," said the Czech.

"Look out for eternal damnation," answered the stranger; "you are talking to a man who last Easter ate hard boiled eggs with the holy father. Don't speak to me in such cold weather about beer; but if you have a flask of wine with you, then give me two or three swallows of it, and I will pardon you a month of purgatory."

"You have not been ordained; I heard you say you had not. How then can you grant me pardon for a month of purgatory?"

"I have not received ordination, but I have my head shaved, because I received permission for that; beside, I am carrying indulgences and relics."

"In the chests?" asked the Czech.

"Yes, in the chests. If you saw all I have there, you would fall on your face, not only you, but all the pines in the forest and all the wild beasts."

But the Czech, being an intelligent and experienced attendant, looked suspiciously at this peddler of indulgences, and said:

"The wolves devoured your horse?"

"Yes, they devoured him, because they are the devil's relatives. If you have any wine, give me some; although the wind has ceased, yet I am frozen, having sat by the road so long."

The Czech would not give him any wine; and they rode along silently, until the stranger began to ask:

"Where are you going?"

"Far. At first to Sieradz. Are you going with us?"

"I must. I will sleep in the stable, and perhaps to-morrow this pious knight will give me a present of a horse; then I will go further."

"Where are you from?"

"From under Prussian lords, not far from Marienburg."

Having heard this, Zbyszko turned and motioned to the stranger to come nearer to him.

"Did you come from Marienburg?" said he

"Yes, sir."

"But are you a German? You speak our language very well. What is your name?"

"I am a German, and they call me Sanderus; I speak your language well, because I was born in Torun, where everybody speaks that language; then I lived in Marienburg, and there it is the same. Bah! even the brothers of the Order understand your language."

"How long since you left Marienburg?"

"I was in the Holy Land, then in Constantinople, and in Rome; thence through France I came to Marienburg and from there I was going to Mazowsze, carrying the holy relics which pious Christians buy willingly, for the salvation of their souls."

"Have you been in Plock or in Warszawa?"

"I was in both cities. May God give good health to both of the princesses! Princess Alexandra is greatly esteemed even by the Prussian lords, because she is a pious lady; the princess Anna Januszowna is also pious."

"Did you see the court in Warszawa?"

"I did not see it in Warszawa but in Ciechanow, where both the princesses received me hospitably, and gave me munificent presents, as God's servant deserves to receive. I left them relics, which will bring them God's blessing."

Zbyszko wanted to ask about Danusia; but he understood that it would be unwise to make a confidant of this stranger, a man of low origin. Therefore, after a short silence, he asked:

"What kind of relics are you carrying?"

"I carry indulgences and relics; the indulgences are different kinds; there are total indulgences, some for five hundred years, some for three hundred, some for two hundred and some for less time, which are cheaper, so that even poor people can buy them and shorten the torments of purgatory. I have indulgences for future and for past sins; but don't think, sir, that I keep the money I receive for them. I am satisfied with a piece of black bread and a glass of water—that is all for me; the rest I carry to Rome, to accumulate enough for a new crusade. It is true, there are many swindlers who carry false indulgences, false relics, false seals and false testimonials; and they are righteously pursued by the holy father's letters; but I was wronged by the prior of Sieradz, because my seals are authentic. Look, sir, at the wax and tell me what you think of them."

"What about the prior of Sieradz?"

"Ah, sir! I fear that he is infected with Wiklef's heresy. If, as your shield-bearer told me, you are going to Sieradz, it will be better for me not to show myself to him, because I do not want to lead him into the sin of blasphemy against holy things."

"This means, speaking frankly, that he thinks that you are a swindler."

"If the question were about myself, I would pardon him for the sake of brotherly love; but he has blasphemed against my holy wares, for which, I am very much afraid, he will be eternally damned."

"What kind of holy wares have you?"

"It is not right to talk about them with covered head; but this time, having many indulgences ready, I give you, sir, permission to keep your cowl on, because the wind is blowing again. For that you will buy an indulgence and the sin will not be counted against you. What have I not? I have a hoof of the ass on which the Holy Family rode during the flight into Egypt; it was found near the pyramids. The king of Aragon offered me fifty ducats for it. I have a feather from the wings of the archangel Gabriel, which he dropped during the annunciation; I have the heads of two quails, sent to the Israelites in the desert; I have the oil in which the heathen wanted to fry St. John; a step of the ladder about which Jacob dreamed; the tears of St. Mary of Egypt and some rust of St. Peter's keys. But I cannot mention any more. I am very cold and your shield-bearer would not give me any wine."

"Those are great relics, if they are authentic!" said Zbyszko.

"If they are authentic? Take the spear from your attendant and aim it, because the devil is near and brings such thoughts to you. Hold him, sir, at the length of the spear. If you do not wish to bring some misfortune on yourself, then buy an indulgence from me; otherwise within three weeks somebody whom you love, will die."

Zbyszko was frightened at this threat, because he thought about Danusia, and said:

"It is not I, but the prior of the Dominicans in Sieradz who does not believe."

"Look, sir, for yourself, at the wax on the seals; as for the prior, I do not know whether he is still living, because God's justice is quick."

But when they came to Sieradz they found the prior alive. Zbyszko went to see him, and purchased two masses; one of which was to be read to insure success for Macko's vow, and the other to insure success for his vow to obtain three peacocks' crests. The prior was a foreigner, having been born in Cylia; but during his forty years' residence in Sieradz, he had learned the Polish language very well, and was a great enemy of the Knights of the Cross. Therefore, having learned about Zbyszko's enterprise, he said:

"A still greater punishment will fall upon them; but I shall not dissuade you, because you promised it upon your knightly honor; neither can there be punishment enough administered by Polish hands for the wrongs they have perpetrated in this land."

"What have they done?" asked Zbyszko, who was anxious to hear about the iniquities of the Knights of the Cross.

CHAPTER III.

106

The old prior crossed his hands and began to recite aloud '"The eternal rest;"[89] then he sat down on a bench and kept his eyes closed for a while as if to collect his thoughts; finally he began to talk:

"Wincenty of Szamotul brought them here. I was twenty years old then, and I had just come from Cylia with my uncle Petzoldt. The Krzyzaks attacked the town and set it on fire. We could see from the walls, how in the market square they cut men and women's heads off, and how they threw little children into the fire. They even killed the priests, because in their fury they spared nobody. The prior Mikolaj, having been born in Elblong, was acquainted with *Comthur* Herman, the chief of their army. Therefore he went accompanied by the senior brothers, to that dreadful knight, and having kneeled before him, entreated him in German, to have pity on Christian blood. *Comthur* Herman replied: "I do not understand," and ordered his soldiers to continue killing the people. They slaughtered the monks also, among them my uncle Petzoldt; the prior Mikolaj was tied to a horse's tail. The next morning there was no man alive in this town except the Krzyzaks and myself. I hid on a beam in the belfry. God punished them at Plowce;[90] but they still want to destroy this Christian kingdom, and nothing will deter them unless God's arm crush them."

"At Plowce," said Zbyszko, "almost all the men of my family perished; but I do not regret it, for God granted a great victory to the king Lokietek,[91] and twenty thousand Germans were destroyed.

"You will see a still greater war and a greater victory," said the prior.

"Amen!" answered Zbyszko.

Then they began to talk about other matters. The young knight asked about the peddler of relics whom he met on the road. He learned that many similar swindlers were wandering on the roads, cheating credulous people. The prior also told him that there were papal bulls ordering the bishops to examine such peddlers and immediately punish those who did not have authentic letters and seals. The testimonials of the stranger seemed spurious to the prior; therefore he wanted to deliver him to the bishop's jurisdiction. If he proved that he was sent by the pope, then no harm would be done him. He escaped, however. Perhaps he was afraid of the delay in his journey; but on account of this flight, he had drawn on himself still greater suspicion.

The prior invited Zbyszko to remain and pass the night in the monastery; but he would not, because he wanted to hang in front of the inn an inscription challenging all knights who denied that *Panna* Danuta Jurandowna was the most beautiful and the most virtuous girl in the kingdom, to a combat on horseback or on foot. It was not proper to hang such a challenge over the gate of the monastery. When he arrived at the inn, he asked for Sanderus.

"The prior thinks you are a scoundrel," said Zbyszko, "because he said: 'Why should he be afraid of the bishop's judgment, if he had good testimonials?'"

"I am not afraid of the bishop," answered Sanderus; "I am afraid of the monks, who do not know anything about seals. I wanted to go to Krakow, but I have no horse; therefore I must wait until somebody makes me a present of one. Meanwhile, I will send a letter, and I will put my own seal on it."

"If you show that you know how to write, that will prove that you are not a churl; but how will you send the letter?"

"By some pilgrim, or wandering monk. There are many people going on a pilgrimage to the queen's tomb."

"Can you write a card for me?"

"I will write, sir, even on a board, anything you wish."

"I think it will be better on a board," said Zbyszko, "because it will not tear and I can use it again later on."

In fact, after awhile the attendants brought a new board and Sanderus wrote on it. Zbyszko could not read what was written on the board; but he ordered it fastened with nails on the door of the inn, under it to be hung a shield, which was watched by the Turks alternately. Whoever struck the shield would declare that he wished to fight. But neither that day nor the following day, did the shield resound from a blow; and in the afternoon the sorrowful knight was ready to pursue his journey.

Before that, however, Sanderus came to Zbyszko and said to him:

"Sir, if you hang your shield in the land of the Prussian lords, I am sure your shield-bearer will buckle your armor."

"What do you mean! Don't you know that a Krzyzak, being a monk, cannot have a lady nor be in love with one, because it is forbidden him."

"I do not know whether it is forbidden them or not; but I know that they have them. It is true that a Krzyzak cannot fight a duel without bringing reproach on himself, because he swore that he would fight only for the faith; but besides the monks, there are many secular knights from distant countries, who came to help the Prussian lords. They are looking for some one to fight with, and especially the French knights."

"*Owa!* I saw them at Wilno, and with God's permission I shall see them in Marienburg. I need the peacocks' crests from their helmets, because I made a vow—do you understand?"

"Sir, I will sell you two or three drops of the perspiration, which St. George shed while fighting with the dragon. There is no relic, which could be more useful to a knight. Give me the horse for it, on which you permitted me to ride; then I will also give you an indulgence for the Christian blood which you will shed in the fight."

"Let me be, or I shall become angry. I shall not buy your wares until I know they are genuine."

"You are going, sir, so you have said, to the Mazowiecki court. Ask there how many relics they bought from me, the princess herself, the knights and the girls for their weddings, at which I was present."

"For what weddings?" asked Zbyszko.

"As is customary before advent, the knights were marrying as soon as they could, because the people are expecting that there will be a war between the Polish king and the Prussian lords about the province of Dobrzyn. Therefore some of them say: 'God knows whether I shall return.'"

Zbyszko was very anxious to hear about the war, but still more anxious to hear about the weddings, of which Sanderus was talking; therefore he asked:

"Which girls were married there?"

"The princess' ladies-in-waiting. I do not know whether even one remained, because I heard the princess say that she would be obliged to look for other attendants."

Having heard this, Zbyszko was silent for awhile; then he asked in an altered voice:

"Was *Panna* Danuta Jurandówna, whose name is on the board, married also?"

Sanderus hesitated before he answered. He did not know anything correctly himself; then he thought that if he kept the knight anxious and perplexed, he would have more influence over him. He wanted to retain his power over this knight who had a goodly retinue, and was well provided with everything.

Zbyszko's youth led him to suppose that he would be a generous lord, without forethought and careless of money. He had noticed already the costly armor made in Milan, and the enormous stallions, which everybody could not possess; then he assured himself that if he traveled with such a knight, he would receive hospitality in noblemen's houses, and a good opportunity to sell his indulgences; he would be safe during the journey, and have abundance of food and drink, about which he cared greatly.

Therefore having heard Zbyszko's question, he frowned, lifted his eyes as if he were trying to recollect, and answered:

"*Panna* Danuta Jurandowna? Where is she from?"

"Jurandowna Danuta of Spychow."

"I saw all of them, but I cannot remember their names."

"She is very young; she plays the lute, and amuses the princess with her singing."

"Aha—young—plays the lute—there were some young ones married also. Is she dark like an agate?"

Zbyszko breathed more freely.

"No, that was not she! Danusia is as white as snow, but has pink cheeks."

To this Sanderus replied:

"One of them, dark as an agate, remained with the princess; the others were almost all married."

"You say 'almost all,' therefore not all. For God's sake, if you wish to get anything from me, then try to recollect."

"In two or three days I could recollect; the best way will be to give me a horse, on which I can carry my holy wares."

"You will get it if you only tell me the truth."

At that moment the Czech, who was listening to the conversation, smiled and said:

"The truth will be known at the Mazowiecki court."

Sanderus looked at him for a while; then he said:

"Do you think that I am afraid of the Mazowiecki court?"

"I do not say you are afraid of the Mazowiecki court; but neither now, nor after three days will you go away with the horse. If it prove that you were lying, then you will not be able to go on your feet either, because my lord will order me to break them."

"Be sure of that!" answered Zbyszko.

Sanderus now thought that it would be wiser to be more careful, and said:

"If I wanted to lie, I would have said immediately whether she was married or not; but I said: 'I don't remember.' If you had common sense, you would recognize my virtue by that answer."

"My common sense is not a brother of your virtue, because that is the sister of a dog."

"My virtue does not bark, as your common sense does; and the one who barks when alive, may howl after death."

"That is sure! Your virtue will not howl after your death; it will gnash its teeth, provided it does not lose its teeth in the service of the devil while living." Thus they quarreled; the Czech's tongue was ready, and for every word of the German, he answered two. Zbyszko having asked about the road to Lenczyca, ordered the retinue to move forward. Beyond Sieradz, they entered thick forests which covered the greater part of the country; but the highways through these forests, had been paved with logs and ditches dug along the sides, by the order of King Kazimierz. It is true that after his death, during the disturbances of the war aroused by Nalenczs and Grzymalits, the roads were neglected; but during Jadwiga's reign, when peace was restored to the kingdom, shovels were again busy in the marshes, and axes in the forests; soon everywhere between the important cities, merchants could conduct their loaded wagons in safety. The only danger was from wild beasts and robbers; but against the beasts, they had lanterns for night, and crossbows for defence during the day; then there were fewer highway robbers than in other countries, and one who traveled with an armed retinue, need fear nothing.

Zbyszko was not afraid of robbers nor of armed knights; he did not even think about them. But he was filled with great anxiety, and longed with his whole soul to be at the Mazowiecki court. Would he find Danusia still a lady-in-waiting of the princess, or the wife of some Mazowiecki knight? Sometimes it seemed to him impossible that she should forget him; then sometimes he thought that perhaps Jurand went to the court from Spychow and married the girl to some neighbor or friend. Jurand had told him in Krakow, that he could not give Danusia to him; therefore it was evident that he had promised her to somebody else; evidently he was bound by an oath, and now he had fulfilled his promise. Zbyszko called Sanderus and questioned him again; but the German prevaricated more and more.

Therefore, Zbyszko was riding along, sad and unhappy. He did not think about Bogdaniec, nor about Zgorzelice, but only how he should act. First, it was necessary to ascertain the truth at the Mazowiecki court; therefore, he rode hastily, only stopping for a short time at the houses of noblemen, in the inns and in the cities to rest the horses. He had never ceased to love Danusia; but while in Bogdaniec and Zgorzelice, chatting almost every day with Jagienka and admiring her beauty, he had not thought about Danusia often. Now she was constantly in his thoughts, day and night. Even in his sleep, he saw her standing before him, with a lute in her hands and a garland on her head. She stretched her hands toward him, and Jurand drew her away. In the morning, when the dreams disappeared, a greater longing came, and he loved this girl more than ever now, when he was uncertain whether they had taken her from him or not.

Sometimes he feared that they had married her against her will; therefore, he was not angry with her, as she was only a child and could not have her own will. But he was angry with Jurand and with Princess Januszowna. He determined that he would not cease to serve her; even if he found her somebody else's wife, he would deposit the peacocks' crests at her feet.

Sometimes he was consoled by the thought of a great war. He felt that during the war, he would forget about everything and that he would escape all sorrows and griefs. The great war seemed suspended in the air. It was not known whence the news came, because there was peace between the king and the Order; nevertheless, wherever Zbyszko went, nothing else was talked about. The people had a presentiment that it would come, and some of them said openly: "Why were we united with Litwa, if not against those wolves, the Knights of the Cross? Therefore we must finish with them once for all, or they will destroy us." Others said: "Crazy monks! They are not satisfied with Plowce! Death is over them, and still they have taken the land of Dobrzyn."

In all parts of the kingdom, they were making preparations, gravely, without boasting, as was customary for a fight for life or death; but with the silent, deadly grudge of a mighty nation, which had suffered wrongs for a long time, and finally was ready to administer a terrible punishment. In all the houses of the nobility, Zbyszko met people who were convinced that at any moment one might be obliged to mount his horse. Zbyszko was pleased to see these hasty preparations which he met at every step. Everywhere other cares gave way to thoughts about horses and armor. Everywhere the people were gravely inspecting spears, swords, axes, helmets and javelins. The blacksmiths were busy day and night, hammering iron sheets and making heavy armor, which could hardly be lifted by the refined western knights, but which the strong noblemen of Wielko and Malopolska could wear very easily. The old people were pulling out musty bags full of *grzywns*[92] from their chests, for the war expedition of their children. Once Zbyszko passed the night in the house of a wealthy nobleman, Bartosz of Bielaw, who having twenty-two sturdy sons, pledged his numerous estates to the monastery in Lowicz, to purchase twenty-two suits of armor, the same number of helmets and weapons of war. Zbyszko now realized that it would be necessary to go to Prussia, and he thanked God that he was so well provided.

Many thought that he was the son of a *wojewoda*; and when he told the people that he was a simple nobleman, and that armor such as he wore, could be bought from the Germans by paying for it with a good blow of an axe, their hearts were filled with enthusiasm for war. Many a knight seeing that armor, and desiring to possess it, followed Zbyszko, and said: "Will you not fight for it?"

In Mazowsze, the people did not talk so much about the war. They also believed that it would come, but they did not know when. In Warszawa there was peace. The court was in Ciechanow, which Prince Janusz rebuilt after the Lithuanian invasion; nothing of the old town remained, only the castle.

In the city of Warszawa, Zbyszko was received by Jasko Socha, the *starosta*[93] of the castle, and the son of the *wojewoda* Abraham, who was killed at Worskla. Jasko knew Zbyszko, because he was with the princess in Krakow; therefore he received him hospitably and with joy; but the young man, before he began to eat or drink, asked Jasko about Danusia. But he did not know anything about her, because the prince and the princess had been in Ciechanow since fall. In Warszawa there were only a few archers and himself, to guard the castle. He had heard that there had been feasts and weddings in Ciechanow; but he did not know which girls were married.

"But I think," said he, "that Jurandowna is not married; it could not be done without Jurand, and I have not heard of his arrival. There are two brothers of the Order, *comthurs*, with the prince; one from Jansbork and the other from Szczytno, and also some foreign guests; on such occasions, Jurand never goes to the court, because the sight of a white mantle enrages him. If Jurand were not there, there would be no wedding! If you wish, I will send a messenger to ascertain and tell him to return, immediately; but I firmly believe that you will find Jurandowna still a girl."

"I am going there to-morrow myself; but may God reward you for your kindness. As soon as the horses are rested, I will go, because I shall have no peace, until I know the truth."

But Socha was not satisfied with that, and inquired among the nobles and the soldiers if they had heard about Jurandowna's wedding. But nobody had heard anything, although there were several among them who had been in Ciechanow.

Meanwhile Zbyszko retired greatly relieved. While lying in bed he decided to get rid of Sanderus; but afterward he thought that the scoundrel might be useful to him because he could speak German. Sanderus had not told him a falsehood; and although he was a costly acquisition, because he ate and drank as much as four men would in the inns, still he was serviceable, and showed some attachment for the young knight. Then he possessed the art of writing, and that gave him a superiority over the shield-bearer, the Czech, and even over Zbyszko himself. Consequently Zbyszko permitted him to accompany his retinue to Ciechanow. Sanderus was glad of this, because he noticed that being in respectable company, he won confidence and found purchasers for his wares more easily. After stopping one night in Nasielsk, riding neither too swiftly nor too slowly, they perceived next day toward evening, the walls of the castle of Ciechanow. Zbyszko stopped in an inn to don his armor, so as to enter the castle according to knightly custom, with his helmet on his head and his spear in his hand; then he mounted his enormous stallion, and having made the sign of the cross in the air, he rushed forward. He had gone only a short distance, when the Czech who was riding behind him, drew near and said:

"Your Grace, some knights are coming behind us; they must be Krzyzaks."

Zbyszko turned and saw about half a furlong behind him, a splendid retinue at the head of which there were riding two knights on fine Pomeranian horses, both in full armor, each of them wearing a white mantle with a black cross, and a helmet having a high crest of peacock's feathers.

"For God's sake, Krzyzacy!" said Zbyszko.

Involuntarily he leaned forward in his saddle and aimed his spear; seeing this the Czech seized his axe. The other attendants being experienced in war, were also ready, not for a fight, because the servants did not participate in single combat, but to measure the space for the fight on horseback, or to level the ground for the fight on foot. The Czech alone, being a nobleman, was ready to fight; but he expected that Zbyszko would challenge before he attacked, and he was surprised to see the young knight aim his spear before the challenge.

But Zbyszko came to his senses in time. He remembered how he attacked Lichtenstein near Krakow, and all the misfortunes which followed; therefore he raised the spear and handed it to the Czech. Without drawing his sword, he galloped toward the Krzyzaks. When he came near them, he noticed that there was a third knight, also with a peacock's crest on his helmet, and a fourth, without armor, but having long hair, who seemed to be a Mazur. Seeing them, he concluded that they must be some envoys to the prince of Mazowiecki; therefore he said aloud:

"May Jesus Christ be praised!"

"For ages and ages!" answered the long-haired knight.

"May God speed you!"

"And you also, sir!"

"Glory be to St. George!"

"He is our patron. You are welcome, sir."

Then they began to bow; Zbyszko told his name, who he was, what his coat of arms was, what his war-cry was and whence he was going to the Mazowiecki court. The long-haired knight said that his name was Jendrek of Kropiwnica and that he was conducting some guests to the prince; Brother Godfried, Brother Rotgier, also Sir Fulko de Lorche of Lotaringen, who being with the Knights of the Cross, wished to see the prince and especially the princess, the daughter of the famous "Kiejstut."

While they were conversing, the foreign knights sat erect on their horses, occasionally bending their heads which were covered with iron helmets ornamented with peacocks' tufts. Judging from Zbyszko's splendid armor, they thought that the prince had sent some important personage, perhaps his own son, to meet them. Jendrek of Kropiwnica said further:

"The *comthur*, or as we would say the *starosta* from Jansbork is at our prince's castle; he told the prince about these knights; that they desired to visit him, but that they did not dare, especially this knight from Lotaringen, who being from a far country, thought that the Saracens lived right beyond the frontier of the Knights of the Cross, and that there was continual war with them. The prince immediately sent me to the boundary, to conduct them safely to his castle."

"Could they not come without your help!"

"Our nation is very angry with the Krzyzaks, because of their great treacherousness; a Krzyzak will hug and kiss you, but he is ready in the same moment to stab you with a knife from behind; and such conduct is odious to us Mazurs. Nevertheless anyone will receive even a German in his house, and will not wrong his guest; but he would stop him on the road. There are many who do this for vengeance, or for glory."

"Who among you is the most famous?"

"There is one whom all Germans fear to meet; his name is Jurand of Spychow."

The heart of the young knight throbbed when he heard that name; immediately he determined to question Jendrek of Kropiwnica.

"I know!" said he; "I heard about him; his daughter Danuta was girl-in-waiting with the princess; afterward she was married."

Having said this, he looked sharply into the eyes of the Mazowiecki knight, who answered with great astonishment:

"Who told you that? She is very young yet. It is true that it sometimes happens that very young girls are married, but Jurandowna is not married. I left Ciechanow six days ago and I saw her then with the princess. How could she marry during advent?"

Zbyszko having heard this, wanted to seize the knight by the neck and shout: "May God reward you for the news!" but he controlled himself, and said:

"I heard that Jurand gave her to some one."

"It was the princess who wished to give her, but she could not do it against Jurand's will. She wanted to give her to a knight in Krakow, who made a vow to the girl, and whom she loves."

"Does she love him?" exclaimed Zbyszko.

At this Jendrek looked sharply at him, smiled and said:

"Do you know, you are too inquisitive about that girl."

"I am asking about my friend to whom I am going."

One could hardly see Zbyszko's face under the helmet; but his nose and cheeks were so red that the Mazur, who was fond of joking, said:

"I am afraid that the cold makes your face red!"

Then the young man grew still more confused, and answered:

"It must be that."

They moved forward and rode silently for some time; but after a while Jendrek of Kropiwnica asked:

"What do they call you? I did not hear distinctly?"

"Zbyszko of Bogdaniec."

"For heaven's sake! The knight who made a vow to Jurandowna, had the same name."

"Do you think that I shall deny that I am he?" answered Zbyszko, proudly.

"There is no reason for doing so. Gracious Lord, then you are that Zbyszko whom the girl covered with her veil! After the retinue returned from Krakow, the women of the court talked about nothing else, and many of them cried while listening to the story. Then you are he! Hej! how happy they will be to see you at the court; even the princess is very fond of you."

"May the Lord bless her, and you also for the good news. I suffered greatly when I heard that Danusia was married."

"She is not married! Although she will inherit Spychow, and there are many handsome youths at the court, yet not one of them looks into her eyes, because all respect your vow; then the princess would not permit it. Hej! there will be great joy. Sometimes they teased the girl! Some one would tell her: 'Your knight will not come back!' Then she would reply: 'He will be back! He will be back!' Sometimes they told her that you had married another; then she cried."

These words made Zbyszko feel very tender; he also felt angry because Danusia had been vexed; therefore he said:

"I shall challenge those who said such things about me!"

Jendrek of Kropiwnica began to laugh and said:

"The women teased her! Will you challenge a woman? You cannot do anything with a sword against a distaff."

Zbyszko was pleased that he had met such a cheerful companion; he began to ask Jendrek about Danusia. He also inquired about the customs of the Mazowiecki court, about Prince Janusz, and about the princess. Finally he told what he had heard about the war during his journey, and how the people were making preparations for it, and were expecting it every day. He asked whether the people in the principalities of Mazowsze, thought it would soon come.

The heir of Kropiwnica did not think that the war was near. The people said that it could not be avoided; but he had heard the prince himself say to Mikolaj of Dlugolas, that the Knights of the Cross were very peaceable now, and if the king only insisted, they would restore the province of Dobrzyn to Poland; or they would try to delay the whole affair, until they were well prepared,

"The prince went to Malborg a short time ago," said he, "where during the absence of the grand master, the grand marshal received him and entertained him with great hospitality; now there are some *comthurs* here, and other guests are coming."

Here he stopped for a while, and then added:

"The people say that the Krzyzaks have a purpose in coming here and in going to Plock to the court of Prince Ziemowit. They would like to have the princes pledge themselves not to help the king but to aid them; or if they do not agree to help the Krzyzaks, that at least they will remain neutral; but the princes will not do that."

"God will not permit it. Would you stay home? Your princes belong to the kingdom of Poland!"

"No, we would not stay home," answered Jendrek of Kropiwnica.

Zbyszko again glanced at the foreign knights, and at their peacocks' tufts, and asked:

"Are these knights going for that purpose?"

"They are brothers of the Order and perhaps that is their motive. Who understands them?"

"And that third one?"

"He is going because he is inquisitive."

"He must be some famous knight."

"Bah! three heavily laden wagons follow him, and he has nine men in his escort. I would like to fight with such a man!"

"Can you not do it?"

"Of course not! The prince commanded me to guard them. Not one hair shall fall from their heads until they reach Ciechanow."

"Suppose I challenge them? Perhaps they would desire to fight with me?"

"Then you would be obliged to fight with me first, because I will not permit you to fight with them while I live."

Zbyszko looked at the young nobleman in a friendly way, and said:

"You understand what knightly honor is. I shall not fight with you, because I am your friend; but in Ciechanow, God will help me to find some pretext for a challenge to the Germans."

"In Ciechanow you can do what you please. I am sure there will be tournaments; then you can fight, if the prince and the *comthurs* give permission."

"I have a board on which is written a challenge for anyone who will not affirm that *Panna* Danuta Jurandowna is the most virtuous and the most beautiful girl in the world; but everywhere the people shrugged their shoulders and laughed."

"Because it is a foreign custom; and speaking frankly, a stupid one which is not known in our country, except near the boundaries. That Lotaringer tried to pick a quarrel with some noblemen, asking them to praise some lady of his; but nobody could understand him, and I would not let them fight."

"What? He wanted to praise his lady? For God's sake!"

He looked closely at the foreign knight, and saw that his young face was full of sadness, he also perceived with astonishment that the knight had a rope made of hairs round his neck.

"Why does he wear that rope?" asked Zbyszko.

"I could not find out, because they do not understand our language, Brother Rotgier can say a few words, but not very well either. But I think that this young knight has made a vow to wear that rope until he has accomplished some knightly deed. During the day, he wears it outside of his armor, but during the night, on the bare flesh."

"Sanderus!" called Zbyszko, suddenly

"At your service," answered the German, approaching

"Ask this knight, who is the most virtuous and the most beautiful girl in the world."

Sanderus repeated the question in German.

"Ulryka von Elner!" answered Fulko de Lorche.

Then he raised his eyes and began to sigh. Zbyszko hearing this answer, was indignant, and reined in his stallion; but before he could reply, Jendrek of Kropiwnica, pushed his horse between him and the foreigner, and said:

"You shall not quarrel here!"

Zbyszko turned to Sanderus and said:

"Tell him that I say that he is in love with an owl."

"Noble knight, my master says that you are in love with an owl!" repeated Sanderus, like an echo.

At this Sir de Lorche dropped his reins, drew the iron gauntlet from his right hand and threw it in the snow in front of Zbyszko, who motioned to the Czech to lift it with the point of his spear.

Jendrek of Kropiwnica, turned toward Zbyszko with a threatening face, and said:

"You shall not fight; I shall permit neither of you."

"I did not challenge him; he challenged me."

"But you called his lady an owl. Enough of this! I also know how to use a sword."

"But I do not wish to fight with you."

"You will be obliged to, because I have sworn to defend the other knight."

"Then what shall I do?" asked Zbyszko.

"Wait; we are near Ciechanow."

"But what will the German think?"

"Your servant must explain to him that he cannot fight here; that first you must receive the prince's permission, and he, the *comthur's*."

"Bah! suppose they will not give permission."

"Then you will find each other. Enough of this talk."

Zbyszko, seeing that he could not do otherwise, because Jendrek of Kropiwnica would not permit them to fight, called Sanderus, and told him to explain to the Lotaringer knight, that they could fight only in Ciechanow. De Lorche having listened, nodded to signify that he understood; then having stretched his hand toward Zbyszko, he pressed the palm three times, which according to the knightly custom, meant that they must fight, no matter when or where. Then in an apparent good understanding, they moved on toward the castle of Ciechanow, whose towers one could see reflected on the pink sky.

It was daylight when they arrived; but after they announced themselves at the gate, it was dark before the bridge was lowered. They were received by Zbyszko's former acquaintance, Mikolaj of Dlugolas, who commanded the garrison consisting of a few knights and three hundred of the famous archers of Kurpie.[94] To his great sorrow, Zbyszko learned that the court was absent. The prince wishing to honor the *comthurs* of Szczytno and Jansbork, arranged for them a great hunting party in the Krupiecka wilderness; the princess, with her ladies-in-waiting went also, to give more importance to the occasion. Ofka, the widow of Krzych[95] of Jarzombkow, was key-keeper, and the only woman in the castle whom Zbyszko knew. She was very glad to see him. Since her return from Krakow, she had told everybody about his love for Danusia, and the incident about Lichtenstein. These stories made her very popular among the younger ladies and girls of the court; therefore she was fond of Zbyszko. She now tried to console the young man in his sorrow, caused by Danusia's absence.

"You will not recognize her," she said. "She is growing older, and is a little girl no longer; she loves you differently, also. You say your uncle is well? Why did he not come with you?"

"I will let my horses rest for a while and then I will go to Danusia. I will go during the night," answered Zbyszko.

"Do so, but take a guide from the castle, or you will be lost in the wilderness."

In fact after supper, which Mikolaj of Dlugolas ordered to be served to the guests, Zbyszko expressed his desire to go after the prince, and he asked for a guide. The brothers of the Order, wearied by the journey, approached the enormous fireplaces in which were burning the entire trunks of pine trees, and said that they would go the next day. But de Lorche expressed his desire to go with Zbyszko, saying that otherwise he might miss the hunting party, and he wished to see them very much. Then he approached Zbyszko, and having extended his hand, he again pressed his fingers three times.

CHAPTER IV.

Mikolaj of Dlugolas having learned from Jendrek of Kropiwnica about the challenge, required both Zbyszko and the other knight to give him their knightly word that they would not fight without the prince and the *comthur's* permission; if they refused, he said he would shut the gates and not permit them to leave the castle. Zbyszko wished to see Danusia as soon as possible, consequently he did not resist; de Lorche, although willing to fight when necessary, was not a bloodthirsty man, therefore he swore upon his knightly honor, to wait for the prince's consent. He did it willingly, because having heard so many songs about tournaments and being fond of pompous feasts, he preferred to fight in the presence of the court, the dignitaries and the ladies; he believed that such a victory would bring greater renown, and he would win the golden spurs more easily. Then he was also anxious to become acquainted with the country and the people, therefore he preferred a delay. Mikolaj of Dlugolas, who had been in captivity among the Germans a long time, and could speak the language easily, began to tell him marvelous tales about the prince's hunting parties for different kinds of beasts not known in the western countries. Therefore Zbyszko and he left the castle about midnight, and went toward Przasnysz, having with them their armed retinues, and men with lanterns to protect them against the wolves, which gathering during the winter in innumerable packs, it was dangerous even for several well armed cavaliers to meet. On this side of Ciechanow there were deep forests, which a short distance beyond Przasnysz were merged into the enormous Kurpiecka wilderness, which on the west joined the impassable forest of Podlasie, and further on Lithuania. Through these forests the Lithuanian barbarians came to Mazowsze, and in 1337 reached Ciechanow, which they burned. De Lorche listened with the greatest interest to the stories, told him by the old guide, Macko of Turoboje. He desired to fight with the Lithuanians, whom as many other western knights did, he had thought were Saracens. In fact he had come on a crusade, wishing to gain fame and salvation. He thought that a war with the Mazurs, half heathenish people, would secure for him entire pardon. Therefore he could scarcely believe his own eyes, when having reached Mazowsze, he saw churches in the towns, crosses on the towers, priests, knights with holy signs on their armor and the people, very daring indeed, and ready for a fight, but Christian and not more rapacious than the Germans, among whom the young knight had traveled. Therefore, when he was told that these people had confessed Christ for centuries, he did not know what to think about the Knights of the Cross; and when he learned that Lithuania was baptized by the command of the late queen, his surprise and sorrow were boundless.

He began to inquire from Macko of Turoboje, if in the forest toward which they were riding, there were any dragons to whom the people were obliged to sacrifice young girls, and with whom one could fight. But Macko's answer greatly disappointed him.

"In the forest, there are many beasts, wolves, bisons and bears with which there is plenty of work," answered the Mazur. "Perhaps in the swamps there are some unclean spirits; but I never heard about dragons, and even if they were there, we would not give them girls, but we would destroy them. Bah! had there been any, the Kurpie would have worn belts of their skins long ago."

"What kind of people are they; is it possible to fight with them?" asked de Lorche.

"One can fight with them, but it is not desirable," answered Macko; "and then it is not proper for a knight, because they are peasants."

"The Swiss are peasants also. Do they confess Christ?"

"There are no such people in Mazowsze. They are our people. Did you see the archers in the castles? They are all the Kurpie, because there are no better archers than they are."

"They cannot be better than the Englishmen and the Scotch, whom I saw at the Burgundian court."

"I have seen them also in Malborg," interrupted the Mazur. "They are strong, but they cannot compare with the Kurpie, among whom a boy seven years old, will not be allowed to eat, until he has knocked the food with an arrow from the summit of a pine."

"About what are you talking?" suddenly asked Zbyszko, who had heard the word "Kurpie" several times.

"About the English and the Kurpiecki archers. This knight says that the English and the Scotch are the best."

"I saw them at Wilno. Owa! I heard their darts passing my ears. There were knights there from all countries, and they announced that they would eat us up without salt; but after they tried once or twice, they lost their appetite."

Macko laughed and repeated Zbyszko's words to Sir de Lorche.

"I have heard about that at different courts," answered the Lotaringer; "they praised your knights' bravery, but they blamed them because they helped the heathen against the Knights of the Cross."

"We defended the nation which wished to be baptized, against invasion and wrong. The Germans wished to keep them in idolatry, so as to have a pretext for war."

"God shall judge them," answered de Lorche.

"Perhaps He will judge them soon," answered Macko of Turoboje.

But the Lotaringer having heard that Zbyszko had been at Wilno, began to question Macko, because the fame of the knightly combats fought there, had spread widely throughout the world. That duel, fought by four Polish and four French knights, especially excited the imagination of western warriors. The consequence was that de Lorche began to look at Zbyszko with more respect, as upon a man who had participated in such a famous battle; he also rejoiced that he was going to fight with such a knight.

Therefore they rode along apparently good friends, rendering each other small services during the time for refreshment on the journey and treating each other with wine. But when it appeared from the conversation between de Lorche and Macko of Turoboje, that Ulryka von Elner was not a young girl, but a married woman forty years old and having six children, Zbyszko became indignant, because this foreigner dared not only to compare an old woman with Danusia, but even asked him to acknowledge her to be the first among women.

"Do you not think," said he to Macko, "that an evil spirit has turned his brain? Perhaps the devil is sitting in his head like a worm in a nut and is ready to jump on one of us during the night. We must be on our guard."

Macko of Turoboje began to look at the Lotaringer with a certain uneasiness and finally said:

"Sometimes it happens that there are hundreds of devils in a possessed man, and if they are crowded, they are glad to go in other people. The worst devil is the one sent by a woman."

Then he turned suddenly to the knight:

"May Jesus Christ be praised!"

"I praise him also," answered de Lorche, with some astonishment.

116

Macko was completely reassured.

"No, don't you see," said he, "if the devil were dwelling in him, he would have foamed immediately, or he would have been thrown to the earth, because I asked him suddenly. We can go."

In fact, they proceeded quietly. The distance between Ciechanow and Przasnysz is not great, and during the summer a cavalier riding a good horse can travel from one city to the other in two hours; but they were riding very slowly on account of the darkness and the drifts of snow. They started after midnight and did not arrive at the prince's hunting house, situated near the woods, beyond Przasnysz, until daybreak. The wooden mansion was large and the panes of the windows were made of glass balls. In front of the house were the well-sweeps and two barns for horses, and round the mansion were many tents made of skins and booths hastily built of the branches of pine trees. The fires shone brightly in front of the tents, and round them were standing the huntsmen who were dressed in coats made of sheepskins, foxskins, wolfskins and bearskins, and having the hair turned outside. It seemed to Sir de Lorche that he saw some wild beasts standing on two legs, because the majority of these men had caps made of the heads of animals. Some of them were standing, leaning on their spears or crossbows; others were busy winding enormous nets made of ropes; others were turning large pieces of urus and elk meat which was hanging over the fire, evidently preparing for breakfast. Behind them were the trunks of enormous pines and more people; the great number of people astonished the Lotaringer who was not accustomed to see such large hunting parties.

"Your princes," said he, "go to a hunt as if to a war."

"To be sure," answered Macko of Turoboje; "they lack neither hunting implements nor people."

"What are we going to do?" interrupted Zbyszko; "they are still asleep in the mansion."

"Well, we must wait until they get up," answered Macko; "we cannot knock at the door and awaken the prince, our lord."

Having said this, he conducted them to a fire, near which the Kurpie threw some wolfskins and urusskins, and then offered them some roasted meat. Hearing a foreign speech, the people began to gather round to see the German. Soon the news was spread by Zbyszko's attendants that there was a knight "from beyond the seas," and the crowd became so great that the lord of Turoboje was obliged to use his authority to shield the foreigner from their curiosity. De Lorche noticed some women in the crowd also dressed in skins, but very beautiful; he inquired whether they also participated in the hunt.

Macko explained to him that they did not take part in the hunting, but only came to satisfy their womanly curiosity, or to purchase the products of the towns and to sell the riches of the forest. The court of the prince was like a fireplace, round which were concentrated two elements—rural and civic. The Kurpie disliked to leave their wilderness, because they felt uneasy without the rustling of the trees above their heads; therefore the inhabitants of Przasnysz brought their famous beer, their flour ground in wind mills or water mills built on the river Wengierka, salt which was very rare in the wilderness, iron, leather and other fruits of human industry, taking in exchange skins, costly furs, dried mushrooms, nuts, herbs, good in case of sickness, or clods of amber which were plentiful among the Kurpie. Therefore round the prince's court there was the noise of a continual market, increased during the hunting parties, because duty and curiosity attracted the inhabitants from the depths of the forests.

De Lorche listened to Macko, looking with curiosity at the people, who, living in the healthy resinous air and eating much meat as was the custom with the majority of the peasants in those days, astonished the foreign travelers by their strength and size. Zbyszko was continually looking at the doors and windows of the mansion, hardly able to remain quiet. There was light in one window only, evidently in the kitchen, because steam was coming out through the gapes between the panes.

In the small doors, situated in the side of the house, servants in the prince's livery appeared from time to time, hurrying to the wells for water. These men being asked if everybody was still sleeping, answered that the court, wearied by the previous day's hunting, was still resting, but that breakfast was being prepared. In fact through the window of the kitchen, there now issued the smell of roasted meat and saffron, spreading far among the fires. Finally the principal door was opened, showing the interior of a brightly lighted hall, and on the piazza appeared a man whom Zbyszko immediately recognized as one of the *rybalts*, whom he had seen with the princess in Krakow. Having perceived him, and waiting neither for Macko of Turoboje, nor for de Lorche, Zbyszko rushed with such an impetus toward the mansion, that the astonished Lotaringer asked:

"What is the matter with the young knight?"

"There is nothing the matter with him," answered Macko of Turoboje; "he is in love with a girl of the princess' court and he wants to see her as soon as possible."

"Ah!" answered de Lorche, putting both of his hands on his heart. He began to sigh so deeply that Macko shrugged his shoulders and said to himself:

"Is it possible that he is sighing for that old woman? It may be that his senses are impaired!"

In the meanwhile he conducted de Lorche into the large hall of the mansion which was ornamented with the horns of bisons, elks and deer, and was lighted by the large logs burning in the fireplace. In the middle of the hall stood a table covered with *kilimek*[96] and dishes for breakfast; there were only a few courtiers present, with whom Zbyszko was talking. Macko of Turoboje introduced Sir de Lorche to them. More courtiers were coming at every moment; the majority of them were fine looking men, with broad shoulders and fallow hair; all were dressed for hunting. Those who were acquainted with Zbyszko and were familiar with his adventure in Krakow, greeted him as an old friend—it was evident that they liked him. One of them said to him:

"The princess is here and Jurandowna also; you will see her soon, my dear boy; then you will go with us to the hunting party."

At this moment the two guests of the prince, the Knights of the Cross, entered: brother Hugo von Danveld, *starosta* of Ortelsburg,[97] and Zygfried von Löve, bailiff of Jansbork. The first was quite a young man, but stout, having a face like a beer drunkard, with thick, moist lips; the other was tall with stern but noble features. It seemed to Zbyszko that he had seen Danveld before at the court of Prince Witold and that Henryk, bishop of Plock, had thrown him from his horse during the combat in the lists. These reminiscences were disturbed by the entrance of Prince Janusz, whom the Knights of the Cross and the courtiers saluted. De Lorche, the *comthurs* and Zbyszko also approached him, and he welcomed them cordially but with dignity. Immediately the trumpets resounded, announcing that the prince was going to breakfast; they resounded three times; and the third time, a large door to the right was opened and Princess Anna appeared, accompanied by the beautiful blonde girl who had a lute hanging on her shoulder.

Zbyszko immediately stepped forward and kneeled on both knees in a position full of worship and admiration. Seeing this, those present began to whisper, because Zbyszko's action surprised the Mazurs and some of them were even scandalized. Some of the older ones said: "Surely he learned such customs from some knights living beyond the sea, or perhaps even from the heathen themselves, because there is no custom like it even among the Germans." But the younger ones said: "No wonder, she saved his life." But the princess and Jurandowna did not recognize Zbyszko at once, because he kneeled with his back toward the fire and his face was in the shadow. The princess thought that it was some courtier, who, having been guilty of some offence, besought her intervention with the prince; but Danusia having keener sight, advanced one step, and having bent her fair head, cried suddenly:

"Zbyszko!"

Then forgetting that the whole court and the foreign guests were looking at her, she sprang like a roe toward the young knight and encircling his neck with her arms, began to kiss his mouth and his cheeks, nestling to him and caressing him so long that the Mazurs laughed and the princess drew her back.

Then Zbyszko embraced the feet of the princess; she welcomed him, and asked about Macko, whether he was alive or not, and if alive whether he had accompanied Zbyszko. Finally when the servants brought in warm dishes, she said to Zbyszko:

"Serve us, dear little knight, and perhaps not only now at the table, but forever."

Danusia was blushing and confused, but was so beautiful, that not only Zbyszko but all the knights present were filled with pleasure; the *starosta* of Szczytno, put the palm of his hands to his thick, moist lips; de Lorche was amazed, and asked:

"By Saint Jacob of Compostella, who is that girl?"

To this the *starosta* of Szczytno, who was short, stood on his toes and whispered in the ear of the Lotaringer:

"The devil's daughter."

De Lorche looked at him; then he frowned and began to say through his nose:

"A knight who talks against beauty is not gallant."

"I wear golden spurs, and I am a monk," answered Hugo von Danveld, proudly.

The Lotaringer dropped his head; but after awhile he said:

"I am a relative of the princess of Brabant."

"*Pax! Pax!*" answered the Knight of the Cross. "Honor to the mighty knights and friends of the Order from whom, sir, you shall soon receive your golden spurs. I do not disparage the beauty of that girl; but listen, I will tell you who is her father."

But he did not have time to tell him, because at that moment, Prince Janusz seated himself at the table; and having learned before from the bailiff of Jansbork about the mighty relatives of Sir de Lorche, he invited him to sit beside him. The princess and Danusia were seated opposite. Zbyszko stood as he did in Krakow, behind their chairs, to serve them. Danusia held her head as low as possible over the plate, because she was ashamed. Zbyszko looked with ecstasy at her little head and pink cheeks; and he felt his love, like a river, overflowing his whole breast. He could also feel her sweet kisses on his face, his eyes and his mouth. Formerly she used to kiss him as a sister kisses a brother, and he received the kisses as from a child. Now Danusia seemed to him older and more mature—in fact she had grown and blossomed. Love was so much talked about in her presence, that as a flower bud warmed by the sun, takes color and expands, so her eyes were opened to love; consequently there was a certain charm in her now, which formerly she lacked, and a strong intoxicating attraction beamed from her like the warm beams from the sun, or the fragrance from the rose.

Zbyszko felt it, but he could not explain it to himself. He even forgot that at the table one must serve. He did not see that the courtiers were laughing at him and Danusia. Neither did he notice Sir de Lorche's face, which expressed great astonishment, nor the covetous eyes of the *starosta* from Szczytno, who was gazing constantly at Danusia. He awakened only when the trumpets again sounded giving notice that it was time to go into the wilderness, and when the princess Anna Danuta, turning toward him said:

"You will accompany us; you will then have an opportunity to speak to Danusia about your love."

Having said this, she went out with Danusia to dress for the ride on horseback. Zbyszko rushed to the court-yard, where the horses covered with frost were standing. There was no longer a great crowd, because the men whose duty it was to hem in the beasts, had already gone forward into the wilderness with the nets. The fires were quenched; the day was bright but cold. Soon the prince appeared and mounted his horse; behind him was an attendant with a crossbow and a spear so long and heavy, that very few could handle it; but the prince used it very easily, because like the other Mazovian Piasts, he was very strong. There were even women in that family so strong that they could roll iron axes,[98] between their fingers. The prince was also attended by two men, who were prepared to help him in any emergency: they had been chosen from among the landowners of the provinces of Warszawa and Ciechanow; they had shoulders like the trunks of oak trees. Sir de Lorche gazed at them with amazement.

In the meanwhile, the princess and Danusia came out; both wore hoods made of the skins of white weasels. This worthy daughter of Kiejstut could *stitch* with a bow better than with a needle; therefore her attendants carried a crossbow behind her. Zbyszko having kneeled on the snow, extended the palm of his hand, on which the princess rested her foot while mounting her horse; then he lifted Danusia into her saddle and they all started. The retinue stretched in a long column, turned to the right from the mansion, and then began slowly to enter the forest.

Then the princess turned to Zbyszko and said:

"Why don't you talk? Speak to her."

Zbyszko, although thus encouraged, was still silent for a moment; but, after quite a long silence, he said:

"Danuska!"

"What, Zbyszku?"

"I love you!"

Here he again stopped, searching for words which he could not find; although he kneeled before the girl like a foreign knight, and showed her his respect in every way, still he could not express his love in words. Therefore he said:

"My love for you is so great that it stops my breathing."

"I also love you, Zbyszku!" said she, hastily.

"Hej, my dearest! hej, my sweet girl" exclaimed Zbyszko. "Hej!" Then he was silent, full of blissful emotion; but the good-hearted and curious princess helped them again.

"Tell her," said she, "how lonesome you were without her, and when we come to a thicket, you may kiss her; that will be the best proof of your love."

Therefore he began to tell how lonesome he was without her in Bogdaniec, while taking care of Macko and visiting among the neighbors. But the cunning fellow did not say a word about Jagienka. When the first thicket separated them from the courtiers and the guests, he bent toward her and kissed her.

During the winter there are no leaves on the hazel bushes, therefore Hugo von Danveld and Sir de Lorche saw him kiss the girl; some of the courtiers also saw him and they began to say among themselves:

"He kissed her in the presence of the princess! The lady will surely prepare the wedding for them soon."

"He is a daring boy, but Jurand's blood is warm also!"

"They are flint-stone and fire-steel, although the girl looks so quiet. Do not be afraid, there will be some sparks from them!"

Thus they talked and laughed; but the *starosta* of Szczytno turned his evil face toward Sir de Lorche and asked:

"Sir, would you like some Merlin to change you by his magic power into that knight?"[99]

"Would you, sir?" asked de Lorche.

To this the Knight of the Cross, who evidently was filled with jealousy, drew the reins of his horse impatiently, and exclaimed:

"Upon my soul!"

But at that moment he recovered his composure, and having bent his head, he said:

"I am a monk and have made a vow of chastity."

He glanced quickly at the Lotaringer, fearing he would perceive a smile on his face, because in that respect the Order had a bad reputation among the people; and of all among the monks, Hugo von Danveld had the worst. A few years previous he had been vice-bailiff of Sambia. There were so many complaints against him there that, notwithstanding the tolerance with which the Order looked upon similar cases in Marienburg, the grand master was obliged to remove him and appoint him *starosta* of the garrison in Szczytno. Afterward he was sent to the prince's court on some secret mission, and having perceived the beautiful Jurandowna, he conceived a violent passion for her, to which even Danusia's extreme youth was no check. But Danveld also knew to what family the girl belonged, and Jurand's name was united in his memory with a painful reminiscence.

De Lorche began to question him:

"Sir, you called that beautiful girl the devil's daughter; why did you call her that?"

Danveld began to relate the story of Zlotorja: how during the restoration of the castle, they captured the prince with the court, and how during that fight Jurandowna's mother died; how since that time Jurand avenged himself on all the Knights of the Cross. Danveld's hatred was apparent during the narration, because he also had some personal reasons for hating Jurand. Two years before, during an encounter, he met Jurand; but the mere sight of that dreadful "Boar of Spychow" so terrified him for the first time in his life that he deserted two of his relatives and his retinue, and fled to Szczytno. For this cowardly act the grand marshal of the Order brought a knightly suit against him; he swore that his horse had become unmanageable and had carried him away from the battlefield; but that incident shut his way to all higher positions in the Order. Of course Danveld did not say anything to Sir de Lorche about that occurrence, but instead he complained so bitterly about Jurand's atrocities and the audacity of the whole Polish nation, that the Lotaringer could not comprehend all he was saying, and said:

"But we are in the country of the Mazurs and not of the Polaks."

"It is an independent principality but the same nation," answered the *starosta*, "they feel the same hatred against the Order. May God permit the German swords to exterminate all this race!"

"You are right, sir; I never heard even among the heathen of such an unlawful deed, as the building of a castle on somebody else's land, as this prince tried to do," said de Lorche.

"He built the castle against us, but Zlotorja is situated on his land, not on ours."

"Then glory be to Christ that he granted you the victory! What was the result of the war?"

"There was no war then?"

"What was the meaning of your victory at Zlotorja?"

"God favored us; the prince had no army with him, only his court and the women."

Here de Lorche looked at the Knight of the Cross with amazement.

"What? During the time of peace you attacked the women and the prince, who was building a castle on his own land?"

"For the glory of the Order and of Christendom."

"And that dreadful knight is seeking vengeance only for the death of his young wife, killed by you during the time of peace?"

"Whosoever raises his hand against a Knight of the Cross, is a son of darkness."

Hearing this, Sir de Lorche became thoughtful; but he did not have time to answer Danveld, because they arrived at a large, snow-covered glade in the woods, on which the prince and his courtiers dismounted.

CHAPTER V.

The foresters under the direction of the head huntsman, placed the hunters in a long row at the edge of the forest, in such a way that being hidden themselves, they faced the glade. Nets were fastened along two sides of the glade, and behind these were the men whose duty it was to turn the beasts toward the hunters, or to kill them with spears if they became entangled in the nets. Many of the Kurpie were sent to drive every living thing from the depths of the forest into the glade. Behind the hunters there was another net stretched; if an animal passed the row of hunters, he would be entangled in it and easily killed.

The prince was standing in the middle in a small ravine, which extended through the entire width of the glade. The head huntsman, Mrokota of Mocarzew, had chosen that position for the prince because he knew that the largest beasts would pass through this ravine. The prince had a crossbow, and leaning on a tree beside him was a heavy spear; a little behind him stood two gigantic "defenders" with axes on their shoulders, and holding crossbows ready to be handed to the prince. The princess and Jurandowna did not dismount, because the prince would not allow them to do so, on account of the peril from urus and bisons; it was easier to escape the fury of these fierce beasts on horseback than on foot. De Lorche, although invited by the prince to take a position at his right hand, asked permission to remain with the ladies for their defence. Zbyszko drove his spear into the snow, put his crossbow on his back and stood by Danusia's horse, whispering to her and sometimes kissing her. He became quiet only when Mrokota of Mocarzew, who in the forest scolded even the prince himself, ordered him to be silent.

In the meanwhile, far in the depths of the wilderness, the horns of the Kurpie were heard, and the noisy sound of a *krzywula*[100] answered from the glade; then perfect silence followed. From time to time the chatter of the squirrels was heard in the tops of the pines.

The hunters looked at the snow-covered glade, where only the wind moved the bushes, and asked themselves what kind of animals would first appear. They expected abundant game, because the wilderness was swarming with urus, bisons and boars. The Kurpie had smoked out a few bears which were wandering in the thickets, angry, hungry and watchful.

But the hunters were obliged to wait a long time, because the men who were driving the animals toward the glade, had taken a very large space of the forest, and therefore they were so far away that the hunters did not even hear the baying of the dogs, that had been freed from the leashes immediately after the horns resounded.

After a while some wolves appeared on the edge of the forest, but having noticed the people, they again plunged into the forest, evidently searching for another pass. Then some boars having emerged from the wilderness, began to run in a long black line through the snowy space, looking from afar like domestic swine. They stopped and listened—turned and listened again: turned toward the nets, but having smelt the men, went in the direction of the hunters, snorting and approaching more and more carefully; finally there resounded the clatter of the iron cranks of the crossbows, the snarl of the bolts and then the first blood spotted the white snow.

Then a dreadful squealing resounded and the whole pack dispersed as if struck by a thunderbolt; some of them rushed blindly straight ahead, others ran toward the nets, while still others ran among the other animals, with which the glade was soon covered. The sounds of the horns were heard distinctly, mingled with the howling of the dogs and the bustle of the people coming from the depths of the forest. The wild beasts of the forest driven by the huntsmen soon filled the glade. It was impossible to see anything like it in foreign countries or even in the other Polish provinces; nowhere else was there such a wilderness as there was in Mazowsze. The Knights of the Cross, although they had visited Lithuania, where bisons attacked[101] and brought confusion to the army, were very much astonished at the great number of beasts, and Sir de Lorche was more astonished than they. He beheld in front of him herds of yellow deer and elks with heavy antlers, mingled together and running on the glade, blinded by fear and searching in vain for a safe passage. The princess, in whom Kiejstut's blood began to play, seeing this, shot arrow after arrow, shouting with joy when a deer or an elk which was struck, reared and then fell heavily plowing the snow with his feet. Some of the ladies-in-waiting were also shooting, because all were filled with enthusiasm for the sport. Zbyszko alone did not think about hunting; but having leaned his elbows on Danusia's knees and his head on the palms of his hands, he looked into her eyes, and she smiling and blushing, tried to close his eyelids with her fingers, as if she could not stand such looks.

Sir de Lorche's attention was attracted by an enormous bear, gray on the back and shoulders, which jumped out unexpectedly from the thicket near the huntsmen. The prince shot at it with his crossbow, and then rushed forward with his boar-spear; when the animal roaring frightfully, reared, he pierced it with his spear in the presence of the whole court so deftly and so quickly, that neither of the "defenders" needed to use his axe. The young Lotaringer doubted that few of the other lords, at whose courts he had visited during his travels, would dare to amuse themselves in such a way, and believed that the Order would have hard work to conquer such princes and such people. Later on he saw the other hunters pierce in the same way, many boars much larger and fiercer than any that could be found in the forest of Lower Lotaringen or in the German wilderness. Such expert hunters and those so sure of their strength, Sir de Lorche had never before seen; he concluded, being a man of some experience, that these people living in the boundless forests, had been accustomed from childhood to use the crossbow and the spear; consequently they were very dexterous in using them.

The glade of the wood was finally covered with the dead bodies of many different kinds of animals; but the hunt was not finished. In fact, the most interesting and also the most perilous moment was coming, because the huntsmen had met a herd of urus and bisons. The bearded bulls marching in advance of the herd, holding their heads near the ground, often stopped, as if calculating where to attack. From their enormous lungs came a muffled bellowing, similar to the rolling of thunder, and perspiration steamed from their nostrils; while pawing the snow with their forefeet, they seemed to watch the enemy with their bloody eyes hidden beneath their manes. Then the huntsmen shouted, and their cries were followed by similar shoutings from all sides; the horns and fifes resounded; the wilderness reverberated from its remotest parts; meantime the dogs of the Kurpie rushed to the glade with tremendous noise. The appearance of the dogs enraged the females of the herd who were accompanied by their young. The herd which had been walking up to this moment, now scattered in a mad rush all over the glade. One of the bisons, an enormous old yellow bull, rushed toward the huntsmen standing at one side, then seeing horses in the bushes, stopped, and bellowing, began to plow the earth with his horns, as if inciting himself to fight.

Seeing this, the men began to shout still more, but among the hunters there were heard frightened voices exclaiming: "The princess! The princess! Save the princess!" Zbyszko seized his spear which had been driven into the ground behind him and rushed to the edge of the forest; he was followed by a few Litwins who were ready to die in defence of Kiejstut's daughter; but all at once the crossbow creaked in the hands of the lady, the bolt whistled and, having passed over the animal's head, struck him in his neck.

"He is hit!" exclaimed the princess; "he will not escape."

But suddenly, with such a dreadful bellowing that the frightened horses reared, the bison rushed directly toward the lady; at the same moment with no less impetus, Sir de Lorche rushed from beneath the trees and leaning on his horse, with his spear extended as in a knightly tournament, attacked the animal.

Those near by perceived during one moment, the spear plunged into the animal's neck, immediately bend like a bow, and break into small pieces; then the enormous horned head disappeared entirely under the belly of Sir de Lorche's horse, and the charger and his rider were tossed into the air.

From the forest the huntsmen rushed to help the foreign knight. Zbyszko who cared most about the princess and Danusia's safety, arrived first and drove his spear under the bison's shoulder blade. He gave the blow with such force, that the spear by a sudden turn of the bison, broke in his hands, and he himself fell with his face on the ground. "He is dead! He is dead!" cried the Mazurs who were rushing to help him. The bull's head covered Zbyszko and pressed him to the ground. The two powerful "defenders" of the prince arrived; but they were too late; fortunately the Czech Hlawa, given to Zbyszko by Jagienka, outstripped them, and having seized his broad-axe with both hands he cut the bison's bent neck, near the horns.

The blow was so powerful that the animal fell, as though struck by a thunderbolt, with his head almost severed from his neck; this enormous body fell on top of Zbyszko. Both "defenders" pulled it away quickly. The princess and Danusia having dismounted, arrived at the side of the wounded youth.

Zbyszko, pale and covered with his own and the animal's blood, tried to rise; but he staggered, fell on his knees and leaning on his hands, could only pronounce one word:

"Danuska."

Then the blood gushed from his mouth. Danusia grasped him by his shoulders, but being unable to hold him, began to cry for help. The huntsmen rubbed him with snow and poured wine in his mouth; finally the head huntsman, Mrokota of Mocarzew ordered them to put him on a mantle and to stop the blood with soft spunk from the trees.

"He will live if his ribs and his backbone are not broken," said he, turning toward the princess. In the meanwhile some ladies of the court with the help of other huntsmen, were attending to Sir de Lorche. They turned him over, searching in his armor for holes or dents made by the horns of the bull; but besides traces of the snow, which had entered between the joints of the iron plates, they could find nothing. The urus had avenged himself especially on the horse, which was lying dead beside the knight; as for Sir de Lorche, he was not seriously injured. He had fainted and his right hand was sprained. When they took off his helmet and poured some wine in his mouth, he opened his eyes, and seeing the sorrowful faces of two pretty young ladies bent over him, said in German:

"I am sure I am in paradise already and the angels are over me."

The ladies did not understand what he said; but being glad to see him open his eyes and speak, they smiled, and with the huntsmen's help raised him from the ground; feeling the pain in his right hand, he moaned and leaned with the left on the shoulder of one of the "angels"; for a while he stood motionless, fearing to make a step, because he felt weak. Then he glanced around and perceived the yellow body of the urus, he also saw Danusia wringing her hands and Zbyszko lying on a mantle.

"Is that the knight who rushed to help me?" he asked. "Is he alive?"

"He is very severely injured," answered a courtier who could speak German.

"From this time, I am going to fight not with him, but for him!" said the Lotaringer.

At this time, the prince who was near Zbyszko, approached Sir de Lorche and began to praise him because he had defended the princess and the other ladies, and perhaps saved their lives by his bold deed; for which, besides the knightly reward, he would be renowned not only then but in all future generations.

"In these effeminate times," said he, "there are few true knights traveling through the world; therefore pray be my guest as long as possible or if you can, remain forever in Mazowsze, where you have already won my favor, and by honest deeds will easily win the love of the people."

Sir de Lorche's heart was filled with joy when he heard the prince's words and realized that he had accomplished such a famous knightly deed and deserved such praise in these remote Polish lands, about which so many strange things were told in the East. He knew that a knight who could tell at the Burgundian court or at the court of Brabant, that when on a hunting party, he had saved the life of the Mazowiecka princess, would be forever famous.

Zbyszko became conscious and smiled at Danusia; then he fainted again. The huntsmen seeing how his hands closed and his mouth remained open, said to one another that he would not live; but the more experienced Kurpie, among whom many an one had on him the traces of a bear's paws, a boar's tusks or an urus' horns, affirmed that the urus' horn had slipped between the knight's ribs, that perhaps one or two of his ribs were broken, but that the backbone was not, because if it were, he could not rise. They pointed out also, that Zbyszko had fallen in a snow drift and that had saved him, because on account of the softness the animal when pressing him with his horns, could not entirely crush his chest, nor his backbone.

Unfortunately the prince's physician, the *ksiondz* Wyszoniek of Dziewanna, was not with the hunting party, being busy in the chateau making wafers.[102] The Czech rushed to bring him immediately, and meanwhile the Kurpie carried Zbyszko to the prince's mansion. The Knight of the Cross, Hugo von Danveld, helped Danusia mount her horse and then, riding beside her and closely following the men who were carrying Zbyszko, said in Polish in a muffled voice, so that she alone could hear him:

"In Szczytno I have a marvelous balm, which I received from a hermit living in the Hercynski forest; I can bring it for you in three days."

"God will reward you," answered Danusia.

"God records every charitable deed; but will you reward me also?"

"What reward can I give you?"

The Krzyzak approached and evidently wished to say something else but hesitated; after a while he said:

"In the Order, besides the brothers there are also sisters. One of them will bring the healing balm, and then I will speak about the reward."

CHAPTER VI.

The *ksiondz* Wyszoniek dressed Zbyszko's wounds and he stated that only one rib was broken; but the first day he could not affirm that the sick man would live, because he could not ascertain whether the heart had been injured or not. Sir de Lorche was so ill toward morning that he was obliged to go to bed, and on the following day he could not move his hand nor his foot, without great pain in all the bones. The princess Danusia and some other ladies of the court nursed the sick men and prepared for them, according to the prescriptions of the *ksiondz* Wyszoniek, different ointments and potions. But Zbyszko was very severely injured, and from time to time blood gushed from his mouth, and this alarmed the *ksiondz* Wyszoniek very much. He was conscious however, and on the second day, although very weak, having learned from Danusia to whom he owed his life, called Hlawa to thank and reward him. He remembered that he had received the Czech from Jagienka and that had it not been for her kind heart, he would have perished. He feared that he never would be able to repay the good-hearted girl for her kindness, but that he would only be the cause of her sorrow.

"I swore to my *panienka*," said Hlawa, "on my honor of a *wlodyka*, that I would protect you; therefore I will do it without any reward. You are indebted to her for your life."

Zbyszko did not answer, but began to breathe heavily; the Czech was silent for a while, then he said:

"If you wish me to hasten to Bogdaniec, I will go. Perhaps you will be glad to see the old lord, because God only knows whether you will recover."

"What does the *ksiondz* Wyszoniek say?" asked Zbyszko.

"The *ksiondz* Wyszoniek says that he will know when the new moon comes. There are four days before the new moon."

"Hej! then you need not go to Bogdaniec, because I will either die, or I will be well before my uncle could come."

"Could you not send a letter to Bogdaniec? Sanderus will write one. Then they will know about you, and will engage a mass for you."

"Let me rest now, because I am very ill. If I die, you will return to Zgorzelice and tell how everything happened; then they can engage a mass. I suppose they will bury me here or in Ciechanow."

"I think they will bury you in Ciechanow or in Przasnysz, because only the Kurpie are buried in the forest, and the wolves howl over their graves. I heard that the prince intends to return with the court to Ciechanow in two days' time, and then to Warszawa."

"They would not leave me here alone," answered Zbyszko.

He guessed correctly, because that same day the princess asked the prince's permission to remain in the house in the wilderness, with Danusia and the ladies-in-waiting, and also with the *ksiondz* Wyszoniek, who was opposed to carrying Zbyszko to Przasnysz. Sir de Lorche at the end of two days felt better, and he was able to leave his bed; but having learned that the ladies intended to remain, he stayed also, in order to accompany them on their journey and defend them in case the "Saracens" attacked them. Whence the "Saracens" could come, the Lotaringer did not know. It is true that the people in the East used thus to call the Litwins; but from them no danger could threaten Kiejstut's daughter, Witold's sister and the first cousin of the mighty "Krakowski king," Jagiello. But Sir de Lorche had been among the Knights of the Cross for so long a time, that notwithstanding all he had heard in Mazowsze about the baptism of the Litwa, and about the union of the two crowns on the head of one ruler, he could not believe that any one could expect any good from the Litwins. Thus the Knights of the Cross had made him believe, and he had not yet entirely lost all faith in their words.

In the meantime an incident occurred which cast a shadow between Prince Janusz and his guests. One day, before the departure of the court, Brother Godfried and Brother Rotgier, who had remained in Ciechanow, came accompanied by Sir de Fourcy, who was a messenger of bad news to the Knights of the Cross. There were some foreign guests at the court of the Krzyzacki *starosta* in Lubowa; they were Sir de Fourcy and also Herr von Bergow and Herr Meineger, both belonging to families which had rendered great services to the Order. They having heard many stories about Jurand of Spychow, determined, to draw the famous warrior into an open field, and ascertain for themselves whether he really was as dreadful as represented. The *starosta* opposed the plan, giving as a reason that there was peace between the Order and the Mazowiecki princes; but finally, perhaps hoping thus to get rid of his terrible neighbor, not only connived at the expedition but even furnished the armed *knechts*. The knights sent a challenge to Jurand, who immediately accepted it under the condition that they would send away the soldiers and that three of them would fight with him and two of his companions on the boundaries of Szlonsk and Spychow. But when they refused to send away the *knechts* or to retire from the land belonging to Spychow, he suddenly fell upon them, exterminated the *knechts*, pierced Herr Meineger dreadfully with a spear, took Herr von Bergow into captivity and put him into the Spychowski dungeon. De Fourcy alone escaped and after three days' wandering in the Mazowiecki forests, having learned from some pitch-burners that there were some brothers of the Order in Ciechanow, he succeeded in reaching them. He and the brothers of the Order made a complaint to the prince, and asked for the punishment of Jurand, and for an order for the deliverance of Herr von Bergow.

This news disturbed the good understanding between the prince and his guests, because not only the two newly arrived brothers but also Hugo von Danveld and Zygfried von Löve, began to beseech the prince to render justice to the Order, to free the boundaries from the plunderer and to punish him once for all his offences. Hugo von Danveld, having his own grievance against Jurand, the remembrance of which burned him with shame and grief, asked for vengeance almost threateningly.

"The complaint will go to the grand master," he said; "and if we be not able to get justice from Your Grace, he will obtain it himself, even if the whole Mazowsze help that robber."

But the prince, although naturally good-tempered, became angry and said.

"What kind of justice do you ask for? If Jurand had attacked you first, then I would surely punish him. But your people were the first to commence hostilities. Your *starosta* gave the *knechts*, permission to go on that expedition. Jurand only accepted the challenge and asked that the soldiers be sent away. Shall I punish him for that? You attacked that dreadful man, of whom everybody is afraid, and voluntarily brought calamity upon yourselves—what do you want then? Shall I order him not to defend himself, when it pleases you to attack him?"

"It was not the Order that attacked him, but its guests, foreign knights," answered Hugo.

"The Order is responsible for its guests, and then the *knechts*, from the Lubowski garrison were there."

"Could the *starosta* allow his guests to be slaughtered?"

Here the prince turned to Zygfried and said.

"You must take heed lest your wiles offend God."

But the stern Zygfried answered:

"Heir von Bergow must be released from captivity, because the men of his family were high dignitaries in the Order and they rendered important services to the Cross."

"And Meineger's death must be avenged," added Hugo von Danveld.

Thereupon the prince arose and walked threateningly toward the Germans; but after a while, evidently having remembered that they were his guests, he restrained his anger, put his hand on Zygfried's shoulder, and said:

"Listen: you wear a cross on your mantle, therefore answer according to your conscience—upon that cross! Was Jurand right or was he not?"

"Herr von Bergow must be released from prison," answered Zygfried von Löve.

There was as a moment of silence; then the prince said:

"God grant me patience!"

Zygfried continued sharply, his words cutting like a sword:

"The wrong which was done to us in the persons of our guests, is only one more occasion for complaint. From the time the Order was founded, neither in Palestine, nor in Siedmiogrod,[103] nor among the heathenish Litwa, has any man wronged us so much as that robber from Spychow. Your Highness! we ask for justice and vengeance not for one wrong, but for thousands; not for the blood shed once, but for years of such deeds, for which fire from heaven ought to burn that nest of wickedness and cruelty. Whose moanings entreat God for vengeance? Ours! Whose tears? Ours! We have complained in vain. Justice has never been given us!"

Having heard this, Prince Janusz began to nod his head and said:

"Hej! formerly the Krzyzaks were received hospitably in Spychow, and Jurand was not your foe, until after his dear wife died on your rope; and how many times have you attacked him first, wishing to kill him, as in this last case, because he challenged and defeated your knights? How many times have you sent assassins after him, or shot at him with a crossbow from the forest? He attacked you, it is true, because vengeance burns within him; but have you not attacked peaceful people in Mazowsze? Have you not taken their herds, burned their houses and murdered the men, women and children? And when I complained to the grand master, he sent me this reply from Marienburg: 'Customary frolic of the boundaries' Let me be in peace! Was it not you who captured me when I was without arms, during the time of peace, on my own land? Had it not been for your fear of the mighty Krakowski king, probably I would have had to moan until now in captivity. Who ought to complain? With such gratitude you repaid me, who belonged to the family of your benefactors. Let me be in peace; it is not you who have the right to talk about justice!"

Having heard this, the Knights of the Cross looked at each other impatiently, angry because the prince mentioned the occurrence at Zlotorja, in the presence of Sir de Fourcy; therefore Hugo von Danveld, wishing to finish the conversation about it, said:

"That was a mistake, Your Highness, and we made amends for it, not on account of fear of the Krakowski king, but for the sake of justice; and with regard to the frolics on the boundaries, the grand master cannot be held responsible, because on every frontier there are some restless spirits."

"Then you say this yourself, and still you ask for the punishment of Jurand. What do you wish then?"

"Justice and punishment!"

The prince clenched his bony fists and repeated:

"God grant me patience!"

"Your Princely Majesty must also remember," said Danveld, further, "that our wantons only wrong lay people who do not belong to the German race, but your men raise their hand against the German Order, and for this reason they offend our Saviour Himself."

"Listen!" said the prince. "Do not talk about God; you cannot deceive Him!"

Then having placed his hands on the Krzyzak's shoulders, he shook him so strongly, that he frightened him. He relented immediately and said, mildly:

"If it be true that our guests attacked Jurand first and did not send away the soldiers, I will not blame him; but had Jurand really accepted the challenge?"

Having said this, he looked at Sir de Fourcy, winking at him, to deny it; but the latter, not wishing to lie, answered:

"He asked us to send our soldiers away, and to fight three against three."

"Are you sure of that?"

"Upon my honor! Herr von Bergow and I agreed, but Meineger did not consent."

Here the prince interrupted:

"*Starosta* from Szczytno! you know better than anybody else that Jurand would not miss a challenge."

Then he turned to all present and said:

"If one of you will challenge Jurand to a fight on horseback or on foot, I give my permission. If he be taken prisoner or killed, then Herr von Bergow will be released without paying any ransom. Do not ask me for anything else, because I will not grant it."

After these words, there was a profound silence. Hugo von Danveld, Zygfried von Löve, Brother Rotgier and Brother Godfried, although brave, knew the dreadful lord of Spychow too well to dare to challenge him for life or death. Only a foreigner from a far distant country, like de Lorche or de Fourcy, would do it; but de Lorche was not present during the conversation, and Sir de Fourcy was still too frightened.

"I have seen him once," he muttered, "and I do not wish to see him any more."

Zygfried von Löve said:

"It is forbidden the monks to fight in single combat, except by special permission from the grand master and the grand marshal; but I do not ask for permission for a combat, but for the release of von Bergow and the punishment by death of Jurand."

"You do not make the laws in this country."

"Our grand master will know how to administer justice."

"Your grand master has nothing to do with Mazowsze!"

"The emperor and the whole German nation will help him."

"The king of Poland will help me, and he is more powerful than the German emperor."

"Does Your Highness wish for a war with the Order?"

"If I wanted a war, I would not wait for you to come to Mazowsze, but would go toward you; you need not threaten me, because I am not afraid of you."

"What shall I say to the grand master?"

"He has not asked you anything. Tell him what you please."

"Then we will avenge ourselves."

Thereupon the prince stretched forth his arm and began to shake his finger close to the Krzyzak's face.

"Keep quiet!" said he, angrily; "keep quiet! I gave you permission to challenge Jurand; but if you dare to invade this country with the army of the Order, then I will attack you, and you will stay here not as a guest but as a prisoner."

Evidently his patience was entirely exhausted, because he threw a cap violently on the table and left the room, slamming the door. The Knights of the Cross became pale and Sir de Fourcy looked at them askance.

"What will happen now?" asked Brother Rotgier, who was the first to break the silence.

Hugo von Danveld turned to Sir de Fourcy and menacing him with his fists, said:

"Why did you tell him that you attacked Jurand?"

"Because it is true!"

"You should have lied."

"I came here to fight and not to lie."

"Well, you fought well, indeed!"

"And you! did you not run away from Jurand of Spychow?"

"*Pax!*" said von Löve. "This knight is a guest of the Order."

"It is immaterial what he said," added Brother Godfried. "They would not punish Jurand without a trial, and in the court, the truth would come out."

"What will be done now?" repeated Brother Rotgier.

There was a moment of silence; then the sturdy and virulent Zygfried von Löve spoke:

"We must finish once for all with that bloody dog!" said he. "Herr von Bergow must be released from his fetters. We will gather the garrisons from Szczytno, Insburk and Lubowa; we will summon the Chelminsk nobility and attack Jurand. It is time to settle with him!"

"We cannot do it without permission from the grand master."

"If we succeed, the grand master will be pleased!" said Brother Godfried.

"But if we do not succeed? If the prince go against us?"

"He will not do that if there is peace between him and the Order."

"There is peace, but we are going to violate it. Our garrisons will not be sufficient to fight against the Mazurs."

"Then the grand master will help us and there will be a war."

Danveld frowned again and became thoughtful.

"No! no!" said he after a while. "If we be successful, the grand master will be pleased. Envoys will be sent to the prince, there will be negotiations and we will go scot-free. But in case of defeat, the Order will not intercede for us and will not declare war. Another grand master is necessary for that. The Polski king is behind the prince, and the grand master will not quarrel with him."

"But we have taken the Dobrzynska province; it is evident that we are not afraid of Krakow."

"There was some pretext—Opolczyk. We took it apparently in pledge, and then——" Here he looked around and said quietly:

"I heard in Marienburg, that if they threaten us with war, we will return the province."

128

"Ah!" said Brother Rotgier, "if we had Markward Salzbach with us, or Shomberg who killed Witold's whelps, he would find some remedy against Jurand. Witold was the king's viceroy and a grand duke! Notwithstanding that, Shomberg was not punished. He killed Witold's children, and went scot-free! Verily, there is great lack among us of people who can find a remedy for everything."

Having heard this, Hugo von Danveld put his elbows on the table, leaned his head on his hands and plunged into deep thought. Then his eyes became bright, he wiped, according to his custom, his moist, thick lips with the upper part of his hand and said:

"May the moment in which you mentioned, pious brother, the name of the valiant Shomberg be blessed."

"Why? Have you found a remedy?" asked Zygfried von Löve.

"Speak quickly!" exclaimed Brother Godfried.

"Listen," said Hugo. "Jurand has a daughter here, his only child, whom he loves dearly."

"Yes, so he has. We know her. The princess Anna Danuta loves her also."

"Yes. Listen then: if you capture this girl, Jurand will give as a ransom for her, not only, Bergow, but all his prisoners, himself and Spychow!"

"By Saint Bonifacius' blood shed in Duchum!" exclaimed Brother Godfried; "it would be as you say!"

Then they were silent, as if frightened by the boldness and the difficulties of the enterprise. But after a while Brother Rotgier turned toward Zygfried von Löve, and said:

"Your judgment and experience are equal to your bravery: what do you think about this plan?"

"I think that the matter is worthy of consideration."

"Because," said Rotgier further, "the girl is a lady-in-waiting with the princess—the princess loves her as if she were her own daughter. Think, pious brother, what an uproar will arise."

But Hugo von Danveld began to laugh:

"You said yourself, that Shomberg poisoned or strangled Witold's whelps, and what happened to him? They will raise an uproar about anything we do; but if we sent Jurand in chains to the grand master, then it is certain that we could expect reward rather than punishment."

"Yes," said von Löve, "there is a good opportunity for an attack. The prince is going away and Anna Danuta will remain here alone with her court. However it is a serious matter to invade the prince's house during the time of peace. The prince's house is not Spychow. It will be the same thing that happened in Zlotorja! Again complaints against the Order will go to all kings and to the pope; again that cursed Jagiello will threaten us, and the grand master; you know him: he is glad to take hold of anything he can, but he does not wish for war with Jagiello. Yes! there will be a great uproar in all the provinces of Mazowsze and of Polska."

"In the meanwhile Jurand's bones will whiten on a hook," answered Brother Hugo. "Then we do not need to take his daughter from the prince's mansion."

"But we cannot do it from Ciechanow either, because there, besides the noblemen, there are three hundred archers."

"No. But Jurand can become ill and send for his daughter. Then the princess would not prevent her going, and if the girl be lost on the road, who will accuse you or me and say to us: 'You captured her!'"

"Bah!" answered von Löve, impatiently. "You must first make Jurand sick and then make him summon the girl."

At this Hugo smiled triumphantly and answered:

"I have a goldsmith, who having been driven from Marienburg for theft, settled in Szczytno and who is able to make a seal; I also have people, who although our bondmen, came from the Mazurski country. Do you understand me yet?"

"I understand," shouted Brother Godfried.

And Rotgier raised his hands and said:

"May God bless you, pious brother, because neither Markward Salzbach, nor Shomberg could find better means."

Then he half closed his eyes, as if he saw something afar.

"I see Jurand," said he, "with a rope around his neck, standing at the Gdansk gate in Marienburg and our *knechts* are kicking him."

"And the girl will become a servant of the Order," said Hugo.

Having heard this, von Löve turned his severe eyes on Danveld; but the latter again rubbed his lips with the upper part of his hand and said:

"And now to Szczytno as soon as we can!"

Before starting on the journey to Szczytno, the four brothers of the Order and de Fourcy went to bid the prince and the princess adieu. It was not a very friendly farewell; but the prince, not wishing to act contrary to the old Polish custom which did not permit the guests to depart with empty hands, made each brother a present of some beautiful marten-fur and of one *grzywna* of silver; they received the presents with great pleasure, assuring the prince that being brothers of an order, and having made a solemn promise to live in poverty, they would not retain the money for themselves, but would distribute it among the poor, whom they would recommend to pray for the prince's health, fame and future salvation.

The Mazurs laughed in their sleeves at such an assurance, because they knew very well how rapacious the Order was, and still better what liars the Knights of the Cross were.

It was a popular saying in Mazowsze: "As the skunk smells, so the Krzyzak lies." The prince waved his hand to such thanks, and after they went out he said that by the intervention of the Knights of the Cross, one would go to heaven as swiftly as the craw-fish walks.

But before that, while taking leave of the princess, at the moment that Zygfried von Löve kissed her hand, Hugo von Danveld approached Danusia, put his hand on her head and caressing her, said:

"Our commandment is to return good for evil, and even to love our enemy; therefore I will send a sister of the Order here, and she will bring you the healing balm."

"How can I thank you for it?" answered Danusia.

"Be a friend of the Order and of the monks."

De Fourcy noticed this conversation, and in the meantime he was struck by the beauty of the young girl; therefore as they traveled toward Szczytno, he asked:

"Who is that beautiful lady of the court with whom you were talking while taking leave of the princess?"

"Jurand's daughter!" answered the Krzyzak.

Sir de Fourcy was surprised.

"The same whom you propose to capture?"

"Yes. And when we capture her, Jurand is ours."

"Evidently everything is not bad that comes from Jurand. It will be worth while to guard such a prisoner."

"Do you think it will be easier to fight with her than with Jurand?"

"I mean that I think the same as you do. The father is a foe of the Order; but you spoke words as sweet as honey to the daughter, and besides you promised to send her the balm."

Evidently Hugo von Danveld felt the need of justification before Zygfried von Löve who, although not better than the others, observed the austere laws of the Order, and very often scolded the other brothers.

"I promised her the balm," said Hugo, "for that young knight, who was injured by the bison and to whom she is betrothed. If they make an outcry when the girl is captured, then we will tell them that we did not wish to harm her any, and the best proof of it will be that on account of Christian mercy we sent her some medicine."

"Very well," said von Löve. "Only we must send somebody whom we can trust."

"I will send a pious woman, entirely faithful to the Order. I will command her to look and to listen. When our people, apparently sent by Jurand, arrive, they will find the road already prepared."

"It will be difficult to get such people."

"No! In our province the people speak the same language. There are in our city, bah! even among the *knechts* of the garrison, some men who left Mazowsze because they were pursued by the law; it is true they are thieves and robbers; but they do not fear anybody and they are ready to do anything. To those men, I will promise, in case they succeed, a large reward; if they fail, a rope."

"Bah! Suppose they betray us?"

"They will not betray us, because in Mazowsze every one of them deserves to be hanged. Only we must give them decent clothes so that they will be taken for Jurand's servants; and we must get the principal thing: a letter with Jurand's seal."

"We must foresee everything," said Brother Rotgier. "It is probable that Jurand will go to see the prince, and justify himself on account of the last war. If he is in Ciechanow, he will go to see his daughter. It may happen that our men when they go to capture Jurandowna, will come in contact with Jurand himself."

"The men whom I am going to choose are sharp. They will know that they will be hanged if they come in contact with Jurand. It will be to their own interest not to meet him."

"But they may be captured."

"Then we will deny them and the letter. Who can prove that we sent them? And then if there be no outrage, there will be no outcry, and it will not harm the Order, if Mazury cut several scoundrels into pieces."

Brother Godfried, the youngest of the monks, said:

"I do not understand your policy, nor your fear that it may be known that the girl was carried off by our command. Because if we have her in our possession, we will be obliged to send some one to Jurand to tell him: 'Your daughter is with us; if you wish her to be set at liberty, give von Bergow and yourself in exchange for her.' You cannot do otherwise, and then it will be known that we ordered the girl to be carried off."

"That is true!" said Sir de Fourcy, who did not like the whole affair. "Why should we hide that which must come out?"

But Hugo von Danveld began to laugh, and turning to Brother Godfried, asked:

"How long have you worn the white mantle?"

"It will be six years the first week after the day of the Holy Trinity."

"When you have worn it six years longer, you will understand the affairs of the Order better. Jurand knows us better than you do. We will tell him: 'Your daughter is watched by Brother Shomberg; if you say a word, remember what happened to Witold's children!'"

"And then?"

"Then von Bergow will be free and the Order also will be free from Jurand."

"No!" exclaimed Brother Rotgier; "everything is planned so cleverly that God ought to bless our enterprise."

"God blesses all deeds whose purpose is the good of the Order," said the gloomy Zygfried von Löve.

Then they rode silently, and before them went their retinue, to open the way, because the road was covered with a heavy snow, which had fallen during the night. The day was cloudy, but warm; therefore the horses were steaming. From the forest flocks of crows were flying toward the villages, filling the air with their gloomy cawing.

Sir de Fourcy remained a little bit behind the Knights of the Cross and rode along in deep thought. He had been the guest of the Order for several years, and had participated in the expeditions against the Zmudz, where he distinguished himself by great bravery. Everywhere he had been received as the Knights of the Cross knew how to receive the knights from remote countries; he became attached to them very strongly, and not being rich, he planned to join their ranks. In the meanwhile he either lived in Marienburg, or visited the commanderies, searching in his travels for distractions and adventures. Having just arrived at Lubowa with the rich von Bergow, and having heard about Jnrand, he desired very much to fight with the man who was regarded with general dread. The arrival of Meineger, who was always victorious, precipitated the expedition. The *comthur* of Lubowa furnished the men for it, but in the meanwhile he told them so much not only about Jurand's cruelty, but also about his cunning and treachery, that when Juvand asked them to send away the soldiers, they refused to do it, fearing that if they did, he would surround and exterminate them or else capture and put them into the Spychowski dungeons. Then Jurand thinking that they cared less about a knightly fight than about plunder, attacked them and defeated them. De Fourcy saw von Bergow overthrown with his horse; he saw Meineger with a piece of a spear in his body, and he saw the men asking in vain for mercy. He escaped with great difficulty, and wandered for several days in the forests, where he would have died of hunger or been destroyed by wild beasts, if by chance he had not reached Ciechanow, where he found Brothers Godfried and Rotgier. From the expedition he emerged with a feeling of humiliation and shame, and with a desire for vengeance and a longing after Bergow, who was his dear friend. Therefore he joined with his whole soul in the complaint of the Knights of the Cross, when they asked for the punishment of the Polish knight and the freedom of his unhappy companion. When their complaint had no effect whatever, in the first moment he was ready to approve of any plan for vengeance against Jurand. But now some scruples were aroused in him. Listening to the conversation of the monks, and especially to what Hugo von Danveld said, he could not refrain from astonishment. It is true, that having become well acquainted during the past few years with the Knights of the Cross, he knew that they were not what they were represented to be in Germany and in the West. In Marienburg, he knew, however, a few honest and upright knights who often complained of the corruption of the brothers, of their lasciviousness and lack of discipline; de Fourcy felt that they were right, but being himself dissolute and lacking in discipline, he did not criticise them for those faults, especially because all knights of the Order redeemed them with bravery. He had seen them at Wilno, fighting breast to breast with the Polish knights; at the taking of castles, defended with superhuman stubbornness by Polish garrisons; he had seen them perishing under the blows of axes and swords, in general assaults or in single combats. They were merciless and cruel toward the Litwa, but at the same time, they were as brave as lions.

But now it seemed to Sir de Fourcy, that Hugo von Danveld advised such actions from which every knight's soul should recoil; and the other brothers not only were not angry with him, but approved of his words. Therefore astonishment seized him more and more; finally he became deeply thoughtful, pondering whether it was proper to join in the performance of such deeds.

If it were only a question of carrying off the girl and then exchanging her for Bergow, he would perhaps consent to that, although his heart had been moved by Danusia's beauty. But evidently the Knights of the Cross wished for something else. Through her they wished to capture Jurand, and then murder him, and together with him,—in order to hide the fraud and the crime—must assuredly murder the girl also.

They had threatened her already with the same fate that Witold's children met, in case Jurand should dare to complain. "They do not intend to keep any promise, but to cheat both and kill both," said de Fourcy, to himself, "although they wear the cross, and ought to guard their honor more than anybody else."

He became more and more indignant at such effrontery, and he determined to verify his suspicions; therefore he rode near Danveld and asked:

"If Jurand give himself up to you, will you set the girl at liberty?"

"If we let her go free, the whole world would immediately say that we had captured both of them," answered Danveld.

"Then, what do you propose to do with her?"

At this Danveld bent toward the knight, and laughing, showed his rotten teeth from beneath his thick lips.

"Do you mean what will be done with her, before or after?"

But Fourcy, surmising already that which he wished to know, became silent; for a while he seemed to struggle with himself; then he raised himself in his stirrups and said so loudly that he could be heard by all four of the monks:

"The pious brother, Ulrych von Jungingen, who is an example and an ornament of knighthood, said to me: 'Among the old knights in Marienburg, one can still find worthy Knights of the Cross; but those who control the commanderies near the frontier, only bring shame upon the Order.'"

"We are all sinful, but we serve the Saviour," answered Hugo.

"Where is your knightly honor? One cannot serve the Saviour by shameful deeds. You must know that I will not put my hand to anything like that, and that I also will prevent you."

"What will you prevent?"

"The artifice, the treachery, the shame!"

"How can you do it? In the fight with Jurand, you lost your retinue and wagons. You are obliged to live on the generosity of the Order, and you will die from hunger if we do not throw you a piece of bread; and then, you are alone, we are four—how could you prevent us?"

"How can I prevent you?" repeated de Fourcy. "I can return to the mansion and warn the prince; I can divulge your plans to the whole world."

Here the brothers of the Order looked at one another, and their faces changed in the twinkling of an eye. Hugo von Danveld, especially, looked questioningly into Zygfried von Löve's eyes; then he turned to Sir de Fourcy:

"Your ancestors," said he, "used to serve in the Order, and you wished to join it also; but we do not receive traitors."

"And I do not wish to serve with traitors."

"Ej! you shall not fulfill your threat. The Order knows how to punish not only the monks——"

Sir de Fourcy being excited by these words, drew his sword, and seized the blade with his left hand; his right hand he put on the hilt and said:

"On this hilt which is in the form of the cross, on St. Denis, my patron's head, and on my knightly honor, I swear that I will warn the Mazowiecki prince and the grand master."

Hugo von Danveld again looked inquiringly at Zygfried von Löve, who closed his eyelids, as if consenting to something.

Then Danveld said in a strangely muffled and changed voice:

"St. Denis could carry his head after he was beheaded, but when yours once falls down——"

"Are you threatening me?" interrupted de Fourcy.

"No, but I kill!" answered Danveld. And he thrust his knife into de Fourcy's side with such strength, that the blade disappeared up to the hilt. De Fourcy screamed dreadfully; for a while he tried to seize his sword which he held in his left hand, with his right, but he dropped it; at the same time, the other three brothers began to pierce him mercilessly with their knives, in the neck, in the back, and in the stomach, until he fell from his horse.

Then there was silence. De Fourcy bleeding dreadfully from several wounds, quivered on the snow. From beneath the leaden sky, there came only the cawing of the crows, which were flying from the silent wilderness, toward human habitations.

Then there began a hurried conversation between the murderers:

"Our servants did not see anything!" said Danveld, panting.

"No. The retinues are in front; we cannot see them," answered von Löve.

"Listen: we will have cause for a new complaint. We will publish the statement that the Mazowiecki knights fell upon us and killed our companion. We will shout aloud—they will hear us in Marienburg—that the prince sent murderers even after his guests. Listen! we must say that Janusz did not wish to listen to our complaints against Jurand, but that he ordered the accuser to be murdered."

In the meanwhile, de Fourcy turned in the last convulsion on his back and then remained motionless, with a bloody froth on his lips and with dread pictured in his widely-opened dead eyes. Brother Rotgier looked at him and said:

"Notice, pious brothers, how God punishes even the thought of treachery."

"What we have done, was done for the good of the Order," answered Godfried. "Glory to those——"

But he stopped, because at that moment, behind them, at the turn of the snowy road, there appeared a horseman, who rushed forward as fast as his horse could go. Having perceived him, Hugo von Danveld quickly exclaimed:

"Whoever this man is—he must die." And von Löve, who although the oldest among the brothers, had very keen eyesight, said:

133

"I recognize him; it is that shield-bearer who killed the bison with an axe. Yes; it is he!"

"Hide your knives, so that he may not become frightened," said Danveld. "I will attack him first, you shall follow me."

In the meanwhile, the Bohemian arrived and reined in his horse at a distance of eight or ten steps. He noticed the corpse lying in the pool of blood, the horse without a rider, and astonishment appeared on his face; but it lasted only for the twinkling of an eye. After a while, he turned to the brothers as if nothing had happened and said:

"I bow to you, brave knights!"

"We recognize you," answered Danveld, approaching slowly. "Have you anything for us?"

"The knight Zbyszko of Bogdaniec, after whom I carry the spear, sent me, because being injured by the bison, he could not come himself."

"What does your master wish from us?"

"My master commanded me to tell you that because you unrighteously accused Jurand of Spychow, to the detriment of his knightly honor, you did not act like honest knights, but howled like dogs; and if any one of you feels insulted by these words, he challenges him to a combat on horseback or on foot, to the last breath; he will be ready for the duel as soon as with God's help and mercy he is released from his present indisposition."

"Tell your master, that the Knights of the Order bear insults patiently for the Saviour's sake, and they cannot fight, without special permission from the grand master or from the grand marshal; for which permission they will write to Malborg."

The Czech again looked at de Fourcy's corpse, because he had been sent especially to that knight. Zbyszko knew that the monks could not fight in single combat: but having heard that there was a secular knight with them, he wanted to challenge him especially, thinking that by doing so he would win Jurand's favor. But that knight was lying slaughtered like an ox, by the four Knights of the Cross.

It is true that the Czech did not understand what had happened; but being accustomed from childhood to different kinds of danger, he suspected some treachery. He was also surprised to see Danveld, while talking with him, approach him closer and closer; the others began to ride to his sides, as if to surround him. Consequently he was upon the alert, especially as he did not have any weapons; he had not brought any, being in great haste.

In the meanwhile Danveld who was near him, said:

"I promised your master some healing balm; he repays me badly for my good deed. But no wonder, that is the usual thing among the Polaks. But as he is severely injured and may soon be called to God, tell him then——"

Here he leaned his left hand on the Czech's shoulder.

"Tell him then, that I—well—I answer this way!——"

And at the same moment, his knife gleamed near the throat of the shield-bearer; but before he could thrust, the Czech who had been watching his movements closely, seized Danveld's right hand, with his iron-like hands, bent and twisted it so that the bones cracked; then hearing a dreadful roaring of pain, he pricked his horse and rushed away like an arrow, before the others could stop him.

Brothers Rotgier and Godfried pursued him, but they soon returned, frightened by a dreadful cry from Danveld. Von Löve supported him with his shoulders, while he cried so loudly that the retinue, riding with the wagons in front at quite a distance, stopped their horses.

"What is the matter with you?" asked the brothers.

But von Löve ordered them to ride forward as fast as they could, and bring a wagon, because Danveld could not remain in his saddle. After a moment, a cold perspiration covered his forehead and he fainted.

When they brought the wagon, they put him on some straw in the bottom and hurried toward the frontier. Von Löve urged them forward because he realized that after what had happened, they could not lose time in nursing Danveld. Having seated himself beside him in the wagon, he rubbed his face with snow from time to time; but he could not resuscitate him. At last when near the frontier, Danveld opened his eyes and began to look around.

"How do you feel?" asked Löve.

"I do not feel any pain, but neither can I feel my hand," answered Danveld.

"Because it has grown stiff already; that is why you do not feel any pain. It will come back in a warm room. In the meanwhile, thank God even for a moment of relief."

Rotgier and Godfried approached the wagon.

"What a misfortune!" said the first. "What shall we do now?"

"We will declare," said Danveld in a feeble voice, "that the shield-bearer murdered de Fourcy."

"It is their latest crime and the culprit is known!" added Rotgier.

CHAPTER VII

In the meanwhile, the Czech rushed as fast as he could to the prince's hunting residence, and finding the prince still there, he told him first, what had happened. Happily there were some courtiers who had seen the shield-bearer go without any arms. One of them had even shouted after him, half in jest, to take some old iron, because otherwise the Germans would get the best of him; but he, fearing that the knights would pass the frontier, jumped on horseback as he stood, in a sheepskin overcoat only and hurried after them. These testimonies dispelled all possible doubts from the prince's mind as to the fact who had murdered de Fourcy; but they filled him with uneasiness and with such anger, that at first he wanted to pursue the Knights of the Cross, capture them and send them to the grand master in chains. After a while, however, he came to the conclusion, that it was impossible to reach them on this side of the boundary and he said:

"I will send, instead, a letter to the grand master, so that he may know what they are doing here. God will punish them for it!"

Then he became thoughtful and after a while he began to say to the courtiers:

"I cannot understand why they killed their guest; I would suspect the shield-bearer if I did not know that he went there without weapons."

"Bah!" said the *ksiondz* Wyszoniek, "why should the boy kill him? He had not seen him before. Then suppose he had had arms, how could he attack five of them and their armed retinues?"

"That is true," said the prince. "That guest must have opposed them in something, or perhaps he did not wish to lie as was necessary for them. I saw them wink at him, to induce him to say that Jurand was the first to begin the fight."

Then Mrokota of Mocarzew said:

"He is a strong boy, if he could crush the arm of that dog Danveld."

"He said that he heard the bones of the German crack," answered the prince; "and taking into consideration what he did in the forest, one must admit it is true! The master and the servant are both strong boys. But for Zbyszko, the bison would have rushed against the horses. Both the Lotaringer and he contributed very much to the rescue of the princess."

"To be sure they are great boys," affirmed the *ksiondz* Wyszoniek. "Even now when he can hardly breathe, he has taken Jurand's part and challenged those knights. Jurand needs exactly such a son-in-law."

"In Krakow, Jurand said differently; but now, I think he will not oppose it," said the prince.

"The Lord Jesus will help," said the princess, who entered just now and heard the end of the conversation.

"Jurand cannot oppose it now, if only God will restore Zbyszko's health; but we must reward him also."

"The best reward for him will be Danusia, and I think he will get her, for when the women resolve to accomplish some object, then even Jurand himself could not prevent them."

"Am I not right, to wish for that marriage?" asked the princess.

"I would not say a word if Zbyszko were not constant; but I think there is no other in the world as faithful as he. And the girl also. She does not leave him now for a moment; she

135

caresses him and he smiles at her, although he is very ill. I cry myself when I see this! I am speaking righteously! It is worth while to help such a love, because the Holy Mother looks gladly on human happiness."

"If it be God's will," said the prince, "the happiness will come. But it is true that he nearly lost his head for that girl and now the bison has injured him."

"Do not say it was for that girl," said the princess, quickly, "because in Krakow Danusia saved him."

"True! But for her sake he attacked Lichtenstein, in order to tear from his head the feathers, and he would not have risked his life for de Lorche. As for the reward, I said before that they both deserve one, and I will think about it in Ciechanow."

"Nothing will please Zbyszko more than to receive the knightly girdle and the golden spurs."

The prince smiled benevolently and answered:

"Let the girl carry them to him; and when the illness leaves him, then we will see that everything is accomplished according to the custom. Let her carry them to him immediately, because quick joy is the best!"

The princess having heard that, hugged her lord in the presence of the courtiers, and kissed his hands; he smiled continually and said:

"You see—A good idea! I see that the Holy Ghost has granted the woman some sense also! Now call the girl."

"Danuska! Danuska!" called the princess.

And in a moment in the side door Danusia appeared; her eyes were red on account of sleepless nights; and she held a pot of steaming gruel, which the *ksiondz* Wyszoniek had ordered to be put on Zbyszko's fractured bones.

"Come to me, my dear girl!" said Prince Janusz. "Put aside the pot and come."

When she approached with some timidity, because "the lord" always excited some fear in her, he embraced her kindly and began to caress her face, saying:

"Well, the poor child is unhappy—*hein?*"

"Yes!" answered Danusia.

And having sadness in her heart, she began to cry but very quietly, in order not to hurt the prince; he asked again:

"Why do you cry?"

"Because Zbyszko is ill," answered she, putting her little hands to her eyes.

"Do not be afraid, there is no danger for him. Is that not true, Father Wyszoniek?"

"Hej! by God's will, he is nearer to the wedding than to the coffin," answered the good-hearted *ksiondz* Wyszoniek.

The prince said:

"Wait! In the meanwhile, I will give you a medicine for him, and I trust it will relieve him or cure him entirely."

"Have the Krzyzaks sent the balm?" asked Danusia quickly, taking her little hands from her eyes.

"With that balm which the Krzyzaks will send, you had better smear a dog than a knight whom you love. I will give you something else."

Then he turned to the courtiers and said:

"Hurry and bring the spurs and the girdle."

After a while, when they had brought them to him, he said to Danusia:

"Take these to Zbyszko—and tell him that from this time he is a belted knight. If he die, then he will appear before God as *miles cinctus*; if he live, then the rest will be accomplished in Ciechanow or in Warszawa."

Having heard this, Danusia seized "the lord" by his knees; then caught the knightly insignia with one hand and the pot of porridge with the other, and rushed to the room where Zbyszko was lying. The princess, not wishing to lose the sight of their joy, followed her.

Zbyszko was very ill, but having perceived Danusia, he turned his pale face toward her and asked:

"Has the Czech returned?"

"No matter about the Czech!" answered the girl. "I bring you better news than that. The lord has made you a knight and has sent you this by me."

Having said this, she put beside him the girdle and the spurs. Zbyszko's pale cheeks flushed with joy and astonishment, he glanced at Danusia and then at the spurs; then he closed his eyes and began to repeat:

"How could he dub me a knight?"

At that moment the princess entered, and he raised himself a little and began to thank her, because he guessed that her intervention had brought such a great favor and bliss to him. But she ordered him to be quiet and helped Danusia to put his head on the pillows again. In the meanwhile, the prince, the *ksiondz* Wyszoniek, Mrokota and several other courtiers entered.

Prince Janusz waved his hand to signify that Zbyszko must not move; then having seated himself beside the bed, he said:

"You know! The people must not wonder that there is reward for good deeds, because if virtue remained without any reward, human iniquities would walk without punishment. You did not spare your life, but with peril to yourself defended us from dreadful mourning; therefore we permit you to don the knightly girdle, and from this moment to walk in glory and fame."

"Gracious lord," answered Zbyszko. "I would not spare even ten lives———"

But he could not say anything more, on account of his emotion; and the princess put her hand on his mouth because the *ksiondz* Wyszoniek did not permit him to talk. The prince continued further:

"I think that you know the knightly duties and that you will wear the insignia with honor. You must serve our Saviour, and fight with the *starosta* of hell. You must be faithful to the anointed lord, avoid unrighteous war and defend innocence against oppression; may God and His Holy Passion help you!"

"Amen!" answered the *ksiondz* Wyszoniek.

The prince arose, made the sign of the cross over Zbyszko and added:

"And when you recover, go immediately to Ciechanow, where I will summon Jurand."

CHAPTER VIII.

Three days afterward, a woman arrived with the Hercynski balm and with her came the captain of the archers from Szczytno, with a letter, signed by the brothers and sealed with Danveld's seal; in that letter the Knights of the Cross called on heaven and earth as witnesses of the wrongs committed against them in Mazowsze, and with a threat of God's vengeance, they asked for punishment for the murder of their "beloved comrade and guest." Danveld added to the letter his personal complaint, asking humbly but also threateningly for remuneration for his crippled hand and a sentence of death against the Czech. The prince tore the letter into pieces in the presence of the captain, threw it under his feet and said:

"The grand master sent those scoundrels of Krzyzaks to win me over, but they have incited me to wrath. Tell them from me that they killed their guest themselves and they wanted to murder the Czech. I will write to the grand master about that and I will request him to send different envoys, if he wishes me to be neutral in case of a war between the Order and the Krakowski king."

"Gracious lord," answered the captain, "must I carry such an answer to the mighty and pious brothers?"

"If it is not enough, tell them then, that I consider them dog-brothers and not honest knights."

This was the end of the audience. The captain went away, because the prince departed the same day for Ciechanow. Only the "sister" remained with the balm, but the mistrustful *ksiondz* Wyszoniek did not wish to use it, especially as the sick man had slept well the preceding night and had awakened without any fever, although still very weak. After the prince's departure, the sister immediately sent a servant for a new medicine apparently—for the "egg of a basilisk"—which she affirmed had the power to restore strength even to people in agony; as for herself, she wandered about the mansion; she was humble and was dressed in a lay dress, but similar to that worn by members of the Order; she carried a rosary and a small pilgrim's gourd at her belt. She could not move one of her hands. As she could speak Polish well, she inquired from the servants about Zbyszko and Danusia, to whom she made a present of a rose of Jericho; on the second day during Zbyszko's slumber, while Danusia was sitting in the dining-room, she approached her and said:

"May God-bless you, *panienko*. Last night after my prayers I dreamed that there were two knights walking during the fall of the snow; one of them came first and wrapped you in a white mantle, and the other said: 'I see only the snow, and she is not here,' and he returned."

Danusia who was sleepy, immediately opened her blue eyes curiously, and asked: "What does it mean?"

"It means that the one who loves you the best, will get you."

"That is Zbyszko!" said the girl.

"I do not know, because I did not see his face; I only saw the white mantle and then I awakened; the Lord Jesus sends me pain every night in my feet and I cannot move my hand."

"It is strange that the balm has not helped you any!"

"It cannot help me, *panienko*, because the pain is a punishment for a sin; if you wish to know what the sin was, I will tell you."

Danusia nodded her little head in sign that she wished to know; therefore the "sister" continued:

"There are also servants, women, in the Order, who, although they do not make any vows, and are allowed to marry, are obliged to perform certain duties for the Order, according to the brothers' commands. The one who meets such favor and honor, receives a pious kiss from a brother-knight as a sign that from that moment she is to serve the Order with words and deeds. Ah! *panienko*!—I was going to receive that great favor, but in sinful obduracy instead of receiving it with gratitude, I committed a great sin and was punished for it."

"What did you do?"

"Brother Danveld came to me and gave me the kiss of the Order; but I, thinking that he was doing it from pure license, raised my wicked hand against him——"

Here she began to strike her breast and repeated several times:

"God, be merciful to me, a sinner!"

"What happened then?" asked Danusia.

"Immediately my hand became motionless, and from that moment I have been crippled. I was young and stupid—I did not know! But I was punished. If a woman fears that a brother of the Order wishes to do something wicked, she must leave the judgment to God, but she must not resist herself, because whosoever contradicts the Order or a brother of the Order, that one will feel God's anger!"

Danusia listened to these words with fright and uneasiness; the sister began to sigh and to complain.

"I am not old yet," said she; "I am only thirty years old, but besides the hand, God has taken from me my youth and beauty."

"If it were not for the hand," said Danusia, "you need not complain."

Then there was silence. Suddenly the sister, as if she had just remembered something, said:

"I dreamed that some knight wrapped you with a white mantle on the snow. Perhaps it was a Krzyzak! They wear white mantles."

"I want neither Krzyzaks nor their mantles," answered the girl.

But further conversation was interrupted by the *ksiondz* Wyszoniek, who entering the room, nodded to Danusia and said:

"Praise God and come to Zbyszko! He has awakened and has asked for something to eat. He is much better."

In fact it was so. Zbyszko was a great deal better, and the *ksiondz* Wyszoniek was almost sure that he would recover, when an unexpected accident upset all his expectations. There came envoys from Jurand with a letter to the princess, containing dreadful news. In Spychow, half of Jurand's *grodek* had been burned, and he himself during the rescue was struck by a beam. It is true that the *ksiondz* Kaleb, who wrote the letter, said that Jurand, would recover, but that the sparks had burned his remaining eye so badly that there was very little sight left in it, and he was likely to become blind.

For that reason, Jurand asked his daughter to come to Spychow as soon as possible, because he wished to see her once more, before he was entirely encompassed by darkness. He also said that she was to remain with him, because even the blind, begging on the roads, had some one to lead them by the hand and show them the way; why should he be deprived of that pleasure and die among strangers? There were also humble thanks for the princess, who had taken care of the girl like a mother, and finally Jurand promised that, although blind, he would go to Warszawa once more, in order to fall at the lady's feet and beg her for further favor for Danusia.

The princess, when the *ksiondz* Wyszoniek had finished reading the letter, could not say a word for some time. She had hoped that when Jurand came to see his daughter and her, she would be able by the prince's and her own influence to obtain his consent for the wedding of the young couple. But this letter, not only destroyed her plans, but in the meanwhile deprived her of Danusia whom she loved as well as she did her own children. She feared that Jurand would marry the girl to some neighbor of his, so as to spend the rest of his life among his own people. It was no use to think about Zbyszko—he could not go to Spychow, and then who knew how he would be received there. The lady knew that Jurand had refused to give him Danusia; and he had said to the princess herself that on account of some secret reason, he would never consent to their marriage. Therefore in great grief she ordered the principal messenger to be brought to her, as she desired to ask him about the Spychowski misfortune, and also to learn something about Jurand's plans.

She was very much surprised when a stranger came instead of the old Tolima, who used to bear the shield after Jurand and usually carried his messages; but the stranger told her that Tolima had been seriously injured in the last fight with the Germans and that he was dying in Spychow; Jurand being very ill himself, asked her to send his daughter immediately, because every day he saw less and less, and perhaps in a few days he would become blind. The messenger begged the princess to permit him to take the girl immediately after the horses were rested, but as it was already dusk she refused; especially as she did not wish to distress Zbyszko and Danusia by such a sudden separation.

Zbyszko already knew all about it, and he was lying like one stricken by a heavy blow; when the princess entered, and wringing her hands, said from the threshold:

"We cannot help it; he is her father!" he repeated after her like an echo: "We cannot help it——" then closed his eyes, like a man who expects death immediately.

But death did not come; but in his breast there gathered a still greater grief and through his head ran sad thoughts, like the clouds which driven by the wind, obstruct the sun and quench all joy in the world. Zbyszko understood as well as the princess did, that if Danusia were once in Spychow, she would be lost to him forever. Here everybody was his friend; there Jurand might even refuse to receive him, or listen to him, especially if he were bound by a vow, or some other unknown reason as strong as a religious vow. Then how could he go to Spychow, when he was sick and hardly able to move in bed. A few days ago, when the prince rewarded him with the golden spurs, he had thought that his joy would conquer his illness, and he had prayed fervently to God to be permitted to soon rise and fight with the Krzyzaks; but now he had again lost all hope, because he felt that if Danusia were not at his bedside, then with her would go his desire for life and the strength to fight with death. What a pleasure and joy it had been to ask her several times a day: "Do you love me?" and to see how she covered her smiling and bashful eyes, or bent and answered: "Yes, Zbyszko."

But now only illness, loneliness and grief would remain, and the happiness would depart and not return.

Tears shone in Zbyszko's eyes and rolled slowly down on his cheeks; then he turned to the princess and said:

"Gracious lady, I fear that I shall never see Danusia again."

And the lady being sorrowful herself, answered:

"I would not be surprised if you died from grief; but the Lord Jesus is merciful."

After a while, however, wishing to comfort him, she added:

"But if Jurand die first, then the tutelage will be the prince's and mine, and we will give you the girl immediately."

"He will not die!" answered Zbyszko.

But at once, evidently some new thought came to his mind, because he arose, sat on the bed and said in a changed voice:

"Gracious lady——"

At that moment Danusia interrupted him; she came crying and said from the threshold:

"Zbyszku! Do you know about it already! I pity *tatus*, but I pity you also, poor boy!"

When she approached, Zbyszko encircled his love with his well arm, and began to speak:

"How can I live without you, my dearest? I did not travel through rivers and forest, I did not make the vow to serve you, that I might lose you. Hej! sorrow will not help, crying will not help, bah! even death itself, because even if the grass grow over me, my soul will not forget you, even if I am in the presence of the Lord Jesus or of God the Father—I say, there must be a remedy! I feel a terrible pain in my bones, but you must fall at the lady's feet, I cannot—and ask her to have mercy upon us."

Danusia hearing this, ran quickly to the princess' feet, and having seized them in her arms, she hid her face in the folds of the heavy dress; the lady turned her compassionate but also astonished eyes to Zbyszko, and said:

"How can I show you mercy? If I do not let the child go to her sick father, I will draw God's anger on myself."

Zbyszko who had been sitting on the bed, slipped down on the pillows and did not answer for a time because he was exhausted. Slowly, however, he began to move one hand toward the other on his breast until he joined them as in prayer.

"Rest," said the princess; "then you may tell me what you wish; and you, Danusia, arise and release my knees."

"Relax, but do not rise; beg with me," said Zbyszko.

Then he began to speak in a feeble and broken voice:

"Gracious lady—Jurand was against me in Krakow—he will be here also, but if the *ksiondz* Wyszoniek married me to Danusia, then—afterward she may go to Spychow because there is no human power that could take her away from me——"

These words were so unexpected to the princess, that she jumped from the bench; then she sat down again and as if she had not thoroughly understood about what he was talking, she said:

"For heaven's sake! the *ksiondz* Wyszoniek."

"Gracious lady! Gracious lady!" begged Zbyszko.

"Gracious lady!" repeated Danusia, embracing the princess' knees.

"How could it be done without her father's permission?"

"God's law is the stronger!" answered Zbyszko.

"For heaven's sake!"

"Who is the father, if not the prince? Who is the mother, if not you, gracious lady?"

And Danusia added:

"Dearest *matuchna*!"[104]

"It is true, that I have been and am still like a mother to her," said the princess, "and Jurand received his wife from my hand. It is true! And if you are once married—everything is ended. Perhaps Jurand will be angry, but he must be obedient to the commands of the prince, his lord. Then, no one need tell him immediately, only if he wanted to give the girl to another, or to make her a nun; and if he has made some vow, it will not be his fault that he cannot fulfill it. Nobody can act against God's will—perhaps it is God's will!"

140

"It cannot be otherwise!" exclaimed Zbyszko.

But the princess, still very much excited, said:

"Wait, I must collect my thoughts. If the prince were here, I would go to him immediately and would ask him: 'May I give Danusia to Zbyszko or not?' But I am afraid without him, and there is not much time to spare, because the girl must go to-morrow! Oh, sweet Jesus, let her go married—then there will be peace. But I cannot recover my senses again—and then I am afraid of something. And you Danusia, are you not afraid?—Speak!"

"I will die without that!" interrupted Zbyszko.

Danusia arose from the princess' knees; she was not only really on confidential terms with the good lady, but also much spoiled by her; therefore she seized her around the neck, and began to hug her.

But the princess said:

"I will not promise you anything without Father Wyszoniek. Run for him immediately!"

Danusia went after Father Wyszoniek; Zbyszko turned his pale face toward the princess, and said:

"What the Lord Jesus has destined for me will happen; but for this consolation, may God reward you, gracious lady."

"Do not bless me yet," answered the princess, "because we do not know what will happen. You must swear to me upon you honor, that if you are married, you will not prevent the girl from going to her father, or else you will draw his curse upon her and yourself.

"Upon my honor!" said Zbyszko.

"Remember then! And the girl must not tell Jurand immediately. We will send for him from Ciechanow, and make him come with Danusia, and then I will tell him myself, or I will ask the prince to do it. When he sees that there is no remedy, he will consent. He did not dislike you?"

"No," said Zbyszko, "he did not dislike me; perhaps he will be pleased when Danusia is mine. If he made a vow, it will not be his fault that he could not keep it."

The conversation was interrupted by the entrance of Danusia and the *ksiondz* Wyszoniek. The princess immediately asked his advice and began to tell him with great enthusiasm about Zbyszko's plan; but as soon as he heard about it, he made the sign of the cross from astonishment and said:

"In the name of the Father and of the Son and of the Holy Ghost! How can I do it? It is advent!"

"For God's sake! That is true!" exclaimed the princess.

Then there was silence; only their sorrowful faces showed what a blow those words of the *ksiondz* Wyszoniek were to all of them.

Then he said after a while:

"If you had a dispensation, then I would not oppose it, because I pity you. I would not ask for Jurand's permission, because our gracious lady consents and, vouches for the prince's consent—well! they are the mother and the father for the whole of Mazowsze. But without a bishop's dispensation, I cannot. Bah! if the *ksiondz* bishop of Kurdwanow were with us, he would not refuse a dispensation, although he is a severe priest, not like his predecessor, Bishop Mamphiolus, who used always to answer: *Bene! Bene!*"

"Bishop Jacob of Kurdwanow loves the prince and myself very much," said the lady.

"Therefore I say he would not refuse a dispensation, more so because there are some reasons for one: the girl must go to her father and that young man is ill and may die—Hm! *in articulo mortis!* But without a dispensation I cannot."

"I could obtain it afterward from Bishop Jacob; no matter how severe he may be, he will not refuse me this favor. I guarantee, he will not refuse," said the princess.

To this the *ksiondz* Wjszoniek who was a good and easy man, replied:

"A word of the Lord's anointed is a great word. I am afraid of the *ksiondz* bishop, but that great word! Then the youth could promise something to the cathedral in Plock. Well, as long as the dispensation will not come, there will be a sin—and nobody's but mine. Hm! It is true that the Lord Jesus is merciful and if any one sin not for his own benefit, but on account of mercy for human misery, he forgives more easily! But there will be a sin, and suppose the bishop should refuse, who will grant me pardon?"

"The bishop will not refuse!" exclaimed Princess Anna.

And Zbyszko said:

"That man Sanderus, who came with me, has pardons ready for everything."

The *ksiondz* Wyszoniek probably did not believe entirely in Sanderus' pardons; but he was glad to have even a pretext so that he could help Danusia and Zbyszko, because he loved the girl, whom he had known from childhood. Then he remembered that at the worst, he would be punished with church penitence, therefore turning toward the princess he said:

"It is true, I am a priest, but I am also the prince's servant. What do you command, gracious lady?"

"I do not wish to command but to beg," answered the lady. "If that Sanderus has pardons——"

"Sanderus has. But there is the question about the bishop. He is very severe with the canons in Plock."

"Do not be afraid of the bishop. I have heard that he has forbidden the priest to carry swords and crossbows and has forbidden different licenses, but he has not forbidden them to do good."

The *ksiondz* Wyszoniek raised his eyes and his hands, and said:

"Let it be according to your wish!"

At this word, joy filled their hearts. Zbyszko again sat on the bed and the princess, Danusia and Father Wyszoniek sat round it and began to plan how they should act.

They decided to keep it secret so that not a soul in the house should know anything about it; they also decided that Jurand must not know until the princess herself told him in Ciechanow about everything.

In the meanwhile, the *ksiondz* Wyszoniek was to write a letter from the princess to Jurand and ask him to come to Ciechanow, where he could find better medicine and where he will not weary. Finally, they decided, that Zbyszko and Danusia will go to confession, that the wedding ceremony will be performed during the night, when everybody will retire.

The thought came to Zbyszko to have his shield-bearer, the Czech, as a witness of the wedding; but he gave up the idea when he remembered that he had received him from Jagienka. For a moment she stood in his memory as though present, so that it seemed to him that he saw her blushing face and her eyes full of tears, and heard her pleading voice say: "Do not do that! Do not repay me with evil for good, nor with misery for love!" Then at once great compassion for her seized him, because he felt that a great wrong would be done her, after which she would find no consolation under the roof of Zgorzelice, nor in the depths of the forest, nor in the fields, nor in the abbot's gifts, nor in Cztan and Wilk's courtship. Therefore he said inwardly: "Girl, may God give you the best of everything, for although I am willing to bend the sky for you, I cannot." In fact, the thought that he could not help it, immediately brought him relief, and tranquillity returned, so that immediately he began to think only about Danusia and the wedding.

But he was obliged to call the Czech to help him; therefore although he determined not to say a word to him about what was going to happen, he summoned him and said:

"To-day I am going to confession as well as to the Lord's table; therefore you must dress me in my best clothing as if I were going to the king's palace."

The Czech was a little afraid and began to look into his face; Zbyszko having noticed this, said:

"Do not be alarmed, people do not go to confession only when they expect to die; the holy days are coming, Father Wyszoniek and the princess are going to Ciechanow, and then there will be no priest nearer than in Przasnysz."

"And are you not going?" asked the shield-bearer.

"If I recover my health, then I will go; but that is in God's hands."

Therefore the Czech was quieted; he hurried to the chests, and brought that white *jaka* embroidered with gold, in which the knight used to dress for great occasions, and also a beautiful rug to cover the bed; then having lifted Zbyszko, with the help of the two

Turks, he washed him, and combed his long hair on which he put a scarlet zone; finally he placed him on red cushions, and satisfied with his own work, said:

"If Your Grace were able to dance, you could celebrate even a wedding!"

"It will be necessary to celebrate it without dancing," answered Zbyszko, smiling.

In the meanwhile the princess was also thinking how to dress Danusia, because for her womanly nature it was a question of great importance, and under no consideration would she consent to have her beloved foster child married in her everyday dress. The servants who were also told that the girl must dress in the color of innocence for confession, very easily found a white dress, but there was great trouble about the wreath for the head. While thinking of it, the lady became so sad that she began to complain:

"My poor orphan, where shall I find a wreath of rue for you in this wilderness? There is none here, neither a flower, nor a leaf; only some green moss under the snow."

And Danusia, standing with loosened hair, also became sorrowful, because she wanted a wreath; after awhile, however, she pointed to the garlands of immortelles, hanging on the walls of the room, and said:

"We must weave a wreath of those flowers, because we will not find anything else, and Zbyszko will take me even with such a wreath."

The princess would not consent at first, being afraid of a bad omen; but as in this mansion, to which they came only for hunting, there were no flowers, finally the immortelles were taken. In the meanwhile, Father Wyszoniek came, and received Zbyszko's confession; afterwards he listened to the girl's confession and then the gloomy night fell. The servants retired after supper, according to the princess' order. Some of Jurand's men lay down in the servants' room, and others slept in the stables with the horses. Soon the fires in the servants' room became covered with ashes and were quenched; finally everything became absolutely quiet in the forest house, only from time to time the dogs were heard howling at the wolves in the direction of the wilderness.

But in the princess', Father Wyszoniek's and Zbyszko's rooms, the windows were shining, throwing red lights on the snow which covered the court-yard. They were waiting in silence, listening to the throbbing of their own hearts—uneasy and affected by the solemnity of the moment which was coming. In fact, after midnight, the princess took Danusia by the hand and conducted her to Zbyszko's room, where Father Wyszoniek was waiting for them. In the room there was a great blaze in the fireplace, and by its abundant but unsteady light, Zbyszko perceived Danusia; she looked a little pale on account of sleepless nights; she was dressed in a long, stiff, white dress, with a wreath of immortelles on her brow. On account of emotion, she closed her eyes; her little hands were hanging against the dress, and thus she appeared like some painting on a church window; there was something spiritual about her; Zbyszko was surprised when he saw her, and thought that he was going to marry not an earthly, but a heavenly being. He still thought this when she kneeled with crossed hands to receive the communion, and having bent her head, closed her eyes entirely. In that moment she even seemed to him as if dead, and fear seized his heart. But it did not last long because, having heard the priest's voice repeat: "*Ecce Agnus Dei,*" his thoughts went toward God. In the room there were heard only the solemn voice of Father Wyszoniek: "*Domine, non sum dignus,*" and with it the crackling of the logs in the fireplace and the sound of crickets playing obstinately, but sadly, in the chinks of the chimney. Outdoors the wind arose and rustled in the snowy forest, but soon stopped.

Zbyszko and Danusia remained sometime in silence; the *ksiondz* Wyszoniek took the chalice and carried it to the chapel of the mansion. After a while he returned accompanied by Sir de Lorche, and seeing astonishment on the faces of those present, he placed his finger on his mouth, as if to stop the cry of surprise, then he said:

"I understand; it will be better to have two witnesses of the marriage; I warned this knight who swore to me on his honor and on the relics of Aguisgranum to keep the secret as long as necessary."

Then Sir de Lorche first kneeled before the princess, then before Danusia; then he arose and stood silently, clad in his armor, on which the red light of the fire was playing. He stood motionless, as if plunged in ecstasy, because for him also, that white girl with a wreath of immortelles on her brow seemed like the picture of an angel, seen on the window of a Gothic cathedral.

The priest put her near Zbyszko's bed and having put the stole round their hands, began the customary rite. On the princess' honest face the tears were dropping one after another; but she was not uneasy within, because she believed she was doing well, uniting these two lovely and innocent children. Sir de Lorche kneeled again, and leaning with both hands on the hilt of his sword, looked like a knight who beholds a vision. The young people repeated the priest's words: "I ... take you ..." and those sweet quiet words were accompanied again by the singing of the crickets in the chimney and the crackling in the fireplace. When the ceremony was finished, Danusia fell at the feet of the princess who blessed them both, and finally intrusted them to the tutelage of heavenly might; she said to Zbyszko:

"Now be merry, because she is yours, and you are hers."

Then Zbyszko extended his well arm to Danusia, and she put her little arms round his neck; for a while one could hear them repeat to each other:

"Danuska, you are mine!"

"Zbyszku, you are mine!"

But soon Zbyszko became weak, because there were too many emotions for his strength, and having slipped on the pillow, he began to breathe heavily. But he did not faint, nor did he cease to smile at Danusia, who was wiping his face which was covered with a cold perspiration, and he did not stop repeating:

"Danuska, you are mine!" to which every time she nodded her fair head in assent.

This sight greatly moved Sir de Lorche, who declared that in no other country had he seen such loving and tender hearts; therefore he solemnly swore that he was ready to fight on foot or on horseback with any knight, magician or dragon, who would try to prevent their happiness. The princess and Father Wyszoniek were witnesses of his oath.

But the lady, being unable to conceive of a marriage without some merriment, brought some wine which they drank. The hours of night were passing on. Zbyszko having overcome his weakness, drew Danusia to him and said:

"Since the Lord Jesus has given you to me, nobody can take you from me; but I am sorry that you must leave me, my sweetest berry."

"We will come with *tatulo* to Ciechanow," answered Danusia.

"If only you do not become sick—or—God may preserve you from some bad accident.—You must go to Spychow—I know! Hej! I must be thankful to God and to our gracious lady, that you are already mine—because we are married and no human force can break our marriage."

But as this marriage was performed secretly during the night and separation was necessary immediately afterward, therefore from time to time, not only Zbyszko, but everybody was filled with sadness. The conversation was broken. From time to time, also the fire was quenched and plunged all heads in obscurity. Then the *ksiondz* Wyszoniek threw fresh logs on the charcoal and when something whined in the wood, as happens very often when the wood is fresh, he said:

"Penitent soul, what do you wish?"

The crickets answered him and the increasing flames which brought out from the shadow the sleepless faces, were reflected in Sir de Lorche's armor, lighting in the meanwhile Danusia's white dress and the immortelles on her head.

The dogs outside again began to howl in the direction of the forest, as they usually do, when they scent wolves.

As the hours of the night flew on, oftener there was silence; finally the princess said:

"Sweet Jesus! We had better go to bed if we are going to sit like this after a wedding, but as it was determined to watch until morning, then play for us, my little flower, for the last time before your departure, on the little lute—for me and for Zbyszko."

"What shall I play?" asked she.

"What?" said the princess. "What else if not the same song which you sang in Tyniec, when Zbyszko saw you for the first time."

"Hej! I remember—and shall never forget it," said Zbyszko. "When I heard that song somewhere else—I cried."

"Then I will sing it!" said Danusia.

And immediately she began to thrum on the lute; then, having raised her little head, she sang:

"If I only could get
The wings like a birdie,
I would fly quickly
To my dearest Jasiek!
I would then be seated
On the high enclosure;
Look, my dear Jasiulku,
Look on me, poor orphan."

But at once her voice broke, her mouth began to tremble and from beneath the closed eyelids the tears began to flow down her cheeks. For a moment she tried not to let them pass the eyelashes, but she could not keep them back and finally she began to cry, exactly as she did the last time she sang that song to Zbyszko in the prison in Krakow.

"Danuska! what is the matter, Danuska?" asked Zbyszko.

"Why are you crying? Such a wedding!" exclaimed the princess. "Why?"

"I do not know," answered Danusia, sobbing. "I am so sad! I regret Zbyszko and you so much."

Then all became very sorrowful; they began to console her, and to explain to her that she was not going to remain in Spychow a long time, but that they would surely be with Jurand in Ciechanow for the holy days. Zbyszko again encircled her with his arm, drew her to his breast and kissed the tears from her eyes; but the oppression remained in all hearts, and thus the hours of night passed.

Finally from the court-yard there resounded such a sudden and dreadful noise, that all shivered. The princess, having rushed from the bench, exclaimed:

"For God's sake. The sweeps of the wells! They are watering the horses!"

And the *ksiondz* Wyszoniek looked through the window, in which the glass balls were growing gray and said:

"The night grows white and the day is coming. *Ave Maria, gratia plena——*"

Then he left the room but having returned after a while, he said:

"The day breaks, but the day will be dark. Jurand's people are watering their horses. Poor girl, you must be ready!"

The princess and Danusia began to cry very loudly and both, together with Zbyszko, began to lament, as simple people do when they have to separate; it was half lamenting and half singing, which flowed from full souls, in a natural way, as the tears flow from the eyes.

"Hej! there is no use of lamenting,
We must separate, my darling,
Farewell—hej!"

Zbyszko nestled Danusia for the last time on his breast and kept her for a long time, as long as he could breathe and until the princess drew her from him, in order to dress her for the journey.

In the meanwhile it was broad daylight.

In the mansion everybody was up and moving round. The Czech came to Zbyszko to ask about his health and to ascertain what were his orders.

"Draw the bed to the window," said the knight to him.

The Czech drew the bed to the window, very easily; but he was surprised when Zbyszko told him to open it. He obeyed, however, only he covered his master with his own fur coat, because it was cold outside, although cloudy, and snow was falling.

Zbyszko began to look; in the court-yard, through the flakes of the falling snow, one could see lights, and round them, on steaming horses, Jurand's people were standing. All were armed. The forest was entirely covered with the snow; one could hardly see the enclosures and the gate.

Danusia, all wrapped up in furs, rushed once more into Zbyszko's room; once more she put her arms around his neck and bade him farewell:

"Although I am going, still I am yours."

He kissed her hands, her cheeks and her eyes, and said:

"May God protect you! May God lead you! You are mine, mine until death!"

When they again separated them, he raised himself as much as he could, leaned his head on the window and looked out; consequently, through the flakes of the snow, as through a veil, he saw Danusia sitting in the sleigh, the princess holding her a long time in her arms, the ladies of the court kissing her and the *ksiondz* Wyszoniek making the sign of the cross for the journey. Before the departure, she turned once more toward him, stretched out her arms and exclaimed:

"Zbyszku, remain with God!"

"May God permit me to see you in Ciechanow!"

But the snow was falling abundantly, as though to deaden every sound, and to cover everything; therefore those last words came muffled to their ears, so that it seemed to each of them that they were already calling to each other from afar.

END OF PART THIRD.

PART FOURTH.

CHAPTER I.

After abundant snowfalls, heavy frost and dry, clear days set in. By day the wood sparkled in the rays of the sun, the ice fettered the rivers and hardened the marshes; serene nights followed in which the frost was intensified to such a degree that the wood in the forest cracked loudly. The birds approached the dwelling-places. Wolves rendered the roads unsafe, gathering in packs and attacking not only solitary people, but also villages. The people however enjoyed themselves at the firesides in their smoky shanties, presaging from the intensely cold winter an abundant year, and they waited gladly for the approaching holidays. The princely Forest Court was deserted. The princess with the court and priest Wyszoniek left for Ciechanow. Zbyszko, who, though considerably improved, was not yet strong enough to ride on horseback, remained in the Forest Court together with Sanderus, his Bohemian armor-bearer and the servants of the place, who were under the superintendence of a noble-woman fulfilling the household duties.

But the knight greatly yearned after his young wife. It is true, it was an immensely consoling thought to him that Danusia was already his, and that no human power could take her from him; but, on the other hand, that same thought intensified his longing. For whole days he hoped for that moment when he should be able to leave the court, and pondered on what he should then do, where to go, and how to appease Jurand. He had, likewise, bad and restless moments. But on the whole the future appeared joyful to him. To love Danusia and pluck peacock plumes from helmets—such a life would he lead. Many a time he desired to speak of it to his Bohemian whom he loved, but he reflected, since the Bohemian, he thought, was with his whole soul Jagienka's, it would be imprudent to speak to him about Danusia, but he, bound to secrecy, could not tell everything that happened.

However, his health improved daily. A week before Vigil (Christmas Eve) he mounted his horse for the first time, and although he felt that he could not do this in his armor, nevertheless he gathered confidence. Besides, he did not expect soon to be obliged to put on the coat of mail and helmet. At the worst he hoped soon to be strong enough to do that too. Indoors, in order to kill time, he attempted to lift up the sword, which he accomplished well, but the wielding of the axe seemed to him yet a difficult task. Nevertheless, he believed that if he grasped the axe with both hands he would be able to wield it effectively.

Finally, two days before the Vigil, he gave orders to repair the carriage, saddle the horses, and notified the Bohemian that they were going to Ciechanow. The faithful armor-bearer was somewhat anxious, the more so on account of the intense frost out-of-doors. But Zbyszko said to him:

"Glowacz,[105] it concerns not your head, there is nothing for us in this court, and even should I happen to be sick, I would not miss seeing the old gentleman in Ciechanow.

Moreover, I shall not ride on horseback, but in a sleigh, up to the neck in hay and under furs, and only when quite near Ciechanow shall I mount my horse."

And so it happened. The Bohemian knew his young master and was aware that it was not good to oppose him, and still worse not to attend scrupulously to his orders. Therefore they started at an early hour. At the moment of departure, Zbyszko seeing Sanderus placing himself and his boxes in the sleigh, said to him: "Why are you sticking to me like burs to sheep's wool?... You told me you wished to go to Prussia."

"Yes, I said so," Sanderus replied. "But can I get there alone in such snows? The wolves would devour me before the first star made its appearance, and I have nothing to stay here for. I prefer the town, to edify the people in godliness, and bestow upon them my holy wares and rescue them from the devil's grasp, as I have sworn to the father of all Christendom in Rome. Besides this, I am exceedingly attached to your grace, whom I shall not leave before my return to Rome, for it may happen that I may be enabled to render you some service."

"He is always for you, sir! He is ready to eat and drink for you," said the Bohemian. "Such service he would be too glad to render, but if a pack of wolves should happen to attack us in the forests near Przasnysz then I shall feed the wolves with him, for he is unfit for anything else."

"Better take care that the sinful words don't freeze to your moustache," replied Sanderus, "for such icicles can only melt in hellfire."

"Owa!" replied Glowacz, reaching with his gauntlet to his incipient moustache, "I shall first try to warm some beer for refreshment, but I'll give none to you."

"But it is forbidden there to give drink to the thirsty,—another sin."

"I shall give you a pail full of water, but meanwhile take what I have in my hand!" Thus saying he gathered as much snow as he could hold with both gauntlets and threw it at Sanderus' beard, but the latter bent aside and said:

"There is nothing for *you* in Ciechanow, for there is already a grown-up bear that plays with snow."

Thus they loved to tease each other. But Zbyszko did not forbid Sanderus to ride with him because that strange man amused him, and at the same time it seemed to him that the man was really attached to him.

They moved from the Forest Court in the bright morning. The frost was so intense that they had to cover the horses. The whole landscape was under snow. The roofs of the cottages were covered and hardly visible. Smoke seemed to issue directly from white hills, shooting up skyward, red-hued in the morning, widening out on the roof like a brush, and looking like the plumes on helmets.

Zbyszko sat in the sleigh, first to gather strength, secondly on account of the severe cold, against which it was easy to protect oneself; he commanded Glowacz to sit down beside him so as to be ready with the crossbow against an attack of wolves, meanwhile he chatted with him merrily.

"In Przasnysz, we shall only feed the horses and warm ourselves a little and then immediately continue our journey."

"To Ciechanow?"

"First to Ciechanow, to pay homage to the court and attend worship."

"After that?" inquired Glowacz.

Zbyszko smiled and replied,

"Afterward, who knows, may be to Bogdaniec."

The Bohemian looked at him with astonishment, the thought crossed his mind: Maybe he has quarrelled with Jurandowna, and this seemed to him most likely, because she had gone away. The Bohemian had also heard in the Forest Court that the lord of Spychow was opposed to the young knight, therefore the honest armor-bearer was glad although he loved Jagienka, but he looked upon her as upon a star in heaven for whose happiness he was willing even to shed his blood. He therefore loved Zbyszko, and from his very soul he longed to serve both of them even unto death.

"Then your grace thinks to settle down on the estate," he exultingly said.

"How can I settle down on my estate," replied Zbyszko, "when I challenged those Knights of the Cross, and even before that, I challenged Lichtenstein. De Lorche said that the Master would invite the king to visit Torun. I shall attach myself to the king's retinue, and I think that at Torun, either *Pan* Zawisza of Garbow or Powala of Taczew will ask permission from our lord to allow me to fight those monks. They will certainly come to fight accompanied by their armor-bearers; in that case you will also have to meet them."

"If I were to kill any one, I should like him to be a monk," said the Bohemian.

Zbyszko looked at him with satisfaction. "Well, he will not fare well who happens to feel your steel. God has given you great strength, but you would act badly if you were to push it to excess, because humility is becoming in the worthy armor-bearer."

The Bohemian shook his head as a sign that he would not waste his strength, but would not spare it against the Germans.

Zbyszko smiled, not on account of what the armor bearer had said, but at his own thoughts.

"The old gentleman will be glad when we return, and in Zgorzelice there will also be joy."

Jagienka stood before Zbyszko's eyes as though she were sitting with him in the sleigh. That always happened, whenever he thought of her he saw her very distinctly.

"Well," he said to himself, "she will not be glad, for when I shall return to Bogdaniec it will be with Danusia. Let her take somebody else...." Here, the figures of Wills of Brzozowa, and young Cztan of Rogow passed through his mind, and suddenly a disagreeable feeling crept over him, because the girl might fall into the hands of one of them, and he said to himself: "I wish I could find some better man, for those fellows are beer-gulpers and gourmands, and the girl is upright." And he thought of this and of that; of his uncle when he should learn what had happened, it would be irksome, no matter how it turned out; but he immediately consoled himself with the thought that with his uncle, matters concerning kinship and wealth were always paramount, and these could advance the interest of the family. Jagienka was indeed nearer, but Jurand was a greater land owner than Zych of Zgorzelice. Moreover the former could easily foresee that Macko could not be long opposed to such a liaison, the more so when he should behold his nephew's love for Danusia and her requital. He would grumble for a while, then he would be glad and begin to love Danuska as his own daughter.

Suddenly his heart was moved with tenderness and yearning toward that uncle who although a severe man, loved him like the pupil of his own eye; that uncle cared for him on the battlefield more than for himself, he took booty for him, and for his sake he was driven out from his estate. Both of them were lonely in the world without near relatives, with only distant ones like the abbot. Moreover, when the time arrived to separate from each other, neither of them knew what to do, particularly the older one, who no more desired anything for himself.

"Hej! he will be glad, he will be glad!" repeated Zbyszko to himself. "Only one thing I should like,—that he should receive Jurand and me as well as he would receive me by myself."

Then he attempted to imagine what Jurand would say and do when he learned of the marriage. There was some alarm in this thought, but not too much of it, for the simple reason that it was an accomplished fact. It would not do for Jurand to challenge him to fight, and even should Jurand oppose, Zbyszko could answer him thus: "Forbear, I ask you; your right to Danuska is human, but mine is divine; she is therefore no more yours, but mine." He once heard from a certain clergyman who was versed in the Scriptures that the woman must leave her father and mother and go with her husband. He felt therefore that the greater part of strength was in his favor; nevertheless he did not expect that intense strife and passion would arise between Jurand and himself, for he counted upon Danusia's petition which would be granted, and quite as much, if not more, upon that which would be obtained by the intercession of the prince under whom Jurand was serving and that of the princess whom Jurand loved as the protectress of his child.

Owing to the severe frosts, wolves appeared in such great packs, that they even attacked people traveling together. Zbyszko was advised to remain over night at Przasnysz, but he took no notice of it, because it happened that, at the inn, they met some Mazovian knights with their trains who were also on their way to meet the prince at Ciechanow, and some armed merchants from that very place convoying loaded wagons from Prussia. There was no danger to travel with such a great crowd; they therefore started toward evening, although a sudden wind arose after nightfall which chased the clouds, and snow began to fall. They traveled keeping close to one another, but they advanced so slowly that it occurred to Zbyszko that they would not arrive in time for the Vigil. They were obliged to dig through the drift in some places where it was impossible for the horses to pass through. Fortunately the road in the woods was not obliterated. It was already dusk when they saw Ciechanow.

Were it not for the fire on the heights where the new castle stood, they would not have known that they were so close to town, and would have strayed much longer in the midst of the blinding snowstorm and gust of wind. They were not sure whether fire was burning there in honor of the guests at Christmas Eve, or whether it was put there according to some ancient custom. But none of Zbyszko's companions thought about it, for all were anxious to find a place of shelter in town as quickly as possible.

Meanwhile the snowstorm constantly increased, the keen, freezing wind carried immense snowclouds; it dragged at the trees, it howled, maddened, it tore whole snowdrifts, carrying them upward, it shifted, heaved up, and almost covered the sleighs and horses and struck the faces of the occupants like sharp gravel; it stifled their breath and speech. The sound of the bells fastened to the poles of the sleighs could not be heard at all, but instead of it there were audible, in the midst of the howling and whistling of the whirlwind, plaintive voices like the howling of wolves, like distant neighing of horses, and at times like human voices in great distress, calling for help. The exhausted horses began to pant, and gradually slacken their pace.

"Hej! what a blizzard! what a blizzard!" said the Bohemian in a choking voice. "It is fortunate, sir, that we are already near the town, and that yonder fires are burning; if it were not for that we should fare badly."

"There is death for those who are in the field," answered Zbyszko, "but even the fire I don't see there any more. The gloom is so thick that even the fire is invisible; perhaps the wood and coal were swept away by the wind."

The merchants and knights in the other wagons were saying: that should the snowstorm carry off anybody from the seat, that one would never hear the morning bell. But Zbyszko became suddenly alarmed and said:

"God forbid that Jurand should be anywhere on the road!"

The Bohemian, although entirely occupied in looking toward the fire, on hearing the words of Zbyszko, turned his head and asked:

"Is the knight of Spychow expected?"

"Yes."

"With the young lady?"

"And the fire is really gone," answered Zbyszko.

And indeed the fire was extinguished, but, instead, several horsemen appeared immediately in front of the horses and sleighs.

"Why dost thou follow?" cried the watchful Bohemian, grasping his crossbow; "Who are you?"

"The prince's people, sent to assist the travelers."

"Jesus Christ be praised!"

"Forever and ever."

"Lead us to town," said Zbyszko.

"Is there nobody left behind?"

"Nobody."

"Whence do you come?"

"From Przasnysz."

"Did you not meet other travelers on the road?"

"We met nobody, but they may be on other roads."

"People are searching on all roads, come with us, you lost your route! To the right."

They turned the horses, and for some time nothing was perceptible but the blast of the storm.

"Are there many guests in the castle?" asked Zbyszko, after a while.

The nearest horseman, who did not hear the question bent toward him.

"What did you say, sir?"

"I asked whether there were many guests at the prince's?"

"As customary: there are enough."

"But is the lord of Spychow there?"

"He is not there, but they expect him. People ware dispatched to meet him too."

"With torches?"

"If the weather permits."

They were unable to continue their conversation, for the boisterous snowstorm was increasing in force.

"Quite a devil's marriage," said the Bohemian. Zbyszko, however, told him to keep quiet, and not to conjure up the evil name.

"Dost thou not know," he said, "that on such a Holy Day, the devil's power is subdued, and the devils hide themselves in the ice-holes? Once the fishermen near Sandomierz on Christmas Eve found him in their net, he had a pike in his mouth, but when the sound of the bells reached his ears, he immediately fainted; they pounded him with their clubs till the evening. The tempest is certainly vehement, but it is with the permission of the Lord Jesus, who desires that the morrow shall be the more joyful."

"Bah! we were quite near the city," said Glowacz. "Yet if it were not for these people, we should have strayed till midnight, since we had deviated from the right path."

"Because the fire was extinguished."

Meanwhile they arrived in town. The snowdrifts in the streets were larger, so big that in some places they even covered the windows, so much so that the wayfarers could not see the light from within. But the storm was not so much felt here. The streets were deserted. The inhabitants were already celebrating the Christmas Eve festival. In front of some houses, boys with small cribs and goats, in spite of the snowstorm, were singing Christmas hymns. In the market-place there were seen men wrapped up in pease straw imitating bears; otherwise the streets were deserted. The merchants who accompanied Zbyszko and the noblemen on the road, remained in town, but they continued their journey toward the prince's residence in the old castle, and, as the windows of the castle were made of glass, the bright light, notwithstanding the blizzard, cast its rays upon the advancing party.

The drawbridge over the moat was lowered, because the Lithuanian incursions of old had diminished, and the Knights of the Cross, who carried on war against the King of Poland, were now themselves seeking the friendship of the Prince of Mazowsze. One of the prince's men blew the horn and immediately the gate was opened. There were in it several archers, but upon the walls and palisades there was not a living soul when the prince permitted the guard to go out. Old Mrokota, who had arrived two days before, went out to meet the guests, and greeted them in the name of the prince and brought them into the house where they could prepare themselves properly for table.

Zbyszko immediately asked him for news of Jurand of Spychow, but he replied that he had not arrived, but was expected because he promised to come, and that if he were very ill he would send word. Nevertheless several horsemen were sent out to meet him, for even the oldest men did not remember such a blizzard.

"Then he may soon be here."

"I believe he will soon be here. The princess ordered dishes for them near the common table."

But Zbyszko, although he was somewhat anxious about Jurand, was nevertheless glad in his heart, and said to himself: "Though I do not know what to do, yet one thing is certain, my wife is coming, my woman, my most beloved Danuska." When he repeated those words to himself, he could hardly believe his own happiness. Why, he reflected, it may be that she has already confessed all to her father, she may have moved him to pity and begged him to give her up at once. "In truth, what else could he do? Jurand is a clever fellow, he knows, that although he keeps her from me, I shall nevertheless take her away, for my right is stronger."

Whilst he was dressing himself he conversed with Mrokota, inquiring after the prince's health and specially that of the princess, whom he loved like his mother since that time when he sojourned in Krakow. He was glad to learn that everybody in the castle was well and cheerful, although the princess greatly yearned after her beloved songstress. Jagienka now played the lute for her and the princess loved her much, but not as much as the songstress.

"Which Jagienka?" inquired Zbyszko with astonishment.

"Jagienka of Wielgolasu, the granddaughter of the old lord of Wielgolasu. She is a fine girl. The Lotarynczyk[106] fell in love with her."

"Then is Sir de Lorche here?"

"Where then should he be? He has been here since he arrived from the Forest Court, for it is well to be here. Our prince never lacks guests."

"I shall be glad to see him, he is a knight with whom none can find fault."

"And he also loves you. But let us go, their Highnesses will soon be at the table."

They went into the dining hall where big fires burned in the two fireplaces and they were taken care of by the servants.

The room was already filled with guests and courtiers. The prince entered first accompanied by the Voyevode and several life guards. Zbyszko knelt and kissed his hands.

The prince pressed Zbyszko's head, then he took him aside and said:

"I know it all already, I was displeased at first, because it was done without my permission, but there was no time, for I was then in Warsaw where I intended to spend the holidays. It is a well-known fact that, if a woman desires anything, opposition is useless, and you gain nothing by it. The princess wishes you well like a mother, and I always desire to please rather than to oppose her wishes, in order to spare her trouble and tears."

Zbyszko bowed again to the prince's knees.

"God grant that I may requite your princely love."

"Praise His name that you are already well. Tell the princess how I received you with good wishes, so that she may be pleased. As I fear God, her joy is my joy! I shall also say a good word in your behalf to Jurand, and I think that he will consent, for he too loves the princess."

"Even if he refused to give her to me, my right stands first."

"Your right stands first and must be acknowledged, but a blessing might fail you. Nobody can forcibly wrest her from you, but without a father's blessing God's is also lacking."

Zbyszko felt uneasy on hearing these words, for he had never before thought about it; but at that moment the princess entered, accompanied by Jagienka of Wielgolasu and other court ladies; he hastened to bow before her, but she greeted him even more graciously than the prince had done, and at once began to tell him of the expectation of Jurand's arrival. "Here are the covers ready for him, and people have been dispatched to guide them through the snowdrifts. We shall not wait any longer for them with the Christmas Eve supper, for the prince does not approve of it, but they will be here before supper is over."

"As far as Jurand is concerned," continued the princess, "he will be here in God's good time. But I shall tell him all to-day or to-morrow after the shepherd service (pasterce), and the prince also promised to say a word in your behalf. Jurand is obstinate but not with those whom he loves, nor those to whom he owes obedience."

Then she began to instruct Zbyszko how he should act with his father-in-law, and that God forbid he should anger him or rouse his obstinacy. It was apparently good advice, but an experienced eye looking at Zbyszko and then at her could discern in her words and looks a certain alarm. It may be because the lord of Spychow was not an accommodating man, and it may also be that the princess was somewhat uneasy at his non-appearance. The storm increased in strength, and all declared that if any one were caught in the open country he would not survive. The princess, however, concluded that Danuska had confessed to her father her marriage to Zbyszko, and he being offended, was resolved not to proceed to

151

Ciechanow. The princess however, did not desire to reveal her thoughts to Zbyszko; there was not even time to do so, for the servants brought in the viands and placed them on the table. Nevertheless Zbyszko endeavored to follow her up and make further inquiries.

"And if they arrive, what will happen then, beloved lady? Mrokota told me that there are special quarters set apart for Jurand; there will be hay enough for bedding for the chilled horses. How then will it be?"

The princess laughed and tapped him lightly on the face with her glove and said: "Be quiet, do you see him?"

And she went toward the prince and was assisted to a chair. One of the attendants placed before the prince a flat dish with thin slices of cake, and wafers, which he was to distribute among the guests, courtiers and servants. Another attendant held before the prince a beautiful boy, the son of the castellan of Sokhochova. On the other side of the table stood Father Wyszoniek who was to pronounce a benediction upon the fragrant supper.

At this moment, a man covered with snow entered and cried: "Most Gracious Prince!"

"What is it?" said the prince. "Is there no reverence; they have interrupted him in his religious ceremonies."

"Some travelers are snowbound on the road to Radzanow, we need people to help us to dig them out."

On hearing this all were seized with fear—the prince was alarmed, and turning toward the castellan of Sokhochova, he commanded:

"Horses and spades! Hasten!"

Then he said to the man who brought the news: "Are there many under the snow?"

"I could not tell, it blew terribly; there are a considerable number of horses and wagons."

"Do you not know who they are?"

"People say that they belong to Jurand of Spychow."

CHAPTER II.

When Zbyszko heard the ill tidings, he did not even ask the prince's permission, but hastened to the stable and ordered his horse to be saddled. The Bohemian, being a noble-born armor-bearer, met Zbyszko in the hall before he returned to the house, and brought him a warm fur coat, yet he did not attempt to detain his young master, for he possessed strong natural sense; he knew that detention would be of no avail, and only loss of time, he therefore mounted the second horse and seized some torches from the guard at the gate, and started at once together with the prince's men who were under the management of the old castellan. Impenetrable darkness enveloped them beyond the gate, but the storm seemed to them to have moderated; were it not for the man who notified them of the accident, they would have lost their way at once; but he had a trained dog with him which being acquainted with the road, enabled him to proceed safely and quickly. In the open field the storm again increased and began to cut their faces. It may be because they galloped. The road was filled with snow, so much so that in some places they were obliged to slacken their speed, for the horses sank up to their bellies in snow. The prince's people lighted their torches and fire-pots and moved on amid smoke and flames; the wind blew with such force as though it endeavored to tear the flames from the torches and carry them over the field and forest. It was a long journey. They passed the settlement near Ciechanow, then they passed Niedzborz, then they turned toward Radzanow.

The storm began really to subside beyond Niedzborz; the gusts of wind were less frequent and no longer carried immense snowclouds. The sky cleared. Some snow yet drifted from the hills, but it soon ceased. The stars appeared here and there between the broken clouds. The horses began to snort, the horsemen breathed freely. The stars came out by degrees and it began to freeze. In a short time the storm subsided entirely.

Sir de Lorche who rode beside Zbyszko began to comfort him, saying, that Jurand undoubtedly in moments of peril thought of his daughter's safety above everything, and although all those buried in the snow should be found dead, she undoubtedly would be discovered alive, probably sleeping in her fur robes. But Zbyszko understood him not, in fact he had no time to listen to him. When, after a little while, the guide who was riding in front of them turned from the road, the young knight moved in front and inquired:

"Why do we deviate from the road?"

"Because they are not covered up on the road, but yonder! Do you observe that clump of alders?"

And he pointed with his hand to the darkening in the distant thicket which could be seen plainly on the white snow-covered expanse, when the clouds unveiled the moon's disk and the night became clear.

"They have apparently wandered from the road; they turned aside and moved in a small circle along the river; in the wind and drifting snow, it is quite easy to go astray. They moved on and on as long as the horses did not give out."

"How did you find them?"

"The dog led us."

"Are there any huts near here?"

"Yes, but they are on the other side of the river. Close here is Wkra."

"Whip up the horses," commanded Zbyszko.

But the command was easier than the execution of the order. The piled up snow upon the meadow was not yet frozen firm, and the horses sank knee-deep in the drifts; they were therefore obliged to move slowly. Suddenly they heard the barking of a dog; directly in front of them there was the deformed thick stump of a willow-tree upon which glistened in the light of the moon a crown of leafless twigs.

"They are farther off," said the guide, "they are near the alder clump, but it seems that here also there might be something."

"There is much drift under the willow-tree. Bring a light."

Several attendants dismounted and lit up the place with their torches. One of them soon exclaimed:

"There is a man under the snow, his head is visible. Here!"

"There is also a horse," said another.

"Dig them out!"

They began to remove the snow with their spades and throw it aside.

In a moment they observed a human being under the tree, his head upon his chest, and his cap pulled down over his face. One hand held the reins of the horse that lay beside him with its nostrils buried in the snow. It was obvious that the man must have left the company, probably with the object of reaching a human habitation as quickly as possible in order to secure help, and when the horse fell he had then taken refuge under the lee of the willow-tree.

"Light!" shouted Zbyszko.

The attendant brought the torch near the face of the frozen man, but his features could not be distinguished. Only when a second attendant lifted the head from the chest, they all exclaimed with one accord:

"It is the lord of Spychow!"

Zbyszko ordered two of his men to carry him to the nearest hut and try to resuscitate him, but himself lost no time but hastened with the rest of the attendants and the guide to rescue the rest of the retinue. On the way it crossed Zbyszko's mind that perhaps he might find his wife Danuska dead, and he urged on his horse who waded up to his breast in snow, to his last breath.

Fortunately it was not distant, a few furlongs at most. In the darkness voices were heard exclaiming: "*Byway.*"[107] They were those who had been left with the snow-covered people.

Zbyszko rushed in and jumped from his horse and shouted:

"To the spades!"

Two sleighs were dug out before they reached those in the rear. The horses and the people in the sleighs were frozen to death, and past all hope of reviving. The place where the other teams were could be recognized by the heaps of snow, though not all the sleighs were entirely covered with snow; in front of some of the sleighs were the horses up to their bellies, in the posture of their last effort to run. In front of one team there stood a man up to his belt in snow, holding a lance and motionless as a post; in front of the others were dead attendants holding the horses by their muzzles. Death had apparently overtaken them at the moment when they attempted to extricate the horses from the drifts. One team, at the very end of the train, was not at all in the drift. The driver sat in front bent, his hands protecting his ears, but in the rear lay two people, who, owing to the continuous, long snow-fall, were completely covered. On their breasts, to escape the drift, they lay closely side by side, and the snow covered them like a blanket. They seemed to be sleeping peacefully. But others perished, struggling hard with the snow-drift to the last moment, their benumbed position demonstrated the fact. A few sleighs were upset, others had their poles broken. The spades now and then uncovered horses' backs, bent like bows, and jaws biting the snow. People were within and beside the sleighs. But there was no woman in any of the sleighs. At times even Zbyszko labored with the spade till his brow was covered with perspiration, and at others he looked with palpitating heart into the eyes of the corpses, perchance to discover the face of his beloved. But all in vain. The faces which the torchlight revealed were those of whiskered soldiers of Spychow. Neither Danusia nor any other woman was there.

"What does it mean?" the young knight asked himself with astonishment.

He hailed those working at a distance and inquired whether they had come across anything else, but they too only found the corpses of men. At last the work was finished. The servants hitched their own horses to the sleighs, placed the corpses in them and drove to Niedzborz, to make an attempt there in the warm mansion, to restore some of the dead to life. Zbyszko, the Bohemian and two attendants remained. It crossed his mind that the sleigh containing Danusia might have separated from the train, or that Jurand's sleigh, as might be supposed, was drawn by his best horses and had been ordered to drive in front; and it might also be that Jurand had left her somewhere in one of the huts along the road. Zbyszko did not know what to do. In any case he desired to examine closely the drifts and grove, and then return and search along the road.

But nothing was found in the drifts. In the grove he only saw several glistening wolves' eyes, but nowhere discovered any traces of people or horses. The meadow between the woods and road now sparkled in the shiny light of the moon, and upon its white mournful cover he really espied dark spots, but those were only wolves that quickly vanished at the approach of people.

"Your grace!" finally said the Bohemian. "Our search is in vain, for the young lady of Spychow was not in the train."

"To the road!" replied Zbyszko.

"We shall not find her there either. I looked well in the sleighs for any baskets containing ladies' finery, but I discovered none. The young lady remained in Spychow."

This supposition struck Zbyszko as correct, he therefore said:

"God grant it to be as you say!"

But the Bohemian penetrated further into his thoughts, and proceeded with his reasoning.

"If she were in one of the sleighs the old gentleman would not have separated from her, or when he left the train he would have taken her with him on horseback, and we should have found her with him."

"Come, let us go there once more," said Zbyszko, in a restless voice. It struck him that the Bohemian might be right, perhaps they had not searched enough where the old man was discovered, perhaps Jurand had taken Danusia with him on horseback, and when the horse fell, she had left her father in search of assistance, in that case she might be somewhere under the snow in the neighborhood.

But Glowacz as though divining his thoughts, said:

"In such a case ladies' apparel would have been found in the sleighs, because she would not have left for the court with only her traveling dress."

In spite of these reasonable suppositions they returned to the willow-tree, but neither there nor for a furlong around did they discover anything. The prince's people had already taken Jurand to Niedzborz, and the whole neighborhood was a complete desolation. The Bohemian observed further, that the dog that ran ahead of the guide and found Jurand would also have discovered the young lady. Then Zbyszko breathed freely, for he was almost sure that Danusia had remained at home. He was even able to explain why she did so. Danusia had confessed all to her father, and he was not satisfied with the marriage, and so purposely left her at home, and went by himself to see the prince and bring an action, and ask for his intercession with the bishop. At this thought Zbyszko could not help feeling a certain sense of relief, and even gladness, when he comprehended that by reason of Jurand's death all hindrances had vanished. "Jurand was unwilling, but the Lord Jesus wants it," said the young knight to himself, "and God's will is always the strongest." Now, he had only to go to Spychow and fetch Danuska as his own and then complete the nuptials. It is even easier to marry her on the frontier than there in the distant Bogdaniec. "God's will! God's will!" he repeated in his soul. But suddenly he felt ashamed of this premature joy and turned to the Bohemian and said:

"Certainly I am sorry for him and I proclaim it aloud."

"They say that the Germans feared him like death," replied the Bohemian.

Presently he inquired:

"Shall we now return to the castle?"

"By way of Niedzborz," answered Zbyszko. When they called at Niedzborz and then left for the court, where the old proprietor Zelech received them, they did not find Jurand, but Zelech told them good news.

"They first rubbed him with snow almost to the bones, then poured wine into his mouth and then put him in a scalding bath where he began to breathe."

"Is he alive?" joyfully asked Zbyszko, who on hearing the news forgot his own interests.

"He lives, but as to his continuing to live God only knows, for the soul that has arrived half way is unwilling to return."

"Why did they remove him?"

"The prince sent for him, and they have wrapped him up in as many feather blankets as they could find in the house and carried him away."

"Did he say anything about his daughter?"

"He only began to breathe but did not recover speech."

"And the others?"

"They are already with God, and the poor fellows will no more be able to attend the *pastene* (Christmas Eve feast) unless at that which the Lord Jesus Himself will prepare in heaven."

"None else survived?"

"None. Come into the entrance hall, the place to converse, and if you wish to see them, they lie along the fireside in the servants' room. Come inside."

But they were in a hurry and did not wish to enter, although old Zelech insisted, for he was glad to get hold of people in order to chat with them. There was yet, quite a considerable distance from Niedzborz to Ciechanow, and Zbyszko was burning like fire to see Jurand as soon as possible and learn something from him.

They therefore rode as fast as they could along the snow-covered road. When they arrived it was already after midnight, and the Christmas feast (lit-Shepherd ceremony) was just ended in the castle chapel. Zbyszko heard the lowing of oxen and the bleating of goats, which voices were produced in accordance with the ancient religious custom, in remembrance that the nativity took place in a stable. After the mass, the princess came to Zbyszko. She looked distressed and frightened, and began to question him:

"And Danuska?"

"Is she not here, has Jurand said nothing, for according to what I gathered she lives?"

"Merciful Jesus!… God's punishment and woe to us! Jurand has not spoken and he lies like a log."

"Fear not, gracious lady. Danuska remained in Spychow."

"How do you know?"

"Because there is no trace of ladies' apparel found in any of the sleighs; she could not have left with only her traveling dress."

"True, as God is dear to me!"

Her eyes immediately were lit up with joy and after a while she exclaimed:

"Hej! It seems that Christ the Infant, who was born to-day is not angry with you, but has a blessing upon us!"

The only thing which surprised her was the presence of Jurand without his daughter. Then she continued questioning him:

"What caused him to leave her at home?"

Zbyszko explained to her his own reason, which seemed to her just, but she did not comprehend it sufficiently.

"Jurand will now be thankful to us for his life," she said, "and forsooth he owes it to you because you went to dig him out. His heart would be of stone if he were still to continue his opposition to you. In this there is also God's warning to him not to oppose the holy sacrament. I shall tell him so as soon as he comes to his senses and is able to speak."

"It is necessary for him first to recover consciousness, because we do not yet know why he has not brought Danuska with him. Perhaps she is sick?"

"Do not say that something has happened I I feel so much troubled that she is not here. If she were sick he would not have left her."

"True!" said Zbyszko.

They went to Jurand. The heat in the room was intense, as in a bath. It was light, because there were big pine logs in the fireplace. Father Wyszoniek kept watch over the patient, who lay in bed, covered with a bear-skin; his face was pale, his hair matted with perspiration, and his eyes closed. His mouth was open, and his chest laboring with difficulty, but with such force that his breathing moved the bear-skin covering up and down.

"How is he doing?" inquired the princess.

"I poured a mug of hot wine into his mouth," replied the priest, "and perspiration ensued."

"Is he asleep, or not?"

"Probably not, for he labors heavily."

"Did you try to speak to him?"

"We tried, but he did not answer, and I believe that he will not speak before dawn."

"We will wait till the dawn," said the princess.

The priest insisted that she should retire but she paid no attention, for she always in everything wished not to fall short of the late Queen Jadwiga, in Christian virtues, in caring for the sick and to redeem with her merits her father's soul; she therefore did not omit any opportunity to make the old Christian country appear no worse than others, and by this means to obliterate the remembrance that she was born in a heathen land.

Besides that, she was burning with desire to hear from Jurand's own lips about Danusia, for she was much concerned about her. She therefore sat by his bedside and began to tell her beads, and then dozed. Zbyszko who had not yet entirely recovered and was moreover greatly fatigued by the night journey, followed her example; and as the hours passed on, both fell asleep, so soundly that they might have slept on till daylight, if they had not awakened by the ringing of the bell of the castle chapel.

But the same sound also awoke Jurand, who opened his eyes and suddenly sat up in bed and began to stare about him with blinking eyes.

"Praised be Jesus Christ!… How do you feel?" said the princess.

But he apparently had not yet regained consciousness, for he looked at her as though he knew her not, and after awhile he exclaimed:

"Hurry! Be quick! Dig open the snowdrift."

"In the name of God, you are already in Ciechanow!" again replied the princess.

Jurand wrinkled his brow like one who with difficulty tries to collect his thoughts, and replied:

"In Ciechanow?… The child is waiting … and … principality …
Danuska! Danuska!"

Suddenly, he closed his eyes and again fell back on the pillow. Zbyszko and the princess feared lest he was dead, but at the same moment his breast began to heave and he breathed deeply like one who is fast asleep.

Father Wyszoniek put his finger to his lips and motioned not to awake him, then he whispered:

"He may sleep thus a whole day."

"So, but what did he say?" asked the princess.

"He said that the child waits in Ciechanow," Zbyszko replied.

"Because he does not remember," explained the priest.

CHAPTER III.

Father Wyszoniek feared that even at Jurand's next awakening, he might be stupefied and might not recover consciousness for a long time. Meanwhile he promised the princess and Zbyszko to let them know when the old knight could speak, and himself retired after they left. In fact Jurand first awoke on the second Holy Day just before noon, but fully conscious. The princess and Zbyszko were present. Therefore, sitting on the bed, he looked at and recognized her and said:

"Your Highness … for God's sake, am I in Ciechanow?"

"And you overslept the Holy Day," replied the lady.

"The snows covered me. Who saved me?"

"This knight: Zbyszko of Bogdaniec. You remember him in Krakow…."

And Jurand gazed with his sound eye at the youth for a moment and said:

"I remember … but where is Danusia?"

"She did not ride with you?" anxiously inquired the princess.

"How could she ride with me, when I did not go to her?"

Zbyszko and the princess looked at each other, believing him to be still speaking under the influence of the fever. Then the lady said: "Wake up, for God's sake! There was no girl with, you?"

"Girl? With me?" inquired Jurand in amazement.

"Because your people perished, but she could not be found among them."

"Why did you leave her in Spychow?"

He then again repeated, but now with alarm in his voice:

"In Spychow? Why, she is with you, Your Highness, not with me!"

"However you sent a letter for her to the Forest Court."

"In the name of the Father and Son!" replied Jurand. "I did not send for her at all."

Then the princess suddenly became pale:

"What is that?" she said, "are you positive that you are speaking in your right senses?"

"For God's mercy, where is the child?" exclaimed Jurand, starting up.

Father Wyszoniek, on hearing this, quickly left the room, while the princess continued:

"Listen: There arrived an armed retinue and a letter from you to the Forest Court, for Danusia. The letter stated that you were knocked down in a conflagration by a falling beam … that you were half blinded and that you wished to see the child…. They took Danusia and rode away…."

"My head swims!" exclaimed Jurand. "As there is a God in Heaven, there was no fire in Spychow, nor did I send for her!"

At that moment Father Wyszoniek returned with the letter, which he handed to Jurand and inquired: "Is not this your clerkly writing?"

"I do not know."

"And the seal?"

"It is mine."

"What does the letter say?"

Father Wyszoniek read the letter while Jurand listened, tearing his hair and finally saying: "The writing is counterfeited! … the seal is false!… my soul! They have captured my child and will destroy her!"

"Who are they?"

"The Teutons!"

"For God's sake! The prince must be informed! He shall send messengers to the master!" exclaimed the princess. "Merciful Jesus, save her and help!" … and she left the room screaming.

Jurand jumped out of bed and began hurriedly to clothe his gigantic frame. Zbyszko sat as if petrified, but in a few moments his tightly set teeth began to gnash with rage.

"How do you know that the Teutons captured her?" asked Father Wyszoniek.

"By the Passion of our Lord, I'll swear!"

"Wait! ... It may be so. They came to complain about you to the Forest Court."

"They wanted to take revenge on you..."

"And they captured her!" suddenly exclaimed Zbyszko. Then he hurried out of the room, and running to the stables he ordered horses to be saddled and harnessed to wagons, not knowing well himself why he did so. He only knew that it was necessary to go to Danusia's assistance—at once—and as far as Prussia—and there to tear her out of the foe's hands or perish.

He then returned to the room to tell Jurand that the weapons and horses would soon be ready. He was sure that Jurand would accompany him. His heart was burning with rage, pain and sorrow,—but at the same time he did not lose hope; it seemed to him that he and the formidable knight of Spychow together would be able to accomplish everything—and that they were equal to attacking the whole Teutonic force.

In the room, besides Jurand, he met Father Wyszoniek and the princess, also the prince and de Lorche, as well as the old knight of Dlugolas, whom the prince, having heard of the affair, summoned also to council on account of his wisdom and extensive knowledge of the Teutons, who had kept him for a number of years in slavery.

"It is necessary to set about it prudently, so as not to commit a sin in blind fury and so lose the girl," said the knight of Dlugolas.

"A complaint must be instantly filed with the master and I will ride thither, if His Highness will give me a letter to him."

"I will give the letter, and go with it," said the prince. "We will not allow the child to be lost, so help me God and Holy Cross! The master dreads war with the Polish king, and he is anxious to win over Semka, my brother and myself.... They did not capture her at his command—and he will order her return."

"And if it was by his orders?" inquired Father Wyszoniek.

"Although he is a Teuton, there is more honesty in him than in the others," replied the prince; "and, as I told you, he would rather accommodate me than make me angry now. The Jagiellonian power is no laughter. Hej! They poured hog's grease under our skin as long as they could, but they did not perceive that if also we Mazurs should assist Jagiello, then it would be bad...."

But the knight of Dlugolas said, "That is true. The Teutons do nothing foolishly; therefore, I think that if they have captured the girl, it is either to disarm Jurand, or to demand a ransom, or to exchange her." Here he turned to the knight of Spychow:

"Whom have you now among your prisoners of war?"

"Herr von Bergow," replied Jurand.

"Is he important?"

"It seems so."

De Lorche, hearing the name von Bergow, began to inquire about him, and, having found out, said: "He is a relative of the Duke of Geldryi, a great benefactor of the Order, and devoted to the Order from his birth."

"Yes," said the knight of Dlugolas, translating his words to those present. "Von Bergow held high rank in the Order."

"Danveld and von Löve strongly demanded him," remarked the prince.

"Whenever they opened their mouths, they said that von Bergow must be free. As God is in Heaven they undoubtedly captured the girl, in order to liberate von Bergow."

"Hence they will return her," said the prince.

"But it would be better to know where she is," replied the knight of Dlugolas. "But suppose the master asks: 'Whom shall I order to return her?' what shall we say then?"

"Where is she?" said Jurand, in a hollow voice. "They certainly are not keeping her on the border, for fear that I might recover her, but they have taken her somewhere to a far secret hold or to the sea."

But Zbyszko said: "I will find and recover her."

The prince now suddenly burst out with suppressed anger: "Villains carried her off from my court, disgracing me as well, and this shall not be forgiven as long as I live. I have had enough of their treacheries! enough of their assaults! I would rather have wolves for neighbors! But now the master must punish these lords and return the girl, and send messengers with apologies to me, otherwise I will send out a call to arms!"

Here he struck the table with his fist and added:

"Owa! The lord of Plock will follow me, and Witold and King Jagiello's forces! Following enough! Even a saint would snort away his patience. I have had enough!"

All were silent, waiting until his anger had quieted down; but Anna Danuta rejoiced that the prince took Danusia's affair so to heart; she knew that he was long-suffering, but stubborn also, and when he once undertook anything he never relinquished it until he attained his object.

Then Father Wyszoniek rose to speak. "There was of old a rule in the Order," he said, "that no lord was permitted to do anything on his own responsibility without the permission of the assembly or the master. Therefore God gave them such extensive territories that they almost exceed all other earthly powers. But now they know neither obedience, truth, honesty, nor belief. Nothing but greed and such ravage as if they were wolves and not human beings. How can they obey the master's commands or those of the assembly, if they do not even obey God's commandments? Each one resides in his castle like an independent prince—and one assists another in doing evil. I shall complain to the master—but they will deny it. The master will order them to restore the girl, but they will refuse to do so, or they will say: 'She is not here, because we have not captured her.' He will command them to take oath and they will do so. What shall we do then?"

"What to do?" rejoined the knight of Dlugolas. "Let Jurand go to Spychow. If they did carry her off for ransom, or to exchange her for von Bergow, then they must and will inform no one but Jurand."

"Those who used to visit the Forest Court captured her," said the priest.

"Then the master will submit them to trial, or order them to give Jurand the field."

"They must give me the field," exclaimed Zbyszko, "because I challenged them first!"

And Jurand removed his hands from his face and inquired: "Which of them were in the Forest Court?"

"There were Danveld, old von Löve, and two brethren, Godfried and Rotgier," replied the priest.

"They made complaint and wished the prince to order you to release von Bergow from imprisonment. But the prince, being informed by de Fourcy that the Germans were the first to attack you, rebuked and dismissed them without satisfaction."

"Go to Spychow," said the prince, "because they will apply to you there. They failed to do it till now, because this young knight's follower crushed Danveld's arm when bearing the challenge to them. Go to Spychow, and if they apply, inform me. They will send your daughter back in exchange for von Bergow, but I shall nevertheless take vengeance, because they disgraced me also by carrying her off from my court."

Here the prince began to get angry again, for the Teutons had entirely exhausted his patience, and after a moment he added:

"Hej! They blew and blew the fire, but they will end by burning their mouths."

"They will deny it," repeated the priest Wyszoniek.

"If they once inform Jurand that the girl is with them, then they will not be able to deny it," somewhat impatiently replied Mikolaj of Dlugolas. "He believes that they are not keeping her on the border, and that, as Jurand has justly pointed out, they have carried her to some distant castle or to the seashore, but if there be proof that they are the perpetrators, then they will not disclaim it before the master."

But Jurand said in a strange and, at the same time, terrible tone: "Danveld, von Löve, Godfried and Rotgier."

Mikolaj of Dlugolas also recommended that experienced and shrewd people be sent to Prussia, to find out whether Jurand's daughter was there, and if not, whither she had been taken; then the prince took the staff in his hand and went out to give the necessary orders; the princess again turned to Jurand to speak encouraging words:

"How are you?" she inquired.

He did not reply for a moment, as if he had not heard the question, but then he suddenly said:

"As if one had struck me in an old wound."

"But trust in God's mercy; Danusia will come back as soon as you return von Bergow to them. I would willingly sacrifice my own blood."

The princess hesitated whether to say anything about the marriage now, but, considering a little, she did not wish to add new worries to Jurand's already great misfortunes, and at the same time she was seized with a certain fear. "They will look for her with Zbyszko; may he find an occasion to tell him," she said to herself, "otherwise he may entirely lose his mind." She therefore preferred to discuss other matters.

"Do not blame us," she said. "People wearing your livery arrived with a writing under your seal, informing us that you were ill, that your eyes were closing, and that you wished to look once more upon your child. How could we oppose it and not obey a father's command?"

But Jurand embraced her feet. "I do not blame anybody, gracious lady."

"And know also that God will return her to you, because His eye is upon her. He will send her succor, as He did at the last hunt, when a fierce wild bull attacked us—and Jesus inspired Zbyszko to defend us. He almost lost his own life, and was ill for a long time afterward, but he saved Danusia and me, for which he received a girdle and spurs from the prince. You see!... God's hand is over her. Surely, the child is to be pitied! I, myself, am greatly grieved. I thought she would arrive with you, and that I should see the dear child, but meanwhile" ... and her voice trembled, tears fell from her eyes, and Jurand's long repressed despair burst out for a moment, sudden and terrible as a tempest. He took hold of his long hair, and began to beat his head against the wall, groaning and repeating in husky tones: "Jesus! Jesus! Jesus!"

But Zbyszko sprang to his side, and shaking him by the shoulders with all his might, exclaimed:

"We must go! To Spychow!"

CHAPTER IV.

"Whose retinue is this?" inquired Jurand, suddenly starting from musing, as if from sleep, beyond Radzanow.

"Mine," replied Zbyszko.

"And did all my people perish?"

"I saw them dead in Niedzborz."

"Have you no old comrades?"

Zbyszko made no reply, and they traveled on in silence, but hurriedly, because they wanted to get to Spychow as quickly as possible, hoping possibly to meet some Teutonic messengers there. To their good fortune the frosts set in again, and the highways were firm, so that they could make haste.

Toward evening Jurand spoke again, and began to inquire about those brethren of the Order who were at the Forest Court, and Zbyszko narrated everything—their complaints, their departure, the death of de Fourcy, his follower's action in crushing Danveld's arm so terribly, and, as he spoke, one circumstance recurred strikingly to his mind, namely the presence in the Forest Court of that woman who brought the healing balsams from Danveld. During the bait, he commenced therefore to inquire of the Bohemian and Sanderus about her, but neither knew exactly what had become of her. It seemed to them, that she had left either in company with those people, who came for Danusia, or soon after them. It now occurred to Zbyszko's mind, that this might have been some one sent for the purpose of warning the people in case Jurand should happen to be at the court in person. In that case they would not claim to have come from Spychow, but could have prepared another missive to give to the princess instead of Jurand's fictitious letter. All this had been arranged with hellish dexterity, and the young knight, who so far had known the Teutons only from the battlefield, thought for the first time, that the fist was not sufficient for them, but that they must be overcome with the head as well. This was a sullen thought for him, because his great sorrow and pain had become concentrated into a desire for fight and

160

blood. Even help for Danusia in his mind took the form of a series of battles either in troops or singly; and now he perceived that it might be necessary to restrain his desire for revenge and splitting of heads, like a bear on a chain, and seek new means of saving and recovering Danusia. While thinking of this, he felt sorry that Macko was not with him. Macko was as cunning as he was brave. He secretly determined to send Sanderus from Spychow to Szczytno, in order to find that woman and to try to learn from her what had happened to Danusia. He said to himself that, even if Sanderus wished to betray him, he could do little harm in the matter, and on the contrary might render great service, because his trade gained admittance for him everywhere. However, he wished to consult Jurand first, but postponed it until their arrival in Spychow, the more so because night came on, and it seemed to him, that Jurand, sitting on a knight's high saddle, had fallen asleep from fatigue, exhaustion and great anxiety. But Jurand rode with a bowed head only because misfortune weighed it down. And it was apparent that he was constantly thinking of it, with a heart full of terrible dread, because he finally said:

"I would rather be frozen under Niedzborz! It was you that dug me out?"

"I, with others."

"And at the hunt, you saved my child?"

"What should I have done?"

"Will you help me now, too?"

And there burst forth in Zbyszko at the same time such love for Danusia and such great hatred toward the Teuton wrongdoers, that he rose in his saddle and began to speak through tightly set teeth, as though with difficulty:

"Listen to what I say: even if I have to bite the Prussian castles with my teeth, I will do it and get her."

Then followed a moment's silence.

The vengeful and uncontrollable nature of Jurand also seemed to awake in full force under the influence of Zbyszko's words, because he began to gnash his teeth in the darkness and after a while to repeat again the names: Danveld, von Löve, Rotgier and Godfried! And he thought in his soul that if they wanted him to restore von Bergow, he would do so; if they demanded an additional payment he would give it, even if he had to throw into the price Spychow entire; but then, woe to those who had raised their hands against this his only child!

Throughout the whole night, sleep did not close their eyelids for a moment. At dawn, they scarcely recognized each other, to such an extent had their faces changed during this single night. At length Jurand was struck by that pain and inveterate hatred on Zbyszko's face and therefore said: "She saved you and snatched you from death—I know. But you also love her?"

Zbyszko looked directly into his eyes with an almost defiant expression and replied: "She is my wife."

Upon that, Jurand stopped his horse and looked at Zbyszko, blinking his eyes with astonishment.

"What do you say?" he inquired.

"I say that she is my wife and I am her husband."

The knight of Spychow brushed his eyes with his sleeve, as if he were dazed by a sudden thunder-stroke, and after awhile, without a word of reply, he urged his horse forward to the head of the troop and rode on silently.

CHAPTER V.

But Zbyszko, riding behind him, could not stand it very long, and said to himself: "I would rather have him burst forth in anger, than become embittered." He therefore rode up to him and jogging his stirrup against his, he commenced to speak: "Listen how it happened. You know what Danusia did for me in Krakow, but you do not know that they proposed to me Jagienka of Bogdaniec, the daughter of Zych of Zgorzelice. My uncle, Macko, was in favor of it, also her parents and Zych; a relative, an abbot, a wealthy man as well.... What is the use of many words?—an honest girl and a beautiful woman and the dowry respectable also. But it could not be. I felt sorry for Jagienka, but still more so for Danusia—and I set out to her to Mazowsze, because, I tell you frankly, I could not live any longer without her.

161

Recollect the time when you yourself loved—recollect it! and it will not seem strange to you."

Here Zbyszko broke off, waiting for a word from Jurand, but as the latter remained silent, he continued:

"God gave me an opportunity at the Forest Court to save the princess and Danusia from a wild bull while hunting. And the princess immediately said: 'Now Jurand will not object any more, because how could he refuse to reward such a deed?' But I did not wish to take her even then without your parental consent. Yet! I was weak,... because the terrible animal injured me so much, that it almost killed me. But then, as you know, those people came for Danusia, in order to take her, as it seemed, to Spychow, and I was still unable to leave my bed. I thought I should never see her again. I thought that you would take her to Spychow and give her to some one else. You objected to me at Krakow ... and I already thought that I should die. Ah! great God, what a night I passed. Nothing but worry; nothing but grief! I thought that if she also left me, the sun would rise no more. Consider human love and human grief!"

And, for a moment, tears almost choked Zbyszko's voice, but, having a courageous heart, he controlled himself and said:

"The people arrived for her in the evening and wanted to take her immediately, but the princess ordered them to wait until morning. Just then Jesus inspired me with the idea of presenting the princess with my compliments and asking her for Danusia. I thought that if I died I should have that consolation at least. Remember that the girl had to leave, while I remained ill and nearly dying. There was also no time to ask for your permission. The prince was no longer in the Forest Court, the princess therefore weighed both sides because she had nobody to take counsel with. But they, together with Father Wyszoniek at last took pity upon me, and Father Wyszoniek performed the ceremony.... God's power, God's right!..."

But Jurand interrupted, gloomily: "And God's punishment!"

"Why should there be punishment?" inquired Zbyszko. "Consider only, they had sent for her before the ceremony, and whether it had been performed or not, they would have carried her off nevertheless."

But Jurand again replied nothing, and rode on alone, gloomy, and with such a stony face, that though Zbyszko at first felt the relief that confession of a long concealed thing always produces, at length he was seized with fear and said to himself, with constantly increasing fear, that the old knight was bitterly angered, and that thenceforth they would be strangers and foes to each other. And there came upon him a moment of great depression. He had never felt so badly since his departure from Bogdaniec. It seemed to him now that there was no hope of reconciliation with Jurand, nor, what was far worse, of saving Danusia, that all was of no avail, and that in the future still greater misfortunes and miseries would befall him. But this depression of spirits lasted a short while only, and, in accordance with his nature, it soon changed into anger, and a desire for quarreling and fight. "He does not want peace," he said to himself, thinking of Jurand, "then let there be discord, let come what will!" And he was ready to fly at Jurand's face. He also longed for a fight with anybody for anything, merely to do something, merely to give vent to his grief, bitterness and anger, and so find some relief.

Meanwhile they arrived at an inn at a ford called Swietlik, where Jurand, on his return from the prince's court, usually allowed his people and horses to rest. He did so now also involuntarily. After a while he and Zbyszko found themselves alone in a separate chamber. Suddenly Jurand stopped before the young knight and, fixing his eyes upon him, inquired:

"Did you wander about for her sake?"

The other almost harshly retorted:

"Do you suppose that I shall deny it?" And he looked straight into Jurand's eyes, ready to meet anger with anger. But there was no indignation in the old warrior's face; there was only almost boundless grief.

"And you saved my child?" he inquired, after a moment, "and dug me out?"

But Zbyszko looked at him in astonishment and fear that his mind was wandering, because Jurand repeated exactly the same questions that he had already asked.

"Be seated," he said, "because it seems to me that you are still weak."

162

But Jurand raised his hands, placed them on Zbyszko's shoulders, and so drew him suddenly with all his strength to his breast; the other, recovering from a momentary amazement, clasped him round the waist and they embraced each other for a long time, because mutual anxiety and mutual woe united them.

After relaxing their hold, Zbyszko again embraced the older knight's knees, and began to kiss his hands with tears in his eyes.

"Will you not object to me?" he asked.

To that Jurand replied: "I did oppose you, because in my soul I consecrated her to God."

"You devoted her to God, and God to me. His will!"

"His will!" repeated Jurand. "But now we need mercy also."

"Whom will God help, if not a father who seeks his daughter; if not a husband who seeks his wife? He will certainly not assist robbers."

"But they captured her nevertheless," answered Jurand.

"Then you will return von Bergow to them."

"I shall return all they wish."

But at the thought of the Teutons, the old passion soon awoke in him and enfolded him like a flame, because he added after a moment through his clenched teeth:

"I shall also add to it what they do not want."

"I also swore their ruin," replied Zbyszko, "but now we must make haste to Spychow."

And he commenced to hasten the saddling of the horses. Accordingly, after they had eaten their oats, and the men had warmed themselves in the rooms, they started out, although it was growing dark outside. As the way was long, and a severe frost had set in for the night, Jurand and Zbyszko, who had not yet regained their strength, traveled in sledges. Zbyszko told about Uncle Macko, for whom his heart yearned, and regretted that he was not present, because his courage as well as craft might be of use, the latter qualification being more necessary against such foes than courage. At last he turned to Jurand and inquired:

"And are you cunning?… Because I am not."

"Neither am I," retorted Jurand. "I did not fight them with craft, but with this hand and that which remained in me."

"I understand that," said the young knight. "I understand it because I love Danusia and because they carried her off. If, God forbid…."

And he did not finish, because the mere thought made him feel not a human but a wolf's heart in his breast. For some time they rode silently over a white, moonlight-flooded road; then Jurand commenced to speak as if to himself:

"If they only had any reason to take revenge on me—I would not say! But gracious God! they had none…. I waged war with them in the field, when sent on an embassy by our prince to Witold, but here I was like a neighbor to neighbors…. Bartosz Natecz captured, chained and imprisoned under ground in Kozmin forty knights who attacked him. The Teutons were compelled to pay half a wagonful of money for them. While I, when a German guest happened to come on his way to the Teutons, received and rewarded him like one knight another. Frequently also, the Teutons came against me across the swamps. I was not hard on them then, and they did to me what I would not do even to-day to my greatest foe…."

And terrible recollections began to tear him with increasing force, his voice died away for an instant in his breast, then he said, half groaning: "I had only one, like a ewe lamb, like the heart in my breast, and they captured her like a dog on a rope, and she died there…. Now again, the child … Jesus, Jesus!"

And again there was silence. Zbyszko raised his youthful, perplexed face toward the moon, then again looked at Jurand and inquired:

"Father!… It would be far better for them to earn men's esteem than their vengeance. Why do they commit so much wrong on all nations and all people?"

But Jurand spread his hands apart as if in despair, and replied with a choked voice: "I do not know…."

Zbyszko meditated for a time over his own question, presently however his thoughts turned to Jurand.

"People say that you wreaked a worthy vengeance," he said.

Jurand meanwhile controlled his anguish, bethought himself and said:

"But I swore their ruin ... and I also swore to God that if He would permit me to glut my vengeance I would surrender to Him the child that was left to me. This is the reason why I objected to you. But now I do not know: was it His will, or did you awaken His anger by your action?"

"No," said Zbyszko. "I told you once before that even if the ceremony had not been performed, yet the scoundrels would have carried her off. God accepted your vow, and presented me with Danusia, because without His will we could accomplish nothing."

"Every sin is against God's will."

"A sin is, but not the sacrament. Because the sacrament is God's matter."

"Therefore there is no help."

"And God be blessed there is not! Therefore do not complain, because nobody would help you against the robbers so well as I will. You will see! In any case I shall pay them for Danusia, but even if one of those who captured your deceased be still alive, leave him to me and you shall see!"

But Jurand shook his head.

"No," he answered, gloomily, "none of those will be alive...."

For a time only the snorting of horses and the smothered echo of the hoofs striking against the beaten road was audible.

"Once at night," continued Jurand, "I heard a voice, as if coming from a wall, saying to me: 'Enough vengeance!' but I did not obey, because it was not the voice of the deceased."

"And whose voice could that be?" inquired Zbyszko, anxiously.

"I do not know. In Spychow frequently something talks in the walls, and sometimes moans, because many have died there in chains underground."

"And what does the priest tell you?"

"The priest sanctified the castle and also ordered me to relinquish vengeance, but that could not be. I became too hard on them, and then they themselves sought revenge. They lay in ambush and challenged me in the field.... And so it was this time. Meineger and von Bergow were the first to challenge me."

"Did you ever accept ransom?"

"Never! Of those I have captured, von Bergow will be the first to come out alive."

The conversation ceased, because they now turned from the broad highway into a narrower road, on which they traveled for a long time in silence on account of its tortuous course, and because in some places the snow formed drifts difficult to traverse. In the spring or summer, on rainy days, this road must have been almost impassable.

"Are we approaching Spychow already?" asked Zbyszko.

"Yes," answered Jurand. "There is a good deal of forest yet, and then begin the morasses, in the centre of which is the castle.... Beyond the morasses are the marshes and dry fields, while the castle can be approached only by the dike. The Germans wished to capture me repeatedly, but they could not, and their bones rot among the forest weeds."

"And it is hard to find," said Zbyszko. "If the Teutons send messengers with letters, how will they find us?"

"They have sent out several times already, and they have people who know the way."

"If we could only meet them at Spychow," said Zbyszko.

This wish was realized sooner than the young knight thought, for issuing from the forest into the open country, where lay Spychow among the swamps, they perceived before them two riders and a low sledge, in which were sitting three dark figures.

The night was very bright, therefore the whole group was perfectly visible against the white background of snow. Jurand's and Zbyszko's heart began to beat faster at this sight, because who else would be riding to Spychow in the middle of the night, but the messengers from the Teutons?

Zbyszko ordered the driver to go faster, and so they soon came so near each other, that they could be heard, and two riders, who apparently watched over the safety of the sledge, turned to them, and, unslinging their crossbows, cried:

"Who is there?"

"Germans!" whispered Jurand to Zbyszko.

Then he raised his voice and said:

"It is my right to ask, and yours to reply!"

"Who are you?"

"Travelers."

"What sort of travelers?"

"Pilgrims."

"Where from?"

"From Szczytno."

"It is they!" again whispered Jurand.

Meanwhile the sledges had come together, and at the same time six horsemen appeared before them. This was the guard of Spychow, which watched the dike leading to the castle day and night. With the horses were very large and savage dogs, exactly resembling wolves.

The guardsmen, having recognized Jurand, began to utter cries of welcome mingled with astonishment that the master had returned so soon and unexpectedly; but he was entirely engaged with the messengers, and therefore turned to them again:

"Where are you traveling to?" he asked.

"To Spychow."

"What do you want there?"

"We can tell that only to the lord himself."

Jurand was about to say: "I am the lord of Spychow;" but he restrained himself, feeling that conversation could not be carried on in the presence of others. He asked them instead, whether they had any letters, and, when they replied that they were ordered to communicate verbally, he gave orders to drive as fast as the horses could go. Zbyszko was equally anxious to hear news of Danusia, and could not turn his attention to anything else. He became impatient when the guards on the dike stopped them twice; and when the bridge was lowered over the moat, behind which rose on the mound a gigantic palisade, and although he had previously often desired to see that castle of ominous fame, at the mention of which the Germans made the sign of a cross, now he saw nothing but the Teuton messengers, from whom he might hear where Danusia was and when she would be set at liberty. He did not foresee though, that a great disappointment was awaiting him. Besides the horsemen, who were given for defence, and the driver, the embassy from Szczytno was composed of two persons: one of these was the same woman who had once brought the healing balsam to the Forest Court; the other was a young *pontnik*.[108] Zbyszko did not recognize the woman, because he had not seen her at the Forest Court; the *pontnik* at once seemed to him to be a disguised warrior. Jurand soon led both into the neighboring room, and halted before them, huge, and almost terrible in the glow of the fire, which fell upon him from the logs burning in the chimney.

"Where is the child?" he asked.

But they were frightened, standing face to face with a menacing man. Although the *pontnik* had an insolent face, he simply trembled like a leaf, and the woman's legs trembled also. She glanced from Jurand to Zbyszko, and then at the shining bald head of the priest Kaleb, and then again at Jurand, as if inquiring what the other two were doing there.

"Sir," she said, finally, "we do not know what you are asking, but we were sent to you on important matters. Yet, the one who sent us ordered us explicitly, that the conversation should be held without witnesses."

"I have no secrets from these!" said Jurand.

"But we have, noble lord," replied the woman, "and if you order them to remain, then we shall ask for nothing but that you allow us to leave to-morrow."

Anger appeared in Jurand's face as he was not used to opposition. For a moment his tawny moustache worked ominously, but he reflected, "For Danusia's sake!" and restrained

165

himself. Moreover, Zbyszko, who wanted above all things that the conversation might be concluded as soon as possible, and felt sure that Jurand would repeat it to him, said:

"If it must be so, then remain alone." And he left, together with the priest Kaleb; but he scarcely found himself in the main hall, in which were hanging targets and weapons, captured by Jurand, when Glowacz approached him.

"Sir," he said, "that is the same woman!"

"What woman?"

"From the Teutons, who brought the balsam. I recognized her at once, and so did Sanderus. She came, at it seems, to spy, and she certainly knows now where the lady is."

"And we shall know," said Zbyszko.

"Do you also know that *pontnik*?"

"No," replied Sanderus; "but do not buy, sir, any remissions from him, because he is a false *pontnik*,"

"If you put him to the torture, you might obtain a lot of information."

"Wait!" said Zbyszko.

Meanwhile, in the next room hardly had the doors closed behind Zbyszko and the priest Kaleb, when the sister of the Order quickly approached Jurand and whispered:

"Robbers captured your daughter."

"With crosses on their robes?"

"No. But God blessed the pious brethren, so that they recovered her, and now she is with them."

"Where is she, I ask."

"Under the care of the religious Brother Shomberg," she answered, crossing her hands on her breast and bowing humbly.

But Jurand, hearing the dreadful name of the hangman of Witold's children, turned as pale as linen; after a moment he sat on a bench, shut his eyes, and began to wipe away the cold perspiration, which collected in beads on his forehead.

Seeing this, the *pontnik*, although he had not hitherto been able to restrain his fear, now put his hands on his hips, lounged on the bench, stretched out his legs and looked at Jurand, with eyes full of pride and scorn. A long silence followed.

"Brother Markward also assists Brother Shomberg in guarding her," again said the woman; "it is a vigilant watch and no harm will happen to the lady."

"What am I to do in order to get her back?" inquired Jurand.

"To humble yourself before the Order!" proudly said the *pontnik*.

At this Jurand arose, went up to him, and bending down over him, said in concentrated, terrible tones:

"Be silent!"

And the *pontnik* was again terror-stricken. He knew, that he could threaten and say what would tame and overwhelm Jurand, but he was terrified lest, before saying a word, something dreadful would happen to him; he therefore remained silent, with dilated eyes, as if petrified with fear, fixed on the threatening face of the lord of Spychow, and sat motionless, only his beard began to quiver with agitation.

Jurand again turned to the sister of the Order:

"Have you a letter?"

"No, sir. We have no letter. What we have to say, we were ordered to say verbally."

"Then speak!"

And she repeated again, as if wishing that Jurand should impress it well in his memory:

"Brother Shomberg and Brother Markward watch over the lady; therefore, you sir, restrain your anger…. But no evil will happen to her, because although you have gravely injured the Order for many years, nevertheless the brethren wish to repay you good for evil if you comply with their just demands."

"What do they wish?"

"They wish you to release Herr von Bergow."

Jurand breathed heavily.

"I will return von Bergow to them," he said.

166

"And the other prisoners that you have in Spychow."

"There are two retainers of Meineger and von Bergow, besides their boys."

"You must release them, sir, and make amends for the imprisonment."

"God forbid that I should bargain for my child."

"The religious friars expected that from you," said the woman, "but this is not all that I was ordered to say. Your daughter, sir, was captured by some men, undoubtedly robbers, and certainly for the purpose of demanding a rich ransom. God permitted the brethren to recapture her, and now they demand nothing but the return of their brother and associate. But the brethren know, and you, too, sir, what hatred there is in this country against them, and how unfairly even their most righteous actions are judged. For this reason the brethren are sure that, if the people here found out that your daughter was with them, they would at once begin to suspect that they had captured her, and would consequently utter only slander and complaints…. O yes, evil and malicious people here have frequently repaid them so, and the reputation of the holy Order has suffered greatly by it, and the brethren are greatly concerned about it, and therefore they add this sole condition that you alone assure the prince of this country and all the mighty knights that it is true, that not the Teutonic knights, but robbers carried off your daughter, and that you had to ransom her from robbers."

"It is true," said Jurand, "that bandits have captured my child, and that I have to buy her back from bandits…."

"You shall tell nobody otherwise, because if only one person should find out that you come to terms with the brethren, if only one living soul or only one complaint were sent to the master, or the assembly, great complications would ensue."

Jurand's face exhibited great alarm. At the first moment it seemed to him quite natural that the knights required secrecy, fearing responsibility and disgrace, but now a suspicion arose in his mind that there might be another reason, but, not being able to account for it, he was seized with such terror as sometimes happens to the most courageous when danger does not threaten them alone, but also their relatives and loved ones.

He determined however to find out more from the Order's servant.

"The knights wish secrecy," he said, "but how can it be kept, when I release von Bergow and the others in return for my child?"

"You will say that you accepted ransom for von Bergow in order to be able to pay the robbers."

"People will not believe it, because I never accepted ransom," gloomily replied Jurand.

"But your child was never in question," hissed the messenger in reply.

And again silence followed, after which the *pontnik*, who, in the meanwhile had gained courage, and judged that Jurand must now restrain himself more, said:

"Such is the will of the brethren Shomberg and Markward."

The messenger continued:

"You will say, that this *pontnik* who came with me, brought you the ransom, we also will leave here with the noble von Bergow and the prisoners."

"How so?" said Jurand, frowning, "do you think that I will give up the prisoners before you return my child?"

"You can act, sir, still differently. You can call personally for your daughter at Szczytno, whither the brethren will bring her to you."

"I? at Szczytno?"

"Because, should the bandits capture her again on the way, your and your people's suspicion would again fall upon the pious knights, and therefore they prefer to give her into your own hands."

"And who will pledge himself for my return, if I walk alone into a wolf's throat?"

"The virtue of the brethren, their justice and godliness!"

Jurand began to walk up and down the room. He began to suspect treason and feared it, but he felt at the same time that the Teutons could impose any conditions they pleased upon him, and that he was powerless before them.

However, an idea struck him, and suddenly halting before the *pontnik*, he gazed at him with a piercing look, and then turned to the messenger and said:

"Well, I will go to Szczytno. You and this man, who is wearing *pontnik* garb, will remain here until my return, after which you will leave with von Bergow and the prisoners."

"Do you refuse, sir, to believe friars." said the *pontnik*; "how then can they trust you to liberate us and von Bergow on your return?"

Jurand's face turned pale with fury, and a critical moment followed, in which it almost seemed that he would catch the *pontnik* by the throat and dash him to the floor; but he suppressed his anger, drew a deep breath and commenced to speak slowly but emphatically.

"Whoever you are, do not strain my patience to the breaking point!"

But the *pontnik* turned to the sister: "Speak! what you were ordered."

"Lord," she said: "we would not dare distrust your oath upon your sword and knightly honor, but it is not proper for you to swear before people of low rank. And we were not sent for your oath."

"What were you sent for?"

"The brethren told us that, without saying anything to anybody, you must appear at Szczytno with von Bergow and the prisoners."

At that, Jurand's shoulders began to draw together, and his fingers to extend like the claws of a bird of prey; at last, stopping before the woman, he bent down, as if to speak into her ear, and said:

"Did they not tell you that I should order you and von Bergow to be broken on the wheel in Spychow?"

"Your daughter is in the power of the brethren, and under the care of Shomberg and Markward," replied the sister, meaningly.

"Robbers, poisoners, hangmen!" burst forth Jurand.

"Who are able to avenge us and who said at our departure: 'Should he not comply with all our orders, it would be far better that the girl should die, as Witold's children died.' Choose!"

"And understand that you are in the power of the knights," remarked the *pontnik*. "They do not wish to do you any harm, and the *starosta* of Szczytno sends you his word by us that you shall go free from his castle; but they want you, for the wrong done to them, to present your respects to the Teuton, and beg for the victor's mercy. They want to forgive you, but they first wish to bend your stubborn neck. You denounced them as traitors and perjurers.—therefore they want you to acknowledge their good faith. They will restore you and your daughter to liberty—but you must beg for it. You trampled upon them—now you must swear that your hand will never, be raised against the white robe."

"The knights wish it so," added the woman, "and Markward and Shomberg with them."

A moment of deathlike silence followed. It seemed only that somewhere among the beams of the ceiling some smothered echo repeated as if in terror: "Markward ... Shomberg."

Outside the windows could be heard the voices of Jurand's archers keeping watch on the mounds near the palisade of the castle.

The *pontnik* and the servant of the Order looked for a long time at each other and Jurand, who sat leaning against the wall, motionless, and with a face deeply shadowed by furs suspended by the window. His brain contained only one thought, that, if he did not do what the Teutons demanded, they would destroy his child; again, if he should do it, he might perhaps even then not save Danusia nor himself. And he saw no help, no way of escape. He felt a pitiless superior force over him which was crushing him. He saw in his soul already the iron hands of a Teuton on Danusia's throat; knowing them thoroughly, he did not doubt for a moment that they would kill her, bury her in the castle yard, and then deny it,—and who would then be able to prove that they had captured her?

It was true that Jurand had the messengers in his power; he could bring them to the prince and get a confession by means of torture, but the Teutons had Danusia, and they might not care about their agents' torture. And for a moment he seemed to see his child stretching out her hands from afar, asking for assistance.... If he at least knew that she was really at Szczytno, then he could go that very night to the border, attack the unsuspecting Germans, capture the castle, destroy the garrison and liberate the child—but she might not be and positively was not in Szczytno. It flashed like lightning through his head, that if he were to seize the woman and the *pontnik*, and take them directly to the grand master, then perhaps the master could draw confessions from them and might order the return of his daughter; but that gleam was extinguished almost as quickly as it took fire.

These people could tell the master that they came to ransom von Bergow and that they knew nothing about a girl. No! that way led to nothing, but what did? He thought, that should he go to Szczytno they would chain him and cast him under ground, while Danusia would not be released, lest it should transpire that they had captured her, if for no other reason. And meanwhile death hung over his only child, death over the last dear head!... And finally his thoughts grew confused, and the pain became so great, that it overpowered itself and became numbness. He sat motionless, for his body became as dead as if cut out of stone. If he wanted to rise now, he would not be able to do so.

Meanwhile the others grew tired of the long waiting, therefore the servant of the Order arose and said:

"It will be soon daylight, therefore permit us, sir, to retire, because we need a rest."

"And refreshment after the long journey," added the *pontnik*. Then they both bowed to Jurand and went out.

But he continued to sit motionless, as if seized by sleep or death.

Presently, however, the door opened and Zbyszko appeared, followed by the priest Kaleb.

"Who are the messengers? What do they want?" inquired the young knight, approaching Jurand.

Jurand quivered, but at first answered nothing; he only began to blink like a man awakened from a sound sleep.

"Sir, are you not ill?" said the priest Kaleb, who, knowing Jurand better, noticed that something curious was taking place within him.

"No!" replied Jurand.

"And Danusia?" further inquired Zbyszko; "where is she and what did they say to you?"

"What did they bring?"

"The ransom," slowly replied Jurand.

"The ransom for von Bergow?"

"For von Bergow...."

"How so, for von Bergow? what is the matter with you?"

"Nothing."

But in his voice there was something so strange and listless that a sudden fear seized those two, especially because Jurand spoke of the ransom and not the exchange of von Bergow for Danusia.

"Gracious God!" exclaimed Zbyszko: "where is Danusia?"

"She is not with the Teutons,—no!" replied Jurand, in a sleepy tone; and suddenly he fell from the bench upon the floor as if dead.

CHAPTER VI.

The following day at noon the messengers saw Jurand, and soon afterward they rode away taking with them von Bergow, two esquires and a number of other prisoners. Jurand then summoned Father Kaleb and dictated a letter to the prince, stating that Danusia had not been carried off by the Knights of the Order, but that he had succeeded in discovering her refuge, and hoped to recover her in a few days. He repeated the same to Zbyszko, who had been wild with astonishment, dread and perplexity since the night before.

The old knight refused to answer any of his questions, telling him instead to wait patiently and not to undertake anything for the liberation of Danusia, because it was unnecessary.

Toward evening he shut himself in again with Father Kaleb, whom he had ordered to write down his last will; then he confessed himself, and after receiving the sacrament, he summoned Zbyszko, and the old taciturn Tolima, who used to accompany him in all his expeditions and fights, and in times of peace administered the affairs of Spychow.

"Here," he said, turning to the old warrior and raising his voice, as if he was speaking to a man who could not hear well, "is the husband of my daughter whom he married at the prince's court, for which he had my entire consent. Therefore, after my death, he will be the master and owner of the castle, the soil, forests, waters, people and all the craft in Spychow...."

Hearing this, Tolima was greatly surprised and began to turn his square head to Jurand and to Zbyszko alternately, he said nothing, however, because he scarcely ever did say anything, he only bowed to Zbyszko and lightly embraced his knees. And Jurand continued:

"This is my will, written by Father Kaleb, and below is my seal in wax; you must testify that you have heard this from me, and that I ordered that the young knight should be obeyed here even as I am. Furthermore, what is in the treasury in booty and money, you will show him, and you will serve him faithfully in peace as well as in war till death. Did you hear?"

Tolima raised his hands to his ears and nodded his head, then, at a sign from Jurand, he bowed and went out; the knight again turned to Zbyszko and said impressively:

"There is enough in the treasury to satisfy the greatest greed and to ransom not one but a hundred captives. Remember!"

But Zbyszko inquired:

"And why are you giving me Spychow already?"

"I give you more than Spychow, in the child."

"And we know not the hour of death," said Father Kaleb.

"Yes, unknown," repeated Jurand, sadly, "a short time ago, the snow covered me up, and, although God saved me, I have no more my old strength...."

"Gracious God!" exclaimed Zbyszko, "something his changed within you since yesterday, and you prefer to speak of death than of Danusia. Gracious God!"

"Danusia will return, she will," replied Jurand; "she is under God's protection. But if she returns ... listen ... take her to Bogdaniec and leave Spychow with Tolima.... He is a faithful man, and this is a wild neighborhood.... There they cannot capture her with a rope ... there she is safer...."

"Hej!" cried Zbyszko, "and you talk already as if from the other world. What is that?"

"Because I went half-way to the other world, and now I seem to be ill. And I also care for my child ... because I have only her. And, you too, although I know that you love her...."

Here he interrupted, and drawing a short weapon from its sheath, called the *misericordia*, he held the handle toward Zbyszko.

"Swear to me now upon this little cross that you will never harm her and that you will love her constantly...."

And tears suddenly started in Zbyszko's eyes; in a moment he fell upon his knees and, putting a finger on the hilt, exclaimed:

"Upon the Holy Passion, I will never harm, and will love her constantly!"

"Amen," said Father Kaleb.

Jurand again put the "dagger of mercy" back into the sheath and extended his arms: "Then you are my child too!..."

They separated then, because it was late, and they had had no good rest for several days. However, Zbyszko got up the following morning at daybreak, because the previous day he had been frightened, lest Jurand were really falling ill, and he wished to learn how the older knight had spent the night. Before the door to Jurand's room he met Tolima, who had just left it.

"How is the lord? well?" he inquired.

The other again bowed, and then, putting his hand to his ear, said:

"What orders, your grace?"

"I am asking how the lord is?" repeated Zbyszko, louder.

"The lord has departed."

"Where to?"

170

"I do not know…. In arms!"

CHAPTER VII.

The dawn was just beginning to whiten the trees, bushes and boulders scattered in the fields, when the hired guide, walking beside Jurand's horse, stopped and said:

"Permit me to rest, knight, for I am out of breath. It is thawing and foggy, but it is not far now."

"You will conduct me to the road, and then return," replied Jurand.

"The road will be to the right behind the forest, and you will soon see the castle from the hill."

Then the peasant commenced to strike his hands against his armpits, because he was chilled with the morning dampness; he then sat on a stone, because this exercise made him still more breathless.

"Do you know whether the count is in the castle?" inquired Jurand.

"Where else could he be, since he is ill?"

"What ails him?"

"People say that the Polish knights gave him a beating," replied the old peasant. And there was a feeling of satisfaction in his voice. He was a Teuton subject, but his Mazovian heart rejoiced over the superiority of the Polish knights.

He presently added:

"Hej! our lords are strong, but they have a hard task with them."

But immediately after saying this, he looked sharply at the knight, as if to convince himself that nothing bad would happen to him for the words which he had heedlessly let slip and said:

"You, lord, speak our language; you are no German?"

"No," replied Jurand; "but lead on."

The peasant arose, and again began to walk beside the horse. On the way, he now and then put his hand into a leathern pouch, pulled out a handful of unground corn, and put it into his mouth, and when he had thus satisfied his first hunger, he began to explain why he ate raw grains, although Jurand was too much occupied with his own misfortune and his own thoughts, to heed him.

"God be blessed for that," he said. "A hard life under our German lords! They lay such taxes upon grist, that a poor man must eat the grain with the chaff, like an ox. And when they find a hand-mill in a cottage, they execute the peasant, take whatever he has, bah! they do not pardon even women and children…. They fear neither God nor the priests. They even put the priest in chains for blaming them for it. Oh, it is hard under the Germans! If a man does grind some grains between two stones, then he keeps that handful of flour for the holy Sunday, and must eat like birds on Friday. But God be blessed for even that, because two or three months before the harvest there will not be even that much. It is not permitted to catch fish … nor kill animals … It is not as it is in Mazowsze."

The Teutonic peasant complained, speaking partly to himself, and partly to Jurand, and meanwhile they passed through a waste country, covered with limestone boulders, heaped with snow, and entered a forest, which looked grey in the morning light, and from which came a sharp, damp coolness. It became broad daylight; otherwise it would have been difficult for Jurand to travel along the forest road, which ran somewhat up hill, and was so narrow that his gigantic battle-horse could, in some places, hardly pass between the trunks. But the forest soon ended, and in a few "*Paters*," they reached the summit of a white hill, across the middle of which ran a beaten road.

"This is the road, lord," said the peasant; "you will find the way alone, now."

"I shall," replied Jurand. "Return home, man." And putting his hand into a leather bag, fastened in front of the saddle, he took from it a silver coin and handed it to the guide. The peasant, accustomed more to blows than to gifts from the local Teutonic knights, could scarcely believe his eyes, and catching the money, dropped his head to Jurand's stirrup and embraced it.

"O Jesus, Mary!" he exclaimed: "God reward your honor!"

"God be with you!"

"God's grace be with you! Szczytno is before you."

171

Then he once more bent down to the stirrup and disappeared. Jurand remained on the hill alone and looked in the direction indicated by the peasant, at a grey, moist veil of fog, which concealed the world before him. Behind this fog was hidden that ominous castle, to which he was driven by superior force and misery. It is already near, then, and what must happen, must happen.... As that thought came into Jurand's heart, in addition to his fear and anxiety about Danusia, and his readiness to redeem her from a foe's hands even with his own blood, he experienced a new, exceedingly bitter, and hitherto unknown feeling of humiliation. And now Jurand, at the mere mention of whose name the neighboring counts trembled, was riding to their command with a bowed head. He who had defeated and trampled under foot so many of them, now felt himself defeated and trampled upon. It is true, they had not overcome him in the field with courage and knightly strength, nevertheless he felt himself subdued. And it was to him something so unusual, that it seemed as if the entire order of the world were subverted. He was going to submit himself to the Teutons, he, who would rather meet single-handed the entire Teuton force, if it were not for Danusia's sake. Had it not happened already, that a single knight, having to choose between disgrace and death had attacked whole armies? But he felt that he might meet disgrace, and, at that thought, his heart groaned with agony as a wolf howls when it feels the dart within it.

But he was a man with not only a body, but also a soul, of iron. He knew how to subdue others, he knew also how to subdue himself.

"I will not move," he said to himself, "until I have overcome this anger with which I should rather lose than deliver my child."

And he wrestled with his hard heart, his inveterate hatred and his desire to fight. Whoever had seen him on that hill, in armor, on a gigantic horse, would have said that he was some giant, wrought out of iron, and would not have recognized that that motionless knight at that moment was waging the hottest of all the battles of his life. But he fought with himself until he had entirely overcome and felt that his will would not fail him. Meanwhile the mist thinned, although it did not disappear entirely, but finally something darker loomed through it.

Jurand guessed that these were the walls of the castle of Szczytno. At the sight of it he still did not move from the place, but began to pray so fervidly and ardently as a man prays, when nothing is left for him in the world but God's mercy. And when his horse did finally move, he felt that some sort of confidence was beginning to enter his heart. He was now prepared to suffer everything that could befall him. There came back to his memory Saint George, a descendant of the greatest race in Cappadocia, who suffered various shameful tortures, and nevertheless not only did not lose any honor, but is placed on the right hand of God and appointed patron of all knighthood. Jurand had sometimes heard tales of his exploits from the abbots, who came from distant countries, and now he strengthened his heart with these recollections.

Slowly even, hope began to awaken in him. The Teutons were indeed famous for their desire of revenge, therefore he did not doubt that they would take vengeance on him for all the defeats which he had inflicted upon them, for the disgrace which had fallen upon them after each encounter, and for the dread in which they had lived for so many years.

But that very consideration increased his courage. He thought that they had captured Danusia only in order to get him; therefore of what use would she be to them, after they had gotten him? Yes! They would undoubtedly seize him, and, not daring to keep him near Mazowsze, they would send him to some distant castle, where perhaps he would have to groan until his life's end under ground, but they would liberate Danusia. Even if it should prove that they had got him insidiously and by oppression, neither the grand master nor the assembly would blame them very much for that, because Jurand was actually very hard on the Teutons, and shed more of their blood than did any other knight in the world. But that same grand master would perhaps punish them for the imprisonment of the innocent girl, who was moreover a foster-daughter of the prince, whose favor he was seeking on account of the threatening war with the Polish king.

And his hope constantly increased. At times it seemed to him almost certain that Danusia would return to Spychow, under Zbyszko's powerful protection.... "He is a strong man," he thought; "he will not permit anybody to injure her." And he began to recall with affection all he knew of Zbyszko: "He defeated the Germans at Wilno, fought single-handed against the Fryzjans whom he challenged with his uncle and quartered, he also beat Lichtenstein, saved the child from the wild bull, and he challenged those four, whom he will surely not pardon." Here Jurand raised his eyes toward heaven and said: "I gave her to you, O Lord, and you to Zbyszko!"

And he gained still more confidence, judging that if God had given her to the youth, then He would certainly not allow the Germans to mock him but snatch her out of their hands, even if the entire Teuton power should oppose it. But then he commenced to think again about Zbyszko: "Bah! he is not only a mighty man but also as true as gold. He will guard her, love her, and Jesus! be good to her; but it seems to me, that, by his side she will neither miss the princely court nor paternal love...." At that thought his eyelids became suddenly moist, and a great yearning filled us heart. He would like to see his child once more at least in his life, and at some future time die in Spychow near those two, and not in the dark Teuton cells. "But God's will be done!" Szczytno was already visible. The walls became more distinct in the mist, the hour of sacrifice was approaching; he therefore began to comfort himself, and said to himself: "Surely, it is God's will! but the end of life is near. A few years more or less, the result will be the same. Hej! I would like to see both children yet, but, justly speaking, I have lived long enough. Whatever I had to experience, I did; whomever to revenge, I revenged. And what now? Rather to God, than to the world; and since it is necessary to suffer, then it is necessary. Danusia with Zbyszko, even when most prosperous, will not forget. Surely, they will sometimes recollect and ask: where is he? is he alive yet, or already in God's court of justice? They will inquire and perhaps find out. The Teutons are very revengeful, but also very greedy for ransom. Zbyszko would not grudge ransoming the bones at least. And they will surely order more than one mass. The hearts of both are honest and loving, for which may God and the Most Holy Mother bless them!"

The road became not only broader but also more frequented. Wagons laden with lumber and straw were on the way to the town. Herders were driving cattle. Frozen fish were carried on sledges from the lakes. In one place four archers led a peasant on a chain to court for some offence, for he had his hands tied behind him, and on his feet were fetters which, dragging in the snow, hardly enabled him to move. From his panting nostrils and mouth escaped breath in the shape of wreaths of vapor, while they sang as they urged him on. Or seeing Jurand, they began to look at him inquisitively, apparently marvelling at the huge proportions of the rider and horse; but, at the sight of the golden spurs and knightly belt, they lowered then crossbows as a sign of welcome and respect. The town was still more populous and noisy, but everybody hastily got out of the armed man's way, while he, traversing the main street, turned toward the castle which, wrapped in clouds, seemed to sleep yet.

Not everything around slept, at least not the crows and ravens, whole flights of which were stirring on the elevation, which constituted the entrance to the castle, flapping their wings and crowing. On coming nearer, Jurand understood the cause of their gathering. Beside the road leading to the gate of the castle, stood wide gallows, on which were hanging the bodies of four Mazovian peasants. There was not the least breath of wind, therefore the corpses, which seemed to be looking at their own feet, did not sway at all, except when the black buds perched upon their shoulders and heads, jostling one another, striking the ropes and pecking the bowed heads. Some of the hanged men must have been there for a long time, because their skulls were entirely naked, and their legs very much lengthened. At Jurand's approach, the flock arose with a great noise, but they soon turned in the air and began to settle on the crossbeam of the gallows. Jurand passed them, crossing himself, approached the moat, and, stopping at the place where the drawbridge was raised before the gate, sounded the horn.

He sounded it a second and a third time and waited. There was no living soul upon the walls, nor could a voice be heard within the gates. After a while though, a heavy flap, visible behind a grate built in stone near the castle gate, was raised with a crash, and in the opening appeared the bearded head of a German servant.

"*Wer da?*" inquired a harsh voice.

"Jurand of Spychow!" replied the knight.

Immediately the flap was closed again and deep silence followed.

Time passed. No movement was heard behind the gate, only the cawing of birds reached his ear from the direction of the gallows.

Jurand stood yet a long time before he raised the horn and sounded it again. But silence again was the sole response.

Now he understood that he was kept before the gate by Teuton pride, which knew no bounds before the defeated, in order to humiliate him like a beggar. He also guessed that he would have to wait thus until evening, or even longer. Consequently his blood began to boil in the first moments; he was suddenly seized with the desire to dismount, pick up one of the rocks which lay near the moat, and cast it at the grate. He and every other Mazovian or Polish knight would have done so, under other circumstances, and let them come then from behind the gate and fight him. But recollecting for what purpose he had come, he bethought himself and desisted.

"Have I not sacrificed myself for my child?" he said in his soul.

And he waited.

Meanwhile something black appeared in the loopholes of the wall. There appeared heads covered with fur, dark hoods and even iron bars, from behind which curious eyes gazed at the knight. More came every moment, because the terrible Jurand, waiting solitarily before the Teuton gate, was an unusual sight for the garrison. Whoever had seen him hitherto, had seen death, but now he could be looked at in safety. The heads constantly multiplied till at last all the loopholes near the gate were occupied by servants. Jurand thought that also the superiors must be looking at him through the grates of the windows in the adjacent tower, and he turned his eyes in that direction, but there the windows were cut in deep walls, and it was impossible to see through them. But in the apertures, the group of people who at first looked at him silently, began to talk. One after another repeated his name, here and there laughter was heard, gruff voices shouted as if at a wolf, louder and more insolently, and when, apparently, nobody among them interfered, they finally began to throw snow at the standing knight. He moved his horse as if involuntarily, and then for a moment the throwing of snow ceased, voices quieted down, and even some heads disappeared behind the walls. Surely, Jurand's name must have been very menacing! Soon, however, even the most cowardly bethought themselves that a moat and a wall separated them from that terrible Mazovian, therefore the rough soldiery again commenced to throw not only small lumps of snow, but also ice, and even shards and stones, which rebounded with a clang from the armor which covered the horse.

"I have sacrificed myself for the child," repeated Jurand to himself.

And he waited. Noontime arrived, the walls were deserted, because the retainers were called to dinner. A few, those that had to be on guard, ate their meal on the wall, and, after having eaten, entertained themselves with throwing the picked bones at the hungry knight. They also began to tease and question each other who would dare to descend and strike him with the fist in the neck, or with the handle of the lance. Others, returning from their meal, called to him that if he disliked waiting he could hang himself, because there was a vacant hook on the gallows with a ready rope. And amidst such mockery, cries, bursts of laughter and cursing, the afternoon hours passed. The short wintry day gradually drew toward evening, and the drawbridge was still up and the gate remained closed.

But toward evening a wind arose, dispersed the mist, cleared the sky and revealed the sunset glow.

The snow became dark-blue, and then violet. There was no frost, but the night promised to be fair. The walls were again deserted by all but the guard; the rooks and crows departed from the gallows to the forests. Finally the sky darkened and complete silence followed.

"They will not open the gate before nightfall," thought Jurand.

And for a moment he thought to return to the city, but he soon gave up that idea. "They want me to stand here," he said to himself. "If I return, they will certainly not let me go home, but surround and capture me, and then they will say that they owe me nothing, because they took me by force, and if I should ride over them, even then I must return...."

The great endurance of the Polish knights for cold, hunger and hardships, so admired by foreign chroniclers, frequently enabled them to perform deeds which the less hardy people from the west could not undertake. Jurand possessed that endurance to a still greater degree than others; therefore, although hunger had long since began to gripe him, and the evening frost penetrated his fur, which was covered with iron plates, he determined to wait, even if he had to die before this gate.

But suddenly, before it became entirely dark, he heard behind him the sound of footsteps in the snow.

He looked back: there were coming toward him, from the direction of the city, six men, armed with lances and halberds; in their midst walked a seventh man supporting himself on a weapon.

"They will perhaps open the gate for them and then I shall ride in with them," thought Jurand. "They will not try to take me by force, nor kill me, because there are too few; should they attack me, however, it will prove that they do not mean to keep their promise, and then—woe to them!"

Thus thinking, he raised the steel axe hanging at his saddle, so heavy, that its weight was too great for the two hands of an ordinary man, and moved toward them.

But they did not think of attacking him. On the contrary, the servants planted their lances and halberds in the snow, and as the night was not entirely dark yet, Jurand saw that the handles somewhat trembled in their hands.

The seventh, who appeared to be the superior, put out his left arm quickly, and turning his hand upward, said:

"Are you the knight Jurand of Spychow?"

"Yes."

"Do you wish to hear my message?"

"I listen."

"The powerful and religious Count von Danveld ordered me to tell you, lord, that until you dismount, the gate will not be opened for you."

Jurand remained motionless for a while, then he dismounted, the horse being instantly taken away by one of the archers.

"The arms must be surrendered to us," again said the man with the weapon.

The lord of Spychow hesitated. Perhaps they would attack him unarmed, and kill him like a beast; or capture and cast him under ground? But after a moment he thought that if it were to be so, they would have sent more men. But should they throw themselves on him, they would not destroy his armor at once, and then he could wrench a weapon from the nearest and kill them all before assistance could arrive. They knew him well.

"And even if they should wish to shed my blood," he said to himself, "I came for no other purpose than that."

Thus thinking, he threw down first the axe, then the sword, and finally the *misericordia*, and waited. They took everything, and then the man who had addressed him previously, withdrawing several steps, stopped and began to speak in an insolent, loud voice:

"For all the wrongs you have done to the Order, you must, by the count's orders, put on this sack cloth which I leave here, tie around your neck the scabbard of your sword with a rope, and wait humbly at the gate until the count's grace orders it to be opened for you."

And the next moment Jurand remained alone in the darkness and silence. In the snow before him the penitential robe and rope showed black while he stood long, feeling something in his soul dissolving, breaking, agonizing, dying, and that shortly he would be a knight no more, Jurand of Spychow no more, but a beggar, a slave without a name, without fame, without respect.

Therefore, a long time passed before he approached the penitential robe, and said:

"How can I do otherwise? Christ, Thou knowest they will kill the innocent child, if I do not do all they order. And Thou also knowest that I would not do that for the sake of my own life! Disgrace is a distasteful thing!... distasteful!—but Thou also wast disgraced of old. Well then, in the name of the Father and of the Son...."

He then bent down, put on the robe in which were cut the openings for the head and hands, then he tied around his neck the scabbard of his sword, and dragged himself to the gate.

He did not find it open; but now it was immaterial to him whether they opened it sooner or later. The castle sank into nocturnal silence, only the guards called now and then to each other on the bastions. In the tower near the gate there was light in one window high up; the others were dark.

The night hours flew one after another, on the sky appeared the crescent moon and threw light upon the gloomy walls of the castle. It became so quiet that Jurand was able to hear his own heart-beats. But he stiffened and became entirely petrified, as if his soul were taken from him, and took no account of anything. One thought remained with him, that he had ceased to be a knight, Jurand of Spychow, but what he was he did not know....
Sometimes it also seemed to him that in the middle of the night death was coming to him across the snow from those hanged men that he had seen in the morning....

Suddenly he quivered and awoke entirely.

"O gracious Christ! what is that?"

From the high window in the adjacent tower, the sounds of a lute, hardly heard at first, reached his ear. Jurand, while on the way to Szczytno, was sure that Danusia was not in the castle, and yet this sound of the lute at night aroused his heart in an instant. It seemed to him that he knew those sounds, and that nobody else was playing but she—his child! his darling.... He therefore fell upon his knees, clasped his hands to pray, and listened shivering, as in a fever.

Just then a half-childish and as if ardently longing voice began to sing:

"Had I the dear little wings
Of a gosling,
I would fly
To Jasiek at Szlonsk."

Jurand wished to reply, to utter the dear name, but his words were imprisoned in his throat, as if an iron band squeezed them. A sudden wave of pain, tears, longing, suffering, collected in his breast; he therefore cast himself down with his face in the snow and began in ecstasy to call upon heaven in his soul, as if in thankful prayer:

"O Jesus! I hear my child once again! O Jesus!" ...

And weeping began to tear his gigantic body. Above, the longing voice continued to sing amid the undisturbed silence of the night:

"Would that I might sit
In the little Szlonsk garden
To gaze upon little Jasiek
The poor orphan!"

In the morning a stout, bearded German retainer began to prod the ribs of the knight lying at the gate.

"Upon your feet, dog!... The gate is open, and the count orders you to appear before him."

Jurand awoke, as if from sleep. He did not catch the man by the throat, he did not crush him in his iron hands, he had a quiet and almost humble face; he arose, and, without saying a word, followed the soldier through the gate.

He had hardly crossed, when a clang of chains was heard, and the bridge began to be drawn up again, while in the gateway itself fell a heavy iron grating.

END OF PART FOURTH.
PART FIFTH.
CHAPTER I.

Jurand, finding himself in the castleyard, did not know at first where to go, because the servant, who had led him through the gate, had left him and gone toward the stables. It is true, the soldiers stood near the palisades, either singly or in groups, but their faces were so insolent, and their looks so derisive, that the knight could easily guess that they would not show him the way, and even if they were to make a reply to his question, it would be a brutal or an indignant one.

176

Some laughed, pointing at him with their fingers, others commenced to throw snow at him, like yesterday. But he, noticing a door larger than the others, over which was cut out in stone Christ on a cross, turned to it, thinking that if the count and the elders were in another part of the castle or in other rooms, somebody must set him right.

And so it happened. The instant Jurand approached that particular door, both halves of it opened suddenly, and there stood before it a youth with a head shaven like the clericals, but dressed in a worldly dress, who inquired:

"Are you Sir Jurand of Spychow?"

"I am."

"The pious count ordered me to guide you. Follow me."

And he commenced to lead him through a great vaulted vestibule toward a staircase. At the stairs though he halted, and casting a glance at Jurand, again inquired:

"But have you no weapon with you? I was ordered to search you."

Jurand threw up his arms, so that his guide might be able to view his whole figure, and replied:

"Yesterday I gave up everything."

Then the guide lowered his voice and said almost in a whisper:

"Be careful then not to break out into anger, because you are under might and superior force."

"But also under God's will," returned Jurand.

Then he looked more carefully at his guide, and observing in his face something in the nature of mercy and sympathy, said:

"Honesty looks through your eyes, young man! Will you answer sincerely to what I question?"

"Make haste, sir," said the guide.

"Will they return the child to me?"

And the youth raised his brows wonderingly.

"Is your child here?"

"My daughter."

"That lady in the tower near the gate?"

"Yes. They promised to send her away if I surrendered to them."

The guide waved his hand to signify that he knew nothing, but his face expressed trouble and doubt.

Then Jurand further asked:

"Is it true, that Shomberg and Markward are watching her?"

"Those brethren are not in the castle. Take her away though, sir, ere the nobleman Danveld regains his health."

Hearing that, Jurand shivered, but there was no time to ask any more questions, because they had arrived at the hall on the upper floor in which Jurand was to face the chief Shchycienski. The youth, after having opened the door, retreated toward the stairs.

The knight of Spychow entered and found himself in a roomy apartment, very dark, because the lead-framed, oval-shaped panes transmitted very little light; furthermore the day was wintry and cloudy. There was, it is true, a fire burning in a large chimney at the other end of the apartment, but the green logs produced little flame. Only after a time, when Jurand's eyes became used to the darkness, he distinguished a table behind which were knights sitting, and behind them a whole group of armed warriors and servants also armed, among whom the castle fool held a tame bear by a chain.

Jurand had frequently met Danveld some time before, and afterward had seen him twice at the court of the prince of Mazowsze, as delegate, but several years had passed since that time; yet, notwithstanding the darkness, he recognized him instantly, because of his obesity, his face, and finally because he sat in the centre behind the table in an armchair, his hand being circled by wooden splints and resting upon the arm of the chair. To his right sat the old Zygfried von Löve of Insburk, an inexorable foe of the Polish race in general, and particularly of Jurand of Spychow; to his left were the younger brethren, Godfried and Rotgier. Danveld had invited them purposely, to witness his triumph over a threatening foe, and at the same time to enjoy the fruits of the treason which they had plotted together, and in the accomplishment of which they had assisted. They sat now comfortably dressed in soft dark cloth, with light swords at their sides. They were joyous and self-confident, and looking upon Jurand with that pride and extreme contempt which they always bore in their hearts toward the weaker and vanquished.

The silence lasted a long while, because they wished to satiate themselves with the sight of the man whom they had previously dreaded, and who stood before them now with his head bowed upon his breast, and dressed like a penitent in sackcloth, and with a rope around his neck, upon which was suspended the scabbard of his sword.

They also apparently wanted as great a number of people as possible to witness his humiliation, for through a side door, leading into other rooms, whoever pleased entered, and the hall was nearly half filled with armed men. They all looked with extreme eagerness at Jurand, conversing loudly and making remarks about him.

But he gained confidence, at the sight of them, because he thought to himself:

"If Danveld did not wish to keep his promise, he would not have ordered so many witnesses."

Meanwhile Danveld raised his hand, and stopped the conversation; he then made a sign to one of the warriors, who approached Jurand, and catching the rope which encircled his neck, dragged him a few steps nearer the table.

And Danveld looked triumphantly at those present and said:

"Look, how the power of religion defeats anger and pride."

"May God always grant it so!" answered those present.

Then again followed a moment of silence, after which Danveld turned to the prisoner:

"You were biting the faith like a mad dog, therefore God has caused you to stand before us, with a rope around your neck, looking for charity and mercy."

"Do not compare me with a dog, count," replied Jurand, "because you thus lower the honor of those who met me and fell under my hand."

At these words the armed Germans commenced to murmur: it was not known whether the daring answer aroused their anger or whether they were struck by its justice.

But the count, dissatisfied at such a turn of the conversation, said:

"Look, even now he spits into our eyes with arrogance and pride!"

Jurand then raised his hands, like a man who calls heaven to witness, and shaking his head, answered:

"God sees that my arrogance remained outside your gate; God sees and will judge, whether in dishonoring my knighthood, you did not dishonor yourself. There is the honor of a nobleman, which every one who has a belt around him, should respect."

Danveld wrinkled his brows, but at that moment the castle fool started to rattle the chain to which he had fastened the bear, and called out:

"Sermon! sermon! the preacher from Mazowsze has arrived! Listen! to the sermon!"

Then turning to Danveld, he said:

"Sir! Duke Rosenheim ordered his sexton to eat the bell-rope from knot to knot whenever the latter awakened him too early for the sermon. This preacher has also a rope around his neck—make him also eat it up before he finishes his sermon."

And, having said this, he gazed at the count in some alarm, being uncertain whether the count would laugh or whether his inappropriate remark would result in an order for a flogging for him. But the religious brethren, gentle, well-behaved, and even humble, whenever they felt they were not in power, did not know any limits before the defeated; therefore, Danveld not only nodded his head at the bear-leader as a sign that he permitted the mockery, but he himself burst out with such unheard-of roughness that the faces of the younger warriors expressed astonishment.

"Don't complain that you were put to shame," he said, "because even if I had made you a dogcatcher, a religious dogcatcher is better than you, knight!"

And the encouraged fool commenced to shout: "Bring the currycomb, comb the bear, and he in turn will comb your shags with his paws."

At that, laughter was heard here and there, and a voice exclaimed from behind the religious brethren:

"You will cut reeds on the lake in the summer!"

"And catch crabs with your carcass!" exclaimed another.

A third added: "And now begin to drive away the crows from the hanging thief! There will always be plenty of work for you."

Thus they made fun of the once terrible Jurand. The assembly gradually became joyous. Some, leaving the table, began to approach the prisoner and look at him closely, saying:

"This is the wild boar of Spychow, whose tusks our count has knocked out; his snout is surely foaming; he would gladly tear somebody, but he cannot!"

Danveld and others of the religious brethren, who at first had wished to give the hearing the solemn appearance of a court, seeing that the affair had turned out differently, also arose from their benches and mingled with those who approached Jurand.

The old Zygfried of Insburk was dissatisfied at that, but the count himself said:

"Be cheerful, there will be a greater joy yet!"

And they also commenced to look at Jurand, for this was a rare opportunity, because when any of the knights or servants had seen him before from so near, they had usually closed their eyes forever. Some of them also remarked:

"He is broad shouldered, although he has a fur beneath his sack; he could be wrapped up with pease straw, and exhibited in country fairs."

Others again commenced to ask for beer in order to make the day a still pleasanter one.

And so in a few moments flowing pitchers began to clink and the dark hall became covered with the foam escaping from under the covers. The good-humored count said:

"That is just right, let him not think that his disgrace is of great importance!"

So they again approached him, and touching his chin with their pewters, said:

"You would like to drink, Mazovian snout!" and others, pouring the beer into their palms, cast it into his eyes, while he stood among them stunned and abused, until at last he moved toward the old Zygfried, and apparently feeling that he could not stand it any longer, he began to cry so loudly as to deafen the noise in the hall:

"By the torture of the Saviour and the salvation of the soul, restore to me my child, as you promised!"

And he attempted to seize the right hand of the old count who quickly withdrew and said:

"Avaunt, prisoner! what dost thou want?"

"I released Bergow from prison, and came myself, because in return you promised to restore my child who is here."

"Who promised you that?" inquired Danveld.

"By the soul and faith, you, count!"

"You will not find any witnesses, but they amount to nothing, if honor and word are in question."

"Upon your honor, upon that of the Order," exclaimed Jurand.

"Then your daughter will be returned to you!" replied Danveld, and, turning to the others, remarked: "All that has happened to him here is an innocent trifle in comparison with his violence and crimes. But since we promised to return his daughter if he should appear and submit himself to us, then know, that the word of a Knight of the Cross is, like God's word, irreproachable, and that that girl, whom we saved from the hands of robbers, shall now be given her liberty, and after an exemplary penance for his sins against the Order, he also shall be allowed to go back to his home."

Such a speech astounded some, because, knowing Danveld and his old hatred for Jurand, they did not expect such honesty from him. Therefore old Zygfried, together with Rotgier and Brother Godfried, looked at him, raising and wrinkling their brows with astonishment, but he pretended not to observe their inquiring looks and said:

"I'll send your daughter back under guard, but you must remain here until our guard returns safely and until you have paid your ransom."

179

Jurand himself was somewhat astonished, because he had ceased to hope that his sacrifice would be of any use to Danusia; he therefore looked at Danveld, almost with thankfulness and replied:

"May God reward you, count!"

"Recognize the Knights of the Cross," said Danveld.

"All mercy from Him!" replied Jurand; "but, since it is long since I saw my child, permit me to see and bless my girl."

"Bah, and not otherwise than before all of us, so that there may be witnesses of our good faith and mercy."

Then he ordered the warriors standing near to bring Danusia, while he himself approached von Löve, Rotgier and Godfried, who surrounded him and commenced a quick and animated conversation.

"I do not oppose you, although this was not your object," said old Zygfried.

And the hot Rotgier, famous for his courage and cruelties, said: "How is this? not only the girl but also that devilish dog is going to be liberated, that he may bite again?"

"He will bite not that way only!" exclaimed Godfried.

"Bah! he will pay ransom!" lazily replied Danveld.

"Even if he should return everything, in a year he will have robbed twice as much."

"I shall not object as to the girl," repeated Zygfried; "but this wolf will yet make the sheep of the Order weep more than once."

"And our word?" queried Danveld, laughingly.

"You spoke differently...."

Danveld shrugged his shoulders. "Did you not have enough pleasure?" he inquired. "Do you wish more?"

Others surrounded Jurand again and commenced to brag before him, praising the upright conduct of Danveld, and the impression it made upon the members of the Order.

"And what bone breaker!" said the captain of the castle-archers. "Your heathen brethren would not have treated our Christian knights so!"

"You drank our blood?"

"And we give you bread for stones."

But Jurand paid no attention either to the pride or to the contempt which their words contained: his heart swelled and his eyelashes were moist. He thought that he would see Danusia in a moment, and that he would see her actually by their favor; he therefore gazed at the speakers almost with humility, and finally said:

"True! true! I used to be hard on you but ... not treacherous."

That instant a voice at the other end of the hall suddenly cried: "They are bringing the girl;" and immediately silence reigned throughout the hall. The soldiers scattered to both sides, because none of them had ever seen Jurand's daughter, and the majority of them did not even know of her presence in the castle on account of the secrecy with which Danveld surrounded his actions; but those who knew, whispered to one another about her admirable grace. All eyes turned with extreme curiosity toward the door through which she was to appear.

Meanwhile a warrior appeared in front followed by the well-known servant of the Order, the same woman that rode to the court in the forest. After her entered a girl dressed in white, with loose hair tied with a ribbon on the forehead.

And suddenly one great outburst of laughter, like the roaring of thunder, rang through the entire hall. Jurand, who at the first moment had sprung toward his daughter, suddenly recoiled and stood as pale as linen, looking with surprise at the ill-shaped head, the bluish lips, and the expressionless eyes of the wench who was restored to him as Danusia.

"This is not my daughter!" he said, in a terrifying voice.

"Not your daughter?" exclaimed Danveld. "By the holy Liboryusz of Paderborn! Then either we did not rescue your daughter from the murderers or some wizard has changed her, because there is no other in Szczytno."

180

Old Zygfried, Rotgier and Godfried exchanged quick glances with each other, full of admiration at the shrewdness of Danveld, but none of them had time enough to speak, because Jurand began to shout with a terrible voice:

"She is, she is in Szczytno! I heard her sing, I heard the voice of dear Danusia!"

Upon that Danveld turned to those assembled and said quietly but pointedly:

"I take you all present as witnesses and especially you, Zygfried of Insburk, and you pious brothers, Rotgier and Godfried, that, according to my word and given promise, I restore that girl, who was said by the robbers whom we defeated, to be the daughter of Jurand of Spychow. If she is not—it is not our fault, but rather the will of our Lord, who in that manner wished to deliver Jurand into our hands."

Zygfried and the two younger brethren bowed to signify that they heard and would testify in case of necessity. Then again they glanced quickly at each other, because it was more than they ever could have expected to capture Jurand, not to restore his daughter, and still ostensibly to keep a promise; who else could do that?

But Jurand threw himself upon his knees and commenced to conjure Danveld by all the relics in Malborg, then by the ashes and heads of his parents, to restore to him his true child and not proceed like a swindler and traitor, breaking oaths and promises. His voice contained so much despair and truth, that some began to suspect treason; others again thought that some wizard had actually changed the appearance of the girl.

"God looks upon your treason!" exclaimed Jurand. "By the Saviour's wounds, by the hour of your death, return my child!"

And arising, he went bent double toward Danveld, as if he wished to embrace his knees; and his eyes glittered with madness, and his voice broke alternately with pain, fear, and dread. Danveld, hearing the accusations of treason and deceit in presence of all, commenced to snort, and at length his features worked with rage; so that like a flame in his desire utterly to crush the unfortunate, he advanced and bending down to his ear, whispered through his set teeth: "If I ever give her up, it will be with my bastard...."

But at that very moment Jurand roared like a bull, and with both hands he caught Danveld and raised him high in the air.

The hall still resounded with the terrible cry: "Save me!" when the body of the count struck the stone floor with such terrible force that the brains from the shattered skull bespattered Zygfried and Rotgier who stood by. Jurand sprang to the wall, near which stood the arms, and snatching a large two-handed weapon, ran like a storm at the Germans, who were petrified with terror. The people were used to battles, butchery and blood, and yet their hearts sank to such an extent that even after the panic had passed, they commenced to retreat and escape like a flock of sheep before a wolf who kills with one stroke of his claws. The hall resounded with the cry of terror, with the sound of human footsteps, the clang of the overturned vessels, the howling of the servants, the growling of the bear, who, tearing himself out of the hands of the trainer, started to climb on a high window, and a terror-stricken cry for arms and targets, weapons and crossbows. Finally weapons gleamed, and a number of sharp points were directed toward Jurand, but he, not caring for anything, half crazed, sprang toward them, and there commenced an unheard-of wild fight, resembling a butchery more than a contest of arms. The young and fiery Brother Godfried was the first to intercept Jurand's way, but he severed his head, hand and shoulder-blade with a lightning swing of his weapon; after him fell by Jurand's hand the captain of the archers, and the castle administrator, von Bracht and the Englishman Hugues, who, although he did not very well understand the cause, pitied Jurand and his sufferings, and only drew his weapon when Danveld was killed. Others, seeing the terrible force and the fury of the man, gathered closely together, so as to offer combined resistance, but this plan brought about a still greater defeat, because he, with his hair standing upright on his head, with maddened eyes, covered all over with blood, panting, raging and furious, broke, tore and cut with terrible strokes of his sword that battered group, casting men to the floor, splashed all over with clotted blood, as a storm overturns bushes and trees. Then followed a moment of terrific fright, in which it seemed that this terrible Mazovian, all by himself, would hew and slay all these people. Like a pack of barking hounds that cannot overpower a fierce boar without the assistance of the hunters, so were those armed Germans; they could not match his might and fierceness in that fight which resulted only in their death and discomfiture.

"Scatter! surround him! strike from behind!" shrieked old Zygfried von Löve.

They consequently dispersed through the hall like a flock of starlings in the field upon which a hawk with crooked beak swoops from a height, but they could not surround him, because, in the heat of the fight, instead of looking for a place of defence, he commenced to chase them around the walls and whoever was overtaken died as if thunderstruck. Humiliation, despair, disappointed hope, changed into one thirst for blood, seemed to multiply tenfold his terrific natural strength. A weapon, for which the most powerful of the Knights of the Cross needed both hands, he managed to wield with one as if it were a feather. He did not care for his life, nor look for escape; he did not even crave for victory; he sought revenge, and like a fire, or like a river, which breaking a dam, blindly destroys everything obstructing its flow, so he, a terrible, blindfolded destroyer, tore, broke, trampled, killed and extinguished human beings. They could not hurt him in his back, because, in the beginning they were unable to overtake him; moreover the common soldiers feared to come near him even from behind; they knew that if he happened to turn no human power could save them from death. Others were simply terror-stricken at the thought, that an ordinary man could cause so much havoc, and that they were dealing with a man who was aided by some superhuman power.

But old Zygfried, and with him Brother Rotgier, rushed to the gallery which extended above the large windows of the hall, and commenced to call others to take shelter after them; these did so in haste, so that, on the narrow stairs, they pushed each other in their desire to get up as quickly as possible and thence to strike the strong knight, with whom any hand to hand struggle appeared to them impossible.

Finally, the last one banged the door leading to the gallery and Jurand remained alone below. From the gallery the sounds of joy and triumph reached him, and soon heavy oak benches and iron collars of torches began to fall upon the nobleman. One of the missiles struck him on the forehead and bathed his face with blood. At the same time the large entrance door opened, and through the upper windows the summoned servants rushed into the hall in a body, armed with pikes, halberds, axes, crossbows, palisades, poles, ropes and all varieties of weapons, which they could hurriedly get hold of. And with his left hand the mad Jurand wiped the blood from his face, so as not to obstruct his sight, gathered himself together, and threw himself at the entire throng. In the hall again resounded groans, the clash of iron, the gnashing of teeth and the piercing voices of the slain men.

In the same hall, behind the table that evening, sat old Zygfried von Löve, who, after the bailiff Danveld, temporarily took command of Szczytno, and near him were Brother Rotgier, and the knight von Bergow, a former prisoner of Jurand's and two noble youths, novices, who were soon to be put on white mantles. The wintry storm was howling outside the windows, shaking the leaden window-frames; the torchlights, which were burning in iron frames, wavered, and now and then the wind drove clouds of smoke from the chimney into the hall. Silence reigned among the brethren, although they were assembled for a consultation, because they were waiting for the word from Zygfried, who, again resting his elbows on the table and running his hands over his grey and bowed head, sat gloomy with his face in the shadow and with sullen thoughts in his soul.

"About what are we to deliberate?" finally asked Brother Rotgier.

Zygfried raised his head, looked at the speaker, and, awakening from thought, said:

"About the defeat, about what the master and the assembly will say, and about this, that our actions may not cause any loss to the Order." He was silent again, but after a while he looked around and moved his nostrils: "There is still a smell of blood here."

"No, count," replied Rotgier; "I ordered the floor to be scrubbed and the place to be fumigated with sulphur. It is the odor of sulphur."

And Zygfried looked at those present with a strange glance, and said:

"God have mercy upon the soul of our brothers Danveld and Godfried!"

They again understood that he implored God's mercy upon their souls, because, at the mention of sulphur, he thought of hell; therefore a chill ran through their bones and all

182

at once replied: "Amen! amen! amen!" After a moment the howling of the wind and the rattling of the window-frames were heard again.

"Where are the bodies of the count and Brother Godfried?" inquired the old man.

"In the chapel: the priests are chanting the litany over them."

"Are they already in coffins?"

"In coffins, only the count's head is covered, because his skull and face are crushed."

"Where are the other corpses, and where are the wounded?"

"The corpses are in the snow so as to stiffen whilst the coffins are being made, and the wounded are being attended to in the hospital."

Zygfried again ran his hands over his head.

"And one man did that!... God, have the Order under Thy care, when it comes to a great war with this wolfish race!"

Upon that Rotgier turned up his eyes, as if recollecting something, and said: "I heard in Wilno, how the bailiff of Samboz spoke to his brother the master: 'If you do not make a great war and get rid of them, so that even their name shall not remain, then woe to us and our nation.'"

"May God give such a war and a meeting with them!" said one of the noble novices.

Zygfried looked at him for some time, as if he wanted to say: "You could have met one of them to-day," but seeing the small and youthful figure of the novice, and perhaps remembering that he himself, although famous for his courage, did not care to expose himself to a sure destruction, refrained and inquired:

"Who saw Jurand?"

"I," replied von Bergow.

"Is he alive?"

"Yes, he lies in the same net in which we entrapped him. When he awoke the servants wanted to kill him, but the chaplain would not allow it."

"He cannot be executed. He is too great a man among his people, and there would be a terrible clamor," replied Zygfried. "It will be also impossible to hide what has happened, because there were too many witnesses."

"What then are we to say and do?" inquired Rotgier.

Zygfried meditated, and finally said:

"You, noble Count von Bergow go to Malborg to the master. You were groaning in Jurand's slavery, and are now a guest of the Order; therefore as such, and because you need not necessarily speak in favor of the monks, they will rather believe you. Tell, then, what you saw, that Danveld, having recovered from a band of rogues a certain girl and thinking her to be Jurand's daughter, informed the latter, who also came to Szczytno, and what happened further you know yourself."

"Pardon me, pious count," said von Bergow. "I suffered great hardships as a slave in Spychow, and as your guest, I would gladly testify for you; but tell me, for the sake of quieting my soul, whether there was not a real daughter of Jurand's in Szczytno, and whether it was not Danveld's treason that drove her father to madness?"

Zygfried von Löve hesitated for a moment with his answer; in his nature lay deep hatred toward the Polish nation, and barbarity in which he exceeded even Danveld, and rapacity, and, when the Order was in question, pride and avarice, but there was no falsehood. It was the greatest bitterness and grief of his life, that lately, through insubordination and riot, the affairs of the Order had turned in such a manner that falsehood had become one of the most general and unavoidable factors of the life of the Order. Therefore von Bergow's inquiry touched the most painful string of his soul, and, after a long silence, he said:

"Danveld stands before God, and God will judge him, while you, duke, should they ask you for conjectures, answer what you please; should they again ask you about what you saw, then say that before we coiled a wild man in a net you saw nine corpses, besides the wounded, on this floor, and among them the bodies of Danveld, Brother Godfried, von Bracht and Hugues, and two noble youths.... God, give them eternal peace. Amen!"

"Amen! Amen!" again repeated the novices.

"And say also," added Zygfried, "that although Danveld wished to subdue the foe of the Order, yet nobody here raised the first weapon against Jurand."

"I shall say only what my eyes saw," replied von Bergow.

"Be in the chapel before midnight; we shall also go there to pray for the souls of the dead," answered Zygfried.

He then extended his hand to him as a sign of gratitude and farewell; he wished to remain for a further consultation alone with Brother Rotgier, whom he loved and had great confidence in. After the withdrawal of von Bergow, he also dismissed the two novices, under the pretence that they might watch the work of the coffins for the common servants killed by Jurand, and after the doors had closed behind them he turned with animation to Rotgier, and said:

"Listen to what I am going to say: there is only one remedy: that no living soul should ever find out that the real daughter of Jurand was with us."

"It will not be difficult," replied Rotgier, "because nobody knew that she was here except Danveld, Godfried, we two, and those servants of the Order who watched her. Danveld ordered the people who brought her here to be made intoxicated and hanged. There were some among the garrison who suspected something, but that affair confused them, and they do not know now themselves whether an error happened on our part, or whether some wizard really exchanged Jurand's daughter."

"This is good," said Zygfried.

"I have been thinking again, noble count, whether, since Danveld lives no longer, we should not cast all the guilt upon him...."

"And so admit before the whole world that we, in a time of peace and concord with the prince of Mazowsze, ravished from his court the pupil of the princess and her beloved courtlady? No, for God's sake! this cannot be!... We were seen at the court together with Danveld; and the grand master, his relative, knows that we always undertook everything together.... If we accuse Danveld, he may desire to avenge his memory...."

"Let us consult on that," said Rotgier. "Let us consult and find good advice, because otherwise woe to us! If we return Jurand's daughter, then she will say herself that we did not capture her from robbers, but that the people who caught her carried her directly to Szczytno."

"That is so."

"And God is witness that I do not care for the responsibility alone. The prince will complain to the Polish king, and their delegates will not fail to clamor at all courts against our outrages, our treason, and our crime. God alone knows how much loss the Order may suffer from it. The master himself, if he knew the truth, ought to order that girl to be hidden."

"And even if so, when that girl is lost, will they not accuse us?" inquired Rotgier.

"No! Brother Danveld was a shrewd man. Do you remember, that he imposed the condition on Jurand, that he should not only appear in Szczytno personally, but also previously proclaim and write to the prince, that he is going to ransom his daughter from the robbers, and that he knows that she is not with us."

"True! but in that case how shall we justify what happened in Szczytno?"

"We shall say that knowing that Jurand was looking for his child, and having captured some girl from the robbers and not being able to tell who she was, we informed Jurand, thinking that this might possibly be his daughter; on his arrival he fell into a fit at the sight of her, and, being possessed with the devil, shed so much innocent blood that more than one battle does not cost so much."

"That is true," replied Rotgier, "wisdom and the experience of age speak through you. The bad deeds of Danveld, even if we should throw the guilt on him, would always go to the account of the Order, therefore, to the account of all of us, the assembly and the master himself; so again our innocence will become apparent, and all will fall upon Jurand, the iniquity of the Poles and their connection with infernal powers...."

"And then whoever wishes may judge us; the Pope, or the Roman Emperor!"

"Yes!" Then followed a moment of silence, after which Brother Rotgier questioned:

"What shall we do then with Jurand's daughter?"

"Let us consult."

"Give her to me."

And Zygfried looked at him and replied:

"No I Listen, young brother! When the Order is in question, do not trust a man, woman nor even your own self. Danveld was reached by God's hand, because he not only wished to revenge the wrongs of the Order, but also to satisfy his own desires."

"You misjudge me!" said Rotgier.

"Do not trust yourself," interrupted Zygfried, "because your body and soul will become effeminate, and the knee of that hard race will some day bear heavily upon your breast, so that you will not be able to arise any more." And he the third time rested his gloomy head on his hand, but he apparently conversed with his own conscience only, and thought of himself only, because he said after a while:

"Much human blood, much pain, many tears weigh heavily on me also … moreover I did not hesitate to seek other means, when the Order was in question, and when I saw I should not succeed by mere force; but when I stand before the Almighty, I shall tell Him: 'I did that for the Order, and for myself—what I chose.'"

And having said this, he put his hands to his breast and opened a dark cloth garment, beneath which appealed a sackcloth. He then pressed his temples with his hands, raised his head and eyes, and exclaimed:

"Give up pleasures and profligacy, harden your bodies and hearts, because even now I see the whiteness of the eagle's feathers in the air and its claws reddened with Teutonic blood!…"

Further speech was interrupted by such a terrible knock of the gate that one window above the gallery opened with a crash, and the entire hall was filled with a howling and whistling of the storm and with snowflakes.

"In the name of God, His Son and the Holy Ghost! this is a bad night," remarked the old Teuton.

"A night of unclean powers," answered Rotgier.

"Are there priests with Danveld's body?"

"Yes…. He departed without absolution…. God have mercy upon him!"

And both ceased speaking. Rotgier presently called some boys, and ordered them to shut the window and light the torches, and after they had gone away, he again inquired:

"What will you do with Jurand's daughter? Will you take her away from here to Insburk?"

"I shall take her to Insburk and do with her what the good of the Order demands."

"What am I to do then?"

"Have you courage in your heart?"

"What have I done to make you doubt it?"

"I doubt not because I know you and love you as my own son for your courage. Go then to the court of the prince of Mazowsze and narrate everything that has happened here, according to our arrangement."

"Can I expose myself to certain destruction?"

"You ought, if your destruction will bring glory to the Cross and Order. But no! Destruction does not await you. They do no harm to a guest: unless somebody should challenge you, as that young knight did who challenged us all … he, or somebody else, but that is not terrible…."

"May God grant it! they can seize me though and cast me under ground."

"They will not do that. Remember that there is Jurand's letter to the prince, and besides that you will go to accuse Jurand. Narrate faithfully what he did in Szczytno, and they must believe you…. We were even the first to inform him that there was a certain girl; we were the first to invite him to come to see her, and he came, went mad, killed the count and slew our people. Thus you will speak, and what can they say to you? Danveld's death will certainly resound throughout the whole Mazowsze. On that account they will fail to bring charges. They will actually look for Jurand's daughter, but, since Jurand himself wrote that she is not here, no suspicion will fall upon us. It is necessary to face them boldly and close their mouths, because they will also think that if we were guilty, none of us would dare to go there."

"True! I will set out on the journey immediately after Danveld's funeral."

"May God bless you, my dear son! If you do all properly, they not only will not detain you, but they will have to disavow Jurand, so that we may not be able to say: 'Look how they treat us!'"

"And so we must sue at all courts."

"The grand master will attend to that for the benefit of the Order, besides being Danveld's relative."

"But if that devil of Spychow should survive and regain his liberty!…"

A dark look came into Zygfried's eyes and he replied slowly and emphatically:

"Even if he should regain his liberty, he will never utter a word of accusation against the Order."

He then commenced again to instruct Rotgier, what to say and demand at the court in Mazowsze.

CHAPTER II.

The rumor of the occurrence in Szczytno arrived in Warsaw however before Brother Rotgier, and there excited amazement and concern. Neither the king himself, nor anybody else at the court, could understand what had happened. Shortly before, just when Mikolaj of Dlugolas was starting for Malborg with the prince's letter, in which he bitterly complained of the capture of Danusia by turbulent border counts and almost threateningly demanded her instant restoration, a letter had arrived from the owner of Spychow stating that his daughter was not captured by the Teutons, but by ordinary border bandits, and that she would be soon released for a ransom. On that account the messenger did not leave; nobody ever dreamed of the Teutons extorting such a letter from Jurand by the threat of his daughter's death. It was difficult to understand what had happened, because the border chiefs, who were subjects of the prince as well as of the Order, attacked one another in the summer, but not in the winter when the snows betrayed their trail. They also usually attacked merchants, or perpetrated robberies in the villages, capturing people and seizing their herds, but to dare to attack the prince himself and to capture his protégée, who was at the same time the daughter of a powerful and universally feared knight, this seemed entirely to exceed human belief. This, as well as other doubts, was answered by Jurand's letter under his own seal, brought this time by a man who was known to come from Spychow; under such circumstances all suspicions became impossible; the prince only became more enraged than he had ever been before, and he ordered a pursuit of the ravishers throughout the border of his principality, at the same time ordering the prince of Plock to do the same and not fail to punish the insolent fellows.

Just then arrived the news of what had happened at Szczytno.

And as it passed from mouth to mouth, it was multiplied tenfold. It was said that Jurand, having arrived all alone in the castle, ran in through the open gate and there committed such slaughter that the garrison was so terrified that it had to send for help to the neighboring castles, to summon the superior knighthood and armed foot-soldiers, who only after a two days' siege succeeded in reentering the castle and there slaying Jurand as well as his associates. It was also said that those forces would probably cross the border, and that a great war would undoubtedly begin. The prince, who knew of how great consequence it was to the grand master in case of war with the Polish king for the powers of both principalities of Mazowsze to remain neutral, did not believe these stories, because it was no secret to him, that should the Teutons declare war on him or the principality of Plock, no human power could keep the Poles back; the master therefore dreaded that war. He knew that it must come, but he wished to postpone it, firstly, because he was of a peaceful disposition, and secondly, because, in order to meet Jagiello's power, it was necessary to gather a strength which the Order until now had never yet possessed, and at the same time to secure the assistance of the princes and knighthood, not only in Germany, but also in the entire West.

The prince, therefore, did not fear the war, but he wished to know what had happened, what he really was to think of the occurrence in Szczytno, of the disappearance of Danusia, and all those stories which arrived from the border; he was also glad, although he hated the Teutons, when on a certain evening the captain of the archers informed him that a knight of the Order had arrived and begged for an audience.

He received him proudly, nevertheless, and although he recognized him instantly as one of the brethren who were in the Forest Court, he pretended not to recollect him and inquired who he was, whence he came, and what caused his arrival in Warsaw.

"I am Brother Rotgier," replied the Teuton, "and a short time ago I had the honor to bow before your Highness."

"Why then, being a brother, do you not wear the insignia of the Order?"

The knight commenced to explain that he did not wear a white cloak, because by so doing he would be undoubtedly captured or killed by the knighthood of Mazowsze: throughout the whole world, in all kingdoms and principalities, the sign of the cross on the cloak is a protection and gains human good-will and hospitality, and only in the principality of Mazowsze does the cross expose the man who wears it to certain death.

But the prince interrupted him angrily:

"Not the cross," he said, "because we also kiss it, but your vices and if they receive you better elsewhere it is, because they do not know you so well."

Then, seeing that the knight was greatly troubled at these words, he inquired: "Were you in Szczytno, do you know what happened there?"

"I was in Szczytno and know what happened there," replied Rotgier, "and I came here not as any one's messenger, but only because the experienced and pious count of Insburk told me: 'Our master loves the pious prince and trusts in his justice, therefore while I hasten to Malborg, you go to Mazowsze and state our grievance, our disgrace, our misery. The just lord will surely not praise a violator of peace and a cruel aggressor, who has shed so much Christian blood, as though he were not Christ's servant but Satan's.'" And then he commenced to narrate everything that had occurred in Szczytno: How Jurand, who had been summoned by them to see whether the girl whom they had taken away from the robbers was not his daughter, instead of repaying that with thankfulness, had fallen into a fit; how he had killed Danveld, Brother Godfried, the Englishmen Hugues, von Bracht and two noble warriors, not counting the servants; how they, remembering God's commandment and not wishing to kill, had finally been compelled to coil the terrible man in a net, who had then turned his sword against himself and wounded himself terribly; how lastly, not only in the castle but also in the tower, there were people, who, in the midst of a wintry gale during the night after the fight, had heard terrible laughter and voices in the air calling: "Our Jurand! Wrongdoer of the cross! Shedder of innocent blood! Our Jurand!"

And the whole story, especially the last words of the Teuton, made a great impression upon all present. Terror fell upon them all. They were simply overwhelmed with fear lest Jurand had actually summoned unclean powers to his assistance, and deep silence followed. But the princess, who was present at the audience, and who, loving Danusia, had a heart full of inconsolable sorrow for her, turned with an unexpected question to Rotgier: "You say, knight," she remarked, "that, after capturing the girl, you thought her to be Jurand's daughter, and therefore summoned him to Szczytno?"

"Yes, beloved lady," replied Rotgier.

"How could you have thought so, since you saw the real daughter of Jurand with me in the Forest Court?"

At that Brother Rotgier became embarrassed, because he was not prepared for such a question. The prince arose and fixed a severe look on the Teuton, while Mikolaj of Dlugolas, Mrokota of Mocarzew, Jasko of Jagielnica and other knights of Mazowsze instantly sprang toward the brother, inquiring alternately with threatening voices:

"How could you have thought so? Speak, German I How could that be?"

And Brother Rotgier recovered himself and said: "We brethren do not raise our eyes to women. In the Forest Court with the beloved princess there were many court ladies, but which among them was Jurand's daughter, none of us knew."

"Danveld knew," said Mikolaj of Dlugolas. "He even talked to her during the hunt."

"Danveld stands before God," replied Rotgier, "and of him I shall only say that the following morning blooming roses were found on his coffin, which, in this wintry weather, could not come there by human hands."

187

Then again followed silence.

"How did you know of the capture of Jurand's daughter?" inquired the prince.

"Only the wickedness and audacity of the deed made it known to us. Therefore on hearing about it, we ordered thanksgiving masses because only a plain court lady, and not one of the children born of your Highness, was captured from the Forest Court."

"But I still wonder, how you could mistake a wench for Jurand's daughter."

"Danveld said: 'Often Satan betrayed his servants, so perhaps he changed Jurand's daughter.'"

"The robbers though, as vulgar men, could not counterfeit Kaleb's writing and Jurand's seal. Who could have done it?"

"The Evil Spirit."

And again nobody could find an answer.

Rotgier glanced searchingly into the prince's eyes and said: "Indeed, these questions are like weapons in my breast, because they contain doubt and suspicion. But I trust in God's justice and the power of truth. I ask of your majesty: even Jurand himself suspected us of that action, and when suspecting, before we summoned him to Szczytno, why did he search for robbers through the whole border in order to buy his daughter back from them?"

"It is true!" said the prince. "Even if you were hiding something from men, you cannot hide it from God. He suspected you in the first moment but then … then he thought differently."

"Behold how the brightness of truth conquers the darkness," said Rotgier, and he glanced triumphantly around the hall; he thought that Teutonic heads had more adroitness and sense than the Polish, and that the latter race would always be the prey and food of the Order, as a fly is the prey and food of the spider.

Therefore, throwing off his previous disguise, he approached the prince and commenced to speak in loud and impetuous tones:

"Requite us, lord, our losses, our grievances, our tears, and our blood! That hellhound was your subject; therefore, in the name of God from whom the power of kings and princes is derived, in the name of justice and the cross, requite us for our grievances and blood!"

But the prince looked at him in astonishment.

"For God's sake!" he said, "what do you want? if Jurand shed your blood in madness, am I to answer for his frenzy?"

"He was your subject, lord," said the Teuton, "in your principality lie his possessions, his villages and his castle, in which he imprisoned the servants of the Order; at least let these possessions, this domain and that wicked castle, become henceforth the property of the Order. Truly this will not be an adequate payment for the noble blood shed! truly it will not revive the dead, but perhaps it will partly appease God's anger and wipe away the disgrace, which will otherwise fall upon this entire principality. O, lord! The Order possesses grounds and castles everywhere, which were given to it by the favor and piety of the Christian princes, and only here in your territory have we no particle of land. Let our grievance, which calls to God for vengeance, be at least so rewarded that we may say that here also live people, who have the fear of God in their hearts!" Hearing this, the prince was still more amazed, and then, after a long silence, replied:

"For God's sake! And through whose clemency, if not through that of my ancestors, does your Order even exist here? The lands, estates and towers, which once upon a time belonged to us and our nation, and which now are your property, do these not suffice for you yet? Jurand's girl is yet alive because nobody has informed you of her death, while you already want to seize the orphan's dower, and requite your grievances with an orphan's bread?"

"Lord, you admit the wrong," said Rotgier, "consequently right it according to what your princely conscience and your honest soul dictates." And he was again glad in his heart, because he thought: "Now, they not only will not sue but they will even consider how to wash their hands and to evade the whole matter. Nobody will blame us for anything, and our fame will be as spotless as the white cloak of the Order."

188

Just then the voice of old Mikolaj of Dlugolas was heard: "They suspect you of being avaricious and God knows whether justly or no, because even in this matter, you care more for the profits than the honor of the Order."

"True!" cried the Mazovian knights in chorus. Then the Teuton advanced a few steps, proudly raised his head, and measuring them with a haughty look, said:

"I do not come here as a messenger, but merely as a witness of the affair and a knight of the Order who is ready to defend the honor of the Order with his own blood to the last gasp! Who, then, in contradiction to Jurand's own words, dares to suspect the Order of having captured his daughter—let him raise this knightly pledge and submit to God's judgment!"

Having said this, he cast before them his knightly glove, which fell upon the floor; they again stood in deep silence, because, although more than one of them would have liked to break his weapon on the Teuton's back, they all feared God's judgment. Every one knew that Jurand had expressly stated that the knights of the Order had not captured his child; so they all thought to themselves, "It is a just cause; consequently Rotgier will be victorious."

He again became so much the more insolent, and leaning upon his loins, inquired:

"If it is so, who will raise that glove?"

Just then, a knight, whose entrance nobody had yet observed, and who for some time had listened at the door to the conversation, advanced to the centre, raised the gauntlet and said:

"I will!" and so saying, he stared directly into Rotgier's face, and then began to speak with a voice which in that universal silence resounded like thunder through the hall:

"Before God, before the august prince and all the honorable knighthood of this land, I tell you, Teuton, that you bark like a dog against justice and truth—and I challenge you to a combat on foot, or horseback, with lance or axe, short or long weapons, and not unto imprisonment but unto the last gasp, unto death!"

A fly could be heard in the hall. All eyes were turned upon Rotgier and the challenging knight, whom nobody recognized, because he had a helmet covering his head, although without a steel cap, but with a circular visor descending below the ear entirely covering the upper part of the face, and casting a deep shadow over the lower part. The Teuton was no less astonished than the rest. Confusion, pallor and raging anger chased each other over his face, as lightning flashes across a mighty heaven.

He caught the gauntlet and attached it to the hook of his armlet, and said:

"Who are you that challenge God's justice?"

The other then unbuckled his gorget, removed the helmet, beneath which appeared a fair, youthful head, and said:

"Zbyszko of Bogdaniec, the husband of Jurand's daughter."

They were all amazed, and Rotgier, with the others, because none of them, except the prince and his wife, Father Wyszoniek and de Lorche, knew of Danusia's marriage; the Teutons moreover were confident that Jurand's daughter had no other natural defender besides her father; but at that moment de Lorche stood up and said:

"Upon my knightly honor I vouch for the truthfulness of his words; should anybody dare to doubt it, here is my guage."

Rotgier, who did not know what fear meant, and whose heart swelled with anger at this moment, would have perhaps accepted even this challenge, but remembering that the man who cast it was powerful, and moreover a relative of Duke Geldryi, he refrained, and the more readily, because the prince himself arose and, wrinkling his brows, said:

"It is forbidden to accept this challenge, because I also declare that this knight has told the truth."

The Teuton, on hearing this, bowed, and then said to Zbyszko:

"If you wish it, then on foot, in closed lists with axes."

"I have already challenged you in all ways," replied Zbyszko.

"May God give the victory to justice!" exclaimed the Mazovian knights.

CHAPTER III.

There was anxiety about Zbyszko in the whole court, among the knights as well as among the ladies, because he was universally liked; but, according to Jurand's letter, nobody doubted that the right was on the side of the Teuton. On the other hand it was known that Rotgier was one of the more famous brethren of the Order. The squire van Krist narrated among the Mazovian nobility, perhaps on purpose, that his lord before becoming an armed monk, once sat at the Honor-Table of the Teutons, to which table only world-famous knights were admitted, those who had accomplished an expedition to the Holy Land, or fought victoriously against giants, dragons, or mighty magicians. Hearing van Krist tell such tales, and, at the same time, boast that his lord had repeatedly met five opponents single-handed with his "dagger of mercy" in one hand and an axe or sword in the other, the Mazurs were disquieted, and some said: "Oh, if only Jurand were here, he could give an account of himself with even two; no German ever escaped him yet, but the youth—bah!—for the other exceeds him in strength, years and experience."

Therefore others regretted that they had not accepted the challenge, asserting that they would undoubtedly have done so, if it had not been for the news from Jurand. "But fear of the judgment of God...." On this occasion, and for mutual entertainment, they recalled the names of Mazovian and more often of Polish knights, who, either in courtly jousts or hunting, had gained numerous victories over the western knights; above all they mentioned Zawisza of Garbow, with whom no knight of the Christian kingdom could cope. But there were also those who cherished great hopes of Zbyszko: "He is not to be despised!" they said "and according to common report he once admirably broke the heads of Germans in fair field." But their hearts were particularly strengthened by the action of Zbyszko's follower, the Bohemian Hlawa, who, on the eve of the combat, hearing how van Krist was talking about Rotgier's unheard-of victories, and being a hasty youth, caught van Krist by the beard, pulled his head up, and said:

"If it is no shame to lie before men, then look up, so that God also may hear you!"

And he kept him long enough to say a "Pater"; while the other, when at length liberated, began to ask him about his lineage, and, having heard that he sprang from the *wlodykas*, challenged him also to fight with axes.

The Mazovians were delighted at such conduct, and again several said:

"Indeed these fellows will not hobble on the barn-floor; even if truth and God be on their side these Teutonic women will not carry away sound bones with them!"

But Rotgier succeeded in throwing dust in the eyes of all, so that many were disquieted as to which had the truth on his side, and the prince himself partook of that fear.

Therefore, on the evening before the combat, he summoned Zbyszko to a consultation at which was present the princess only, and asked:

"Are you positive that God will be with you? How do you know that they captured Danusia? Did Jurand perchance tell you any thing? Because, you see, here is Jurand's letter, by the hand of the priest Kaleb, and his seal, and in this letter Jurand says that he knows that it was not the Teutons. What did he tell you?"

"He said that it was not the Teutons."

"How then can you risk your life and appeal to the judgment of God?"

Then Zbyszko was silent, and only his jaws worked for some time and tears gathered in his eyes.

"I know nothing, gracious lord," he said. "We left here together with Jurand, and on the way I admitted our marriage. He then began to lament that this might be a sin against God, but when I told him it was God's will, he quieted down and forgave me. Along the whole way he said that nobody captured Danusia but the Teutons, and what happened afterward I do not know myself! That woman who brought certain medicines for me to the Forest Court, came to Spychow, accompanied by another messenger. They shut themselves up with Jurand and deliberated. Neither do I know what they said, only after the interview his own servants could not recognize Jurand, because he looked as if he had risen from the grave. He told us: 'Not the Teutons,' but he released von Bergow and all the prisoners he had underground, God knows why! he himself again rode away without any warrior or servant.... He said that he was riding after robbers to ransom Danusia, and ordered me to wait. And I waited until the news from Szczytno arrived, that Jurand had slain Germans and fallen himself. Oh! gracious lord! The soil in Spychow almost scorched me and I nearly ran mad. I made people mount horses in order to revenge Jurand's death, and then the priest

Kaleb said: 'You will not be able to take the castle, and do not commence war. Go to the prince, perhaps they know something about Danusia there.' Hlawa and I arrived, and just heard how that dog was barking about Teutonic grievances and Jurand's frenzy.... My lord, I accepted his challenge, because I had challenged him before, and although I know nothing, this much I know, that they are hellish liars—without shame, without honor and without belief! Look, gracious lord, they stabbed de Fourcy to death and tried to cast the guilt upon my follower! By God! they stabbed him like an ox, and then they came to you, lord, for vengeance and retribution! Who will swear then, that they did not lie to Jurand before, and now do the same to you, lord?... I know not, I know not where Danusia is but I challenged him, because, even if I were to lose my life, I prefer death to life without my love, without the one who is clearest to me in the whole world."

Saying this in rapture, he tore off a band from his head, so that his hair fell about his shoulders, and clutching it, he began to weep bitterly, until the princess Anna Danuta was moved to the bottom of her soul for the loss of Danusia, and, pitying him for his sufferings, laid her hands upon his head, and said:

"May God help you, console and bless you!"

CHAPTER IV.

The prince did not object to the duel, because, according to the customs of that time, he had no power to do so. He only prevailed upon Rotgier to write a letter to the master and to Zygfried von Löve, stating that he was the first to throw down the gauntlet to the Mazovian knights, in consequence of which he appeared at a combat with the husband of Jurand's daughter, who had already challenged him once before.

The Teuton also explained to the grand master, that if he appeared at the duel without permission, he did it for the sake of the honor of the Order, and to avert ugly suspicions, which might entail disgrace, and which he, Rotgier, was always prepared to redeem with his own blood. This letter was sent instantly to the border by one of the knight's footmen, to be sent thence to Malborg by mail, which the Teutons, some years before others, invented and introduced into their possessions.

Meanwhile the snow in the courtyard was leveled and strewn with ashes, so that the feet of the fighters should neither clog nor slip upon the smooth surface. There was unusual excitement in the whole castle.

The knights and court ladies were so agitated that on the night preceding the fight nobody slept. They said, that a fight on horseback with spears, and even with swords, frequently terminates in wounds; on foot on the contrary, and particularly with terrible axes, it always terminates in death. All hearts were with Zbyszko, but the very ones who felt most friendly toward him or Danusia recollected with so much more fear the stories about the fame and dexterity of the Teuton. Many ladies spent the night in church, where also Zbyszko confessed to the priest Wyszoniek. They said one to another as they looked at his almost boyish face: "Why, he is a child yet! how can he expose his head to the German axe?" And they prayed the more fervently for aid for him. But when he arose at daybreak and walked through the chapel, in order to put on his arms in the hall, they again gained courage, because, although Zbyszko's features were indeed boyish, his body was of an extraordinary size, and strong, so that he seemed to them to be a picked man, who could take care of himself against even the most powerful.

The fight was to take place in the castle yard, which was surrounded by a porch. When it was broad daylight, the prince and princess arrived together with their children and took their seats in the centre between the pillars, from where the whole yard could best be overlooked. Next to them were the principal courtiers, noble ladies, and the knighthood. All the corners of the vestibule were filled: the domestics gathered behind the wall which was made from the swept snow, some clung to the posts, and even to the roof. There the vulgar muttered among themselves: "God grant that our champion may not be subdued!"

The day was cold, moist, but clear; the sky swarmed with daws, which inhabited the roofs and summits of the bastions, and which, scared by the unusual bustle, moved in circles, with great clapping of wings, over the castle. Notwithstanding the cold, the people perspired with excitement, and when the first horn sounded to announce the entrance of the combatants, all hearts began to beat like hammers.

They entered from opposite sides of the arena and halted at the barriers. Every one of the onlookers then held his breath, every one thought, that very soon two souls would escape to the threshold of the Divine Court and two dead bodies remain on the snow, and the lips, as well as the cheeks of the women turned pale and livid at that thought; the eyes of the men again gazed steadfastly at the opponents as at a rainbow, because every one was trying to forecast, from their postures and armament alone, which side would be victorious.

The Teuton was dressed in an enameled blue cuirass, with similar armor for the thighs, as also the helmet with raised visor, and with a magnificent bunch of peacock feathers on the crest. Zbyszko's breast, sides and back were encased in splendid Milanese mail, which he had once captured from the Fryzjans. He had on his head a helmet with an open visor, and without feathers; on his legs was bull's hide. On their left shoulders, they carried shields with coat of arms; on the Teuton's at the top was a chessboard, at the bottom, three lions rampant; on Zbyszko's, a blunt horseshoe. In the right hand they carried broad, huge, terrible axes, set in oaken, blackened helves, longer than the arm of a grown man. The warriors who seconded them were: Hlawa, called by Zbyszko, Glowacz, and van Krist, both dressed in dark iron mail, both equally with axes and shields: van Krist had on his shield a St. John's wort; the shield of the Bohemian resembled that of the *Pomian*, with this difference, that instead of an axe stuck in a bull's head, it had a short weapon half sunk in the eye.

The horn sounded the second time, and, at the third, the opponents, according to agreement, were to advance against each other. A small space strewn with grey ashes now only separated them; over that space hovered in the air like an ominous bird—death. But before the third signal was given, Rotgier approached the pillars between which sat the prince's family, raised his steel-encased head, and began to speak in such a loud voice that he was heard in all corners of the vestibule:

"I take God, you, worthy lord, and the whole knighthood of this soil, as witness that I am not guilty of the blood that is about to be shed."

At these words their hearts were again ready to break with grief, seeing that the Teuton was so confident of himself and his victory. But Zbyszko, having a simple soul, turned to his Bohemian, and said:

"That Teutonic boasting stinks; it would be more appropriate after my death than while I am alive. That boaster moreover has a peacock's plume on his helmet, and at the very outset I made a vow to obtain three of them and afterward as many fingers of the hand. God grant it!"

"Lord ..." said the Bohemian, bending down and picking up in his hands some ashes from the snow, to prevent the axe-handle from slipping in his hand; "perhaps Christ will permit me quickly to despatch that vile Prussian, and then perhaps, if not to defeat this Teuton, at least put the handle of the axe between his knees and upset him."

"God save you!" hastily exclaimed Zbyszko; "you would cover me and yourself with disgrace."

But at that moment the horn sounded the third time. On hearing it, the seconds sprang quickly and furiously at each other, while the knights moved slowly and deliberately, as their dignity and gravity demanded, for the first bout.

Very few paid attention to the seconds, but those of the experienced men and of the domestics who looked at them understood at once how great were the odds on Hlawa's side. The German wielded the heavier axe and his shield was cumbersome. Below the shield were visible his legs which were longer, though not so strong nor active as the sturdy and tightly covered legs of the Bohemian.

Hlawa moreover pressed so vigorously that van Krist, almost from the first moment, was compelled to retreat. It was instantly understood that one of the adversaries would fall upon the other like a tempest; that he would attack and strike like lightning, while the other, under the conviction that death was already upon him, would merely defend himself so as to postpone the terrible moment as long as possible.

And so it actually was. That boaster, who generally stood up to fight only when he could not do otherwise, now recognized that his insolent and heedless words had led him into a fight with a terrible giant whom he ought to have avoided like a perdition; and so, when he now felt that every one of these blows could kill an ox, his heart began to fail entirely. He almost forgot that it is not sufficient to catch the blows on the shield, but that it was also necessary to return them. He saw above him the lightning of the axe and thought that every gleam was the last. Holding up the shield, he involuntarily half closed his eyes with a feeling of terror and doubt whether he would ever open them again. Very rarely he gave a blow himself, but without any hope of reaching his opponent, and raised the shield constantly higher over his head, so as to save it yet for a little.

Finally he began to tire, but the Bohemian struck on constantly more powerfully. Just as from a tall pine-tree great chips fly under the peasant's axe, so under the Bohemian's strokes fragments began to scale off and fly from the German warrior's armor. The upper edge of the shield was bent and shattered, the mail from the right shoulder rolled to the ground, together with the cut and already bloody strap of leather. This made van Krist's hair stand on end—and a deadly fear seized him. He struck with all the force of his arm once and again at the Bohemian's shield; finally, seeing that he had no chance against his adversary's terrible strength and that only some extraordinary exertion could save him, he threw himself suddenly with all the weight of his armor and body against Hlawa's legs. Both fell to the ground and tried to overcome each other, rolling and struggling in the snow. But the Bohemian soon appeared on top; for a moment he still checked the desperate efforts of his opponent; finally he pressed his knee upon the chain-armor covering his belly, and took from the back of his belt a sharp three-edged "dagger of mercy."[109]

"Spare me!" faintly gasped van Krist, raising his eyes toward those of the Bohemian.

But the latter, instead of answering, stretched himself upon him the easier to reach his neck, and, cutting through the leather fastening of the helmet under the chin, stabbed the unfortunate man twice in the throat, directing the sharp edge downward toward the centre of the breast.

Then van Krist's pupils sank in their sockets, his hands and legs began to beat the snow, as if trying to clean it of the ashes, but after a moment he stiffened out and lay motionless, breathing only with red, foam-covered lips, and bleeding profusely.

But the Bohemian arose, wiped the "dagger of mercy" on the German's clothing, then raised the axe, and, leaning against it, he began to look at the harder and more stubborn fight between his knight and Brother Rotgier.

The western knights were already accustomed to comforts and luxuries, while the landowners in Little Poland and Great Poland, as also in Mazowsze, led a rigorous and hardy life, wherefore they awoke admiration by their bodily strength and endurance of all hardships, whether constant or occasional, even among strangers and foes. Now also it was demonstrated that Zbyszko was as superior to the Teuton in bodily strength as his squire was superior to van Krist, but it was also proven that his youth rendered him the inferior in knightly training.

It was in some measure favorable for Zbyszko that he had chosen a combat with axes, because fencing with that kind of weapon was impossible. With long and short swords, with which it was necessary to know the strokes, thrusts, and how to ward off blows, the German would have had a considerable superiority. But even so, Zbyszko, as well as the spectators, recognized from his motions and management of the shield, that they had before them an experienced and formidable man, who apparently was not entering a combat of this kind for the first time. To each of Zbyszko's blows Rotgier offered his shield, slightly withdrawing it at the concussion, by which means even the most powerful swing lost its force, and could neither cleave nor crush the smooth surface. He at times retreated and at times became aggressive, doing it quietly, though so quickly that the eyes could hardly follow his motions.

The prince was seized with fear for Zbyszko, and the faces of the men looked gloomy; it seemed that the German was purposely trifling with his opponent. Sometimes he did not even interpose the shield, but at the moment when Zbyszko struck, he turned half aside, so that the sharp edge of the axe cut the empty air. This was the most terrifying thing, because Zbyszko might thereby lose his balance and fall, and then his destruction would be inevitable. Seeing this, the Bohemian, standing over the slain van Krist, also became alarmed, and said to himself: "My God! if my master falls, I will strike him with the hook of my axe between the shoulder-blades, and overthrow him also."

However, Zbyszko did not fall, because, being very strong upon his legs and separating them widely, he was able to support the entire weight of his body on either as he swung.

Rotgier observed that instantly, and the onlookers were mistaken in supposing that he underestimated his opponent. On the contrary, after the first strokes, when, in spite of his utmost skill in withdrawing the shield, his hand almost stiffened under it, he understood that he would have a hard time with this youth, and that, if he did not knock him down by some clever manoeuvre, the combat would prove long and dangerous. He expected Zbyszko to fall upon the snow after a vain stroke in the air, and as that did not happen, he immediately became uneasy. He saw, beneath the steel visor, the closely-drawn nostrils and mouth of his opponent, and occasionally his gleaming eyes, and he said to himself that the other would fly into a blind rage and forget himself, lose his head, and madly think more of striking than of defending himself. But he was mistaken in this also. Zbyszko did not know how to avoid a stroke by a half-turn, but he did not forget his shield, and, while raising the axe, did not expose himself more than was necessary. His attention was apparently redoubled, and having recognized the experience and skill of his opponent, instead of forgetting himself he collected his thoughts and became more cautious; and there was that premeditation in his blows which not hot but cool anger only can conquer.

Rotgier, who had fought in many wars and battles, either in troop or singly, knew by experience that there are some people, like birds of prey, who are born to fight, being specially gifted by Nature, who bestows all things, with what others only attain after years of training, and he at the same time observed that he was now dealing with one of those. He understood from the very first strokes that there was in this youth something as in a hawk, who sees in his opponent only his prey, and thinks of nothing but getting him in his claws. Notwithstanding his own strength, he also noticed that it was not equal to Zbyszko's, and should he get exhausted before succeeding in giving a final stroke, the combat with this formidable, although less experienced, stripling, might result in his ruin. Thus reflecting, he determined to fight with the least possible effort, drew the shield closer to him, did not move much either forward or backward, restricted his motions, and gathered all the power of his soul and arm for one decisive stroke, and awaited his opportunity.

The terrible fight lasted longer than usual. A deathlike silence reigned in the porches. The only sounds heard were the sometimes ringing and sometimes hollow blows of the sharp points and edges of the axes against the shields. Such sights were not strange to the princes, knights and courtiers; and nevertheless a feeling, resembling terror, seemed to clutch all hearts as if with tongs. It was understood that this was not a mere exhibition of strength, skill and courage, but that in this fight there was a greater fury and despair, a greater and more inexorable stubbornness, a deeper vengeance. On one side terrible wrongs, love and fathomless sorrow; on the other, the honor of the entire Order and deep hatred, met on this field of battle for the Judgment of God.

Meanwhile the wintry, pale morning brightened, the grey fog cleared away, and the sunrays shone upon the blue cuirass of the Teuton and the silver Milanese armor of Zbyszko. The bell rang in the chapel for early mass, and at the sounds of the bell flights of crows again flew from the castle roofs, flapping their wings and crowing noisily, as if in joy at the sight of blood and the corpse lying motionless in the snow. Rotgier looked at it once and again during the fight, and suddenly began to feel very lonesome. All the eyes that were turned upon him were those of enemies. All the prayers, wishes and silent vows which the women were offering were in Zbyszko's favor. Moreover, although the Teuton was fully convinced that the squire would not cast himself upon him from behind, nor strike him treacherously, nevertheless, the presence and nearness of that terrifying figure involuntarily inspired him with such fear as people are subject to at the sight of a wolf, a bear or a buffalo, from which they are not separated by bars. And he could not shake off this feeling, especially as the Bohemian, in his desire to follow closely the course of the battle, constantly changed his place, stepping in between the fighters from the side, from behind, from the front—

bending his head at the same time, and looking at him fiercely through the visor of the helmet, and sometimes slightly raising his bloody weapon, as if involuntarily.

At last the Teuton began to tire. One after another, he gave two blows, short but terrible, directing them at Zbyszko's right arm, but they were met by the shield with such force that the axe trembled in Rotgier's hand, and he himself was compelled to retreat suddenly to save himself from falling; and from that moment, he retreated steadily. Finally, not only his strength but also his coolness and patience began to be exhausted. At the sight of his retreating, a few triumphant shouts escaped from the breasts of the spectators, awakening in him anger and despair. The strokes of the axes became more frequent. Perspiration flowed from the brows of both fighters, and panting breath escaped from their breasts through their clenched teeth. The spectators ceased keeping silence, and now every moment voices, male or female, cried: "Strike! At him!... God's judgment! God's punishment! God help you!"

The prince motioned with his hand several times to silence them, but he could not restrain them! Every moment the noise increased, because children here and there began to cry on the porches, and finally, at the very side of the princess, a youthful, sobbing, female voice called out:

"For Danusia, Zbyszko! for Danusia!"

Zbyszko knew well that it was for Danusia's sake. He was sure that this Teuton had assisted in her capture, and in fighting him, he fought for her wrongs. But being young and eager for battles, during the combat he had thought of that only. But suddenly, that cry brought back to his mind her loss and her sufferings. Love, sorrow and vengeance poured fire into his veins. His heart began to call out with suddenly awakened pain, and he was plainly seized with a fighting frenzy. The Teuton could not any longer catch nor avoid the terrible strokes, resembling thunderbolts. Zbyszko struck his shield against his with such superhuman force, that the German's arm stiffened suddenly and fell…. He retreated in terror and half crouched, but that instant there flashed in his eyes the gleam of the axe, and the sharp edge fell like a thunderbolt upon his right shoulder.

Only a rending cry reached the ears of the onlookers: "Jesus!"—then Rotgier retreated one more step and fell upon his back on the ground. Immediately there was a noise and buzz on the porches, as in a bee-garden in which the bees, warmed by the sun, commence to move and swarm. The knights ran down the stairs in whole throngs, the servants jumped over the snow-walls, to take a look at the corpses. Everywhere resounded the shouts: "This is God's judgment … Jurand has an heir! Glory to him and thanksgiving! This is a man for the axe!" Others again cried: "Look and marvel! Jurand himself could not strike more nobly." A whole group of curious ones stood around Rotgier's corpse, and he lay on his back with a face as white as snow, with gaping mouth and with a bloody arm so terribly shorn from the neck down to the armpit, that it scarcely held by a few shreds.

Therefore, others again said: "He was alive just now and walked upon the earth with arrogance, but now he cannot even move a finger." And thus speaking, some admired his stature, because he took up a large space on the battlefield, and appeared even larger in death; others again admired his peacock plume, changing colors beautifully in the snow; others again his armor, which was valued at a good village. But the Bohemian, Hlawa, now approached with two of Zbyszko's retainers in order to take it off from the deceased, therefore the curious surrounded Zbyszko, praising and extolling him to the skies, because they justly thought that his fame would redound to the credit of the whole Mazovian and Polish knighthood. Meanwhile the shield and axe were taken from him, to lighten his burden, and Mrokota of Mocarzew unbuckled his helmet and covered his hair, wet with perspiration, with a cap of scarlet cloth.

Zbyszko stood, as if petrified, breathing heavily, with the fire not fully extinguished yet in his eyes, and a face pale with exhaustion and determination and trembling somewhat with excitement and fatigue. But he was taken by the hand and led to the princely family, who were waiting for him in a warm room, by the fireside. There Zbyszko kneeled down before them and when Father Wyszoniek gave him a blessing and said a prayer for the eternal rest of the souls of the dead, the prince embraced the young knight and said:

"God Almighty decided between you two and guided your hand, for which His name be blessed. Amen!"

Then turning to the knight de Lorche and others, he added:

"You, foreign knight and all present I take as witnesses to what I testify myself, that they met according to law and custom, and as the 'Judgment of God' is everywhere performed, this also was conducted in a knightly and devout manner."

The local warriors cried out affirmatively in chorus; when again the prince's words were translated to de Lorche, he arose and announced that he not only testified that all was conducted in knightly and devout style, but should anybody in Malborg or any other princely court dare to question it, he, de Lorche, would challenge him instantly to fight either on foot or horseback, even if he should not merely be a common knight, but a giant or wizard, exceeding even Merlin's magical power.

Meanwhile, the princess Anna Danuta, at the moment when Zbyszko embraced her knees, said as she bent down to him:

"Why do you not feel happy? Be happy and thank God, because if He in His mercy has granted you this suit, then He will not leave you in the future, and will lead you to happiness."

But Zbyszko replied:

"How can I be happy, gracious lady? God gave me victory and vengeance over that Teuton, but Danusia was not and still is not here, and I am no nearer to her now than I was before."

"The most stubborn foes, Danveld, Godfried and Rotgier live no longer," replied the princess, "and they say that Zygfried is more just than they, although cruel. Praise God's mercy at least for that. Also de Lorche said that if the Teuton fell he would carry his body away, and go instantly to Malborg and demand Danusia from the grand master himself. They will certainly not dare to disobey the grand master."

"May God give health to de Lorche," said Zbyszko, "and I will go with him to Malborg."

But these words frightened the princess, who felt it was as if Zbyszko said he would go unarmed among the wolves that assembled in the winter in packs in the deep Mazovian forests.

"What for?" she exclaimed. "For sure destruction? On your arrival, neither de Lorche nor those letters, written by Rotgier before the fight, will help you. You will save nobody and only ruin yourself."

But he arose, crossed his hands and said: "So may God help me, that I shall go to Malborg and even across oceans. So may Christ bless me, that I shall look for her until the last breath of my nostrils, and that I shall not cease until I perish. It is easier for me to fight the Germans, and meet them in arms, than for this orphan to moan under ground. Oh, easier! easier!"

And he said that, as always when he mentioned Danusia, with such rapture, with such pain, that his words broke off as if some one had clutched him by the throat.

The princess recognized that it would be useless to turn him aside, and that if anybody wanted to detain him it must be by chaining him and casting him under ground.

But Zbyszko could not leave at once. Knights of that day were not allowed to heed any obstacles, but he was not permitted to break the knightly custom that required the winner in a duel to spend a whole day on the field of combat, until the following midnight, and this in order to show that he remained master of the field of battle and to show his readiness for another fight, should any of the relatives or friends of the defeated wish to challenge him to such.

This custom was even observed by whole armies, which thus sometimes lost advantages which might accrue from haste after the victory. Zbyszko did not even attempt to evade that inexorable law, and refreshing himself, and afterward putting on his armor, he lingered until midnight in the castle yard, under the clouded wintry sky, awaiting the foe that could not come from anywhere.

At midnight, when the heralds finally announced his victory by sound of trumpet, Mikolaj of Dlugolas invited him to supper and at the same time to a council with the prince.

CHAPTER V.

The prince was the first to take the floor at the consultation and spoke as follows:

"It is bad that we have no writing nor testimony against the counts. Although our suspicions may be justified, and I myself think that they and nobody else captured Jurand's daughter, still what of it? They will deny it. And if the grand master asks for proofs, what shall I show him? Bah! even Jurand's letter speaks in their favor."

Here he turned to Zbyszko:

"You say that they forced this letter from him with threats. It is possible, and undoubtedly it is so, because if justice were on their side, God would not have helped you against Rotgier. But since they extorted one, then they could extort also two. And perhaps they have evidence from Jurand, that they are not guilty of the capture of this unfortunate girl. And if so, they will show it to the master and what will happen then?"

"Why, they admitted themselves, gracious lord, that they recaptured her from bandits and that she is with them now."

"I know that. But they say now that they were mistaken, and that this is another girl, and the best proof is that Jurand himself disclaimed her."

"He disclaimed her because they showed him another girl, and that is what exasperated him."

"Surely it was so, but they can say that these are only our ideas."

"Their lies," said Mikolaj of Dlugolas, "are like a pine forest. From the edge a little way is visible, but the deeper one goes the greater is the density, so that a man goes astray and loses his way entirely."

He then repeated his words in German to de Lorche, who said:

"The grand master himself is better than they are, also his brother, although he has a daring soul, but it guards knightly honor."

"Yes," replied Mikolaj. "The master is humane. He cannot restrain the counts, nor the assembly, and it is not his fault that everything in the Order is based upon human wrongs, but he cannot help it. Go, go, Sir de Lorche, and tell him what has happened here. They are more ashamed before strangers than before us, lest they should tell of their outrages and dishonest actions at foreign courts. And should the master ask for proofs, then tell him this: 'To know the truth is divine, to seek it is human, therefore if you wish proofs, lord, then seek them.' Order the castles to be summoned and the people to be questioned, allow us to search, because it is foolishness and a lie that this orphan was stolen by bandits of the woods."

"Folly and lies!" repeated de Lorche.

"Because bandits would not dare to attack the princely court, nor Jurand's child. And even if they should have captured her, it would be only for ransom, and they alone would inform us that they had her."

"I shall narrate all that," said the Lotaringen, "and also find von Bergow. We are from the same country, and although I don't know him, they say that he is a relative of Duke Geldryi's. He was at Szczytno and should tell the master what he saw."

Zbyszko understood a few of his words, and whatever he did not, Mikolaj explained to him; he then embraced de Lorche so tightly that the knight almost groaned.

The prince again said to Zbyszko:

"And are you also absolutely determined to go?"

"Absolutely, gracious lord. What else am I to do? I vowed to seize Szczytno, even if I had to bite the walls with my teeth, but how can I declare war without permission?"

"Whoever began war without permission, would rue it under the executioner's sword," said the prince.

"It is certainly the law of laws," replied Zbyszko. "Bah! I wished then to challenge all who were in Szczytno, but people said that Jurand slaughtered them like cattle, and I did not know who was alive and who dead.... Because, may God and the Holy Cross help me, I will not desert Jurand till the last moment!"

"You speak nobly and worthily," said Mikolaj of Dlugolas. "And it proves that you were sensible not to go alone to Szczytno, because even a fool would have known that they would keep neither Jurand nor his daughter there, but undoubtedly would carry them away to some other castle. God rewarded your arrival here with Rotgier."

"And now!" said the prince, "as we heard from Rotgier, of those four only old Zygfried is alive, and the others God has punished already either by your hand or Jurand's. As for Zygfried, he is less of a rascal than the others, but perhaps the more ruthless tyrant. It is bad that Jurand and Danusia are in his power, and they must be saved quickly. In order that no accident may happen to you, I will give you a letter to the grand master. Listen and understand me well, that you do not go as a messenger, but as a delegate, and write to the master as follows: Since they had once made an attempt upon our person, in carrying off a descendant of their benefactors, it is most likely now, that they have also carried off Jurand's daughter, especially having a grudge against Jurand. I ask therefore of the master to order a diligent search, and if he is anxious to have my friendship, to restore her instantly to your hands."

Zbyszko, hearing this, fell at the prince's feet, and, embracing them, said:

"But Jurand, gracious lord, Jurand? Will you intercede also in his behalf? If he has mortal wounds, let him at least die in his own home and with his children."

"There is also mention made of Jurand," said the prince, kindly. "He is to appoint two judges and I two also to investigate the counts' and Jurand's actions, according to the rules of knightly honor. And they again will select a fifth to preside over them, and it will be as they decide."

With this, the council terminated, after which Zbyszko took leave of the prince, because they were soon to start on their journey. But before their departure, Mikolaj of Dlugolas, who had experience and knew the Teutons well, called Zbyszko aside and inquired:

"And will you take that Bohemian fellow along with you to the Germans?"

"Surely, he will not leave me. But why?"

"Because I feel sorry for him. He is a worthy fellow, but mark what I say: you will return from Malborg safe and sound, unless you meet a better man in combat, but his destruction is sure."

"But why?"

"Because the dog-brothers accused him of having stabbed de Fourcy to death. They must have informed the master of his death, and they doubtless said that the Bohemian shed his blood. They will not forgive that in Malborg. A trial and vengeance await him because, how can his innocence be proven to the master. Why, he even crushed Danveld's arm, who is a relative of the grand master. I am sorry for him, I repeat, if he goes it is to his death."

"He will not go to his death, because I shall leave him in Spychow."

But it happened otherwise, as reasons arose whereby the Bohemian did not remain in Spychow. Zbyszko and de Lorche started with their suites the following morning. De Lorche, whose marriage to Ulryka von Elner, Father Wyszoniek dissolved, rode away happy and, with his mind entirely occupied with the comeliness of Jagienka of Dlugolas, was silent. Zbyszko, not being able to talk with him about Danusia also, because they could not understand each other very well, conversed with Hlawa, who until now had known nothing about the intended expedition into the Teutonic regions.

"I am going to Malborg," he said, "but God knows when I shall return…. Perhaps soon, in the spring, in a year, and perhaps not at all, do you understand?"

"I do. Your honor also is surely going to challenge the knights there.
And God grant that with every knight there is a shield-bearer!"

"No," replied Zbyszko. "I am not going for the purpose of challenging them, unless it comes of itself; but you will not go with me at all, but remain at home in Spychow."

Hearing this, the Bohemian at first fretted and began to complain sorrowfully, and then he begged his young lord not to leave him behind.

"I swore that I would not leave you. I swore upon the cross and my honor. And if your honor should meet with an accident, how could I appear before the lady in Zgorzelice! I swore to her, lord! Therefore have mercy upon me, and not disgrace me before her."

"And did you not swear to her to obey me?" asked Zbyszko.

"Certainly! In everything, but not that I should leave you. If your honor drives me away, I shall go ahead, so as to be at hand in case of necessity."

"I do not, nor will I drive you away," replied Zbyszko; "but it would be a bondage to me if I could not send you anywhere, even the least way, nor separate from you for even one day. You would not stand constantly over me, like a hangman over a good soul! And as to the combat, how will you help me? I do not speak of war, because these people fight in troops, and, in a single combat, you certainly will not fight for me. If Rotgier were stronger than I, his armor would not lie on my wagon, but mine on his. And besides, know that I should have greater difficulties there if with you, and that you might expose me to dangers."

"How so, your honor?"

Then Zbyszko began to tell him what he had heard from Mikolaj of Dlugolas, that the counts, not being able to account for de Fourcy's murder, would accuse him and prosecute him revengefully.

"And if they catch you," he said, finally, "then I certainly cannot leave you with them as in dogs' jaws, and may lose my head."

The Bohemian became gloomy when he heard these words, because he felt the truth in them; he nevertheless endeavored to alter the arrangement according to his desire.

"But those who saw me are not alive any more, because some, as they say, were killed by the old lord, while you slew Rotgier."

"The footmen who followed at a distance saw you, and the old Teuton is alive, and is surely now in Malborg, and if he is not there yet he will arrive, because the master, with God's permission, will summon him."

He could not reply to that, they therefore rode on in silence to Spychow. They found there complete readiness for war, because old Tolima expected that either the Teutons would attack the small castle, or that Zbyszko, on his return, would lead them to the succor of the old lord. Guards were on watch everywhere, on the paths through the marshes and in the castle itself. The peasants were armed, and, as war was nothing new to them, they awaited the Germans with eagerness, promising themselves excellent booty.

Father Kaleb received Zbyszko and de Lorche in the castle, and, immediately after supper, showed them the parchment with Jurand's seal, in which he had written with his own hand the last will of the knight of Spychow.

"He dictated it to me," he said, "the night he went to Szczytno". And—he did not expect to return."

"But why did you say nothing?"

"I said nothing, because he admitted his intentions to me under the seal of confession."

"May God give him eternal peace, and may the light of glory shine upon him...."

"Do not say prayers for him. He is still alive. I know it from the Teuton Rotgier, with whom I had a combat at the prince's court. There was God's judgment between us and I killed him."

"Then Jurand will undoubtedly not return ... unless with God's help!..."

"I go with this knight to tear him from their hands."

"Then you know not, it seems, Teutonic hands, but I know them, because, before Jurand took me to Spychow, I was priest for fifteen years in their country. God alone can save Jurand."

"And He can help us too."

"Amen!"

He then unfolded the document and began to read. Jurand bequeathed all his estates and his entire possessions to Danusia and her offspring, but, in case of her death without issue, to her husband Zbyszko of Bogdaniec. He finally recommended his will to the prince's care; so that, in case it contained anything unlawful, the prince's grace might make it lawful. This clause was added because Father Kaleb knew only the canon law, and Jurand himself, engaged exclusively in war, only knew the knightly. After having read the document to Zbyszko, the priest read it to the officers of the Spychow garrison, who at once recognized the young knight as their lord, and promised obedience.

They also thought that Zbyszko would soon lead them to the assistance of the old lord, and they were glad, because their hearts were fierce and anxious for war, and attached to Jurand. They were seized with grief when they heard that they would remain at home, and that the lord with a small following was going to Malborg, not to fight, but to formulate complaints.

The Bohemian Glowacz, shared their grief, although on the other hand, he was glad on account of such a large increase of Zbyszko's wealth.

"Hej! who would be delighted," he said, "if not the old lord of Bogdaniec! And he could govern here! What is Bogdaniec in comparison with such a possession!"

But Zbyszko was suddenly seized with yearning for his uncle, as it frequently happened to him, especially in hard and difficult questions in life; therefore, turning to the warrior, he said on the impulse:

"Why should you sit here in idleness! Go to Bogdaniec, you shall carry a letter for me."

"If I am not to go with your honor, then I would rather go there!" replied the delighted squire.

"Call Father Kaleb to write in a proper manner all that has happened here, and the letter will be read to my uncle by the priest of Krzesnia, or the abbot, if he is in Zgorzelice."

But as he said this, he struck his moustache with his hand and added, as if to himself:

"Bah! the abbot!..."

And instantly Jagienka arose before his eyes, blue-eyed, dark-haired, tall and beautiful, with tears on her eyelashes! He became embarrassed and rubbed his forehead for a time, but finally he said:

"You will feel sad, girl, but not worse than I."

Meanwhile Father Kaleb arrived and immediately began to write. Zbyszko dictated to him at length everything that had happened from the moment he had arrived at the Forest Court. He did not conceal anything, because he knew that old Macko, when he had a clear view of the matter, would be glad in the end. Bogdaniec could not be compared with Spychow, which was a large and rich estate, and Zbyszko knew that Macko cared a great deal for such things.

But when the letter, after great toil, was written and sealed, Zbyszko again called his squire, and handed him the letter, saying:

"You will perhaps return with my uncle, which would delight me very much."

But the Bohemian seemed to be embarrassed; he tarried, shifted from one foot to another, and did not depart, until the young knight remarked:

"Have you anything to say yet, then do so."

"I should like, your honor ..." replied the Bohemian, "I should like to inquire yet, what to tell the people?"

"Which people?"

"Not those in Bogdaniec, but in the neighborhood.... Because they will surely like to find out!"

At that Zbyszko, who determined not to conceal anything, looked at him sharply and said:

"You do not care for the people, but for Jagienka of Zgorzelice."

And the Bohemian flushed, and then turned somewhat pale and replied:

"For her, lord!"

"And how do you know that she has not got married to Cztan of Rogow, or to Wilk of Brzozowa?"

"The lady has not got married at all," firmly answered the warrior.

"The abbot may have ordered her."

"The abbot obeys the lady, not she him."

"What do you wish then? Tell the truth to her as well as to all."

The Bohemian bowed and left somewhat angry.

"May God grant," he said to himself, thinking of Zbyszko, "that she may forget you. May God give her a better man than you are. But if she has not forgotten you, then I shall tell her that you are married, but without a wife, and that you may become a widower before you have entered the bedchamber."

But the warrior was attached to Zbyszko and pitied Danusia, though he loved Jagienka above all in this world, and from the time before the last battle in Ciechanow, when he had heard of Zbyszko's marriage, he bore pain and bitterness in his heart.

"That you may first become a widower!" he repeated.

But then other, and apparently gentler, thoughts began to enter his head, because, while going down to the horses, he said:

"God be blessed that I shall at least embrace her feet!"

Meanwhile Zbyszko was impatient to start, because feverishness consumed him,— and the affairs of necessity that occupied his attention increased his tortures, thinking constantly of Danusia and Jurand. It was necessary, however, to remain in Spychow for one night at least, for the sake of de Lorche, and the preparations which such a long journey required. He was finally utterly worn out from the fight, watch, journey, sleeplessness and worry. Late in the evening, therefore, he threw himself upon Jurand's hard bed, in the hope of falling into a short sleep at least. But before he fell asleep, Sanderus knocked at his door, entered, and bowing, said:

"Lord, you saved me from death, and I was well off with you, as scarcely ever before. God has given you now a large estate, so that you are wealthier than before, and moreover the Spychow treasury is not empty. Give me, lord, some kind of a moneybag, and I will go to Prussia, from castle to castle, and although it may not be very safe there, I may possibly do you some service."

Zbyszko, who at the first moment had wished to throw him out of the room, reflected upon his words, and after a moment, pulled from his traveling bag near his bed, a fair-sized bag, threw it to him and said:

"Take it, and go! If you are a rogue you will cheat, if honest—you will serve."

"I shall cheat as a rogue, sir," said Sanderus, "but not you, and I will honestly serve you."

Zygfried von Löve was just about to depart for Malborg when the postman unexpectedly brought him a letter from Rotgier with news from the Mazovian court. This news moved the old Knight of the Cross to the quick. First of all, it was obvious from the letter that Rotgier had perfectly conducted and represented the Jurand affair before Prince Janusz. Zygfried smiled on reading that Rotgier had further requested the prince to deliver up Spychow to the Order as a recompense for the wrong done. But the other part of the letter contained unexpected and less advantageous tidings. Rotgier further informed him that in order better to demonstrate the guiltlessness of the Order in the abduction of the Jurands, the gauntlet was thrown down to the Mazovian knights, challenging everybody who doubted, to God's judgment, i.e., to fight in the presence of the whole court. "None has taken it up," Rotgier continued, "because all saw that in his letter Jurand himself bears testimony for us, moreover they feared God's judgment, but a youth, the same we saw in the forest court, came forward and picked up the gauntlet. Do not wonder then, O pious and wise brother, for that is the cause of my delay in returning. Since I have challenged, I am obliged to stand. And since I have done it for the glory of the Order, I trust that neither the grand master nor you whom I honor and heartily love with filial affection will count it ill. The adversary is quite a child, and as you know, I am not a novice in fighting, it will then be an easy matter for me to shed his blood for the glory of the Order, especially with the help of Christ, who cares more for those who bear His cross than for a certain Jurand or for the wrong done to a Mazovian girl!" Zygfried was most surprised at the news that Jurand's daughter was a married woman. The thought that there was a possibility of a fresh menacing and revengeful enemy settling at Spychow inspired even the old count with alarm. "It is clear," he said to himself, "that he will not neglect to avenge himself, and much more so when he shall have received his wife and she tells him that we carried her off from the forest court! Yes, it would be at once evident that we brought Jurand here for the purpose of destroying him, and that nobody ever thought of restoring his daughter to him." At this thought it struck Zygfried that owing to the prince's letters, the grand master would most likely institute an investigation in Szczytno so that he might at least clear himself in the eyes of the prince, since it was important for the grand master and the chapter to have the Mazovian prince on their side in case of war with the powerful king of Poland. To disregard the strength of the prince in face of the multitude of the Mazovian nobility was not to be lightly undertaken. To be at peace with them fully insured the knights' frontiers and permitted them better to concentrate their strength. They had often spoken about it in the presence of Zygfried at Malborg, and often entertained the hope, that after having subdued the king, a pretext would be found later against the Mazovians and then no power could wrest that land from their hands. That was a great and sure calculation. It was therefore certain that the master would at present do everything to avoid irritating Prince Janusz, because that prince who was married to Kiejstut's daughter was more difficult to reconcile than Ziemowit of Plock, whose wife, for some unknown reason, was entirely devoted to the Order.

In the face of these thoughts, old Zygfried, who was ready to commit all kinds of crimes, treachery and cruelty, only for the sake of the Order and its fame, began to calculate conscientiously:

"Would it not be better to let Jurand and his daughter go? The crime and infamy weigh heavily on Danveld's name, and he is dead; even if the master should punish Rotgier and myself severely because we were the accomplices in Danveld's deeds, would it not be better for the Order?" But here his revengeful and cruel heart began to rebel at the thought of Jurand.

To let him go, this oppressor and executioner of members of the Order, this conqueror in so many encounters, the cause of so many infamies, calamities and defeats, then the murderer of Danveld, the conqueror of von Bergow, the murderer of Meineger, Godfried and Hugue, he who even in Szczytno itself shed more German blood than one good fight in war. "No, I cannot! I cannot!" Zygfried repeated vehemently, and at this thought his rapacious fingers closed spasmodically, and the old lean breast heaved heavily. Still, if it were for the great benefit and glory of the Order? If the punishment should fall in that case upon the still living perpetrators of the crimes, Prince Janusz ought to be by this time reconciled with the foe and remove the difficulty by an arrangement, or even an alliance. "They are furious," further thought the old count; "but he ought to show them some kindness, it is easy to forget a grievance. Why, the prince himself in his own country was an abductor; then there is fear of revenge…."

Then he began to pace in the hall in mental distraction, and then stopped in front of the Crucifix, opposite the entrance, which occupied almost the whole height of wall between the two windows, and kneeling at its feet he said: "Enlighten me, O Lord, teach me, for I know not! If I give up Jurand and his daughter then all our actions will be truly revealed, and the world will not say Danveld or Zygfried have done it but they will lay the blame upon the Knights of the Cross, and disgrace will fall upon the whole Order, and the hatred of that prince will be greater than ever. If I do not give them up but keep them or suppress the matter, then the Order will be suspected and I shall be obliged to pollute my mouth with lying before the grand master. Which is better, Lord? Teach and enlighten me. If I must endure vengeance, then ordain it according to Thy justice; but teach me now, enlighten me, for Thy religion is concerned, and whatever Thou commandest I will do, even if it should result in my imprisonment and even if I were awaiting death and deliverance in fetters."

And resting his brow upon the wooden cross he prayed for a long time; it did not even for a moment cross his mind that it was a crooked and blasphemous prayer. Then he got up, calmed, thinking that the grace of the wooden cross sent him a righteous and enlightened thought, and that a voice from on high said to him: "Arise and wait for the return of Rotgier." "So! I must wait. Rotgier will undoubtedly kill the young man; it will then be necessary to hide Jurand and his daughter, or give them up. In the first instance, it is true, the prince will not forget them, but not being sure who abducted the girl he will search for her, he will send letters to the grand master, not accusing him but inquiring, and the affair will be greatly prolonged. In the second instance, the joy at the return of Jurand's daughter will be greater than the desire to avenge her abduction. Surely we can always say that we have found her after Jurand's outrage." The last thought entirely calmed Zygfried. As to Jurand himself there was no fear; for he and Rotgier had long before come to an understanding that in case Jurand were to be set free, he could neither avenge himself nor harm them. Zygfried was glad in his terrible heart. He rejoiced also at the thought of God's judgment which was to take place in the castle at Ciechanow. And as to the result of the mortal combat he was not in the least alarmed. He recollected a certain tournament in Königsberg when Rotgier overcame two powerful knights, who passed in their Andecave country as unconquerable fighters. He also remembered the combat near Wilno, with a certain Polish knight, the courtier Spytko of Melsztyn, whom Rotgier killed. And his face brightened, and his heart exulted, for when Rotgier to a certain extent was already a celebrated knight, he first had led an expedition to Lithuania and had taught him the best way to carry on a war with that tribe; for this reason he loved him like a son, with such deep love, that only those who must have strong affections locked up in their hearts are able to do. Now that "little son" will once more shed hated Polish blood, and return covered with glory. Well, it is God's judgment, and the Order will at the same time be cleared of suspicion. "God's judgment...." In the twinkling of an eye, a feeling akin to alarm oppressed his old heart. Behold, Rotgier must engage in mortal combat in defence of the innocence of the Order of the Knights of the Cross. Yet, they are guilty; he will therefore fight for that falsehood.... What then if misfortune happen? But in a moment it occurred to him again that this was impossible. Yes! Rotgier justly writes: "That by the help of Christ who cares more for those who bear the cross than for a certain Jurand or the wrong done to one Mazovian girl." Yes, Rotgier will return in three days, and return a conqueror.

Thus the old Knight of the Cross calmed himself, but at the same time he wondered whether it would not be advisable to send Danusia to some out of the way, distant castle, from which in no possible manner the stratagems of the Mazovians could rescue her. But after hesitating for a moment he gave up that idea. To take overt action and accuse the Order, only Jurandowna's husband could do that. But he will perish by Rotgier's hand. After that, there will only be investigations, inquiries, correspondence, and accusations from the prince. But this very procedure will greatly retard the affair, and it will be confused and obscured, and it goes without saying, it will be infinitely delayed. "Before it comes to anything," said Zygfried to himself, "I shall die, and it may also be that Jurandowna will grow old in the prison of the Knights of the Cross. Nevertheless, I shall order that everything in the castle be prepared for defence, and at the same time to make ready for the road, because I do not exactly know what will be the result of the meeting with Rotgier. Therefore I shall wait."

Meanwhile two of the three days, in which Rotgier had promised to return, passed by; then three and four, yet no retinue made its appearance at the gates of Szczytno. Only on the fifth day, well-nigh toward dark, the blast of the horn resounded in front of the bastion at the gate of the fortress. Zygfried, who was just finishing his vesper prayer, immediately dispatched a page to see who had arrived.

After a while the page returned with a troubled face. This Zygfried did not observe on account of the darkness, for the fire in the stove was too far back to illuminate the room sufficiently.

"Have they returned?" inquired the old Knight of the Cross.

"Yes!" replied the page.

But there was something in his voice which alarmed the old knight, and he said:

"And Brother Rotgier?"

"They have brought Brother Rotgier."

Then Zygfried got up and for a long while he held on to the arm of the chair to prevent himself from falling, then in a stifled voice he said:

"Give me the cloak."

The page placed the cloak on his shoulders. He had apparently regained his strength, for he put on the cowl himself without assistance, then he went out.

In a moment he found himself in the courtyard of the castle, where it was already quite dark; he walked slowly upon the cracking snow toward the retinue which was coming through the gate. He stopped near it where a crowd had already gathered, and several torches, which the soldiers of the guard brought, illuminated the scene. At the sight of the old knight the servants opened a way for him. By the light of the torches could be seen the terrified faces, and the whispering of the people could be heard in the dark background:

"Brother Rotgier...."

"Brother Rotgier has been killed...."

Zygfried drew near the sleigh, upon which the corpse was stretched on straw and covered with a cloak; he lifted one end of it.

"Bring a light," he said, whilst drawing aside the cowl.

One of the servants brought a torch which he held toward the corpse and by its light the old knight observed the head of Rotgier; the face was white as if frozen and bandaged with a black kerchief fastened under the beard, evidently for the purpose of keeping the mouth closed. The whole face was drawn and so much altered that it might be mistaken for somebody else's. The eyes were closed, and around them and near the temples were blue patches, and the cheeks were scaly with frost. The old knight gazed at it for a long while amid complete silence. Others looked at him, for it was known that he was like a father to Rotgier, and that he loved him. But he did not shed even a single tear, only his face looked more severe than usual, but there was depicted in it a kind of torpid calm.

"They sent him back thus!" he said at last.

But he immediately turned toward the steward of the castle and said:

"Let a coffin be prepared by midnight, and place the body in the chapel."

"There is one coffin left of those which were made for those Jurand killed; it wants only to be covered with cloth, which I shall order to be done."

"And cover him with a cloak," said Zygfried, whilst covering the face of Rotgier, "not with one like this but with one of the Order."

After a while he added:

"Do not close the lid."

The people approached the sleigh. Zygfried again pulled the cowl over his head, but he recollected something before leaving, and he asked:

"Where is van Krist?"

"He also was killed," replied one of the servants, "but they were obliged to bury him in Ciechanow because putrefaction set in."

"Very well."

Then he left, walking slowly, entered the room and sat down upon the same chair where he was when the tidings reached him; his face was as if petrified and motionless and he sat there so long that the page began to be alarmed; he put his head halfway in the door now and then. Hour after hour passed by. The customary stir ceased within the castle, but from the direction of the chapel came a dull indistinct hammering; then nothing disturbed the silence but the calls of the watchmen.

It was already about midnight when the old knight awoke as from sleep, and called the servant.

"Where is Brother Rotgier?" he asked.

But the servant, unnerved by the silence, events and sleeplessness, apparently did not understand him, but looked at him with fear and replied in a trembling voice:

"I do not know, sir...."

The old man burst out into laughter and said mildly:

"Child, I asked whether he is already in the chapel."

"Yes, sir."

"Very well then. Tell Diedrich to come here with a lantern and wait until my return; let him also have a small kettle of coals. Is there already a light in the chapel?"

"There are candles burning about the coffin."

Zygfried put on his cloak and left.

When he entered the chapel, he looked around to see whether anybody else was present; then he closed the door carefully, approached the coffin, put aside two of the six candles burning in large brazen candlesticks in front of him, and knelt down before it.

As his lips did not move, it showed that he was not praying. For some time he only looked at the drawn yet still handsome face of Rotgier as though he were trying to discover in it traces of life.

Then amid the dead silence in the chapel he began to call in suppressed tones:
"Dear little son! Dear little son!"

Then he remained silent; it seemed as though he were expecting an answer.

Then he stretched out his hand and pushed his emaciated talon-like fingers under the cloak, uncovered Rotgier's breast and began to feel about it, looking everywhere at the middle and sides below the ribs and along the shoulder-blades: at last he touched the rent in the clothing which extended from the top of the right shoulder down to the armpit, his fingers penetrated and felt along the whole length of the wound, then he cried with a loud voice which sounded like a complaint:

"Oh!... What merciless thing is this!... Yet thou saidst that fellow was quite a child!... The whole arm! The whole arm? So many times thou hast raised it against the Pagans in defence of the Order.... In the name of the Father, the Son and the Holy Ghost. Thou foughtest falsely, and so succumbed in a false cause; be absolved and may thy soul...."

The words were cut short on his lips which began to tremble, and deep silence reigned once more in the chapel.

"Dear little son! Dear little son!"

Now there was something like a petition in Zygfried's voice, and at the same time it seemed as he lowered his voice as though his petition contained some important and terrible secret.

"Merciful Christ!... If thou art not condemned, give a sign, move thy hand, or give one twitch of the eye, for my old heart is groaning within my breast.... Give a sign, I loved thee, say one word!..."

And supporting himself with his hands upon the edge of the coffin, he fastened his vulture-like eyes upon the closed eyelids of Rotgier and waited.

"Bah! How couldst thou speak?" said he, at last, "when frost and evil odor emanate from thee. But as thou art silent, then I will tell thee something, and let thy soul, flying about here among the flaming candles, listen!"

Then he bent down to the face of the corpse.

"Dost thou remember how the chaplain would not permit us to kill Jurand and how we took an oath. Well, I will keep that oath, but I will cause thee to rejoice wherever thou art, even at the cost of my own damnation."

Then he retreated from the coffin, replaced the candlesticks, covered the corpse with the cloak, and left the chapel.

At the door of the room, overpowered with deep sleep, slept the servant, and according to Zygfried's orders Diedrich was already waiting inside. He was of low stature thickly set, with bowed legs and a square face which was concealed by a dark cowl falling to his arm. He was dressed in an untanned buffalo jacket, also a buffalo belt upon his hips from which was hanging a bunch of keys and a short knife. In his right hand he held a membrane-covered lantern; in the other, a small kettle and a torch.

"Are you ready?" inquired Zygfried.

Diedrich bowed silently.

"I gave orders for you to bring with you a kettle with coal in it."

The short fellow was still silent; he only pointed to the burning wood in the fireplace and took the iron shovel standing at the fireside, and filled the kettle with the burning coal, then he lit the lantern and waited.

"Now listen, dog," said Zygfried; "you have never revealed what Count Danveld commanded you to do; the count also ordered the cutting out of your tongue. But you can still motion to the chaplain with your fingers. I therefore forewarn you, if you show him even with the slightest motion of your hand what you are to do now by my command, I shall order you to be hanged."

Diedrich again bowed in silence, but his face was drawn on account of the terrible, ominous recollection; for his tongue was torn out for quite another reason than what Zygfried said.

"Now proceed, and lead to the underground cell where Jurand is."

The executioner grasped the handle of the kettle with his gigantic hand, picked up the lantern and then left. At the door they passed by the guard who was asleep, descended the stairs, and turned, not toward the principal entrance, but directed their steps to the small corridor in the rear of the stairs, extending through the whole width of the edifice, and terminating in a heavy iron door which was concealed in a niche in the wall. Diedrich opened it and they found themselves again in the open air in a small courtyard surrounded on its four sides by high walled granaries where they kept their stores in case the castle should be besieged. Underneath one of these stores, on the right, was an underground prison. There was not a single guard standing there, because even if a prisoner should succeed in breaking through from the underground prison, he would then find himself in the courtyard which only gave exit through the door in the niche.

"Wait," said Zygfried, and leaning against the wall, he rested, for he felt that something was the matter with him; he was short of breath, as though his breast was too much tightened under the straight coat of mail. In plain terms, considering what had happened, he felt his old age, and his brow under the cowl was covered with drops of perspiration; he therefore stopped for a moment to recover breath.

The night following the gloomy day became extraordinarily clear and the little courtyard was brightly illuminated by the rays of the moon which caused the snow to glisten with a yellowish tint. Zygfried inhaled with pleasure the cool invigorating air, but he forgot that on a similar bright night Rotgier left for Ciechanow whence he did not return alive.

"And now thou liest in the chapel," he murmured to himself.

Diedrich thought that the count was talking to him; he therefore lifted up his lantern and threw its light upon his face which had a terrible and cadaverous appearance, but at the same time it looked like the head of an old vulture.

"Lead on," said Zygfried.

Diedrich lowered the lantern again which cast upon the snow a yellow circle of light and they proceeded. In the thick wall of the storehouse there was a recess in which several steps led to a large iron door. Diedrich opened it and went down the stairs in the deep dark aperture, raising the lantern so as to show the way to the count. At the end of the stairs there was a corridor in which, to the right and left, were exceedingly low doors leading to the cells of the prisoners.

"To Jurand!" said Zygfried.

And in a moment the bars creaked and they entered, but there was perfect darkness in the cell. But Zygfried, who could not see well in the dim light from the lantern, ordered the torch to be lighted, and in a moment he was enabled by its bright light to see Jurand lying on the straw. The prisoner's feet were fettered, but the chains on the hands were somewhat longer so as to enable him to carry food to his mouth. Upon his body was the same coarse sackcloth which he had on when he was arraigned before the court, but now it was covered with dark blood-stains, because, that day when the fight ended, only when maddened with pain the frantic knight was entangled in the net, the soldiers then tried to kill him, struck him with their halberds and inflicted upon him numerous wounds. The chaplain interfered and Jurand was not killed outright, but he lost so much blood that he was carried to prison half dead. In the castle they expected his death hourly. But owing to his immense strength he prevailed over death, although they did not attend to his wounds, and he was cast into the terrible subterranean prison, in which during the daytime when it thawed drops fell from the roof, but when there was frost the walls were thickly covered with snow and icicles.

On the ground on the straw lay the powerless man in chains, but he looked like a piece of flint shaped in human form. Zygfried commanded Diedrich to throw the light directly upon Jurand's face, then he gazed at it for a while in silence. Then he turned to Diedrich and said:

"Observe, he has only one eye—destroy it."

There was something in his voice like sickness and decrepitude, and for that very reason, the horrible order sounded more terrible, so that the torch began somewhat to tremble in the hand of the executioner. Yet he inclined it toward Jurand's face, and in a moment big drops of burning tar began to fall upon the eye of Jurand, covering it entirely from the brow down to the projecting cheek bone.

Jurand's face twitched, his grey mustachios moved, but he did not utter a single word of complaint. Whether it was from exhaustion, or the grand fortitude of his terrible nature, he did not even groan.

Zygfried said:

"It has been promised that you shall be freed, and you shall be, but you shall not be able to accuse the Order, for your tongue, which you might use against it, shall be torn out."

Then he again signaled to the executioner who replied with a strange guttural sound and showed by signs that for this he roust employ both hands, and therefore wanted the count to hold the light.

Then the old count took the torch and held it in his outstretched, trembling hand, but when Diedrich pressed Jurand's chest with his knees Zygfried turned his head and looked at the hoarfrost covered wall.

For a while resounded the clank of the chains, followed by the suppressed panting of a human breast which sounded like one dull, deep groan—and then all was still.

Finally Zygfried said:

"Jurand, the punishment which you have suffered you have deserved; but I have promised to Brother Rotgier, whom your son-in-law has killed, to place your right hand in his coffin."

Diedrich, who had just got up from his last deed, bent again upon the prostrate form of Jurand, when he heard Zygfried's words.

After a little while, the old count and Diedrich found themselves again in that open courtyard which was illuminated by the bright moon. When they reëntered the corridor, Zygfried took the lantern from Diedrich, also a dark object wrapped up in a rag, and said to himself in a loud voice,

"Now to the chapel and then to the tower."

Diedrich looked keenly at the count, but the count commanded him to go to sleep; he covered himself, hanging the lantern near the lighted window of the chapel and left. On his way he meditated upon what had just taken place. He was almost sure that his own end had also arrived and that these were his last deeds in this world, and that he would have to account for them before God. But his soul, the soul of a "Knight of the Cross," although naturally more cruel than mendacious, had in the course of inexorable necessity got accustomed to fraud, assassination and concealing the sanguinary deeds of the Order, he now involuntarily sought to cast off the ignominy and responsibility for Jurand's tortures, from both himself and the Order. Diedrich was dumb and could not confess, and, although he could make himself understood with the chaplain, he would be afraid to do so. What then? Nobody would know. Jurand might well have received all his wounds during the fight. He might have easily lost his tongue by the thrust of a lance between his teeth. An axe or a sword might have easily cut off his right hand. He had only one eye; would it be strange therefore that the other eye was lost in the fracas, for he threw himself madly upon the whole garrison of Szczytno. Alas! Jurand! His last joy in life trembled for a moment in the heart of the old Knight of the Cross. So, should Jurand survive, he ought to be set free. At this, Zygfried remembered a conversation he had had once with Rotgier about this, when that young brother laughingly remarked: "Then let him go where *his eyes will carry him*, and if he does not happen to strike Spychow, then let him *make inquiries* on the road." For that which had now happened was a part of the prearranged programme between them. But now Zygfried reentered the chapel and, kneeling in front of the coffin, he laid at Rotgier's feet Jurand's bleeding hand; that last joy which startled him was only for a moment and quickly disappeared, for the last time, from his face.

"You see," he said, "I have done more than we agreed to do. For King John of Luxemburg, although he was blind, kept on fighting and perished gloriously. But Jurand can stand no more and will perish like a dog behind the fence."

At this he again felt that shortness of breath that had seized him on his way to Jurand, also a weight on his head as of a heavy iron helmet, but this only lasted a second. Then he drew a deep breath and said:

"Ah! My time has also come. You were the only one I had; but now I have none. But if I lived longer, I vow to you, O little son, that I would also place upon your grave that hand which killed you, or perish myself. The murderer who killed you is still alive...."

Here his teeth clinched and such an intense cramp seized him that he could not speak for some time. Then he began again, but in a broken voice:

"Yes, your murderer still lives, but I will cut him to pieces ... and others with him, and I will inflict upon them tortures even worse than death itself...."

Then he ceased.

In a moment he rose again and approaching the coffin, he began to speak in quiet tones,

"Now I take leave of you ... and look into your face for the last time; perhaps I shall be able to see in your face whether you are pleased with my promises.... The last time."

Then he uncovered Rotgier's face, but suddenly he retreated.

"You are smiling, ..." he said, "but you are smiling terribly...."

In fact, the frozen corpse, which was covered with the mantle, had thawed. It may be from the heat of the burning candles, it had begun to decompose with extraordinary rapidity, and the face of the young count looked indeed terrible. The enormously swollen, and livid mouth looked something monstrous, the blue and swollen curled lips had the appearance of a grinning smile.

Zygfried covered that terrible human mask as quickly as possible.

Then he took the lantern and left the chapel. Here again, for the third time, he felt shortness of breath; he entered the house and threw himself upon his hard bed of the Order and lay for a time motionless. He thought he would fall asleep, when suddenly a strange feeling overpowered him; it seemed to him that he would never again be able to sleep, and that if he remained in that house death would soon follow.

Zygfried, in his extreme weariness, and without hope of sleep, was not afraid of death; on the contrary he regarded it as an exceedingly great relief. But he had no wish to submit himself to it that evening. So he sat up in his bed and cried:

"Give me time till to-morrow."

Then he distinctly heard a voice whispering in his ear:

"Leave this house. It will be too late to-morrow and you will not be able to accomplish your promise. Leave this house!"

The count got up with difficulty and went out. The guards were calling to one another from the bastions upon the palisades. The light emanating from the windows of the chapel illuminated the snow in front with a yellow gleam. In the middle of the court near the stone wall were two black dogs playing and tugging at a black rag. Beyond this the courtyard was empty and silent.

"It is yet necessary this night!" said Zygfried. "I am exceedingly tired, but I must go.... All are asleep. Jurand, overcome by torture, might also be asleep. I only am unable to sleep. I will go. I will go, for there is death within, and I have promised you.... Let death come afterward; sleep will not come. You are smiling there, but my strength is failing me. You are smiling, you are apparently glad. But you see that my fingers are benumbed, my hands have lost their strength, and I cannot accomplish it by myself ... the servant with whom she sleeps will accomplish it...."

Then he moved on with heavy steps toward the tower situated near the gate. Meanwhile the dogs which were playing near the stone wall came running up and began to fawn upon him. In one of them Zygfried recognized the bulldog which was so much attached to Diedrich that it was said in the castle that it served him as a pillow at night.

The dog greeted the count, it barked low once or twice; and then returned toward the gate acting as though it had divined his thoughts.

After a while Zygfried found himself in front of the narrow little doors of the tower, which at night were barred on the outside. Removing the bars, he felt for the balustrade of the stairs which commenced quite near the doors and began to ascend. In his absentmindedness he forgot the lantern; he therefore went up gropingly, stepping carefully and feeling with his feet for the steps.

Having advanced a few steps, he suddenly halted, when below quite near him he heard something like the breathing of a man, or beast.

"Who is there?"

But there was no answer, only the breathing grew quicker.

Zygfried was not a timid man; he was not afraid of death. But the preceding terrible night had quite exhausted his courage and self-control. It crossed his mind that Rotgier or the evil spirit was barring his way, and his hair stood up on his head and his brow was covered with cold sweat.

He retreated to the very entrance.

"Who is there?" he asked, with a choked voice.

But at that moment something struck him a powerful blow on his chest, so terrible that the old man fell through the door upon his back and swooned. He did not even groan.

Silence followed, after which there could be seen a dark form, stealthily issuing from the tower and making off toward the stable which was situated on the left side of the courtyard near the arsenal. Diedrich's big bulldog followed that figure silently. The other dog also ran after him and disappeared in the shadow of the wall, but shortly appeared again with its head to the ground, scenting as it were the trail of the other dog. In this manner the dog approached the prostrate and lifeless body of Zygfried, which it smelled carefully, then crouched near the head of the prostrate man and began to howl.

The howling continued for a long while, filling the air of that sombre night with a new kind of dolefulness and horror. Finally the small door concealed in the middle of the gate creaked and a guard armed with a halberd appeared in the courtyard.

"Death upon that dog," he said, "I'll teach you to howl during the night."

And he aimed the sharp end of the halberd so as to hit the animal with it, but at that moment he observed something lying near the little open door of the bastion.

"Lord Jesus! what is that?..."

He bent his head so as to look in the face of the prostrate man, and began to shout: "Help! Help! Help!"

Then he rushed to the gate and pulled with all his strength at the bell-rope.

END OF PART FIFTH.

PART SIXTH.

CHAPTER I.

Although Glowacz was somewhat anxious to hasten to Zgorzelice, he could not make the progress he wished, because the road was exceedingly bad. A general thaw had followed the severe winter, keen frost, and immense snowdrifts which covered whole villages.

Luty (February), in spite of its name,[110] by no means showed itself formidable. First there were thick, continuous fogs, succeeded by torrential rains, which melted the white snowdrifts before one's eyes; and in the intervals there were very high winds as is usual in the month of March; then the tempestuous clouds were suddenly torn asunder by the wind which now drove them together, and now scattered them, whilst on the earth the wind howled in the thickets, whistled in the forests and dispersed the snow beneath which only a short time before the boughs and trunks had slept their silent, wintry sleep.

The woods assumed a dark color. The meadows were inundated with broad sheets of water. The rivers and streams overflowed. Only the fishermen were glad at the abundance of the watery element, but the rest of humanity were confined as within a prison, sheltering themselves within their houses and huts. In many places communication between village and village could only be effected by means of boats. There was no lack of dams, dykes and roads through the forests and swamps, constructed of trunks, of trees and logs, but now the dykes became soft and the stumps in the low, wet places endangered travel, or the roads were rendered altogether impracticable. The most difficult part for the Bohemian to traverse was the lake-land region of Wielkopolska, where every spring the thaw was greater than in any other part of Poland. Consequently the road was specially difficult for horses.

He was therefore obliged to wait whole weeks, sometimes in small towns, sometimes in villages and farms, where he and his men were hospitably received, according to custom, by the people, who were willing listeners to the tale of the "Knights of the Cross," and paid for it with bread and salt. For this reason spring was already far advanced, and the greater part of March had already passed before he found himself in the neighborhood of Zgorzelice and Bogdaniec.

He longed to see his mistress as soon as possible, although he knew that he could never gain her, even as he could not gain the stars of heaven; nevertheless he adored and loved her with his whole soul. Yet he resolved first to go and see Macko; first, because he was sent to him; secondly, because he was bringing men with him who were to be left at Bogdanice. Zbyszko, having killed Rotgier, according to established rules, became the owner of his following, which consisted of ten men and as many horses. Two of them had been sent back with the body of Rotgier to Szczytno. Knowing how anxious his uncle was to obtain colonists, he sent the remaining eight men by Glowacz as a present to old Macko.

The Bohemian, on his arrival at Bogdaniec, did not find Macko at home; he was informed that Macko had gone with his dogs and crossbow to the forest; but he returned the same day, and having heard that an important retinue was waiting for him, he hastened to salute the guests and offer them hospitality. He did not recognize Glowacz at first, but when he gave his name, Macko was greatly agitated, and throwing down his hat and crossbow he cried:

"For God's sake! tell me, have they killed him? Tell what you know."

"They have not killed him," replied the Bohemian. "He is enjoying good health."

On hearing this, Macko was somewhat ashamed of himself, and began to puff; at last he drew a deep breath.

"Praised be the Lord Christ," he said. "Where is he now?"

"He left for Malborg and sent me here with news."

"And why did he go to Malborg?"

"To fetch his wife."

"Be careful, boy, in the name of God what wife did he go for?"

"For Jurand's daughter. There is much to be told about it, enough for a whole night, but, honored sir, allow me to rest a little, for I have been constantly traveling since midnight."

Macko ceased questioning for a little while, for his great surprise deprived him of speech. When he had somewhat recovered, he shouted to the servant to throw some wood on the fire and bring food for the Bohemian; then he began to pace up and down, gesticulating and talking to himself:

"I cannot believe mine own ears…. Jurand's daughter…. Zbyszko married…."

"He is married and not married," said the Bohemian.

Then he began slowly to relate what had happened, while Macko listened eagerly, only interrupting with questions when what the Bohemian related was not quite clear to him. For instance, Glowacz could not give the exact time when Zbyszko had got married, as there had been no public marriage. Nevertheless he affirmed that that marriage had surely taken place, and that it had come to pass owing to the instigation of Princess Anna Danuta, and had been made public only after the arrival of the Knight of the Cross, Rotgier, when Zbyszko had challenged him to the judgment of God, in the presence of the entire Mazovian court.

"Ah! He fought?" Macko exclaimed, his eyes sparkling with intense curiosity. "What followed?"

"He cut the German in two, and God also made me happy by delivering the armor-bearer into my hands."

Macko again began to puff, but this time with an air of satisfaction.

"Well!" he said. "He is a fellow not to be trifled with. He is the last of the Gradys, but so help me God, not the least. He was that already in the fight with the Fryzjans … when he was a mere stripling…."

Here he glanced sharply once and again at the Bohemian, then he continued:

"And so you tried to imitate him, and it seems you tell the truth. I doubted your words, but, as you yourself say, you had little work with the armor-bearer. But if he chopped off the arm of that dog-brother after killing the Aurochs, those are valiant deeds."

Then he suddenly asked:

"Is there rich spoil?"

"We have taken the arms, horses and ten men, eight of whom, the young lord sends you."

"What has he done with the other two?"

"He sent them back with the corpse."

"Why did not the prince send two of his own servants? Those two will not return."

The Bohemian smiled at Macko's greed which often betrayed him.

"The young lord need not consider such trifles now," he said, "Spychow is a large estate."

"It is a large estate; what of it, it is not yet his."

"Then whose is it?"

Macko rose from his seat.

"Speak! and Jurand?"

"Jurand is a prisoner, and dying, in the hands of the Knights of the Cross. God knows whether he will survive, and even if he survives and returns, what of it? Did not Father Caleb read Jurand's testament, announcing to all that the young lord is to be their master?"

The last words obviously made a great impression upon Macko; because he was too much amazed to thoroughly grasp the news. That Zbyszko had got married was painful to him at the first moment, for he loved Jagienka with a fatherly love, and heartily wished to see Zbyszko united to her. But, on the other hand, he had already grown accustomed to regard the affair as lost; moreover Jurandowna brought with her so much that Jagienka could never bring; the prince's favor, and being an only daughter her dower was many times greater. Macko already saw Zbyszko, as the prince's friend, the master of Bogdaniec and of Spychow; nay, in the near future, a castellan. That was not at all unlikely. For it was told in those days of a certain poor nobleman who had twelve sons, six fell in battle and the other six became castellans and were advancing toward greatness; only a reputation could assist Zbyszko in this career, so that Macko's ambition and greed for a pedigree might be realized according to his wishes. The old man, however, had much cause for alarm. He, himself, had once gone to the Knights of the Cross, to save Zbyszko and brought back with him an iron splinter between the ribs; now Zbyszko had gone to Malborg, into the very throat of the wolf. Was it to get his wife there or death? They would not look upon him there with a favorable eye, thought Macko. He had just destroyed one of their famous knights and before that he had killed Lichtenstein. Those dog-blooded men loved vengeance. That thought made the old knight very uneasy. It also occurred to him that Zbyszko, being quick tempered, would engage in a fight with some German; or what he most feared was that they would kidnap him as they had old Jurand and his daughter. At Zlotorja they did not scruple to kidnap even the prince himself. Why then should they be scrupulous with Zbyszko?

Then he asked himself what would happen if the youngster should escape the knights, but not find his wife? This thought pleased him, because even if Zbyszko should not recover her, he would still be the owner of Spychow, but that pleasure only lasted for a moment. For while the old man was much concerned about the property, yet Zbyszko's offspring interested him quite as much. If Danusia were to be lost, like a stone in the water and nobody knew whether she were alive or dead, Zbyszko could not marry another, and then there would be no heir to the Gradys of Bogdaniec. Ah! It would be quite another thing if he were married to Jagienka!... Moczydoly was not to be scorned; it was spacious and well stocked. Such a girl, like an apple-tree in the orchard, would bring forth every year without fail. Thus Macko's regret was greater than his joy at the prospect of the possession of the new estate. His regret and agitation caused him to renew his questions, and he again inquired of the Bohemian how and when the marriage had taken place.

But the Bohemian replied:

"I have told you already, honored sir, that I do not know when it happened, and what I conjecture I cannot confirm with an oath."

"What do you conjecture?"

"I have never left my young master and we slept together. On one evening only, he ordered me to leave him when I saw them all visit him: the princess accompanied by the lady Jurandowna, (Danusia,) Lord de Lorche and Father Wyszoniek. I was even surprised to see the young lady with a wreath on her head; but I thought they had come to administer the sacrament to my master.... It may be that the marriage took place then.... I recollect that the master commanded me to attire myself as for a wedding ceremony, but then I also thought that that was to receive the eucharist."

"And after that, did they remain by themselves?"

"They did not remain alone; and even if they had remained by themselves the master was then so feeble that he could not even eat without assistance. And there were already people sent by Jurand waiting for the young lady, and she left the following morning...."

"Then Zbyszko has not seen her since?"

"No human eye has seen her."

Then silence reigned for a while.

"What do you think?" asked Macko, presently. "Will the Knights of the Cross give her up, or not?"

The Bohemian shook his head, then he waved his hand discouragingly.

"I think," he said, slowly, "she is lost forever."

"Why?" asked Macko in terror.

"Because, when they said they had her there was yet hope, one could yet contend with them, either to ransom her, or take her from them by force. 'But,' they said, 'we had a girl retaken from robbers and we notified Jurand; he did not recognize her, and he killed of our people, in our very presence, more than fall in one good fight in war.'"

"Then they showed Jurand some other girl."

"So it is said. God knows the truth. It may not be true, and it may be that they showed him some other girl. But it is a fact that he killed people, and the Knights of the Cross are ready to swear that they never abducted Panna Jurandowna, and that is an exceedingly difficult affair. Even should the grand master order an investigation, they would reply that she was not in their hands; especially since the courtiers of Ciechanow spoke of Jurand's letter in which he said that she was not with the Knights of the Cross."

"It may be she is not with them."

"I beg your pardon, sir!... If they had recaptured her from the robbers, it would have been for no other motive than for ransom. The robbers, before that happened could neither write a letter nor imitate the signature of the lord of Spychow, nor send an honorable messenger."

"That is true; but what do the Knights of the Cross want her for?"

"Revenge on Jurand's race. They prefer vengeance to mead and wine; and if they want a pretext, they have one. The lord of Spychow was terrible to them, and his last deed completely finished them.... My master, I also heard, had lifted up his hand against Lichtenstein; he killed Rotgier.... God helped me, too, to shatter that dog-brother's arm. Wait, I pray, let us consider. There were four of them to be exterminated; now hardly one is alive, and that one is an old man, and your grace must bear in mind that we yet have our teeth."

There was again silence for a moment.

"You are a discreet armor-bearer," said Macko, at last; "but what do you think they are going to do with her?"

"Prince Witold, they say, is a powerful prince, even the German emperor bows to him; and what did they do to his children? Have they but few castles? Few underground prisons? Few wells? Few ropes and halters for the neck?"

"For the living God's sake!" exclaimed Macko.

"God grant that they may not also detain the young lord, although he went there with a letter from the prince, and accompanied by de Lorche who is a powerful lord and related to the prince. Ah, I did not want to set out for this place. But he commanded me to go. I heard him once say to the old lord of Spychow: 'It is to be regretted that you are not cunning, for I shall get nothing by craft, and with them that is a necessary thing. O Uncle Macko! he would be useful here;' and for that reason he dispatched me. But as for Jurandowna, even you, sir, will not find her, for probably she is already in the other world, and where death is concerned, even the greatest cunning cannot prevail."

Macko was absorbed in thought for a long while, after which he said:

"Ha! Then there is no counsel. Cunning cannot prevail against death. But if I were to go there and only get assurance that she has been removed, then in that case Spychow as well as Zbyszko remain. He will be able to return here and marry another maiden."

Here Macko breathed freely, as though a burden were removed from his heart, and Glowacz asked in a bashful, subdued voice:

"Do you mean the young lady of Zgorzelice?"

"Well!" replied Macko, "especially as she is an orphan, and Cztan of Rogow and Wilk of Brzozowa continually press their court to her."

At that the Bohemian straightened himself up.

"Is the young lady an orphan?... The knight Zych?..."

"Then you do not know."

"For the love of God! What has happened?"

"Well you are right. How could you know, since you have just arrived; and our only conversation has been about Zbyszko. She is an orphan. Unless he had guests, Zych of Zgorzelice never remained at home; otherwise he avoided Zgorzelice. He wrote about you to his abbot that he was going to visit Prince Przemka of Oswiecemia and ask him to give you to him. Zych did it because he was well acquainted with the prince and they have often frolicked together. Consequently Zych called upon me and said as follows: 'I am going to Oswiecemia, then to Glewic; keep your eye on Zgorzelice.' I at once suspected something wrong and said: 'Don't go! I will keep good watch over Jagienka and the estate,' for I know that Cztan and Wilk intend to do you some wrong, and you ought to know that the abbot out of spite against Zbyszko, preferred Cztan or Wilk for the girl. But he subsequently learned to know them better and rejected both of them, and turned them out of Zgorzelice; but not effectually, for they obstinately persisted. Now they have quieted down for a while, for they have wounded each other and are laid up, but before that occurred there was not a moment of security. Everything is upon my head, protection and guardianship. Now Zbyszko wishes me to come.... What will happen here to Jagienka—I don't know, but now I will tell you about Zych; he did not follow my advice—he went. Well, they feasted and frolicked together. From Glewic they went to see old Nosak, Prince Przemka's father, who rules in Cieszyn; till Jasko, the prince of Racibor, out of hatred for Prince Przemka, set upon them the robber band under the leadership of the Bohemian Chrzan; Prince Przemka and Zych of Zgorzelice perished in the affray. The robbers stunned the abbot with an iron flail, so that even now his head shakes and he knows nothing of what is going on in the world and has lost his speech, God help him, forever! Now old Prince Nosak bought Chrzan from the owner of Zampach, and tortured him so much that even the oldest inhabitants never heard of such cruelty,—but the cruelty did not lessen the sorrow of the old man for his son; neither did it resuscitate Zych, nor wipe away the tears of Jagienka. This is the result of the frolic.... Six weeks ago they brought Zych here and buried him."

"Such a hard master!..." sorrowfully said the Bohemian. "Under Boleslaw I was comfortably situated when he took me into captivity. But such was the captivity that I would not have exchanged it for freedom.... He was a good and worthy master! May God grant him eternal glory. Ah, I am very sorry! But I must grieve for the helpless young lady."

"Because the poor thing is a good girl, she loved her father more than a man loves his mother. Then too she is not safe in Zgorzelice. After the funeral, scarcely had the snow covered Zych's grave, when Cztan and Wilk stepped into the mansion of Zgorzelice. My people were informed of it beforehand. Then I, with the farm hands went to the rescue; we arrived in good time and with God's help we gave them a good thrashing. Immediately after the fight, the girl fell on her knees and begged me to save her. 'If I cannot belong to Zbyszko,' she said, 'I will belong to nobody else; only save me from those torturers, I prefer death to them....' I tell you that I made a real castle out of Zgorzelice. After that, they appeared twice on the premises, but believe me, they could not succeed. Now there will be peace for some time, for as I told you: they hurt each other badly, so much so, that neither is able to move head or foot."

Glowacz made no observation upon this, but when he heard of the conduct of Cztan and Wilk, he began to gnash his teeth so loudly, that it sounded like the creaking caused by the opening and closing of a door, then he began to rub his strong hands upon his thighs as though they were itching. Finally, he uttered with difficulty only one word:

"Villains!"

But at that moment, a voice was heard in the entrance-hall, the door suddenly opened and Jagienka rushed into the house, and with her was Jasko, her oldest brother, who was fourteen years old and looked as like her, as though they were twins.

She had heard from some peasants at Zgorzelice, that they had seen the Bohemian Hlawa, at the head of some people, journeying to Bogdaniec, and like Macko, she also was terrified, and when they informed her that Zbyszko was not among them she was almost sure that some misfortune had happened. She therefore lost no time and hastened to Bogdaniec to ascertain the truth.

"What has happened?... For God's sake tell me," she shouted, when yet upon the threshold.

"What should happen?" replied Macko. "Zbyszko is alive and well."

The Bohemian hastened toward the young lady, knelt upon one knee and kissed the hem of her dress, but she paid no attention to it; only when she heard the reply of the old knight she turned her head from the fireplace to the darker side of the room, and only after a while, as if having forgotten that it was necessary to salute the Bohemian, she said:

"The name of Jesus Christ be praised!"

"Forever and ever," replied Macko.

Then she observed the kneeling Bohemian at her feet and bent toward him.

"From my soul I am glad to see you, Hlawa, but why did you leave your master behind?"

"He sent me away, most gracious lady."

"What were his orders?"

"He ordered me to go to Bogdaniec."

"To Bogdaniec?... What else?"

"He sent me to get counsel.... He also sends his compliments and good wishes."

"To Bogdaniec? Very well, then. But where is he himself?"

"He left for Malborg, and is now among the Knights of the Cross."

Jagienka's face again assumed an expression of alarm.

"Why, is he tired of life?"

"He is in quest, gracious lady, of that which he will not be able to find."

"I believe he will not find it," interrupted Macko. "Just as one cannot drive a nail without a hammer, so are man's wishes without the will of God."

"What are you talking about?" cried Jagienka. But Macko replied with another query.

"Did he say to you that Zbyszko went for Jurandowna? It seems to me that he did."

Jagienka at first did not reply, and only after awhile, catching her breath, she replied:

"Ay! He said! But what hindered him telling?"

"Well, then, now I can talk freely."

And he began to tell to her all that he had heard from the Bohemian. He wondered at himself why his words came haltingly and with difficulty, but being a clever man, he tried to avoid any expression that might irritate Jagienka, and he dwelt strongly upon what he himself believed, that Zbyszko was never the husband of Danusia in reality and that she was already lost to him forever.

The Bohemian confirmed Macko's words now and then, sometimes by nodding his head in approval, sometimes repeating "By God, true, as I live," or: "It is so, not otherwise!" The young lady listened, with eyelashes lowered till they touched her cheeks; she asked no more questions, and was so quiet that her silence alarmed Macko.

"Now, what do you say to that?" he enquired when he had ended.

But she did not reply, only two tears glistened between her eyelids and rolled down her cheeks.

After a while she approached Macko, and kissing his hand, said:

"The Lord be praised."

"Forever and ever," replied Macko. "Are you so much needed at home? Better stay with us."

But she refused to remain, giving as a reason that she had not given out the provisions for supper. But Macko, although he knew that there was the old lady, Sieciechowa, at Zgorzelice, who could easily fulfil Jagienka's duties, did not persuade her to remain, for he knew that sorrow does not like the light on human tears, and that a man is like a fish, when it feels the penetrating harpoon in its body it sinks to the depths.

Then he only regarded her as a girl, so he led her and the Bohemian into the courtyard.

But the Bohemian brought the horse from the stable, harnessed him, and departed with the young lady.

But Macko returned to the house, shook his head, and murmured:

"What a fool that Zbyszko is?... Why, her presence seems to have filled the whole house with perfume."

The old man lamented to himself. "Had Zbyszko taken her immediately after he returned, by this time there might have been joy and delight! But what of it now? If they should speak of him her eyes would immediately be filled with tears of longing, and the fellow is roaming about the world and may break the head of some of the knights at Malborg, provided they do not break his; and now the house is empty, only the arms on the wall glitter. There is some benefit in husbandry. Running about is nothing, Spychow and Bogdaniec are nothing. Very soon none will remain to whom they might be left."

Here Macko became angry.

"Wait, you tramp," he exclaimed, "I will not go with you, you may do as you like!"

But at that very moment he was seized with an exceeding yearning after Zbyszko.

"Bah! shall I not go," he thought. "Shall I remain at home? God forbid!... I wish to see that rascal once more. It must be so. He will again fight one of those dog-brothers—and take spoil. Others grow old before they receive the belt of knighthood, but he already has received the belt from the prince.... And rightly so. There are many valorous youths among the nobility; but not another like him."

His tender feelings entirely subdued him. First he began to look at the arms, swords and axes which had become blackened by the smoke, as though considering which to take with him, and which to leave behind; then he left the house; first, because he could not stay there; secondly, to give orders to prepare the carriage and give the horses double provender.

In the courtyard where it was already beginning to grow dark, he remembered Jagienka, who only a moment ago sat here on horseback, and he again became uneasy.

"I must go," he said to himself, "but who is going to protect the girl against Cztan and Wilk. May thunder strike them."

But Jagienka was on the road with her little brother, Jasko, crossing the woods leading to Zgorzelice, and the Bohemian accompanied them in silence, with love and grief in his heart. A moment since he saw her tears, now he looked at her dark form, scarcely visible in the darkness of the forest, and he guessed her sorrow and pain. It also seemed to him that at any moment Wilk or Cztan's rapacious hands might dart from the dark thicket and grasp her, and at that thought, he was carried away by wild anger and longed for a fight. At times the desire for fight was so intense that he wanted to grasp his axe or sword and cut down a pine tree on the road. He felt that a good fight would comfort him. Lastly he would be glad, even if he could let the horse go at a gallop. But he could not do it, they rode silently in front of him, and at a very slow gait, foot by foot, and little Jasko, who was of a talkative disposition, after several attempts to engage his sister in conversation, seeing that she was unwilling to speak, desisted, and also sank into deep silence.

But when they were approaching Zgorzelice, the sorrow in the Bohemian's heart turned to anger against Cztan and Wilk: "I would not spare even my blood in your behalf," he said to himself, "provided it comforted you. But what can I, unfortunate, do? What can I tell you? Unless I tell you that he ordered me to kneel before you. And, God grant that that might be of some comfort to you."

Thinking thus, he urged his horse close to Jagienka's.

"Gracious lady...."

"Are you riding with us?" enquired Jagienka, as though awaking from sleep. "What do you say?"

"I forgot to tell you what my master commanded me to say to you. When I was about to depart from Spychow, he called me and said 'I bow at the feet of the young lady of Zgorzelice, for whether in good or bad fortune, I shall never forget her; and for what she did for my uncle and myself, may God recompense her, and keep her in good health.'"

"May God also recompense him for his good words," replied Jagienka.

Then she added, in such a wonderful tone, that it caused the Bohemian's heart to melt:

"And you, Hlawa."

The conversation ceased for a while. But the armor-bearer was glad for himself and for her words. For he said to himself: "At least it shall not be said that she has been fed with ingratitude." He also began to rack his brains for something more of the same nature to tell her; and after a moment he said:

"Lady."

"What?"

"This ... as it were ... I want to say, as the old *pan* of Bogdaniec also said: 'That the lady there is lost forever, and that he will never find her, even if the grand master himself assist him.'"

"Then she is his wife...."

The Bohemian nodded his head.

"Yes, she is his wife."

Jagienka made no reply to this, but at home, after supper, when Jasko and the younger brother were put to bed, she ordered a pitcher of mead. Then she turned to the Bohemian and asked:

"Perhaps you want to retire. I wish to continue our conversation."

The Bohemian, although tired, was ready to chatter even till morning. So they began to talk, and he again related in general terms all that had happened to Zbyszko, Jurand, Danusia and himself.

CHAPTER II.

Macko prepared for his journey, and Jagienka did not show herself at Bogdaniec for two days after her consultation with the Bohemian. It was only on the third day that the old knight met her on his way to church. She was riding with her brother Jasiek to church at Krzesnia, and with her was a considerable number of armed servants in order to protect her from Cztan and Wilk, because she was not sure whether Cztan and Wilk were still sick or were planning to harm her.

"Any way, I intended to call upon our own people at Bogdaniec," she said, greeting Macko, "because I have to consult you about a very important affair, but since you are here we can talk about it now."

Then she advanced in front of the retinue, obviously to prevent the servants overhearing their conversation. When Macko was near her she inquired:

"Are you surely going?"

"If God will, not later than to-morrow."

"Are you going to Malborg?"

"To Malborg, or any other place, according to circumstances."

"Now then listen to me. I have thought a long time about what I ought to do. I want to ask your advice, too. You well know that as long as papa was alive, and the abbot was powerful, it was quite different. Cztan and Wilk also thought that I should choose one of them, so they kept their temper. But now I stand alone without a protector; then either I shall remain at Zgorzelice in a fortress, like a prisoner, or they will do us some harm without fail. Is it not so?"

"Yes," said Macko, "I thought of it myself."

"And what did you devise?"

"I devised nothing, but I must tell you one thing, that we are in Poland and the law of this country punishes severely those who are guilty of acts of violence."

216

"Very well, but the transgressors have no difficulty in crossing the frontier. Indeed, I know that Szlonsk is also in Poland, yet there the princes themselves quarrel and attack each other. If it were not so, my beloved father would still be alive. There are already Germans there and the times are stormy; they are mischievous, so that if any one of them wishes to conceal himself, he does. It would be easy for me to avoid Cztan and Wilk, but it concerns my little brother. If I should be absent there would be peace, but if I remained in Zgorzelice, God only knows what ill luck might happen. There would be outrages and fights; and Jasiek is already fourteen years old, and nobody, not even myself, can detain him. Upon the last occasion when you came to our assistance he flew to the front, and when Cztan used his club upon the crowd he nearly hit him on the head. 'O,' Jasko said to the servants, 'those two I will prosecute to the very end.' I tell you that there will not be a single peaceful day and some evil might befall the youngster."

"Faith. Cztan and Wilk are dog-brothers," said Macko, "although they would not dare lift up their hands against children. Bah! only a Knight of the Cross would do that."

"They will not lift up their hands against children, but in case of tumult, or, God forbid, in an incendiary fire, there will be no lack of accidents. Why talk! I love the brother of old Sieciechowa as my own parents, and protection for them from the dear old woman is not wanting, yet, without me ... would they be safer without me?"

"May be," replied Macko.

Then he looked slyly at the girl.

"Then, what do you want?"

And she replied in a low tone:

"Take me with you."

Then Macko, although he easily understood the drift of the conversation, was much surprised. He checked his horse, and exclaimed:

"Fear God, Jagienka."

But she dropped her head and replied bashfully and sadly:

"You may think so, but as far as myself is concerned, I would rather speak out than be silent. Hlawa and yourself said that Zbyszko will never find Danusia, and the Bohemian's hope of finding her is even less. God is my witness that I do not wish her evil in the least. Let the mother of God watch over that poor girl and keep her. Zbyszko loved her more than myself. Well, I cannot help it. Such is my lot. But observe this, so long as Zbyszko does not find her, or as you believe, he will never find her, then, then ..."

"What then?" asked Macko, seeing that the girl was getting more and more confused and stammering.

"Then I do not wish to be Madame Cztan, nor Madame Wilk, nor madame anybody."

Macko breathed freely.

"I thought that you had already forgiven him."

But she, still in a sad tone, replied: "Ah!..."

"Then what are your wishes? How can we take you among the Knights of the Cross?"

"Not exactly among the Knights of the Cross, I should like to be now with the abbot who is confined in the hospital at Sieradz. He has not a single friendly soul with him. The servants care more for the pitcher than they do for him. Moreover, he is my godfather and benefactor. If he were well I would have sought his protection all the same because the people fear him."

"I shall not dispute that," said Macko, who as a matter of fact, would be glad that Jagienka should not go with him, for he well knew the Knights of the Cross, and he was thoroughly convinced that Danuska would never come out alive from their hands. "But only this I tell you, that to travel with a girl is very troublesome."

"May be with others, but not with me. Nothing has occurred to me so far, but I am accustomed to go about with the bow and can endure hardship in the chase. When it is necessary, it is necessary. Don't be afraid. I shall take Jasiek's clothing and a net for my hair and I shall go. Jasiek, although younger than I am, with the exception of his hair looks exactly like myself, so much so that when we disguised ourselves last carnival our departed father could not tell one from the other. Observe, neither the abbot nor anybody else recognized me."

"Neither Zbyszko?"

"If I shall see him...."

Macko thought for a moment, then suddenly smiled and said:

"But Wilk of Brzozowa and Cztan of Rogow would be furious."

"Let them! It might be worse if they came after us."

"Well! Fear not. I am an old man, but let them beware of my fist. All the Gradys are of the same mettle!... However, they have already tested Zbyszko...."

Meanwhile they arrived at Krzesnia. Old Wilk of Brzozowa, who also happened to be at church, from time to time cast gloomy glances at Macko, but he did not mind it, and with a light heart he returned with Jagienka immediately after mass.... Then they took leave of each other and parted. When Macko was by himself at Bogdaniec, less happy thoughts passed through his mind. He understood that neither the people at Zgorzelice nor the relatives of Jagienka would really object to her departure. "But as to the girl's admirers," he said to himself, "that is quite another affair, but against the orphans and their property they would not dare to lift up their hand, because they would cover themselves with excessive infamy. Everybody would be against them as one is against a wolf. But Bogdaniec is left to God's favor!... The quarries will be filled up, the flocks will be seized, the peasants will be enticed away!... If God permit me to return, then I will fight them. I shall send out bans, and fight them not with the fist but with the law!... Only let me return, and if I do?... They will combine against me, because I have spoiled their love affair, and if she goes with me they will yet be more rancorous."

He was much grieved about his estate at Bogdaniec which he had improved. Now he felt sure that on his return he would find it desolate and in ruins.

"Now then, it is necessary to take counsel," he thought.

Accordingly, after dinner, he ordered his horse to be saddled and left directly for Brzozowa.

It was already dark when he arrived. Old Wilk was sitting in the front room drinking mead from a pitcher. Young Wilk, who was wounded by Cztan, was lying on a skin-covered bench, and was also drinking mead. Macko entered unexpectedly and remained standing upon the threshold with a stern look on his face; tall, bony, armed only with a big sabre at his side. They recognized him at once, because his face was lit up by the bright flame of the fireplace, and at the first moment, both the father and son jumped up, lightning-like, and running toward the wall seized the first arms that were at hand.

But the old experienced Macko, well knowing the people and their customs, did not interfere in the least, he did not even reach his hand to his sword. He only put his hands on his hips, and said quietly in a somewhat sarcastic voice:

"How is it? Is this the kind of hospitality which the nobles in Brzozowa practice?"

These words had the desired effect; their hands fell, and in a moment the old man let fall the sword with a clash, the young man dropped his pike, and they stood with their necks craned toward Macko, their faces still expressing hatred, but already amazed and ashamed of themselves.

Macko smiled and said:

"May the name of Christ be praised!"

"Forever and ever."

"And Saint Jerzy."

"We serve him."

"I come to visit my neighbors with good will."

"With good will we greet you, the guest of his holy person."

Then old Wilk rushed toward Macko, and with his son, both of them pressed his right hand, they made him sit at a comfortable place at the table; in a second they threw another log on the fireplace, spread the table and put upon it a dish full of food, a jug of beer, a pitcher of mead, and began to eat and drink. Young Wilk glanced now and then at Macko, which, happily for the guest, contributed to lessen his hatred against him. But he served him, however, so diligently that he became pale from fatigue, because he was wounded and deprived of his wonted strength. The father and son burned with curiosity to know the object of Macko's call. None, however, asked him why, but waited for him to speak.

But Macko, as a man of manners, praised the meat, drink and hospitality. Only when he had filled himself well, he looked up and spoke with dignity:

"People often quarrel. But neighborly peace above all."

"There is not a better thing than peace," replied old Wilk, with equal composure.

"It also often happens," said Macko, "when one wants to undertake a long journey, he wants to make up and bid good-bye even to his adversaries."

"God reward you for your candid words."

"Not mere words, but deeds, for I actually came to wish you good-bye."

"From our soul we wish you might visit us daily."

"I wish I could feast you in Bogdaniec in a manner suitable to people who are acquainted with knightly honor. But I am in a hurry to go."

"Is it to war, or to some holy place?"

"I should like to go to one of the two, but the place I am going to is worse, for I am going among the Knights of the Cross."

"Among the Knights of the Cross," exclaimed both father and son.

"Yes!" replied Macko. "And one who is their enemy is going to them. It is well for him to be reconciled with God and men, so that he may not forfeit, not only his life, but everlasting salvation."

"It is wonderful," said old Wilk. "I have never yet seen any man who has not suffered from their wrongs and oppression."

"So it is in the whole fatherland," added Macko. "Neither Lithuania before its conversion to Christianity, nor even the Tartars were such a burden to the Polish kingdom as those devilish monks."

"Quite true, but this you also know, they gathered and gathered. It is time now to finish with them."

Then the old man spat in his hands, and young Wilk added:

"It cannot be otherwise now."

"It will come to pass, surely, but when? We cannot do it, it is the king's affair. It may be soon or not ... God only knows. But meanwhile I must go to them."

"Is it not with ransom for Zbyszko?"

As his father mentioned Zbyszko's name young Wilk's face became pale with hatred. But Macko replied quietly:

"May be with ransom but not for Zbyszko."

These words intensified the curiosity of both lords of Brzozowa. Old Wilk, who could no more contain himself, said:

"Can you tell us, or not, the reason for your going there?"

"I will tell you! I will!" he said, nodding assent, "but first let me tell you something else. Take notice then. After my departure Bogdaniec will be under God's care.... When Zbyszko and myself were fighting under Prince Witold, the abbot, also Zych of Zgorzelice, looked somewhat after our small property. Now we shall miss even that little. It pains me terribly to think that my endeavor and labor will be in vain.... You can well form an idea how much this troubles me. They will entice away my people, plough up the boundaries; they will take away my herds. Even should God permit me to return, I shall find my property ruined.... There is only one remedy, only one help ... good neighbor. For this reason I came to ask you as a neighbor that you would take Bogdaniec under your protection and see that no harm is done."

Listening to Macko's request, old Wilk and his son exchanged looks; both of them were amazed beyond measure. They were silent for a moment, and neither could muster courage enough to reply. But Macko lifted another cup of mead to his mouth, drank it, then continued his conversation in as quiet and confiding a manner as though the two had been his most intimate friends for years.

"I have told you candidly from whom most damage is expected. It is from no other quarter but from Cztan of Rogow. Although we were hostile to each other, I fear nothing from you because you are noble people who would face your adversaries, yet would not revenge yourselves by acting meanly. You are quite different. A knight is always a knight. But Cztan is a *prestak* (churl). From such a fellow anything might be expected, as you know. He is very bitter against me because I spoiled his game with Jagienka."

"Whom you reserve for your nephew," burst out young Wilk.

Macko looked at him and held him under his cold gaze for a moment, then he turned to the old man and said quietly:

"You know, my nephew married a rich Mazovian proprietress and took considerable dower." Silence more profound than before again reigned for a while. Both father and son gazed at Macko with their mouths wide open, for some time.

Finally the old man said:

"O! how is that? Tell us...."

Macko appeared not to notice the question and continued:

"This is the very reason why I must go, and why I also ask you, as worthy and upright neighbors, to take care of Bogdaniec when I go, and see to it that nobody damages my property. Have your eye especially upon Cztan and protect me against him."

During that time young Wilk, who was quick to understand, reflected that since Zbyszko had got married it would be better to be in friendship with Macko, because Jagienka confided in him, and did nothing without asking his advice. Thus new prospects suddenly presented themselves before his eyes. "It is not enough, we must not only not oppose Macko, but endeavor to be reconciled with him," he said to himself. Therefore, although he was somewhat under the influence of drink, he quickly stretched his hand under the table and grasped his father's knee and pressed it vigorously as a sign for his father to be careful in his speech, but said himself:

"Ay! we do not fear Cztan! Let him only try. He wounded me with the platter, true, but I too have given him such a sound drubbing that his own mother could not recognize him. Fear nothing! Be at your ease. Not even one crow shall be lost at Bogdaniec!"

"I see you are upright people. Do you promise me?"

"We promise!" both exclaimed.

"Upon your knightly honor?"

"Upon knightly honor."

"And upon your escutcheon?"

"Upon the escutcheon; yea, upon the cross too. So help us God!"

Macko smiled with satisfaction, and said:

"Well, this is now with you, and I am confident you will do it. If so, let me tell you something more. Zych, as you know, appointed me guardian of his children. I have, therefore, spoiled both Cztan's incursions and your young man at Zgorzelice. But now when I arrive at Malborg, or, God knows where, what then will become of my guardianship?... It is true, that God is a father of the fatherless; and woe to him who shall attempt to harm her; not only will I chop off his head with an axe, but also proclaim him an infamous scoundrel. Nevertheless I feel very sorry to part, sorry indeed. Then promise me I pray, that you will not only yourself not do any harm to Zych's orphans, but see too that others do not harm them."

"We swear! We swear!"

"Upon your knightly honor and your escutcheon?"

"Upon knightly honor and escutcheon."

"Also upon the cross?"

"Upon the cross too."

"God hears it. Amen," concluded Macko, and he breathed deeply, because he was sure that they would not break such an oath. Even if they were provoked they would rather gnaw their fists with anger than perjure themselves.

Then he began to take leave, but they insisted upon his remaining. He was obliged to drink and fraternize with old Wilk. But young Wilk, contrary to his custom to look for quarrels when drunk, this time limited his anger to threats against Cztan, and ran around

Macko so assiduously as though he were to obtain Jagienka from Macko the following morning. Toward midnight he fainted from over-exertion, and after they revived him, he fell asleep like a log. Old Wilk followed the example of his son, so that when Macko left them they were lying under the table like corpses. Yet Macko himself had an extraordinary head and was not so much affected by the drink, but was cheerful. When he returned home he reflected with joy upon what he had accomplished.

"Well!" he said to himself, "Bogdaniec is safe and so is Zgorzelice. They will be raging when they hear of Jagienka's departure. But she and my property are safe. The Lord Jesus has endowed men with skill, so that when one cannot make use of his fist, he uses his mind. The old man will surely challenge me when I return home, but it is not worth while to think about it…. Would to God that I might entrap the Knights of the Cross in such manner…. But it will be a difficult task with them. With us, even when one has an affair with a 'dog brother,' nevertheless if he takes an oath on his knightly honor and escutcheon he will keep it. But with them an oath has no value; it is like spitting upon the water. But may the mother of Jesus assist me, that I may be as serviceable to Zbyszko as I have been to Zychow's children, and Bogdaniec…."

Here, it crossed his mind, that perhaps it might be advisable not to take Jagienka, because the two Wilks would care for her as the apple of their eye. But the next moment he rejected that plan. "The Wilks might care for her, true, but Cztan will persist in his attempts, and God knows who will prevail. But it is a sure thing that there will be a succession of fights and outrages from which Zgorzelice, Zych's orphans, and even the girl might suffer. It will be an easy matter for Wilk to guard Bogdaniec. But by all means it will be better for the girl to be as far away from the two murderers as possible, and at the same time to be as near the rich abbot as possible. Macko firmly believed that Danusia would never be rescued from the Knights of the Cross, alive. And the hope that Zbyszko would return home as a widower and most likely take to Jagienka, never left him."

"Ah! Mighty God!" he said to himself. "In such a case he will be the owner of Spychow, then he will get Jagienka and Moczydoly, and in addition to it he will acquire that which the abbot will bequeath. I would not even spare him wax for candles."

Occupied with such thoughts, the road from Brzozowa seemed to be shortened, yet he arrived at Bogdaniec after nightfall, and was surprised to see his windows brightly illuminated. The servants, too, were awake, for he had scarcely entered the courtyard when the stable boy came rushing to him.

"Are there some guests?" asked Macko, dismounting.

"There is the young gentleman of Zgorzelice with the Bohemian," replied the stable boy.

This information astonished Macko, for Jagienka had promised to arrive next day, very early, when they were to start immediately. Then, why had Jasko come and that so late? It struck the old knight that something must have occurred at Zgorzelice, and he entered his house with a certain amount of anxiety. But within he found a bright fire burning in the large clay oven in the centre of the room. And upon the table were two iron cradles and two torches in them, by which light Macko observed Jasko, the Bohemian, Hlawa, and another young servant with a face as red as an apple.

"How are you, Jasko? and what is the matter with Jagienka?" asked the old nobleman.

"Jagienka ordered me to tell you," he said, whilst kissing Macko's hand, "that she has reconsidered the matter and she prefers to stay at home."

"For God's sake! What do you say? How? What has happened to her?"

But the boy looked at him with his beautiful blue eyes and smiled.

"What are you prating about?"

But at this moment, the Bohemian and the other boy also burst out laughing.

"You see!" exclaimed the disguised boy. "Who could recognize me. You even have failed to recognize me!"

Then Macko looked at the lovely figure carefully and exclaimed:

"In the name of the Father and Son! It is a true carnival! You also here, croaking thing. Why?"

"Yes! Why? Those who are on the road have no time to lose."

"Is it not to-morrow at dawn, that you were to leave?"

"Certainly! to-morrow at dawn, so that all may know. To-morrow they will think at Zgorzelice that I am your guest, and they will not notice it till the day after to-morrow. Sieciechowa and Jasiek know it. But Jasko promised, upon knightly honor, that he will tell only then, when the people begin to be restless. How is it you did not recognize me?"

Now it was Macko's turn to laugh.

"Let me have a good look at you; you are an excessively fine boy!... and singularly so. From such one might expect to raise a good breed.... I justly declare, if this fellow were, (pointing at himself) were not old,—well! But, even thus I tell you, keep off, girl, from creeping under my eyes, stand back!..."

And he began to threaten her with his finger, but looked at her with much pleasure. Because such a girl he never saw before. Upon her head she had a silken red net, and a yellow jacket upon her body and the breeches ample round her hips and tighter above them, of which one little leg was of the same color as the cap (net) upon her head, the other had longwise stripes, with a richly covered little sword at her side, smiling and bright like the dawn. Her face was so exquisite that he could not take his eyes off her.

"My God!" said the overjoyed Macko. "She looks like some marvelous young lady or like a flower, or something else!"

"And this one here—I am sure it must also be somebody in disguise?"

"This is Sieciechowa," answered Jagienka. "It would be improper for me to be alone among you. How could I? Therefore I have taken Anulka[111] with me so that two courageous women will be of help and service. Her also, nobody can recognize."

"There, old woman, you have a marriage feast. One is bad enough, now there will be two."

"Don't tease."

"I am not teasing, but everybody will recognize you and her, in the daytime."

"Pray, and why?"

"In order to go on their knees to you and to her also."

"O, give us peace!..."

"You shall have it, I am not in a hurry. But will Cztan or Wilk let you have peace? God knows. Do you know, birdie, where I have just been? Why, at Brzozowa."

"For God's sake! What are you saying?"

"It is true as truth itself that the Wilks protect Bogdaniec and Zgorzelice against Cztan. Well, it is an easy matter to challenge an enemy and fight him. But to make your enemy into a protector of your own property is a very difficult task."

Then Macko related his adventures with the Wilks, how they had become reconciled to each other. How he had got advantage over them; to this she listened with the greatest wonder, and when he concluded she said:

"The Lord Jesus did not stint you in craftiness, and I observe that you will always be successful in your undertakings."

But Macko shook his head, as though he felt sorry.

"Ay, daughter! If that were so, you would have long ago become the lady of Bogdaniec!"

Upon hearing that, Jagienka looked at him with her lovely blue eyes for a moment, then she approached him, and kissed his hand.

"Why do you kiss me?" inquired the old knight.

"Nothing.... I only wish to bid you goodnight, because it is getting late and to-morrow we must get up early for our journey."

She then embraced Sieciechowa and left, and Macko led the Bohemian to his room, where they stretched themselves upon aurochs' skins and both fell sound asleep.

CHAPTER III.

After the destruction, conflagration and slaughter which the Knights of the Cross had committed in 1331, at Sieradz, Casimir the Great rebuilt the razed town. The place, however, was not exceedingly splendid and could not keep pace with the other towns of the realm. But Jagienka, who hitherto had spent her time among the people of Zgorzelice and Krzesnia, was beside herself with admiration and astonishment at the sight of the houses, towers, town hall, and especially the churches; the wooden structure at Krzesnia could not be compared with them. At first she lost her wonted resolution, so much so that she dared not talk aloud, and only inquired of Macko in a whisper about those wonderful things which dazzled her eyes. But when the old knight assured her that there was as much difference between Sieradz and Krakow as there is between a firebrand and the sun, she would not believe her own ears, because it appeared to her an impossibility that another city could be found in the world which could be equal to Sieradz.

They were received in the cloister by the same shriveled old prior, who still remembered in his childhood the butchery by the Knights of the Cross, and who had previously received Zbyszko. The news of the abbot occasioned them sorrow and trouble; he lived in the cloister for a long while, but he left a fortnight before their arrival to visit his friend, the bishop of Plock. He was constantly ill. He was generally conscious in the morning; but toward the evening he lost his head, he stormed and he asked to put on a coat of mail, and challenged Prince John of Racibor. The clergy were obliged to apply force to keep him in bed; that was not accomplished without considerable trouble and even much risk. About a fortnight ago he had entirely lost his reason, and in spite of his serious illness, he had given orders to be taken to Plock immediately.

"He said that he confided in nobody so much as in the bishop of Plock, and that he wished to receive the sacrament from him alone and leave his testament with him. We opposed his journey as much as we could, for he was very faint, and we feared that he would not survive even one mile's journey. But to oppose him was not an easy task. So the attendants prepared a wagon and carried him away. May God direct it to a happy issue."

"If he had died somewhere near Sieradz you would have heard of it," said Macko.

"We would have surely heard of it," replied the little old prior. "We therefore are of opinion that he did not die, and we think that he had not yet when he reached Lenczyca. What may have happened beyond that place, we are unable to tell. You will get information on the road if you go after him."

Macko felt uneasy when he received the tidings, and he went to take counsel with Jagienka, who had already got information from the Bohemian whither the abbot had gone.

"What is to be done?" he asked her; "and what are you going to do with yourself?"

"Come to Plock, and I will go with you."

"To Plock!" repeated Sieciechowa, in a piping voice.

"Look how things go! Is it as easy for you to go to Plock as to handle the sickle?"

"How can I and Sieciechowa return by ourselves? If I cannot continue my journey with you, it would have been preferable to have remained at home. Do you not think that Wilk and Cztan will be more obstinate in their intrigues against me?"

"Wilk will protect you against Cztan."

"I fear Wilk's protection as much as Cztan's open violence. I see that you too are opposing me; if it were only simple opposition I should not mind it, but not when it is in earnest."

Indeed Macko's opposition was not in earnest; on the contrary he preferred that Jagienka should accompany him, than return, so when he heard her words, he smiled and said:

"She has got rid of her petticoats, and now she wants reason too."

"Reason is only to be found in the head."

"But Plock is out of the way."

"The Bohemian said that it is not out of the way, but it is nearer to Malborg."

"Then you have already consulted the Bohemian?"

"Surely; moreover, he said: 'If the young lord got into trouble at Malborg, then we could get much help from Princess Alexandra, for she is a relative of the king; besides that, being a personal friend of the Knights of the Cross, she has great influence among them.'"

"It is true, as God is dear to me!" exclaimed Macko. "It is a fact well known to all, that if she wished to give us a letter to the master we could travel with perfect safety in all lands of the Knights of the Cross. They love her because she loves them. That Bohemian boy is not a fool, his advice is good."

"And how much so!" Sieciechowa exclaimed with warmth, lifting up her little eyes.

Macko suddenly turned toward her and said:

"What do you want here?"

The girl became much confused, lowered her eyelashes and blushed like a rose.

However, Macko saw that there was no other remedy but to continue his journey and take both girls with him. This he much desired. The following morning he took leave of the little old prior and then they continued their journey. Owing to the thawing of the snow and inundations they progressed with greater difficulty than before. On the road they inquired after the abbot, and they found many courts, and parsonages, where there were none of the former, even inns, where he had remained for a night's lodging. It was quite easy to follow in his track, because he had lavishly distributed alms, bought missals, contributed to church bells and subscribed to funds for the repair of churches. Therefore every beggar, sexton, yea even every priest they met remembered him with gratitude. They generally said: "He traveled like an angel," and prayed for his recovery, although here and there were heard more expressions of apprehension that his everlasting rest was drawing nigh, than hopes of temporary recovery. In some places he had taken supplies enough for two or three days. It seemed to Macko that most likely he would be able to overtake him.

Yet Macko was mistaken in his calculations. The overflow of the rivers Ner and Bzur prevented them from arriving at Lenczyca. They were obliged to take up their quarters for four days at a deserted inn, whose owner apparently had fled on account of the threatening floods. The road leading from the inn to the town which to a certain extent was repaired with stumps of trees was submerged for a considerable stretch in the muddy flood. Macko's servant, Wit, a native of that locality, had some knowledge of the road leading through the woods, but he refused to act as guide, because he knew that the marshes of Lenczyca were the rendezvous of unclean spirits, especially the powerful Borut who delighted in leading people to bottomless swamps, whence escape was only possible by forfeiture of the soul. Even the inn itself was held in bad repute, so that travelers used to provision themselves with victuals to avoid hunger. Even old Macko was scared of this place. During the night they heard skirmishing upon the roof of the inn; at times there were also rappings at the door. Jagienka and Sieciechowa, who slept in the alcove near the large room, also heard the sound of little footsteps upon the ceiling and walls during the night-time. They were apparently not afraid of it, because at Zgorzelice they were accustomed to croaking birds. Old Zych, in his time, fed them, according to the then prevailing custom there were not wanting those who would provide them with crusts, and they were not mischievous. But on a certain night, from the neighboring thickets resounded a dull ominous bellowing, and the following morning they discovered huge cloven-foot traces upon the mud. They might have been of aurochs or bison, but Wit was of opinion that the traces were those of Borut, and although his outward appearance is that of a man, even of a nobleman, he has cloven instead of human feet. But owing to parsimony he takes off his boots when crossing the swamps. Macko was informed that one could appease him with drink; he considered during the whole day whether it would be sinful to gain the friendship of the evil spirit. He even took counsel with Jagienka on the same subject.

"I should like to suspend upon the fence a bull's bladder full of wine or mead," he said, "and if it were found that something of the drink were missing, then it would be conclusive proof that the evil spirit was present."

"But that might displease the heavenly powers," replied Jagienka, "of whose blessing we stand in need to assist us in succoring Zbyszko successfully."

"I, too, am afraid, but I think that a little mead is not the soul. I shall not give him my soul. One bladder full of wine or mead, I think, is of little significance in the eyes of the heavenly powers!"

Then he lowered his voice and added:

"One nobleman entertains another even if he is a useless fellow, and they say he is a nobleman."

"Who?" asked Jagienka.

"I do not want to mention the name of the unclean spirit."

Nevertheless, Macko, with his own hands suspended the same evening a large bull's bladder in which drink is usually carried, and it was found empty the following morning.

When that was related to the Bohemian, he laughed heartily, but nobody paid attention to it. Macko, however, was filled with joy, because he expected that when he should attempt to cross the swamp no mishap would occur on that account.

"Unless they told an untruth when they said that he knows honor," he said to himself. Above all things it was necessary to investigate if there was a passage through the woods. It might have been so, because where the soil was made firm by the roots of the trees and other growths, it did not easily soften by the rains; although Wit, who belonged in the locality, could best perform that service, he refused to go, and when his name was suggested, he shouted: "Better kill me. I shall not go."

Then they explained to him that the unclean spirits are powerless during the daytime. Macko himself was willing to go, but it was finally arranged that Hlawa should venture, because he was a bold fellow, agreeable to all, specially to the ladies. He put an axe in his belt, and in his hand a scythe, and left.

He left early in the morning and was expected to return about noon, but he did not, and they began to be alarmed. Later on, the servants were watching at the edge of the forest, and in the afternoon Wit waved his hand as a sign that Hlawa had not returned, and should he return the danger is greater for us, for God knows whether, owing to a wolf's bite, he is not transformed into a werewolf. Hearing this, all were frightened; even Macko was not himself. Jagienka turned toward the forest and made the sign of the cross. But Anulka searched in vain in her skirt and apron for something with which to cover her eyes, but finding nothing she covered them with her fingers, from between which tears began to trickle in big drops.

However, toward evening time, just at the spot where the sun was about to set, the Bohemian appeared, and that, not by himself, but accompanied by a human figure whom he drove in front of him on a rope. All rushed out toward him with shouts of joy. But at the sight of the figure they became silent; it was dwarfed, monkey-like, hairy, black and dressed in wolf skin.

"In the name of the Father and Son tell me; what is this figure you have brought," shouted Macko.

"How do I know?" replied the Bohemian. "He said that he was a man and a pitch-burner, but I don't know whether he told me the truth."

"Oh, he is not a man, no," said Wit.

But Macko ordered him to be quiet; then he looked carefully around him and suddenly said:

"Cross yourself. We are accustomed to cross ourselves when with the spirits...."

"Praised be Jesus Christ!" exclaimed the prisoner, and crossed himself as fast as he could. He breathed deeply, looked with great confidence at the group and said:

"Praised be Jesus Christ. I too, O Jesus, was uncertain whether I was in Christian or in the devil's power."

"Fear not, you are among Christians, who attend the holy Mass. What are you then?"

"I am a pitch-burner, sir, dwelling in a tent. There are seven of us who dwell in tents with our families."

"How far are you from here?"

"Not quite ten furlongs."

"How do you get to town?"

"We have our private road along the 'Devil's Hollow.'"

"Along what? The Devil's?... then cross yourself again."

"In the name of the Father, Son, and the Holy Ghost. Amen."

"Very well. Is that road practicable for vehicles?"

"Now there is quagmire everywhere, although there is less near the Hollow than upon the regular road; owing to the access of the wind the mud is quickly dried up. But farther on to Buda the road is bad. But those who know the track push through it slowly."

"Will you lead us for a florin or two?"

The pitch-burner accepted the offer willingly, but begged for half a loaf of bread, which he said is very scarce in the woods and he had seen none for some time past. It was arranged that they should start very early the next morning, because it was "not good to travel in the evening," he said. "There at Boruca ghosts storm terribly, but they do no harm. But being jealous for the Lenczyca principality they chase away other devils into the bushes. It is only bad to meet them during the night, especially when a man is drunk, but the sober need not be afraid."

"You were afraid nevertheless," said Macko.

"Because that knight unexpectedly grasped me with such strength that I took him for another being."

Then Jagienka smiled that all of them took the pitch-burner to be the devil, and he thought them to be the same. Anulka and Sieciechowa laughed at Macko's words, when he said:

"Your eyes are not yet dry from weeping for Hlawa; now you are laughing?"

The Bohemian looked at the girl, he observed her eyelids which were still moist, then he asked:

"Did you cry for me?"

"Of course not," replied the girl. "I was only scared."

"You ought to be ashamed. Are you not a noblewoman, and a noblewoman like your mistress is not afraid. Nothing evil could happen to you in the middle of the day, and among people."

"Nothing to me, but to you."

"Yet you said that you did not cry for me."

"I insist, not for you."

"Then why did you cry?"

"From fear."

"You are not afraid now?"

"No."

"Why?"

"Because you have returned."

Then the Bohemian looked at her with gratitude, smiled, and said:

"Bah! If we kept on talking in that manner we might have continued till morning. What a smart woman you are!"

"Make no fun of me," quietly replied Sieciechowa. In fact she was as smart as any woman; and Hlawa who was himself a cunning fellow understood it well. He knew that the girl's attachment to him was daily increasing. He loved Jagienka, but the love was that of a subject for his king's daughter, and with great humility and reverence, and without any other motive. Meanwhile the journey brought him in closer contact with Sieciechowa. When on the march old Macko and Jagienka usually rode side by side in front, while Hlawa and Sieciechowa were together in the rear. He was as strong as a urus and hot-blooded, so that when looking straight into her lovely bright eyes, at her flaxen locks which escaped from under her bonnet, upon her whole slender and well-shaped figure, especially at her admirably shaped limbs gripping the black pony, his whole frame trembled. He could restrain himself no longer. The more he looked upon those charms the more intense and longing his gaze became. He involuntarily thought that if the devil were to assume the form of that girl he would have no difficulty in leading one into temptation. She was moreover of a sweet temperament, very obedient, and lively, like a sparrow upon the roof. Sometimes strange thoughts crossed the Bohemian's mind; once when he and Anulka remained somewhat in the rear near the packhorses, he suddenly turned toward her and said:

"Do you know I shall devour you here as a wolf devours a lamb."

She heartily laughed, and showed her pretty little white teeth.

"Do you want to eat me?" she asked.

"Yes I even with the little bones."

And he cast such a look at her that she melted under his glances. Then they lapsed into silence, only their hearts were beating intensely, his with desire, and hers with pleasurable intoxication tinged with fear.

But the Bohemian's passion at first entirely prevailed over his tenderness, and when he said that he looked at Anulka like a wolf at a lamb, he told the truth. Only on that evening when he observed her eyelids and cheeks moistened with tears, his heart became softened She seemed to him as good, as though near to him and as though she were already his own, and as he himself was upright by nature, and at the same time a knight, he not only was elated with pride, and not hardened at the sight of the sweet tears, but he courageously continued gazing at her. His wonted gaiety of conversation left him, and although he continued to jest in the evening with the timid girl, yet it was of a different nature. He treated her as a knightly armor-bearer ought to treat a noblewoman.

Old Macko was chiefly occupied in thinking of the journey, and the crossing of the swamps, and he only praised him for his noble manners which, as he observed, he must have learned when he was with Zbyszko at the Mazovian court.

Then he turned to Jagienka and added:

"Hey! Zbyszko!… His deportment befits even a king's presence."

But his work was over in the evening, when it was time to retire. Hlawa, after having kissed the hand of Jagienka, lifted in turn the hand of Sieciechowa to his lips and said:

"Not only need you not fear me, but whilst you are with me you need fear nothing, for I shall not give you to anybody."

Then the men went into the front room whilst Jagienka and Anulka retired to the alcove and slept together in a wide and comfortable bed. Neither fell asleep readily, especially Sieciechowa, who was restless and turned from side to side. At length Jagienka moved her head toward Anulka and whispered:

"Anulka?"

"What is it?"

"It seems to me that you are much taken with that Bohemian…. Is it so?"

Her question remained unanswered.

But Jagienka whispered again:

"I understand it all…. Tell me."

Sieciechowa did not reply, but instead, pressed her lips to the cheeks of her mistress and showered kisses upon them.

At Anulka's kisses, poor Jagienka's breast heaved.

"Oh, I understand, I understand," she whispered, so low that Anulka's ear scarcely caught her words.

CHAPTER IV.

After a mild and foggy night, a windy and gloomy day came. At times the sky was bright, at others it was covered with broken clouds which were driven before the wind like flocks of sheep. Macko ordered the train to move by daybreak. The pitch-burner, who was hired as guide to Buda, affirmed that the horses could pass everywhere, but as to the wagons, provisions and baggage, it would be necessary in some places to take them apart and carry them piecemeal, and that could not be done without tedious work. But people accustomed to hard labor preferred hardship to lounging in the deserted inn. Therefore they moved on willingly. Even the timid Wit was not scared by the words and presence of the pitch-burner.

They left the inn and entered at once between high-trunked forest trees, free from undergrowth. They led their horses, and could pass along without taking the wagons to pieces. Occasionally a storm arose, and at times it increased to such extraordinary force that it struck the branches of the bending pines as with gigantic wings, bending, twisting and shaking and breaking them as it were with the fans of a windmill. The forest bent under the unchained elements. Even in the intervals between the gusts it did not cease to howl and thunder, as if angry with their rest at the inn, and the forced march they had undertaken. Now and then the clouds entirely obscured the daylight. Drenching rain mingled with hail came down in torrents, and it became as dark as nightfall. Wit was short of breath, and shouted that "evil was bent to do harm and is doing it." But nobody paid attention to it, even the timid Anulka did not take his words to heart because the Bohemian was so near that her stirrup touched his, and he looked ahead with such a brave air that he seemed to want to challenge the very devil.

Behind the tall pine trees where the undergrowth began, the thickets were impassable. There they were obliged to take the wagons in sections; they did it dexterously and quickly. The strong servants transported the wheels, axle-tree, front of the wagon, packages and stores, upon their shoulders. The bad road continued about three furlongs. However they arrived at Buda about nightfall; there the pitch-burner received them as his guests, and they were assured by him that along the Devil's Hollow, correctly speaking, they could reach the town. These people, inhabitants of the pathless forest seldom saw bread or flour, yet they were not starving. Because all kinds of smoked meat, especially eels, which abounded in all swamps and mud holes, they had in plenty. They treated them liberally, in exchange, holding out greedy hands for the biscuits. There were among them women and children, all blackened from the smoke. There was also a peasant, more than one hundred years old, who remembered the massacre of Lenczyca, which happened in 1331, and the complete destruction of the town by the "Knights of the Cross." Although Macko, the Bohemian, and the two girls, had already heard the narrative from the prior of Sieradz, nevertheless they listened with much interest to the tale of the old man who was sitting at the fireside scraping in the cinders. It seemed as if he discovered among them the events of his earlier days. At Lenczyca, as well as at Sieradz, they spared not even the churches and clergy, and the knives of the conquerors were covered with the blood of old men, women and children. Always the Knights of the Cross, the everlasting Knights of the Cross! The thoughts of Macko and Jagienka were constantly directed toward Zbyszko, who was living in the very jaws of the wolves, in the midst of a hardened clan who knew neither pity nor the laws of hospitality. Sieciechowa was faint at heart, because she feared that their hunt after the abbot might lead them among those terrible Knights of the Cross.

But the old man, to counteract the unfavorable impression which the stories made upon the women, told them of the battle near Plowce, which put an end to the incursions of the Knights of the Cross, and in which he took part as a soldier in the infantry raised by the peasants, and armed with an iron flail. In that battle perished almost the whole clan of the Gradys; Macko knew all the particulars of it, nevertheless he listened now as though it were a recital of a new terrible calamity caused by the Germans, when like cornfields before the storm they were mowed down by the sword in the hands of the Polish knighthood and the forces of King Lokietek....

"Ha! I just recollect," said the old man, "when they invaded this country, they burned the town and castles. Yes, they even massacred the infants in the cradles, but their terrible end came. Hey! It was a fine fight. I can see the battle now with my eyes closed...."

He closed his eyes and was silent, gently moving the ashes until Jagienka, who could wait no longer, asked:

"How was it?"

"How was it?..." repeated the old man. "I remember the battlefield, it seems that I am now looking at it; there were bushes, and patches of stubble to the right. But after the battle nothing was visible but swords, axes, pikes and fine armor, one upon another, as though the whole blessed land was covered with them.... I have never seen so many slain in one heap, and so much human blood shed...."

Macko's heart was strengthened anew by the recollection of these events, then he said:

"True. Merciful Lord Jesus! They had then encompassed the kingdom like a conflagration or like a plague. Not only Sieradz and Lenczyca, but they destroyed many other towns. What now? Are not our people mighty and indestructible? And although those dog-brothers, the Knights of the Cross, were severely chastised, yet if you cannot crush them they will attack you and break your teeth.... Only see, King Kazimierz rebuilt Sieradz and Lenczyca so that they are better now than ever before, yet the incursions occur there as of old, and the Knights of the Cross are laid low and rot there as they were at the battle of Plowce. May God always grant them such an end!"

When the old peasant heard these words he nodded assent; finally he said:

"Perhaps they don't lie and rot. We of the infantry were ordered by the king, after the battle was over, to dig ditches; the peasants from the neighborhood came to assist us in our labor. We worked industriously, so that the spades groaned. Then we laid the Germans in trenches and covered them well, to avoid pestilence. But they did not remain there."

"What happened? Why did they not remain there?"

"I did not see it, but the people said afterward that after the battle there came a fierce storm which lasted about twelve weeks, but only at night-time. The sun shone during the daytime, but at night the wind was so fierce that it almost tore the hair from off the head. The devils, like thick clouds, came down in great numbers, whirling like a hurricane; every one of them held a pitchfork, and as soon as one of them reached the earth he thrust the pitchfork into the ground and carried off one Knight of the Cross to hell. At Plowce they heard a hurly-burly of human voices which sounded like the howling of whole packs of dogs, but they did not know what it all meant, whether it were the noise of the Germans, who were howling with terror and pain, or the devils with joy. That continued as long as the trenches were not consecrated by the priest, and the ground was not frozen, so that there was no need even for pitchforks."

Silence followed for a moment, then the old man added:

"But God grant, Sir Knight, such an end to them as you said, and although I shall not live to see it, but such young lasses as these two will live, but they shall not see what mine eyes have seen."

Then he turned his head, now looking at Jagienka, now at Sieciechowa, wondering at their marvelous faces and shaking his head.

"Like poppies in corn," he said. "Such beautiful faces I have never seen."

Thus they chattered during a part of the night. Then they went to sleep in the shanties and lay down upon mosses as soft as down and covered themselves with warm fur; then after a refreshing sleep, they arose early in the morning and continued their journey. The road along the hollow was not an easy passage, but it was not a very bad road. So that before sunset they descried the castle of Lenczyca. The city had arisen from its ashes, it was rebuilt; part of it was built of brick and part of stone, its walls were high, the towers armed. The churches were even larger than those of Sieradz. There they had no difficulty in getting information from the Dominican friars concerning the abbot. He was there, he said that he felt better, and he hoped to recover his health entirely; and only a few days ago he left for his onward journey. Macko was not bent on overtaking him on the road, so he had already procured conveyance for both girls to Plock, where the abbot himself would have taken them. But Macko was much concerned about Zbyszko, and other news distressed him. The rivers had arisen after the departure of the abbot, and it was impossible to continue the journey. Seeing that the knight was accompanied by a considerable retinue and was proceeding to the court of Prince Ziemowit, the Dominicans offered him their hospitality; they had even provided him with an olive-wood tablet upon which there was inscribed a Latin prayer to the angel Raphael, the patron of travelers.

Their compulsory sojourn at Lenczyca lasted a fortnight, during which time a servant of the castle discovered that the two young pages accompanying the knight were females in disguise, and at once fell deeply in love with Jagienka. The Bohemian was about to challenge him at once, but as it happened on the eve of their departure Macko dissuaded him from taking such a step.

When they moved on toward Plock, the wind had already somewhat dried the road, and although it rained often, yet the rainfall, as is usual in the spring, consisted of larger drops, but warm, and of short duration. The furrows upon the fields glistened with water. The moist, sweet smell from the cultivated fields was wafted by the strong wind. The marshes were covered with buttercups and the violets blossomed in the woods, and the grasshoppers joyfully chirped among the branches. The hearts of the travelers were also filled with new hope and longing, especially as they were now progressing well. After sixteen days' travel they were at the gates of Plock.

But they arrived at night, when the gates of the city were closed. They were obliged to pass the night with a weaver outside the wall.

The girls retired late, and after the fatigue of the long journey they fell sound asleep, but Macko, who was not troubled by fatigue, got up early; he did not wish to wake them and he entered the town by himself at the opening of the gates. He found the cathedral and the

229

bishop's residence without difficulty. There he was informed that the abbot had died a week ago, but according to the prevailing custom they had celebrated mass before the coffin from the sixth day, and the funeral was to take place on the day of Macko's arrival, after which would be obsequies and last honors in memory of the defunct.

Owing to intense grief, Macko did not even look about the town, but he knew something already from that time when he had passed through that city with a letter from the princess Alexandra to the grand master. He returned to the weaver's place as fast as he could, and on his way home he said to himself:

"Ha! He is dead. Eternal repose to him. There is nothing in the world to remedy it. But now what shall I do with the girls?"

Then he reflected whether it were not better to leave them with the princess Alexandra, or with the princess Anna Danuta, or to take them to Spychow. It struck him more than once, that if Danuska were dead, it would be advisable to have Jagienka close to Zbyszko at Spychow, since Zbyszko, who loved Danuska above all other things would greatly mourn after his beloved. He was also sure that Jagienka's presence at Zbyszko's side would have the desired effect. He also remembered that Zbyszko in his boyhood, although his heart was after the woods in Mazowsze, was constantly longing for Jagienka. For these reasons, and fully believing that Danusia was lost, he often thought that in case of the abbot's demise, he would not send Jagienka to any other place; but as he was greedy to acquire landed property, he was therefore concerned about the property of the abbot. Surely, the abbot was displeased with them and promised to bequeath nothing to them; but after that he must have felt sorry, and, before he died left something for Jagienka. He was sure that the abbot had bequeathed something to her, because he frequently spoke about it at Zgorzelice, and he would not overlook Zbyszko on account of Jagienka. Macko was also thinking of remaining for sometime at Plock, so as to investigate the will and attend to the matter, but other thoughts crossed his mind, and he said: "Should I longer be here looking after property, whilst my boy yonder is stretching out his hand and waiting for my help from some Knight of the Cross dungeon?"

In truth, there was only one course, and that was: to leave Jagienka under the care of the princess and the bishop, and beg them to look after her interest. But that plan did not please Macko. The girl has already considerable property of her own, and when her estate is increased by that which the abbot has bequeathed her, then as sure as there is a God some Mazur will take her, for she cannot hold out any longer. Zych, her defunct father, used to say of her, that she was in danger[112] even then. In such case, the old knight thought that both Danusia and Jagienka might fail Zbyszko. That of course was not to be thought of.

He will take one of the two, whichever God had decreed. Finally that plan to rescue Zbyszko he preferred to the others; and as to Jagienka, he resolved either to leave her in the care of Princess Danuta, or at Spychow, but not at the court at Plock where there was much glitter, and which was filled with handsome knights.

Overwhelmed with these thoughts, he proceeded quickly to the dwelling of the weaver, to inform Jagienka of the abbot's death. He was determined not to break the news to her suddenly, as it might greatly endanger her health. When he reached home both ladies were properly dressed and appeared as gay as birds; he sat down and ordered the servants to bring him a jug of brown beer; then he assumed a doleful air, and said:

"Do you hear the bells ringing in town? Guess, why are they ringing, since to-day is not Sunday, and you slept during matins. Would you like to see the abbot?"

"Surely! What a question?" answered Jagienka.

"Well, you shall see him as the king sees Cwiék."[113]

"Has he left the city?"

"He has left, but do you not hear the bells ringing?"

"Is he dead?" exclaimed Jagienka.

"Yes! say 'God rest his soul.' …"

Both ladies knelt down and began to chant: "God rest his soul," in a bell-like voice. Then tears streamed down Jagienka's cheeks, for she was very fond of the abbot, who, though of a violent temper, never harmed anybody, but did much good; he specially loved Jagienka, for he was her godfather, he loved her as one loves his own daughter. Macko remembered that the abbot was related to him and Zbyszko; he was also moved to tears and even cried. After his grief had subsided a little, he took the ladies and the Bohemian with him and went to the funeral services in the church.

It was a magnificent funeral. The bishop himself, Jacob of Kurdwanow, conducted it. There were present all the priests and monks of the diocese of Plock, all the bells were ringing, and prayers were said which none else but the clergy understood, for they were said in the Latin. Then the clergy and the laity went to the banquet at the bishop's palace.

Macko and his two girls (disguised as boys) also went to the banquet; he, as a relative of the deceased, and known to the bishop, was fully entitled to be present. The bishop also willingly received him as such, but immediately after the invitation he said to Macko:

"There is here a bequest of some forests for the Gradys of Bogdaniec. The rest he did not bequeath to the abbey and the cloister, but to his goddaughter, a certain Jagienka of Zgorzelice."

Macko, who did not expect much, was glad for the woodlands. The bishop did not observe that one of the youths accompanying the old knight at the mentioning of the name of Jagienka of Zgorzelice lifted up her tearful eyes, and said:

"May God recompense him, but I wish he were alive."

Macko turned and said angrily:

"Be silent, otherwise you will shame yourself."

But he suddenly stopped, his eyes glistened with amazement, then his face assumed wolfish fierceness, when at a distance from him opposite the door, through which the princess Alexandra had just entered, he observed the figure, dressed in court uniform, of Kuno of Lichtenstein, the very man by whom Zbyszko had nearly lost his life in Krakow.

Jagienka had never seen Macko in such a condition. His face was contracted like the jaws of a fierce dog, his teeth glistened beneath his moustache, and in a moment he tightened his belt and moved toward the hateful Knight of the Cross.

But when about midway he checked himself and began to pass his broad hands through his hair; he reflected in time, that Lichtenstein might only be a guest in the court of Plock, or an envoy, therefore, if he were to strike him without apparent reason, the very thing which happened to Zbyszko on his way from Tyniec to Krakow might be repeated here.

Thus possessing more reason than Zbyszko, he restrained himself, adjusted the belt to its previous place, relaxed the muscles of his face and waited, and when the princess, after greeting Lichtenstein, entered into a conversation with the bishop, Macko approached her and bowed deeply. He reminded her who he was, and that he had been once engaged in the service of his benefactress as the carrier of letters.

The princess did not recognize him at first, but she remembered the letters and the whole affair. She also was acquainted with the occurrences in the neighboring Mazovian court. She had heard of Jurand, of the imprisonment of his daughter, of Zbyszko's marriage, and of his deadly fight with Rotgier. These things interested her greatly, so much so that it seemed to her one of those knight-errant stories or one of the minstrel songs in Germany, and the *rybalt* songs in Mazowsze. Indeed, the Knights of the Cross were not inimical to her, as they were to princess Anna Danuta, the wife of Prince Janusz, more especially because they wished to get her on their side, they strove to outvie each other in rendering her homage and adulation, and overwhelmed her with munificent gifts, but in the present case her heart beat for her favorite, whom she was ready to help; above all, she was glad that she had before her a man who could give her an accurate account of the events.

But Macko, who had already resolved to obtain, by whatever means possible, the protection and the princely influence, seeing that she was listening attentively, told her Zbyszko's and Danusia's ill luck. The narrative brought tears to her eyes, specially when she felt more than anybody the misfortune of her niece, and from her very soul she pitied her.

"I have never heard a more woeful story," said the princess, at last, "the greatest sorrow to my mind is, that he has married her, that she was already his, yet he knew no happiness. However, are you sure that he knew her not."

"Hey! Almighty God!" exclaimed Macko. "If he only knew her, he was bed-ridden when he married her in the evening, and the following morning she was carried off."

"And, do you think that the Knights of the Cross did it? It was said here, that those who actually did it were robbers, and the Knights of the Cross recaptured her, but it turned out to be another girl. They also spoke of a letter which Jurand had written...."

"Human justice did not decide it, but divine. That was a great thing, that knight Rotgier, who conquered the strongest, fell by the hand of a comparative child."

"Well, a fine child he is," said the princess, with a smile, "his valor is a safeguard in his travels. It is a grievance, true, and your complaints are just, but three out of those four opponents are dead, and the remaining old one has also, according to the information I have received, been nearly killed."

"And Danuska? And Jurand?" replied Macko. "Where are they? God only knows whether something ill has happened to Zbyszko, who was on the road to Malborg."

"I know, but the Knights of the Cross are not such out-and-out dog-brothers as you think them to be. In Malborg nothing evil can happen to your nephew, whilst he is at the side of the grand master and his brother Ulrych, who is an honorable knight. Your nephew undoubtedly is provided with letters from Prince Janusz. Unless whilst there he challenged one of the knights and succumbed. At Malborg there are always present a great number of the most valorous knights from all parts of the world."

"Ay! My nephew does not fear them much," said the old knight. "If they only did not cast him in prison, or kill him treacherously, as long as he has an iron weapon in his hand he is not afraid of them. Only once he found himself facing one stronger than himself, but he stretched him in the lists, and that was the Mazovian Prince Henryk who was bishop here and who was enamored of the handsome Ryngalla. But Zbyszko was then a mere youth. For this reason he would be the only one, as sure as amen in prayer, to challenge this one whom I also have vowed to challenge and who is present here."

Saying this, he glanced in the direction of Lichtenstein, who was conversing with the governor (Waywode) of Plock.

But the princess wrinkled her brow and said in stern and dry tones, as she always did when in an angry mood:

"Whether you vowed or not, you must remember that he is our guest and whosoever wishes to be our guest must observe decorum."

"I know, most gracious lady," replied Macko. "For that reason when I adjusted my belt and went to meet him, I restrained myself and thought of obedience."

"He will obey. He is important among his own people, even the master builds upon his counsel and nothing is denied to him. May God grant that your nephew does not meet him at Malborg, especially as Lichtenstein is a determined and revengeful person."

"He could not well recognize me because he did not see me often. We had helmets on when we were at Tyniec, after that I went only once to see him in the Zbyszko affair and that was in the evening. I observed just now that he looked at me, but seeing that I was engaged in a lengthy conversation with Your Grace, he turned his eyes in an opposite direction. He would have recognized Zbyszko, but he only looked at me and very likely he did not hear of my vow, and has to think of more important challenges."

"How so?"

"Because it may be that other powerful knights challenged him, such as Zawisza of Garbow, Powala of Taczew, Marcin of Wrocimowice, Paszko Zlodziej, and Lis of Targowisko. Every one of those, gracious lady, and ten like them. So much the more so if they are numerous. It would be better for him not to have been born, than to have one of those swords over his head. I shall not only try to forget the challenge, but I have resolved to endeavor to go with him."

"Why?"

Macko's face assumed a cunning expression like that of a fox.

"That he might give me a safe conduct to travel through the country belonging to the Knights of the Cross, that will enable me to render assistance to Zbyszko in case of need."

"Does such proceeding deserve praise?" inquired the princess with a smile.

"Yes! It does," replied Macko. "If for instance in time of war I were to attack him from the rear without warning him to face me I should disgrace myself; but in time of peace if one hangs the enemy upon a hook no knight need be reproached for such an act."

"Then I will introduce you," replied the princess. She beckoned to Lichtenstein and introduced Macko; she was of opinion that even if Lichtenstein should recognize Macko nothing serious would result.

But Lichtenstein did not recognize him, because when he had seen him at Tyniec he had his helmet on, and after that he had spoken to Macko only once, and that in the evening, when Macko had begged him to forgive Zbyszko.

However he bowed proudly, the more so because when he saw the two exquisitely dressed youths, he thought that they were not Macko's, his face brightened up a little and he assumed a haughty demeanor as he always did when he spoke to inferiors.

Then the princess pointing at Macko, said: "This knight is going to Malborg. I have given him a recommendation to the grand master, but he heard of your great influence in the Order; he would also like to have a note from you."

Then she went to the bishop, but Lichtenstein fixed his cold, steely eyes upon Macko, and asked:

"What motive induces you, sir, to visit our religious and sober capital?"

"An upright and pious motive," replied Macko, looking at Lichtenstein. "If it were otherwise the gracious princess would not have vouched for me. But apart from pious vows, I wish also to know your grand master, who causes peace in the land and who is the most celebrated knight in the world."

"Those whom your gracious and beneficent princess recommends will not complain of our poor hospitality. Nevertheless, as far as your wishes to know the master is concerned, it is not an easy matter. About a mouth ago, he left for Danzig, thence he was to go to Königsberg, and from that place proceed to the frontier, where, although a lover of peace, he is obliged to defend the property of the Order against the violence of the treacherous Witold."

Hearing this, Macko was apparently so much grieved, that Lichtenstein, who noticed it, said:

"I see that you were quite as anxious to see the grand master as to fulfil your religious vows."

"Yes! I am, I am," replied Macko. "Is war against Witold a sure thing?"

"He, himself, began it; he has sworn to help the rebels."

There was silence for a moment.

"Ha! May God help the Order as it deserves!" said Macko. "I see I cannot make the grand master's acquaintance; let me at least fulfil my vow."

But in spite of these words, he did not know what to do, and with deep grief he asked himself:

"Where shall I look for Zbyszko, and where shall I find him?"

It was easy to foresee that if the grand master had left Malborg and gone to war, it was useless to look for Zbyszko there. In any case it was necessary to get the most accurate information of his whereabouts. Old Macko was very anxious about it, but he was a man of ready resource, and he resolved to lose no time, but continue his march next morning. Having obtained a letter from Lichtenstein with the aid of Princess Alexandra in whom the *comthur* had boundless confidence, it was not a difficult task to obtain. He therefore received a recommendation to the *starosta* of Brodnic, and to the Grand Szpitalnik of Malborg, for which he presented a silver goblet to Lichtenstein, a treasure procured in Breslau, like that which the knights were accustomed to have near their beds filled with wine, so that in case of sleeplessness they might have at hand a remedy for sleep and at the same time pleasure. This act of Macko's liberality somewhat astonished the Bohemian, who knew that the old knight was not too eager to lavish presents on anybody, especially on Germans, but Macko said:

"I did it because I have vowed, and must fight him, and by no means could I do it to one who has done me some service. To recompense good with evil is not our custom."

"But such a magnificent goblet! It is a pity," replied the Bohemian, apparently vexed.

"Don't fear. I do nothing without premeditation," said Macko; "for if the Lord enables me to overthrow (kill) that German, I shall get back not only the goblet, but a great many good things I shall acquire with it."

Then they, including Jagienka, began to take counsel among themselves concerning further action. Macko thought of leaving Jagienka and Sieciechowa with Princess Alexandra at Plock, owing to the abbot's will, which was in the possession of the bishop. But Jagienka was entirely opposed to it; she was even determined to travel by herself; there was no necessity to have a separate room for night quarters, neither to observe politeness, nor safety, and various other causes. "Surely I did not leave Zgorzelice to rusticate at Plock. The will is at the bishop's and cannot be lost, and as far as they are concerned, when it will be shown that there is need to remain on the road, it will be of greater advantage to be left in the care of Princess Anna, than with Princess Alexandra, because at the former court the Knights of the Cross are not frequent visitors, and Zbyszko is more appreciated there." Upon that Macko truly observed that reason does not belong to women, and that it is unbecoming for a girl "to command" as though she possessed reason. Nevertheless he did not persist in his opposition, and relented entirely when Jagienka had taken him aside and, with tears in her eyes, said:

"You know!… God sees my heart, that every morning and evening I pray for that young lady, Danuska, and for Zbyszko's welfare. God in heaven knows it best. But you and Hlawa said that she had perished already, that she would never escape the hands of the Knights of the Cross alive. Therefore if this has to be so, then I…."

Here she somewhat hesitated and tears streamed down her checks and she became silent.

"Then I want to be near Zbyszko…."

Macko was moved by the tears and words, yet he replied:

"If Danusia is lost, Zbyszko will be so much grieved, that he will care for none else."

"I don't wish that he should care for me, but I would like to be near him."

"You know well that I should like to be myself near him as well as you do, but he would in the first instance be unmindful of you."

"Let him be unmindful," she replied, with a smile, "for he will not know that it was myself."

"He will recognize you."

"He will not know me. You did not recognize me. You will tell him too that it was not I but Jasko, and Jasko is exactly like myself. You will tell him that I have grown up and it will never occur to him that it is anybody else but Jasko…."

Then the old knight remembered somebody upon his knees before him and that kneeling one had the appearance of a boy; then there was no harm in it, specially that Jasko really had exactly the same face, and his hair after the last cutting had again grown up and he carried it in a net just as other noble young knights. For this reason Macko gave way, and the conversation turned to matters concerning the journey. They were to start on the following day. Macko decided to enter into the country of the Knights of the Cross, to draw near to Brodnic to get information there, and if the grand master was still, in spite of Lichtenstein's opinion, at Malborg, to proceed there, and if not there, to push on along the frontiers of the country of the Knights of the Cross in the direction of Spychow, inquiring along the road about the Polish knight and his suit. The old knight even expected that he would easily get more information of Zbyszko at Spychow, or at the court of Prince Janusz of Warsaw, than elsewhere.

Accordingly, they moved on the following day. Spring was fully ushered in, so that the floods of the Skrwy and Drwency obstructed the way, so much so that it took them ten days to travel from Plock to Brodnic. The little town was orderly and clean. But one could see at a glance the German barbarity by the enormously constructed gallows,[114] which was erected out of town on the road to Gorczenice, and which was occupied by the hanging corpses of the executed, one of which was the body of a woman. Upon the watch-tower and upon the castle floated the flag with the red hand on a white field. The travelers did not find the count at home, because he was at the head of the garrison which was drafted of the neighboring noblemen, at Malborg. That information Macko got from a blind old Knight of the Cross, who was formerly the count of Brodnic, but later on he attached himself to the place and castle, and he was the last of his line. When the chaplain of the place read Lichtenstein's letter to the count, he invited Macko as his guest; he was very familiar with the Polish language, because he lived in the midst of a Polish population, and they easily carried on their conversation in that language. In the course of their conversation Macko was informed that the count had left for Malborg six weeks before, being summoned as an experienced knight to a council of war. Moreover he knew what happened in the capital. When he was asked about the young Polish knight, he had heard of such a one, he said, who at first had roused admiration because, in spite of his youthful appearance, he already appeared as a belted knight. Then he was successful at a tourney which, according to custom, the grand master ordained, for foreign guests, before his departure for the war. Little by little he even remembered that the manly and noble, yet violent brother of the master, Ulrych von Jungingen, had become very fond of the young knight and had taken him under his care, provided him with "iron letters," after which the young knight apparently departed toward the east. Macko was overjoyed at the news, because he had not the slightest doubt that the young knight was Zbyszko. It was therefore useless to go to Malborg, for although the grand master, as well as other officials of the Order, and knights who remained at Malborg might furnish more accurate information, they could by no means tell where Zbyszko actually was. On the other hand Macko himself knew better where Zbyszko might be found, and it was not difficult to suppose that he was at that moment somewhere in the neighborhood of Szczytno; or in case he had not found Danusia there, he was making research in distant eastern castles and county seats.

Without losing any more time, they also moved toward the east and Szczytno. They progressed well on the road, the towns and villages were connected by highways which the Knights of the Cross, or rather the merchants of the towns, kept in good condition, and which were as good as the Polish roads, which were under the care of the thrifty and energetic King Kazimierz. The weather was excellent, the nights were serene, the days bright, and about noon a dry and warm zephyr-like wind blew which filled the human breast with health-giving air. The cornfields assumed a green hue, the meadows were covered with abundant flowers, and the pine forests began to emit a smell of rosin. Throughout the whole journey to Lidzbark, thence to Dzialdowa, and further on to Niedzborz, they did not see a single cloud. But at Niedzborz they encountered a thunderstorm at night, which was the first one of the spring, but it lasted only a short time, and in the morning it cleared up and the horizon was brightened with rosy golden hues. It was so brilliant that the land, as far as the eye could reach, appeared like one carpet brocaded with jewels. It seemed as though the whole country smiled back to the sky and rejoiced because of abundant life.

In such a pleasant morning they wended their course from Niedzborz to Szczytno. It was not far from the Mazovian frontier. It was an easy matter to return to Spychow. There was a moment when Macko wanted to do it, but considering the whole matter he desired to push onward toward the terrible nest of the Knights of the Cross, in which Zbyszko's loss was terribly guarded. He then engaged a guide and ordered him to lead them directly to Szczytno; although there was no need of a guide, because the road from Niedzborz was a straight one, marked with white milestones.

The guide was a few steps in advance. Behind him were Macko and Jagienka on horseback; some distance behind them were the Bohemian and Sieciechowa, and farther back were the wagons surrounded by armed men. It was an exquisite morning. The rosy glow had not yet disappeared from the horizon, although the sun had already risen and changed into opals the dewdrops upon the trees and grasses.

"Are you not afraid to go to Szczytno?" asked Macko.

"I am not afraid," replied Jagienka, "God is with me, because I am an orphan."

"There is no faith there. The worst dog was Danveld whom Jurand killed together with Godfried.... The Bohemian told me so. The second after Danveld, was Rotgier, who succumbed by Zbyszko's axe, but the old man is a ruthless tyrant, and is sold to the devil.... They know not kindness. However, I am of opinion that if Danuska has perished she did so by his own hands. They also say that something happened to her. But the princess said in Plock that she extricated herself. It is with him that we shall have to contend at Szczytno....

It is well that we have a letter from Lichtenstein, and as it appears they, the dog-brothers, are afraid of him more than they are of the master himself.... They say that he has great authority and is particularly strict, and is very revengeful, he never forgives even the slightest offence.... Without this safe conduct I would not travel so peacefully to Szczytno...."

"What is his name?"

"Zygfried von Löve."

"God grant that we may manage him too."

"God grant it!"

Macko smiled for a moment and then said:

"The princess also told me in Plock: 'Ye grieve and complain like lambs against wolves, but in this instance three of the wolves are dead, because the innocent lambs strangled them.' She spoke the truth; it is actually so."

"What about Danuska and her father?"

"I told the princess the very same thing. But I am really glad, since it is demonstrated that it is not safe to harm us. We know already how to handle the helve of an axe, and fight with it. As to Danuska and Jurand, it is true, I think, and so does the Bohemian, that they are no more in this world, but in reality nobody can tell. I am very sorry for Jurand, for he grieved very much for his daughter, and if he perished, it was a hard death."

"If such a thing is mentioned to me," said Jagienka, "I always think of papa, who also is no more."

Then she lifted up her eyes and Macko nodded his head and said:

"He rests with God in everlasting bliss, for there is not a better man than he was in our whole kingdom...."

"Oh there was none like him, none!" sighed Jagienka.

Further conversation was interrupted by the guide, who suddenly checked his stallion, turned and galloped toward Macko and shouted in a strange and frightened voice:

"O, for God's sake! Look there, Sir Knight; who is there on the hillside advancing toward us?"

"Who? Where?" asked Macko.

"Look there! A giant or something of that kind...."

Macko and Jagienka reined in their horses, looked in the direction indicated by the guide, and they indeed descried, about the middle of the hill, a figure, which appeared to be of more than human proportions.

"To tell the truth the man seems to be huge," murmured Macko.

Then he frowned, and suddenly spat and said:

"Let the evil charm be upon the dog."

"Why are you conjuring?" asked Jagienka.

"Because I remember that it was on just such a fine morning when Zbyszko and I were on the road from Tyniec to Krakow we saw such a giant. They said then that it was Walgierz Wdaly. Bah! It was shown afterward that it was the lord of Taczew. Still, nothing good resulted from it. Let the evil charm be upon the dog."

"This one is not a knight, because he is not on horseback," said Jagienka, straining her eyes. "I even see that he is not armed, but holds a staff in his left hand...."

"And he is groping in front of him, as though it were night."

"And can hardly move; surely he must be blind?"

"As sure as I live, he is blind—blind!"

They urged their horses forward, and in a little while they halted in front of the beggar who was slowly coming down the hill and feeling his way with his staff. He was indeed an immense old man, and appeared to them, even when they were near him, a giant. They were convinced that he was stone blind. Instead of eyes he had two red hollows. His right hand was wanting; instead of it he carried a bandage of dirty rags. His hair was white and falling down upon his shoulders, and his beard reached his belt.

"He has neither food, nor companion, not even a dog, but is feeling the way by himself," exclaimed Jagienka. "For God's sake, we cannot leave him here without assistance. I do not know whether he will understand me, but I shall try to talk to him in Polish."

Then she jumped from her horse and approached the beggar, and began to look for some money in her leather pouch which was suspended from her belt.

The beggar, when he heard the noise and tramping of the horses, stretched his staff in front of him and lifted up his head as blind men do.

"Praised be Jesus Christ," said the girl. "Do you understand, little grandfather, in the Christian fashion?"

But on hearing her sweet, young voice, he trembled; a strange flush appeared on his face as though from tender emotion; he covered his hollow orbits with his eyebrows, and suddenly threw down his staff and fell on his knees, with outstretched arms, in front of her.

"Get up! I will assist you. What ails you?" asked Jagienka in astonishment.

But he did not reply, but tears rolled down his cheeks, and he groaned:

"A!—a!—a!..."

"For the love of God—Can you not say something?"

"A!—a!"

Then he lifted up his hand, with which he made first the sign of the cross, then passed his left hand over his mouth.

Jagienka understood it not, and she looked at Macko, who said:

"He seems to indicate that his tongue has been torn out."

"Did they tear out your tongue?" asked the girl.

"A! a! a! a!" repeated the beggar several times, nodding his head.

Then he pointed with his fingers to his eyes; then he moved his left hand across his maimed right, showing that it was cut off.

Then both understood him.

"Who did it?" inquired Jagienka.

The beggar again made signs of the cross repeatedly in the air.

"The Knights of the Cross," shouted Macko.

As a sign of affirmation the old man let his head drop upon his chest again.

There was silence for a moment. Macko and Jagienka looked at each other with alarm, because they had now before them sufficient proof of their cruelty and the lack of means to chastise those knights who style themselves "the Knights of the Cross."

"Cruel justice!" said Macko, finally. "They punished him grievously, and God knows whether deservedly. If I only knew where he belongs, I would lead him there, for surely he must be from this neighborhood. He understands our language, for the common people here are the same as in Mazowsze."

"Did you understand what we said?" asked Jagienka.

The beggar nodded his head.

"Are you of this neighborhood?"

"No!" The beggar shook his head.

"Perhaps he comes from Mazowsze?"

"Yes!" he nodded.

"Under Prince Janusz?"

"Yes!"

"But what were you doing among the Knights of the Cross?"

The old man could give no answer, but his face assumed an air of intense suffering, so much so that Jagienka's heart beat with greater force out of sympathy. Even Macko who was not subject to emotion, said:

"I am sure the dog-brothers have wronged him. May be he is innocent."

Jagienka meanwhile put some small change in the beggar's hand.

"Listen," she said, "we will not abandon you. Come with us to Mazowsze, and in every village we will ask you whether it is yours. May be we shall guess it. Meanwhile, get up, for we are no saints."

But he did not get up, nay, he even bowed lower and embraced her feet as much as to place himself under her protection and show his gratitude. Yet there were marks of certain astonishment, yea even disappointment on his face. May be that from the voice he thought he was in the presence of a young woman; but his hand happened to touch the cowskin gaiters which the knights and armor-bearers were accustomed to wear.

But she said:

"It shall be so; our wagons will soon be here, then you will rest and refresh yourself. But we are not going to take you now to Mazowsze because we must first go to Szczytno."

When the old man heard this, he jumped straight up, terror and amazement were depicted on his face. He opened his arms as though desiring to obstruct their way, and strange, wild ejaculations proceeded from his throat, full of terror and dismay.

"What is the matter with you?" exclaimed Jagienka, much frightened.

But the Bohemian, who had already arrived with Sieciechowa, and for some time had his eyes riveted upon the old beggar, suddenly turned to Macko, and with a countenance changed, and in a strange voice, said:

"For God's sake, permit me, sir, to speak to him, for you do not know who he may be."

After this he begged for no further permission, but rushed toward the old man, placed his hands upon his shoulders, and asked him:

"Do you come from Szczytno?"

The old man appeared to be struck by the sound of his voice, quieted himself and nodded affirmatively.

"Did you not look there for your child? …"

A deep groan was the only reply to this question.

Then the Bohemian's face paled a little, he looked sharply for a moment at the outlines of the old man's face, then he said slowly and composedly:

"Then you are Jurand of Spychow."

"Jurand!" shouted Macko.

But Jurand was overcome at that moment and fainted. Protracted torture, want of nourishment, fatigue of the road, swept him from his feet. The tenth day had now passed since he left, groping his way, erring and feeling his way with his stick, hungry, fatigued and not knowing where he was going, unable to ask the way, during the daytime he turned toward the warm rays of the sun, the night he passed in the ditches along the road. When he happened to pass through a village, or hamlet, or accidentally encountered people on the road, he only could beg with his hand and voice, but seldom a compassionate hand helped him, because as a rule he was taken for a criminal whom law and justice had chastised. For two days he had lived on bark and leaves of trees; he was already giving up all hope of reaching Mazowsze, when suddenly compassionate voices and hearts of his own countrymen surrounded him; one of whom reminded him of the sweet voice of his own daughter; and, when at last his own name was mentioned, he was greatly agitated and unable to bear it any longer; his heart broke. His thoughts whirled through his head; and, were it not for the strong arms of the Bohemian which supported him, he would have fallen with his face in the dust of the road.

Macko dismounted, then both took hold of him, and carried him to the wagons and laid him upon the soft hay. There, Jagienka and Sieciechowa nursed him. Jagienka observed that he could not carry the cup of wine to his lips by himself so she helped him. Immediately after this he fell into a profound sleep, from which he did not awake till the third day.

Meanwhile they sat down to deliberate.

"To be brief," said Jagienka, "we must go now to Spychow instead of Szczytno, so that by all means we place him in security among his own people."

"Look, how can that be carried out," replied Macko. "It is true that we must send him to Spychow, but there is no necessity for all of us to accompany him, one wagon is enough to carry him there."

"I do not order it, I only think so, because there we might get much information from him about Zbyszko, and Danusia."

"But how can you procure information from one who has no tongue?"

"But the very information that he has no tongue, we got from himself. Do you not see that even without speech we got all that information necessary. How much more shall we derive when we communicate with him by motions of the head and hands? Ask him, for instance, whether Zbyszko has returned from Malborg to Szczytno. You will then see that he will either nod assent, or deny it."

"It is true," said the Bohemian.

"I too do not dispute it," said Macko. "I know it myself, but I am accustomed to think first and then talk."

Then he ordered the train to return to the Mazovian frontier. On the way Jagienka visited now and then the wagon where Jurand slept, fearing that death might ensue.

"I did not recognize him," said Macko, "but it is no wonder. He was as strong as an auroch! They said of him that he was among those who could fight with Zawisza, and now he is reduced to a skeleton."

"We are accustomed to hear all sorts of things," said the Bohemian, "but nobody would believe it if they were told that Christians had acted thus with a belted knight, whose patron is also Saint Jerzy."

"God grant that Zbyszko may at least avenge part of his wrongs. Now, look what a difference there is between them and us. It is true, that three out of those four dog-brothers are dead, but they died in fight, and none of them had his tongue or his eyes plucked out in captivity."

"God will punish them," said Jagienka.

But Macko turned to the Bohemian and said:

"How did you recognize him?"

"I did not recognize him at first, although I saw him later than you did. But it struck me, and the more I looked at him the more so…. Though when I first saw him he had neither beard nor white hair; he was then a very powerful lord. How then could I recognize him in the old beggar. But when the young lady said that we were going to Szczytno, and he began to howl my eyes were opened at once."

Macko was absorbed in thought, then he said:

"From Spychow, it is necessary to take him to the prince, who will not leave the wrong perpetrated on such an important person, unpunished."

"They will excuse themselves. They treacherously abducted his child and they defended themselves. And as to the lord of Spychow they will say that he lost his tongue, eyes and hand in the fight."

"You are right," said Macko. "They once carried off the prince himself. He cannot fight them, because he is no match for them; perhaps our king will assist him. The people talk and talk of a great war, but here we don't even have a little one."

"He is with Prince Witold."

"Thank God, that at least he thinks that they are worthless. Hey! Prince Witold is my prince! In craftiness he is unsurpassable. He is more crafty than all of them together. Those dog-brothers had him cornered once, the sword was over his head and he was about to perish, but, like a serpent, he slipped from their hands and bit them…. Be on your guard when he strikes, but be exceedingly careful when he is patting you."

"Is he so with everybody?"

"He is only so with the Knights of the Cross, but he is a kind and liberal prince with everybody else."

At this Macko pondered, as though making an effort to recall Prince Witold.

"He is an entirely different man to the prince here," he said, suddenly. "Zbyszko ought to have joined him, for under him and through him, one might achieve the most against the Knights of the Cross."

Then he added:

"Both of us might be found there. Who can tell? For it is there where we can revenge ourselves most properly."

Then he spoke of Jurand, of his misfortunes and of the unheard of injuries, inflicted upon him by the Knights of the Cross, who first, without any cause, murdered his beloved wife, then, revenge for revenge, they carried off his child, and then mangled him in such a cruel manner, that even the Tartars could not invent worse torture. Macko and the Bohemian gnashed their teeth at the thought that even when they set him free it was with malicious intent of inflicting additional cruelty in order to frustrate the old knight's intention,

239

who most likely promised himself that when he was free he would take proper steps to make an inquest and get information of the whole affair, and then pay them out with interest.

On the journey to Spychow they passed their time in such dialogues and thoughts. The clear fine day was succeeded by a quiet starry night; they therefore did not halt for night quarters, but stopped thrice to feed the horses. It was yet dark when they passed the frontier, and in the morning, led by the hired guide, they arrived upon the land of Spychow.

There Tolima apparently held everything with an iron hand, for no sooner did they enter the forest of Spychow, than two armed men advanced against them. These, seeing that the newcomers were not soldiers, but a simple train, not only let them pass without questioning, but placed themselves in front to show the way, which was inaccessible to those unacquainted with the moats and marshes.

Tolima and the priest Kaleb received the guests when they arrived in town. The news that the lord had arrived, and was brought back by pious people spread like lightning through the garrison. But when they saw him in the condition as he looked when he left the Knights of the Cross, there was such an outburst of raging and wild threatening that if there had yet been any Knights of the Cross confined in the prison of Spychow, no human power would have been able to save them from a terrible death.

The retainers wished to mount their horses at once and start to the frontier to capture any Germans and cut off their heads and throw them under the feet of the master. But Macko restrained them because he knew that the Germans lived in the towns and cities, whilst the country people were of the same blood, but lived against their own will under foreign superior force. But neither the din and noise nor the creaking of the well-sweeps could awake Jurand, who was carried upon a bearskin into his own house and put to bed. Father Kaleb was Jurand's intimate friend; they grew up together and loved each other like brothers; he remained with him, and prayed that the Redeemer of the world might restore to the unfortunate Jurand, his eyes, tongue, and hand.

The fatigued travelers went to bed also. Macko who awoke about noon, ordered Tolima to be called.

He knew from the Bohemian that Jurand, before his departure, had ordered all his servants to obey their young master, Zbyszko, and that the priest had informed him of his ownership of Spychow. Macko therefore spoke to the old man with the voice of a superior:

"I am the uncle of your young master, and as long as he is away, I am the commander here."

Tolima bowed his grey head, which had something wolfish, and surrounding his ear with his hand, asked:

"Then you are, sir, the noble knight from Bogdaniec?"

"Yes!" replied Macko. "How do you know it?"

"Because the young master Zbyszko expected and inquired after you here."

Hearing this, Macko stood up straight, and forgetting his dignified manner, he exclaimed:

"What, Zbyszko in Spychow?"

"Yes, he was here, sir; only two days ago since he left."

"For the love of God! Whence did he come and where did he go?"

"He came from Malborg, and on the road he was at Szczytno. He did not say where he was going."

"He did not say, eh?"

"May be he told the priest Kaleb."

"Hey! Mighty God, then we crossed each other on the road," he said, putting his hands on his ribs.

But Tolima put his hand to the other ear:

"What did you say, sir?"

"Where is Father Kaleb?"

"He is at the bedside of the old master."

"Call him, but stop ... I will go myself to see him."

"I will call him," said Tolima, and he left. But before he brought the priest, Jagienka entered.

"Come here," said Macko. "Do you know the news? Zbyszko was here only two days ago."

Her face changed in a moment and she almost tottered.

"He was, and left?" she asked, with quickly beating heart. "Where to?"

"It is only two days since he left, but where to I do not know. May be the priest knows."

"We must go after him," she said, peremptorily.

After a while Father Kaleb entered. Thinking that Macko wanted him for information concerning Jurand, he anticipated his question by saying:

"He is still asleep."

"I heard that Zbyszko was here?" said Macko.

"He was, but he left two days ago."

"Where to?"

"He did not know himself…. Searching…. He left for the frontier of Zmudz, where there is war now."

"For the love of God, tell us, father, what you know about him!"

"I only know what I heard from himself. He was at Malborg. May be he obtained protection there. Because with the order of the master's brother, who is the first among the knights, Zbyszko could search in all castles."

"For Jurand and Danuska?"

"Yes; but he does not search for Jurand, because he was told that he was dead."

"Tell us from the beginning."

"Immediately, but let me first catch breath and regain presence of mind, for I come from another world."

"How so?"

"From that world which cannot be reached on horseback, but through prayer…. I prayed at the feet of the Lord Jesus that He may have mercy upon Jurand."

"You have asked for a miracle. Have you that power?" asked Macko, with great curiosity.

"I have no power whatever, but I have a Saviour, who, if He wished, could restore to Jurand his eyes, tongue and hand…."

"If He only wanted to do so He could," replied Macko. "Nevertheless you asked for an impossible thing."

Father Kaleb did not reply; possibly because he did not hear it; his eyes were still closed, as if absent-minded, and in reality it was obvious that he was meditating on his prayer.

Then he covered his eyes with his hands and remained so for a while in silence. Finally he shook himself, rubbed his eyes with his hands, and said:

"Now, ask."

"In what manner did Zbyszko attack the Justice of Sambinsk?"

"He is no more the Justice of Sambinsk…."

"Never mind that…. You understand what I am asking; tell me what you know about it."

"He fought at a tourney. Ulrych liked to fight in the arena. There were many knights, guests at Malborg, and the master ordered public games. Whilst Ulrych was on horseback the strap of the saddle broke and it would have been an easy matter for Zbyszko to throw him from his horse; but he lowered his spear to the ground and even assisted him."

"Hey! You see!" exclaimed Macko, turning toward Jagienka. "Is this why Ulrych likes him?"

"This is the reason of his love for Zbyszko. He refused to tilt against him with sharp weapons, neither with the lance, and has taken a liking to him. Zbyszko related his trouble to him, and he, being zealous of his knightly honor, fell into a great passion and led Zbyszko to his brother, the master, to lodge a complaint. May God grant him redemption for this deed, for there are not many among them who love justice. Zbyszko also told me that de Lorche, owing to his position and wealth, was of much help to him, and testified for him in everything."

241

"What was the result of that testimony?"

"It resulted in the vigorous order of the grand master to the *comthur* of Szczytno, to send at once to Malborg all the prisoners who were confined in Szczytno, including even Jurand. Concerning Jurand, the *comthur* replied that he had died from his wounds and was buried there in the church-yard. He sent the other prisoners, including a milkmaid, but our Danusia was not among them."

"I know from the armor-bearer Hlawa," said Macko, "that Rotgier, whom Zbyszko killed whilst at the court of Prince Janusz, also spoke in the same manner about a certain milkmaid whom they captured whom they took for Jurand's daughter, but when the princess asked: 'How could they mistake Danusia for a common girl, since they knew and had seen the true one, Danusia?'" "You are right," he replied, "but I thought they had forgotten the real Danusia." "This same thing the *comthur* had written to the master that that girl was not a prisoner but she was under their care, that they had at first rescued her from the robbers, who had sworn that she was Jurand's daughter, but transformed."

"Did the master believe it?"

"He did not know whether to believe or not, but Ulrych was more incensed than ever, and influenced his brother to send an official of the Order with Zbyszko to Szczytno, which was done. When they arrived at Szczytno, they did not find the old *comthur*, because he had departed to the eastern strongholds against Witold, to the war; but a subordinate, whom the magistrate ordered to open all prisons and underground dungeons. They searched and searched, but found nothing. They even detained people for information. One of them told Zbyszko that he could get much information from the chaplain, because the chaplain understood the dumb executioner. But the old *comthur* had taken the executioner with him, and the chaplain left for Königsberg to attend a religious gathering…. They met there often in order to lodge complaints against the Knights of the Cross to the pope, because even the poor priests were oppressed by them…."

"I am only surprised that they did not find Jurand," observed Macko.

"It is obvious that the old *comthur* let him go. There was more wickedness in that than if they had cut his throat. They wished that he should suffer excruciatingly more than a man of his standing could endure.—Blind, dumb and maimed.—For God's sake!… He could neither find his home, nor the road, not even ask for a morsel of bread…. They thought that he would die somewhere behind a fence from hunger, or be drowned in some river…. What did they leave him? Nothing, but the means of discerning the different degrees of misery. And this meant torture upon torture…. He might have been sitting somewhere near the church, or along the road, and Zbyszko passed by without recognizing him. May be he even heard Zbyszko's voice, but he could not hail him…. Hey!… I cannot keep myself from weeping!… God wrought a miracle, and that is the reason why I think that He will do a great deal more, although this prayer proceeds from my sinful lips."

"What else did Zbyszko say? Where did he go to?" asked Macko.

"He said: 'I know that Danuska was at Szczytno, but they have carried her off, or starved her. Old von Löve did it, and so help me God, I will not rest until I get him.'"

"Did he say so? Then it is sure that the *comthur* left for the east, but now there is war."

"He knew that there was a war, and that is the cause why he left for the camp of Prince Witold. He also said, he would succeed sooner in scoring a point against the Knights of the Cross through him, than through the king."

"So, to Prince Witold!" exclaimed Macko.

Then he turned to Jagienka.

"Did I not tell you the very same thing. As I live, I said: 'that we should also have to go to Witold.' …"

"Zbyszko hoped," said Father Kaleb, "that Prince Witold would make an inroad into Prussia and take some of the castles there."

"If time were given to him, he would not delay," replied Macko. "Praise God now, we know at least where to look for Zbyszko."

"We must press on at once," said Jagienka.

"Silence!" said Macko. "It is not becoming for a boy to interrupt the council."

Then he stared at her, as though to remind her that she was a boy; she remembered and was silent.

Macko thought for awhile, and said:

"Now we shall surely find Zbyszko, for he is not moving aimlessly; he is at the side of Prince Witold. But it is necessary to know whether he is still searching for something in this world, besides the heads of the Knights of the Cross which he vowed to get."

"How can that be ascertained?" asked Father Kaleb.

"If we knew that the priest of Szczytno had already returned from the synod. I should like to see him," said Macko. "I have letters from Lichtenstein to Szczytno and I can go there without fear."

"It was not a synod gathering, but a congress," replied Father Kaleb, "and the chaplain must have returned long ago."

"Very well. Everything is upon my own shoulders. I shall take Hlawa with me, and two servants, with proper horses and go."

"Then to Zbyszko?" asked Jagienka.

"Then to Zbyszko," replied Macko. "But you must wait for me here until I return. I also think that I shall not be detained there for more than three or four days. I am accustomed to mosquitoes and fatigue. Therefore, I ask you, Father Kaleb, to give me a letter to the chaplain of Szczytno. He will believe me without hesitation if I show your letter, for there is always great confidence among the clergy."

"The people speak well of that priest," said Father Kaleb, "and if there is one who knows something, it is he."

He prepared a letter in the evening, and in the morning, before sunrise, old Macko left Spychow.

CHAPTER V.

Jurand awoke from his long sleep in the presence of the priest; he forgot what had happened to him and where he was; he began to feel around in bed and at the wall. The priest caught him in his arms and wept, tenderly kissing him, and said:

"It is I! You are at Spychow! Brother Jurand!... God tried you.... But you are now among your own.... Good people brought you here. Brother, dear brother, Jurand."

Then he repeatedly pressed him to his breast, kissed his brow and his hollow eyes; but Jurand appeared to be stupefied and unconscious. At last he moved his left hand toward his head and brow as though wishing to dispel the cloud of sleep and stupor from his mind.

"Do you hear and understand me?" asked Father Kaleb.

Jurand moved his head affirmatively. Then he stretched his hand toward the silver crucifix on the wall which he had once taken from the neck of a powerful German knight, pressed it to his lips and heart and then gave it to Father Kaleb.

"I understand you, brother!" said the priest. "He remained with you. He is able to restore to you all you lost, just as He delivered you from captivity."

Jurand pointed with his hand heavenward, a sign that all will there be returned to him. Then his hollow eyes were filled with tears, and an indescribable pain was depicted upon his tortured face.

Father Kaleb having observed his painful emotion concluded that Danuska was dead. He therefore knelt at the bedside and said:

"O Lord! Grant her eternal rest in peace, and everlasting bliss be hers. Amen."

Then Jurand lifted himself up and began to twist his head and move his hand as though wishing to check the priest, but the priest did not understand. At that moment old Tolima entered, and with him were the garrison of the town, the former and present elders of the peasants of Spychow, foresters, fishermen, etc., because the news of Jurand's return had rapidly spread throughout Spychow. They embraced his feet, kissed his hand and bitterly wept when they saw the old and maimed cripple who looked like another being, not in the least the once invincible knight, the terror of the Knights of the Cross. But some of them, especially those who used to accompany him on his expeditions, were enraged; their faces grew pale and determined. After a while they crowded together and whispered, pulled, and pushed each other. Finally, a certain Sucharz, a member of the garrison and village blacksmith, approached Jurand, clasped his feet and said:

"We intended to go to Szczytno, as soon as they brought you here, but that knight, who brought you, hindered us. Permit us, sir, now. We cannot leave them unpunished. Let it be now as it was long ago. They shall not disgrace us and remain scathless. We used to fight them under your command. Now we will march under Tolima, or without him. We must conquer Szczytno and shed the dog-blood. So help us God!"

"So help us God!" repeated several voices.

"To Szczytno!"

"We must have blood!"

Forthwith a burning fire took hold of the inflammable Mazur hearts, their brows began to wrinkle, their eyes to glisten. Here and there was heard the sound of gnashing teeth. But in a moment the noise ceased, and all eyes were turned toward Jurand, whose cheeks reddened and he assumed his wonted warlike appearance. He rose and again felt for the crucifix upon the wall. The people thought that he was looking for a sword. He found it and took it down. His face paled, he turned toward the people, lifted his hollow eyes heavenward and moved the crucifix in front of him.

Silence reigned. It was beginning to get dark; the twittering of birds retiring upon the roofs and trees of the village, penetrated through the open windows. The last red rays of the setting sun penetrated into the room and fell upon the raised cross and upon Jurand's white hair.

Sucharz, the blacksmith, looked at Jurand, glanced at his comrades and looked again at Jurand. Finally, he bid them good-bye and left the room on tiptoe. The others followed suit. When they reached the courtyard they halted, and the following whispered conversation ensued:

"What now?"

"We are not going. How then?"

"He did not permit."

"Leave vengeance with God. It is obvious that even his soul has undergone a change."

It was so indeed.

Those who remained were Father Kaleb and old Tolima. Jagienka with Sieciechowa, who were attracted by the armed crowd in the courtyard, came to learn what was the matter.

Jagienka, who was more daring and sure of herself than her companion, approached Jurand.

"God help you, Knight Jurand," she said. "We are those who brought you here from Prussia."

His face brightened at the sound of her young voice. It was obvious that it brought back to his mind in proper order all the events which had happened upon the road from Szczytno, because he showed his thankfulness by inclining his head and placing his hand upon his chest several times. Then she related to him how they first met him, how Hlawa, the Bohemian, who was Zbyszko's armor-bearer, recognized him, and finally how they brought him to Spychow. She also told him about herself, that she and her companion bore a sword, helmet and shield for the knight Macko of Bogdaniec, the uncle of Zbyszko, who left Bogdaniec to find his nephew, and now he had left for Szczytno and would return to Spychow within three or four days.

At the mention of Szczytno, Jurand did not fall down nor was he overcome as he was when upon the road to that place, but great trouble was depicted upon his face. But Jagienka assured him that Macko was as clever as he was manly, and would not let himself be fooled by anybody. Besides that, he possessed letters from Lichtenstein, which enabled him to travel in safety everywhere.

These words quieted him considerably. It was obvious that he wished to get information about many other things. But as he was unable to do it, he suffered in his soul. This the clever girl at once observed and said:

"We shall often, talk about things. Then everything will be told."

244

Then he smiled and stretched out his hand and placed it upon her head for a while; it seemed he was blessing her. He thanked her indeed very much, but as a matter of fact he was touched by the youthful voice like the warbling of a bird.

When he was not engaged in prayer, as he was almost all day, or asleep, he wished to have her near him, and when she was not there, he yearned to hear her speak, and endeavored by all means in his power to call the attention of the priest and Tolima that he wished to have that delightful boy near him.

She came often, because her tender heart sincerely pitied him. Besides that, she passed the time in waiting for Macko, whose stay at Szcytno seemed to her uncommonly long.

He was to return within three days, and now the fourth and fifth have passed by and it is already the evening of the sixth, and he has not yet returned. The alarmed girl was ready to ask Tolima to send a searching party, when suddenly the guard upon the watch-oak signalled the approach of some horsemen, and in a few moments was heard the tramp of the horses upon the drawbridge, and Hlawa accompanied by a courier appeared in the courtyard. Jagienka who had left her room, to watch in the courtyard before their arrival, rushed toward Hlawa before he dismounted.

"Where is Macko?" she asked, with beating heart and alarmed.

"He went to Prince Witold, and he ordered you to stay here."

CHAPTER VI.

When Jagienka realized the import of Macko's message, that she was to remain at Spychow, she was almost stunned. Grief and anger rendered her speechless for a while, and with wide opened eyes she stared at the Bohemian, which told him how unwelcome was the information he brought her. He therefore said:

"I should also like to inform you, what we heard at Szcytno. There is much and important news."

"Is it from Zbyszko?"

"No, from Szcytno. You know...."

"Let the servant unsaddle the horses, and you come with me."

The order was executed and they went into her room.

"Why does Macko leave us here? Why must we remain at Spychow, and why did you return here?" she asked in one breath.

"I returned," replied Hlawa, "because the knight Macko ordered me. I wished to go to the war, but an order is an order. Knight Macko told me thus: 'Return, take care of the lady of Zgorzelice, and wait for news from me. You may have to escort her to Zgorzelice, since she cannot go there by herself.'"

"For the love of God, tell me what happened! Did they find Jurand's daughter? Has Macko gone there to search for Zbyszko? Did you see her? Have you spoken to her? Why have you not brought her with you? Where is she now?"

Hearing such an avalanche of questions, the Bohemian bowed to the girl's feet and said:

"Let it not displease your grace if I do not reply to all questions at once, for it is impossible for me to do so, but, I shall if nothing hinders, endeavor to answer them one by one in the order according as they were put."

"Well, did they find her?"

"No, but there is sure information that she was at Szczytno, and that she was probably removed to a distant castle in the east."

"But why must we remain at Spychow?"

"Bah! If she were found?... It is true, as your grace is aware.... There would be no reason for remaining here...."

Jagienka was silent, only her cheeks reddened. But the Bohemian said;

"I thought and am still of the opinion, that we shall not be able to rescue her alive from the talons of those dog-brothers. But everything is in God's hands. I must relate to you from the beginning. We arrived at Szczytno. Well. Knight Macko showed Lichtenstein's letter to the bailiff, who kissed the seal in our presence, and received us as guests. He did not suspect us in the least and had full confidence in us, so that if we had had a few of our men

245

in the neighborhood we could easily have taken possession of the castle. There was no hindrance to our interview with the priest. We conversed for two nights; we informed ourselves of strange things which the priest got from the executioner."

"But the executioner is dumb."

"He is, but the priest speaks to him by signs, and he understands him perfectly well. They are strange things. It must have been the finger of God. That executioner cut off Jurand's hand, tore out his tongue, and put out his eyes. That executioner is such that where men are concerned he would not shrink from inflicting any torture, even if he were ordered to pull the teeth of the victim; but, where girls are concerned, he would not lift up his hand to kill them, or to assist in torturing them. The reason for this determination is, because he too had an only daughter whom he loved dearly, and whom the Knights of the Cross have...."

Here Hlawa stopped; he knew not how to continue his narrative. This Jagienka observed, and she said:

"What do I care about the executioner?"

"Because this is in order," he replied. "When our young master quartered the knight Rotgier the old *comthur* Zygfried almost raved. They said at Szczytno that Rotgier was the *comthur's* son. The priest confirmed the story, that no father ever loved his son as much as Zygfried loved Rotgier; for his thirst for vengeance he sold his soul to the devil. All this the executioner saw. The *comthur* talked with the slain Rotgier, as I am talking to you, and the corpse smiled; then he gnashed his teeth, and for joy he licked his livid lips with his black tongue when the old *comthur* promised him Zbyszko's head. But as he could not then get Zbyszko, he ordered Jurand to be tortured in the meanwhile and then placed Jurand's tongue and hand in Rotgier's coffin, who began to devour it...."

"It is terrible to hear. In the name of the Father, Son and Holy Ghost, amen," said Jagienka. Then she got up and threw a log of wood on the fire because it was night already.

"How," continued Hlawa, "how will it be in the day of judgment? Because then everything belonging to Jurand must be restored to him. But that surpasses human understanding. The executioner then saw everything. Gorged with human flesh, the old *comthur* went to take Jurand's daughter, because the other, it seems, whispered to him that he wanted to drink innocent human blood, after his meal. But the executioner, as I have already told you, who did everything, but would not hurt or kill a girl, placed himself upon the staircase.... The priest said that otherwise the executioner is stupid and half a brute, but in that matter he was wide awake, and when necessary he has no equal in cunning. He sat on the stairs and waited, until the *comthur* arrived and heard the breathing of the executioner. He saw something shining and started back for he thought it was the devil. The executioner struck him in the neck with his fist, so that he thought the bones were completely shattered. He did not die, but fainted, and became sick with fright. When he recovered, he was afraid to repeat this attempt upon Jurandowna."

"But they have carried her off."

They have, but they have taken the executioner with her. The *comthur* did not know that it was he who defended Jurandowna. He thought that some supernatural power, good or evil, did it. He had taken the executioner with him and would not leave him at Szczytno. He was afraid of his testimony, for although dumb, he could in case of a trial testify by signs that which he told the priest. Moreover, the priest finally told Macko that old Zygfried no more threatens Jurandowna, because he is afraid; and although he ordered somebody else to harm her, nothing will happen to her as long as Diedrich lives; he will not permit it, especially as he has already protected her once."

"But does the priest know where they have taken her?"

"Not exactly, but he heard them talk of a certain place called Ragniec, which castle is situated not far from the Lithuanian or Zmudz frontiers."

"What did Macko say concerning that?"

"Pan Macko told me the following day: 'If it is so, then I can and will find her, but I must hasten to Zbyszko, to see that he is not entrapped by them through Jurandowna as they did with Jurand. They have only to tell him that if he comes by himself they will give her up to him and he would not hesitate to go; then old Zygfried would wreak his vengeance upon him, for the death of Rotgier, in unheard-of tortures.'"

"True! It is true!" exclaimed Jagienka, alarmed. "If that is the reason of his hurried departure, then he is right."

But after a moment she turned to Hlawa and said:

"Nevertheless he made a mistake in sending you here. There is no need to guard us here. Old Tolima can do it as well. You, being strong and intrepid, could be of much help to Zbyszko there."

"But who would guard you in case you were to go to Zgorzelice?"

"In such a case they would have to convey the news by somebody; they will do it through you. You will precede them and take us home."

The Bohemian kissed her hand, and asked, with emotion:

"But during the time of your sojourn here?"

"God watches over orphans! I shall remain here."

"Will you not find it tedious? What will you do here?"

"I shall ask the Lord Jesus to restore happiness to Zbyszko and keep all of you in good health."

Then she burst out weeping, and the armor-bearer bowed again at her feet, and said:

"You are indeed like an angel in heaven."

CHAPTER VII.

But she wiped away her tears, took the armor-bearer with her and went to Jurand to tell him the news. She found him in a bright room, the tame she-wolf at his feet, sitting with Father Kaleb, old Tolima and Sieciechowa. Supporting their heads with their hands, absorbed in thought, and sorrowful, they were listening to a poem which the village beadle, who was also the *rybalt*, accompanied by his lute, sang of Jurand's former exploits against the "abominable Knights of the Cross." The room was lit up by the moon. A very warm and quiet night followed a scorching day. The windows were open, and beetles from the linden in the courtyard, were seen crawling upon the floor. In front of the fireplace, where there were yet glimmering a few embers, sat the servant sipping a mixture of hot mead, wine and spices.

The *rybalt*, or beadle, and servant of Father Kaleb, was about to begin another song, entitled "The Happy Encounter." "Jurand is riding, riding, upon a chestnut-colored horse," when Jagienka entered and said:

"The Lord Jesus be praised!"

"Forever and ever," replied Father Kaleb. Jurand sat in an armchair, with his elbows upon the arms, but when he heard her voice he immediately turned toward her, and began to greet her, nodding his milk white head.

"Zbyszko's armor-bearer has arrived from Szczytno," said the girl, "and has brought news from the priest. Macko will not return to this place. He went to Prince Witold."

"Why will he not return here?" asked Father Kaleb.

Then she told all she had heard from the Bohemian. She related how Zygfried avenged himself for Rotgier's death; how the old *comthur* intended to destroy Danusia for Rotgier to drink her innocent blood; and how the executioner defended her. She even told them of Macko's hopes to find Danusia, with Zbyszko's assistance, rescue her, bring her to Spychow; and for that very reason he had gone to Zbyszko and ordered her to remain here.

Be it from grief or sorrow her voice trembled at the end. When she finished, silence prevailed for a while in the room and only the chirping of the crickets, from the linden in the courtyard, penetrated through the open windows and sounded like a heavy rainfall. All eyes were directed toward Jurand, who with closed eyelids and head bent backward, showed no sign of life.

"Do you hear?" finally asked the priest.

But Jurand kept on bending his head, lifted up his left hand and pointed toward the sky. The light of the moon fell directly upon his face, upon the white hair, upon the blind eyes; and there was depicted in that face such indescribable suffering, together with complete hope and resignation in God's will, that it appeared to all present that he only saw with his soul which was freed from the fetters of the body, and had renounced once for all earthly life, in which nothing was left for him.

Silence again reigned and the noise of the crickets was still audible.

But almost with filial love, Jagienka was suddenly overcome with great pity for the unhappy old man. At the first impulse she rushed to his side, grasped his hand and covered it with kisses and tears.

"And I too am an orphan!" she exclaimed, with swelling heart. "I am not a boy, but am Jagienka of Zgorzelice. Macko took me in order to protect me from bad people. Now I shall remain with you until God restores Danusia to you."

Jurand was not at all surprised; he seemed to know it already; he only took hold of her and pressed her to his breast, and she continued to kiss his hand and spoke in a broken and sobbing voice:

"I will remain with you. Danuska will return…. Then I shall return to Zgorzelice. God protects the orphans! The Germans have also killed my father. But your beloved one is alive and will return. Grant this, O most merciful God! Grant this, O most holy and compassionate Mother!…" Then Father Kaleb suddenly knelt and with a solemn voice began to pray:

"Lord have mercy upon us!"

"Christ have mercy upon us!" immediately responded the Bohemian and Tolima. Then all knelt down, because it was the Litany, which is not only said at the moment of death, but also for the delivery of dear and near persons from the danger of death. Jagienka knelt; Jurand slipped down from his seat and knelt, and all began to pray in chorus:

"Lord have mercy upon us!"

"Christ have mercy upon us!"

"O God the Father in Heaven, have mercy upon us!"

"Son of God, Redeemer of the world, have mercy upon us!"

Their praying voices, "Have mercy upon us!" were mingled with the chirping of the crickets.

The tame she-wolf suddenly got up from the bearskin upon which she was crouching, in front of Jurand, approached the open window, supported herself upon the sill, turned her triangular jaws toward the moon and howled in a low and plaintive voice.

END OF PART SIXTH.
PART SEVENTH
CHAPTER I.

To a certain extent the Bohemian adored Jagienka, but his love for the charming Sieciechowna was on the increase, nevertheless his young and brave heart caused him to be eager above all for war. He returned to Spychow with Macko's message, in obedience to his master, and therefore he felt a certain satisfaction that he would be protected by both masters, but when Jagienka herself told him what was the truth, that there was none to oppose him in Spychow and that his duty was to be with Zbyszko, he gladly assented. Macko was not his immediate authority. It was therefore an easy matter to justify himself before him, that he had left Spychow at the command of his mistress to go to Zbyszko.

But Jagienka did it purposely, that the valiant and clever armor-bearer might always be of assistance to Zbyszko and save him in many dangerous situations. He had already shown his ability at the prince's hunting party in which Zbyszko nearly perished from the attack of a urus; much more so would he be useful in war, specially such as the present one on the Zmudz frontier. Glowacz was so eager for the field, that when he left Jurand with Jagienka he embraced her feet and said:

"I desire to kneel before you at once and beg you for a good word for my journey."

"How is that?" asked Jagienka. "Do you want to go to-day?"

"Early to-morrow, so that the horses may rest during the night, for the expedition to Zmudz is very far."

"Then go so that you may easily overtake Macko."

"It will be a hard task. The old gentleman is hardy in all kinds of toil, and he is several days ahead of me. In order to shorten my way I shall have to travel through Prussia, through pathless forests. Pan Macko has letters from Lichtenstein which he can show when necessary; but I have nothing to show, I shall therefore be obliged to make a free road for myself."

Then he placed his hand upon his sword. At that Jagienka exclaimed:

"Be careful! It is necessary to travel as fast as possible, but on the other hand you must be careful to avoid being caught and imprisoned by the Knights of the Cross. Also be careful whilst you are in the wild forests, for there are just now all kinds of gods whom the people of that land who have not been converted to Christianity worship. I remember what Macko and Zbyszko said about them in Zgorzelice."

"I too remember what they said about those gods, but I am not afraid of them; they are puny things and no gods, and they have no power whatever. I shall manage them as well as the Germans whom I shall meet in the field and make it hot for them."

"But you can't kill gods! Tell me, what did you hear of them among the Germans?"

Then the discreet Bohemian wrinkled his brow, stopped for a moment, and said:

"Killing or no killing, we informed ourselves of everything, specially Pan Macko, who is cunning and able to circumvent every German. He asks for one thing or another, or pretends to salute, and says nothing that might betray him, and whatever he says is to the point and draws his information as the angler draws out the fish. If your grace will listen patiently I will tell you: Some years ago, Prince Witold planned an expedition against the Tartars, but wished to be at peace with the Germans; he therefore ceded to them the province of Zmudz. Then there was great friendship and peace. He allowed them to build castles. Bah, he even assisted them. They, including the master, met at an island, where they ate, drank and showed each other much friendship. They were even permitted to hunt in those wild forests. When the poor people of Zmudz rose in arms against the rule of the Order, Prince Witold helped the Germans with his own soldiers. The people throughout Lithuania murmured that the prince was against his own blood. All this the under-bailiff of Szczytno related to us; he praised the courts of the Knights of the Cross in Zmudz because they sent priests to that country to convert the people to Christianity and feed them in time of dearth. Something of that kind was done, for the grand master, who fears God more than the others, ordered it. But instead of it, they gathered together the children and sent them to Prussia, and they outraged the women in the presence of their husbands and brothers; whoever dared to oppose it was hanged. This, lady, is the cause of the present war."

"And Prince Witold?"

"The prince had his eyes shut for a long time to the wrongs of the oppressed people of Zmudz, and he loved the Knights of the Cross. It is not long since the princess, his wife, went to Prussia to visit Malborg. They received her with great pomp, as though she were the queen of Poland. That happened quite recently! They showered gifts upon her, and gave numerous tourneys, feasts, and all kinds of fêtes wherever she went. The people thought that it would result in everlasting friendship between the Knights of the Cross and Prince Witold. But suddenly his heart was changed...."

"This confirms what I heard from my lamented father and Macko more than once, that the prince often changed his heart."

"Not often toward the upright, but frequently toward the Knights of the Cross, owing to the very reason that they themselves keep no faith, and are unreliable in everything. They asked him to give up deserters to them. His reply was that he would give up only those of ill repute, but free men he would not, because, as such, they were entitled to live wherever they chose. Just now they are soured and engaged in writing letters, complaining against each other. The people of Zmudz, now in Germany, heard of it; they left the garrisons, stirred up the people in the small castles, and now they make raids in Prussia itself and Prince Witold not only does not hinder them any longer, but he also laughs at the German trouble, and assists the Zmudzians secretly."

"I understand," said Jagienka. "But if he assists them secretly, open war is not yet declared."

"There is open war with the Zmudz people, but as a matter of fact there is also war against Prince Witold. Germans are coming from all parts of the country to defend their strongholds on the frontier and are contemplating a great expedition to invade Zmudz. But they cannot execute it before the winter season arrives, because it is a swampy country and impossible for them to fight in, and where a Zmudz warrior could pass, a German knight would stick fast. Winter, therefore, would be favorable to the Germans. As soon as it begins to freeze, the whole German forces will move, but Prince Witold will come to the aid of the Zmudz people. He will come with the permission of the king of Poland, since the king is the head of all great princes and, above all, Lithuania."

"Then there will be war against the king?"

"The people here, as well as in Germany, say that there will be war. The Knights of the Cross are probably now collecting forces in all courts, with cowls upon their heads like thieves. For every Knight of the Cross knows that the king's army is no joke, and, most likely, the Polish knights would easily vanquish them."

Jagienka sighed, and said:

"A boy is always more happy than a girl is. Here is proof of what I say. You will go to the war, as Zbyszko and Macko went, and we shall remain here, in Spychow."

"How can it be otherwise, lady? It is true that you remain here, but perfectly secure. The name of Jurand I have learned in Szczytno, is still a terror to the Germans, and if they learn that he is now at Spychow they will be terrified at once."

"We know that they will not dare to come here, because the swamps and old Tolima defend this place, but it will be hard to sit here without news."

"I will let you know if anything occurs. Even before we departed for Szczytno, two good young noblemen volunteered to start for the war. Tolima was unable to prevent it, because they are noblemen and come from Lenkawice. We shall now depart together and if anything occurs, one of them will be sent to you with the news."

"May God reward you. I have always known that you are wise in any adventure, but for your willingness and good heart toward me I shall thank you as long as I live."

Then the Bohemian knelt upon one knee and said:

"I have had nothing but kindness from you. Pan Zych captured me near Bolesławce, when I was a mere boy, and set me free without any ransom. But I preferred captivity under you to freedom. God grant that I might shed my blood for you, my lady."

"God lead you and bring you back!" replied Jagienka, holding out her hand to him.

But he preferred to bow to her knees and kiss her feet to honor her the more. Then he lifted up his head and said submissively and humbly:

"I am a simple boy, but I am a nobleman and your faithful servant. Give me therefore some token of remembrance for my journey. Do not refuse me this request; war time is approaching and I take Saint Jerzy to witness that I shall always try to be one of those in front, but never in the rear."

"What kind of souvenir do you ask for?"

"Girdle me with a strip of cloth for the road, so that if I fall in the field my pain may be lessened in having, when dying, the belt you fastened round my body."

Then he bowed again at her feet, folded his arms and gazed into her eyes imploringly. But Jagienka's face assumed a troubled look, and after a while she replied as if with involuntary bitterness:

"O, my dear! Ask me not for that, my girdling will be of no use to you. Whoever is happy can impart happiness to you. Only such an one can bring you fortune. But I, surely, have nothing but sorrow! Alas! I can give happiness neither to you nor others; for that which I do not possess myself I cannot impart to others. I feel so, Hlawa. There is nothing, now, for me in the world, so, so that…."

Then she suddenly ceased, because she knew that if she said another word it would cause her to burst into tears, even so her eyes became clouded. But the Bohemian was greatly moved, because he understood that it would be equally bad for her, in case she had to return to Zgorzelice and be in the neighborhood of the rapacious villains Cztan and Wilk: or to remain in Spychow, where sooner or later Zbyszko might come with Danusia. Hlawa seemed to understand Jagienka's troubles, but he had no remedy for them. He therefore embraced her knees again and repeated.

"Oh! I will die for you! I will die!"

"Get up!" she said. "Let Sieciechowna gird you for the war, or let her give you some other keepsake, because you have been friends for some time past."

Then she began to call her, and Sieciechowna entered from the neighboring room immediately. She had heard before she entered, but she dared not enter although she burned with desire to take leave of the handsome armor-bearer. She therefore was frightened and confused, and her heart was beating violently when she entered; her eyes were glistening with tears, and with lowered eyelashes she stood before him; she looked like an apple blossom, and could not utter a single word.

Hlawa worshipped Jagienka, but with deepest respect, and he dared not reach her even in mind. He often thought familiarly about Sieciechowna because the blood in his veins coursed rapidly at the very sight of her and he could not withstand the presence of her charms. But now his heart was taken by her beauty, especially when he beheld her confusion and tears, through which he saw affection as one sees the golden bed of a crystal stream.

He therefore turned toward her and said:

"Do you know that I am going to war. Perchance I shall perish. Will you be sorry for me?"

"I shall feel very sorry for you!" replied the girl, in soft tones. Then she shed copious tears as she was always ready to do. The Bohemian was moved and began to kiss her hands, smothering his desire for more familiar kisses in the presence of Jagienka.

"Gird him or give him something else as a memento for the road, so that he may fight under your colors and in your name."

But Sieciechowna had nothing to give him, because she was attired in boy's clothes. She searched for something but found neither ribbon, nor anything that could be fastened, because her women's dresses were still packed up in the baskets, which had not been touched since they left Zgorzelice. She was therefore greatly perplexed until Jagienka came to her rescue by advising her to give him the little net upon her head.

"My God!" Hlawa joyously exclaimed, "let it be the net, attach it to the helmet, and woe betide that German who attempts to reach it."

Then Sieciechowna took it down with both hands and immediately her bright golden hair fell upon her shoulders and arms. At the sight of her beautiful disheveled hair, Hlawa's face changed, his cheeks flamed and then paled. He took the net, kissed it, and hid it in his breast. Then he embraced Jagienka's feet once more, and did the same, though a little more strongly than was necessary, to Sieciechowna. Then with the words: "Let it be so," he left the house without another word.

Although he was about to travel and in want of rest, he did not go to sleep. With his two companions who were to accompany him to Zmudz, he drank throughout the whole night. But he was not intoxicated, and at the first ray of light he was already in the courtyard where the horses were ready for the journey.

From the membrane window above the carriage house two blue eyes were looking upon the courtyard. When the Bohemian observed them, he wished to approach and show the net which he had attached to his helmet, then wish her good-bye once more, but Father Kaleb and old Tolima, who came to give him advice for his journey, interrupted him.

"Go first to the court of Prince Janusz," said the priest. "Perhaps Pan Macko stopped there. At all events, you will get there proper information; you will find there numerous acquaintances. Also the road there to Lithuania is known, and it is not difficult there to procure guides for the wilderness. If you are indeed bent on seeing Pan Zbyszko, then do not go directly to Zmudz, for there is the Prussian reservation, but go via Lithuania. Remember that the Zmudzians themselves might kill you even before you could shout to them who you were. But it is quite a different matter in Lithuania in the direction where Prince Witold is. Finally, may God bless you, and those two knights. May you return in good health and bring the child with you. I shall daily lie prostrate before the cross from vespers to the rising of the first star in prayer for this cause."

"I thank you, father, for your blessing," replied Hlawa. "It is not an easy task to rescue one alive from their devilish hands. But since everything is in God's hands, it is better to hope than to sorrow."

251

"It is better to hope, for this reason I do not despair. Hope lives, although the heart is full of anxiety.... The worst is, that Jurand himself, when his daughter's name is mentioned, immediately points with his finger toward heaven as though he already sees her there."

"How could he see her without eyes?"

The priest then replied, partly to himself and partly to Hlawa:

"Perchance he who has lost his bodily vision sees more with his spiritual eyes.... It may be so. It may be! But this, that God should permit so much wrong to be done to such an innocent lamb I do not understand clearly. Why should she suffer so much, even if she had offended the Knights of the Cross. But there was nothing against her and she was as pure as the divine lily, loving to others and lovely as yonder little free singing bird. God loves children, and is compassionate. Bah! If they were to kill her, He is able to resuscitate her as He did Piotrowina, who after having risen from the grave lived for many long years.... Depart in peace, and may God's hand protect you all!"

Then he returned to the chapel to say early Mass. The Bohemian mounted his horse, for it was already broad daylight, and bowed once more toward the window and departed.

CHAPTER II.

Prince and Princess Janusz had left with part of the court for the spring fishing at Czerska, of which sport he was extremely fond, and loved it above all others. The Bohemian got much important information from Mikolaj of Dlugolas, treating of private affairs as well as of the war. First he learned that Macko had apparently given up his intended route to Zmudz, the "Prussian enclosure," that a few days ago he had left for Warsaw where he found the princely pair. As to the war, old Mikolaj informed him all that he had already heard in Szczytno. All Zmudz, as one man, had risen in arms against the Germans, and Prince Witold not only had refused to help the Order against the unhappy Zmudzians, but had not yet declared war against them, and was negotiating with them; but meanwhile he supplied the Zmudzians with money, men, horses and corn. Meanwhile, he, as well as the Knights of the Cross, sent ambassadors to the pope, to the emperor, and to other Christian lords, accusing each other of breach of faith, and treachery. The ambassador carrying the letters of the prince was the clever Mikolaj of Rzeniewa, a man of great ability who could unravel the thread which was woven by the artifice of the Knights of the Cross, convincingly demonstrating the great wrongs done to the lands of Lithuania and Zmudz.

Meantime when at the diet in Wilno the ties between the Poles and Lithuanians were strengthened, it acted like poison in the hearts of the Knights of the Cross. It was easy to foresee that Jagiello as the supreme lord of all the lands under the command of Prince Witold, would stand at his side in time of war. Count Jan Sayn, the *comthur* of Grudzia, and Count Schwartzburg of Danzig, went, at the request of the grand master, to see the king and asked him what might be expected from him. Although they brought him falcons and costly presents, he told them nothing. Then they threatened him with war, without really intending it, because they well knew that the grand master and the chapter were terribly afraid of Jagiello's forces, and were anxious to avert the day of wrath and calamity.

All their schemes were broken like cobwebs, especially with Prince Witold. The evening after Hlawa's arrival, fresh news reached Warsaw. Bronisz of Ciasnoc, courtier of Prince Janusz, whom the prince had previously sent for information from Lithuania, arrived, and with him were two important Lithuanian princes. They brought letters from Witold and the Zmudzians. It was terrible news. The Order was preparing for war. The fortresses were being strengthened, ammunition manufactured, soldiers, (knechts) and knights were gathering at the frontier, and the lighter bodies of cavalry and infantry had already crossed the frontier near Ragnety, Gotteswerder and other border strongholds. The din of war was already heard in the forests, fields and villages, and during the night the woods were seen on fire along the dark sea. Witold finally received Zmudz under his overt protection. He sent his governors, and wagons with armed people he placed under the most famous warrior Skirwoillo. He broke into Prussia, burned, destroyed and devastated. The prince himself approached with his army toward Zmudz. Some fortresses he provisioned; others, Kowno, for instance, he destroyed, so that the Knights of the Cross might find no support. It was no more a secret, that at the advent of winter, when the swamps should be frozen, or even earlier than that, if the season was dry, a great war would break out, which would embrace all the lands of Lithuania, Zmudz, and Prussia. But should the king rush to the assistance of Witold then a day must follow in which the flood would inundate the German or the other half of the world, or would be forced back for long ages into its original river-bed.

But that was not to happen yet. Meanwhile, the sighs of the Zmudzians, their despairing complaints of the wrongs done to them, and their appeals for justice were heard everywhere. They also read letters concerning the unfortunate people in Krakow, Prague, in the pope's court and in other western countries. The nobleman brought an open letter to Prince Janusz, from Bronisz of Ciasnoc. Many a Mazovian involuntarily laid his hand on his sword at his side and considered seriously whether voluntarily to enroll under the standard of Witold. It was known that the great prince would be glad to have with him the valiant Polish nobles, who were as valorous in battle as the Lithuanian and Zmudzian nobility, and better disciplined and equipped than they. Others were also impelled by their hatred toward the old enemies of the Polish race, whilst others wanted to go out of compassion.

"Listen! Oh listen!" They appealed to the kings, princes and to the whole Zmudzian nation. "We are people of noble blood and free, but the Order wants to enslave us! They do not care for our souls, but they covet our lands and wealth. Our need is already such that nothing remains for us but to gather together, or kill ourselves! How can they wash us with Christian water when they themselves have unclean hands. We wish to be baptized, but not with blood and the sword. We want religion, but only such as upright monarchs shall teach,—Jagiello and Witold.

"Listen to us and help us, for we perish! The Order does not wish to christen us for our enlightenment. They do not send us priests, but executioners. Our beehives, our flocks, and all the products of our land they have already carried away. We are not even allowed to fish or hunt in the wilds.

"We pray you: Listen to us! They are just bending our necks under the yoke and force us to work during the night in the castles. They have carried off our children as hostages; our wives and daughters they ravish in our presence. It behooves us to groan, but not to speak. Our fathers they have burned at the stake; our lords have been carried off to Prussia. Our great men, Korkucia, Wasigina, Swolka and Songajle, they have destroyed."

"Oh listen! for we are not wild beasts but human beings. We earnestly call upon the Holy Father to send us Polish bishops to baptize us, for we thirst for baptism from the very depth of our heart. But baptism is performed with water and not with shedding of human living blood."

This was the kind of complaint the Zmudzians made against the Knights of the Cross, so that when they were heard by the Mazovian court, several knights and courtiers immediately presented themselves ready to go and help them; they understood that it was not even necessary to ask for permission from Prince Janusz, even if only for the reason that the princess was the sister of Prince Witold. They were specially enraged when they learned from Bronisz and the noblemen, that many noble Zmudzian young ladies, who were hostages in Prussia, but could not endure dishonor and cruelty, had taken their own lives when the Knights of the Cross were about to attack their honor.

Hlawa was very glad to learn of the desire of the Mazovian knights, because he thought that the more men from Poland that joined Prince Witold, the more intense would be the war, and the affair against the Knights of the Cross would be more potent. He was also glad of his chances of meeting Zbyszko, and the old knight Macko, to whom he was much attached and whom, he believed, he was worthy to meet, and together see new wild countries, hitherto unknown cities, and see knights and soldiers never seen before, and, finally, that Prince Witold whose great fame resounded then throughout the world.

Those thoughts decided him to undertake the long and hurried journey—not stopping upon the road more than was necessary for the horses to rest.

The noblemen who arrived with Bronisz of Ciasnoc and other Lithuanians who were present at the prince's court, and who were acquainted with the roads and all passes, were to guide him and the Mazovian knights, from hamlet to hamlet, from city to city and through the silent, immense, deep wilderness which covered the greater part of Mazovia, Lithuania and Zmudz.

CHAPTER III.

In the woods, about a mile to the east of Kowno, which Witold had destroyed, were stationed the principal forces of Skirwoillo, extending in time of need from point to point in the neighborhood. They made quick expeditions sometimes to the Prussian frontier, and at others against the castles and smaller fortified places which were still in the hands of the Knights of the Cross, and filled the country with flame of war. There the faithful armor-bearer found Zbyszko and Macko only two days after the latter arrived. After greetings, the Bohemian slept like a rock the whole night, only on the following evening he went out to greet the old knight who looked fatigued and ill-humored and received him angrily, and asked him why he had not remained at Spychow as ordered. Hlawa restrained himself till Zbyszko had left the tent, when he justified his conduct, which was owing to Jagienka's command.

He also said that apart from her order, and his natural inclination for war, he was urged by the desire, in case of emergency, to carry the news to Spychow at once. "The young lady," he said, "who has a soul like an angel, is praying against her own interest for Jurandowna. But there must be an end to everything. If Danusia is not alive, then let God give her eternal glory, because she was an innocent lamb. But should she be found, then it will be necessary to let Jagienka know it immediately, so that she may at once leave Spychow, and not wait until the actual return of Jurandowna, which would seem as though she were driven away in shame and dishonor."

Macko listened unwillingly, repeating from time to time: "It is not your business." But Hlawa had resolved to speak openly; he did not entirely agree in this with Macko; at last he said:

"It would have been better if the young lady had been left at Zgorzelice. This journey is in vain. We told the poor lady that Jurandowna was dead and that something else might turn up."

"Nobody but you said that she was dead," exclaimed the knight, with anger. "You ought to have held your tongue. I took her with me because I was afraid of Cztan and Wilk."

"That was only a pretext," replied the armor-bearer. "She might have safely remained at Zgorzelice, and those fellows would have hurt each other. But, you feared, sir, that, in case of Jurandowna's death Jagienka might escape Zbyszko. That is the reason why you took her with you."

"How dare you speak so? Are you a belted knight and not a servant?"

"I am a servant, but I serve my lady; that is the reason why I am watching that no evil betide her."

Macko reflected gloomily, because he was not satisfied with himself. More than once he had blamed himself for taking Jagienka with him, because he felt that in any case, under such circumstances, it would be, to a certain extent, to her disadvantage. He also felt that there was truth in the Bohemian's bold words, that he had taken the girl with him in order to preserve her for Zbyszko.

"It never entered my head," he said, nevertheless, to deceive the Bohemian. "She was anxious to go herself."

"She persisted because we said that the other was no more in this world, and that her brother would be safer without than with her; it was then that she left."

"You persuaded her," shouted Macko.

"I did, and I confess my guilt. But now, sir, it is necessary to do something; otherwise we shall perish."

"What can one do here?" said Macko, impatiently, "with such soldiers, in such a war?... It will be somewhat better, but that cannot be before July, because the Germans have two favorable seasons for war, viz: winter when everything is frozen, and the dry season. Now it is only smouldering, but does not burn. It seems that Prince Witold went to Krakow to interview the king and ask his permission and help."

"But in the neighborhood are the fortresses of the Knights of the Cross. If only two could be taken, we might find there Jurandowna, or hear of her death."

"Or nothing."

"But Zygfried brought her to this part of the country. They told us so at Szczytno, and everywhere, and we ourselves were of the same opinion."

"But did you observe these soldiers; go into the tents and look for yourself. Some of them are armed with clubs, whilst others with antiquated swords made of copper."

"Bah! As far as I have heard they are good fighters."

"But they cannot conquer castles with naked bodies, especially those of the Knights of the Cross."

Further conversation was interrupted by the arrival of Zbyszko and Skirwoillo, who was the leader of the Zmudzians. He was a small man and looked like a boy, but broad shouldered and strong, his chest protuded so much that it looked like a deformity, his hands were long, they almost reached his knees. In general he resembled Zyndram of Maszkow, a famous knight, whom Macko and Zbyszko had formerly known in Krakow, because he also had a tremendous head and bowed legs. They said that he too understood the art of war very well. He had spent a lifetime in fighting the Tartars in Russia, and the Germans, whom he hated like the plague. In those wars he had learned the Russian language, and later on, at the court of Witold, he had learned some Polish. He knew German, at least he repeated only the three words: "Fire, blood and death." His big head was always filled with ideas and stratagems of war, which the Knights of the Cross could neither foresee nor prevent. He was therefore banished from the lands on the other side of the frontier.

"We were talking of an expedition," said Zbyszko to Macko, with unusual animation, "and that is the reason why we came here so that we too might learn your opinion."

Macko sat down with Skirwoilla upon a pine stump covered with a bear skin. Then he ordered the servants to bring little tubs full of mead from which the knights drew with tin cups and drank. Then after they had taken refreshment, Macko asked:

"Do you want to undertake an expedition?"

"Burn the German castles...."

"Which?"

"Ragnety, or Nowe (new) Kowno."

"Ragnety," said Zbyszko. "We were three days in the neighborhood of Nowe Kowno, and they beat us."

"Just so," said Skirwoilla.

"How so?"

"Well."

"Wait," said Macko, "I am a stranger here, and do not know where Nowe Kowno and Ragnety are."

"From this place to Old Kowno is less then a mile,"[115] replied Zbyszko, "and from that place to Nowe Kowno, is the same distance. The castle is situated upon an island. We wanted to cross over yesterday, but we were beaten in the attempt; they pursued us half the day, then we hid ourselves in the woods. The soldiers scattered and only this morning some of them returned."

"And Ragnety?"

Skirwoilla stretched his long arms, pointed toward the north, and said:

"Far! Far...."

"Just for the reason that it is distant," replied Zbyszko, "there is quiet in the neighborhood, because all the soldiers were withdrawn from there and sent to this place. The Germans there expect no attack; we shall therefore fall upon those who think themselves secure."

"He speaks reasonably," said Skirwoilla.

Then Macko asked:

"Do you think that it will also be possible to storm the castle?"

Skirwoillo shook his head and Zbyszko replied:

"The castle is strong, therefore it can only be taken by storm. But we shall devastate the country, burn the towns and villages, destroy provisions, and above all take prisoners, among whom we may find important personages, for whom the Knights of the Cross will eagerly give ransom or exchange...."

Then he turned toward Skirwoillo and said:

"You yourself, prince, acknowledged that I am right, but now consider that Nowe Kowno is upon an island, there we shall neither stir up the people in the villages, drive off

255

the herds of cattle, nor take prisoners, the more so because they have repulsed us here. Ay! Let us rather go where they do not expect us."

"Conquerors are those who least expect an attack," murmured Skirwoillo.

Here Macko interrupted and began to support Zbyszko's plans, because he understood that the young man had more hope to hear something near Ragnety than near Old Kowno, and that there were more chances to take important hostages at Ragnety who might serve for exchange. He also thought that it was better to go yonder at all events and attack an unguarded land, than an island, which was a natural stronghold and in addition was guarded by a strong castle and the customary garrison.

He spoke as a man experienced in war, he spoke in a clear manner, he adduced such excellent reasons that convinced everybody. They listened to him attentively. Skirwoillo raised his brows now and then as an affirmative sign; at times he murmured: "Well spoken." Finally he moved his big head between his broad shoulders so that he looked like a hunchback, and was absorbed in thought.

Then he rose, said nothing, and began to take leave.

"How then will it be, prince?" inquired Macko. "Whither shall we move?"

But he replied briefly:

"To Nowe Kowno."

Then he left the tent.

Macko and the Bohemian looked at each other for some time in surprise; then the old knight placed his hands upon his thighs and exclaimed:

"Phew! What a hard stump!… He listens, listens and yet keeps his mouth shut."

"I heard before that he is such a man," replied Zbyszko. "To tell the truth all people here are obstinate; like the little fellow, they listen to the reasoning of others, then … it is like blowing in the air."

"Then why does he consult us?"

"Because we are belted knights and he wants to hear the thing argued on both sides. But he is not a fool."

"Also near Nowe Kowno we are least expected," observed the Bohemian, "for the very reason that they have beaten you. In that he is right."

"Come, let us see the people whom I lead," said Zbyszko, "because the air in the tent is too close. I want to tell them to be ready."

They went out. A cloudy and dark night had set in, the scene was only lit up by the fire around which the Zmudzians were sitting.

CHAPTER IV.

Macko and Zbyszko had seen enough of Lithuanian and Zmudz warriors when serving under Prince Witold. The sights of the encampment were nothing new to them. But the Bohemian looked at them with curiosity. He pondered both upon the possibility of their fighting qualities and compared them with the Polish and German knights. The camp was situated on a plain surrounded by forests and swamps, which rendered it impregnable, because none could wade through that treacherous marsh land. Even the place where the booths were situated was quaggy and muddy, but the soldiers had covered it with a thick layer of chips and branches of fir and pine-trees, which enabled them to camp upon it as upon perfectly dry ground. For Prince Skirwoillo they had hastily constructed a Lithuanian *numy*, constructed of earth and logs, and for the most important personages scores of booths of twisted branches. But the common soldiers were squatting in the open around the camp-fires, and for shelter against bad weather they only had goatskin coats, and skins upon their naked bodies. None had gone to sleep yet; they had nothing to do, after yesterday's defeat, and had thrown up earthworks during the day. Some of them were sitting or lying around the bright fire which they fed with dry juniper branches. Others were scraping in the ashes and cinders from which proceeded a smell of baked turnips, which form the ordinary food of the Lithuanians, and the strong odor of burned meat. Between the camp-fires were piles of arms; they were close at hand so that in case of need it would be an easy matter for everybody to reach his own weapon. Hlawa looked with curiosity upon the lances with narrow and long heads made of tempered iron, and the handles of oak saplings, studded with flint or nails, hatchets with short handles like the Polish axes used by travelers,

256

and others with handles almost as long as those of the battle-axes used by the foot-soldiers. There were also among them some bronze weapons from ancient times when iron was not yet employed in that low country. Some swords were entirely made of bronze, but most of them were of good steel of Novgorod. The Bohemian handled the spears, swords, hatchets, axes and tarred bows, examining them closely by the light of the camp-fires. There were a few horses near the fires, whilst the cattle grazed at a distance in the forests and meadows, under the care of vigilant ostlers; but the great nobles liked to have their chargers close at hand, hence there were about twoscore horses within the camp, fed by hand by the slaves of the noblemen in a space enclosed by stacked arms. Hlawa was amazed at the sight of the extraordinarily small shaggy chargers, with powerful necks, such strange brutes that the western knights took them to be quite another species of wild beast, more like a unicorn than a horse.

"Big battle horses are of no use here," said the experienced Macko, recollecting his former service under Witold, "because large horses would at once stick in the mire, but the native nag goes everywhere, like the men."

"But in the field," replied the Bohemian, "the native horse could not withstand that of the German."

"True, he may not be able to withstand, but, on the other hand, the German could not run away from the Zmudzian, neither could he catch him; they are very swift, swifter than those of the Tartars."

"Nevertheless I wonder; because when I saw the Tartar captives whom Lord Zych brought to Zgorzelice, they were small and matched their horses; but these are big men."

The men were tall indeed; their broad chests and strong arms could be seen under their goatskin coats; they were not stout, but bony and sinewy, and as a rule they excelled the inhabitants of other parts of Lithuania, because they lived in better and more productive lands, and were seldom subject to the dearth which often afflicted Lithuania. On the other hand they were wilder than the other Lithuanians. The court of the chief prince was at Wilno, whither the princes from the east and west, and ambassadors and foreign merchants came, and that contributed somewhat to lessen the roughness of the inhabitants of the city and neighborhood. There the stranger only appeared in the form of a Knight of the Cross or a sworded cavalier, carrying to the settlements in the deep forests fire, slavery and baptism of blood. That was the reason that the people in that part of the country were very coarse and rude, more like those of ancient times, and very much opposed to everything new, the oldest custom and the oldest warrior clan were theirs, and the reason that paganism was supported was that the worship of the cross did not bring the announcement of good tidings with apostolic love, but armed German monks instead, possessing souls of executioners.

Skirwoilla and the most notable princes and nobles were already Christians, because they followed the example of Jagiello and Witold. Others even among the common and uncivilized warriors felt in their hearts that the death-knell of the old world and religion had sounded. They were ready to bend their heads to the cross, but not to that cross which the Germans carried, not to the hand of the enemy. "We ask baptism," they proclaimed to all princes and nations, "but bear in mind that we are human beings, not beasts, that can be given away, bought or sold." Meanwhile, when their old faith was extinguished, as a fire goes out for lack of fuel, their hearts were again turned away simply because the religion was forced upon them by the Germans, and there was a general sense of deep sorrow for the future.

The Bohemian, who had been accustomed from his infancy to hear the jovial noise of the soldiers, and had grown up among songs and music, observed for the first time the unusual quiet and gloom in the Lithuanian camp. Here and there, far away from the camp-fires of Skirwoilla, the sound of a whistle or fife was heard, or the suppressed notes of the song of the *burtenikas*, to which the soldiers listened with bent heads and eyes fixed on the glowing fire. Some crouched around the fire with their elbows upon their knees and their faces hidden in their hands, and covered with skins, which made them look like wild beasts of the forest. But when they turned their heads toward the approaching knights, one saw from their mild expression and blue pupils that they were not at all savage or austere, but looked more like sorrowful and wronged children. At the outskirts of the camp the wounded of the last battle lay upon moss. *Labdarysi* and *Sextonowi*, conjurers and soothsayers, muttered exorcisms over them or attended to their wounds, to which they applied certain healing herbs; the wounded lay quietly, patiently suffering pain and torture. From the depth of the forest, across the marshes and lakes, came the whistling of the ostlers; now and then the wind arose, driving the smoke of the camp-fires and making the dark forest resound. The night was already far advanced and the camp-fires began to burn down and extinguish, which increased the dominating silence and intensified the impression of sadness, almost to a crushing extent.

Zbyszko gave orders to the people he led, who easily understood him because there were a few Poles among them. Then he turned to his armor-bearer and said:

"You have seen enough, now it is time to return to the tent."

"I have seen," replied Hlawa, "but I am not satisfied with what I have observed, for it is obvious that they are a defeated people."

"Twice,—four days in front of the castle, and the day before yesterday at the crossing. Now Skirwoilla wants to go a third time to experience another rout."

"How is it that he does not see that he cannot fight the Germans with such soldiers? Pan Macko told me the same thing, and now I observe myself that they are a poor lot, and that they must be boys in battle."

"You are mistaken in that, because they are a brave people and have few equals, but they fight in disordered crowds, whilst the Germans fight in battle array. If the Zmudzians succeed in breaking the German ranks, then the Germans suffer more than themselves. Bah, but the latter know this and close their ranks in such a manner that they stand like a wall."

"We must not even think about capturing the castles," said Hlawa.

"Because there are no engines of war whatever to attempt it," replied Zbyszko. "Prince Witold has them, but as long as he does not arrive I am unable to capture them, unless by accident or treachery."

Then they reached the tent, in front of which burned a huge fire, and within they found smoking dishes of meat, which the servants had prepared for them. It was cold and damp in the tent, therefore the knights and Hlawa lay down upon skins in front of the fire.

When they had fortified themselves, they tried to sleep, but they could not; Macko turned from side to side, and when he observed Zbyszko sitting near the fire covering his knees with twigs, he asked:

"Listen! Why did you give advice to go as far as Ragnety against Gotteswerder, and not near here? What do you profit by it?"

"Because there is a voice within me which tells me that Danuska is at Ragnety, and they are guarded less than they are here."

"There was no time to continue the conversation then, for I too was fatigued and the people after the defeat gathered in the woods. But now, tell me, how is it? Do you mean to search for the girl forever?"

"I say that she is not a girl, but my wife," replied Zbyszko.

There was silence, for Macko well understood that there was no answer to that. If Danuska were still Jurandowna (Miss Jurand) Macko might have advised his nephew to abandon her: but in the presence of the Holy Sacrament, his search for her was his simple duty. Macko would not have put the question to him if he had been present.

Not having been there he always spoke of her at the betrothal or marriage as a girl.

"Very well," he said, after a while. "But to all my questions during the last two days, you replied that you knew nothing."

"Because I do know nothing, except that the wrath of God is probably upon me."

Then Hlawa lifted up his head from the bearskin, sat up and listened with curiosity and attention.

And Macko said:

"As long as sleep does not overpower you, tell me what have you seen, what have you done, and what success have you had at Malborg?"

Zbyszko stroked his long, untrimmed hair from his brow, remained silent for a moment, and then said:

"Would to God that I knew as much of Danuska as I do of Malborg. You ask me what I have seen there? I have seen the immense power of the Knights of the Cross; it is supported by all kings and nations, and I do not know any one who could measure himself with it. I have seen their castles, which even Caesar of Rome does not possess. I have seen inexhaustible treasures, I have seen arms, I have seen swarms of armed monks, knights, and common soldiers,—and as many relics as one sees with the Holy Father in Rome, and I tell you that my soul trembled within me at the thought of the possibility of fighting them. Who can prevail against them? Who can oppose them and break their power?"

"We must destroy them," exclaimed the Bohemian, who could restrain himself no longer.

Zbyszko's words appeared strange also to Macko, and although he was anxious to hear all the adventures of the young man, nevertheless, he interrupted him and said:

"Have you forgotten Wilno? How many times we threw ourselves against them, shield against shield, head against head! You have also seen that, how slow they were against us; and, at our hardiness, they exclaimed that it was not enough to let the horses sweat and break the lances, but it was necessary to take the strangers by the throat or offer their own. Surely there were also guests who challenged us. But all of them went away with shame. What has caused you to change?"

"I am not changed, for I fought at Malborg where also they tilted with sharp weapons. But you don't know their whole strength."

But the old knight got angry and said:

"Do you know the whole strength of Poland? Did you see all the regiments together? Well, you did not. But their strength consists in the people's wrongs and treachery; there, they do not even possess one span of land. They received our princes there in the same manner as a beggar receives in his house, and they presented gifts, but they have grown powerful, they have bitten the hand which fed them, like abominable mad dogs. They seized the lands and treacherously captured the city; that is their strength. The day of judgment and vengeance is at hand."

"You requested me to tell you what I have seen, and now you get angry; I prefer to tell no more," said Zbyszko.

But Macko breathed angrily for a while, then he quieted down and said:

"But this time, thus it will be: You see a tremendous tower-like pine-tree in the forest; it seems as it will stand there forever; but strike it fairly with your axe and it will reveal hollowness and punk will come out. So is it with the strength of the Knights of the Cross. But I commanded you to tell me what you have done and what you have accomplished there. Let me see, you said you fought there with weapons, did you not?"

"I did. They received me at first in an ungrateful and arrogant manner; they knew of my fight with Rotgier. Perhaps they had planned some evil against me. But I came provided with letters from the prince; and de Lorche, whom they honor, protected me from their evil designs. Then came feasts and tourneys in which the Lord Jesus helped me. You have already heard how Ulrych, the brother of the grand master, loved me, and obtained an order from the master himself to surrender Danuska to me."

"We were told," said Macko, "that when his saddle-girdle broke, you would not attack him."

"I helped him up with my lance, and from that moment he became fond of me. Hey! Good God! They furnished me with such strong letters, that enabled me to travel from castle to castle and search. I thought then that my sufferings were at an end, but now I am sitting here, in a wild country, without any help, in sorrow and perplexity, and it is getting worse daily."

He remained silent for a moment, then he forcibly threw a chip into the fire which scattered sparks among the burning brands, and said:

"If that poor child is suffering in a castle, somewhere in this neighborhood, and thinks that I don't care for her, then let sudden death overtake me!"

His heart was evidently so full of pain and impatience that he began again to throw chips into the fire, as though carried away by a sudden and blind pain; but they were greatly astonished because they had not realized that he loved Danusia so much.

"Restrain yourself," exclaimed Macko. "How did you fare with those letters of safe conduct. Did the *comthurs* pay no attention to the master's command?"

"Restrain yourself, sir," said Hlawa. "God will comfort you; perhaps very soon."

Tears glistened in Zbyszko's eyes, but he controlled himself, and said:

"They opened different castles and prisons. I have been everywhere; I searched up to the breaking out of this war. At Gierdaw I was told by the magistrate, von Heideck, that the laws of war differ from those in time of peace, and that my safe conduct was of no avail. I challenged him at once, but he did not accept, and he ordered me to quit the castle."

"What happened in other places?" inquired Macko.

"It was the same everywhere. The Count Könizsberg, who is the chief magistrate of Gierdaw, even refused to read the letter of the master, saying that 'war is war,' and told me to carry my head—while it was intact—out of the place. It was everywhere the same."

"Now I understand," said the old knight, "seeing that you got nothing, you came here at least to avenge yourself."

"Exactly so," replied Zbyszko. "I also thought that we should take prisoners, and also invest some castles. But those fellows could not conquer castles."

"Hey! It will be otherwise when Prince Witold himself comes."

"May God grant it!"

"He will come; I heard at the Mazovian court that he will come, and perhaps the king and all the forces of Poland will come with him."

Further conversation was interrupted by the appearance of Skirwoilla who unexpectedly appeared from the shadow, and said:

"We must be on the march."

Hearing that, the knights got up with alacrity. Skirwoilla approached his tremendous head to their faces, and said in low tones:

"There is news: A relief train is moving toward New Kowno. Two knights are at the head of the soldiers, cattle and provisions. Let us capture them."

"Shall we cross the Niemen," inquired Zbyszko.

"Yes! I know a ford."

"Do they know at the castle of the relief train?"

"They know and will come to meet them, but we shall pounce upon them too."

Then he instructed them where they were to lie in ambush, so as to attack, unexpectedly, those hurrying from the castle. His intentions were to engage the enemy in two battles at the same time, and avenge himself for the last defeat, which could easily be effected, considering that owing to their last victory the enemy considered himself perfectly safe from an attack. Therefore Skirwoilla appointed the place and time where they should meet; as for the rest, he left it with them, for he relied upon their courage and resource. They were very glad at heart because they appreciated the fact that an experienced and skilful warrior was speaking to them. Then he ordered them to start, and he went to his *numy* where the princes and captains were already waiting. There he repeated his orders, gave new ones, and finally put to his lips a pipe, carved out of a wolf's bone, and whistled shrilly, which was heard from one end of the camp to the other.

At the sound of the whistle they gathered around the extinguished camp-fires; here and there sparks shot up, then little flames which increased momentarily, and wild figures of warriors were visible gathering around the stands of arms. The forest throbbed and moved. In a moment there were heard the voices of the ostlers chasing the herd toward the camp.

CHAPTER V.

They arrived very early at Niewiazy where they crossed the river, some on horseback, some upon bundles of osier. Everything went with such dispatch that Macko, Zbyszko, Hlawa and the Mazovian volunteers were astonished at the skilfulness of the people; only then they understood why neither woods, nor swamps, nor rivers could prevent Lithuanian expeditions. When they emerged from the river none had taken off his wet clothing, not even the sheep and wolfskin coats, but exposed themselves to the rays of the sun until they steamed like pitch-burners, and after a short rest they marched hastily toward the north. At nightfall they arrived at the Niemen.

260

The crossing of the great river at that place, swollen in the spring, was not an easy matter. The ford, which was known to Skuwoilla, changed in places into deep water, so that the horses had to swim more than a quarter of a furlong. Two men were carried away quite near Zbyszko, and Hlawa tried to rescue them, but in vain; owing to the darkness and the rushing water they lost sight of them. The drowning men did not dare to shout for help, because the leader had previously ordered that the crossing should be effected in the most quiet manner possible. Nevertheless all the others fortunately succeeded in reaching the other side of the river, where they remained without fires till the morning.

At dawn, the whole army was divided into two divisions. Skirwoilla at the head of one went toward the interior to encounter the knights at the head of the relief train for Gotteswerder. The second division was led back by Zbyszko, toward the island, in order to attack the people coming from the castle to meet the expedition, upon the elevated ground.

It was a mild and bright morning, but down in the woods the marshes and bushes were covered with a thick white steam which entirely obscured the distance. That was just a desirable condition for Zbyszko, because the Germans coming from the castle would not be able to see them in time to retreat. The young knight was exceedingly glad of it, and said to Macko:

"Let us get to our position instead of contemplating the mist yonder. God grant that it is not dissipated before noon."

Then he hurried to the front to give orders to the *setniks*,[116] and immediately returned and said:

"We shall soon meet them upon the road coming from the ferry of the island toward the interior. There we shall hide ourselves in the thicket and watch for them."

"How do you know about that road?" asked Macko.

"We got the information from the local peasants, of whom we have quite a number among our people who will guide us everywhere."

"At what distance from the castle do you intend to attack?"

"About one mile from it."

"Very well; because if it were nearer, the soldiers from the castle might hurry to the rescue, but now they will not only not be able to arrive in time, but will be beyond hearing distance."

"You see I thought about that."

"You thought about one thing, think also about another: if they are reliable peasants, send two or three of them in front, so as to signal when they descry the Germans coming."

"Bah! That also has been attended to."

"Then, I have yet something else to tell you; order one or two hundred men, as soon as the battle begins, not to take part in the fight, but hasten to the rear and cut off their retreat to the island."

"That is the first thing," replied Zbyszko. "Those orders have been given. The Germans will fall into a trap and be snared."

Hearing this, Macko looked approvingly at his nephew; he was pleased that in spite of his youth, he understood much of warfare; therefore he smiled and murmured:

"Our true blood!"

But Hlawa, the shield-bearer, was more glad than Macko, because there was nothing he loved more than war.

"I don't know the fighting capacity of our people," he said, "but they march quietly, they are dexterous, and they seem to be eager. And if Skirwoilla yonder has well devised his plans, then not a single foot shall escape."

"God grant that only a few may escape," replied Zbyszko. "But I have given orders to capture as many prisoners as possible; and if there should happen to be a knight or a religious brother among them, he must absolutely not be killed."

"Why not, sir?" inquired the Bohemian.

"You also take care," Zbyszko replied, "that it be so. If there be a knight among them, he must possess much information, owing to his wanderings in many cities and castles, seeing, and hearing much; much more so if he is a religious member of the Order. Therefore

261

I owe to God my coming to this place so that I might learn something about Danusia, and exchange prisoners. If there be any, this is the only measure left for me."

Then he urged his horse and galloped again to the front to give his final orders and at the same time to get rid of his sad thoughts; there was no time to be lost, because the spot where they were to lie in ambush was very near.

"Why does the young lord think that his little wife is alive, and that she is somewhere in this neighborhood?" asked the Bohemian.

"Because if Zygfried, at the first impulse, did not kill her at Szczytno," replied Macko, "then one may rightly conclude that she is still alive. The priest of Szczytno would not have told us what he did, in the presence of Zbyszko, if she had been killed. It is a very difficult matter; even the most cruel man would not lift up his hand against a defenceless woman. Bah! Against an innocent child."

"It is a hard thing, but not with the Knights of the Cross. And the children of Prince Witold?"

"It is quite true, they have wolfish hearts. Nevertheless, it is true that they did not kill her at Szczytno, and Zygfried himself left for this part of the country; it is therefore possible that he had hid her in some castle."

"Hey! If it turns out so, then I shall take this island and the castle."

"Only look at this people," said Macko.

"Surely, surely; but I have an idea that I will communicate to the young lord."

"Even if you have ten ideas, I do not care. You cannot overthrow the walls with pikes."

Macko pointed toward the lines of pikes, with which most of the warriors were provided; then he asked:

"Did you ever see such soldiers?"

As a matter of fact, the Bohemian had never seen the like. There was a dense crowd in front of them marching irregularly. Cavalry and infantry were mixed up and could not keep proper steps while marching through the undergrowth in the woods. In order to keep pace with the cavalry the infantry held on to the horses' manes, saddles and tails. The warriors' shoulders were covered with wolf, lynx and bearskins; some had attached to their heads boars' tusks, others antlers of deer, and others still had shaggy ears attached, so that, were it not for the protruding weapons above their heads, and the dingy bows and arrows at their backs, they would have looked from the rear and specially in the mist like a moving body of wild beasts proceeding from the depths of the forest, driven by the desire for blood or hunger, in search of prey. There was something terrible and at the same time extraordinary in it: it had the appearance of that wonder called *gnomon*, when, according to popular belief, wild beasts and even stones and bushes were moving in front of them.

It was at that sight that one of the young nobles from Lenkawice, who accompanied the Bohemian, approached him, crossed himself, and said:

"In the name of the Father and Son! I say I am marching with a pack of wolves, and not with men."

But Hlawa, although he had never before seen such a sight, replied like an experienced man who knows all about it and is not surprised at anything.

"Wolves roam in packs during the winter season, but the dog-blood of the Knights of the Cross they also taste in the spring."

It was spring indeed, the month of May; the hazel-trees which filled the woods were covered with a bright green. Among the moss, upon which the soldiers stepped noiselessly, appeared white and blue anemones as well as young berries and dentillated ferns. Softened by abundant rains, the bark of the trees produced an agreeable odor, and from the forest under foot, consisting of pine-needles and punk, proceeded a pungent smell. The sun displayed a rainbow in the drops upon the leaves and branches of the trees, and above it the birds sang joyfully.

They accelerated their pace, because Zbyszko urged them on. At times Zbyszko rode again in the rear of the division with Macko, the Bohemian and the Mazovian volunteers. The prospect of a good battle apparently elated him considerably, for his customary sad expression had disappeared, and his eyes had regained their wonted brightness.

"Cheer up!" he exclaimed. "We must now place ourselves in the front—not behind the line."

He led them to the front of the division.

"Listen," he added. "It may be that we shall catch the Germans unexpectedly, but should they make a stand and succeed in falling in line, then we must be the first to attack them, because our armor is superior, and our swords are better."

"Let it be so," said Macko.

The others settled themselves in their saddles, as if they were to attack at once. They took a long breath, and felt for their swords to see whether they could be unsheathed with ease.

Zbyszko repeated his orders once more, that if they found among the infantry any knights with white mantles over the armor, they were not to kill but capture them alive; then he galloped to the guides, and halted the division for a while.

They arrived at the highway which from the landing opposite the island extended to the interior. Strictly speaking, there was no proper road yet, but in reality the edge of the wood had been recently sawed through and leveled only at the rear so much as to enable soldiers or wagons to pass over them. On both sides of the road rose the high trunked trees, and the old pines cut for the widening of the road. The hazelnut growths were so thick in some places that they overran the whole forest. Zbyszko had therefore chosen a place at the turning, so that the advancing party would neither be able to see far, nor retreat, nor have time enough to form themselves in battle array. It was there that he occupied both sides of the lane and gave commands to await the enemy.

Accustomed to forest life and war, the Zmudzians took advantage of the logs, cuts and clumps of young hazelnut growths, and fir saplings—so that it seemed as if the earth had swallowed them up. No one spoke, neither did the horses snort. Now and then, big and little forest animals passed those lying in wait and came upon them before seeing them and were frightened and rushed wildly away. At times the wind arose and filled the forest with a solemn, rushing sound, and then again silence fell and only the distant notes of the cuckoo and the woodpecker were audible.

The Zmudzians were glad to hear those sounds, because the woodpecker was a special harbinger of good fortune. There were many of those birds in that forest, and the pecking sound was heard on all sides persistent and rapid, like human labor. One would be inclined to say, that each of those birds had its own blacksmith's forge where it went to active labor very early. It appeared to Macko and the Mazovians that they heard the noise of carpenters fixing roofs upon new houses, and it reminded them of home.

But the time passed and grew tedious; nothing was heard but the noise of the trees and the voice of birds. The mist hovering upon the plain was lifting. The sun was quite high and it was getting hot, but they still lay in wait. Finally Hlawa who was impatient at the silence and delay, bent toward Zbyszko's ear and whispered:

"Sir, if God will grant, none of the dog-brothers shall escape alive. May we not be able to reach the castle and capture it by surprise?"

"Do you suppose that the boats there are not watching, and have no watchwords?"

"They have watchmen," replied the Bohemian, in a whisper, "but prisoners when threatened with the knife will give up the watchword. Bah! they will even reply in the German language. If we reach the island, then the castle itself...."

Here he stopped, because Zbyszko put his hand upon his mouth, because from the roadside came the croak of a raven.

"Hush!" he said. "That is a signal."

About two "paters" later, there appeared at the border a Zmudzian, riding upon a little shaggy pony, whose hoofs were enveloped in sheepskin to avoid the clatter and traces of horses' hoofs in the mud. The rider looked sharply from side to side and, suddenly hearing from the thicket an answer to the croaking, dived into the forest, and in a moment he was near Zbyszko.

"They are coming!" ... he said.

CHAPTER VI.

263

Zbyszko inquired hurriedly, how many horsemen and infantry were among them, in what manner they were advancing, and above all the exact distance; and he learned from the Zmudzian that their number did not exceed one hundred and fifty warriors and that about fifty of that number were horsemen led by a Knight of the Cross, who appears to be of the secular knights; that they were marching in ranks and had empty wagons with a supply of wheels upon them; and that at a distance in front of the detachment were bodies of archers composed of eight men who frequently left the road and searched the woods and thickets, and finally that the detachment was about one quarter of a mile distant.

Zbyszko was not particularly pleased with the information of the manner of their advancing in battle array. He knew by experience how difficult it was to break the ordered German ranks, and how such a crowd could retreat and fight in the same manner as a wild-boar that defends itself when brought to bay by dogs. On the other hand, he was glad of the news that they were only a quarter of a mile distant, because he calculated that the people who were detached to cut off their retreat had already done so,—and, in case of the Germans being routed, not a single soul could escape. As to the outpost at the head of the detachment he did not care much, because he knew from the first that such would be the case and was prepared for them; he had given orders to his men to allow them to advance, and if they were engaged in searching the thickets to capture them quietly one by one.

But the last order seemed unnecessary; the scouts advanced without delay. The Zmudzians who were hidden in the growths near the highway had a perfect view of the advancing party when they halted at the turning and took counsel. The chief, a powerful red-bearded German, who signalled to them to keep silence, began to listen. It was visible for a moment that he hesitated whether to penetrate the forest or not. At last, as there was only audible the hammering of the woodpeckers, and he apparently thought that the birds would not be working so freely if people were hidden among the trees. Therefore he waved his hand for the detachment to go forward.

Zbyszko waited until they were near the second turning, then he approached the road, at the head of his well-armed men, including Macko, the Bohemian, and the two noble volunteers from Lenkawice, and three young knights from Ciechanow, and a dozen of the better armed Zmudzian nobles. Further concealment was not necessary. Nothing remained for Zbyszko but to station himself in the middle of the road and, as soon as the Germans appeared, to fall upon them, and break their ranks. If that might be accomplished, he was sure that his Zmudzians would take care of the Germans.

There was silence for a little while, which was only disturbed by the usual forest noises, but soon there were heard the voices of people proceeding from the east side; they were yet a considerable distance away but the voices grew little by little more distinct as they approached.

Without losing a moment's time, Zbyszko and his men placed themselves in the form of a wedge in the middle of the road. Zbyszko himself formed the sharp end and directly behind him were Macko and the Bohemian, in the row behind them were three men, behind those were four; all of them were well armed. Nothing was wanting but the "wooden" lances of the knights which could greatly impede the advance of the enemy in forest marches, instead of those long handled lances; theirs were shorter and lighter. Zmudzian weapons were well adapted for the first attack, and the swords and axes at their saddles were handy for combat at close quarters.

Hlawa was wide awake and listening; then he whispered to Macko:

"They are singing, they shall be destroyed."

"But what surprises me is that the woods obscure them from our sight," replied Macko.

Then Zbyszko, who considered further hiding and silence unnecessary, replied:

"Because the road leads along the stream; that is the reason for its frequent windings."

"But how merrily they are singing!" repeated the Bohemian.

One could judge from the melody that the Germans were singing profane songs indeed. It could also be distinguished that the singers were not more than about a dozen, and that they all repeated only one burden which resounded far and wide in the forest, like a thunderstorm.

Thus they went to death, rejoicing and lusty.

"We shall soon see them," said Macko.

Then his face suddenly darkened and assumed a wolf-like and savage expression. He had a grudge against the knights for the shots which he had received at the time when he went to Zbyszko's rescue, on that occasion when he was the carrier of letters from Prince Witold's sister to the grand master. Therefore his blood began to boil, and a desire for vengeance overflowed his soul.

The fellow who first attacks will not fare well, thought Hlawa, as he looked at the old knight.

Meanwhile the wind carried the sound of the phrase which the singers repeated:

"Tandaradei! Tandaradei!" The Bohemian at once recognized the song known to him:
"Bi den rôsen er wol mac

Tandaradei!

Merken wa mir'z houlet lac...."

Then the song was interrupted, because upon both sides of the road was heard such a croaking noise that it seemed as if the crows were holding parliament in that corner of the forest. The Germans were wondering whence so many crows came, and why they proceeded from the ground and not from the tops of the trees. In fact the first line of the soldiers appeared at the turning and halted as though nailed to the spot, when they observed unknown horsemen facing them.

At the same moment Zbyszko sat down in his saddle, spurred his horse, and rushed forward, crying:

"At them!"

The others galloped with him. The terrible shouting of the Zmudzian warriors was heard from the woods. Only a space of about two hundred feet separated Zbyszko from the enemy, who, in the twinkling of an eye, lowered a forest of lances toward Zbyszko's horsemen; the remaining lines placed themselves with the utmost dispatch on both sides to protect themselves against an attack from the direction of the forest. The Polish knights might have admired the dexterity of the German tactics, but there was no time for contemplation, owing to the great speed and impetus of their horses in their charge upon the close phalanx of the Germans.

Happily for Zbyszko, the German cavalry were in the rear of the division near the wagon train; in fact, they hastened at once to their assistance, but they could neither reach them in time nor pass beyond them so as to be of any assistance at the first attack. The Zmudzians, pouring from the thickets, surrounded them like a swarm of poisonous wasps upon whose nest a careless traveler had trod. Meanwhile Zbyszko and his men threw themselves upon the infantry.

The attack was without effect. The Germans planted the ends of their heavy lances and battle-axes in the ground, held them fast and even so that the Zmudzian light horses could not break the wall. Macko's horse, which received a blow from a battle-axe in the shin, reared and stood up on his hind legs, then fell forward burying his nostrils in the ground. For a while death was hovering above the old knight; but he was experienced and had seen many battles, and was full of resources in accidents. So he freed his legs from the stirrups, and grasped with his powerful hand the sharp end of the pike which was ready to strike him, and instead of penetrating his chest it served him as a support. Then he freed himself, and, springing among the horsemen, he obtained a sword and fell upon the pikes and battle-axes with such fury as an eagle swoops upon a flock of long-beaked cranes.

At the moment of attack Zbyszko sat back on his horse, charged with his spear—and broke it; then he also got a sword. The Bohemian, who, above all, believed in the efficacy of an axe, threw it in the midst of the Germans. For a while he remained without arms. One of two *wlodykas* who accompanied him was slain in the onset; at the sight of that, the other lost his reason and raved so that he began to howl like a wolf, stood up upon his blood-covered horse and charged blindly into the midst of the throng. The Zmudzian noblemen cut with their sharp blades the spearheads and wooden handles, behind which they observed the faces of the *knechts* (common soldiers) upon which was depicted alarm, and at the same time they were frowning with determination and stubbornness. But the ranks remained unbroken.

Also the Zmudzians, who made a flank attack, quickly retreated from before the Germans, as one runs away from a venomous snake. Indeed they returned immediately with yet greater impetuosity, but they did not succeed. Some of them climbed up the trees in the twinkling of an eye and directed their arrows into the midst of the *knechts*, but when their leader saw this he ordered the soldiers to retreat toward the cavalry. The German ranks also began to shoot, and from time to time a Zmudzian would fall down and tear the moss in agony, or wriggle like a fish drawn from the water. The Germans, indeed, could not count upon a victory, but they knew the efficacy of defending themselves, so that, if possible, a small number, at least, might manage to escape disaster and reach the shore.

Nobody thought of surrendering, because they did not spare prisoners, they knew that they could not count upon mercy from people who were driven to despair and rebellion. They therefore retreated in silence, in close rank, shoulder to shoulder, now raising, now lowering their javelins and broad axes, hewing, shooting with their crossbows as much as the confusion of the fighting permitted them, and continuing to retreat slowly toward their horsemen, who were engaged in life and death battle with another section of the enemy.

Meanwhile something strange occurred which decided the fortune of the stubborn fight. It was caused by the young *wlodyka* of Lenkawice, who became mad at the death of his companion; he did not dismount, but bent down and lifted up the body of his companion with the object of depositing it in a safe place to save it from mutilation, and so that he might find it after the battle was over. But at that very moment a fresh wave of madness came over him and he entirely lost his mind, so that instead of leaving the road, he rushed toward the German soldiers and threw the body upon the points of their pikes, which penetrated the corpse in various parts, and the weight caused them to bend, and before the Germans were able to withdraw their weapons, the raving man fell in, breaking the ranks and overturning the men like a tempest.

In the twinkling of an eye, half a score of hands were extended toward him and as many pikes penetrated the flanks of his horse, but the ranks were thrown into disorder, and one Zmudz noble who was near, rushed through and immediately after him came Zbyszko, then the Bohemian, and the terrible confusion increased every moment.
Other *bojars* followed the example, seized corpses and thrust them against the enemies' arms, whilst the Zmudzians again attacked the flanks. The order which had hitherto reigned in the German ranks wavered; it began to shake like a house whose walls are cracked; it was cleft like a log by a wedge, and finally it burst open.

In a moment the fighting turned to slaughter, the long German pikes and broad axes were of no use at close quarters. Instead of it the swords of the horsemen fell upon helmet and neck. The horses pressed into the midst of the throng, upsetting and trampling the unfortunate Germans. It was easy for the horsemen to strike from above and they took advantage of the opportunity and ceaselessly cut the enemy. From the woods on both sides continually arrived wild warriors, clothed in wolves' skins, and with a wolfish desire for blood in their hearts. Their howling drowned the voices praying for mercy and those of the dying. The conquered threw away their arms; some tried to escape into the forest, others feigned death and fell to the earth, others stood erect, their faces white as snow, and bloodshot eyes, whilst others prayed. One of them, apparently demented, began to play the pipe, then looked upward and smiled, until a Zmudzian crushed his head with a club. The forest ceased to rustle and death dominated it.

Finally the small army of the Knights of the Cross melted away; only at times there were heard voices of small bands fighting in the woods, or a terrible cry of despair. Zbyszko, Macko and all their horsemen now galloped toward the cavalry. They were still defending themselves, placing themselves in the form of a wedge. The Germans were always accustomed to adopt that manoeuvre when surrounded by an overwhelming force of the enemy. The cavalry were mounted upon good horses and were better armed than the infantry; they fought manfully and obstinately and deserved admiration. There was none with a white mantle among them, but they were of the middle classes and small nobility of the Germans who were obliged to go to war when called upon by the Order. Most of their horses were also armed, some had body armor; but all had iron head covers with a spike of steel protruding from the centre. Their leader was a tall, sturdy knight; he wore a dark blue coat of mail and a helmet of the same color, with a lowered steel visor.

A rain of arrows was showered upon them from the depths of the forest. But they did but little harm. The Zmudzian infantry and cavalry came nearer and surrounded them like a wall, but they defended themselves, cutting and thrusting with their long swords so furiously that in front of the horses' hoofs lay a ring of corpses. The first lines of the attackers wanted to retire, but they were unable to do so. There was a press and confusion all around. The eyes became dazzled by the glint of the spears and the flash of the swords. The horses began to neigh, bite, rear and kick. Then the Zmudz noblemen charged down; Zbyszko, Hlawa and the Mazovians fell upon them. By dint of the press, the German throng began to waver, and swayed like trees before a storm, but they hewed like choppers of firewood in the forest thickets, and advanced slowly amidst fatigue and excessive heat.

But Macko ordered his men to gather together the long-handled German battle-axes from the battlefield, and armed with them thirty of his wild warriors pressed on eagerly toward the Germans. "Strike the horses' legs!" he shouted. A terrible effect was soon apparent. The German knights were unable to reach the Zmudzians with their swords, at the same time the battle-axes were crushing the horses' legs. It was then that the blue knight recognized that the end of the battle was at hand, and that he had only two resources left— either to fight his way through the army and retreat, or to remain and perish.

He chose the first plan, and in a moment his knights turned their faces in the direction whence they came. The Zmudzians fell upon their rear. Nevertheless the Germans threw their shields upon their shoulders and cut in front and to the sides, and broke through the ranks of the attacking party, and hurricane-like, fled toward the east. But that division which had been despatched for that purpose, rushed to meet them; but by dint of superior fighting and the greater weight of the horses, they fell in a moment like flax before a storm. The road to the castle was open, but escape thither was insecure and too far away, because the Zmudzian horses were fleeter than those of the Germans. The blue knight was quite aware of it.

"Woe!" he said to himself. "Here none will escape; perhaps I may purchase their salvation with my own blood."

Then he shouted to his men to halt, and himself turned around toward the foe, not caring whether any one overheard his command.

Zbyszko galloped up to him first, the German struck him upon the visor, but without breaking it or harming Zbyszko. At the same time, Zbyszko, instead of giving stroke for stroke, grasped the knight by the middle, but, in the attempt to take him alive, engaged in a close struggle, during which the girth of his horse gave way from the intense strain of the contest, and both fell to the ground. For a while they wrestled; but the extraordinary strength of the young man soon prevailed against his antagonist; he pressed his knees against his stomach, holding him down as a wolf does a dog who dares to oppose him in the woods.

But there was no need to hold him, because the German fainted. Meanwhile Macko and the Bohemian arrived at a gallop. Zbyszko shouted: "Quick, here! A rope!"

The Bohemian dismounted, but seeing the helplessness of the German, he did not bind him, but disarmed him and unbuckled his armlets and his belt, and with the attached "*misericordia*," (dagger of mercy) cut the gorget, and lastly he unscrewed the helmet.

But he had scarcely glanced in the face of the knight, when he started back and exclaimed:

"Master! master! please only look here!"

"De Lorche!" shouted Zbyszko.

And there lay de Lorche pale and motionless as a corpse, with closed eyes and face covered with perspiration.

CHAPTER VII.

Zbyszko gave orders for him to be laid upon one of the captured wagons which were laden with spare wheels and axles for the expedition coming to relieve the castle. He mounted another horse, and with Macko they continued the pursuit of the fleeing Germans. It was not a difficult pursuit, because the German horses were not speedy enough, particularly upon the ground softened by the spring rains, more especially for Macko, who had with him a light and fleet mare which belonged to the deceased *wlodyka* of Lenkawice. After a distance of several furlongs he passed almost all the Zmudzians. He soon reached the first German trooper, whom he at once challenged according to the then prevailing custom among the knights, to surrender or fight. But the German feigned deafness. He even threw away his shield to relieve the horse, and bent in the saddle and spurred his horse. The old knight struck him with his broad axe between the shoulder-blades, and he fell to the ground.

Thus Macko avenged himself upon the fleeing Germans for the treacherous shot he had once received. They ran before him like a herd of frightened deer. They had no thought of continuing the fight or defending themselves, but of fleeing before that terrible man. Some dashed into the forest, but one stuck fast near the stream: him the Zmudzians strangled with a halter. Then a hunt as if after wild beasts began after the crowd of fugitives which sprang into the woods.

The depths of the forests rang with the shouts of the hunters and the shrieks of the hunted until the latter were exterminated. Then the old knight, accompanied by Zbyszko and the Bohemian, returned to the battlefield upon which lay the hacked bodies of the German infantry. They were already stripped naked. Some were mutilated by the revengeful Zmudzians. It was an important victory, and the soldiers were drunk with joy. After the last defeat suffered by Skirwoilla near Gotteswerder, a sort of apathy had seized the Zmudzians, more especially because the promised relief from Prince Witold had not yet arrived as quickly as expected. However, now hope revived and the fire was kindled anew as when wood is thrown upon glowing embers. The number of slain Germans, as well as Zmudzians to be buried, was very great, but Zbyszko ordered a special grave to be dug for the *wlodykas* of Lenkawice, who contributed so much toward the victory. They were buried there among the pine-trees, and Zbyszko cut a cross with his sword upon the bark. Then he ordered the Bohemian to keep watch over de Lorche who was still unconscious; he stirred up the people and hurried on along the road toward Skirwoilla to lend him affective assistance in case of emergency.

But after a long march he came across a deserted battlefield that resembled the former, being covered with German and Zmudzian corpses. It was easy for Zbyszko to conclude that the terrible Skirwoilla had also gained an equally important victory over the enemy, because if he had been defeated, Zbyszko would have met the victorious Germans marching to the castle. But the victory must have been a bloody one, because for some distance a great number of dead were met with. The experienced Macko was able to deduce from this that some Germans had even succeeded in retreating from the defeat.

It was difficult to tell whether Skirwoilla was pursuing them or not, because the tracks were mingled and confused. He also concluded that the battle had taken place quite early, perhaps earlier than Zbyszko's fight, for the corpses were livid and swollen, and some of them torn by wolves, that scattered in the thickets at the approach of armed men.

In face of these circumstances Zbyszko resolved not to wait for Skirwoilla, but to return to the original safe camp. He arrived there late at night and found the leader of the Zmudzians who had arrived somewhat early. His face, which usually wore a sullen expression, was now lighted with fiendish joy. He asked at once about the result of the fight, and when he was told of the victory he said in tones that sounded like the croaking of a crow:

"I am glad of your victory, and I am glad of mine. They will send no more relief expeditions for some time, and when the great prince arrives there will be more joy, for the castle will be ours."

"Have you taken any prisoners?" inquired Zbyszko.

"Only small fry, no pike. There was one, there were two but they got away. They were pikes with sharp teeth! They cut the people and escaped."

"God granted me one." replied the young knight. "He is a powerful and renowned knight, although a Swede—a guest!"

The terrible Zmudzian raised his hands to his neck and with the right hand made a gesture like the up-jerk of a halter:

"This shall happen to him," he said, "to him as well as to the other prisoners ... this!"

Then Zbyszko's brow furrowed.

"Listen, Skirwoilla," he said. "Nothing will happen to him, neither *this* nor *that* because he is my prisoner and my friend. Prince Janusz knighted both of us. I will not even permit you to cut off one finger from his hand."

"You will not permit?"

"No, I will not."

Then they glared fiercely into each other's eyes. Skirwoilla's face was so much wrinkled that it had the appearance of a bird of prey. It appeared as if both were about to burst out. But Zbyszko did not want any trouble with the old leader, whom he prized and respected; moreover his heart was greatly agitated with the events of the day. He fell suddenly upon his neck, pressed him to his breast and exclaimed:

"Do you really desire to tear him from me, and with him my last hope? Why do you wrong me?"

Skirwoilla did not repel the embrace. Finally, withdrawing his head from Zbyszko's arm, he looked at him benignantly, breathing heavily.

"Well," he said, after a moment's silence. "Well, to-morrow I will give orders for the prisoners to be hanged, but if you want any one of them, I will give him to you."

Then they embraced each other again and parted on good terms—to the great satisfaction of Macko, who said:

"It is obvious that you will never be able to do anything with him by anger, but with kindness you can knead him like wax."

"Such is the whole nation," replied Zbyszko; "but the Germans do not know it."

Then he gave orders for de Lorche, who had taken rest in the booth, to be brought to the camp-fire. A moment later the Bohemian brought him in; he was unarmed and without a helmet, having only his leather jacket upon which the marks of the coat of mail were visible. He had a red cap on his head. De Lorche had already been informed by Hlawa that he was a prisoner and therefore he came in looking cool and haughty, and the light of the flames revealed defiance and contempt in his countenance.

"Thank God," Zbyszko said, "that He delivered you in my hands, because nothing evil shall happen to you by me."

Then he extended a friendly hand; but de Lorche did not even move.

"I decline to give my hand to knights who outrage knightly honor, by joining pagans in fighting Christian knights."

One of the Mazovians present, who could not restrain himself, owing to Zbyszko's importance, on hearing this became excited and his blood boiled.

"Fool!" he shouted and involuntarily grasped the handle of his "*misericordia.*"

But de Lorche lifted up his head.

"Kill me," he said. "I know that you do not spare prisoners."

"But, do you spare prisoners?" the Mazur who could not restrain himself, exclaimed: "Did you not hang on the shore of the island all the prisoners you took in the last fight? That is the reason why Skirwoilla will hang all his prisoners."

"Yes! they did hang them, but they were pagans."

There was a certain sense of shame in his reply; it could easily be seen that he did not entirely approve of such deeds.

Meanwhile, Zbyszko controlled himself, and in a quiet and dignified manner said:

"De Lorche, you and I received our belts and spurs from the same hand, you also know well that knightly honor is dearer to me than life and fortune. Listen, therefore, to my words which I say under oath to Saint Jerzy: There are many among this people whose Christianity does not date from yesterday, and those who have not yet been converted stretch out their hands toward the Cross for salvation. But, do you know who hinder them and prevent their salvation and baptism?"

The Mazur translated all Zbyszko's words to de Lorche, who looked into the young knight's face questioningly.

"The Germans!" said Zbyszko.

"Impossible," shouted de Lorche.

"By the spear and spurs of Saint Jerzy, the Germans! Because if the religion of the Cross were to be propagated here, they would lose a pretext for incursions, and domination and oppression of this unhappy people. You are well acquainted with these facts, de Lorche! You are best informed whether their dealings are upright or not."

"But I think that in fighting with the pagans they are only banishing them to prepare them for baptism."

"They are baptizing them with the sword and blood, not with water that saves. Read this letter, I pray, and you will be convinced that you yourself are the wrongdoer, plunderer and the hell-*starosta* of those who fight religion and Christian love."

Then he handed him the letter which the Zmudzians had written to the kings and princes, which was distributed everywhere; de Lorche took it and perused it rapidly by the light of the fire. He was greatly surprised, and said;

"Can all that be true?"

"May God, who sees best, so help you and me that I am not only speaking the truth but I also serve justice."

De Lorche was silent for a moment and then said:

"I am your prisoner."

"Give me your hand," replied Zbyszko. "You are my brother, not my prisoner."

Then they clasped hands and sat down in company to supper, which the Bohemian ordered the servant to prepare.

De Lorche was greatly surprised when he was informed on the road that Zbyszko, in spite of his letters, had not got Danusia, and that the *comthurs* had refused important and safe conduct on account of the outbreak of the war.

"Now I understand why you are here," he said to Zbyszko, "and I thank God that He delivered me into your hands, because I think that through me the Knights of the Order will surrender to you what you wish. Otherwise there will be a great outcry in the West, because I am a knight of importance and come from a powerful family...."

Then he suddenly threw down his cap and exclaimed:

"By all the relics of Akwizgran! Then those who were at the head of the relief train to Gotteswerder, were Arnold von Baden and old Zygfried von Löve. That we learned from the letters which were sent to the castle. Were they taken prisoners?"

"No!" said Zbyszko, excitedly. "None of the most important! But, by God! The news you tell me is important. For God's sake, tell me, are there other prisoners from whom I can learn whether there were any women with Zygfried?"

Then he called the men to bring him lit resinous chips and he hastened to where the prisoners were gathered by order of Skirwoilla. De Lorche, Macko and the Bohemian ran with him.

"Listen," said de Lorche to Zbyszko, on the way. "If you will let me free on parole I will run and seek her throughout the whole of Prussia, and when I find her, I will return to you and you will exchange me for her."

"If she lives! If she lives!" replied Zbyszko.

Meanwhile they reached the place where Skirwoilla's prisoners were. Some were lying upon their backs, others stood near the stumps of trees to which they were cruelly fastened with fibre. The bright flame of the chips illuminated Zbyszko's face. Therefore all the prisoners' looks were directed toward him.

Then from the depths of the road there was heard a loud and terrible voice:

"My lord and protector! Oh, save me!"

Zbyszko snatched from the hands of the servant a couple of burning chips and ran into the forest toward the direction whence the voice proceeded, holding aloft the burning chips, and cried:

"Sanderus!"

"Sanderus!" repeated the Bohemian, in astonishment.

But Sanderus, whose hands were bound to the tree, stretched his neck and began to shout again.

"Mercy!... I know where Jurand's daughter is!... Save me."

CHAPTER VIII.

The soldiers unbound him at once, but his limbs were benumbed and he fell; when they lifted him up he was seized with successive fainting fits. In spite of Zbyszko's orders for him to be taken to the fire and given food and drink, and rubbed over with fat and then covered with warmed skins, Sanderus did not recover consciousness, but lapsed into a very deep sleep, which continued until noon of the following day when the Bohemian succeeded in awakening him.

Zbyszko, who was burning with fiery impatience, immediately went to him, but at first he could get no information from him, because either from his terrible experiences or from the relaxation which usually overpowers weak natures when the threatening danger has passed, Sanderus burst into long and uncontrollable weeping, so that for some time he could give no answer to the questions put to him. He was choked with sobs, his lips trembled, and tears flowed down his cheeks so copiously that it seemed as though his very life was flowing out with them.

Finally he succeeded to some extent in controlling himself, and he strengthened himself a little with mares' milk, which mode of refreshing themselves the Lithunians learned from the Tartars. He began to complain that the "sons of Belial" had thrust him with their pikes against a wild apple-tree; that they had taken away his horse which was laden with relics of priceless virtue; and finally when they had bound him to the tree, the ants had attacked his feet and body so that he expected to die from it, if not to-day, to-morrow.

Zbyszko's anger overcame him and he could restrain himself no longer, and he interrupted Sanderus and said:

"You vagabond, answer the questions I am going to put to you and take care that you tell the truth, or you will fare worse."

"There are red ants yonder," said the Bohemian, "order them to be pat upon him, and he will soon find a tongue in his mouth."

Hlawa did not say this seriously; he even smiled as he spoke, for his heart was well inclined toward Sanderus. The latter, however, was terror-stricken, and shouted.

"Mercy! Mercy! Give me some more of that pagan drink and I will tell you all that I have and that I have not seen."

"If you tell lies, even one word that is not true, I will drive a wedge between your teeth," said the Bohemian.

They brought him another skin full of mares' milk; he grasped it and fastened his lips to it with the avidity that a child does to its mother's breast, and began to gulp it down, alternatively opening and closing his eyes. When he had drank from it about half a gallon or more, he shook himself, placed the skin upon his knees, and as if submitting himself to the inevitable, he said:

"Vile stuff!..." Then he turned toward Zbyszko. "Now, deliverer! ask."

"Was my wife in that division with you?"

Sanderus' face assumed a certain air of surprise. In fact he had heard that Danusia was Zbyszko's wife, but it had been a secret marriage, and immediately afterward she had been abducted, and he had always thought of her as Jurandowna, (Miss Jurand).

He replied quickly:

"Yes, *voyevode!* She was! But Zygfried von Löve and Arnold von Baden broke through the enemy's ranks and escaped."

"Did you see her?" asked Zbyszko, with beating heart.

"I did not see her face, sir, but I saw a closed litter made of brushwood, suspended between two horses, in which there was somebody, led by that very lizard, the same servant of the Order who came from Danveld to the Forest Court. I also heard sad singing proceeding from the litter...."

Zbyszko grew pale with emotion; he sat down on the stump and was unable to ask another question for a while. Macko and the Bohemian were also much moved at this great and important news. The latter, probably, thought about his beloved lady who remained at Spychow, and upon whom this news would fall like a doom.

There was silence for a moment. Finally, the shrewd Macko who did not know Sanderus, and who had scarcely heard of him previously, looked at him with suspicion, and asked:

"Who are you and what were you doing among the Knights of the Cross?"

"Who am I, powerful knight?" replied Sanderus. "Let this valiant prince answer for me," (here he pointed toward Zbyszko), "and this manly Bohemian noble who has known me long."

The effect of the kumys (mares' milk) upon Sanderus apparently began to show itself, for he grew lively, and turning to Zbyszko he spoke in a loud voice and showed no trace of his previous feeble condition.

"Sir, you have saved my life twice. If it were not for you, the wolves would have devoured me, or the punishment of the bishops who were misguided by my enemies. (Oh, what a wicked world this is!) They issued an order to hunt me for selling relics which they thought were not genuine, simply because they took me for one of your people. But you, O lord, protected me, and thanks to you I was not destroyed by the wolves, nor shall their persecution harm me. Food and drink was never lacking whilst I was with you—better than the mares' milk here which makes me sick, but I drink it in order to show how a poor but pious pilgrim can stand all kinds of privations."

"Speak, you bear-trainer; tell us quickly what you know, and do not play the fool," exclaimed Macko.

But he lifted the skin to his mouth again and entirely emptied it; apparently not hearing Macko's words, he turned again to Zbyszko: "This is another reason why I love you. The saints, as it is written in the Scriptures, sinned nine times an hour, consequently, sometimes also Sanderus transgresses, but Sanderus never was nor shall be ungrateful. Therefore, when misfortune came upon you, you remember, sir, what I told you; I said, 'I will go from castle to castle, and, instructing the people along the road, I will search for your lost one.' Whom did I not ask? Where did I not go?—It would take me a long time to tell you.—But, suffice it to say, I found her; and from that moment on, burrs do not cling as tenaciously to the cloak as I attached myself to old Zygfried. I became his servant, and from castle to castle, from one *comthur* to another, from town to town I went with him without intermission until this last battle."

Zybszko meanwhile mastered his emotion and said:

"I am very thankful to you and I shall surely reward you. But now, answer my questions. Will you swear, by the salvation of your soul, that she is alive?"

"I swear by the salvation of my soul that she is alive," replied Sanderus, with a serious air.

"Why did Zygfried leave Szczytno?"

"I do not know, sir. But I surmise that as he was never the *starosta* of Szczytno, he left it; perhaps he feared the grand master's orders, which were, they say, to give up the little lamb to the Mazovian court. Perhaps that very letter was the cause of his flight, because his soul burned within him with pain and vengeance for Rotgier who, they say now, was Zygfried's own son. I cannot tell what happened there, but this I do know, that something turned his head and he raved, and determined not to surrender Jurand's daughter—I meant to say, the young lady—as long as he lives."

"All this seems to me very strange," suddenly interrupted Macko. "If that old dog thirsts so much for the blood of all who belong to Jurand, he would have killed Danuska."

"He wanted to do so," replied Sanderus, "but something happened to him and he became very sick, and was at the point of death. His people whisper much over that affair. Some say that upon a certain night when he went to the tower intending to kill the young lady he met the Evil Spirit—some say it was an angel whom he met—well—they found him lying upon the snow in front of the tower wholly lifeless. Now, when he thinks about it, his hair stands up upon his head like oak-trees; this is the reason why he does not himself dare to lift up his hand against her, he even fears to order others to do it. He has with him the dumb executioner of Szczytno, but it is not known why, because the executioner as well as others, are equally afraid to harm her."

These words made a great impression. Zbyszko, Macko and the Bohemian came near Sanderus, who crossed himself and then continued:

"It was not well to be among them. More than once I heard and saw things that made my flesh creep. I have told your lordship already that something was wrong with the old *comthur's* head. Bah! How could it be otherwise, when spirits from the other world visit him. He would have remained there, but some presence is always near him which sounds like one who is breathless. And that is that very Danveld, whom the terrible lord of Spychow killed. Then Zygfried says to him: 'What shall I do? I cannot avenge you on anything; what profit will you get?' But the other (the ghost) gnashes his teeth and then pants again. Very often Rotgier appears, and the odor of sulphur is noticeable, and the *comthur* has a lengthy conversation with him. 'I cannot,' he says to him. 'I cannot. When I come myself then I will do it, but now I cannot.' I also heard the old man asking: 'Will that comfort you, dear son,' and other expressions of the same character. When this happens, the old *comthur* speaks to nobody for two or three days in succession, and his face seems as if he is suffering intense pain. He and the woman servant of the Order watch the litter carefully, so that the young lady is always unable to see anybody."

"Do they not torture her?" asked Zbyszko, in hollow tones.

"I will tell your lordship the candid truth, that I did not hear any beating or crying; the only thing I heard proceeding from the litter was sad melodies; sometimes it seemed to me like sweet, sad warblings of a bird...."

"That is terrible," exclaimed Zbyszko, his voice hissing between his set teeth.

But Macko interrupted further questioning.

"That is enough," he said. "Speak now of the battle. Did you see how they departed and what became of them?"

"I saw and will give a faithful account. At first they fought terribly. But when they saw that they were surrounded on all sides, then only they thought of escape. Sir Arnold, who is quite a giant, was the first to break the ring, and opened such a road, that he, the old *comthur* and some people with the horse-litter succeeded in passing through it."

"How is it that they were not pursued?"

"They were pursued, but nothing could be done, because when they came too near them, then Sir Arnold faced the pursuers and fought them all. God protect those who meet him, because he possesses such extraordinary strength; he considers it a trifle to fight against a hundred. Thrice he thus turned, thrice he kept the pursuers in check. All the people who were with him perished. It seems to me that he too was wounded, and so was his horse, but he escaped, and meanwhile the old *comthur* succeeded in making good his escape."

When Macko heard the story he thought that Sanderus was telling the truth, for he recollected that when he entered the field where Skirwoilla had given battle, the whole stretch of the road on the line of the Germans' retreat, was covered with dead Zmudzians, so terribly hacked as though it had been done by giant hands.

"Nevertheless, how could you observe all that?" he asked Sanderus.

"I saw it," replied the vagabond, "because I grasped the tail of one of the horses which carried the litter, and held on until I received a kick in my stomach. Then I fainted, and that was the reason that you captured me."

"That might happen," said Hlawa, "but take care, if anything you say turns out to be false; in such case you shall fare badly."

"There is another proof," replied Sanderus; "let one who wishes take a note of it; yet it is better to believe a man's word than to condemn him as one who does not tell the truth."

"Although you sometimes unwillingly tell the truth, you will howl for simony."

And they began to tease each other as they formerly did, but Zbyszko interrupted their chatter.

"You have passed through that region, then you must be acquainted with the localities in the neighborhood of the castles; where do you suppose Zygfried and Arnold hide themselves?"

"There are no strongholds whatever in that neighborhood; all is one wilderness, through which a road was recently cut. There are neither villages nor farms. The Germans burned those that were there, for the reason that the inhabitants of those places who are also

Zmudzians, had also risen in arms against the Knights of the Cross with their brethren here. I think, sir, that Zygfried and Arnold are now wandering about the woods; either they are trying to return to the place whence they came, or attempting furtively to reach that fortress whither we were going to before that unfortunate battle."

"I am sure that it is so," said Zbyszko. He became absorbed in thought so that he contracted his brows; he was obviously trying to find some plan, but it did not last long. After a while he lifted up his head and said:

"Hlawa! See that the horses and men get ready; we must move at once."

The Bohemian, whose custom was never to ask for reasons when commanded, without saying a single word, got up and ran toward the horses; then Macko opened wide his eyes at his nephew and said with surprise:

"And ... Zbyszko? Hey! Where are you going? What?... How?..."

But he answered his questions with another:

"And what do you think? Is it not my duty?"

The old knight had nothing to say. His looks of astonishment disappeared little by little from his face; he shook his head once or twice and finally drew a deep breath and said as though replying to himself:

"Well! there you are.... There is no other remedy!"

And he also went to the horses, but Zbyszko returned to de Lorche, and by means of a Mazovian interpreter spoke to him thus:

"I cannot ask you to go with me against the people with whom you served. You are therefore free and you may go wherever you please."

"I cannot serve you now with my sword against my knightly honor," replied de Lorche; "but as to your granting me my freedom, I cannot accept that either. I remain your prisoner on parole and shall be at your command whithersoever you send me. And in case you want to exchange prisoners, remember that the Order will exchange for me any prisoner, because I am not only a powerful knight, but I am a descendant of a line of Knights of the Cross of great merit."

Then they embraced each other according to custom, placing their hands on each other's arms and kissing each other on the cheeks, and de Lorche said:

"I will go to Malborg or to the Mazovian court, so that you may know if I am not in one place you can find me in the other. Thy messenger need only tell me the two words, '*Lotaryngia-Geldria*'"

"Well," said Zbyszko, "still I will go to Skirwoilla to obtain a pass for you which the Zmudzians will respect."

Then he called upon Skirwoilla; the old leader gave the pass for his departure without any difficulty, for he knew all about the affair and loved Zbyszko; he was grateful to him for his bravery in the last battle, and for this very reason he made no objection whatever to the departure of the knight who belonged to another country and came on his own account. Then, thanking Zbyszko for the great services which he had rendered, he looked at him in surprise at his courage in undertaking a journey in the wild lands; he bid him good-bye, expressing his wishes to meet him again in some greater and more conclusive affair against the Knights of the Cross.

But Zbyszko was in a great hurry, for he was consumed as with a fever. When he arrived at the post he found everybody ready, and his uncle, Macko, on horseback, among them; he was armed and had on his coat of mail and his helmet upon his head. Zbyszko approached him and said:

"Then you too go with me!"

"But what else could I do?" replied Macko, a little testily.

Zbyszko did not reply, but kissed the right hand of his uncle, then mounted his horse and proceeded.

Sanderus went with them. They knew the road as far as the battlefield very well, but beyond that he was to guide them. They also counted upon the local inhabitants whom they might meet in the woods; who, out of hatred of their masters, the Knights of the Cross, would aid them in tracking the old *comthur* and the knight, Arnold von Baden, to whom Sanderus attributed such superhuman strength and bravery.

CHAPTER IX.

The road to the battlefield where Skirwoilla had routed the Germans was easy, because they knew it, and so they soon reached it. Owing to the insufferable stench arising from the unburied dead, they crossed it in a hurry. As they did so, they drove away wolves, and large flights of crows, ravens and jackdaws. Then they began to look for traces along the road. Although a whole division had passed over it on the previous day, nevertheless, the experienced Macko found upon the trampled road without trouble, the imprint of gigantic hoofs leading in an opposite direction. Then he explained to the younger and less experienced companions-in-arms:

"It is fortunate that there has been no rainfall since the battle. Only look here. Arnold's horse carrying an unusually big man must also be exceedingly large; this too is easily observed, that the imprint of the horse's feet on this side of the road is much deeper, owing to the galloping in his flight; whilst the tracks marking the previous march on the other side of the road are not so deep, because the horse walked slowly. Let those who have eyes look how the marks of the horseshoes are visible. God grant that we may track those dog-brothers successfully, provided they have not already found shelter somewhere behind walls!"

"Sanderus said," replied Zbyszko, "that there are no forts in this neighborhood, and it is actually so; because the Knights of the Cross have only recently taken possession of this region and have not had enough time to build in it. Then where can they hide themselves? All the peasants who dwelt in these lands joined Skirwoilla, because they belong to the same stock as the Zmudzians…. The villages, Sanderus said, these same Germans destroyed by fire and the women and children are hidden in the thick forest. Provided we do not spare our horses we shall yet overtake them."

"We must spare the horses, for even if we overtake them our safety afterward depends upon our horses," said Macko.

"Sir Arnold," interrupted Sanderus, "received a blow between his shoulder-blades in battle. He took no notice of it at first, but kept on fighting and slaying, but they were obliged to dress it afterward; as is always the case, at first one does not feel the blows but they pain later on. For this reason he cannot exert himself too much to run fast and it may be that he is even obliged to rest himself."

"You said that there are no other people with them?" inquired Macko.

"There are two who lead the litter, the *comthur* and Sir Arnold. There were quite a number of men with them, but the Zmudzians killed them."

"Let our men lay hold of the two fellows who are with the litter," said Zbyszko. "You, uncle, manage old Zygfried, and I will pounce upon Arnold."

"Well," replied Macko, "I shall be able to manage Zygfried, because, thank God, there is still strength in these bones. But as far as your task is concerned, I should say, do not be so self-confident, for that knight seems to be a giant."

"O well! We shall see," replied Zbyszko.

"You are strong, that I don't dispute, but there are stronger men than you are. Did you observe our own knights whom we met at Krakow? Could you conquer Pan Powala of Taczew, Paszko Zlodziej of Biskupice, and Zawisza Czarny, eh? Don't be too rash, but consider the facts."

"Rotgier also was a strong man," murmured Zbyszko.

"Will there be any work for myself?" asked the Bohemian. But he received no reply, because Macko was thinking about something else.

"If God blesses us we shall be able to reach the Mazowiecki wilderness. We shall be safe there, and all trouble will be at an end."

But after a while he sighed when he reflected that even there affairs would not be entirely ended, there would yet be something to attend to for the unfortunate Jagienka.

"Hey!" he murmured, "God's decrees are wonderful. I had often thought about it. Why did it not occur to you to get married quietly, and let me live with you peacefully. That would have been the most happy course. But now we are the only ones among the noblemen of the kingdom, who are wandering in various regions and wilds, instead of attending to our homes as God commands."

"Well, that is true, but it is God's will," replied Zbyszko.

Then they proceeded on their journey for a while in silence. The old knight turned again to his nephew:

"Do you rely on that vagabond? Who is he?"

"He is a fickle man and perhaps he is a rogue, but he wishes me well, and I am not afraid of treachery from him."

"If so let him ride in front, for if he overtakes them he will not be scared. Let him tell them that he is fleeing from captivity, and they will easily believe him. This is the best way, because if they chanced to see us they might evade us and hide themselves, or have time enough to prepare for defence."

"He is afraid and will not travel by himself at night," replied Zbyszko. "But during the daytime I am sure that that plan is the best one to adopt. I will tell him to stop and wait for us three times during the day. If we do not find him at the appointed places then it will be a sign that he is already with them, and following up his tracks we will fall upon them unexpectedly."

"But will he not warn them?"

"No. He is more friendly to me than to them. I will also tell him that when we surprise them we will also bind him, so that he may escape their revenge later on. Let him not recognize us at all...."

"Do you intend to preserve those fellows alive?"

"How else should it be?" replied Zbyszko, somewhat anxiously. "You see.... If it were in our country, at home in Mazowsze, we would challenge them, as I challenged Rotgier, to mortal combat; but this cannot be here in their own country.... What concerns us here is Danuska and speed. In order to avoid trouble all must be done quietly afterward we will do as you said and push on as fast as our horses can go, to the wilds of Mazowsze. But attacking them unexpectedly we might find them unarmed, yes, even without their swords. Then how could we kill them? I am afraid of reproach. We are now both of us, belted knights, so are they...."

"It is so," said Macko. "Yet it may lead to an encounter."

But Zbyszko contracted his brow and in his face was depicted that determination so characteristic of the looks of the men of Bogdaniec, for at that moment he looked as if he were Macko's own son.

"What I should also like," he said, in low tones, "is to have that bloody dog Zygfried crushed under Jurand's feet! May God grant it!"

"Grant it, God! grant it!" immediately repeated Macko.

Whilst conversing, they covered a considerable stretch of the road until nightfall. It was a starry night, but there was no moon. They were obliged to halt the horses, breathe, and refresh the men with food and sleep. Zbyszko informed Sanderus before resting that he was to proceed in front in the morning. Sanderus willingly assented; but reserved to himself, in case of an attack by wolves or people, the right to run back to Zbyszko. He also asked him for permission to make four stations instead of three, because in solitude fear always took hold of him, even in pious countries. How much more so in such an abominable wilderness as the one where they found themselves now?

When they had refreshed themselves with food, they lay down to sleep upon skins near a small camp-fire, which they built about half a furlong from the road. The servants alternately guarded the horses, which, after they were fed, rolled upon the ground and then slept, resting their heads upon each other's necks. But no sooner did the first ray illuminate the woods with a silvery hue, than Zbyszko arose and awoke the others, and at dawn they continued their march. The tracks of the hoofs of Arnold's immense stallion were easily recovered, because the usual muddy ground had dried up from drought. Sanderus went on ahead and soon disappeared. Nevertheless, they found him about half way between sunrise and noon, at the waiting place. He told them that he had not seen any living soul, only one large aurochs, but was not scared and did not run away, because the animal got out of his way. But he declared that shortly before, he had seen a peasant bee-keeper, but had not detained him, for fear that in the depths of the forest there might be more of them. He had attempted to question him, but they had not been able to make themselves understood.

As time went by, Zbyszko became somewhat troubled.

"What will happen," he said, "if I arrive in the higher and drier region, where, owing to the hard, dry road, the traces of the fugitives will be lost? or, if the pursuit shall last too long and lead to an inhabited region where the people have long since accustomed themselves to the servitude of the Knights of the Cross; an attack and capture of Danusia by them is more than probable, because, although Arnold and Zygfried did not erect forts, or fortify their towns, the inhabitants would surely take their part."

Happily that fear turned out to be groundless, because they did not find Sanderus at the appointed second post, but found instead an incision in the form of a cross, apparently newly cut into the bark of an adjacent pine tree. They looked at each other and their hearts began to beat faster. Macko and Zbyszko immediately dismounted, in order to discover the tracks upon the ground; they examined carefully, but it did not last long, because they were plainly discernible.

Sanderus had apparently deviated from the road into the forest, and followed the prints of the huge horse-hoofs, which, owing to the dry condition of the turfy soil, were not so deeply impressed, but sufficiently visible. The heavy horse disturbed at every step the pine needles which were blackened at the margins of the impressions.

Other marks did not escape Zbyszko's keen sight. Then he and Macko mounted their horses, and, together with the Bohemian, silently began taking counsel as though the enemy were quite near them.

The Bohemian's advice was that they should advance on foot at once, but they did not agree to that, because they did not know the distance they would have to traverse in the woods. The footmen, however, had to proceed carefully in advance, and signal in case something occurred, so that they might be in readiness.

They moved onward among the woods in some trepidation, and another incision upon a pine tree assured them that they had not lost Sanderus' tracks. Very soon they also discovered a path, showing that people frequently passed that way, and they were convinced that they were in the neighborhood of some forest habitation, and within it was the object of their search.

The sun was getting low, and shed a golden hue upon the trees of the forest. The evening promised to be serene; silence reigned in the woods because beast and birds had retired to rest, only here and there, among the little top branches of the trees, squirrels moved to and fro looking quite red in the last beams of the sun. Zbyszko, Macko, the Bohemian and the attendants, closely followed each other, knowing that their men were considerably in advance and would warn them in proper time; the old knight spoke to his nephew in not very subdued tones.

"Let us calculate from the sun," he said. "From the last station to the place where we found the first incision, we covered a great distance. According to Krakow time it would be about three hours…. Then Sanderus must be by this time among them, and has had time enough to tell them his adventure, provided he has not betrayed us."

"He has not betrayed us," replied Zbyszko.

"Provided they believe him," continued Macko; "if they do not, then it will be bad for him."

"But why should they not believe him? Do they know of us? Him they know. It often happens that prisoners escape from captivity."

"But what concerns me is this: if he told them that he ran away they might fear he would be pursued, and they would move on at once."

"No, he will succeed in casting dust in their eyes by telling them that such a long pursuit would not be undertaken."

They were silent for a while, then it seemed to Macko that Zbyszko was whispering to him; he turned and asked:

"What do you say?"

But Zbyszko had said nothing to Macko, but looking upward, said:

"Only if God would favor Danuska and the courageous enterprise in her behalf."

Macko also began to cross himself; but he had scarcely made the first sign of the cross, when from the hazelnut thickets one of the scouts approached him suddenly and said:

"A pitch-burning cabin! They are there!"

"Stop!" whispered Zbyszko, and dismounted at once. Macko, the Bohemian, and the attendants, also dismounted; three of the latter received orders to hold the horses in readiness and take care that they, God forbid, did not neigh. "I left five men," said Macko. "There will be the two attendants and Sanderus, whom we shall bind in a moment, and, should any one show fight, then, at his head!"

Then they advanced, and, as they moved on, Zbyszko said to his uncle:

"You take the old man, Zygfried; and I, Arnold."

"Only take care!" replied Macko. Then he beckoned to the Bohemian, reminding him to be ready at a moment's notice to be on hand to assist his master.

The Bohemian nodded assent. Then he breathed deeply and felt for his sword to see whether it could be easily unsheathed.

But Zbyszko observed it and said:

"No! I command you to hasten at once to the litter and not move from it for a single moment whilst the fight is going on."

They went quickly but silently through the hazelnut thickets. But they had not gone far, when at a distance of not quite two furlongs, the growth ceased suddenly, revealing a small field upon which were extinguished pitch-burning heaps, and two earthen shanties, or huts, where the pitch-burners had dwelt before the war. The setting sun brightly illuminated the lawn, the pitch-burning heaps, and the two detached shanties—in front of one of which the two knights were sitting upon the ground; and in front of the other were Sanderus and a bearded, red-headed fellow. These two were occupied in polishing the coats of mail with rags. Besides this, the two swords were lying at Sanderus' feet ready to be cleaned afterward.

"Look," said Macko, forcibly grasping Zbyszko's arm to detain him if possible for another moment, "he has taken the coats of mail and swords purposely. Well, that one with the grey head must be...."

"Forward!" suddenly shouted Zbyszko.

And like a whirlwind he rushed into the clearing; the others did the same, but they only succeeded in reaching Sanderus. The terrible Macko caught hold of old Zygfried by the breast, bent him backward and in a moment held him under him. Zbyszko and Arnold grasped each other like two hawks, with their arms intertwined and began to struggle fiercely with each other. The bearded German, who was with Sanderus, sprang toward the sword, but he did not use it. Wit, Macko's servant, struck him with the back of his axe, and stretched him upon the ground. Then they began to bind Sanderus, according to Macko's order, but he, although he well knew that it was so arranged beforehand, began to bellow as terribly as a yearling calf whose throat is being cut by the butcher's knife.

But Zbyszko, though so strong that he could squeeze a branch of a tree and cause the sap to run out, felt that he was not grasped by human hands, but was in the hug of a bear. He also felt that if it were not for the cost of mail which he had on, in case of having to fight with the sword, the German giant would have crushed his ribs and perhaps the spinal column too. The young knight lifted him a little from the ground, but Arnold lifted him up higher still, and gathering all his strength he tried to throw him to the ground so that he might not be able to rise again.

But Zbyszko also clutched him with such terrible force that blood issued from the German's eyes. Then he crooked his leg between Arnold's knees, bent him sideways and struck him in the hollow of the knee, which threw him to the ground. In reality both fell to the ground, the young knight underneath; but at the same moment, Macko, who was observing all this, threw the half doubled-up Zygfried into the hands of an attendant, and rushed toward the prostrate fighters, and in the twinkling of an eye he had bound the feet of Arnold with a belt; then he jumped, and sat down upon him as upon a wild boar, took the *misericordia* from his side, and plunged it deep into his throat.

Arnold screamed horribly, and his hands involuntarily withdrew from Zbyszko's sides. Then he began to moan not only with the pain of the wound, but he also felt an indescribable pain in his back: where he had received a blow from a club in his previous fight with Skirwoilla.

Macko grasped him with both hands and dragged him off Zbyszko, and Zbyszko got up from the ground and sat down; he tried to stand up but could not; he sat thus without being able to rise, for some time. His face was pale and covered with perspiration. His eyes were bloodshot and his lips were blue; and he looked in front of him as though half dazed.

"What is the matter?" asked Macko, in alarm.

"Nothing, but I am very tired. Help me to get up."

Macko put his hands under Zbyszko's arms and lifted him up at once.

"Can you stand?"

"I can."

"Do you feel pain?"

"Nothing, but I am short of breath."

Meanwhile the Bohemian, seeing apparently that the struggle in the farm yard was all over, appeared in front of the hut, dragging the woman servant of the Order by the neck. At that sight, Zbyszko forgot his fatigue, his strength returned to him at once, and he rushed to the hut as though he had never struggled with the terrible Arnold.

"Danuska! Danuska!" cried Zbyszko; but no answer came.

"Danuska! Danuska!" he repeated; then he remained silent. It was dark within, for that reason he could see nothing at first. But instead, he heard, proceeding from behind the stones which were heaped up behind the fireplace, a quick and audible panting, like that of a little animal hiding.

"Danuska! For God's sake. It is I! Zbyszko!"

Then he observed in the darkness, her eyes, wide open, terrified and bewildered.

He rushed toward her and pressed her in his arms, but she did not entirely recognize him, and tore herself away from his embrace, and began to repeat in a subdued whisper:

"I am afraid! I am afraid! I am afraid!"

END OF PART SEVENTH.

PART EIGHTH.

CHAPTER I.

Neither loving words nor tender persuasion availed. Danusia recognized nobody and did not regain consciousness. The only feeling which pervaded her whole being was fear, a kind of fear shown by captured birds. When food was brought to her she refused to eat it in the presence of others. In the glances of rejection which she cast upon the food one could detect habitual hunger. Left alone, she sprang upon the eatables like a ravenous little wild beast. But when Zbyszko entered she rushed into the corner and hid herself under a bundle of dry hops. Zbyszko opened his arms in vain, he stretched out his hands in vain, with tears he begged her, but unavailingly. She refused to issue from her hiding-place even when the light was so arranged that she could recognize the outlines of Zbyszko's face. It seemed as though she had lost her memory along with her senses. He therefore gazed upon her emaciated pale face in which was depicted an expression of dismay, her hollow eyes, her tattered dress, and his heart cried out within him from pain at the thought in whose hands she had been and how she had been treated. He was finally seized with such a terrible rage that he grasped his sword and rushed toward Zygfried, and he would have certainly killed him, had not Macko grasped him by the arm.

Then like enemies they struggled with each other. But the young man was so much fatigued from his previous fight with the gigantic Arnold, that the old knight prevailed. Twisting Zbyszko's wrist, he exclaimed:

"Are you mad?"

"Let me go!" he begged, gnashing his teeth, "for my heart bursts within me."

"Let it burst! I will not let you go. It is better to dash your head to pieces than disgrace yourself and the whole family."

And, clutching Zbyszko's hand, as with iron tongs, he said threateningly:

"See, revenge will not escape you; and you are a belted knight. How then dare you kill a prisoner in bonds? You cannot help Danusia. What will be the result? Nothing but disgrace. You say that kings and princes think it proper to destroy their prisoners. Bah! That is not the case with us; and what is feasible with them is not so with you. They have a kingdom, cities, castles. But what have you? Knightly honor. Those who find no fault with them will spit in your face. Consider, for God's sake!"

There was silence for a moment.

"Let me go!" Zbyszko repeated gloomily. "I will not kill him."

"Come to the fire, let us consult."

Macko led him by the hand to the fire which the servant stirred up near the tar-ovens. There they sat down and Macko reflected for a moment, and then said:

"You must also remember that you have promised this old dog to Jurand, who will avenge his own and his daughter's tortures. He is the one who will pay him, and do not you fear! In this you must please Jurand. It is his affair and not yours. Jurand may do it, but you must not; he did not capture him but will receive him as a present from you; he can even flay him alive and none will blame him for it. Do you understand me?"

"I understand," replied Zbyszko. "You are right."

"You are evidently coming to your senses again. Should you again be tempted by the devil, bear this also in your mind, that you have also challenged Lichtenstein and other Knights of the Cross, and if you should kill a defenceless captive and the men should publish your action, no knight would accept your challenge, and he would be justified. God forbid! We have enough misfortunes, but spare us shame. Let us rather talk about what concerns our present doings and movements."

"Give your advice," said the young man.

"My advice is this: that serpent who was with Danusia ought to be killed; but it does not become a knight to kill a woman. We shall therefore deliver her into the hands of Prince Janusz. She plotted treason whilst at the forest court of the prince and princess. Let the Mazovian courts judge her. If they do not crush her upon the wheel for her crimes, then they will offend God's justice. As long as we find no other woman to wait upon Danusia, as long as she is wanted to serve her we must keep her until some other old woman be found; then we will tie her to a horse's tail. But now we must push on toward the Mazovian wilderness as soon as possible.

"It cannot be done at once, it is dark already. By to-morrow, if God will, Danusia may come to her senses."

"Let the horses rest well, and at daybreak we will start."

Further conversation was interrupted by Arnold von Baden, who was stretched on his back at a distance, trussed by his own sword; he said something in German. Old Macko got up and went to him, but as he did not understand him he called the Bohemian.

But Hlawa could not come at once because he was busy about something else. During the conversation, near the fire, he went directly to the servant of the Order, put his hands around her neck, shook her like a pear-tree, and said:

"Listen, you slut! Go into the shanty and prepare the fur bedding for the young lady. But before you do that, dress her in your good apparel, whilst you put upon your carcass the tattered rags which you have given her…. May your mother suffer perdition!"

He was so angry that he could not control himself, and shook her so savagely that her eyes bulged out. He would have twisted her neck, but he thought better of it since she was still of some use; finally he let her go, saying:

"After that I will hang you to a branch."

She embraced his knees in terror, but he kicked her. She rushed into the shanty, threw herself at Danusia's feet and began to scream:

"Protect me. Do not permit!"

But Danusia closed her eyes, and uttered her customary suppressed whisper: "I am afraid, I am afraid, I am afraid."

Then she lapsed into perfect silence, because that was the effect whenever the woman approached her. She permitted the woman to undress, wash and dress her in the new clothes. The woman prepared the bedding and laid upon it Danusia, who had the appearance of a wooden or wax figure; after which she sat down near the fireplace fearing to go out.

But the Bohemian entered after awhile. First he turned toward Danusia and said:

"You are among friends, lady, so in the name of the Father, Son and Holy Ghost, sleep peacefully!"

Then he made the sign of the cross. Then not wishing to disturb her he said to the servant in a low voice:

"You shall lie bound at the threshold; you must keep quiet and do not frighten her; if not, I will break your neck. Get up, and come."

He led her out and bound her tightly, then he went to Zbyszko.

"I have ordered that lizard to dress the lady in her own garments, to make her a soft bed, and the lady is asleep; better leave her alone because she is scared. God grant that by to-morrow, after repose, she may regain her presence of mind. You too must think of refreshment and rest."

"I shall sleep at her threshold," replied Zbyszko.

"Then I shall withdraw the slut from the threshold and place her near that corpse with curled locks. But you must take refreshment now, because there is a long road and no little fatigue before you."

Then he went and got some smoked meat and dried turnips which they had procured in the Lithuanian camp; but he had scarcely put the meal in front of Zbyszko when Macko called him to come to Arnold.

"Notice carefully, what this mass wishes, although I know a few German words, I am unable to understand him."

"Bring him to the fire, sir, and have your conversation there," replied the Bohemian.

Then he unbelted himself and placed the belt under Arnold's arms and lifted him upon his shoulders; he bent much under the heavy weight of the giant, but as the Bohemian was a powerful man, he carried him near the fireplace and threw him down, as one throws a sack of peas, at the side of Zbyszko.

"Take off the fetters from me," said Arnold.

"That might be done if you swore on knightly honor, that you would consider yourself a prisoner. Nevertheless, I will order the sword to be taken from under your knees, the bonds of your hands to be loosened, so as to enable you to sit with us, but the rope binding your feet shall remain until we have discussed the affair." And he nodded to the Bohemian, who cut the bonds away from Arnold's hands and assisted him to sit down. Arnold looked haughtily at Macko and Zbyszko and asked:

"Who are you?"

"How do you dare to ask? It is not your business. Go and inform yourself."

"It concerns me, because to swear upon the honor of a knight can only be done to knights."

"Then look!"

And Macko opened his cloak and showed his knightly belt upon his loins.

Seeing that, the Knight of the Cross was greatly amazed, and after awhile said:

"How is it? and you prowl in the wilderness for prey and assist the pagans against the Christians?"

"You lie!" exclaimed Macko.

Then the conversation began in an unfriendly and arrogant manner, which seemed like quarreling. But when Macko vehemently shouted that the very Order prevented Lithuania from embracing Christianity, and when all proofs were adduced, Arnold was again amazed and became silent, because the truth was so obvious that it was impossible not to see it, or to dispute it. What specially struck him was Macko's words which he uttered whilst making the sign of the cross: "Who knows whom ye actually serve, if not all at least some among you." It specially struck him because there were certain *comthurs* in the very Order who were suspected of having given themselves over to Satan. Steps were not taken against them for fear of public reproach of the whole Order. But Arnold knew it well because these things were whispered among the brethren of the Order and happenings of such a character reached his ears. Therefore, Macko's narrative which he had heard from Sanderus, concerning the inconceivable conduct of Zygfried, greatly disturbed the mind of the candid giant.

"Oh, that very Zygfried, with whom you marched to war," he said. "Does he serve Christ? Have you never heard how he communicates with evil spirits, how he whispers to them, smiles and gnashes his teeth at them?"

"It is true!" murmured Arnold.

But Zbyszko, whose heart was filled with new waves of grief and anger, suddenly exclaimed:

"And you, who speak of knightly honor? Shame upon you, because you help a hangman, a devilish man. Shame upon you, because you quietly looked upon the torture of a defenceless woman, and a knight's daughter. Maybe you also outraged her. Shame upon you!"

Arnold closed his eyes, and making the sign of the cross, said:

"In the name of the Father, the Son, and the Holy Ghost.... How is that?... That fettered girl in whose head dwell twenty-seven devils? I?..."

"Oh, horrible! horrible!" interrupted Zbyszko, groaning.

And, grasping the handle of his *misericordia* he again looked savagely toward the dark corner where Zygfried lay on his back.

Macko placed his hand quietly upon Zbyszko's arm, which he pressed with his whole strength, so as to bring him back to his senses; whilst he himself, turning toward Arnold, said:

"That woman is the daughter of Jurand of Spychow, and wife of this young knight. Do you understand now, why we followed you up, and why we have captured you?"

"For God's sake!" said Arnold. "Whence? How? she is insane...."

"Because the Knights of the Cross kidnapped that innocent lamb and subjected her to torture."

When Zbyszko heard these words: "Innocent lamb," he put his fist to his mouth, gnashed his teeth, and was not able to restrain his tears.

Arnold sat absorbed in thought; but the Bohemian told him in a few words of Danveld's treachery, the kidnapping of Danusia, the torture of Jurand, and the duel with Rotgier. Silence reigned when he concluded. It was only disturbed by the rustling of the trees of the forest and the crackling of the brands in the fireplace.

In that manner they sat for a while. Finally Arnold lifted up his head and said:

"I swear to you not only upon my knightly honor, but also upon the crucifix, that I have not seen that woman, that I did not know who she was, and that I have not taken the least part in her tortures and never laid my hand upon her."

"Then swear also that you will go with us willingly and that you will make no attempt to escape, then I will order your bonds to be entirely unloosed," said Macko.

"Let it be as you say. I swear! Whither are you going to take me?"

"To Mazovia, to Jurand of Spychow."

Then Macko himself cut the rope from Arnold's feet, and ordered meat and turnips to be brought. After a while Zbyszko went out and sat upon the threshold of the hut to rest, where he no longer found the servant, for the hostler boys had carried her off and put her among the horses. Zbyszko lay down upon the fur which Hlawa brought. He resolved to keep awake and wait until daybreak; peradventure then some happy change might take place in Danusia!

But the Bohemian returned to the fireplace where he wished to converse with the old knight of Bogdaniec about a certain affair and take off the burden which pressed so heavily upon his heart. He found him also absorbed in troubled thought, and not noticing the snoring of Arnold who, after having consumed an immense quantity of baked turnips and meat, was much fatigued and slept the sleep of a stone. "And why do you not take a rest?" inquired the Bohemian.

"Sleep has fled from my eyelids," replied Macko. "May God grant a good morning." Then he looked at the stars and said:

"The Wagoner is already visible in the sky, and I am continually thinking about how all these things shall be arranged. And I shall not go to sleep either because the young lady of Zgorzelice occupies my mind."

"Ah! that is true. More trouble. But she, at least, is at Spychow."

282

"But we brought her to Spychow from Zgorzelice, not knowing why."

"It was at her own request," replied Macko, impatiently, because he knew in his heart that he was wrong and he hated to talk about it.

"Yes! But what now?"

"Ha! Well? I shall carry her back to her home; then let God's will be done!"

But after a moment he added:

"Yes! God's will be done, that at least Danuska be restored to health, one might then know what to do. But as it is now, the deuce knows! What will it be if she neither recovers nor dies? The Devil knows."

But the Bohemian was thinking all the time of Jagienka.

"Your honor should understand that when I left Spychow and bade her good-bye, she told me this: 'If anything should happen, come and inform me before Zbyszko and Macko arrive. And as they will be obliged to send information by somebody, let them send it by you, then you will take me to Zgorzelice.'"

"Hey!" replied Macko. "Surely, it would be improper for her to stay at Spychow when Danusia arrives. Surely she ought now to be taken back to Zgorzelice. I pity the little orphan, I sincerely regret it. But God's will must be done. But now how shall I arrange the matter? Let me see. Did you say that she commanded you to come ahead of us with the news, and then take her to Zgorzelice?"

"She did. I repeated to you her words exactly."

"Now, you may move ahead of us. Old Jurand must also be informed that his daughter has been found, but it must be done carefully so that the sudden joy may not kill him. As I love God, I declare that it is the most practical thing to do."

"Return! Tell them that we have rescued Danusia, and that we shall bring her home without delay. Then take that other poor girl to Zgorzelice!"

Then the old knight sighed, because he was really sorry for Jagienka, whom he had fostered.

After a while he asked again:

"I know that you are a valiant and powerful man, but see that you keep her out of harm's way or accident. Things of that character are often met with on the road."

"I shall do my best, even if I lose my head! I shall take with me a few good men, whom the lord of Spychow will not grudge, and I shall bring her safely even to the end of the world."

"Well, do not have too much confidence in yourself. Bear also in mind that even there, at Zgorzelice, it will be necessary to watch Wilk of Brzozowa and Cztan of Rogow. But, I confess, in speaking of Wilk and Cztan, I am out of order; for, it was necessary to watch them when there was nothing else to think of. But now, things have changed and there is no more hope, and that which is going to happen must happen."

"Nevertheless, I shall protect the young lady from those knights, seeing Danusia is very weak and consumptive. What if she should die?"

"As God is dear to me you are right. The emaciated lady is scarcely alive. If she should die?"

"We must leave that with God. But we must now think only of the young lady of Zgorzelice."

"By rights, I ought to convey her myself to her fatherland. But it is a difficult task. I cannot now leave Zbyszko for many potent reasons. You saw how he gnashed his teeth, how he strove to get at the old *comthur* to kill him, and my wrangling with him. Should that girl die on the road, even I should be unable to restrain him. And if I shall not be able to prevent him, nobody else could, and everlasting shame would fall upon him and upon our clan, which God forbid. Amen!"

Then the Bohemian replied:

"Bah! There is, I am sure, a simple means. Give me the hangman and I will keep him and bring him to Jurand at Spychow and shake him out of the sack."

"How clever you are! May God grant you health," exclaimed Macko, joyfully. "It is a very simple thing, quite simple. Should you succeed in bringing him to Spychow alive then do with him as you please."

"Then let me also have that Szczytno bitch, and if she is not troublesome on the road, I will bring her too to Spychow, if she is, then I shall hang her on a tree."

"The removal of the pair, whose presence causes much fear to Danusia, may contribute to her speedy recovery. But if you take the female servant with you, who is going to nurse Danusia?"

"You may find some old woman in the wilderness, or one of the fugitive peasant women; take hold of the first one you meet, for any one will be better than this. Meanwhile, you must take care of lady Zbyszko."

"You speak to-day somewhat more prudently than usually. Seeing that Zbyszko is constantly with her, he will also succeed in filling the double position, that of father and mother, for her. Very well, then. When do you intend to start?"

"I shall not wait for the dawn; now I must lie down for a while, it is scarcely midnight yet."

"The Wagoner[117] is already in the sky, but the chickens[117] had not yet made their appearance."

"Thank God that we have taken some counsel together, for I was very much troubled."

Then the Bohemian stretched himself near the expiring fire, covered himself over with the long furred robe and in a moment he fell asleep. However, the sky had not yet paled and it was still deep, dark night when he awoke, crept from under the skin, looked at the stars, and stretching his somewhat benumbed limbs, he awoke Macko.

"It is time for me to move," he said.

"Whither?" asked the semi-conscious Macko, rubbing his eyes with his fists.

"To Spychow."

"True, I quite forgot. Who is there snoring so loud as to awake the dead?"

"The knight Arnold. Let me throw a few branches upon the embers, then I will go to the men."

Then he left, and hastily returned in a little while, and from a distance he called in a low voice:

"Sir, there is news, bad news!"

"What has happened?" Macko exclaimed, jumping to his feet.

"The servant has escaped. The men took her among the horses. May thunder strike them, and when they fell asleep, she sneaked like a serpent from among them and escaped. Come, sir!"

Macko, in alarm, moved quickly with the Bohemian toward the horses, where they found only one man, the others had scattered in pursuit of the fugitive. But, considering the darkness of the night and the thickets of the forest, the search was a foolish undertaking, and after a while they returned with hanging heads. Macko began to belabor them quietly with his fists. Then he returned to the fireplace, for there was nothing to be done.

Zbyszko, who was watching in the hut and did not sleep, came in, hearing the movements, to ascertain the reason. Macko told him all about his consultation with the Bohemian, then he also informed him of the woman's escape.

"It is not a great misfortune," he said. "Because she will either die of starvation, or fall into the hands of the peasants who will flay her; that is, if she succeeds first in escaping the wolves. It is only to be regretted that she escaped the punishment at Spychow."

Zbyszko also regretted her escaping punishment at Spychow; otherwise he received the news quietly. He did not oppose the departure of the Bohemian with Zygfried, because he was indifferent to anything which did not directly concern Danusia. He began to talk about her at once.

"I shall take her in front of me on horseback to-morrow, then we shall proceed."

"How is it there? Is she asleep?" inquired Macko.

"At times she moans, but I do not know whether she does it in sleep or whilst she is awake, but I don't want to disturb her, lest I frighten her."

Further conversation was interrupted by the Bohemian, who observing Zbyszko, exclaimed:

"O! your honor, also here! It is now time for me to start. The horses are ready and the old devil is fastened to the saddle. It will soon begin to dawn because now the nights are short. Good-bye, your grace!"

"God be with you, and health!"

But Hlawa pulled Macko aside again and said:

"I wish also to ask you kindly, that in case anything should happen…. You know, sir … some misfortune or another … you would dispatch a courier posthaste to Spychow. If we have left Spychow, let him overtake us."

"Well," said Macko, "I have also forgotten to tell you to take Jagienka to Plock. Do you understand? Go there to the bishop, and tell him who she is, that she is the goddaughter of the abbot, for whom there is a will in the bishop's possession; then ask his guardianship for her, as that is also mentioned in the abbot's will."

"But if the bishop orders us to remain in Plock?"

"Then obey him in everything and follow his counsel."

"It shall be so, sir! Good-bye!"

"Good-bye!"

CHAPTER II.

Sir Arnold was informed in the morning of the flight of the servant of the Order; he chuckled at the news, on the other hand he held the same opinion as Macko, viz, that she might fall a prey to the wolves, or be slain by the Lithuanians. The latter was not at all improbable, since the inhabitants of that locality who were descendants of the Lithuanians abhorred the Order and all those who came in contact with it. Some of the male population had joined Skirwoillo, others had risen in arms and slaughtered the Germans here and there; they, their families and their cattle hid themselves in the inaccessible fastnesses of the forest. They searched the following day for the servant, but without success, because Macko and Zbyszko were occupied with more important matters; hence the lack of indispensable ardor in the searchers.

They were obliged to push on toward Mazowsze; they wished to start at once, at the rising of the sun, but they were unable to do so because Danuska was in a profound sleep, and Zbyszko would not permit her to be disturbed.

He listened to her moanings during the night-time and thought that she was not asleep. He, therefore, promised himself good results. Twice he stealthily went into the hut; twice he saw by the light falling through crevices of the logs her closed eyes, open mouth and glowing face, as little children are wont to have when asleep. His tears melted his heart at that sight, and he said to her:

"May God grant you health my most beloved little flower." Then he continued: "Your troubles are ended, your tears are ended. May the most merciful Lord Jesus grant that your happiness may be as inexhaustible as the flowing river."

Then, lifting up his simple and upright heart heavenward, he asked himself: "With what can I thank Thee? What shall I render to Thee for Thy favors? Shall I offer to the Church some of my wealth, grain, herds, wax, or something of the same nature acceptable to God?" He was even about to vow and name accurately his offerings, but he wished to wait and see the result when Danusia awoke, whether she had recovered her senses so that there might be reason for thanksgiving.

Although Macko knew well that there would be perfect safety when once in the domains of Prince Janusz, nevertheless he was also of the opinion that it was better not to disturb Danusia's rest. He therefore kept his horses and servants in readiness but waited.

Nevertheless when it was past noon and Danusia continued to sleep, they were somewhat alarmed. Zbyszko, who was incessantly watching, looking through the crevices and door, entered suddenly for the third time into the hut and sat down upon the block where the servant had dressed Danusia yesterday.

He sat and gazed at her, but she had her eyes closed. But after the lapse of a short time, not more than it takes to say one "Pater" and "Ave Maria," her lips began to twitch a little, and she whispered as though she saw through her closed eyelids:

"Zbyszko…."

In an instant he threw himself upon his knees in front of her, grasped her emaciated hands, which he kissed in ecstasy. Then he addressed her in a broken voice:

"Thank God! Danuska! You recognize me."

His voice awoke her completely. Then she sat up in the bed and with open eyes she repeated:

"Zbyszko!"

Then she began to blink and look around her in amazement.

"You are no more in captivity," said Zbyszko. "I have rescued you from their hands and I am taking you to Spychow."

But she withdrew her hands from Zbyszko's and said:

"All this came to pass because there was no permission from dear papa. Where is the princess?"

"Awake, then, dear little berry! The princess is far away and we have rescued you from the Germans."

Then she appeared not to notice his words but seemed to try to recollect something.

"They have also taken away my little lute and have broken it against the wall. Hey!"

"O God!" exclaimed Zbyszko.

He then observed that she was absent-minded and her eyes were glassy and her cheeks were glowing, and it struck him that she must be very ill, and the mention of his name twice was due to feverish hallucinations.

This caused his heart to tremble within him with despair and a cold sweat covered his brow.

"Danuska!" he said. "Do you see and understand me?"

But she replied in a low voice:

"Drink! Water!"

"Gracious Lord!"

And he rushed out, and at the door encountered Macko, who was coming to ascertain her condition. Zbyszko could only tell him hurriedly, "Water;" and then hastened to the stream which ran among neighboring bushes.

He returned after a moment with a full pitcher of water and handed it to Danusia who drank it with much avidity. Macko entered the hut before Zbyszko and seeing the patient he became gloomy.

"She is feverish?" he said.

"Yes!" groaned Zbyszko.

"Does she understand what you say?"

"No."

The old knight furrowed his brow, then he began to rub his neck and nape with his hands.

"What is to be done?"

"I do not know."

"There is only one thing to be done," said Macko.

But Danusia, who finished drinking, interrupted him at that moment; she fixed her dilated pupils on him, and said:

"You too I have not offended, have mercy upon me!"

"We have pitied you already, child. We only desire your welfare," replied the old knight, somewhat agitated.

Then he turned to Zbyszko:

"Listen, there is no use to leave her here. The wafting of the wind and the rays of the sun will probably benefit her. Do not lose your head, boy, but take her to the same cradle wherein she was when they brought her here—or upon the saddle and let us move on! Do you understand?"

Then he left the hut to give the last orders, but he had scarcely looked in front of him, when he suddenly stood still—as if nailed to the spot.

A numerous host of infantry armed with pikes and spears was surrounding the huts, ovens and clearing, on all sides like a wall.

"Germans!" thought Macko.

286

He was greatly terrified, but in a moment he grasped the hilt of his sword, clenched his teeth, and had the appearance of a wild beast at bay, ready to defend himself desperately.

Then the giant-like Arnold, and another knight, advanced toward them from the shanty, and when he approached Macko, Arnold said:

"Fortune's wheel turns rapidly. I was your prisoner yesterday; you are mine to-day."

Then he looked haughtily at the old knight as one looks upon an inferior person. He was neither a very bad man, nor a very cruel one, but he had the defect common to all Knights of the Cross, who in spite of their being well-bred and even humane, looked with contempt upon those whom they conquered, neither could they suppress their great pride when they felt themselves the stronger.

"You are prisoners," he repeated, haughtily.

The old knight looked around gloomily; he was very serious but audacious in his heart.

Were he armored, upon his charger, and with Zbyszko at his side;—if both had swords in their hands and were armed with axes, or the terrible "woods," which the Polish noblemen knew how to wield dexterously, he would then have probably attempted to break through, that wall of lances and spears. Not without reason did the foreign knights, quoting it as an objection, exclaim to the Polish in the fight near Wilno: "You scorn death too much."

But Macko was on foot facing Arnold, alone, without his coat of mail. He therefore looked around and observed that his men had already thrown down their arms, and he thought that Zbyszko too was with Danusia in the hut, entirely unarmed. As an experienced man, and much accustomed to war, he knew that there was no chance whatever.

Therefore he slowly drew the short sword from its sheath and threw it at the feet of the knight who stood at Arnold's side, who without the least of Arnold's haughtiness, but at the same time with benevolence, replied in excellent Polish:

"Your name, sir? I shall not put you in bonds but shall parole you, because I see you are a belted knight, and you treated my brother well."

"My word!" replied Macko.

Having informed him who he was, Macko inquired whether he would be permitted to go to the hut and warn his nephew against any mad action. His request was granted. He entered and remained there for a while and emerged with the *misericordia* in his hands.

"My nephew is even without a sword, and he begs you to permit him to remain with his wife as long as you intend to stay here."

"Let him remain," said Arnold's brother. "I shall send him food and drink; we shall not move soon, because the people are tired out and we too are in need of refreshment and rest. Sir, we also invite you to accompany us."

Then they turned and went to the same fireplace near which Macko had spent the night. But either from pride, or from ignorance they permitted him to walk behind them. But he, being a great warrior, knowing how it ought to be, and adhering strictly to custom, inquired:

"Pray, sir, am I your guest or a prisoner?"

Arnold's brother was shamed at first; he halted and said:

"Proceed, sir."

The old knight went in front, not wishing to hurt the self-respect of the very man from whom he expected much.

"It is evident, sir, that you are not only acquainted with courteous speech, but your behavior is also courtly."

Then, Arnold, who only understood a few words, asked:

"Wolfgang, what are you talking about?"

"I am doing the right thing," said Wolfgang, who was evidently flattered by Macko's words.

They sat down at the fireside, and began to eat and drink. The lesson which Macko had given to the German was not in vain. Wolfgang regaled Macko first at the repast.

The old knight learned, from the conversation which followed, how they were caught in the trap. Wolfgang, the younger brother of Arnold, led also the Czluch infantry to

Gotteswerder, against the rebellious Zmudzians. Those, however, proceeding from distant counties could not arrive in time to assist Arnold. The latter did not think it necessary to wait for them because he expected to meet on the road other bodies of infantry proceeding from the towns and castles situated on the adjacent Lithuanian frontier. This was the reason that his younger brother delayed his march several days, and thus it happened that he found himself on the road in the neighborhood of the tar-burners, where the fugitive woman-servant of the Order informed him of the ill-luck which had happened to his older brother. Arnold, whilst listening to the narrative which was told him in German, smiled with satisfaction; finally he affirmed that he expected such a result.

But the crafty Macko, who, in whatever situation he was, always tried to find some remedy, thought that it would be of advantage to him to make friends with the Germans, therefore he said after a while:

"It is always hard to fall into captivity. Nevertheless, thank God, I am fortunate to have been delivered into nobody else's hands but yours, because, I believe, that you are real knights and mindful of its honor."

Then Wolfgang closed his eyes and nodded his head somewhat stiffly but evidently with a feeling of satisfaction.

The old knight continued:

"That you speak our language well. God has given you understanding in everything."

"I know your language, because the Czluchs speak Polish, and my brother and I served for seven years in those counties."

"You will in time take office after him. It cannot be otherwise, because your brother does not speak our language."

"He understands it a little, but cannot speak it. My brother is more powerful, although I am not a weakling either, but of duller wit."

"Hey! He does not seem to me dull."

"Wolfgang, what does he say?" asked Arnold again.

"He praises you," replied Wolfgang.

"True, I praised him," added Macko, "because he is a true knight, and that is the reason. I tell you frankly that I intended to let him go entirely free to-day on parole, so that he might go wherever he wished to, even if he were to present himself in a year's time. Such treatment is customary among belted knights."

Then he looked attentively into Wolfgang's face, but it was wrinkled, and he said:

"Were it not for the assistance you have given to the pagan dogs against us, I also might have let you go on parole."

"This is not true," replied Macko.

Then the same asperity of discussion as in yesterday's dispute between Arnold and himself was repeated. However, although right was on the old knight's side, it went on with more difficulty, because Wolfgang was of a more severe disposition than his older brother. Nevertheless, one good thing resulted from the dispute, that Wolfgang learned of all the abominable practices of the Order at Szczytno, their crooked actions and treachery—at the same time he learned of Danusia's misfortunes and tortures. To those very iniquities which Macko had thrown in his teeth he had no reply. He was obliged to acknowledge that the revenge was justifiable, and that the Polish knights were right in their acts, and finally said:

"Upon the glorified bones of St. Liborus! I swear, that I also will not pity Danveld. They said of him that he practiced black magic, but God's power and justice is mightier than black magic. As to Zygfried, I am not sure whether he also served the devil or not. But I shall not hunt for him, because first, I have no horses, and on the other hand, if what you said is true that he outraged that girl, then let him also never return from Hades!"

Here he stretched himself and continued:

"God! Help me till the hour of my death."

"But how will it be with that unfortunate martyr?" inquired Macko. "Are you not going to permit us to take her home? Has she to suffer agony in your underground prisons? Remember, I beseech you, God's wrath!…"

"I have nothing against the woman," replied Wolfgang, roughly. "Let one of you take her home to her father, on condition that he present himself afterward, but the other must remain here."

"Bah! But what if he swears upon his knightly honor and upon the lance of St. Jerzey?"

Wolfgang hesitated a little because it was a great oath; but at that moment Arnold asked a third time:

"What does he say?"

When he informed himself of the matter he opposed it vehemently and rudely. He had his private reasons for it. First, he was conquered by Skirwoillo, then in single combat, by the Polish knight. He also knew that owing to the destruction of the army at the previous engagement it would be impossible for his brother to advance with his infantry to Gotteswerder and he would be obliged to return to Malborg. Moreover he knew that he would be obliged to give an account to the Master and marshal for the defeat, and that it would be to his advantage if he were able to show even one important prisoner. To produce one knight alive is of more value than to explain that two such were captured....

When Macko heard the loud protestations and oaths of Arnold, he resolved, since nothing else could be obtained, to take what was previously offered. Turning to Wolfgang he said:

"Then, I beg one more favor—permit me to acquaint my nephew; I am sure he will see the wisdom of remaining with his wife, while I go with you. At all events, permit me to let him know that he has nothing to say against it, for it is your will."

"Well, it is all the same to me," replied Wolfgang. "But let us talk about the ransom which your nephew must bring for himself and you. Because all depends on that."

"About ransom?" inquired Macko, who would have preferred to postpone that conversation to a later period. "Have we not time enough to talk about it? Where a belted knight is concerned his word is of equal value with ready money, and as to the sum it can be left to conscience. There, near Gotteswerder, we captured one of your important knights, a certain de Lorche. And my nephew (it was he who captured him) paroled him. No allusion whatever was made to the amount of ransom."

"Have you captured de Lorche?" inquired Wolfgang, sharply. "I know him. He is a powerful knight. But why did we not meet him on the road?"

"He, evidently, did not go this way, but went to Gotteswerder, or to Ragniec," replied Macko.

"That knight comes from a powerful and renowned family," repeated Wolfgang. "You have made a splendid capture! It is well then, that you mentioned it. But I cannot let you go for nothing."

Macko chewed his mustache; nevertheless he lifted up his head haughtily, and said: "Apart from that, we know our value."

"So much the better," said the younger von Baden, and immediately added:

"So much the better. It is not for us, for we are humble monks, who have vowed poverty, but for the Order that will enjoy your money, to God's praise."

Macko did not reply to that but only looked at Wolfgang, with such an expression as to say: "Tell that to somebody else." After awhile they began to bargain. It was a difficult and irritable task for the old knight. On the one hand he was very sensitive to any loss, and on the other hand, he understood that he would not succeed in naming a too small sum for Zbyszko and himself. He therefore wriggled like an eel, especially when Wolfgang, in spite of his polished words and manners, had shown himself excessively grasping and as hard hearted as a stone. Only one thought comforted Macko and that was, that de Lorche would have pay for all, but even that, the loss of de Lorche's ransom, worried him. Zygfried's ransom he did not count in the affair because he thought that Jurand, and even Zbyszko, would not renounce his head for any price.

After long haggling they finally compromised upon the sum in *grzywiens* and the time of payment, and stipulated upon the number of horses and men Zbyszko should take with him. Macko went to inform Zbyszko, and advised him not to tarry but depart at once, for something else might meanwhile come into the German's head.

"So it is with knightly conditions," said Macko, sighing. "Yesterday you held them by the head, to-day they hold you. Well, it is a hard lot. God grant that our turn may come. But now, it is necessary not to lose time. If you hasten on, you may yet overtake Hlawa and you will be safer together, and once out of the wilderness and in the inhabited region of Mazowsze you will find hospitality and assistance in every nobleman's or *wlodyka's* house. In our country they do not refuse those things even to a foreigner, how much more to one of their own people! The condition of the poor woman might also be improved thereby."

Then he looked at Danusia, who was in feverish half-sleep, breathing quickly and loudly, with her transparent hands stretched upon the black bearskin, trembling with fever. Macko made the sign of the cross at her and said:

"Hey, take her and go! May God restore her, for it appears to me that her thread of life is being spun very thin."

"Do not say that!" exclaimed Zbyszko, in a distressed tone.

"God's power! I will order your horses to be brought here—and you must leave at once!"

He went out and arranged everything for the journey. The Turks, whom Zawisza had presented to them, led the horses and the litter, filled with mosses and fur, and they were headed by Zbyszko's man, Wit. Zbyszko left the hut in a moment, carrying Danusia in his arms. There was something touching in that, so that even the brothers von Baden, whose curiosity had drawn them to the hut, looked curiously into the childlike face of Danuska. Her face was like that of the holy images in the churches of Our Lady, and her sickness was so great that she could not hold up her head which lay heavily on the young knight's arm. They looked at each other with astonishment, and in their hearts arose a feeling against the authors of her woes.

"Zygfried has the heart of a hangman, and not that of a knight," whispered Wolfgang to Arnold, "and that serpent, although she is the cause of your liberty, I will order to be beaten with rods."

They were also touched when they saw Zbyszko carrying her in his arms, as a mother is wont to carry her child. They comprehended how great was his love for her, for youthful blood coursed in the veins of them both.

He hesitated for awhile whether to keep the patient on horseback near his breast on the road or to lay her in the litter. Finally he resolved upon the latter course, thinking that she might feel more comfortable in a recumbent posture. Then he approached his uncle and bowed to kiss his hand and bid him good-bye. But Macko, who, as a matter of fact, loved Zbyszko as the apple of his eye, was somewhat disinclined to show his agitation in the presence of the Germans; nevertheless he could not restrain himself, and embracing him strongly, pressed his lips to his abundant golden hair.

"May God guide you," he said. "But remember the old man, for it is always a hardship to be in captivity."

"I shall not forget," replied Zbyszko. "May the most Holy Mother comfort you."

"God will recompense you for this and for all your kindness."

Zbyszko mounted his horse immediately, but Macko recollected something and hastened to his side, and placing his hand upon Zbyszko's knee, he said:

"Listen, if you should overtake Hlawa, remember not to molest Zygfried, otherwise you will bring down reproach upon yourself and upon my gray head. Leave him to Jurand, but do nothing to him yourself. Swear to me upon your sword and honor."

"As long as you do not return," replied Zbyszko, "I shall even prevent Jurand from harming him in order to prevent the Germans from injuring you on Zygfried's account."

"So, and you seem to care for me?"

And the young knight smiled sadly. "You well know that, I am sure."

"Move on and good-bye."

The horses moved on, and in a little while disappeared in the hazelnut thickets. Macko felt suddenly very much troubled and lonely and his heart was torn for that beloved boy in whom rested the entire hope of the family. But he soon got rid of his sorrow, for he was a man of valor and could master his emotions.

"Thank God that I am a prisoner and not he."

Then he turned toward the Germans and said:

"And you, gentlemen, when will you start and whither are you going?"

"When it is agreeable to us," replied Wolfgang, "but we go to Malborg, where, sir, you must first appear before the Master."

"Hey! I shall yet have to forfeit my head there, for the help I have given to the Zmudzians," said Macko to himself.

Nevertheless his mind was at rest when he thought that de Lorche was in reserve; the Baden knights themselves would protect his head even if it were only for the ransom.

"Otherwise," he said to himself, "Zbyszko will neither be obliged to present himself nor lessen his fortune."

That thought caused him a certain relief.

CHAPTER III.

Zbyszko was unable to overtake Hlawa, because the latter traveled day and night, and only rested as much as was absolutely necessary to avoid the breaking down of the horses, which only subsisted on grass, and were consequently faint and unable to withstand such long marches as they could in regions where oats could be easily procured. Hlawa neither spared himself, nor took into consideration the advanced age and weakness of Zygfried. The old knight suffered terribly, especially because the sinewy Macko had previously wrenched his bones. But still worse were the mosquitoes which swarmed in the humid wilderness, and as his hands were bound and his legs fastened beneath the horse's belly, he was unable to drive them away. Hlawa did not directly torture him in the least, but he had no compassion for him, and only unfastened his right hand to enable him to eat when he stopped for refreshment.

"Eat, ravening wolf, so that I may bring you alive to the lord of Spychow." Such were the words of inducement to stimulate Zygfried's appetite. At first Zygfried resolved to starve himself to death; but when he heard the announcement that in such case Hlawa would forcibly open his teeth with a knife and stuff the food down his throat, he gave up his intention in order to avoid such a degradation of the Order and knightly honor.

But the Bohemian was particularly anxious to arrive at Spychow before his master, so that he might spare his adored young lady from shame. Simple, but courageous and fearless, he was not void of knightly noble sentiment, and he well understood that Jagienka would be humiliated if she were at Spychow together with Danusia. "It will be possible to tell the bishop, in Plock (he thought) that the old knight of Bogdaniec, owing to his guardianship, thought it necessary to take her with him, and then, as soon as it was known that she was the bishop's ward, and besides Zgorzelice she was also entitled to the abbot's estate, then even the *wojewoda's* son would not be too great for her." That thought contributed to soothe his troubled mind. The very reason of his conveying good news to Spychow troubled his mind, as it would be the source of misfortune to Jagienka.

The beautiful face of Sieciechowna, as red as an apple, often appeared before his eyes. On such occasions, he would, if the road permitted, tickle the horse's sides with his spurs, because he wanted to reach Spychow as soon as possible.

They traveled along intricate roads, or rather no roads at all, through the woods, going straight ahead as the reaper does. The Bohemian knew that by pushing on a little toward the west and constantly in a southerly direction, he would reach Mazowsze and then all would go well. During the daytime he followed the sun, and at night he marched by the stars. The wilderness in front of him appeared endless. Days and nights passed by. More than once he thought that Zbyszko would not succeed in bringing the woman through the terrible wilderness alive, where there was no food to be procured, and where the horses must be guarded by night from wolves and bears. During the daytime they had to get out of the way of herds of bison and aurochs; where the terrible wild-boar sharpens his crooked tusks against the roots of the pine-trees, and very often it happened that those who made no use of the crossbow, or did not strike with the pike into the sides of a deer or young boar, such passed whole days without food.

"How will it be here," thought Hlawa, "with a maiden who is already almost tortured to death!"

Now and then, it happened that they had to cross swamps and deep ravines, which continuous spring rains filled for days with rushing streams. Lakes, too, were not wanting in the wilderness, in which they saw at sunset whole flocks of deer and elk disporting in the red transparent waters.

Often they also perceived smoke which showed the presence of people. On several occasions Hlawa approached such forest settlements, whence wild people would issue, clothed with skins upon their naked bodies, armed with clubs and bows, and looking from under their shaggy-tangled hair; the men took them to be werewolves. It was necessary to take advantage of their first astonishment whilst they were looking at the knights, and leave them in the greatest haste.

Arrows whistled twice near the Bohemian's ears, and he heard the shouts of "Wokili" (Germans!) But he preferred to run away rather than to make himself known. Finally, after a few days he began to think that perhaps he had already crossed the frontier, but there was nobody from whom he could ascertain. Only when he met some colonists who spoke the Polish language did he get the information, that he finally stood upon Mazowszian soil.

There it was better, although the whole eastern part of Mazowsze was also one wilderness. But it did not terminate uninhabited as the other did. When the Bohemian arrived at a colony they were less shy—perhaps because they were not so much brought up in constant hatred, or that the Bohemian could converse with them in Polish. The only trouble with them was the boundless curiosity of the people who surrounded the travelers, and overwhelmed them with questions. When they were informed that he carried a prisoner, a Knight of the Cross, they said:

"Give him to us, sir, we will take care of him!"

They importuned the Bohemian so much, that he often became very angry with them, but at the same time, he explained, that he could not grant their request because the prisoner belonged to the prince. Then only they relented. Later on when he arrived in the inhabited places among the nobles and land-owners, he did not get off so easily. The hatred against the Order was raging, because everywhere they still remembered vividly the wrongs which the prince had suffered at its hands when, in time of peace, the Knights of the Cross had kidnapped the prince near Zlotorja and imprisoned him. They did not wish to dispatch Zygfried at once. But here and there, one of the doughty Polish nobles would say: "Unbind him and we will give him arms, and then challenge him to deadly combat." To such the Bohemian would give a potent reason: that the right to vengeance belonged to the unfortunate lord of Spychow, and one must not deprive him of that privilege.

The journey through the inhabited region was easy; because there were good roads and there was plenty of provender for the horses. The Bohemian continued his uninterrupted march until after ten days' travel he arrived before Corpus Christi day at Spychow.

He arrived in the evening, at the same time as when he had brought the news from Macko, that he had left Szczytno for the Zmudz country. It also happened now as before, that Jagienka, observing him through the window, rushed toward him, and he fell at her feet. He was speechless for a while. But she soon lifted him up and took him aside, as she did not wish to interrogate him in the presence of others.

"What news?" she asked, trembling with impatience, and scarcely able to catch her breath. "Is she alive? Well?"

"Alive! Well!"

"Has she been found?"

"She has. They rescued her."

"Praised be Jesus Christ!"

But whilst she spoke these words her face assumed a deathly pallor, because all her hopes crumbled into dust.

However, her strength did not forsake her, neither did she lose consciousness. After a moment she mastered herself entirely and enquired again:

"When will she be here?"

"Within a few days! She is sick and the road is very bad."

"Is she sick?"

"Martyred. Her reason is confused with her tortures."

"Merciful Jesus!"

Silence reigned for a moment. Jagienka's lips became pale and they moved as though in prayer.

"Did she recognize Zbyszko?" she asked again.

"She may have done so, but I am not sure, because I left at once, in order to inform you, lady, of the news. That is the reason why I am standing here."

"God reward you. Tell me how it happened!"

The Bohemian related briefly how they rescued Danusia, how they captured the giant Arnold together with Zygfried. He also informed them that he had brought Zygfried with him, because the young knight wished to present him to Jurand so that the latter might avenge himself.

"I must now go to Jurand," said Jagienka, when he had finished.

Then she left, but Hlawa had not been long alone when Sieciechowna rushed toward him from the next apartment; but either because not entirely conscious, owing to the fatigue and exceeding great troubles he had passed through, or owing to his yearning for her, he entirely forgot himself when he saw her; suffice it to say he caught her by the waist, pressed her to his breast and kissed her eyes, cheeks and mouth in such a manner as though he had previously informed her of everything that was necessary for her to know before the kissing began.

Perhaps he had already told her everything in spirit, when upon the road, therefore he kissed her and kept on kissing endlessly. He embraced her so strongly that she lost her breath. Yet she did not defend herself, at first from surprise and then, from faintness, so that were it not for Hlawa's powerful grasp she would have fallen to the ground.

Fortunately this did not last too long because distant steps were heard on the stairs, and after a moment, Father Kaleb rushed into the room.

They then quickly separated, and the priest began to overwhelm him with questions. But Hlawa was unable to catch his breath and replied with difficulty. The priest thought that his condition was owing to fatigue. But when the news of the finding of Danusia, her rescue and the presence of her torturer in Spychow was confirmed by Hlawa, he fell upon his knees to thank God for it. Meanwhile Hlawa quieted down a little, and when the priest got up, he was able to repeat his story in a more intelligent and quiet manner in what way Danusia had been found and how they had rescued her.

"God did not deliver her," the priest said, whilst listening to his narrative, "in order that her reason and soul should be restored whilst she was in the darkness and in the power of the unclean. Let Jurand only lay his saintly hand upon her, and offer only one of his prayers, and he will restore her reason and health."

"Knight Jurand?" asked the Bohemian, with astonishment. "Does he possess so much power? Can he become a saint whilst he is alive?"

"Before God he is considered a saint even whilst he is alive. But when he dies the people will have one more patron saint in heaven;—a martyr."

"But you said, reverend father,'that if he were only to lay his saintly hands upon the head of his daughter.' Has his right hand grown again? for I know you prayed for it."

"I said: 'the hands,' as it is customary to say," replied the priest. "But one hand is enough, if God will."

"Surely," answered Hlawa.

But in his voice there was something discouraging when he thought that it appeared like a miracle. Jagienka's entrance interrupted further conversation.

"Now I have informed him carefully of the news," she said. "To avoid the death, which sudden joy might cause, but he fell with the cross in his hands and prayed."

"I am sure that he will be in such a condition till morning, as he is accustomed to lie prostrate in prayer whole nights," said Father Kaleb.

And so it happened; they called to see him several times and each time they found him stretched on the ground, not asleep but in such a fervent prayer that it bordered on perfect ecstasy. Now the watchman, whose duty it was to watch according to custom over

Spychow from the top of the tower, said afterward that he observed that night an extraordinary brightness in the house of the "Old lord."

Very early on the following morning when Jagienka called again to see him, he showed his desire to see Hlawa and the prisoner. The prisoner was brought before him immediately from the dungeon. He was tightly bound with his hands crossed upon his chest. All, including Tolima, advanced toward the old man.

But owing to a dark, cloudy day and the insufficient light of a threatening tempest, which penetrated the bladder panes, the Bohemian was unable to see Jurand well. But as soon as his keen eyes grew accustomed to the darkness and looked upon him, he scarcely recognized him. The gigantic man had dwindled to a giant skeleton. His face was so white that it did not much differ from his snow-white hair, and when he bowed on the arm of his chair, with his eyelids closed, he appeared to Hlawa like a real corpse.

In front of the chair stood a table; upon it were a crucifix, a pitcher of water, and a loaf of black bread in which stuck the *misericordia*, that terrible knife which the knights made use of in dispatching the wounded. Besides bread and water, Jurand enjoyed no other nourishment. His only garment consisted of coarse sackcloth upon his naked body fastened with a straw girdle. Such was the manner of living of that once powerful and terrible knight of Spychow, since his return from his captivity in Szczytno.

Now, when he heard them arrive, he kicked aside the tame she-wolf which gnawed at his bare feet, It was then that Jurand appeared to the Bohemian like a real corpse. There was suspense for a moment, because they expected some sign from him ordering them to talk: but he sat motionless, pale, and peaceful; his mouth, a little opened, had the real appearance of one who is plunged in the everlasting sleep of death.

Jagienka finally announced that Hlawa was there, and gently enquired:

"Do you wish to hear him?"

Old Jurand nodded his head affirmatively, and the Bohemian began, for the third time, to narrate briefly the story of the battles with the Germans near Gottes800werder. He told him of the fight with Arnold von Baden and how they had rescued Danusia. Not wishing to add new pains to the sufferings of the old martyr and destroy the effect produced by the good news of Danusia's rescue, he purposely avoided relating that her mind suffered for a long time on account of terrible distress. But, on the other hand, as his heart was filled with rancor against the Knights of the Cross, and thirsting to see Zygfried receive his deserved terrible chastisement, he purposely mentioned the fact that when they found her she was terrified, emaciated and sick, and it was evident that they must have treated her as executioners do, and had she remained longer in their terrible hands she would have withered and perished as a little flower withers and perishes when trodden under foot.

Whilst Hlawa recited the news, the sky was overcast and the clouds grew darker, which showed the approach of a storm. The copper-colored masses of clouds which hung over Spychow rolled more heavily upon one another.

Jurand was motionless and listened to the recital without any trembling, so that he appeared to be in deep sleep. Nevertheless, he heard and understood everything, for when Hlawa told the story of Danusia's woes, two large drops of tears rolled down his cheeks from the hollows of his eyes. Only one earthly feeling still remained in his breast, and that was love for his child.

Then his blue lips began to move in prayer. The first distant thunderclaps were heard outside. Now and then lightning illuminated the windows. He prayed long, and again the tears trickled down upon his white beard. When he finally ceased to pray, long silence reigned, which was so much prolonged as to cause uneasiness to those present because they did not know what to do.

Finally, old Tolima, who was Jurand's right hand, his companion in all battles, and the chief guard of Spychow, said:

"That man of Hades, that werewolf Knight of the Cross who tortured you and your child stands now before you. Give a sign what shall be done to him, and in what manner we shall chastise him!"

Upon hearing these words, rays of light crossed Jurand's face and he nodded to them to bring the prisoner near him. And in the twinkling of an eye, two men grasped him by the shoulders and placed him in front of the old man, who stretched out his hand to Zygfried's face, which he touched as though to feel the outlines and recognize it for the last time. Then he lowered his hand to Zygfried's chest upon which he felt his bound hands, touched the fastening ropes, again closed his eyelids and bowed his head.

They thought that he was absorbed in thought, but whether that was so or not, it was not of long duration, because after a while he started out of his reverie and pointed with his hand in the direction of the loaf of bread, in which the ill-omened *misericordia* stuck.

Then, Jagienka, the Bohemian, even old Tolima and all present held their breath. It was a hundredfold well-deserved punishment, a righteous revenge. Yet their hearts palpitated at the thought that the half-alive old man should be groping to slash the bound prisoner.

But Jurand, seizing the knife in the middle, ran his finger along its sharp edge, so that he might feel the thing he was cutting, and began to sever the bonds upon Zygfried's arms.

At that sight, all were seized with amazement, because they understood his desire and could scarcely believe it. However, that was too much for them. Hlawa was the first to murmur; he was followed by Tolima and the other men. Only the priest Kaleb began to ask, in a voice broken with unrestrained weeping:

"Brother Jurand, what are your wishes? Do you intend to give the prisoner his liberty?"

"It is so!" replied Jurand, nodding his head affirmatively.

"No punishment for him, nor vengeance? Is that your desire?"

"It is!" and he nodded again.

Open discontent was shown in the murmurs and anger of the men, but the priest did not wish to belittle such an unheard-of deed of mercy. He turned to the murmurers and exclaimed:

"Now who dares to oppose the saint? Down upon your knees!"

Then he knelt down himself and began to say:

"Our Father who art in heaven, hallowed be Thy name. Thy kingdom come...."

And he repeated the Lord's Prayer to the end. At the words: "And forgive us our trespasses as we forgive those who trespass against us," he directed his eyes involuntarily toward Jurand, whose face actually assumed an unearthly radiance.

That sight, and that expressive prayer crushed the hearts of all present; even old Tolima, the confirmed, hardened warrior, made the sign of the Holy Cross, and immediately embraced Jurand's feet and said:

"Lord, if you want your wishes to be accomplished, then the prisoner should be led to the frontier."

"Yes!" nodded Jurand.

The storm approached nearer and nearer and the lightning more frequently illuminated the windows.

CHAPTER IV.

Two horsemen, in the midst of the storm and pouring rain, reached the frontier of Spychow. They were Zygfried and Tolima. The last mentioned accompanied the German to protect him from the waylaying peasants and the servants of Spychow, who burned with hatred and revenge toward him. Zygfried was unarmed, but he was not fettered. The rainstorm, driven by the tempest, had already overtaken them. Now and then, when it suddenly thundered, the horses reared. They traveled in deep silence in a ravine. Owing to the narrowness of the road, they were at times so near that they struck each other's stirrups. Tolima, who had been accustomed to guard prisoners for many years, frequently looked at Zygfried watchfully, as though he were guarding against his escaping suddenly, and an involuntary shudder seized him every time he looked at Zygfried, because his eyes appeared to him to be shining in the darkness like the eyes of an evil spirit, or of a vampire. It struck Tolima that it would be advisable to make the sign of the cross over Zygfried, but he refrained from doing so, because, he thought, that under the sign of the cross, he would hear unearthly voices, and Zygfried would be transformed into a hideous being. His teeth chattered and his fear increased. The old soldier who could fight singly against a whole band of Germans and fall fearlessly upon them, as a hawk swoops upon a flock of partridges, was nevertheless afraid of unclean spirits, and wanted to have nothing to do with them. He would have preferred simply to point out to the German the road and return; but he was ashamed of himself, therefore he led him as far as the frontier.

It was then, when they had drawn near the border of the Spychow forest, that the rain ceased, and the clouds were lit up with a strange yellowish light, that Zygfried's eyes lost that above-mentioned unnatural glare. But Tolima was seized with another temptation: "They ordered me," he said to himself, "to lead this mad dog safely as far as the frontier. I have done that; but must the torturer of my master and his daughter leave without revenge and punishment? Would it not be a proper and God-pleasing deed to kill him? Ay! I should like to challenge him to deadly combat, but he is not armed. Very soon at *Pan* Warcimow's farm, about a mile from here, they will supply him with some weapon, and then I will challenge him. With God's help I shall overthrow him, then kill him, and fitly, cut off his head and bury it in the dung!" These were the words which Tolima said to himself. Then looking greedily at the German he began to dilate his nostrils as if he already smelt fresh blood. He fought hard in his mind with that desire; it was hard wrestling with himself, until he reflected that Jurand had not only granted to the prisoner his life and freedom as far as the frontier, but also beyond it, otherwise Jurand's holy deed would have no merit and the heavenly reward for him would thereby be lessened. He finally prevailed over himself, and reining in his horse, said;

"Here is our border; your side is not far from here; proceed, you are free; and if the qualms of conscience do not take you off, or God's thunder does not strike you, then you need not fear man."

Then Tolima returned; and Zygfried proceeded. His face looked as if petrified and a savage expression was depicted upon it. He did not reply a single word, as though he heard nothing that was said to him. He continued his journey now upon a wider road and had the appearance of one who is fast asleep.

The break in the storm and the brightening of the sky only lasted a short time. It darkened again; so much so that it looked like the darkness of night. The clouds traveled so low that they quite enveloped the forest and from the hills came down an ill-boding obscurity, a kind of hissing and growling of impatient vampires, who were kept back by the angel of the storm. Blinding lightning illuminated the threatening sky every moment and terrified the land. Then one could see the broad highway extending between the two black walls of forest, and upon it a lonely horseman. Zygfried moved on in a semi-conscious condition, consumed by fever. Despair had lacerated his heart since Rotgier's death and filled it with crimes of revenge. Remorse, awful visions, soul stirrings had already tortured his mind in the past to such a degree that with great effort he had to fight madness; there were even moments when he could fight no longer and he surrendered. But the new troubles, fatigue upon the road under the strong hand of the Bohemian, the night he had passed in the dungeon of Spychow, the uncertainty of his fate, and above all, that unheard-of and almost superhuman deed, had quite terrified him. All this had brought him to a climax. There were moments when his mind became so stupefied that he entirely lost his judgment and he did not know what he was doing. Then the fever awoke him and, at the same time awoke within him a certain dull feeling of despair, destruction, and perdition,—a feeling that all hope was already gone, extinguished and ended. He felt that about him was only night, night and darkness, a horrible abyss into which he must plunge.

Suddenly a voice whispered in his ear:

"Go! Go!"

And he looked around him and saw the very image of death, a skeleton mounted upon a skeleton horse, pressing closely beside him, with his white rattling bones.

"Is it you?" asked Zygfried.

"Yes it is. Go! Go!"

But at that moment he glanced to the other side and observed that he had another companion there. Stirrup to stirrup rode a form, appearing somewhat like a human being but for his face and head. It had the head of an animal, with raised long pointed ears, covered with black shaggy hair.

"Who are you?" asked Zygfried.

But the being, instead of replying, showed its teeth and growled.

Zygfried closed his eyes, but in a moment he heard a louder clattering of bones and the voice speaking to him in the same ear:

"Time! Time! Hurry on, go!"

"I go!" he replied.

But that last reply came from his breast and seemed to have been uttered by somebody else. Then, impelled as it were by an external unconquerable power, he dismounted and took off his high knight's saddle, and then the bridle. His companions also dismounted, and did not leave him for a moment. They left the middle of the road and went toward the margin of the wood. There, the black being bent down a branch of a tree and assisted him in fastening to it the strap of the bridle.

"Hurry!" whispered Death.

"Hurry!" whistled some voices from the tops of the trees.

Zygfried, who was like one plunged in deep sleep, drew through the buckle the other end of the strap so as to form a noose. Then he stepped upon the saddle which he had placed in front of the tree, and adjusted the noose upon his neck.

"Push back the saddle! ... Already! Ah!"

The saddle, which he pushed with his feet, rolled away several paces and the body of the unfortunate Knight of the Cross hung heavily. It seemed to him, only for a short moment, that he heard a kind of smothering, snorting and roaring, and that abominable vampire threw itself upon him, shook him and then began to tear his breast with its teeth to rend his heart. Then, as the light of his eyes was about extinguished he yet saw something else; for lo, death dissolved into a whitish cloud, which slowly approached him, embraced him, and finally surrounded and covered all with a dismal and impenetrable veil.

At that moment the storm broke with great fury. Thunder roared in the middle of the road with such a terrible crash that it seemed as though the earth was shaken to its very foundations. The whole forest bent under the tempest. The noise of whistling, hissing, howling, creaking of the trunks, and cracking of the broken branches, filled the depths of the woods. The tempest-driven sheets of rain hid the world from sight. Only at short intervals, when lit up by blood-colored lightning, could be seen the wild dangling body of Zygfried by the roadside.

* * * * *

The following morning, advancing upon the same road, a numerous train might be seen. In front was Jagienkna, with Sieciechowna and the Bohemian. Behind them moved the wagons, surrounded by four servants, armed with bows and swords. Every driver had also a spear and an axe near him, not counting forged hayforks and other cutting arms suitable upon the road. Those arms were necessary for protection against wild beasts, as well as robbers, who always swarmed upon the border of the Knights of the Cross. This caused Jagiello to complain in his letters to the Grand Master of the Order, and when they met at Racionza.

But being provided with skilful men and good arms, the retinue traveled without fear.

The stormy day was succeeded by a wonderful one; cheerful, silent and so bright that the eyes of the travelers were blinded when not in the shade. Not a single leaf stirred; from each of them hung large drops of rain which the sun changed into a rainbow. Among the pine-needles they had the appearance of large glistening diamonds. The rainfall produced small streams upon the road, which ran with glad sound toward the lower places, where they formed shallow little lakes. The whole neighborhood was wet and bedewed, but smiling in the morning brightness. On such mornings, also, the human heart is filled with gladness. Therefore the ostlers and servants began to sing; they marveled at the silence which reigned among those riding in front of them.

But they were quiet because a heavy burden oppressed Jagienka's heart. There was something which had ended in her life, something broken. Although she was not experienced in meditation and could not determine distinctly the cause and what was going on in her mind, yet she felt that all that had lived hitherto had vanished, that all her hopes had dissipated as the morning mist upon the fields is dissipated. She felt that she must now renounce and give up everything and forget, and begin almost a new life. She also thought that although, with God's will, her present position was not of the worst, yet it could not be otherwise than sad, and in no way could the new life turn out to be as good as that which had just terminated. And an immense sorrow had taken hold of her heart, so that, at the thought that every past hope was gone forever, tears came to her eyes. But not wishing to add shame to her other troubles, she restrained herself from weeping. She wished that she had never left Zgorzelice; in that case she would not now have to return thither. Then, she thought, it was not only to remove the cause for attacks upon Zgorzelice by Cztan and Wilk that Macko brought her to Spychow. That she could not believe. "No," she said, "Macko also knew that that was not the only cause for taking me away. Perhaps Zbyszko will also know it." At that thought, her cheeks became crimson and bitterness filled her heart.

"I was too daring," she said to herself, "and now I have what I deserved. Trouble and uncertainty to-morrow, suffering and deep sorrow in the future and with it humiliation."

But the train of oppressing thoughts was interrupted by a man coming hastily from the opposite direction. The Bohemian, whose eyes nothing escaped, rushed toward the man, who with crossbow upon his shoulder and badger-skin pouch at his side, and with a feather of a black woodcock in his cap, was recognized as a forester.

"Hey! Who are you? Stop!" exclaimed the Bohemian.

The man approached quickly, his face was agitated, and had the expression of those who have something extraordinary to communicate. He cried:

"There upon the road ahead of you is a man hanging on a tree!"

The Bohemian was alarmed, thinking that it might be a murder, and he asked the man quickly:

"How far from here is it?"

"A bowshot distance, and upon this road."

"Is there nobody with him?"

"Nobody; I frightened away a wolf that was smelling around him."

The mention of a wolf quieted Hlawa, for it told him that there were neither people nor farms in the neighborhood.

Then Jagienka said:

"Look there, what is that?"

Hlawa rushed ahead, and soon returned hurriedly.

"Zygfried is hanging there!" he exclaimed while reining in his horse in front of Jagienka.

"In the name of the Father, Son and Holy Ghost! You do not mean Zygfried, the Knight of the Cross?"

"Yes, it is he. He hung himself with the bridle."

"Did you say by himself?"

"It seems so, because the saddle lies alongside him, and if there were robbers they would have killed him outright and made off with the saddle, because it is valuable."

"Shall we proceed?"

"Let us not go that way! No!" cried Anula Sieciechowna, afraid. "Something evil might happen to us!"

Jagienka was also somewhat afraid, because she believed that the body of a suicide is surrounded by crowds of evil spirits. But Hlawa, who was fearless and bold, said:

"Bah! I was near him, and even pushed him with the lance, and do not feel any devil upon my neck."

"Do not blaspheme!" cried Jagienka.

"I am not blaspheming," replied the Bohemian, "I only trust in God's power. Nevertheless, if you are afraid we will go around it."

Sieciechowna begged him to do so; but Jagienka, having reflected for a moment, said:

"It is not proper to leave the dead unburied. It is a Christian act commanded by the Lord. Anyhow it is the body of a man."

"Yes, but it is the body of a Knight of the Cross, a hangman and executioner! Let the crows and wolves occupy themselves with his body."

"It was not specified. God will judge for his sins, but we must do our duty; and if we fulfil God's commandment nothing evil will befall us."

"Well, then, let it be done according to your wishes," replied the Bohemian.

Accordingly he gave the order to the servants, who were reluctant. But they feared Hlawa, to oppose whom was a dangerous thing. Not having the necessary spades to dig a hole in the ground, they therefore gathered pitchforks and axes for that purpose and left. The Bohemian also went with them and to give them an example, he crossed himself and cut with his own hands the leather strap upon which the body was hanging.

Zygfried's face had become blue whilst hanging; he had an awful appearance, because his eyes were open and terror-stricken, his mouth was also open as though in the act of trying to catch his last breath. They quickly dug a pit near by and pushed therein the corpse of Zygfried with the handles of their pitchforks; they laid him with his face downward and covered it first with dust, then they gathered stones and placed them upon it, because it was an immemorial custom to cover the graves of suicides with stones; otherwise they would come out during the night and frighten the passers-by.

As there were many stones upon the road and under the mosses, the grave was soon covered with a considerable mound. Then Hlawa cut a cross with his axe upon the trunk of the pine-tree near. He did that, not for Zygfried, but to prevent evil spirits from gathering at that place. Then he returned to the retinue.

"His soul is in hell and his body is already in the ground," he said to Jagienka. "We can travel now."

They started; but Jagienka, whilst passing along, took a small branch of pine-tree and pressed it upon the stones. Then everybody of the train followed the example of the lady. That, too, had been an old custom.

They traveled for a long while absorbed in thought, thinking of that wicked monk and knight. Finally Jagienka said:

"God's justice cannot be escaped. It does not even permit the prayer, 'Everlasting rest'[118] to be offered up because there is no mercy for him."

"You have shown by your order to bury him that you possess a compassionate soul," replied the Bohemian.

Then he spoke hesitatingly: "People talk. Bah! maybe they are not people, but witches and wizards—that a halter or a strap taken from the hanging body secures to the possessor certain luck in everything. But I did not take the strap from Zygfried, because I wish that your luck should proceed from the Lord Jesus and not from necromancers."

Jagienka did not reply to that at once, but after awhile she sighed several times and said as it were to herself:

"Hey! My happiness is behind, not in front of me."

CHAPTER V.

It was not until the end of the ninth day after Jagienka's departure that Zbyszko reached the frontier of Spychow, but Danusia was already so near death that he entirely lost all hope of bringing her alive to her father.

On the following day, when she began to be incoherent in her replies, he observed that not only her mind was out of order, but that she was also suffering from a certain malady against which that childlike frame, exhausted by so much suffering, prison, torture and continuous fright, could not fight. Perhaps the noise of the fight of Macko and Zbyszko with the Germans contributed to fill her cup of terror, and it was just about that time that she was taken ill with that malady. Suffice it to say that the fever never left her from that moment until they reached the end of the journey. So far it was successfully accomplished, because throughout the terrible wilderness, in the midst of great troubles, Zbyszko carried her as though she were dead. When they left the wilderness and reached inhabited regions, among farmers and nobles, trouble and danger ceased. When the people were informed that he carried one of their own daughters whom he had rescued from the Knights of the Cross, especially when they knew that she was the daughter of the famous Jurand, of whose exploits the minstrels sang in the villages, hamlets, and huts, they vied with each other in rendering help and service. They procured proper horses and supplies. All doors stood open for them. It was no more necessary for Zbyszko to carry her in a cradle when the strong young men carried her from one village to another in a litter. They carried her as carefully as though she were a saint. The women surrounded her with the most tender care. The men, upon hearing the account of her wrongs, gnashed their teeth, and not a few put on the steel cuirass, grasped the sword, axe, or lance and went along with Zbyszko, in order to take revenge with interest. Because, the valiant race considered even retribution, wrong for wrong, insufficient.

But revenge did not then occupy Zbyszko's mind; his only thought was for Danusia. He lived between flashes of hope when there were momentary signs of improvement, and gloomy despair when she got worse, and as far as her latter condition was concerned, he could not deceive himself. A superstitious thought struck him more than once at the beginning of the journey, that there was, somewhere in the pathless regions they were passing, death, riding along with them, step by step, lying in wait for the moment when he might fall upon Danusia and wring from her the last breath of life. That vision or feeling became especially pronounced at dark midnight, so much so, that more than once he was seized with a despairing desire to return and challenge death to a combat to a finish, in the same fashion as knights are wont to do toward each other. But at the end of the journey it became worse, because he felt that death was not following them, but was in the very midst of the retinue; invisible truly, but so near that its cold breath could be felt. Then he understood that against such an enemy, courage, strength and arms are counted as nothing and that he would be obliged to surrender the most precious head as a prey without even a struggle.

And that was a most terrible feeling, because it roused within him a tempestuous, irresistible sorrow, a sorrow, bottomless as the sea. Could therefore Zbyszko restrain himself from groaning, could his heart remain unbroken by pain, when he looked at his most beloved? He spoke to her as in terms of involuntary reproach: "Was it for this that I loved you? Was it for this that I searched and rescued you in order that you should be put under ground to-morrow and I should never see you again?" Then he would look at her cheeks which glowed with fever, at her expressionless and dull eyes, and ask her again:

"Are you going to leave me? Are you not sorry for it? You prefer going to staying with me." Then he thought that something was happening in his own head, and his breast swelled with immense sadness which seared it, but he could not give vent to his feeling with tears, because of a certain feeling of anger and hatred against that compassionless power which was consuming the innocent, blind, and cold child. If that wicked enemy, the Knight of the Cross, were present, he would have fallen upon him and torn him to pieces like a wild beast.

When they arrived at the forest court, he wished to halt, but as it was the spring season the court was deserted. There he was informed by the keepers that the princely pair had gone to their brother, Prince Ziemowita, at Plock. He therefore resolved, instead of going to Warsaw where the court physician might have given him some relief, to go to Spychow. That plan was terrible, because it seemed to him that all was over with her and that he would not be able to bring her alive to Jurand.

But just as they were only a few hours distant from Spychow the brightest ray of hope shone again in his heart. Danuska's cheeks became paler, her eyes were less troubled, her breathing not so loud and quick. Zbyszko had observed it immediately, and had given orders to stop, so that she might rest and breathe undisturbed.

It was only about three miles from the inhabited part of Spychow, upon a narrow road winding between fields and meadows. They stopped near a wild pear-tree whose branches served to the sick as a protection from the rays of the sun. The men dismounted and unbridled their horses so as to facilitate their grazing. Two women, who were hired to attend Danusia and the youths who carried her, fatigued with the road and heat, lay down in the shade and slept. Only Zbyszko remained watching near the litter and sat close by upon the roots of the pear-tree, not taking his eyes off her even for a moment.

She lay in the midst of the afternoon silence, her eyelids closed. It seemed to Zbyszko that she was not asleep,—when at the other end of the meadow a man who was mowing hay stopped and began to sharpen his scythe loudly upon the hone. Then she trembled a little and opened her eyelids for a moment, but immediately closed them again. Her breast heaved as though she was deeply inspiring, and in a hardly audible voice she whispered:

"Flowers smell sweetly...."

These were the first words, clear and free from fever, spoken since they had left, because the breeze really wafted from the sun-warmed meadow a strong, redolent hay and honey perfume, fragrant with the scent of herbs. This caused Zbyszko to think that reason had returned to her. His heart trembled within him for joy. He wished to throw himself at her feet at the first impulse. But fearing lest that might frighten her, he desisted. He only knelt in front of the litter, and bending over her, said in a whisper:

"Dear Danusia! Danusia!"

She opened her eyes again, and looked at him for a while. Then a smile brightened up her face, the same as when she was in the tar-burner's shanty, but far from consciousness, but she pronounced his name:

"Zbyszko!..."

She attempted to stretch her hands toward him, but owing to her great weakness she was unable to do it. But he embraced her, his heart was so full that it seemed as if he were thanking her for some great favor he had received.

"I praise the Lord," he said, "you have awoke ... O God...." Now his voice failed him, and they looked at each other for some time in silence. That silence was only interrupted by the gentle wind which moved the leaves of the pear-tree, the chirping of the grasshoppers among the grass and the distant indistinct song of the mower.

It seemed as though her consciousness was gradually increasing, for she continued to smile and had the appearance of a sleeping child seeing angels in its dream. Little by little her face assumed an air of astonishment.

"Oh! where am I?" she cried. He was so much overcome with joy that he uttered numerous short and abrupt questions.

"Near Spychow. You are with me, and we are going to see dear papa. Your sorrow is ended. Oh! my darling Danusia, I searched for you and rescued you. You are no more in the power of the Germans. Be not afraid. We shall soon be at Spychow. You were ill, but the Lord Jesus had mercy upon you. There was so much sorrow, so many tears! Dear Danusia. Now, everything is well. There is nothing but happiness for you. Ah I how much did I search for you!... How far did I wander!... Oh! Mighty God!... Oh!..."

He sighed deeply and groaned as though he had thrown off the last heavy burden of suffering from his breast.

Danusia lay quiet trying to recall something to her mind and reflecting upon something. Then finally she asked:

"So, you cared for me?"

Two tears which were gathering in her eyes slowly rolled down her cheeks upon the pillow.

"I, not care for you?" cried Zbyszko.

There was something more powerful in that smothered exclamation than in the most vehement protestations and oaths, because he had always loved her with his whole soul. And from the moment when he had recovered her she had become more dear to him than the whole world.

Silence reigned again. The distant singing of the mowing peasant ceased and he began to whet his scythe again.

Danusia's lips moved again, but with such a low whisper that Zbyszko could not hear it. He therefore bent over her and asked:

"What do you say, darling?"

But she repeated:

"Sweet smelling blossoms."

"Because we are near the meadows," he replied. "But we shall soon proceed and go to dear papa, whom we have also rescued from captivity, and you shall be mine even unto death. Do you hear me well? Do you understand me?"

Then he suddenly became alarmed, for he observed that her face was gradually paling and was thickly covered with perspiration.

"What ails you?" he asked in great alarm.

And he felt his hair bristling and frost creeping through his bones.

301

"What ails you, tell me," he repeated.

"It darkens," she whispered.

"It darkens? Why, the sun shines and you say: 'it darkens'?" he said with a suppressed voice. "Up to this time you have spoken rationally. In God's name I beseech you, speak, even if it is only one word."

She still moved her lips, but she was unable even to whisper. Zbyszko guessed that she tried to pronounce his name and that she called him. Immediately afterward, her emaciated hands began to twitch and flutter upon the rug covering her. That lasted only for a moment. No doubt was left now that she had expired.

Horrified and in despair, Zbyszko began to beg her, as though his entreaties could avail:

"Danuska! Oh, merciful Jesus!... Only wait till we come to Spychow! Wait! Wait, I beseech you! Oh, Jesus! Jesus! Jesus!"

The appeal awoke the sleeping women, and the men who were stretched with the horses upon the lawn came running. They guessed at a glance what had happened; they knelt down and began loudly to recite the litany.

The breeze ceased, even the leaves upon the pear-tree did not rustle. Only the voices reciting the litany sounded throughout that profound silence.

Danusia opened her eyes once more at the very end of the litany, as though she wished to look upon Zbyszko and upon the sunlit world for the last time. Then she lapsed into an everlasting sleep.

* * * * *

The women closed her eyelids; then they went to the meadow to gather flowers. The men followed them in file. Thus they walked in the sunshine among the luxuriant grass and had the appearance of field spirits bowing now and then, and weeping, for their hearts were filled with pity and sorrow. Zbyszko was kneeling in the shade beside the litter, with his head upon Danusia's knees, speechless and motionless, as if he too were dead. But the gatherers kept on plucking here and there, marigolds, buttercups, bellflowers and plenty of red and white sweet-smelling little blossoms. They also found in the small moist hollows in the meadow, lilies of the valley, and upon the margin near the fallow ground, they got St. John's wort until they had gathered their arms full. Then they sadly surrounded the litter and began to adorn it, until they had covered the dead with flowers and herbs; they only left the face uncovered, which in the midst of the bellflowers and lilies looked white, peaceful, calm, as in eternal sleep, serene, and quite angelic.

The distance to Spychow was less than three miles. Then, when they had shed copious tears of sorrow and pain, they carried the litter toward the forest where Jurand's domains began.

The men led the horses in front of the retinue. Zbyszko himself carried the litter upon his head, and the women loaded with the surplus of the bunches of flowers and herbs, sang hymns. They moved very slowly along the herb-covered meadows and the grey fallow fields and had the appearance of a funeral procession. Not a cloudlet marred the blue clear sky, and the region warmed itself in the golden rays of the sun.

The further adventures of Zbyszko will be found in a subsequent volume.

FOOTNOTES:

[Footnote 1: The Benedictine Abbey at Tyniec was in Poland as important and rich, relatively, as the Abbey of Saint-Germain des Près in France. In those times the order organized by Saint Benoit (Benedictus) was the most important factor in the civilization and material prosperity of the country. The older contained 17,000 abbeys. From it came 24 Popes; 200 Cardinals; 1,600 Archbishops; 4,000 Bishops; 15,000 Writers; 1,500 Saints; 5,000 Beatified; 43 Emperors, and 44 Kings. These figures are material facts showing the importance of the order. About its influence on art, literature and culture one could write a volume.]

[Footnote 2: Two powerful families.]

[Footnote 3: Lithuania.]

[Footnote 4: Historical fact.]

[Footnote 5: Prince.]

302

[Footnote 6: Lithuanian.]

[Footnote 7: Money—it is difficult to tell the value exactly.]

[Footnote 8: Bishop.]

[Footnote 9: Priests.]

[Footnote 10: An exclamation of trifling.]

[Footnote 11: Prince Kiejstut's daughter.]

[Footnote 12: Slave minstrels.]

[Footnote 13: A kind of guitar.]

[Footnote 14: The names of the noblemen of every country are derived from the estates which they possess—hence the particles before the name of a true nobleman: *de* in France, for instance, de Nevers, means that the name comes from the place called Nevers; *of* in England, for instance, Duke of Manchester; *von* in Germany has the same signification; in Poland z, for instance Macko z Bogdanca—means that the estate Bogdaniec belonged to his family and to him;—in the following centuries the z was changed to *ski*, put on the end of the name and instead of writing z Bogdanca, a man of the same family was called Bogdanski; but it does not follow that every Pole, whose name ends in *ski* is a nobleman. Therefore the translation of that particular z into English *of* is only strictly correct, although in other cases z should be translated into English *from*: to write: Baron de Rothschild is absurd and ridiculous, because the sign "red shield" was not an estate, and one cannot put *de* before it.]

[Footnote 15: A wealthy possessor of land—they were freemen and had serfs working for them—some of them were noblemen, and had the right to use coats of arms.]

[Footnote 16: Pan—Lord]

[Footnote 17: A man coming from Mazowsze—the part of Poland round Warsaw.]

[Footnote 18: Count.]

[Footnote 19: Back side of the axe.]

[Footnote 20: A town surrounded with walls and having a peculiar jurisdiction or a kind of a castle.]

[Footnote 21: Inhabitants of Rus'—part of Poland round Lwow—Leopol (Latin), Lemberg (German).]

[Footnote 22: Money;—marks.]

[Footnote 23: Hail—the war-cry of the family, either because it was numerous like hail or struck sharply like hail.]

[Footnote 24: Count.]

[Footnote 25: Wdaly—in old Polish—handsome.]

[Footnote 26: Beautiful.]

[Footnote 27: Abbot of a hundred villages.]

[Footnote 28: Ordinary German soldiers.]

[Footnote 29: A nobleman holding an estate of the Crown, with or without jurisdiction.]

[Footnote 30: Knight of the Cross in Polish.]

[Footnote 31: Vocative from Zbyszko.]

[Footnote 32: Pater-noster—the Lord's prayer.]

[Footnote 33: Historical fact.]

[Footnote 34: A military title with jurisdiction—corresponding to general.]

[Footnote 35: Historical fact.]

[Footnote 36: Bonebreaker.]

[Footnote 37: Historical fact.]

[Footnote 38: A large building which served for different purposes, but especially, as a depot of broadcloth; in Polish *sukno*, hence its name: *sukiennice*.]

[Footnote 39: Noblemen in Lithuania and Russia.]

[Footnote 40: The Tartars were divided into Ords—it was a fancy division, without any precise number.]

[Footnote 41: Anjou in French.]

[Footnote 42: Piasts is family name—the first kings of Poland were
Piasts.]

[Footnote 43: Mountains in Poland—sometimes improperly called Carpathian
Mountains.]

[Footnote 44: Priest—or prince in the old Slav language.]

[Footnote 45: In Poland they use in the churches a sprinkling brush made of thin
shavings of a certain wood—such a brush is called, "kropidlo."]

[Footnote 46: The Province of Dobrzyn was seized by the Knights of the
Cross on the ground of an unlawful agreement with Wladyslaw Opolczyk.]

[Footnote 47: Allusion to beehives on the trees; to take honey from them, the keeper
was obliged to climb a rope.]

[Footnote 48: Famous battle in which the Germans were defeated by King
Wladyslaw Lokietek.]

[Footnote 49: Ksiondz—priest.]

[Footnote 50: We will go to dissipate.]

[Footnote 51: Marienburg in German.]

[Footnote 52: King.]

[Footnote 53: Friend.]

[Footnote 54: Diminutive of *kniaz*—prince.]

[Footnote 55: Diminutive from *bojar*—Lord.]

[Footnote 56: Marienburg in German.]

[Footnote 57: A sort of coat.]

[Footnote 58: The bison of Pliny; the urus of Caesar. The bison, destroyed in all other
countries of Europe, is only to be found in Poland in the forest of Bialowieza, where a
special body of guards takes care of this rare animal.]

[Footnote 59: It means here a fort, a stronghold, a castle.]

[Footnote 60: Grzywna or mark was equal to half pound of silver.]

[Footnote 61: High sharp pointed hat.]

[Footnote 62: Crooked.]

[Footnote 63: Polish *tata* = papa; hence the diminutive and endearing terms *tatus*,
tatutu and *tatulku* = "dear papa," "dear little papa," etc.]

[Footnote 64: Another form of diminutive from *tata*—father.]

[Footnote 65: Church with certain special privileges. It is a popular expression for the
church called *collegiata*, in Latin.]

[Footnote 66: Silesia.]

[Footnote 67: A popular exclamation of joy—sometimes of distress if it is put with
another word.]

[Footnote 68: An exclamation of mirth, especially in songs; and while dancing, they
exclaim in Poland: hoc! hoc!]

[Footnote 69: Wooden beehive excavated in a tree.]

[Footnote 70: Kind of fur jacket—bolero.]

[Footnote 71: Both words are diminutives of *tata*—father.]

[Footnote 72: Diminutive of mother.]

[Footnote 73: In 1331.]

[Footnote 74: Stronghold—castle.]

[Footnote 75: Miss.]

[Footnote 76: Breslau in German.]

[Footnote 77: Diminutive of *tata* father.]

[Footnote 78: Abbreviation of Przeclaw.]

[Footnote 79: Podhale is part of the mountains of Karpaty.]

[Footnote 80: Nickname given to bears.]

[Footnote 81: Popular name for bear.]

[Footnote 82: Wolf.]

[Footnote 83: Seminarists students.]

[Footnote 84: Diminutive of *wlodyka*.]

[Footnote 85: Piece of money; it is twenty-fourth part of *grzywna* or mark, which was worth half pound of silver; one *skojeg* was worth about one-third of an ounce.]

[Footnote 86: "Bold Mountain"—a place in Poland, where one of the first three Benedictine monasteries was built by the king, Boleslaw Chrobry (the Valiant) 1125. In this monastery is a part of our Saviour's cross—hence pilgrimages to that place.]

[Footnote 87: Diminutive of *wlodyka*.]

[Footnote 88: Another form of *pan*—lord; when one speaks in commiseration or in sympathy, any noun can take this form.]

[Footnote 89: A short prayer for the dead.]

[Footnote 90: The famous victory over the Knights of the Cross by the king Wladyslaw Lokietek.]

[Footnote 91: Lokiec means an ell in Polish. King Wladyslaw was of the family Piasts, but he was called Lokietek on account of his short stature.]

[Footnote 92: Marks.]

[Footnote 93: Here it means a commandant.]

[Footnote 94: A part of Poland. The people were called Kurpie, on account of their shoes made of the bark of trees. They were all famous marksmen.]

[Footnote 95: Krystyn.]

[Footnote 96: A woolen material, made by Polish peasants. In some provinces *kilimeks* are very artistic on account of the odd designs and the harmony of the colors.]

[Footnote 97: Szczytno in Polish.]

[Footnote 98: Cymbaska who married Ernest Iron Habsburg.]

[Footnote 99: The knight Uter, being in love with the virtuous Igerna, wife of Prince Gorlas, with Merlin's help assumed the form of Gorlas, and with Igerna begot the king Arthur.]

[Footnote 100: Kind of horn.]

[Footnote 101: Wigand of Marburg mentions such cases.]

[Footnote 102: There is a custom in Poland, Hungary, Bohemia and some other countries, to break wafers at receptions and parties, on Christmas eve and the following two days, expressing in the meantime good wishes for all manner of prosperity and happiness. The wafers are distributed by the parish that is to say by the priest or sexton. The author refers to that custom.]

[Footnote 103: Siebenkirchen in German, a province which now belongs to Hungary, it was then an independent principality.]

[Footnote 104: Diminutive of mother; it is a charming expression. The Polish language, like the Italian, has a great variety of diminutives.]

[Footnote 105: *Glowacz* the Polish for the Bohemian *Hlawa*, the latter means "head," but the former means also "big" or "thick head."—(S.A.B.)]

[Footnote 106: Lotarynczyk means the man from Lotaringen.]

[Footnote 107: *Byway* means, in this instance, "here we are".]

[Footnote 108: *Pontnik*, "Pardoner," one who dispenses indulgences.—(S.A.B.)]

[Footnote 109: Called: *Misericordia*.]

[Footnote 110: February is called in Polish "Luty," meaning also dreadful, awful, etc.]

[Footnote 111: The diminutive of Anna.]

[Footnote 112: Lit., She was walking on live coals.]

[Footnote 113: Meaning never.]

[Footnote 114: Relics of the gallows were preserved down to the year 1818.]

[Footnote 115: One Polish mile is about three American miles.]

[Footnote 116: *Setnik*, captain over one hundred.]

[Footnote 117: The Greater Bear, or Charleswain ... other names are hen and chickens, dipper, etc. Arabic, *Dhiba*.]

[Footnote 118: *Wieczny odpoczynek racz mu daj Panie*. "God rest his soul."]